I0822320

THE SAFE LANDS

Complete Collection

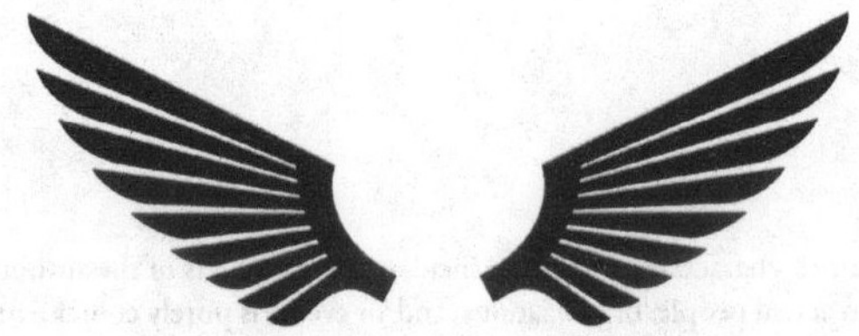

Book 1: Captives
Book 2: Outcasts
Book 3: Rebels

JILL WILLIAMSON

This is a work of fiction. Names, characters, places, and incidents are products of the author's imagination or are used fictitiously. Any similarity to actual people, organizations, and/or events is purely coincidental.

Cover Design by Emilie Hendryx and Luke Williamson

Map Design by Jill Williamson

The author is represented by MacGregor Literary Inc. of Hillsboro, OR.

International Standard Book Number: ISBN: 978-1-955843-47-8

Printed in the United States of America

TABLE OF CONTENTS

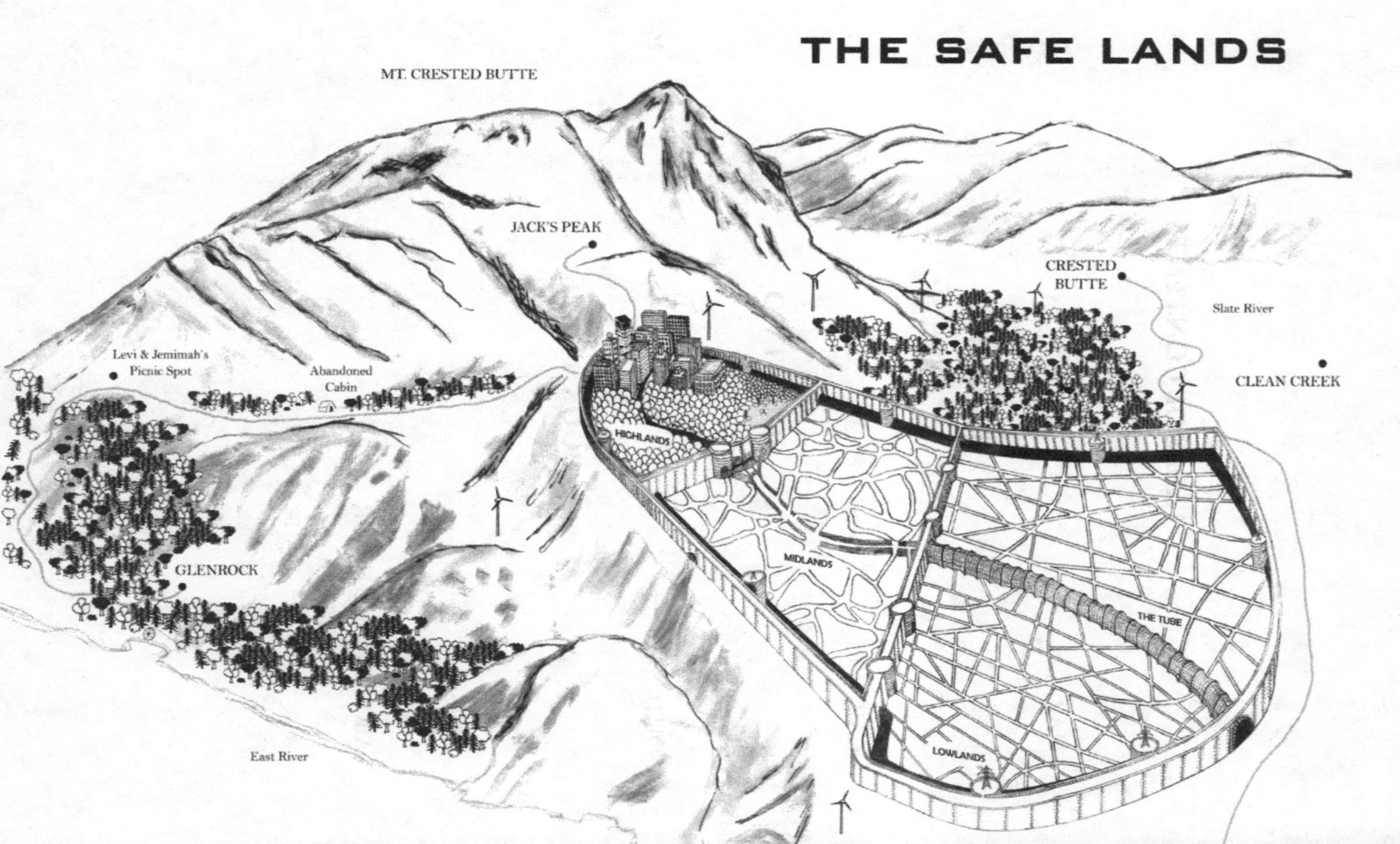
THE SAFE LANDS
MT. CRESTED BUTTE
JACK'S PEAK
CRESTED BUTTE
Slate River
CLEAN CREEK
Levi & Jemimah's Picnic Spot
Abandoned Cabin
HIGHLANDS
MIDLANDS
THE TUBE
LOWLANDS
GLENROCK
East River

BOOK ONE

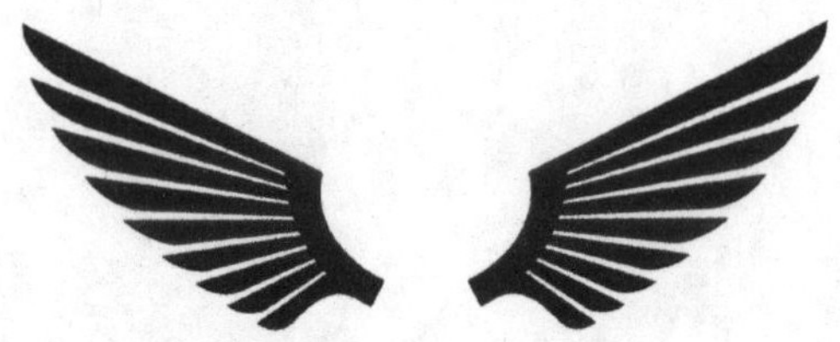

CAPTIVES

To Greg Bremner, for teaching me how to shoot a rifle.
You're my hero.

PROLOGUE

MAY 2088

King Nebuchadnezzar of Babylon declared war on Jerusalem and besieged the city. The king told Ashpenaz, head of the palace staff, to get some Israelites from the
royal family and nobility—young men who were healthy and handsome,
intelligent and well-educated, good prospects for leadership positions in the
government, perfect specimens!
—Daniel 1:1, 3–5, *The Message*

"They're ready for you, Miss Rourke."

Ciddah looked up at the enforcer and took a deep breath. She hugged her CompuChart and stood from her seat on the bench, wobbling on her stilettos. The enforcer pulled open the door, a yawning maw that expelled a breath of frigid air into the warm hallway. Ciddah tottered toward the entrance but stopped on the threshold.

The auditorium loomed before her, a vast and silent cube. She'd seen it on the ColorCast before: a purple concrete floor; a field of orange velvet bucket seats; walls painted in gradient: lime green at the bottom to black at the top. A spider's web of pin lights hung under the vast ceiling. Though the room had looked vibrant and cheerful when she'd seen it on her Wyndo, in person it was dull and cold.

The hooded Ancients of the Safe Lands Guild sat behind three tables on raised platforms that stretched along the front and side walls, their predatory eyes fixed on Ciddah.

"Miss Rourke?"

Ciddah spun to face the enforcer, who was holding the door partially open. No. He was trying to close it, and she was standing in the way.

She stumbled forward, and the enforcer shut her inside. Another deep breath, and she started down the center aisle, each step a crack that echoed through the vast chamber as she made her way toward the witness podium in front.

"The Director of Medical Care's Public Health Report has changed little since our discussion six months ago when this guild approved the requisition of Miss Kendall Collin from Wyoming. We still face a lack of healthy children born within our walls."

Lawten's familiar voice was somewhat comforting, and Ciddah searched for him on the platform. He sat at the center of the front table. His face—the only one uncovered—looked small among the hooded Ancients.

"Then present your case, Mr. Task Director," a grizzled voice said from the left wall, "and we will determine a course of action."

"I call Ciddah Rourke to the witness podium to give her report on the status of Miss Collin's pregnancy." Lawten aimed his calculating gaze down on Ciddah as if to remind her, *Just like we practiced*.

Ciddah reached the "podium," a short platform that sat in front of the head table. She climbed three steps to the top and sat in the chair facing Lawten, relieved not to have fallen on her face.

The air-conditioning being pumped into the auditorium was meant to compensate for several hundred bodies, not the nineteen now present. Ciddah shivered. It didn't help that her blouse had a low back and capped sleeves, or that she was about to testify before so many faceless Ancients.

"Miss Rourke," Lawten said, "please inform the Guild how Miss Collin is doing. Take your time."

Ciddah didn't need long. There was little to say. Still, she took a deep breath to calm her sparking nerves. "Kendall and her unborn baby are both infected."

Everyone seemed to speak at once. "What do you mean?" "Surely not!" "How could this have happened?" "Where did we go wrong?"

Lawten struck the gavel against the sound block. "Please hold your questions until Miss Rourke completes her report." He looked down to Ciddah. "Continue, Miss Rourke."

She focused on Lawten's face, as if speaking to him alone, which eased her nerves. "The goal with this transfer was to discover whether we could match an infected donor male with an uninfected female. As you know, it seemed successful at first. But the virus appeared in Miss Collin in the twenty-first week of her pregnancy. We still held out hope for the baby, but just last week, in week thirty-five, tests showed the fetus is now carrying the virus as well."

"Is there any chance that once the child is born...?" a hooded Ancient asked her.

"I cannot imagine that the virus will disappear, sir."

"What's to be done, then?" the Ancient asked. "Is there no way to irradiate this virus from our populace?"

"I cannot speak to cures, sir, as that is not my area of expertise," Ciddah said. "But if you want to produce a healthy child, you must have two healthy donors."

A stunned pause. "But there are none!"

"There are the Naturals," another said.

"A myth!"

"Naturals are no myth."

"If they are real, why do they never enter the city?"

"They abhor our city and our way of life."

Ciddah sat back and waited as the faceless Ancients argued.

"Forget the Naturals. How much will it cost us to trade for more people from Wyoming?"

"Kendall Collin cost more credits than we all make in a year."

"What a waste."

"We might be able to afford a half dozen more uninfected trades from Wyoming, but will six-to-eighteen children a year, if Fortune favors us, be enough to save our land? And what after that? How will we ensure these people remain uninfected? That they serve more than one successful term as conscripted surrogates?"

"Kendall Collin received status as a national, a citizen of our land. In the future, we mustn't allow outsiders to fully integrate into our world."

"We cannot imprison innocent people. And Fortune would not favor us if we did. We are not barbarians."

"Hang Fortune! She has not favored us either way."

"We *must* provide national status to outsider women. The public will be watching."

"Agreed. The publicity of our 'queens' through the ColorCast is too important to morale in the Safe Lands."

"No one need know what happen to the queens postpartum."

"Too dangerous. We need our past queens long after a successful delivery. They are the faces of the future."

"Some future."

"I have another suggestion, gentlemen," Lawten said.

All heads turned to the task director general. Good. Lawten would add some reason to this senseless debate.

"One of our enforcer patrols happened upon an outsider a few weeks back." Lawten's clear voice echoed around the room. "A young male, clearly uninfected. After some discussions, we learned it had always been this outsider's desire to come inside our fair city, and so the enforcers brought him to Otley, who brought him to me."

"Now we have a male donor and no females?" an Ancient asked. "So we attempt another trade with Wyoming and hope that the next girl remains healthy?"

"Hear me out, sir," Lawten said. "I am suggesting something on a grander scale. Enticement. Recruitment. Enrollment."

"I'm not following you, Mr. Task Director."

"We visit this young man's village and encourage his people to relocate."

The Ancient's brow lowered. "A large number of outsiders in the Safe Lands?"

"If they haven't wanted to live here for the past eight decades, why would they now?" asked another.

"Why give them a choice?" Lawten said, as if just coming up with the idea.

Ciddah's breath caught. How could he suggest such a thing?

"This Guild will not lock innocent people in cages, Mr. Task Director," an Ancient said.

"Please, hear me out," Lawten said. "This young man had been told lies about our people and our way of life. Once he saw our city with his own eyes, he wanted to live here more than anything. And he believes that, once his people visit, they will too."

A thoughtful pause. "So you propose bringing people here, possibly against their will, in order to show them what they really desire?"

"In a way. I truly believe the outsiders will enjoy living here, in time. We only need to require the men to donate for a month or two," Lawten said. "That would give us enough uninfected samples to last for years. With the procedure, of course, the women will have to make greater sacrifices."

"Spoken like a man." This was the first female voice to come from the Ancients.

"I cannot help the facts of biology, madam," Lawten said. "But this sacrifice also means the women will become queens, with the adoration of the Safe Lands public heaped upon them. Their surrogacy terms will be filled with luxury."

Ciddah had heard Lawten's ambition before and never cared for it, but here, now, she found his words terrifying. How could she have trusted such a man? How could anyone?

"There are at least three villages in the very shadow of our city—Jack's Peak, Glenrock, and Clean Creek," an Ancient said. "Maybe more. That could provide hundreds of surrogates. An entire new generation of uninfected."

Ciddah's hopes flared at the very idea. If they could convince the people to come willingly...

"What's to ensure they remain uninfected?" an Ancient asked.

"Fortune's numbers. We add a zero, then create a law that only zero can match with zero."

"We can't add a zero, and you know it."

"Nor can we allow the uninfected the freedom to become infected," another Ancient said. "And we'd still have to number the outsiders to avoid consanguinity."

Ciddah frowned. Were Fortune's numbers based on something other than which life a person was currently living? Based on DNA? She'd have to investigate this possibility.

"If we would simply remove the stimulant from the ACT treatment each person receives, we would go a long way toward managing this virus and living longer lives."

Another shock. There was stimulant in the treatment? Ciddah's mind spun with this new information.

"That is not a real option. No one wants to grow old," a very Ancient voice said. "Our people want youth, to enjoy this life as much as possible before going on to the next."

No one spoke for a moment. Ciddah was sure they could all hear her heart pounding.

The Ancient on Lawten's left spoke. "We will try it your way, Mr. Task Director. Take your troops to one village. *One.* Present the benefits of relocation. Should these people refuse the offer, you are to leave."

"Naturals owe no allegiance to our enforcers," the female Ancient said. "What if they should open gunfire upon our troops?"

"We want no bloodshed. Arm the enforcers with sleepers only. Bring back those willing to relocate and no one else. If this mission is a success, perhaps we can approach the other villages in the area."

The group seemed to consider the proposal.

"May I speak?" a familiar voice asked.

Ciddah spun to her right. At the very end of the table sat General Otley. Ciddah had forgotten that there were two guild members under age forty who were allowed to show their faces: the task director general and the enforcer general.

Lawten nodded. "Go ahead, General Otley."

"Outsiders are aggressive," Otley said. "Permission to take dual-action pistols as well? I hope to avoid such force and bring the outsiders in quietly, but sleeper downtime can take as long as two-and-a-half minutes between shots. One outsider can take out a lot of enforcers in that time. I need a way to protect my men in case the worst happens."

Lawten pursed his lips. "As long as your men understand the goal, General Otley. Uninfected people do us no good if they're dead."

"Understood, sir," Otley said.

"Thank you for your time, Miss Rourke," Lawten said to Ciddah. "You are directed to keep this meeting to yourself. If we learn that this discussion has leaked, the consequence will be premature liberation. Is that understood?"

Now Lawten was threatening her? Ciddah clutched the sides of her chair to keep from leaping to her feet. She managed to say, "Yes, Mr. Task Director."

"We look forward to a time when you bring us good news," Lawten said.

"As do I," she said.

"You are dismissed."

Ciddah left the podium and walked across the auditorium, feeling as though all eighteen Guild members were watching her go. Her legs felt rubbery, and she fought to contain her composure. Once the doors shut behind her, she collapsed upon the nearby bench and puzzled over all she'd heard from the leaders of her nation... and Lawten's coldness.

Stimulant in the ACT treatments? Fortune's numbers assigned for genetic purposes? She couldn't fathom any motivation behind such measures and fully intended to look into the matter as soon as possible. And this new attempt to find uninfected donors... only Fortune knew if the Safe Lands had a future. Ciddah could only hope the people of the outsider village would be open to change.

Chapter 1

JUNE 2088

Father invaded Mason's bedroom like a hornet. He yanked the psychology textbook from Mason's hands and tossed it on the floor. "You hear me calling for Omar, boy? Stop wasting time, and go find your brother. And don't take all day doing it."

"Yes, sir." Avoiding eye contact, Mason leaped off his bed and darted into the dark hallway, heading for the front of the house. He had indeed heard his father bellowing Omar's name, but since it was Omar's name and not his own, Mason had made the logical assumption that the solicitation was not for him. Unfortunately, logic had never been Father's companion.

Father's footsteps clomped behind him, and Mason walked faster, not wanting to become the focus of Father's anger. Three more steps to the door...

"Now that Levi's getting married, it's your turn."

That announcement stopped Mason completely. He glanced at his mother—who stood at the kitchen table, drying jars for canning—then looked at his father. "Me marry? Now? I'm only seventeen."

"Why wait?"

"Because there's no one I feel particularly drawn to in Glenrock *or* Jack's Peak."

"No matter," Father said. "I've made arrangements with Mia's mother."

Mason felt as if his father had slammed him into a brick wall. He glanced at his mother, but she turned her attention to the jars before he could make eye contact. "Father, there's no sense in my marrying Mia. I'd be more compatible with any other girl, in fact. We should exhaust all options before making such a rash pairing."

"Everyone else is too young."

"I can wait."

"Mia needs a husband. Her mother needs a son." Father shrugged. "No reason to wait."

"But she and I would be terrible together. We're not even friends."

"Focus on her pretty face." Father slapped Mason on the back and stepped toward the front door. "Now stop arguing, and go find your brother. I may have managed to marry him off as well, but it's no good if I can't find him. And I don't want to keep Elsu waiting. Need to leave now if I want to get to Jack's Peak in time."

Mason stared at the open door, listening to Father's footsteps pound across the porch, down the steps, and crunch across the rocky path that led to the village square. Mason's face burned over the nonsense of Mia becoming his wife. "I don't want to marry Mia. I won't."

"Mason," his mother said, "you're smart enough to find a way to make this work."

"But she despises me. And from what I gather from the books Levi brought me, and from my observations here in Glenrock, marriage is difficult enough when the pair have strong affections for one another. I don't want a future of misery for myself or for Mia."

"It's been two years since Mia's mother lost her husband. This marriage will mend the hole in their family. They'll have a man in their home again."

Mason stared at her. "But Mother, I will never love Mia." He doubted he could even force himself to like her.

"Since when has love ever been important to your father? He values strength. Show your strength by making this work." Mother went back to drying the jars. "You'd best go find your brother before your father catches you dawdling."

Mason pushed out the front door into the afternoon heat and crossed the porch in three steps. He jumped off the side and kept moving, the wild grass and flowers tickling his bare feet. Grazer's claws scraped over the plank porch as the dog chased him and soon bounded alongside.

Mason leaned over to scratch behind Grazer's ears. "Where's Omar, huh, boy? Go fetch Omar."

The dog panted and squinted his eyes, in no apparent hurry to lend assistance. Mason swallowed the tightness in his throat.

Mia? Really?

Glenrock consisted of a dozen log homes scattered in a forest of pine around the village square's clearing. Their house faced the entrance road that ended at a roundabout in front of the square and meeting hall. On the distant road, Father was a mere puff of dust as he headed up the mountain trail to meet Elsu.

Mason strode toward the hall, his gaze sweeping over the village, searching for the Old Colorado State Patrol hat his little brother, Omar, always wore. The sun lit the square and illuminated billions of dust motes. This was the time of day when everyone tried to remain indoors to keep cool.

Mason saw no one besides his older brother Levi and Levi's friend Jordan. Both were sitting on their ATVs, which were parked in front of an elevated plank stage. Levi and Jemma's engagement celebration would happen tonight on this stage, and members of the village would sit on the split log benches that surrounded the area and cheer the future union. All hail perfect Levi and his perfect fiancée, the future elders of Glenrock.

Mason had no desire for perfection. *But... Mia?*

He skulked toward the stone fire pit at the center of the square and soon was close enough that he could hear Levi and Jordan mumbling. Mason wasn't surprised they didn't acknowledge him. Typical behavior for the heir to the patriarchy of Glenrock and his loyal adherent.

With a long breath, Mason entered the meeting hall, which was easily ten degrees cooler than outside. Jemma, Jordan's sister and Levi's intended, was decorating tables with wildflowers. Some of the younger boys were playing a scavenged Old video game on the television in the far corner. No sign of Omar.

"Hi, Mason." Jemma looked up from the flowers and smiled. "How are you today?"

"Fine. Looking for Omar." Unlike most people, when Jemma asked, "How are you?" she truly wanted to know. But if Mason had answered truthfully, Jemma would insist on more information. And Mason had no time for Jemma's compassion today. "Have you seen him?"

"Not since the harvest field this morning," she said. "Levi says your father might have made him a match."

"Yes, well, my father and Levi's enthusiasm in the matter only enforces my skepticism."

"*Mason.*" After staring at the centerpiece for a moment, Jemma pulled a mule's ear from her hand and threaded the flower into the arrangement. "You should be happy for Omar. Getting married would be wonderful for him."

"I'm not unhappy. I simply see no point in celebrating that which has not yet taken place."

Jemma practically sang her reply. "'You can nearly always enjoy things if you make up your mind firmly that you will.'"

Mason frowned, pondering her words. "That's not yours, is it?"

"*Anne of Green Gables*, one of my favorite Old books. And Anne is right. So go find Omar so you can celebrate."

Mason left without offering a reply and made his way back across the square to the stage. He suspected Levi would have many baffling encounters with his new bride. How women could find joy in the marriage of complete strangers, Mason would never understand.

The ATVs now sat empty. Levi and Jordan stood on opposite sides of the stage, throwing a little ball to one another so fast it passed through the air as a red blur.

Levi pitched the ball at Jordan. "Find Omar yet?"

Mason stopped in front of Levi. "I thought I'd check the square again, but the only ones out here are you two not helping me."

Jordan flung the ball, and it bounced off the side of Levi's head.

"Ow, you maggot!" Levi chased after the ball and tossed it back at Jordan, who was laughing so hard he barely managed to catch it before it hit the ground.

"Forget Omar. Let's take Mason instead." Jordan threw the ball over the stage.

Levi ducked, letting it fly past the side of the meeting hall. He slouched and sighed, hands on his hips the way Father did when he was disappointed. "Mason's not a good trade."

"I'm standing right here," Mason said.

Jordan ran around the stage. "No, listen. They're all about nature and healing up in Jack's Peak. They'd love Mason. Then I wouldn't have to worry about him messing with my wife."

"Jordan," Levi said. "I meant that Mason is too valuable to trade."

"I never imposed upon anyone's wife," Mason said. "And what happened last week had nothing to do with yours. Cody gave Mother—*a doctor*—permission to allow me—*her assistant*—to observe his wife's labor process for educational purposes."

"For edu— Well, you're never going to educate *my* wife, let alone observe her."

"Your comment is backward," Mason said. "And it was for *my* education, not—"

"*You're* backward."

"I won't belabor my point." Mason walked away. He might have to take his Father's abuse, but he didn't have to take it from Jordan.

"I don't even know what that means," Jordan yelled.

"Not surprising," Mason said.

As he stretched the distance between him and the square, Mason heard Jordan ask Levi, "Did he just insult me?"

Mason chuckled and whistled for Grazer, wondering where the dog had run off to. Jordan wasn't the only man in Glenrock who disliked Mason training to be a doctor. The village doctor had always been female. Mason found their fears ridiculous and insulting. Some of the women went hunting, and no one treated them any differently.

He passed by Mia's house—the house that would become his if Father got his way. Women's clothing hung on the line in back. A flower garden ran along the side, and bees buzzed softly as they drank nectar. Mason walked a little faster, entered the forest, and continued down the river path, scanning for his brother.

Grazer returned to Mason's side, head down, sniffing the ground. They traversed all of Glenrock in their search for Omar, the dog nibbling grass at each stop. They passed by the waterwheel and the generator as it purred along. They searched the garden and greenhouse, doubled back to the smokehouses where Omar sometimes sketched from the rooftops, checked the kissing trees and the outhouses, cut through the woods and the graveyard, crossed the cattle field, and finally walked out of the village.

No Omar. And no clue to his whereabouts.

Instead of returning to the village, Mason headed west through the forest toward the compound. Grazer ran ahead, abandoning Mason to the aspens and pines. It was a two-mile hike to the field that separated the compound from the forest. Birdsong and the rustle of leaves encouraged Mason to take his time under the shaded trees.

Papa Eli, the patriarch of Glenrock and Mason's great grandfather, had forbidden the people to go near the compound that declared itself the Safe Lands, claiming it was populated with people who would lead them astray. Despite the warnings, Mason and

Omar had stood near the perimeter many times—Mason to forage plants for his mother's medicinal stock, Omar to sketch the compound's walls with his art tools.

Branches cracked to Mason's right. He froze until he spotted Grazer, a brown blur winding between the trees. He hoped the dog stayed clear of the medusaheads today. Mason had spent hours picking awns from Grazer's coat yesterday.

He thought back to what he'd been reading in the Old psychology book before Father had interrupted. According to the writer, the definition of family had been changing even in the year of 2006. The age of *first* marriage—as they called it, since divorce had been commonplace then—had been at an all-time high of 27.5 for men and 25.5 for women. Mason could not fathom how people could have waited so long. How ever did they keep their society running?

He was now about ten yards from the tree line. Beyond the shadowed branches, he could see the colorful expanse of wildflowers in the field.

Marriage and procreation were vital to the people of Glenrock, and while Mason saw no logic in waiting to marry until he reached 27.5 years, reaching at least twenty would offer him so much more knowledge and life experience. Plus, in three years, one or more of the younger girls would come of age. Why couldn't his father see the logic in—

A chorus of female screams broke the peace of the forest. Grazer sped away like a superhero from one of Omar's prized comic books. Mason's heart lurched. Was someone in trouble? Bear or cougar, perhaps? Mason followed the dog, praying whatever he was running toward was relatively harmless.

The moment he left the forest, the sun's heat struck him. He slowed to a stop and squinted across the clearing, following the ripple in the waist-high grass that marked Grazer's path. The dog was headed toward three girls who were running from... some strange vehicle. It looked like a giant beetle made of black and blue glass, and it rocked and bounced over the waves of the field like a boat. What in all the lands?

The girls ran toward Mason. They were close enough now that he recognized the threesome as his cousins Nell and Penelope and their friend Shaylinn, Jordan and Jemma's little sister. The vehicle veered after the girls; it could have only come from the Safe Lands.

Mason sprinted, the thin flower stalks whipping his legs. Just as he reached the girls they darted past, leaving Mason and the invader on a collision course if one of them didn't turn aside. Mason came to a jarring stop, took one long breath, then turned back toward the trees. He jogged, hoping it might give the girls more time to reach the forest.

Grazer bounced around the vehicle, barking as he circled in front of Mason and back to his adversary. The vehicle continued to plow forward, producing no sound beyond a soft whirr and the crunch of tires over the grass.

The girls stood off to the side of the trail's head, watching from behind a grove of aspen trees.

"Hurry, Mason!" Penelope yelled.

The vehicle stopped. Mason glanced behind him, and a uniformed man climbed out the passenger side. An enforcer! Mason slowed, curious, but when he saw the man wore a gun belt, he sped up and ran into Grazer, who'd been threading around him again.

Mason lifted his knees, trying not to step on the dog. His legs tangled in the wildflowers, and he went down like a felled tree. The thick vegetation caught him like a blanket.

He took a few panting breaths, contemplating whether he should get up and run or remain in the grass. Was he hidden? His heartbeat slowed. Movement in the grasses to his left and Grazer's growl on his right made him tense. Mason squeezed his eyes shut, waiting, hoping, praying that the man did not see him.

"You Omar?" a voice asked from above.

Omar? Mason rolled over and looked up into the enforcer's face. He wore a navy blue uniform like the law enforcement officers of Old. A gray helmet covered his head, only exposing the features of his face. Mason noted the man's pale, cracked skin. *The plague!*

Mason held his breath, but remembered Papa Eli's warning that the plague was a bloodborne virus, not airborne, which made Mason suddenly aware of a scratch on his arm.

"I'm talking to you, shell! Are you Omar?"

The enforcer's voice brought Mason back to his senses. His brother knew this man? He was about to say, "Yes," that he was Omar, to see what the man would say, or even ask what "shell" was supposed to mean, but someone else spoke first.

"That's not Omar. He's Mason," Shaylinn's said.

Mason scrambled to his feet. Shaylinn and Penelope were standing a few yards away, clutching each other's hands. Nell still hid behind the aspen trees. He could hear her sobbing.

"Why are you looking for Omar?" Mason asked.

"Not your interest." The enforcer walked back toward the vehicle.

Mason searched for something to say that might gain him more information. "He's my brother. Can I take him a message?"

The enforcer grabbed the top of the vehicle and pulled himself up, standing on the side. "Nice effort, shell." He slid inside, and a black window slid over the door opening, blocking any chance for further questions.

Mason stood with the girls, watching as the strange vehicle turned around and glided away. Grazer chased after it, but Mason whistled him back.

Omar had always loved sketching the compound walls, but apparently his fascination with the Safe Lands went deeper than Mason had realized. When had Omar connected with this person? What had their talks entailed? Mason found himself oddly jealous, wondering if Omar had been inside the walls and, if so, what he might have seen.

"I thought he was going to kill you!" Penelope said.

"We wanted to come back to you sooner," Shaylinn said, "but Nell tried to stop us."

"Penelope hit me!" Nell yelled from the tree line.

"Mason was trying to help us!" Penelope hollered back. "I wasn't going to let those guys shoot him."

"Like we could have stopped a gun," Shaylinn said.

"They're little guns," Penelope said. "They look like toys."

Shaylinn folded her arms. "My papa says all guns are for killing."

"Nobody was shooting at me," Mason said, hoping to end the argument.

"Why did he ask for Omar?" Shaylinn asked.

"I don't know," Mason said. "What were you all doing out here, anyway?"

"Following Omar," Penelope said. "He promised to draw us yesterday, then he changed his mind. When we asked again this morning and he said no, we followed him."

"And he was speaking with a Safe Lands enforcer?" Mason asked.

Penelope shrugged. "We lost Omar in the woods and were trying to find him in the field when that truck came out of nowhere and chased us."

"Why are you guys so mean to me?" Nell yelled, drawing Mason's gaze back to the trees.

Penelope rolled her eyes. "She can be so dramatic. We'd better go before she pretends to faint." She ran to Nell, who hugged her tightly.

Mason and Shaylinn followed. They reached the trailhead where Penelope and Nell were still locked in an embrace, Nell sobbing and gasping in hitches of air.

"Your cousins are strange sometimes," Shaylinn said to Mason.

"Are they?" Mason looked at Shaylinn. She was tall and thick, her torso like a tree trunk. She had the same dark brown eyes as Jordan and Jemma. "Don't all girls cry?"

"Not me," Shaylinn said. "And I've even got a cut on my arm from when I fell."

An injury! Mason might be useless in an enforcer encounter, but at least he could use his medical training to help someone. "May I see?"

Shaylinn turned her back and pointed over her shoulder to her left tricep, where a piece of wood was imbedded in her skin.

"It's not a cut. You've got a sliver. Hold still."

It was a big one, so Mason pinched her arm to make the wood stand up, then used his thumbnail to scrape it free. "All done."

"That was fast," Shaylinn said, rubbing her arm. "Thanks."

"You're welcome."

Once Nell calmed down, the foursome started back toward the village. The girls, all in their early teens, were rarely seen apart and were often sillier than toddlers. Penelope led their pack, brave and careless, while Shaylinn followed in silent wonder and Nell in deplorable protest. The girls all wore loose, sleeveless dresses pieced together from rabbit skins and Old print fabrics—whatever the men had scavenged from the Old dilapidated cities or the women had made in the village. Mason wore the same cattail vest he wore every day with his summer deerskin pants that were shredded below the knee. No one wore shoes in the summer unless they were riding an ATV, which meant Mason didn't wear shoes often. The ethanol used for the scavenged ATVs took a great deal of effort to create, so riding privileges were only given to those who went out to hunt or gather supplies.

Mason's, Penelope's, and Nell's fathers were Justin, Colton, and Ethan, the three brothers of tribe Elias, the ruling family in the village. Like most of Elias, the three cousins looked alike with light brown hair, blue eyes, and pale skin that burned in the sun.

Mason studied Shaylinn as they walked. She had darker features and skin like her older sister, Jemma, but she was thick where Jemma was thin, flat where Jemma curved, and frizzy where Jemma had curls. Shaylinn was not unpleasant to look upon, though his father had already said he couldn't wait for another girl to grow up. Plus, Mason doubted Jordan would approve of Mason marrying his kid sister. Still, the idea lingered.

Mason jogged to catch up with Shaylinn. "Slivers can sometimes become infected, you know. If your arm is bothering you, I can take another look."

"It's fine."

Of course it was; Mason had gotten it all. He groped for something else to say. "So, your sister and my brother... How's it going to feel to get Jemma out of your house?"

Shaylinn's folded her arms. "I don't want things to change."

"Oh. I guess I'm not really looking forward to it either. With Levi gone, Omar and I will receive all of my father's attention."

"Is it hard to live with him?"

Mason shrugged. "I've learned ways to avoid his temper."

"He told me I was fat," Shaylinn said.

Mason didn't doubt it. "Father is rarely positive."

"Do *you* think I'm fat?"

Mason considered her question. "The word *fat* is relative. Compared to Penelope, some might consider you overweight. But if you stand beside my grandma Marian, you'd look quite thin."

Shaylinn's eyebrows—eyebrows that were thicker than Father's—sank low over her eyes, giving Mason the impression that he had said the wrong thing.

Penelope suddenly ran off the trail and into the forest. Grazer took off after her.

"Be careful of the berberis thorns!" Mason yelled, then said to Shaylinn, "She's going to hurt herself."

"She doesn't care," Shaylinn replied.

Nell stopped in the middle of the road. When Mason and Shaylinn reached her, she stepped between them and took Shaylinn's hand. "Penelope dared me, but I'm not racing."

They were almost back to the village now. Mason caught sight of Mia weaving a cattail hide on the table in back of her house. She was barefoot and wore an Old flower print dress that cinched at the waist, her body the definition of the hourglass shape. She *was* very pretty. Perhaps he should consider his knowledge of Mia's personality as tentative and maintain an open mind.

Considering the circumstances, it was only fair.

Chapter 2

That night, Mason again got lost in his Old psychology book. This time his mother found him.

"You're not even dressed?" she said, peeking into his room. "Everyone else is already in the meeting hall."

Mason shut his book and stood, hoping she didn't notice the reluctance he felt inside. "Sorry, Mother. I'll be right there."

He changed into what his mother considered his formal outfit—an Old black suit jacket over a woven cattail and red nylon shirt with his long deerskin pants—and left the house. He could hear the sound of chanting as he crossed the square.

"Elder Eli, bless my face.
Elder Eli, give me grace.
Elder Eli, teach me more.
Elder Eli gets the floor!"

Mason entered the hall. The smell of fresh bread filled his lungs. He stopped just inside the door and leaned against the wall, hoping he'd be allowed to remain outside the proceedings for at least a few more minutes.

The hall was warm and bright. The entire population of Glenrock—some four dozen people—sat at four long tables that were filled with platters of food and drink and Jemma's wildflowers. The head table stretched across the center of the longest wall, right in front of the hearth. The other three tables ran perpendicular to it.

Omar sat at the end of the head table, his State Patrol hat making him stand out. Mason never had found him earlier. Though he'd heard Father yelling once he'd returned from the trade with Elsu, furious that Omar had missed his chance to meet a girl from Jack's Peak. Mason had stayed in his room, as far from the conflict as possible.

The thought of conflict pulled Mason's gaze to Mia. She sat with her mother at the table on the far right. Mia was now wearing an Old red-and-black-print dress. Mia liked Old clothing, and Mason often wondered how the other women felt about Mia claiming so many that could be used for fabric.

Papa Eli stood, front and center, at the head table, wearing his cattail cape over his formal deerskins. A fire in the hearth behind him rimmed his body in orange fire glow. At ninety-two, he was still tall and spry. Wrinkles and age spots covered his face, and his hair was thick and white, but his gaze—green and sharp—flitted around the room like a bird seeking its next meal.

"My question is for my grandson Justin. Stand up, boy," Papa Eli said.

Since Grandpa Seth had died a few years back, Mason's father was next in line for patriarch of the village. As such, he sat to Papa Eli's right. Father pushed back his chair and stood. "Ask your question, Elder, and I will answer true."

Mason smiled at how Papa Eli could get Father to play along with the puzzles and songs of celebration festivities. He doubted Father would carry on such traditions once he was the patriarch.

"Riddle me this," Papa Eli said. "The more you take, the more you leave behind. What are they?"

"Pictures?" Father guessed immediately.

Papa Eli shook his head, a wide grin stretching the wrinkles across his cheeks.

Father took longer to come up with his second answer. "Smiles?"

"No, Justin, my boy," Papa Eli said. "When you *take* smiles, you keep them."

The people laughed, and Nell's squeal rose above the others. Father's face darkened a shade at his grandfather's chide, but he quickly said, "Omar's blunders?" and smiled at the words that poked fun at his youngest son.

The laughter dwindled into groans of pity for Omar, who sat staring at his plate. Mother's lips squeezed into a thin line. Father would no doubt hear her thoughts on that "joke" later.

"Three false answers must take his seat, and I will ask another." Papa Eli glanced around the room as Father sat down. His gaze settled on Mason. "Let's see if my great-grandson can fare better. Mason?"

Mason pushed off the wall and straightened his posture. "Ask your question, Elder, and I will answer true."

"The more you take, the more you leave behind. What are they?"

"Footsteps," Mason said, trying not to smile, which would only aggravate his father.

A handful of people responded with an "Ahh!" and the crowd applauded.

As the clapping died down, Mason overheard his father say, "Sissy word games won't put food on the table."

Papa Eli gripped Father's shoulder but smiled at Mason. "Right you are, Mason. And since you answered correctly, *you* have the floor."

Mason took that moment to walk to the head table and sit between Levi and Omar. He nudged his little brother. "You okay?"

Omar shrugged one shoulder. "Why wouldn't I be?" He picked up a roll from a basket and ripped it in half.

"Mason, we're waiting. The floor is now yours," Papa Eli said.

Why had he answered correctly? Mason quickly stood and spat out the simplest riddle he could think of. "Wisdom of the aged, with the length of days. Elder of the line, what youngest is thine? Uhh…" He searched the faces until he made eye contact with Jemma's father. "Harvey."

All heads turned to the far left table as Harvey stood. "The youngest in my line is Shaylinn," he said, setting his hand on Shaylinn's head.

"No!" Shaylinn, who was sitting beside her father, pointed across the table to where Jordan and his wife, Naomi, sat, their hands interlocked and resting on her belly, which was very large so late in her pregnancy. "Your youngest heir is there, Papa."

The crowd laughed.

"True as that may be, Shay, my youngest heir cannot yet speak for himself—"

"It's a girl!" Shanna, Shaylinn's mother, said.

"—or herself," Harvey added with a nod to his wife. "So the floor goes to you, my daughter."

Shaylinn stood and smoothed out her dress. "A wise old owl lived in an oak. The more he saw, the less he spoke. The less he spoke, the more he heard… Omar, finish it." Shaylinn fell back into her chair and grinned at Omar.

An owl rhyme for the moody boy who was obsessed with owls. Mason admired Shaylinn for wanting to cheer Omar and for the clever way she'd done it.

Omar set down his mutilated roll and said, his voice raspy as always, "Why can't we all be like that wise old bird?"

The crowd clapped.

Omar pushed off the tabletop as he stood. "My question is for my father."

And just like that, Omar threw away Shaylinn's gift. The room went silent. Mason lowered his gaze and held his breath.

"I already went," Father said. "Pick someone else."

Papa Eli slapped the tabletop. "Stand up, Justin. Your son has a question for you."

"Fine." Father pushed back his chair and stood, staring at Omar with raised brows. "Ask your question, boy." He didn't bother with the traditional reply.

Omar's neck and ears flushed pink. "Will you take me with you to Denver City?"

"No."

"But you promised I could go."

"Someday, yes. This time, no."

"But Levi went when he was only fourteen. I'm sixteen."

"As everyone in Glenrock knows, *you're* not Levi. My answer is final."

Omar sat down, leaving Father as the focus of everyone's attention. He cleared his throat. "Well, now that everyone is here, uh… Before we start the engagement proceedings, I do have an announcement. Jennifer of James and I have made a match. My son Mason and her daughter Mia will marry."

Mason's heart slid into his stomach. He stared at the empty plate before him, unable to look at the table on the far right, unable to bear seeing Mia's face. A deep, silent breath, which Mason blew out in a short puff, helped him hold his tongue. How typical of Father to announce this publicly before Mason had even a chance to get used to the idea.

The crowd applauded politely; Nell didn't even squeal. Mason noted how different the reaction was compared to when Father had announced Levi and Jemma's engagement. This was what happened to the leftovers after the people who actually loved each other paired off.

"Will you serve as elder to this young couple?" Papa Eli asked Father.

"Jennifer will serve as their elder as I'm already mentoring Levi and Jemma."

A blessing, in Mason's opinion. He could only imagine what advice Father would give a soon-to-be husband who didn't hunt.

Jennifer added a chair between hers and Mia's. "Come, then, my son, and sit at my table."

Mason got up. Moved across the room. Offered those around him a tight smile in return for their warm ones. He would keep an open mind, focus on Mia's positive attributes, her looks. The chair beside Jennifer was only six yards away, but the journey felt like miles. He sat down. Again, everyone applauded. Polite. Obligatory.

Mia whispered in his ear, "Don't look so excited," and spoiled her beauty by speaking.

"I don't see you beaming with delight," Mason said.

"Because *I* had to settle. *I* wanted a hunter for a husband."

Mason ran his tongue along his bottom row of teeth to keep from saying something cruel. He settled on, "It's not too late to marry Omar."

"Omar is *not* a hunter. And he's always sniffling or rubbing his eyes like some dumb toddler."

"He's allergic to pollen."

Papa Eli's raised voice silenced any rebuttal from Mia. "And now let's focus on tonight's festivities. Levi of Elias, you have a request of the elders of Glenrock?"

"I do," Levi said.

"Then stand and make your request known."

Levi stood. "It is my wish to marry Jemma of Zachary two weeks from today."

Jordan wolf-whistled, which set off an infectious round of laughter and applause.

See? How could I do that? How could I stand before all of Glenrock and declare my intentions to marry Mia when I want no part of it?

"Jemma of Zachary, your favor has been petitioned," Papa Eli said. "Stand and tell this community how you respond."

Jemma pushed up from her seat and faced Papa Eli. "I accept the offer."

Nell squealed. More applause.

"Does anyone have reason to speak against this union?"

Levi glanced at Omar, and Mason prayed Omar would not say anything rude. But no one spoke. No one ever said anything during this part.

"What elder will speak for this couple?" Papa Eli asked. "Who has seen their commitment and helped to mold it by offering guidance and mentoring?"

Father stood up, shoulders back, proud. "I have."

Papa Eli looked around the room. "People of Glenrock, you have witnessed an offer of marriage, an acceptance, and an endorsement by a village elder. I hereby declare Levi of Elias and Jemma of Zachary engaged to be married in two weeks' time. You are all invited to the celebration. Levi and Jemma, come before me to receive your blessing."

Levi stepped out from behind the high table and waited for Jemma. He took her hand, and they walked to stand before Papa Eli.

Papa Eli placed his hands on their heads. "May God be with you and bless you. May you see your children's children. May you be poor in misfortunes, rich in blessings. And may you know nothing but happiness from this day forward."

Yet another round of applause filled the meeting hall, but Mason's silent scream was a roar between his ears that drowned all other noise. He was happy for Levi and Jemma, sure. But he couldn't imagine that Papa Eli's beautiful words would come true in his own situation.

"Father God, we thank you for the fine company of family and friends and for the blessing of this feast. Amen," Papa Eli said then took his seat.

Jennifer passed Mason a platter of chicken. "I'm thankful to have a man in the family again. James has been gone two years. It's a comfort to know his line won't die with Mia."

Mason nodded, unable to manage a verbal response. He passed the platter to Mia without taking any meat.

"There's no way I'm becoming a vegetarian like you just because you can't stomach being a man," Mia said. "I don't suppose you'll even butcher a chicken."

Would every word from her lips be poison? It hadn't been a question, really, so Mason didn't answer. This might be the first day of his new life of self-imposed silence.

As people talked around them, the volume of his father's raised voice was a welcome distraction for the first time in his life. "I'm *not* taking him, Grandfather," Father said to Papa Eli. "He's a useless extra mouth to feed."

"No one is useless in this world if they lighten the burden of another," Papa Eli said.

"That's just it. Omar *is* the burden on a trip like this. He can't shoot. He can't follow simple instructions. He eats more than the rest of us combined and is too much of a weakling to help carry the haul. The boy only wants to come so he can look for owls or find more art materials for his sissy drawings."

"You'll have many days on the journey to teach him what you feel he lacks."

"Then you teach him. I'm *not* taking him anywhere until he proves he has a brain in that round head of his."

Omar jumped up and ran out of the hall.

"See! Off he runs to cry. Denver City is a trip for men of strength, and Omar has a long way to go."

Mason pushed back his chair and stood.

Mia grabbed his wrist. "Where do you think you're going?"

"To talk to Omar."

"You better come back. You're my dance partner."

"Mia, I don't dance."

"Of course you don't. Mason, everything about you embarrasses me." Her eyes were cold and angry.

"You may as well get used to it." Mason pulled free from Mia's grip and left.

He found Omar in his room, kneeling on the floor before one of his notepads, blackening the eyes of an owl with a charcoal pencil. He'd removed his Colorado State Patrol hat, and his hair was sticking up. Omar's artwork wallpapered his room. Mostly close-ups of animals or people. They made Mason feel like he was being stared at by a million eyes.

Omar ripped away the owl drawing and scraped the charcoal pencil over a fresh sheet again and again, creating the soft lines of a wing. "Go away, Mase. I'm fine."

"*I* wouldn't be."

Another owl materialized on the paper under Omar's skilled strokes, this one soaring. "He's said the same about you before."

"Naw. About me, he says, 'If it weren't for Mason's brain, he'd have no muscles in his body.' Or my personal favorite, 'Don't mind you talking so much, sissy boy, so long as you don't mind me not listening.'"

Omar tossed his shard of charcoal into a tray of pencils, ripped the page from the notebook, and crumpled it. "He never calls Levi a sissy."

"That's because Levi came out of the womb holding a rifle. In regards to Father, I refuse to engage in a battle of wits with an unarmed man. I suggest you do the same."

Omar snorted a laugh. "That's mad good, Mase."

Mason leaned against the doorframe and crossed his arms. "I met an enforcer today."

Omar's hand jerked, drawing a dark line across his sketch. "Oh?"

"Why would an enforcer be asking for you by name?"

Omar went back to shading in the owl's wings. "None of your business."

"So, when I inform Father, it will be none of his business either?" Mason asked.

Omar sighed. "I met them in Crested Butte when I was scavenging. It's not a big deal."

That only raised more questions. "Papa Eli might disagree."

Omar sat back and stared at the wall. "I bet I could find a girl in the Safe Lands."

The words brought a chill over Mason. "Don't say that, Omar. Don't even joke about it. You shouldn't be talking to those people at all."

"Have you really looked at what's inside those walls? From the mountain with my binoculars, I can see women. Lots of them. And lots of color. I bet they have fresh paints."

Was Omar seriously thinking about going into the Safe Lands? The place Papa Eli had almost died trying to get away from? "You know what Papa Eli says about that place. Why he left and came here. They're immoral there. They withhold water as punishment."

"Papa Eli is older than dirt."

"Hey, now. Papa Eli just stuck up for you in there."

Omar rubbed the scar on the bridge of his nose. "A lot of good it did. His *help* only made Father insult me in front of the whole village. They're probably all laughing."

"No one's laughing," Mason said. "Why do you want to go to Denver City, anyway?"

"I want to draw the ruins. It doesn't matter though. Father hates me. Levi hates me. Jemma is marrying Levi. Mia is marrying *you*. Shaylinn is fat. Everyone else is my cousin or lives in Jack's Peak."

"*Omar...*"

Omar pitched his wadded-up owl at Mason. "It's true! I should just move to Jack's Peak. Then everyone would be happy. Except I blew that too, because I missed meeting the girl Father found for me, and now she doesn't want me either. Even if she did, it would be worse up there. Jack's Peak men are all about killing animals with their bare hands. I'm no good at any of that."

"What do you want?"

"I don't know. To feel strong. Like I matter. Like someone cares."

Omar looked so small sitting on the floor with Mason standing over him. A child wanting to be loved. "*I* care."

Omar rolled his eyes. "I can't marry *you*."

"You really want a wife?"

Omar moved to his bed, lying on his back and staring at the drawing of a woman's face—a face that looked suspiciously like Jemma's. "If I don't find a wife, Father says I'll starve, since I'm such a bad shot. He wanted me to marry the Jack's Peak girl so *she* could hunt for the both of us. Plus, he's trying to get rid of me."

"Ignore him. And stop feeling sorry for yourself. I'd trade you Shaylinn for Mia if I could."

"Really?" Omar pushed himself to one elbow. "Why?"

"Because Shaylinn is kind. I'd take kind over thin or pretty any day. Haven't you noticed? Mia is just a female version of Father."

Omar sniffed in a long breath and rubbed his nose. "She's prettier than Father."

"Beauty only exists in perception."

Omar raised his eyebrows at Mason. "You don't think Mia is prettier than Shaylinn?"

Mason did, but he couldn't imagine living with Mia's cruelty. "Jemma once said, 'It's beauty that captures your attention, but it's personality that captures your heart.' She likely read it somewhere, but I think it validates my point."

Omar heaved a sigh. "Jemma."

"Don't start. Jemma belongs to Levi now, and you'd be wise to take down that drawing before he sees it."

"Just go away, Mase."

"Fine." Mason walked to the doorway and took one last glance at Omar, who'd closed his eyes as if he might go to sleep.

Mason left the cabin and sat on the porch, gazing out toward the square. People had left the hall and were now dancing to music being played by Elder Harvey and Uncle Ethan. A handful of older women stood in a circle around the dancers, laughing and singing.

"Do the twist, do the twirl,
every boy, grab your girl

Twist and twirl, boy and girl,
whirl and whirl and whirl!"

Levi and Jemma were dancing on the stage. Mason didn't see Mia, but she was likely still cross about her first glimpse of what it would be like to marry him. Her husband would never dance and would often go into hiding.

Mason prayed Omar wouldn't do anything foolish, like run away to the Safe Lands or follow Father's group when they left for Denver City. Papa Eli might think that Omar and Father would be forced to bond if Omar went on the trip, yet Mason didn't think there could be anything worse than Omar and their father together for two whole weeks.

He was wrong.

Chapter 3

The view of the valley from where Levi had spread the picnic blanket on the eastern side of Mt. Crested Butte was one of the best, but Levi couldn't stop staring at Jemma. He'd gone to Denver City for only ten days, but being apart from her had felt like months.

"I don't like leaving you," he said.

Strands of her hair danced around her face in the wind, and she brushed them aside. "I don't like you leaving."

"I brought you something." He reached over his rifle and under the edge of the blanket where he'd stashed the little box, then handed it to Jemma.

She gave him with a curious smile. He leaned forward as she opened it, eager to see her reaction.

She gasped and fingered the necklace of pink pearls. "I've never seen anything like it." She handed the pearls back to Levi and twisted her hair to one side.

Levi drew the strand around her throat, clasped them together, then he kissed the back of her neck and breathed her in.

"*Levi.*" She giggled and dropped her hair back into place. "Where did you find it?"

He tucked his chin over her right shoulder and spoke softly in her ear. "Denver City. I found wedding rings too, but you can't see those yet." He settled back beside her on the blanket and offered a coy smile.

"Wedding rings too?"

"I know few people wear them these days since we all know who is married to whom and rings are hard to come by, but I thought you'd like to."

"I'd love to." She slid her arms around his neck. "I can't wait to marry you. Are you excited?"

He pulled her close. "You have no idea."

The sun hung low in the sky. From where they sat on their picnic blanket on the lower hills of Mt. Crested Butte, the whole valley lay before them. Green and brown mountains stood guard on all sides, the Slate River glimmered in the distance, but the bell-shaped walls that traced the outline of the Safe Lands scarred the beauty of this place. A concrete and barbed-wire reminder that all was not right in the world.

Jemma leaned against Levi, head tucked under his chin. "Tell me about Denver City."

"It's huge, Jem. Buildings sit side by side for miles, and in the center, they're five times as tall as the ones in the Safe Lands." He eyed the cluster of buildings at the top of the bell. "When you stand in the middle of Denver City, you can see nothing but towering buildings, Old vehicles, streetlamps, traffic signals... There are a few trees on each street, and patches of grass and saplings grow in cracks in the asphalt, but the ground is mostly concrete for miles."

"*Traffic* and *asphalt*... those words sound so odd. I find it impressive that those tall buildings are still standing."

"They have deep foundations. And they're built of steel, not wood. Someday I'll lead my own expedition to Denver City, and I'll stay longer. So many houses have never been scavenged. The things we could use! Toys for the children. More gifts for you."

Jemma fingered the pink pearl necklace and smiled.

Levi bumped his shoulder against hers. "I knew you'd like it. Found it in a store filled with jewelry. Father has enough treasure to trade for years."

"I can't begin to think how people made such things."

"Gold and silver are just metals people melted down and reshaped. But Mother once told me pearls came from the oceans. Grew inside the mouths of sea creatures."

"And people captured the creatures to steal the pearls from their lips?" Jemma pressed her shoulder back against Levi's. "It sounds like a children's story. Like the one with the tiny world that lived on a flower."

"*Horton Hears a Who!* I love that one. Oh, Jem! We found a bookstore too. Father only let me stop a few minutes, but I was able to grab some of the books with the horses on the—" A plume of dust rose like chimney smoke on the road, and Levi straightened. "Someone's coming." Jemma drew in a sharp breath as Levi grabbed the rifle and looked through the scope. "An ATV." He lowered the weapon and the tone of his voice. "Omar. He's driving my rig."

Omar was supposed to be at the village's lookout all morning. He better not have left the perch empty. When Levi needed Omar, the boy couldn't be found. But when Levi wanted to be alone, Omar was always the first to show up.

"I wondered what was taking him so long." Jemma smirked. "Our picnic is almost over."

Levi set down his rifle and groaned. "Why must he follow me everywhere?"

"I'm sure it's important if he's driving your cart."

"Omar invents trouble."

"He admires you. Perhaps you should encourage him in some way."

Levi looked to Jemma. "You think I'm cruel?"

She cocked one eyebrow. "I know you don't intend to be, but a sharp word from you sends Omar sulking like a chastened puppy."

"I just don't think he should look up to me the way he does."

"Why wouldn't he look up to you? You're his brother. And you're perfect."

If she only knew.

Jemma snuggled against Levi's side and took hold of his hand. "I feel badly about what happened with the Jack's Peak girl. Do you think she'll reconsider him?"

"No." And if Levi had known which girl Elsu had been trying to marry off, he never would have gone along. The whole thing had been terribly awkward.

Jemma frowned and sent Levi a pleading look, as if he could force some girl to marry Omar. "If she can't find a husband among her own people, why refuse one of ours?"

Levi coughed on his own breath. *Because this girl only wants me.* "I don't know, love." He squinted down the valley. The trail of dust from the ATV was larger now. Omar was rounding the final switchback that led up to the ridge.

"Poor Omar," Jemma said. "He's not *that* awful, you know. I considered him once."

Levi's gaze jerked to meet hers. "When?"

"The day my mother said, 'You chose the best of the brothers, Jemma.' I thought it over, and I had to agree."

Levi chuckled. "And what about Mason? Did you consider him too?"

Jemma took Levi's other hand so that she was holding both. "I love your brothers well enough—as brothers. But I'm worried for Mason. Mia will rule him like an evil queen. They're a poor match, and his agreeing to marry her makes me question his sanity."

"How was he to refuse after Father announced it to all of Glenrock? Mason will find a way to make it work. He's smart."

"Book smart. Have you seen him try and talk to girls? Information about poisonous mushrooms and rashes don't exactly warm a girl's heart."

Levi chuckled at the idea of Mason showing Mia which mushrooms to avoid. "You're full of opinions on my brothers today, Jemma of Zachary. I'm not sure how to feel about this."

"Feel blessed to have found true love in a world with so little of it, *farm boy*."

"As you wish." He kissed her hand, and Jemma giggled.

Omar arrived then, stopping Levi's ATV and attached cart three feet from the picnic blanket and sending a cloud of dust over Levi, Jemma, and what remained of their food. He was wearing Old jeans, his blue and yellow striped shirt, and his Old policeman hat. Without the hat, he didn't look all that different from Levi and Mason. Just younger.

Omar dismounted and approached their picnic blanket. "Hello, Jemma," he said, his voice airy as usual whenever he was in her presence.

Jemma offered him a sympathetic smile. "Hello."

Levi didn't budge from Jemma's side. "What are you doing here, Omar? Who's at the lookout?"

Omar wiped a hand under his nose, which never ceased to water. "Penelope took my place. A message came in from Beshup over in Jack's Peak. He has some ammo he thinks you'll want to see."

Ammo? How had Beshup come into such a trade, and why did he want to share it? Levi mumbled, "We *are* low on ammo. The Old stuff is more accurate than any we make ourselves." He glanced at Jemma. "Do you mind if I go?"

She reached ran her finger down his forehead. "Come see me when you get back?"

"Of course." He jumped up and helped Jemma stand. "I don't want you going back alone. We'll drop you at the village, then Omar and I will go meet Beshup."

"That'll take too long," Omar said, sniffling.

"And we're closer to the cabin now," Jemma said.

"I can take her back on the motorcycle," Omar said. "You don't need me there to trade with Beshup. I'll just be in the way."

"A ride would be nice," Jemma said, nudging Levi's side. He could tell by the look on her face that she wanted him to be nice to Omar.

Levi sighed. "Give us a moment, Omar." He took Jemma's hand and pulled her a few steps away from his brother. "I don't like sending you off with him. If by some chance you encounter a mountain lion or a bear, he's not the best shot and tends to panic in a crisis."

Jemma brushed Levi's hair out if his eyes. "Our village needs ammunition. I'll be fine."

"Still..." He threaded his fingers with hers and frowned. "I have a bad feeling."

She squeezed his hand. "You always have a bad feeling. Don't worry so much. I'll see you tonight at dinner."

He slid his hands around her waist and pulled her close. "Two more days."

Her gaze sank into his.

"This is true love, Jemma of Zachary," Levi said. "You think this happens every day?"

She smiled. "You're like a fairy-tale prince. We shall live happily ever after."

"Yes. Just like the prince. But I dress better."

She stepped back and took in his appearance. "I don't know. You might look nice in a doublet and tights." Before he could respond, Jemma stretched on her tiptoes and gave him a quick kiss. If Omar hadn't been staring, she would've been more generous.

Jemma quickly packed their picnic. Levi helped her fold the blanket, then roped it and the basket to the rack on the back of the motorcycle.

Levi walked to where Omar stood beside his ATV, and they traded keys. "Drive *slowly*. And watch out for mountain lions."

"Don't worry, brother. I won't let anything happen to your precious Jem."

Jemma climbed on the back of the motorcycle behind Omar and wrapped her arms around his waist. Levi scowled at the smile that spread across his brother's face. Jemma gave him one last wave before Omar started the motorcycle and drove away.

Levi shook off his annoyance with his little brother and climbed onto his ATV. It was time to trade.

Chapter 4

Mason and his mother sat at the table, shucking the peas they'd picked that morning. Father sat in the living room, oiling his gun. It was early afternoon, the hottest time of the day, and a blessing to be indoors.

"It's been a good year for peas," Mother said. "I'd like to can at least one hundred pounds this year."

"You should have more than enough." Confident with his declaration, Mason hulled the next pod right into his mouth.

"Don't eat the harvest," Father said.

Because without that one pea pod, all of Glenrock would surely starve.

"Papa Eli!" Penelope's voice came from outside, distant and shrill.

Mason cocked his head at the sound then made eye contact with his mother as she stood and approached the door.

"Something's wrong," she said.

"Papa Eli!" Penelope's voice was nearer now.

"Sit. I'll get it." Father shooed Mother back and opened the door just as Penelope bounded up the steps.

The hair around her face stuck to her flushed cheeks. "Safe Landers are coming, Uncle Justin." She panted. "Three big trucks."

Father paced back to the sofa and picked up his gun. "Where's Omar? Why didn't he bring this news?"

"He asked me to watch the perch while he got a fresh sketch pad," Penelope said. "About a half hour ago."

Father loaded his rifle and headed for the door. "Mason, get your gun."

"I'm not going to shoot any—"

"Now!"

"Yes, sir." Mason pushed back his chair and approached the gun rack.

As he reached out to grab his rifle—the one that had accidently taken Joel's life—Father stepped in Mason's way and grabbed his shoulder, looking him in the eye. "I need you, son. Just stand beside me and look tough. You don't have to shoot."

A deep breath filled Mason's chest. He nodded and lifted the weapon from the wall.

"Should I wake Papa?" Mother asked.

"Let him sleep, Tamera. I can handle this." Father traded guns with Mason and loaded Mason's gun. "Round up the women and children and get them into the meeting hall just in case. If there is a threat, it might be easier to defend one location rather than the whole village." Father returned Mason's gun and took back his own. "Penelope, fetch Harvey and Jordan. They should be down at the river. And if you see your dad or your uncle Ethan—any men you see—tell them to get their rifles and come to the square."

Penelope fled. Father left the house and headed toward the village square. Mason trailed after him, his heartbeat throbbing between his ears. Mother closed the door and followed.

"Omar never came for paper, did he?" Father asked over his shoulder.

"No, sir." Mason had no idea what his brother was up to, but it didn't look good.

"He'd better not be in the hall playing video games. I always said that thing was a waste on our generator."

Mason jogged to keep up with his father. A cluster of Glenrock men stood before the stage, guns in hand. There were maybe a dozen—about half the men in the village. Women and children scurried around the square, most headed to the hall.

Aunt Susan ran up to Mason. "Have you seen Sophie?"

"No, ma'am."

"Sophie!" Aunt Susan ran toward the outhouses.

"We got a man in the perch?" Father asked when they reached the square. "How far out are they?"

"Richard's up there." Uncle Colton lifted a handheld two-way radio to his mouth. "Colt to Rich Man, what's the ETA?"

The two-way radio emitted a string of static, then Elder Richard's voice. "They're just getting to the forest now. My guess is you've got maybe five to ten minutes."

"Where's Levi?" Uncle Ethan asked as he walked toward the group.

"Went off to have lunch with Jemma somewhere," Father said.

"And Papa Eli?"

Father aimed his gun at the road and looked through the scope. "Taking a nap."

"I'll go wake him," Uncle Colton said.

Father lowered his gun and grabbed his brother's arm. "We can handle this without Grandpa. The worry will do him more harm. Let him sleep."

Mason disagreed. No one was calmer in the face of conflict that Papa Eli. And no one knew more about the Safe Lands either. Should he speak up? Run fetch Papa Eli on his own? Instead, he simply stood there, frozen, gun trembling in his hand.

Jordan sprinted into the square just ahead of his father and Penelope. "Enforcers?"

"Looks like," Uncle Colton said.

Jordan spun around. "Pen, go get my mother and Shay."

"I want to fight!" Penelope said.

"No one is fighting," Uncle Ethan said.

Mason adjusted the gun against his shoulder and hoped that was true.

"The house is right there, crowbait," Jordan said, pointing to his family's cabin.

Penelope scowled at Jordan. "You don't have to call names."

"*Penelope!*" Uncle Colton raised one eyebrow, and his daughter stomped toward the Zachary home.

Harvey came to stand beside Father. "How many men you think they've got?"

"Can't say," Uncle Colton said. "Richard said three trucks."

"Could be they're not coming to fight," Naomi's father, Sam, said.

"Seeing as we haven't seen them this close in years, we have no way of knowing. But they must want something," Uncle Ethan said.

Jordan glared down the road. "Whatever they want, we can handle it."

"Two dozen against an army? How do you figure we'll handle that?" Uncle Ethan asked.

"One less than that." Sam eyed Mason. "He ain't going to shoot."

Mason's stomach twisted. *Please, God, protect us.*

"Let's not jump to the worst-case scenario here," Uncle Colton said.

"No, we prepare for the worst," Father said. "Sam, take ten men and spread out on the east side. Ethan, you take the others west. Be my snipers. Harvey, you and Jordan get on the roofs and cover the square. Colton and Mason, stay with me. Go, go!"

As the men ran off, Shaylinn and her mother fled the Zachary home and ran toward the outhouses.

"Where you going?" Harvey called.

"Susan can't find Sophie," his wife said. "We're going to help look for her daughter."

"Well, be quick about it," Harvey said.

Penelope came out of the house and walked straight to her father's side. "I know how to shoot. Levi taught me."

"I don't care if Levi taught you to build a bomb." Uncle Colton pointed to the water spout where Uncle Ethan's children were getting a drink. "Get those boys into the hall, now!"

Penelope stomped toward Jake and Joey.

Movement in the trees above revealed Jordan creeping down the incline of his family's roof, gun clutched in one hand.

"There they come," Uncle Colton said, nodding at the road.

Mason looked past his father, expecting to see Levi and Jemma returning. Instead, a convoy of strange trucks entered the village.

The first resembled an Old ambulance. The other two were as big as Old semi trucks. All three were yellow and silver with metal grids on the sides instead of windows and doors. Like the vehicle Mason had seen a few weeks ago, these were almost silent but for the crunch of their tires over the gravel.

The trucks drove into the roundabout, one behind the other. The ambulance-like vehicle rolled to a stop near the meeting hall. Mason backed against the fire pit, trying to get into a position where he could see all three vehicles at once, but they were too close.

The metal grids of the ambulance vehicle slid up into the roof, and the driver and passenger climbed out. The back grid slid away as well, and enforcers trickled into the square one by one. No movement from the other two vehicles.

Father lifted his gun. Uncle Colton followed suit, so Mason lifted his, keeping his finger away from the trigger. His body throbbed with adrenaline and heat. *I can't do this.*

There were a dozen enforcers total. They wore navy blue uniforms, gray helmets, and tall black boots. All were emblazoned with the golden bell crest of the Safe Lands and a small name patch. The helmets had eye shades that hid the men's faces from view. Holsters strapped handguns to their hips.

One man stood out from the rest, towering over the others like a monstrous bat. His eye shade had been pushed to the top of his helmet, though a pair of sunglasses and a thick beard covered most of his face. The skin that did show was pale and flaky. He had the thin plague, a disease that—according to Papa Eli—killed a person's immune system over time.

His name patch said "Otley." Gold rings looped through each eyebrow and the center of his bottom lip, and a gold spike curled out of each nostril like a section of the barbed wire that topped the Safe Lands walls. A small white number eight was tattooed on his cheek.

"Help you boys?" Father asked.

Otley ambled around the front of the stage. "We're having a membership drive. Wondering if your people are ready for a life with a little more... fun."

"Not interested," Father said.

"Not surprised, but I'm afraid I can't take that answer. See, we need people to join us in the Safe Lands. Need them to join now. But since I'm a nice guy, I'm going to give you a choice." Otley reached toward his holster.

"Hey, hey, hey!" Uncle Colton said.

He and Father both aimed at Otley, which caused half of the enforcers to draw their weapons as well. All those guns made Mason's nerves so jittery he about wet his pants. *But that would be normal*, he told himself. *A neurobiological response to a life-threatening situation.*

Otley raised his hands and chuckled. "Cool off, shells! Just trying to show you that our pistols hold sleepers *and* killers. The guns have a switch. Blue for sleep, red for kill. Question is, which way do you want us to flick the switch?"

"Can't imagine the dead would make good members for your commune, Safe Lander," Father said. "We only shoot one way in Glenrock, and it ain't for sleeping."

"And you refuse to come take a look at our fine city?" Otley asked.

"That's right," Father said.

Otley sighed. "Remember what I said, men." He turned in a circle, pointing his finger over the enforcers. "One kill each. Sleep the rest of the village."

Otley spun and fired twice. The discharge was like the pop of an electric nail gun. Father crumpled. As did Uncle Colton.

Mason screamed and raised his rifle, but gunfire rained over the enforcers from above. Jordan and Harvey. Mason dropped to his stomach and crawled under the stage, dragging his rifle into darkness. Sharp rocks stabbed his knee caps and palms. Gunfire spat into the dirt behind him, and he crawled faster. All around him men were crying out. Glenrock rifle fire exploded against the airy pops of Safe Lands handguns.

Mason stopped under the middle of the stage. His arms were shaking badly, but he pushed to a kneeling position and looked back. Sunlight lit the edge of the stage. He could see the toe of his father's boot and the top of Uncle Colton's head as both lay on the ground.

Mason threw up. The first of it landed in his lap. He leaned over and heaved and heaved, his mind a blur of questions.

One kill each, Otley had said. How had he drawn so quickly? Had he fired sleepers or killers? What did a sleeper do? Should Mason go back? Try to help? He didn't see any movement from his father or uncle, but he had to know. He crept toward them, got close enough to look...

A girl's scream forced Mason to look away from his father. Suddenly, he was crawling to the back of the stage. He had to help her. Needed to.

"Get away from me!" the girl screamed.

Mason peeked out from under the stairs. Shaylinn, running from an enforcer toward the tree line. The enforcer shot his gun. Shaylinn fell. The enforcer continued toward her. She pushed up to her hands and knees. Fell. Writhed and tried again to rise. Screamed for help.

Mason could only stare from his safe haven. Accusations assaulted his mind in time with the gunfire. *Coward. Sissy. Gutless. Weakling.*

The crack of a gun brought the enforcer to his knees, then to his face, prostrate in the grass a few yards from Shaylinn.

Jordan. Shooting from the trees. But Mason could still help.

He pushed out from under the stage and sprinted toward Shaylinn, his muscles tense, knowing he could be shot at any moment.

"Shaylinn." He knelt beside her. "Can you move?"

She panted in a few long breaths. "I think... so." She got to her feet.

Mason pulled her arm around his shoulders and helped her stand. "Behind the sick house," he said.

They started for it, but after a few steps, Shaylinn sagged against him. Mason held her up and dragged her along.

"My legs won't work," she said. "I can't make them move."

Mason squatted and lifted her the way men did in Old movies. A groan escaped him as he struggled with her weight. He sucked in a deep breath and staggered to the sick house, certain he'd drop her any moment. Somehow, he managed to reach the far side of the structure before collapsing.

"Shaylinn? Talk to me," he said. "Where does it hurt?"

Her eyes were glassy, liquid with unshed tears. "My back."

Mason knelt beside her and rolled her body against his knees. He patted her back to look for a wound and found a small hole in the back of her dress, just to the right of her spine. "There's no blood." A sleeper?

"What's no blood mean?" Shaylinn asked, her voice slow.

Best guess? "I assume it means you're going to go to sleep."

"What if I don't wake up?"

Mason struggled for something uplifting to say as he rolled her to her back. "Whether you wake on earth or in heaven, I can't say. Either would be good, though, right?"

Her eyes flew wide. "But I don't want to die! I've... never been in love." Her eyelids fluttered. "Never kissed... a boy. Never been beautiful. Everyone here thinks I'm... I'm ugly. Omar said..."

But Mason didn't discover what Omar had said, because Shaylinn's eyes drifted shut.

Mason sank against the wall of the sick house, listening to the sounds around him. It was quieter now. He could hear men talking but couldn't tell what they were saying or whether they were friend or foe.

Mason glanced toward the square just as the front door to his house swung in. Papa Eli stepped onto the porch, clutching his rifle in one hand. He wore a plain white T-shirt and a pair of black shorts that bared his knobby knees.

Mason scrambled to his feet and sprinted toward his great-grandfather. The old man started to lift his gun in Mason's direction, then recognized him.

"What's going on out here?" Papa asked.

"Safe Lands enforcers asked us to move into the compound. Father refused and they shot him and Uncle Colton. The men fought back, but I don't know who won." Mason sucked in a quick breath. "Some are dead, but some are only sleeping. The enforcers had two kinds of ammo, and I... I don't know which kind they used on each person."

Papa Eli looked over Mason's shoulder. "Why didn't someone come get me?"

A sob stole its way out Mason's throat. "Father said to let you sleep."

Papa Eli pursed his lips and sighed out his nose. "Get your gun, and let's go take a look."

Mason ran back to where he'd left Shaylinn and picked up his rifle. Papa Eli met him there, and they peeked past the edge of the sick house. Enforcers milled around the square. Two lifted Jordan's body off the ground and carried it toward the back of the second transport.

Did that mean Jordan was alive? "What are we going to do?" Mason asked.

"Where is everyone?" Papa asked.

"Father sent the women into the meeting hall. He split up the men to shoot from the forest and the roofs." Mason took a deep breath, feeling a hint better with Papa Eli by his side.

"So the women are trapped and no one's shooting." Papa Eli stepped out from behind the sick house. "Cover me."

Mason grappled with his rifle until he was holding it correctly, though the barrel quivered like a branch in the wind. Behind him, footsteps rustled through the ferns. Mason glanced over his shoulder, hoping to see one of the village men or even Grazer. But it was Otley and an enforcer whose name badge read *Lemuel*.

"Papa!" Mason yelled.

Papa Eli spun around, gun ready, and he and Otley held each other in their sights.

Otley frowned. "You're an abomination, old man! How long have they let you live?"

"I was there when they built your Safe Lands, boy," Papa Eli said to Otley. "I didn't want any part of it then, and I still don't."

"Men like you disgust me," Otley said. "To take resources from the young and refuse liberation..."

Papa chuckled—a gun pointed at his head and he laughed! "You'll think differently someday."

"Not likely, you stimming Ancient."

Otley and Papa Eli fired at the same time. The bullet's impact sent Otley flying, and he landed on his back a few yards away. Papa Eli crashed against the sick house wall and slid down it. Blood bloomed red and bright against his white shirt.

"*No!*" Mason pointed his rifle at Lemuel, the barrel a blur from his trembling.

Lemuel raised his pistol to Mason's head. He too had a number tattooed to his cheek. A number three. "I don't think you've got the juice to pull the trigger, shell."

"Don't kill him!" Otley whispered from where he lay on the ground, clutching his stomach. "We need the young ones alive."

How could the man still be breathing?

"Don't worry, general. My gun's on sleep," Lemuel said.

Mason pulled his trigger, but it didn't budge. *The safety.* He fumbled with the switch, certain he was about to feel a bullet enter his skull; instead, a gun went off. Mason cowered, his ears ringing. The enforcer Lemuel fell, a hole between his eyes.

Mason whipped around. Papa Eli's arm fell, his pistol clutched in his hand. Mason lunged to his great-grandfather's side and helped him lie down. The bullet had entered just below Papa Eli's right shoulder and looked to have pierced his pectoral muscle and possibly his right lung. Mason lifted Papa Eli until he spotted the exit wound in his center back.

Control the bleeding, staunch if possible. It didn't matter if his hands were dirty. An infection could be treated later. There was no pressure point for the shoulders, so all Mason could do was apply direct compression and pray God sent a miracle. He tried to pull up Papa Eli's shirt. No good. So, he shrugged off his cattail vest, folded it, and pressed it over the entrance wound.

Papa Eli gasped. "Careful, boy!"

Good. He was talking, which meant his airway was clear, but there could still be issues with his lungs and his breathing. Plus, the exit wound was extremely close to the spine. "Turn your head to the side, Papa, so you can breathe better."

"I can breathe fine."

The blood quickly soaked through Mason's vest and coated his hands in a glossy red sheen. He needed something else for the exit wound, and fast. All the blood was likely draining out the back. He tucked his vest under the exit wound on Papa Eli's back and pressed his hands over the shoulder wound. "Can you move your hands and feet?"

"You're worse than my Hannah." A dreamy smile claimed Papa Eli's face. "You would have liked your great-grandmother, Mason—tenacious in her ministrations, she was. And I'll tell you the same thing I'd tell her; if it's my time to go, your efforts won't matter."

Tears flooded Mason's eyes. He didn't want anyone else to die. *Get it together, Mason—focus!* His body grew heavy with the realization that until the bleeding stopped or until another pair of hands came along, there wasn't anything else he could do .

Papa shivered and sucked in a series of weak breaths—he was going into shock. Mason needed to get a blanket, something, but he didn't dare leave Papa's side.

A sting between his shoulder blades knocked him forward, and he barely kept himself from collapsing on Papa Eli. A burning tingle throbbed out from his center back. He looked over his shoulder and his head swam.

Otley was watching him. Smiling. Pistol in hand. "Nightie-night, shell."

Mason turned back to Papa Eli, bloody, blurry… two Papas, three.

The sky was bright blue above him. Fat white clouds. How had he gotten on his back? He needed to help Papa Eli. Stop the bleeding.

But Papa Eli's face appeared above him, dark, backlit by the light of day. He grabbed Mason's hand and squeezed. "Don't let them change you, boy. No matter what. Stay true to…"

Mason's eyelids slid closed.

Chapter 5

The motorcycle jerked over the ruts of the mountain trail. Omar tried to steer carefully, but his efforts only seemed to make the ride bumpier. He liked the feel of Jemma's arms around his waist though, and how they tightened whenever he hit a bump. He hoped it wouldn't be long until he found a fiancée of his own.

Omar slowed to turn onto the valley road, and the ride became much smoother. He sped over the thick treads the Safe Lands vehicles had dug into the dirt. Were the tracks one-way or two? Were the enforcers still in the village? He hoped so.

Once they entered the forest, the shade cooled the air, which made him shiver despite the hot muffler warming his leg. The question of what was happening in Glenrock overwhelmed his thoughts. What would the people say when the enforcers made their offer?

It was a mad good idea, relocating. Omar had been inside the Safe Lands only at night, but that had been enough to see that the city was amazing. So modern. To have to work only a few hours each day? To not have to hunt or grow your own food? The ability to do whatever you wanted? And the conveniences! Surely the people of Glenrock would at least want to go inside to see for themselves. Omar couldn't be the only curious about the place.

The task director had said the enforcers would come right away. Then three weeks passed, and Omar had begun to think they weren't coming at all. He'd spent every moment he could watching from the perch, even volunteering for more shifts. He'd almost thought he'd been imagining those trucks when he saw them coming today.

Thankfully Penelope, Shay, and Nell had followed him, begging him to draw their portraits. Omar had tricked Penelope into watching the perch, promising her an extra drawing for her trouble, then went to fetch Jemma and send Levi away. Something told him Levi wouldn't like the Safe Lands, but if Jemma visited first... Well, she could talk Levi into anything.

Plus, Jemma was worth a million credits to Omar. The task director had promised him a referral fee for every new citizen he brought into the compound. Females were worth a million credits each while males were worth only ten thousand. So, if Levi never came, Omar wasn't out much. Things would move smoother without his interference anyway.

Omar downshifted as he steered the motorcycle into the village square. The three Safe Lands trucks he'd seen from the perch were parked in the roundabout. Pairs of enforcers were carrying bodies to the trucks.

Bodies? Omar's stomach turned inside out. No one was supposed to get hurt! The task director had promised a peaceful offer and negotiation. He'd promised.

Several enforcers aimed guns at Omar as he approached. He let the motorcycle coast to a stop and lifted his hands above his head, but his gaze fell on two motionless bodies on the ground in front of the stage.

With a sharp cry, Jemma climbed off to bike and sprinted to the stage. The enforcers tracked her with their guns but didn't fire. She knelt beside the bodies. "Oh! Omar, come quick!"

Omar must have followed, because he suddenly found himself at her side, looking down on the face of his father.

Dead.

His skin prickled, and he felt lightheaded. He shuffled back a few steps. Father couldn't be dead. He couldn't be. Father was supposed to move into the Safe Lands and be proud of Omar for coming up with the brilliant idea of relocating the people of Glenrock. How could Father be proud if he were dead? And Uncle Colton too?

This couldn't be real. He must have fallen asleep in the perch. Once he woke, Penelope would be begging him to draw her, and he'd laugh about all of this.

Voices muttered nearby. That had to be Penelope and Shay and Nell. He rubbed his forefinger along the scar on the bridge of his nose until it was sore.

"Omar."

His head snapped back. Jemma was shaking him by his shoulders.

"They want us to go into the hall." Her voice was weepy.

Why was she crying? He ran the back of his hand under his nose. His gaze again fell to the bodies. "Is that... my father?" His voice came out in a hoarse whisper.

"Omar, I'm so sorry." Jemma sniffed in a deep breath and hugged him. The warmth of her body confused him. Felt real.

Suddenly she was gone. "No! Let go," Jemma yelled. "Omar, please... Stay with me!"

With her? Stay? He shook his head. "What?" He looked up in time to see an enforcer drag Jemma into the meeting hall.

"Okay, shell, let's go inside." Another enforcer took Omar's arm and led him away from his father. Omar glanced back to make sure his father was... Yes. There he lay. On the ground with Uncle Colton. What a horrible nightmare.

Inside the meeting hall, the air felt cool. The lull of men's voices and the high-pitched wail of a girl crying met his ears.

When his eyes adjusted to the darkness, Omar saw that at least three dozen people occupied the meeting hall. The banquet tables had been taken down, leaving the floor bare. His female friends, neighbors, and their children sat along the wall, wrists bound in their laps, half of them weeping, half of them asleep or dead. A sea of navy blue uniforms stood before them: Safe Lands enforcers, armed with black pistols. The enforcer holding Jemma pushed her toward the women.

"No!" Mother yelled. "Omar, get Jemma out of here!"

"Jemma, run!" Naomi screamed from her place along the wall.

Jemma wheeled around and ran back to the doors, where Omar was standing. "Back outside, Omar. Hurry!"

Then came a pop, followed by the metallic clink of a shell casing hitting the floor. Jemma gasped and stumbled. Someone screamed. Omar lunged forward and caught her under her arms. Behind her, an enforcer stood, his gun pointed at her back.

Fire seared Omar's chest. "Why'd you shoot her?"

Jemma's eyes filled with liquid. "Getting shot doesn't hurt as much as I thought it would," she mumbled.

"It's just a sleeper, shell," the enforcer said to Omar. "She'll be fine."

Two other enforcers dragged Jemma away from Omar and set her against the wall by the door. Omar felt somewhat relieved that she'd live but still didn't know what to do.

Kruse, the task director general's assistant, glided to Omar's side. He was thin, bald, had a pinkish hue to his skin, and smelled like flowers. The man held a flat piece of glass in his black-gloved hands and tapped his finger against words that were displayed on the surface. "What took you so long?"

Blood tingled inside Omar's head, making him dizzy. He hoped no one had heard—

"What!" The word came out like a scream torn from Mother's throat. "Omar? You knew about this?"

Omar swallowed and lowered his voice. "Mother, it's okay. I had to go and—"

"What's that femme's name?" Kruse asked.

Femme? Oh, right—their term for girl. "Jemma," Omar said, staring at the strange tattoo on the side of Kruse's head. It looked like a black arm that reached out of the man's collar, ran up the side of his neck, and splayed its hand over the side of his shiny scalp.

"G-e-m-m-a?"

Omar focused on Kruse's face, on the white number five on his cheek. "Um... J-e-m-m-a."

"*Omar*," Jemma said, her voice slurred. "Don't help them."

Kruse tapped the glass and spoke softly. "Jemma. Done."

Omar could feel the women staring at him.

"See anyone missing?" Kruse asked. "General Otley wants to get as many of you outsiders as he can. We've already loaded the males and given you the referrals. And we've credited you for each femme here. You're rich, shell. Anyone else we need to get?"

"Just my brother, Levi. But I have a feeling he'll come on his own." Omar glanced at Jemma.

"That's right," Jemma whispered, her eyes glistening. "Levi *will* come, Omar. And you'll forever regret this betrayal."

"It's not like that." Omar felt like he was falling and only words could save him. "We were supposed to be able to choose... to get a chance for a better life." He looked to Kruse. "Why did you kill people?"

"*That* is an excellent question, shellie," Kruse said. "And I can promise you there will be an inquiry."

An inquiry. His father was *dead*. "Is that supposed to make me feel better?"

"What's he saying, Jemma?" Mother yelled from across the room. "Omar?"

Kruse removed a gold paper envelope from his front pocket. "Take this to the Registration Department to get your task station and post. They'll also assign your home." He pointed to a short, muscled enforcer with longish, frizzy brown hair and a tiny mustache. "You can ride back with Skottie. See you around, shellie." Kruse exited the meeting hall.

"Omar?" Mother yelled. "Don't listen to them."

The enforcers got the women and girls to their feet and led them out the door in a line. One picked up Shay and tossed her over his shoulder like she was a ragdoll. Another carried Jemma with about as much care.

When Mother neared the door, she tried to approach Omar, but an enforcer held her back. "Omar, why?" she asked. "You plan to work for them? *Live* with them?"

Tears pooled in the corners of Omar's eyes. He sniffed in a short breath and stepped back. "You'll like it there, Mother. You'll see. It's *amazing* inside the Safe Lands."

"What about the thin plague?" Mother asked, her voice laced with tears. "The slavery Papa Eli told us about?"

"Papa Eli was wrong about the Safe Lands," Omar said. "Things are different there now. Better than here. No drafty cabins."

Naomi, who was in line in front of Mother, yelled, "Maybe if you built one, you'd appreciate them more, you lazy slug!"

Omar flinched and focused on Naomi. Like her husband, Jordan, she had a way with quick insults. "They have stable electricity in the Safe Lands," he said. "Better health care for you and your baby. TVs in every home. Indoor showers with hot water. Air conditioning. This will make everything better for our people. Once all this is sorted out, it's going to be mad good."

Naomi slipped past an enforcer and trotted up to Omar, her pregnant belly no hindrance to her speed. She cuffed her bound hands against his ear. Omar put his hands over his head and ducked out of reach, but Naomi managed to knock off his hat and grab hold of his hair. Two enforcers dragged her back to the line. "Our fathers are dead, Omar!" Naomi screamed. "You think that's good?"

Omar looked away as an enforcer led Naomi and his mother out the door. He picked up his hat, and his gaze landed on Jemma as she was carried past. His chin quivered. "Don't look at me like that." He put his hat back on. "Levi will come—we both know he will. Once he sees how g-good..."

The enforcer shifted Jemma in his arms, and her head lolled to face Omar. "You're wrong. You won't get away with this." As the enforcer took her outside, she yelled, "Levi will save us!"

Omar stood by the wall across from the door until all the women had been taken outside.

Skottie approached. His frizzy brown hair looked like a helmet, but unlike the other enforcers, this guy didn't have one. He did have a white number seven on his cheek. Omar realized he'd never asked about the numbers during his visit. All Safe Landers seemed to have them on their faces and right hands. They must mean something.

"Some crazy flames, huh?" Skottie said. "I mean, we were told these people *wanted* to relocate, but then they showed up with guns and everything went crazy."

"Why'd you shoot them?" Omar practically yelled.

"Walls!" Skottie lifted his hands. "Not me, shell. I just drive the truck. But between you and me, Otley thinks he runs the Safe Lands. He got hit, you know, by some ancient. Maybe that will humble him a bit. We can hope." He walked toward the door. "Let's get out of here. It's dead hot, and my truck has air."

Omar followed Skottie to the third truck in the line. He tried to see his father's body once more, but the stage blocked it from view. Swallowing a lump, he turned to open the door to the truck but found no handle. Before he could decide what to do, the metal grid that covered the door slid up onto the roof.

Inside the cab, Skottie sat on the driver's side, his door grid already sliding down. "Sorry, shell. I forgot you don't have a SimTag. Jump in."

Omar climbed up into the cab. Skottie tapped his right fist on the dashboard, and Omar's door closed.

The dashboard was black with a grid of square indentations, some vent slots, and the imprint of a steering wheel. The push of a button started the vehicle. Another button made the steering wheel rise from the dash. Electric green gauge lights lit up in a line across the top of the windshield: RPM, MPH, Gas, Time.

"Dashboard-air-eight," Skottie said, and cool air shot out from the vents. "Let me know if that gets too cold."

Omar turned to look out the grid and found it clear glass—tinted—but there was no sign of the metal crosshatch. "I thought the doors were metal."

"Yeah, that's one-way ballistic SimGlass. Only looks like metal from the outside."

The truck ahead of Skottie's started to move, and Skottie steered after it. Omar watched out his window, craning to get one last glimpse of Father's body.

He straightened, facing the back of the truck before them, wishing he could see through the grid on the back to know who was inside. Naomi had said her father was dead. How many others had died? He hoped Mason was okay. His brother wouldn't have fired a gun. But he could have gotten hit trying to help someone.

Please. He closed his eyes. *Please let Mason be alive.*

Chapter 6

Levi steered his ATV and cart up the mountain. The image of Jemma with her arms around Omar's waist kept a scowl on his face, despite his attempts to focus on the coming trade. Omar had been right to arrange this meeting, though. The people of Glenrock were dangerously low on ammunition and gunpowder. If anyone should attack the village... Well, Levi didn't want to think about such a scenario.

Instead, he imagined how pleased his dad would be when he returned with enough ammunition to last the winter. Such a prize might soften the man enough to allow Levi to travel to Denver City alone next time. The delight on Jemma's face when Levi had given her the pearls filled his thoughts. He liked giving her things, seeing her eyes light up, being the cause of her beautiful smile. And there were thousands more treasures for her in Denver City.

Enough to last a lifetime.

When Levi reached the trading cabin, Beshup hadn't arrived yet. So Levi checked over his ATV, organized his trader cart, and visited the outhouse behind the cabin. When he returned to the yard, he was disappointed not to see Beshup waiting or even approaching. His impatience increased his agitation. The abandoned cabin stood closer to Jack's Peak than to Glenrock. Where was the man?

Hurry up, Beshup. I've got stuff to do. I could be with Jemma right—

The sound of distant gunfire straightened Levi's posture. Several single-shot rifles firing at once. Levi jogged down the driveway to an outcropping of rock that enabled him to see much of the valley.

Another few rounds of gunfire rang out from the northeast, far from where the walls of the Safe Lands split the countryside. His stomach tightened.

The gunfire was coming from home. Who or what were they shooting at?

He paced back to the cabin, then returned to the rocky ledge as more gunfire pattered in the valley below. He walked back and forth a few more times, squeezing his fists and frowning.

Where was Beshup?

As Levi reached the rocky viewpoint for the fourth time, he picked up his two-way radio to call the perch in Glenrock. "Jackrabbit to Rich Man, come in."

He waited... listened to the static... and hammered a fist against the side of his rig. He called again, then called his dad's two-way radio, his uncle's, Harvey's. No answer.

Maybe Beshup would answer. "Jackrabbit to Thunder Cry. Come in, Thunder Cry. Over."

Only a moment passed before the two-way radio clicked. "Ten four, Jackrabbit. This is Thunder Cry. How are you this fine afternoon? Over?"

"Where you been, Thunder Cry? I've been waiting at the bird's nest for a while now. Over."

"Why you waiting?"

That was a strange question. "Omar said you have fire to trade."

"Who told you that? We've barely got enough for ourselves."

Levi gritted his teeth. "Omar said you called him."

Static. "I haven't talked to your brother in over a month."

Levi closed his eyes. *What are you up to, Omar?*

"You still there, Jackrabbit?"

"I'm hearing gunfire over in Glenrock," Levi said. "Going to go take a look."

"Let me know what you find."

"Will do. Over and out." Levi tossed his two-way radio into his cart and started the ATV. The mile-and-a-half trek down the mountain had never seemed so long. He wanted to take the shortcut past the Safe Lands, but he'd do his village no good if he were captured. Every minute was agony to him. The men couldn't be target shooting. There wasn't enough ammo for sport.

He steered onto the village road, and the fresh dual-axle tracks he saw in the dirt made him push the ATV even faster. Levi veered onto the waterwheel trail so he could come around the back of the village.

He parked at the river. The only sound was the hydro-generator puttering away. He grabbed his rifle and ran up the hill through the forest, darting past trees and over moss and mushrooms, cutting across the trail's switchbacks. As the hill carried him higher, his legs grew weak, forcing him to slow down.

Something lay across the path before him. A body. He sprinted toward it and knelt beside the form of a man. Elder Sam, Naomi's father, dead, a pistol still clutched in his hand. His body was matted with grass and dirt and looked to have rolled down the incline. Levi's mind screamed, knowing this was real, yet at the same time certain only nightmares contained such horror. His pulse thudded in his head like drums.

As if someone else were controlling him, his hands tugged the gun from Elder Sam's hand and checked it for ammunition. Empty. He tucked it into the back of his pants anyway.

"I'll come back for you, Elder Sam." Levi crept farther up the hill. As he neared the village square, he found three more bodies in the woods: Elder Mark, Elder Devin, and Elder Michael. All had been shot. All were out of ammo. They had died fighting.

Levi also found Grazer, Mason's dog, lifeless near a tree. The mutt had been incredibly friendly—why would someone have shot him?

He left the dog and took off through the forest toward his house. Levi's family home stood on the far side of the square. He went in through the back door and made his way to the front, checked all the bedrooms. No one home.

He ran out the front door and scanned the area. A body lay on the ground halfway between him and the sick house.

Papa Eli.

Levi sprinted across the grass and fell to his knees beside his great-grandfather. Papa Eli, founder of Glenrock and the oldest living member of the Elias tribe, lay on his stomach in the grass. Blood coated the back of his white T-shirt.

Levi set down his rifle. "Papa Eli?" He tucked the old man's arm close and rolled him over. The grass beneath him was red and wet. So much blood. A bullet had passed through at an angle, leaving a hole in Papa Eli's shoulder. Or maybe the bullet had entered from the front and passed out the back. Mother would know.

Mother!

Levi wanted to find his mother, his father, his brothers. Help Papa Eli. Find out who'd done this and—

Papa Eli wheezed. His eyes flashed open, wide and bloodshot. They rolled around in their sockets and fixed on Levi. Recognition softened the look of pain on the old man's face. His voice came out in a raspy whisper. "Didn't get you?"

"No, sir." Levi fought to keep his voice steady. "Who shot you?"

"Enforcers." Papa Eli grimaced. "Killed our men... Took our women and young ones."

Ice pooled in Levi's heart, sending chills down every vein. "To the compound?"

"Afraid so." He reached out and patted Levi's thigh. "Thought we'd be safe... Thought they'd leave us alone... We were wrong. *I* was wrong. You have to... get them back."

"Yes, sir. I won't let you down."

Papa Eli slapped Levi's thigh the way he slapped the tabletop to get everyone's attention at mealtimes. "Good. Good." He closed his eyes and took a few deep breaths.

"What can I do?" Levi asked. "Mother and Mason are the doctors. I don't know how to—"

"Don't fret." Papa Eli opened his eyes and focused on Levi. "My Hannah's... gone... twenty years now."

Levi swallowed hard. "That's a long time to be missing someone."

Papa Eli nodded slightly. "I was... looking forward... your wedding. That Jemma... a pretty girl. Kind too. You're smart to grab... her."

Rage filled Levi's chest at the idea of Jemma in the Safe Lands. "I'll get her back, sir."

"I know." He took a ragged breath. "And I'm going... leave you to it. Head to eternity... with my God and... my Hannah."

Tears flooded Levi's eyes.

Papa Eli patted Levi's thigh again, this time much softer. "Good man. Lord knows best." He closed his eyes. "Been with me all these..." The life left his great-grandfather's face.

Levi fell onto his back in the grass, staring up at the hazy pine trees, wondering if Papa Eli's soul was floating to heaven this very moment. His throat burned. His eyes burned too.

No one had earned a proper burial more than Papa Eli. The man had survived the Great Pandemic and escaped the Safe Lands. Founded Glenrock as an answer to the Safe Land's tyranny and governed the village with wisdom and grace. Served God as best he could. Trained up three generations to follow in his footsteps. Outlived his wife and their son.

Was Levi truly the only one left? Papa Eli has said they'd taken the women and young ones—which meant Mason, Jordan, and Omar likely lay dead on the grass somewhere too.

A fat drop of water struck Levi's cheek. Summer storms were common, but as distant thunder crackled, Levi wondered if God had looked down on Glenrock and shed tears for the death of its people. For Papa Eli.

Levi lay on the grass, letting the rain soak him. He gave in to tears and prayed for help, for guidance, for sanity. The storm cloud passed quickly, and Levi decided he too should get moving. He pushed himself up and went looking for survivors, his mind racing, trying to piece together the truth. Omar had lied to him about Beshup's trade, and he couldn't fathom why.

Just when Levi thought he'd finished crying, he found his father's body. Elder Justin had been shot once in the forehead. Likely hadn't suffered, which was some consolation.

Levi found no survivors in the village. There were eighteen dead—thirteen elder men, four elder women, and little Sophie, who'd been only six. No sign of Jordan, Mason, or Omar.

Levi couldn't dig eighteen graves himself. But he couldn't leave the bodies to the wolves, either. Over the next two hours, he moved the dead, including Grazer, to the square where he could keep an eye on them. He piled the weapons in the back of his cart. Then he decided to dig three graves in the cemetery: one for his father, one for Papa Eli, and one for Sophie.

The digging took him well into the afternoon.

Several times, the horror gripped him, and Levi lost himself in a fit of rage, beating the shovel against a tree or the ground until finally the spade separated from the shaft.

Once he'd buried the three and said a prayer for their lives, he sat against a tree to catch his breath. His palms stung with blisters. His arms ached. He nodded off once, told himself to get up and do something about the other bodies. But he eventually nodded off again and fell into a full slumber.

Chapter 7

Omar was shaking now. How had everything gone so wrong? His whole body felt numb and tingly like he was going to throw up. As much as he tried not to think about it, Father's face was burned on his brain. Relocation was supposed to gain Omar acceptance with his people, not further cast him out. He fought to steady his breath, crossed his arms to fight the shaking.

"You juicing, shell?" Skottie asked.

Skottie's mustache looked like two strokes of paint going out from each nostril. "What?"

"Stims, joy juice, hard candy, vapes. Uh... narcots?

"Narcotics?" Omar recalled the word from Old movies.

Skottie bobbed his head. "That's what I said."

And the guy thought Omar was on drugs? "Someone killed my father. And it was because of me."

"Ahh, premie lib," Skottie said.

Omar looked over at Skottie. "Premie what?"

"Going on to the next life before reaching your limit. I hear having someone go through that can be tough. How old was your friend?"

Omar rubbed his scar. "My father was forty-six."

Skottie shrugged. "Past his time then. Safe Lands used to liberate at fifty, but they changed it to forty back in seventy-two. It's for the best. No one wants to get old."

The best? "But I just left him there. I should go back. Bury him maybe. And the others. Can we turn around?"

"Walls, no, shell." The truck bounced over a hole in the dirt road. "Ask the Tasker G when you take in your fancy gold ticket. No way I'm putting my skin under fire for an ancient."

Would Omar ever understand what these people were saying? "You keep calling me a shell. What does that mean?"

"It's what we call someone who's so sick with the plague that their mind is gone. They do weird things like eat dirt or forget to get dressed. But we also use the word to describe clueless outsiders. You won't be a shell much longer."

As they drove through the forest, it was silent but for the air conditioning and Omar's raspy breathing.

"So." Skottie tapped his fingers on the steering wheel. "You tasked a deal. What did they promise?"

"Uh... I'm supposed to get a position with the enforcers." A position that would have shown his father he wasn't worthless. A position that didn't seem to matter anymore.

"Ah, we'll be seeing each other then. You'll have to take basic. I'm in there now. Then you'll be assigned a task internship somewhere. They made me a driver. But they let me carry a gun, which about liberated my friend Charlz when he found out. Charlz collects guns, but he's interning in patrol and only gets to carry a stunner. Charlz already has ten different stunners."

The task director had promised Omar an officer's rank within the enforcers. He hoped Skottie wouldn't be offended when he found out that Omar was jumping ahead in rank. Now that he'd alienated his entire village, he needed any friends he could get.

"What else?" Skottie asked. "Got to get your mind off your friend. What do you do for fun?"

Omar forced the image of Father's face away. "I draw and paint."

"Ooh, an artist. Check out this store called Task for Art in the Highlands. They're got all kinds of real paint in there. I'm assuming you meant Old art and not SimArt."

"What's SimArt?"

"Like the window of my truck. SimTech illusion." Skottie tapped the iridescent number seven on his cheek. "Same way this works. Same way that black hand on Kruse's head works."

They left the forest, and sunlight brightened the cab. "I don't understand."

"I'll show you." Skottie unbuttoned his jacket and shrugged it off his shoulders. He held out his right arm. "Pull my sleeve."

Omar did. Once Skottie's arm was free from his jacket, he held it out again. It was solid with bright tattoos. Green, red, yellow, blue, silver images melded together in a combination of abstract art: a cat's face, a dagger, a pair of dice, a skull, a net stocking, a thorny rose.

"Did it hurt?" Omar asked, studying the colors. "The needle?"

"No needles. SimTags itch a little when you get them, but that's it. No one wants to be tagged for life. It's all simulation. Electronic ink."

Omar studied Skottie's arm again. "How does electronic ink work?"

"I'll do my best, peer, but there's a reason I don't task in tech." Skottie turned the wheel, following the truck ahead. The Safe Lands walls rose in front of them. "Every national gets two SimTags for identification. One here"—he tapped his cheek—"and one here." He held up his fist, and Omar could see another number seven on the back of his right hand. "Each SimTag covers a three-inch diameter. You can get more, then they 'talk' to each other to create bigger images."

Like tiny computers? "How many did it take to do your arm?"

"Twenty-five. I also got ten in my chest and twelve on my back."

"How do you choose the pictures?"

"In any SimArt store, or, if you like art and get the right adds, you can change them yourself. Some people even design their own."

Ideas for what Omar could do with SimTags filled his thoughts.

The truck slowed to a stop before a massive gate. On either side of the road, a concrete pillar rose into the sky like a grain silo. Enforcers stood on the tops, weapons pointed down toward the truck. A concrete wall stretched from each pillar into the distance.

A huge boom of metal made Omar jump. The noise was followed by metallic clanking. When the sound ceased, the truck rolled forward again. They passed under a gate. All went dark, and then the bright sky appeared overhead again, separated by a tunnel of mesh wire the truck was driving through. The Safe Lands in the daytime was all new to Omar.

He peered out his window at blurred figures that were wading in a vast field of green that reached their knees, stooping to pick from the plants. The scent of livestock was thick on the air. Every so often they passed a mishmash of buildings and intersections before returning to endless fields spread out on either side of the tunnel.

"Some people work in the fields?"

"Sure. Not everyone can get tasked to the enforcers, right?"

The truck passed under another gate and tunnel, this time without stopping. On the other side, they drove through a grid of streets similar to the Old neighborhoods in Crested Butte but in much better condition.

A massive TV screen, bigger than the truck, loomed on the side of the road. It showed a man and woman in matching outfits. The woman had chin-length, smooth black hair and was wearing a pale yellow dress with black dots. The man wore a black suit with a ruffly yellow bow tie. Words scrolled beneath their image: *Finley and Flynn discuss Lonn liberation.*

"They show movies on the road?" Omar asked.

"Expos," Skottie said. "That's a DigiBoard."

"What's a Lonn liberation?" Omar asked.

"Ooh, Richark Lonn the rebel. He Xed out years ago, but they finally caught him. He's way overage, so he's due to get liberated and move on to the next life."

"They're going to execute him?"

"Death is life, peer."

Omar had no response for that. He wished Mason were here. His brother was smart and always knew what to say.

They were traveling uphill now and soon stopped before a third gate. This one had pillars like the main gate and a dividing wall that ran across the land.

"Why so many gates?"

"The people in the three areas keep mostly to themselves. A lot of Midlanders task in the Highlands, since no one who lives in the ritzy Highlands ever manages to test for service positions—nothing suspicious there, ha ha. But there's only so much room up here, so lots have to live in the Midlands and commute in. The gates keep everyone where they belong at the end of the day."

The truck lurched forward again. It passed between two massive steel doors that were as tall as the concrete pillars, then they entered a thick forest.

They approached another DigiBoard, but this one flashed still images. One showed a woman with pale blue, sparkling skin. Text flashed across the screen that said, "Veins showing through your makeup? Try Roller Paint. Available in over two hundred colors, textures, and prints. Smoothes all flakes and completely covers varicose and spider veins."

The truck departed the forest and made its way toward the buildings clustered at the top of the bell—buildings taller than the concrete pillars at the last gate. The city rose against the bright sky; the sight stole the breath from Omar's lungs.

The truck carried them into the middle of the towers, joining more vehicles on the road. People walked along the sidewalks, many wearing black and pale yellow like the people from the DigiBoard. Omar swore he saw someone with green skin, then realized that with SimTags and Roller Paint, he probably had.

Electric signs displayed words in lighted, moving letters: *Savoy. Westwall. Golden Lily. Monogram Room*. Omar could only assume they were the clubs he'd been told about on his first visit. Skottie turned into a covered loading zone—the ceiling solid with round lights the size of apples—and stopped before a wall of dark glass doors that reflected the massive vehicle. Omar could see his own eyes looking out through the grid illusion. Two men dressed in gold and blue uniforms with shiny gold buttons stood on either side of the glass doors, staring ahead like statues.

"If you wait, I'll drop you by City Hall," Skottie said. "It might be a while, though. Or you could walk. It's just two blocks to the right from the end of this driveway."

Omar didn't want to stand around and watch the enforcers carry his kin into the building. "I'll walk. Thanks." He turned to the door and realized again that he had no means of opening it.

Skottie laughed and tapped his fist on a square on the dashboard. Omar's door started to rise. "You want me to show you around tonight? I can take you to a glossy dance club."

"Really?" Had Omar made a friend? "Sure. Thanks."

"If they don't give you a Wyndo, ask your doorman to tap me. The number's 7–67–18."

"7–67–18." Omar committed the number to memory.

"That's right. Talk to you later, peer, and stay out of trouble."

Omar walked to where the driveway met the main road. Cars sped past in blurs of color and glass. He felt as if he were standing in a movie. He turned right and started walking but soon forgot his plan to enjoy the sights, lost in the memory of how he'd left his father dead on the ground. He should have spoken up. Should've done something. His father had been right: Omar *was* a sissy coward.

The next time he noticed his surroundings, he'd nearly passed City Hall. He craned his neck all the way back to look up the side of the building. It was made of ten silvery glass cubes, one stacked on top of the other like giant building blocks. Each block was turned slightly so that the corners jutted out at different angles—an impressive example of cubist architecture. The light hit it in ways that Omar thought would be interesting to sketch in charcoal.

The elevator to the tenth floor didn't thrill Omar as much today as it had a few weeks back. The task director general's receptionist sent him right in. Omar took a deep breath and entered.

The rectangular room had a shiny wooden floor, sparse chrome and red suede furniture, and floor-to-ceiling windows on three walls. Clean, sharp, simple—minimalist design. This was another reason the Safe Lands so intrigued Omar. So much beauty and architecture. There was none of this in Glenrock. Until Omar had visited the Safe Lands, he'd never seen anything from the Old art books Levi had given him.

Lawten Renzor, the Task Director General of the Safe Lands, sat at his desk. Kruse, his pink-skinned, bald assistant, stood beside him. The task director looked no different than the first time Omar had met him. He was tall and hunched with a tiny head, a glowing yellow nine on his cheek, a large nose, and almost no muscle on his bones. He had ink-black hair and eyebrows that looked even darker against his papery, white skin.

If Omar were to draw a caricature of the task director, he'd make him look like a vulture. But the man's lips were so full, he could also pass for an ugly woman. A vulture in a dress, perhaps.

"Ah, it's our outsider friend," the task director said. "Come sit. We have much to discuss."

That's right, they did. Omar just needed to work up the courage to say so. He needed to be strong and brave like his father and brothers. The enforcers had broken their promise, and it was up to Omar to make sure the task director understood how unacceptable that was. He sat on a red suede chair on the other side of the task director's desk.

The man's tiny, shrewd eyes searched Omar's face, omniscient eyes that seemed to know more than they should. Omar avoided looking at them now; instead, he focused on a mobile sculpture hanging above the task director's desk. It had nine black leaves and one red one, and shifted hypnotically.

"We have a problem, Omar of Glenrock," the task director said.

His words captured Omar's full attention, and he dared to meet those black pupils with his own. "We do?"

"Kruse informed me that several were killed in the attempt to relocate your village, including two women of childbearing age and one female child."

One blow after another. Who? Who else had died in Omar's quest for a better life? A child?

"Nine fertile males were also killed," the task director said, drawing Omar's focus to the number nine on the man's cheek. "And one of the two we have in custody is being difficult."

Nine males killed. Omar pinched his leg, trying not to think about the deaths he was responsible for. His curiosity won out, however. He had to know. "Who lives? Of the men?"

The task director glanced at Kruse, who picked up his glass computer from the edge of the task director's desk. "The outsiders named Jordan and Mason."

A chill gripped Omar, causing his arm hair to stand on end. Mason lived. Praise God. Then he flinched—*could* he praise God after what he'd done? Would God welcome his prayers at all?

"This loss changes things," the task director said, pulling Omar back to the present.

Omar crossed his arms, trying to look like his father—tough and intolerant. "How so? It was the, uh, enforcers who killed my people. And after you had promised a peaceful visit."

The task director sighed. "Yes, I confess: things got out of hand. But Kruse tells me you were not present when the enforcers arrived. How were they to explain their offer to the people without your help? From what I was told, our men were met with a militia that refused to listen. This was your idea, Omar of Glenrock. And you let your people down."

The words melted Omar's spine, and he slouched in the plush chair. So much for being tough. "But you said women were the most important. And I had to fetch one who wasn't in the village. I was trying to help."

"I understand. But there are consequences to your actions. First, because of the lack of males harvested and the refusals to cooperate from the one we're dealing with now, you'll be required to make donations twice a week."

Omar cringed. He didn't fully understand the Safe Lands' way of procreating, but knew it was vastly different from how things worked in Glenrock. "For how long?"

"As long as I deem necessary. And you must not to pair up with any women."

Pair up meant romance. "That wasn't part of our deal! I want a wife."

The task director's brow furrowed over his large nose. "And *I* don't want you infecting yourself with the thin plague. You'd be useless to me then."

Omar stared at the task director, unable to utter a sound for several moments. "So you never intended to let me marry? Even though you knew that's what I wanted above all else?" His heart slammed inside his chest. "There must be *some* women who aren't infected."

"Why, yes, there are. Eight of pairing age, in fact," the task director said. "I believe you know them already as they're from your village."

"What? No!" Omar fumed. "You promised me a wife!"

"I told you there were many women here, not that I would assist you in finding a lifer. But the fact that you are the only male able or willing to donate at this time—as I've said already—has changed our original agreement. Our mission is top priority. You're welcome to any of the uninfected women, though."

"The girls from Glenrock—they all hate me! And none of them are my age." A thought struck him. "Where do you come up with eight?"

"I pre-registered eight women between the ages of fourteen and thirty-six for the surrogacy pool we quaintly refer to as the harem," Kruse said. "Those too young for the harem were placed in the boarding school or nursery, and the other women were too old."

"Half those women are already married!"

"Were," the task director said. "And that's not my problem."

"It is! Your men killed their husbands. You think their wives would want to marry the guy who made it happen? This is your fault, not mine. My being there wouldn't have kept your men from shooting people."

"You imply that our people fired first?"

"I don't know!" Omar was losing control of the situation, but he couldn't have betrayed his village for nothing. There had to be some way to save this. "What about that other place? Wyoming. Can I visit Wyoming to find a wife?"

The task director rubbed the loose skin on his neck. "If you report to the Donation Center when summoned, avoid liaisons with our women, and keep the Safe Lands' laws... I'll consider it."

Omar swallowed his anxiety. "I can do that." *I've got to look tough, like Father. Strong.*

"Now, for the loss of the women who died, you'll be demoted one rank."

That wasn't so bad. Omar didn't understand the ranks anyway. "Will I still get to live in the Highlands? Will I still get the credits I was promised?"

"Yes, but I'm watching you, Omar of Glenrock." And those eyes seemed to say, *Now and wherever you go.* "See that you sever all ties to the ways of your people. Their insistence on clinging to outdated beliefs will get in the way of our mission, and it's likely some will try to hold you to them."

"I want nothing to do with Glenrock's ways." Ways that had always left him behind, alone, and the source of his father's scorn.

His dead father.

"Good. Your uniform is waiting with my receptionist, *Captain*. Report to the Registration Department on the second floor to receive your residence and schedule. You'll also need a physical and your SimTag implants. General Otley is your task director, so, if he's mended, he'll assign you to a task tomorrow morning."

"You have an appointment at ten o'clock in the Enforcers' Office," Kruse said.

"Well, there you go," the task director general said.

"Okay, thanks. Sir." Omar stood and walked toward the door, feeling foolish for not knowing how to properly address the task director. He reached the door and turned the knob, but the task director general's voice stopped him.

"Thank you for seeking us out and putting this opportunity before us. I hope you find pleasure in life here, Omar. You're one of us now."

Chapter 8

Shaylinn opened her eyes to a bright white ceiling. She must be in heaven, because in Old movies, heaven was always white and glowing. But Papa Eli had said there would be no mourning or pain in heaven, and the ache in Shaylinn's chest hurt.

"Hello?" she called, her voice barely a croak.

She lay on a stiff, narrow bed. When she tried to sit, she found her arms were bound to the bed. Her heart tumbled within her. "Help! Someone help me!" The words resulted in nothing but a break in the silence around her.

She lifted her head in hopes of getting some sort of bearings. A tall cupboard hung on the wall on her right. Down past her feet, a door without a handle or knob. To her left, a glowing blue sheet of glass covered the wall. The surface seemed to ripple with low light.

Her cheek itched, and she turned her head to scratch it with her shoulder. That was when she realized she was wearing a thin white dress. Who would take her clothes? What was going on? "Hello? Is someone there? Please, help me!"

The door swung slowly inward. Shaylinn stared at it. *Please be a woman. Please be a woman. God, please make it be a woman.*

A short, blonde woman entered, and Shaylinn almost cried in relief. She wore a baggy shirt and pants that were pink with tiny red hearts all over them. In her hand, she carried a little red box the size of an Old paperback book.

"Hello," the woman said. "My name is Ciddah. I'm glad to see you awake."

"Why am I here? Where are my clothes? Why am I tied to this bed?"

"Try to remain calm," Ciddah said. "Can you tell me your name and age?"

"Shaylinn of Zachary. I'm fourteen."

"It's nice to meet you, Shaylinn." Ciddah walked all the way to Shaylinn's bed and looked down on her. She had a nice figure and long hair like shiny corn silk.

Ciddah smiled, and it seemed genuinely kind. "You're here because you were struck with a sleeper. It's protocol to monitor sleeper victims, as we never know how long they'll remain unconscious. We took your clothes so we could examine you fully. You can have them back. The restraints were to keep you from thrashing about and hurting yourself or one of our medics. I'll remove them, if you'd like."

"Yes, please."

Ciddah touched the side of Shaylinn's bed, and the restraints retracted. Shaylinn slid off the end of the table and backed into the corner by the door.

"There's no need to be frightened, Shaylinn. That's a lovely name, by the way."

Ciddah's friendliness confused her, and Shaylinn could barely think. She needed to get away. How did that door open without a handle?

"I need to explain some things before you get dressed," Ciddah said. "Of all the new female nationals, there were two who were ready for egg retrieval. You're one of them. Fortune blessed us, and we were able to collect two eggs from you without any fertility stims—drugs that we normally use to speed the process along. So we're going to have you come back in a few days for an embryo transfer."

Shaylinn's mind raced to understand what this woman was talking about. "I'm pregnant? But I've never..."

Ciddah fought a smile. "You're not pregnant, Shaylinn. Not yet, at least. We're hoping to change that in a few days' time."

Shaylinn fought to fill her lungs with air. She hugged herself, squeezed. "Pick somebody else."

"Fortune has chosen you," Ciddah said. "You'll receive a summons when we're ready to do the procedure."

Shaylinn shivered. "But I don't want the procedure. I don't want to be pregnant."

"Don't be silly. It's the greatest honor to be had in the Safe Lands. You'll be given privileges beyond your imagination. Now, let me show you how to take your meds."

Tears filled Shaylinn's eyes. She blinked them away. "I don't want any."

"It's absolutely necessary. You can learn to take them yourself with a personal vaporizer, or I can inject them into your arm with a needle. Your choice."

Shaylinn sniffled, swallowed, glanced at the door again. "What will they do to me?"

"They won't harm you. It's simply a combination of hormones to help your body become receptive for the embryo."

Shaylinn squirmed. Tamera, Omar's mother, had taken Shaylinn, Penelope, and Nell aside two years ago and told them how babies were created, and nothing Ciddah was telling her felt right. Especially since she didn't appear to have any choice in what was happening.

"Why are you doing this to me?" Shaylinn asked. "Where's my mama? My sister?"

Ciddah moved closer to Shaylinn. Her skin was creamy white, perfect, like it had been painted. Not one blemish. "I understand this is a lot to take in. That's why we've assigned Kendall Collin as your suite mentor. She's gone through this already. She'll help you understand how it all works." She held out the little red box. "Can I show you this, please?"

Shaylinn shrugged one shoulder. Maybe if she listened, Ciddah would go away.

Ciddah opened the box and turned it so Shaylinn could see the contents. Inside was a thick black cylinder, like an Old lipstick, and three clear tubes filled with yellow liquid.

"These three are your hormone meds." Ciddah lifted the black cylinder out of the box. "This is a personal vaporizer—some call it a PV. They're so much nicer than swallowing pills or getting injections. You open it like this." She twisted and pulled it apart at the middle. "Then insert one of the vials." She set one of the clear tubes inside the PV with the pointed side down. "When you put the PV back together and twist, it punctures the vial, and you're ready to go. Take one long breath from the PV three times a day. With each meal is fine. When it runs out, this little light will turn red. That means you need to put in a new vial. Think you can do that?"

Shaylinn shook her head. "I'd rather swallow a pill."

Ciddah frowned. Her lips were perfect too. "Are you sure? PVs are very easy to use."

"I don't want it." It looked like the pipes the men from Jack's Peak smoked. And her mother had told her smoking was a nasty thing to do.

Ciddah nodded and stood. "All right. Why don't you get dressed and meet me out front? Your clothes are in the cupboard. I'll get some pills ready for you. Would you like help?"

Shaylinn shook her head. "I'm okay."

"I'll see you in a few minutes, Shaylinn. Just come out the door and walk to the right."

Shaylinn stayed perfectly still as she watched Ciddah tap her fist against a black square beside the door to open it.

The door whooshed closed behind Ciddah, and Shaylinn jumped up and opened the cupboard. Her dress was hanging on a hook inside. She grabbed it and went to stand in front of the door, changing with one foot pressed against it in case anyone tried to enter. Once she was dressed, she set her left fist against the pad by the door like Ciddah had. Nothing happened. She lifted her right fist and gasped. It had a white number four on it. *When did I get that?* She rubbed the number, but it didn't come off. She set her right fist against the pad, and the door popped open.

A bright hallway stretched in both directions, lined with doors spaced evenly along each side. She could hear voices coming from the right, the way Ciddah had told her to go. At the end of the hallway to the left, a glowing green exit sign hung from the ceiling. Shaylinn slipped into the hall and ran towar exit sign. There was no door, but the hallway took a turn to the right, and Shaylinn could see another exit sign at the end of a shorter hall.

She ran to it and slammed her fist against the pad in hopes this door worked like the others. Slowly, it opened into a cool cement stairwell with steps going up and down. She ran down, winding around and around. She tired quickly, certain her heart was going to give out altogether.

Suddenly, she reached the bottom. Shaylinn paused to catch her breath and listen for footsteps behind her. Silence. Satisfied that she'd escaped, Shaylinn used her fist to open the final door.

She exited into the night and let the door close behind her. Buildings towered overhead, higher than any tree, so tall they blurred against the dark sky and made Shaylinn feel dizzy. She wandered forward, staring up at the structures, feeling like she was floating in outer space.

She was in the city. She'd always dreamed of coming inside. Now... where should she go? Which way was home?

A siren howled and faded in a breath, like some kind of electric bird call. Lights flooded the area, blinding her. She raised her arm to block the glare and stumbled back toward the exit door.

"Shaylinn Zachary?" a man's voice called. It sounded tinny and came from above her head.

She spun, pressed against the exit door, and tried to see who was out there. It was no use. The lights were too bright. She inched to the right, sliding along the door, then the wall of the building. *Please, God! Keep me safe.*

"Don't move," the voice warned.

But she couldn't stay there and let them impregnate her. On the count of three, she'd run. Once she got away from the lights, she'd be able to see. Then she could make a better decision of where to go. Anywhere had to be better than this building.

One... two... three!

Shaylinn ran blindly. Before her, the shape of a road materialized. But just as she sped toward it, she heard a buzz like the sound of a rattlesnake. Something pinched her hand, cramping every muscle, and she fell. Her face struck the ground. She told the rattlesnake to let go, but the words never came out. She couldn't move or speak or even breathe.

"Why you shells won't listen..." the voice said.

The next thing Shaylinn knew, she awoke to a man helping her out of the back of a car. When she stood, her limbs trembled. Her hands and face stung. Thick scrapes dotted with spots of blood covered both palms.

Tears stung her eyes, but she blinked them back. Shaylinn didn't cry. She was tough like her dad and Jordan, not girly like Jemma. She could get through whatever this was.

"Come on, femme. Let's get you back where you belong." The man was one of those enforcers, dressed in the dark blue uniform. He had pale, papery skin and a frizz of carrot-red hair. The patch on his uniform said *Ewan*.

Shaylinn followed Ewan through the revolving glass door of a building. The ceiling was so low she was sure it would fall down and crush her. The place was filled with various sitting areas of dark wood furniture cushioned in forest green brocade. Stiff carpet in a pattern of gold, blue, and orange covered the floor. Lights made of crystals dripped from the ceiling.

It was simultaneously ugly and beautiful.

There were people too, dressed in clothing that looked new and clean and strange. Quite a few wore combinations of black and pale yellow, making Shaylinn think of a room filled with swallowtail butterflies. A frail woman looked Shaylinn up and down with a gaze of surprise and disapproval. She wore a black fitted dress with a thick yellow belt, and her skin looked yellower than normal. The woman lifted a slender, black cylinder to her lips and blew out a plume of black smoke.

Smoking black things? No wonder the poor woman looked so unhealthy. Shaylinn was glad she'd refused Ciddah's pipe.

Ewan led Shaylinn to three sets of polished wooden doors evenly spaced along one wall. He pressed a button on the wall. A soft bell chimed, and one of the doors slid open.

"An elevator," Shaylinn whispered to herself.

Ewan raised his eyebrows and motioned her inside. She obeyed. Ewan followed her in and pressed the button with a number five on it, and soon the door glided closed. The floor didn't seem to move, though her body felt like it was being stretched upward. She set her hand on the wall. Was this the same building she'd escaped from? Were they going back?

Moments later, a queasy flutter ran through her stomach, and the door slid open, accompanied by the soft ding of the bell. Shaylinn trailed Ewan out into another wide hallway; this one had red and black swirly carpeting with gold accents. The ceiling was three times as high as the one downstairs and dripped with fancy crystal lights. The hallway led to a set of wide golden doors carved with an image of a creature with hooves that was a woman and a cat and a bird all at once.

Shaylinn didn't like her.

Ewan touched his fist to the wall, and when he pulled back his hand, Shaylinn saw the little black square on the wall beside the door.

Moments later, the door opened, and a tall, shapely woman looked down her nose like Shaylinn was rotten apples. She wore a silky purple jacket and skirt and black high-heeled shoes that made Shaylinn grin and blurt out, "I didn't know anyone still wore those."

The woman gripped the open door with one hand and held her other hand out to the side, a gold pipe as long and thin as one of Omar's paintbrushes tucked between her fingers.

"This the one you lost?" she asked Ewan.

"I didn't lose her, Matron. She ran off from the Surrogacy Center."

Matron frowned and looked Shaylinn over. "Praise Fortune they all don't look like her." She sucked on her paintbrush pipe and exhaled purple smoke in Shaylinn's face.

Shaylinn held her breath, expecting to choke, but there was no smokiness or smell at all to the purple cloud—simply moisture.

"Well, don't just stand there, outsider girl. Come in!"

Shaylinn stepped through the door and into a fairy-tale palace. She stood on white, plush carpet that was so very soft on her feet, nothing like the flat, stained rugs in Glenrock homes. The room was a humongous rectangle with a ceiling as high as the one in the hallway that was painted gold and dripping with gold and crystal lights. All kinds of little round tables of dark wood and fancy chairs and couches with red and gold cushions filled the space. Two doors took up the left wall. A stairway with a banister made of curling, polished wood stretched along the right wall with a landing halfway up and another one at the top. Straight ahead, a wall of glass scooped out in a half circle as tall as the ceiling and looked out over a green field.

Matron walked past Shaylinn with little steps, holding her arms bent at the elbows with her hands dangling as if they were wet and she didn't want to drip on her clothing.

"I've done the spiel already for all your ungrateful friends, so I'll be brief. If you have questions, ask your suitemates. Understood?"

What a grouch. "Yes, ma'am."

Matron rolled her eyes. "I'm twenty-seven years old. Do *not* call me ma'am. In fact, don't call anyone in the Safe Lands ma'am, *understood*?"

"Sorry," Shaylinn said.

Matron tossed her head and exhaled. "This is the harem, otherwise known as the home for women with a ticket to paradise. While you're conscripted here, you do not leave the harem unaccompanied. If you need anything, call Sona. She's the harem's housekeeper." Matron inhaled from her pipe and blew out a puff. "You're fortunate to be here. Minors are rarely admitted to the harem, but the task director general has made an exception for reasons he has not disclosed to me. Should you conceive, like your darling friend Naomi, you'll become an icon in the Safe Lands. Royalty among women."

She leveled an unfriendly glance at Shaylinn. "I understand you're one of the first to undergo the procedure. But from where I'm standing, it looks like we'll have to get you more than a makeover. More like a renovation." She chuckled and let it end in a singsong sigh. "Never fear. Our Tyra is a miracle worker. Believe it or not, I've seen her transform women much worse off than you."

This should have felt like a slap to the face, but the idea of a makeover thrilled Shaylinn more than she cared to admit even to herself.

"I'm Matron Dlorah, by the way. The administrator of this establishment." She took a long puff from her pipe and blew it into the air, looking at the far wall. "I'm not climbing those stairs again today, so you're on your own to find your room. I'd ask Sona to help, but she's run to the G.I.N.—an everything store of sorts—to buy blueberries. Naomi said they were her favorite. You're in the Blue Diamond Suite. It's on the second floor. Take the stairs halfway and go down the hall. Kendall Collin is your suite mentor, so Fortune's blessed you there if nowhere else. Off you go, then."

Shaylinn followed Matron's instructions and found her way to a door with a plaque proclaiming the room to be the Blue Diamond Suite. She was tired, and her hands and face hurt. She pressed her fist to the black square beside the door, and it swung inward, revealing a very pregnant teenage girl. Stunningly pretty, really, with golden brown hair, a peaches-and-cream complexion, and bright green eyes.

"Hello," the girl said. "You must be Shaylinn, yes?"

"I am."

"Shay!" The door jerked open wider, and Jemma pushed past the pregnant girl and gabbed Shaylinn in a fierce hug. "Oh, Shay! Thank God. I was so worried! Where have you been? What happened to your face?" Jemma let go and pulled Shaylinn inside. "Come in and sit. I'll get something to help you clean up."

Jemma dragged Shaylinn inside what seemed like a house. Everything was bright blue or white or polished wood. The carpet was the same soft white plush. There was a gleaming wooden table and chairs, a small kitchen that filled one side of the room, and a sheet of glass that took up most of one wall and was so thin it looked to be painted onto the surface. There were also two couches. Mia and Naomi were each sitting on a different one. Shaylinn was so relieved to see their familiar faces.

Jemma sat Shaylinn on the sofa beside their sister-in-law Naomi, who turned Shaylinn's chin from side to side. A pearly number eight on Naomi's cheek caught Shaylinn's gaze. Shaylinn looked to Jemma, who had the number four. Mia, a number eight. The pregnant teen who'd welcomed her had a number one.

"They put numbers on our faces and hands?" Shaylinn asked. "Like the enforcers?

"Everyone who lives here has them," Mia said.

Shaylinn looked at her hand. "There's a four on my face?"

"Just like me," Jemma said, sitting down and gently rubbing a wet cloth over Shaylinn's scraped cheek. It stung a little.

Naomi and Mia were cousins. "Because we're related?" Shaylinn asked.

"Maybe," Jemma said.

Shaylinn touched her other cheek. It felt a little swollen, but maybe it was just scraped up too. "What do you think they mean?" she asked her sister.

"I don't know." Jemma starting to wipe Shaylinn's right palm. "We didn't ask for the number, and if the Safe Landers have them, I worry they have some terrible meaning. Hopefully everything will be revealed soon."

"Shay, this is Kendall," Naomi said, referring to the pregnant girl. "She's very nice and has been trying to help us understand what goes on in this crazy place."

"Hi," Shaylinn said. "You're so pretty."

Kendall blushed. "They've done a lot of work on me."

"Really?" Shaylinn couldn't believe it. "You weren't so pretty before?"

"Well, I don't know." Kendall sat on a chair at the table. "They're very good at enhancing what you've got."

Mama used to say to use what God gave you. "Where's Mama?" Shaylinn asked Jemma.

"We figured they'd be in a different suite, but the only other people from Glenrock in the harem are Aunt Mary, Chipeta, Jennifer, and Eliza. They're in the Fire Opal suite, if you want to go talk to them."

"What about Penelope and Nell?"

Jemma started to clean Shaylinn's other hand. "What happened to you, Shay? Where have you been?"

The way her sister changed the subject made Shaylinn wonder what she wasn't saying. Shaylinn told them about waking in the medical room and how Ciddah said she'd get pregnant. And about running away and getting caught.

"That explains who was number one in their lineup," Mia said.

Shaylinn held up her hand. "No, I'm number four."

"Not *that* number," Mia said. "The number you are in line to have a baby. Matron told each of us our surrogacy number. Chipeta is six. I'm five. My mom is four. Jemma's three. Eliza is two."

"And I'm one," Shaylinn said. "Of course."

"They mean to force my baby sister to bear a child?" Jemma clapped her hand over her chest. "That's not acceptable. You're not old enough!"

"When I first heard the word *harem*, I panicked," Shaylinn said. "All I could think of was the harem in the book *Anna and the King of Siam.*"

"Such a good book," Jemma said.

"That's one reason I ran," Shaylinn said. "But when Matron explained the harem, it didn't seem like that at all. I don't understand."

"The people in the Safe Lands have trouble conceiving," Kendall said. "Living in the harem is meant to be an incentive; giving women a posh environment, not to mention fame, so they'll produce babies for the government. But lately every woman inside the walls has failed to bring an uninfected child to term. Even me."

"What does that mean—failed?" Shaylinn asked. "Your baby is going to die?"

"No. Just that both my baby and I have the thin plague."

Shaylinn looked to Jemma, suddenly chilled. "What Papa Eli warned us about."

"They were hoping that, since I was uninfected, my baby would be healthy too. But the plague infected both of us instead," Kendall said.

"I will *not* let this happen to you, Shay!" Jemma stood and marched between the couches. "We'll find a way out before this happens. And of course Levi will come for us."

"Who's Levi?" Kendall asked.

"My fiancé." Jemma fingered a necklace of small pink beads she was wearing around her neck, and her eyes filled with tears. "He's the Westley to my Princess Buttercup. We're to be married in two days." She sniffed and smiled.

"They're perfect for each other," Naomi said, grinning.

Mia rolled her eyes.

"Marriage doesn't exist in the Safe Lands," Kendall said. "Sometimes lifers pair up exclusively, which is sort of the same." She sighed. "There was a boy back home... Roger. He had golden hair that always hung down to his nose. I used to imagine we got married and that I kept his hair cut short enough so I could see his eyes."

"You're not from the Safe Lands?" Shaylinn asked.

"I'm from Casper," Kendall said. "That's in Wyoming."

"How can anyone live so far from the safe water source?" Naomi asked. "Elder Eli—he was our village leader. He always told us the only safe water was near Mount Crested Butte."

"There was a water bottling plant in Casper before the Great Pandemic," Kendall said. "The survivors lived off that for years until they invented a purifier that filters out the virus."

Shaylinn hadn't known that any other settlements existed. How many more might there be across the globe? "But if you can live there, why come to the Safe Lands?"

"My uncle traded me to drug lords, who traded me here."

"Betrayed by family," Jemma mumbled. "Just like us and Omar."

Shaylinn's heart tightened at the mention of Omar's name. "What do you mean?"

"Omar is responsible for everything that happened today," Naomi said.

Shaylinn couldn't breathe, but managed to ask, "How?"

Jemma shook her head. "I don't know. But when he and I arrived at the meeting hall, the enforcers knew him. And they gave him some fancy gold paper."

"A golden ticket," Kendall said. "That's what they call a special provision from the task director general himself. Still, I doubt this Omar is wholly responsible. They would have come for you at some point anyway. Most of the people who live inside these walls don't know how bad off things are. Since the government raises the children elsewhere, people tend to forget the kids even exist."

Wait. "They raise the children *where?*" Shaylinn asked.

"There are no families in the Safe Lands," Kendall said. "Children are raised by those tasked to caregiving. Older children live in the Safe Lands Boarding School."

"That's where they took Glenrock's children," Jemma said, meeting Shaylinn's gaze. "Penelope, Nell, the boys and girls—all of them. The babies went to a nursery."

"We about had a riot when we figured it out," Naomi said. "And half of us got shot with those electrical guns. We tried to start our own war, clawing and lashing out at the guards with whatever we could get our hands on. We lost."

"This battle only," Jemma said.

"Yeah, Eliza and Chipeta and Jennifer are probably plotting their next attack," Naomi said. "Mary just cries and cries."

Shaylinn wished she could cry. It was all too horrible to be real. Children taken from their parents? Forced pregnancies? She prayed for God's deliverance and protection, that Levi would come—along with her father and brother—and rescue them before she received Ciddah's summons. And she begged God that Jemma was wrong about Omar, that he'd had nothing to do with any of this.

It just couldn't be true. Could it?

Chapter 9

"You sure he's awake?" a man's voice asked. "We're practically carrying him."

Mason shivered. He opened his eyes, and a hallway came into focus. Halos of yellow light gleamed down on gray walls and a series of black doors. His feet moved across the floor as though disconnected from his body. He tried to stop his forward momentum, but someone jerked his arm.

"Keep moving, shell."

Mason blinked and fought the nausea roiling in his gut. Two enforcers were pulling him along. "Where are you taking me?" he asked, his voice raspy.

The enforcer on his right chuckled. "He speaks!"

"We're having some trouble with your peer, shell," the enforcer on his left said. "We want you to talk to him."

"My peer?"

The enforcers stopped in front of a black door with a silver number seven on it.

"We've had to stun him. Twice." The enforcer on Mason's right was thick with muscle. His face was thick too, with a wrinkled forehead, thick brows, and curly black hair. The name on his uniform proclaimed him Hale. "The task director general wants you and your peer in there to become nationals. When you agree, we'll take you to the Registration Department. Until then, welcome home."

The slender guy on Mason's left nudged him slightly. "Just calm him down enough so that we can explain things." His name tag read Bentzon. He somehow had gray camouflaged skin.

Mason blinked and squinted at Bentzon again. Still camouflage. As his vision cleared further, he also noticed the iridescent numbers on both men's right cheeks. Mason glanced up and down the hall. Both directions looked identical: black doors, gray walls, halo lights.

Where was he? The Safe Lands? Actually inside the compound?

"E72 to Highland Gatekeeper, requesting entry to holding cell seven," Hale said.

"Please verify identification," a muted woman's voice replied.

Mason examined the men, curious when he didn't see any radios. Where had the voice come from?

Hale set his fist against a black square on the wall next to the door. Bentzon lifted the side of Mason's hand against the square, then dropped it and held up his own.

"Identifications verified," the woman said.

The door clicked and swung inward.

"Here we go," Hale said.

"Let me out of here, you maggots!" Jordan yelled.

If Jordan was the man the enforcers thought would listen to Mason, they were in for a disappointment.

"We'll be back in ten, shell." Bentzon pushed Mason inside. The door clicked shut.

Mason reached for the handle but found none. He stood in a gray icebox with a concrete floor. He shivered and noticed for the first time that he wore a thin gray jumpsuit and black canvas slip-on shoes. Who had dressed him?

There were two metal chairs in the room. Jordan was bound to one. Shackles held his wrists to the sides of the chair, and a chain belt encircled his waist.

"Mason! Unhook me, quick!"

Mason stumbled to the chair and studied the shackles. "They're locked."

Jordan screamed and pulled against the bindings until his face flushed red and veins popped out on his neck.

Mason noticed a pale number four on Jordan's right cheek. The milky color seemed to move, as if the number were made of liquid that had been imbedded under transparent skin. "You have a number four on your face. How did that happen?"

Jordan stopped struggling and stared at Mason. "You have a number nine. And you tell me. What's with these people?" He yanked at his shackles again.

Finally, Mason's brain began recalling what had happened in the village. Gunfire. His father was dead. Uncle Colton too. Shaylinn had been hurt. Then Otley had shot Mason.

Mason perched on the edge of the other chair. "We're in the compound?"

"How'd you guess, genius?"

"What happened?"

"I woke up tied to a table in some hospital," Jordan said. "I yelled until the doctor came and untied me. Then I ran. They didn't like that. Some enforcers chased me and shot me with some kind of electrocution gun. Burned like mad. They brought me here, told me I was being given the great honor of becoming a national, and that my cooperation would save their pitiful city. When I tried to get away, they shot me again and hooked me to this chair. End of story. Why's it so cold?"

Mason located a vent in the ceiling. "Must be air-conditioning. Papa Eli told me about it. It used to be everywhere before the Pandemic." A bright yellow camera looked down from the corner of the ceiling. "They must have implanted the numbers while we were in the hospital."

"Pull me to the door," Jordan said.

"What?"

"Come on! Get me close."

Mason got up and dragged Jordan's chair over to face to door, cringing as the metal legs scraped over the floor. When Mason got him close enough, Jordan kicked the door.

"*Jordan.*"

He kicked the door again. "Open up, you bowels of a dead skunk!"

"Jordan, stop," Mason said.

But Jordan kicked again, growling this time.

Mason sat back down and watched Jordan assault the door. Jordan might be nineteen years old, but he had a tendency to act like he was five. "The enforcers are well aware of your displeasure."

"Good." Jordan lifted his feet and kicked the door so hard that his chair tipped back. It paused on two legs for one second before gravity won out. Mason winced as the chair slammed against the floor. Jordan kept his chin against his chest and managed to keep his head from hitting anything.

"Feel better?" Mason asked.

Jordan eased down his head. "No." He slammed his feet against the door, one at a time, like he was running.

What was he trying to accomplish? "You do realize the door swings inward?"

"Shut up, dog face."

So Mason did. He could think of nothing helpful to say anyhow. His pulse was still throbbing in his ears; it had been since the first gun had fired. Shock, no doubt. His body trying to compensate for the horror of seeing so many killed. He thought over the five stages of grief he'd read about in his psychology book. How could shock not be one of them? And when would he start denying that any of this had taken place? "Why kill some of us, but not all? I don't understand."

Jordan let his legs fall limp and turned his head, craning his neck and rolling his eyes up so he could see Mason. "Think she's okay?" he asked, his voice a low croak.

Mason didn't know if Jordan meant one of his sisters, his mother, or his wife.

"I mean, she's already pregnant. So they wouldn't hurt her, right?"

Ah, Naomi, his wife. "You saw them take the women?" Mason asked.

"The enforcer said the women were going to bear children for the Safe Lands. Do you think *all* of the women? And *whose* children?"

Mason cringed. Surely, they didn't intend to force the women... Only monsters would do such a thing. Almost as unsettling: the Safe Lands enforcers, though violent with their gunfire today, hadn't bothered Glenrock in seventy years. Why now? And why were he and Jordan so important?

Mason thought through what had happened. "The last thing I remember... Papa Eli!" *Please, Lord, let someone have helped him.* Mason looked at his hands. They were clean. No blood. "Someone washed my hands." He held one out to Jordan. "I was trying to stop Papa Eli's bleeding when I got shot." His eyes stung, his vision clouded. He coughed and sucked in a breath.

"Hey!" Jordan said. "None of that. We have to keep it together. My dad's dead too, but do you see me crying? Huh? We've got to get out of this place, find the others. As hard as it is... buck up."

Elder Harvey dead too? "What if there are no others? And why not kill us?"

"When they were loading the women and kids into a truck, I heard an enforcer say they wanted the young people."

"But why?" All Mason truly knew of Safe Landers was that they were inflicted with a terminal disease that stemmed from the original virus that had entered the world's water supply and caused the Great Pandemic. According to the stories Papa Eli had told, the Safe Lands had started as a haven for the uninfected because of the clean water coming from the mountain. But when the waterborne strain mutated into a bloodborne one and Safe Lands leaders neglected the warnings from doctors, many people left, which was how the outlying villages had come to exist, keeping close to the clean water, but far from Safe Lands' dangers. Papa Eli had warned the people of Glenrock never to marry a Safe Lands national or they'd become infected.

"If they hurt Naomi," Jordan said. "If they hurt my boy..."

"What makes you so certain your child is male?"

Jordan flubbed his lips. "It's a boy."

Mason smiled. It was a bit forced, but even a half-hearted smile felt good at this point. "If you say so."

Reality suddenly hung heavily on Mason's heart, and his eyes stung. He needed to think. The enforcers would be coming back soon. One had told Jordan that the women would bear children for the Safe Lands. Why? And what were the men to do?

"Think Levi's dead?" Jordan asked.

The very idea brought another smile to Mason's lips. "No way. Not Levi."

Jordan straightened his neck and gazed at the ceiling. "He'll come for us, then. And when he does, we're going to kill them all."

Mason had no doubt his big brother would bring fire and brimstone upon this place, but he searched for the right words to curb talk of more death. "That will only make you just like them."

"Don't turn into Papa Eli on me right now, Mason. Just leave me to my murderous daydreams, will you?"

The door opened, whacking against the side of Jordan's chair. Two people entered: Hale and Otley, the giant pierced bat who'd killed Mason's father and uncle and Papa Eli.

But Papa Eli had shot him in the chest. He should be dead.

"How?" Mason stood, fists clenched, heart throbbing. "Papa Eli shot you."

"Takes more than one round to take me out, rat," Otley said.

Jordan kicked Otley's leg. "Where is my wife, you son of a cockroach's vomit?"

Hale drew his gun, and Jordan stopped kicking.

Otley bent over Jordan. "Your woman's in the harem, rat. I intend to visit her myself."

Jordan's face went red in the space of a breath. "If you *touch* her... If you even *breathe* on her..."

"You'll chase after me, and I'll stomp on you." Otley smacked Jordan's face softly—slap, slap, slap—then walked to the door and turned. "Last chance for compliance, rats. Become Safe Lands nationals. Give us what we need to create healthy children. Refuse, and you'll be sent to the rehabilitation center. You have ten minutes to decide." He ducked out the open doorway, and Hale followed, closing the door behind him.

Jordan screamed and pulled against his restraints, cursing and kicking until he ran out of breath.

Mason sank onto his chair. "I think we should comply."

Jordan turned his head to glare at Mason. "Are you crazy?"

"Our best chance is to play along and see what they want."

"I will *not* become one of them," Jordan said.

Mason took a deep breath. "We're not one of them—ever. But we can pretend to be. We can't do anything from in here."

"If I can get that enforcer's gun, I could get us free."

"You're secured to a chair, lying on the floor, Jordan. You can't get anyone's gun."

"I could get it."

Mason's father had always admired such foolish brawn over thoughtful logic. Mason glanced quickly at the camera then lowered himself to the ground and whispered in Jordan's ear. "Listen to me. Violence against these people will only lead us to our graves. We have to think." Mason inched a little closer. "Playing along will give us a chance at freedom inside these walls. Then we can find out where the women and children are being held, where to get weapons, and how we might escape."

"You're a coward!" Jordan yelled. "You've always been a coward, ever since Joel died."

The words sent fire through Mason's chest. "I sat by your brother's side until his last breath. The rest of you ran off to kill something. So, who was the coward, Jordan?"

Jordan's voice came softly. "You used to hunt with us. You used to eat meat."

Mason clenched his teeth, then finally said, "*Don't* start this. I never liked to hunt. I'm not a killer. It was that way long before the accident."

Jordan turned his head so he could see Mason. "Naomi would've married him. You know that? She and Joel were close."

Mason huffed a silent laugh. "They both liked to climb trees."

"The kissing trees."

"Jordan, stop." But Mason closed his eyes, thinking of the one time he'd climbed those trees with a girl. Eliza. He'd been so young. He still felt bad about how things had ended between them. He shuddered at the memory.

Jordan's voice softened. "Sometimes I think, what if he'd lived? If he'd lived, then I wouldn't have her. So I'm glad he'd dead, right, Mason? My own brother. I'm glad."

Mason squeezed his eyes tight before opening them. "You're *not* glad he's gone. You're thankful to be blessed with a good wife. That's different."

"I'd die without her. I can't live without her. What if these maggots do something to her?" Jordan broke down this time. No kicking the door. Just sobbing.

"Hey," Mason stood and heaved Jordan's chair up, grunting with the effort. Once the chair was on all fours, he walked around front. "You said no crying. You told me to buck up."

The door opened. Otley and Hale entered the room. Mason backed against the wall, fighting the urge to run at Otley. *Anger won't help. Anger won't help.*

But Jordan kicked at Otley with renewed vigor. "Why don't you untie me, fight me man to man, you doe-kissing, dog-licking pile of fish guts—you coward!"

Hale drew his gun and fired. Jordan uttered a short cry, then his body went rigid. No bullets. No wires or rays. Yet Jordan lay silent and limp. How?

Hale unhooked Jordan, kicked the metal chair aside, and dragged him by the ankles out the door. The last Mason saw of his brother's best friend was his fingertips trailing around the doorframe.

Bentzon stepped into the doorway, stunning gun pointed at Mason.

"And you, little rat?" Otley asked, looking down on Mason. "Going to the rehabilitation center as well?"

"No." Mason had to do what he felt was right. He couldn't help anyone Jordan's way. "I'll cooperate."

Otley motioned to Bentzon in the doorway. "Take him to Registration."

Bentzon waved his gun at Mason. "Let's go, shell."

Mason walked into the hallway. No sign of Jordan. He wanted to ask where they'd taken him but thought better of it. His words and actions needed to look compliant.

It was time to join the Safe Lands.

Chapter 10

Bentzon transported Mason to a building the guard referred to as City Hall. On the third floor, they entered the Men's Health and Wellness Department and went strait to the Donation Center. A guard gave Mason a plastic cup, then sent him into a small room with a shower-like stall and sink. Mason paced as he tried to figure out why he'd been brought here. Bentzon hadn't given any hint as to what happened at the Donation Center, like he assumed Mason already knew. Based on what Jordan had said about the Glenrock women needing to bear children, Mason reasoned the Donation Center was the male's version of the harem.

Mason remembered something his mother once said: that, in the Old Days, doctors had been able to use different scientific methods to impregnate a woman. Such procedures had been lost over time, but Mason had read in one of Mother's medical textbooks about surrogacy, artificial insemination, and in vitro fertilization. Could the Safe Lands have regained that lost knowledge?

Mason looked again at the cup in his hands. He couldn't do it.

The cup was opaque, so he put a little water inside and spit into it, then snapped on the lid and hoped it would be enough to get him out of the center. He carried the cup to a man at the front desk, then the enforcer led him to the elevator.

Mason held his breath as he and the enforcer waited. Surely, any moment, the man would discover Mason's cheat. To his relief, the elevator arrived, and Bentzon pushed him inside.

Mason was escorted down to the second floor Registration Department, an open room with a counter at one end and a dozen desks to the left of it.

The man at the counter had yellow and black striped hair. "I'm Dallin. I need to take your picture before we start. Can you back up against that wall and stand on those black footprints?"

Mason saw no reason to refuse. Dallin used a rectangle of glass to snap a picture, then returned to his desk. "Have a seat."

Mason sat and tried to relax. If someone was coming to capture him for his faulty sample, they likely would have arrived by now. Acting like a nervous wreck wouldn't gain him much acceptance amidst these strange people. "Um, Dallin, how did your hair get that way?"

"The To Dye For salon," Dallin said. "He comes up with the best mimic looks. Now, I'm going to work up your identification, then you'll take the task test, which will determine your schedule. Since you're new to all this, let me explain. Each national must perform a task to help our city operate—a basic job we assign based on your test performance. We understand some tasks are desired over others, but all must be done to ensure the pleasure and survival of each national. Your test will generate a list of several tasks you're suited for, and you'll work each task for a six-month shift before rotating to the next on your list. After three years, you can retest and see if your list changes. If you find you love a certain task, you can apply to prolong your assignment in that area, but there's no guarantee your request will be approved. Do you understand?"

"Yes, sir," Mason said.

Dallin set a little black pad on the counter. "Press your right fist on the pad." When Mason did, Dallin took away the pad and asked, "Do you have a last name?"

"Our people identify with tribes. I'm from the Elias tribe."

"How about we make Elias your last name? Unless there's another name you'd prefer."

"Elias is fine."

"Okay." Dallin tapped on his computer screen, which was nothing more than a sheet of glass on an elevated base. He turned the glass so that Mason could see the surface. Mason's picture, name, and number appeared like on TV screen. The words *task*, *task director*, *task start date*, *region*, and *residence* were displayed below.

"This will all get filled in after you task test," Dallin said. "I'm all done here, so you can sit at any station to test. Go ahead."

Mason moved to the nearest desk. The surface was black glass. Mason looked back to Dallin, not sure what he was supposed to do.

"It's a GlassTop touchscreen," Dallin said, coming over beside Mason. He tapped the screen with his finger. A picture slowly faded from black into a bright blue. The words *TaskTest 6.0* hovered in a white rectangle in the center of the screen. Dallin touched it with his finger, and the screen changed to a series of blanks.

"Tap the screen to type in your name and number and to answer each question."

"Thank you," Mason said, marveling at the machine. Clearly, the Safe Landers had managed to hold on to a lot of technology from the Old Days.

The test was multiple choice with questions about cooking, drawing, architecture, machines, cleaning, driving, and teaching. Some questions Mason needed Dallin to explain before he could answer.

Around question thirty, the test became more specific, as if the computer were starting to learn Mason's interests. Most questions were now medical or mathematical in nature. Mason didn't understand most of the math questions.

When he expected question sixty-eight to appear, the screen displayed *TaskTest complete. Please report to your test director.*

Mason returned to Dallin's desk.

"All done?"

"Yes, sir."

Dallin tapped around on his glass screen. "Huh," he said. "You're a smart guy. Got a list of high-level tasks here, but the system flagged you since you're an outsider. That means the task director general will have to approve your task list. That doesn't happen very often." He looked at Mason, then spoke to the enforcers, who were practically dozing in the waiting area. "Why don't you take him to the cafeteria while I figure out what to do?"

Mason followed the enforcers to a vast room packed with people, noise, and savory smells. The enforcers took him through a line where he had to press his fist against another black pad before someone operating a glass screen would let him pass. Mason examined the side of his fist and found a small puncture, bloodless. Some sort of implant?

The food was set out in long metal trays. There were many choices, even for a vegetarian. Mason chose foods he recognized: green salad, peas, biscuits, sweet potatoes, rice, and two slices of pie—apple and one made of gooey nuts. When he finished eating, the enforcers took him to the tenth floor where he was sent in to meet the task director general.

Mason entered a modern palace decorated in black and red with hardwood floors and windows that wrapped around three walls, exposing a vast view of the valley below. Mason felt like he was walking among the clouds.

A large desk sat in front of the only true wall. A bald man stood beside it, blocking Mason's view of the man seated there. Mason closed the door behind him, drawing the bald man's attention.

"Well, Hay-o, Mr. Elias," the man said, walking toward him. "My name is Kruse." He extended his hand, and Mason shook it. "Come meet the task director general, Lawten Renzor."

The man behind the desk was slender with a hunched posture and a large nose that was flaking badly. His dark and protruding eyes instantly unsettled Mason. They seemed too eager, too knowing.

"This is Mason Elias, the smart one." Kruse winked at Mason.

Kruse's behavior startled Mason, but he forced himself to stay focused on the task director. This man ruled the Safe Lands. The murderer Otley answered to him. If Mason's people were to have any chance, he needed to find some way of negotiating with this man. "It's nice to meet you, sir."

The task director nodded in greeting, then motioned for Mason to sit on a red leather chair. Mason complied.

"Your test results show you to be a clever young man, Mr. Elias," the task director said.

"Thank you, sir."

"He's so polite!" Kruse said. "Let him task for me. I could use an assistant who doesn't complain."

With no reaction to Kruse at all, the task director said, "I'd like to place you as a medic."

"I don't know enough to be a doctor." Working with the medical staff, though, might give him access to some valuable information.

"Which is why you'll task as an assistant to a lower-level lead medic. In six months, when you rotate, we could also place you in low-level research. Would you like that?"

Mason had no plans to be within the compound by the time the next rotation came around. "What kind of research?"

"Medical, of course."

The idea sent a thrill through Mason. Of course he'd love to study medical research. He reminded himself that his priority was helping the people of Glenrock.

"That said, while your test results were impressive, I have two concerns," the task director said. "First, your education. You learned from outsiders and may not understand our medical procedures. This, however, can be taught. My second concern is honesty. You're smart enough to know what the donation cup was for and either pretended not to know or thought you could lie to us. Now, *I'd* be the fool if I placed a dishonest man in a sensitive position, don't you agree?"

Well, Mason had figured he'd be caught at some point. "You would, sir."

"Then why should I allow you to task as a medic and not send you to sweep the streets?"

Mason took a deep breath—if the task director wanted honesty, he would have it. "Because I'm not a violent man. I've only ever wanted to save lives. I'm also a cautious man. You asked me to do something I didn't fully understand. To fulfill a role I hadn't agreed to take on. I learned many things while I was in my village, and have plenty of common sense, but until I grasp an adequate understanding of your ways, don't expect me to conform. I'm willing to learn, but not willing to be forced."

Lawten's dark eyes stared back. "It's quite simple. Male nationals are required to leave a donation once a month. What will it take for you to comply?"

All male nationals? "Explain why I must do this. Why it's so important." Mason couldn't very well come up with an alternative solution unless he understood the problem.

The task director chuckled, a wheezing sound that made the folds of skin on his neck twitch. "You want full disclosure, is that it?"

"I think it's only fair."

The task director turned to Kruse. "Place him in his fifth option, as a level two medic under Ciddah Rourke. And schedule a meeting with Ciddah so I can explain." He turned to Mason. "Ms. Rourke is a Level Nine Medic in the Surrogacy Center. They deal mostly with reproductive appointments, so you'll have access to our process, which should answer most of your questions. And since they're located in City Hall, they also arrange private medical appointments for people in my office, so you will also get to do regular first aid, see how simple procedures differ from those in your village. Ask whatever questions you like, though I suggest you watch your tone. I'll make sure Ciddah knows you've been given permission to look into how things operate in the facility."

Having that much free rein in the Surrogacy Center was more than Mason had dared hope for, though he wished the task director would have answered his questions outright. Yet the fact that he had not been taken to the Rehabilitation Center—whatever that was—with Jordan told him that he had value here. He could use that to his advantage.

"Thank you," Mason said. "I appreciate your giving me this chance to learn."

"I'll be watching you, Mr. Elias. Don't give me reason to doubt your sincerity."

Mason entered the Surrogacy Center's reception area and, as he had been doing all day, approached a desk. Unlike the other buildings he'd seen, the floors, walls, and ceiling here were sterile white.

A full-figured woman with pale yellow skin and spiky black hair sat behind the desk. She was tapping on her GlassTop while talking to herself. "Will Friday the second work?"

Mason stopped before the desk. "Excuse me. How do you make your skin yellow?"

The woman looked up, and her eyes bulged. She held up a finger. "Great. You're all set then." She tapped on the image of a keypad on her desk, made it disappear, then looked up at Mason. "*Hay-o, Valentine*. How can I help you?"

"Um, you could answer my question about your skin." Mason could feel himself turning warm. Of all the things to ask, and he had to ask twice. He should instead ask who she'd been speaking to.

"Oh, it's Roller Paint. I've been doing yellow along with Luella Flynn. Kind of getting tired of it, though. She's coming in here today, you know. Filming another check-up with Kendall Collin. It's getting close to Kendall's delivery." Her gaze traveled down his body.

Mason frowned, understanding little of her answer. "I'm here to task with Ciddah Rourke. The task director general sent me. Are you Miss Rourke?"

The woman cackled, her mouth so wide Mason could see her the back of her throat. "I'm Rimola. I task in reception. But I am *so* glad you're here. Not only are you yummy to look at, now I won't have rotate to a task where I need to take vitals or stock the rooms with— You're going to be here every week for six months, right?"

Mason fumbled for the sheet of paper Dallin had given him. "I suspect that is the Registration Department's intention for me." Though Mason planned to be back in Glenrock long before then.

Rimola gasped. "Are you an outsider?"

"I'm not from the Safe Lands, no."

She reached out. "Can I shake your hand?"

Mason extended his arm. Rimola clasped his hand and pulled him toward her, rubbing her thumb and fingers over his skin. "Fortune be praised, you're soft! I heard outsiders were rough and leathery."

Mason pulled free and stepped back from the desk. "Miss Rimola, I... well... Please let Ciddah Rourke know that I've arrived." He walked to the farthest chair from the desk and sat down.

Rimola tapped her fingers over her GlassTop and spoke to someone through what must be an ear device, though Mason could see none.

He tried to ignore her and spent the time focusing on ways he could use this opportunity to help his people, even praying at one point that God would show him what to do. This position could bring him closer to the information he sought.

"Mason Elias?"

Halfway between Rimola's desk and where Mason sat stood an angel. This young woman was achingly pretty, more so than even Mia. She had long, golden hair, creamy skin, and huge, sapphire-blue eyes. Once Mason tore his gaze away from her face, he noticed she wore scrubs, like nurses and doctors of Old. They were solid purple, and while most people likely drowned in such baggy clothes, this woman made them look like a former ensemble.

He stood to greet her. She was short and curvy and perfect. He shook the thought away.

"I'm Ciddah Rourke. You can call me Ciddah."

She stuck out her hand, and he took it, pleased for an invitation to touch such a lovely woman. Suddenly, he wasn't quite as offended with Rimola for her actions as he let his fingers hold on a little longer than was likely appropriate.

"Why don't you come on back, Mason, and I'll give you a tour. Luella Flynn is coming in today, so we won't have much time." Ciddah pulled her hand free and walked toward the reception desk.

Mason followed, kicking himself for behaving like a fool. He didn't have time to be drooling over any woman, especially a Safe Lands national. He needed to focus.

Ciddah showed him the exam rooms, the supply room, and the restrooms. Everything was white and gray and spotless, with the exception of the yellow security cameras in the hallway and reception area. Next, Ciddah led him to her office. It too was white and gray, though portraits of bright flowers hung on the walls, the images changing every few seconds to different flowers. Despite the stark walls, the place looked like a dog had chased a squirrel through it. Mason could barely see a desk and three chairs under a mess of scattered papers and stacks of handheld computer screens. Wads of paper lay on the floor around the trashcan. The only thing he didn't see within the office was a security camera.

Ciddah whisked a stack of papers off a chair in front of her desk. "Take a seat."

Mason sat on the edge of the chair, and resisted the urge to straighten the stack of handheld computers on the desk in front of him.

Ciddah lifted one of the computers off the stack and handed it to Mason. It was about six by eight inches and quite light. She stood beside him and regarded it. "This is a CompuChart," she said. "Any data you input under a national's ID goes straight to his or her file on the grid. That way, we have each patient's history at our fingertips."

Mason studied the screen. "Convenient."

"Yes, well, you start by inputting a national's ID. I'll use mine as an example." Ciddah set her hand on his shoulder and reached over him with her other arm; he was extremely aware of her side brushing against his. She smelled like vanilla and cinnamon.

She set her fist against the glass, and the screen flashed to a new page. Across the top, the it said *NAME: Ciddah Rourke; DOB: 5-2-2069; AGE: 19*

"The ID will bring up the national's information and histories: medical, obstetrical, gynecological, genetic, social, allergies, medications and—"

"Luella Flynn is here." Rimola's voice came from somewhere on Ciddah's desk.

Ciddah sighed and moved a pile of papers, revealing a small black speaker. She pressed a button. "Show them to exam room three. I'll be right there." She took the CompuChart from Mason. "Thank Fortune there won't be many more of these silly visits. Luella—she's famous, in case you don't already know. She's been coming in almost constantly to film ColorCast specials on Kendall's pregnancy. The nationals have a fascination with our queens. Once Kendall delivers, they'll start focusing on Naomi, since she's due next. I've arranged it so you'll replace me as the medical consultant for those little spectacles."

"Replace you? But I don't know how to—"

"Don't worry. I'll make sure you know what to say. I just abhor being on the ColorCast. And Safe Landers will love that our new queen wants her friend as her medic. Come on."

Mason could not be Naomi's medic. Jordan would never approve. He followed Ciddah out of the office, not understanding what Ciddah had meant about ColorCast until they reached exam room four.

Bright lights spilled out the door. Mason shielded his eyes as he followed Ciddah into the sweltering room. Powerful bulbs and a camera were focused on the exam table where a young pregnant girl lay, looking bored and hot. A woman stood beside her. She had short, spiral burgundy curls clipped with a sparkly flower, and she wore a burgundy pants suit.

"How's the lighting, Byran?" the cameraman asked, though Mason saw no other men.

"Luella?" Ciddah called from the doorway. "We're here."

"Hay-o!" Luella sang. "Make way for the medics!"

The cameraman stepped aside so that Ciddah and Mason could squeeze into the end of the room, which felt more like an oven than the doorway had.

"We're live in sixty!" the cameraman said.

"You're Mason, is that right?" Luella asked.

Mason nodded, captivated by the thickness of the makeup on Luella's face.

"Well, speak, Valentine, so we can get your voice on the boom. Have you met Kendall?"

"No," Mason said.

Luella fixed Mason with a glare. "Speak more than that!"

"Sorry. No, I have not met Kendall. Hello, Kendall," Mason said.

Kendall giggled. "Hello, Mason."

"Marvelous! Byran? We'll need to do makeup and wardrobe on Mason in the future. He's looking a little drab." She turned to Mason. "But you've got a face viewers will love, trigger. Kendall's shows bring in seventy-two percent female viewers."

Luella touched her ear and said, "Will do." She took hold of Mason's arm and pulled him around the end of the exam table. "Byran wants you on Ciddah's left, just behind the foot of the table... That's right. How we sound, Byran?"

"Do I have to speak?" Mason asked.

"No, trigger," Luella said. "In fact, don't speak unless you're spoken to. This is just a facial for you. We want the audience to get used to seeing you on screen."

"Ten seconds!" the cameraman said.

Mason wanted to ask if Kendall was in labor, but didn't dare speak after Luella's instructions. He caught Kendall looking his way, and her friendly smile eased his nervousness somewhat. No wonder Ciddah didn't want to do this. Mason already wanted to run out of the room.

"In five, four, three, two..." The cameraman pointed at Luella.

Luella came to life, talking directly into the camera. "I'm live at the Surrogacy Center with Kendall Collin for her very last routine check-up." She turned and set her hand on Kendall's belly. "Tell us, Kendall, are you in labor?"

Kendall laughed a little. "I don't think so. Ciddah says I'll know if it happens, so... I guess not."

"Are you excited or scared or nervous, or all three?"

"Kind of all three," Kendall said, her smile now looking a bit forced.

Luella turned back to the camera. "Medic Ciddah Rourke is training Mason Elias today in how to listen to the baby's heartbeat. We've heard our boy's heart dozens of times, but, Ciddah, tell us how this miracle machine works."

Ciddah's face flushed, but she lifted what looked like a thick blanket off a table behind her. "This is a mimeo imager," Ciddah said, draping it over Kendall's belly. "We use it to take pictures of the baby and to find the heartbeat. It's programmed to this exam room's Wyndo." She turned to a blue screen of glass that covered half the wall and tapped the word *audio*. "Hear that?" Whirring came from a speaker in the ceiling. "That's the placenta's blood flow. That's good." A pattering, like a distant, galloping horse, replaced the whir. "There's our boy."

Several seconds passed as they listened to the baby's heartbeat.

"That's fascinating," Mason said, amazed.

"Simply magical!" Luella exclaimed, turning back to look into the camera. "Stay tuned for our continuing coverage of Kendall Collins' delivery week. We'll be shopping for new clothes, helping her pack her hospital bag, meeting her surgeon, and talking more with Ciddah Rourke about the entire process. Until then, Safe Lands, find pleasure in life."

"Clear," the cameraman said.

Luella sighed. "Don't speak means don't speak, Mason. I know this is your first day and all, but we're going to have to work on that mouth of yours if you're going to be our new medic." Luella raised her eyebrow at Mason, then strode out the door. "Bye-o, peers!"

Mason cheeks burned. He didn't want to be their new medic. He had work to do, and this, while intriguing, had been a waste of time. The lights, blessedly, went out, which instantly cooled the air. The cameraman started to pack his gear.

"Now that *that's* over," Ciddah said. "How's our queen?"

Kendall wiped the corner of her eye. "Just a little emotional."

"I can give you something for that." Ciddah picked up a CompuChart from the counter and tapped on it. "Be sure and tap me right away if you feel any contractions, Kendall."

"What will the delivery be like?" Kendall asked.

"The surgeon and I will meet you at the Treatment Center next Monday morning. Luella will be there with her cameraman, as there's no way they'll miss the birth. I'll be the one to put you under; you won't feel a thing. Before you know it, you'll wake up in the Recovery Center. And that's that. Nothing to worry about."

They were going to film the delivery? "How can the mother be unconscious during labor?" Mason asked.

"She won't go into labor if we can help it," Ciddah said. "We scheduled a C-section."

Mason had read about that procedure. "Is the baby breech? Or is this because of the plague?"

Both women looked at him as if he had twelve eyes.

"All births are C-section in the Safe Lands, Mason," Ciddah said. "It makes everything easier."

"But I get to see him, right? After recovery?" Kendall asked.

Ciddah's forehead wrinkled. "Of course not, Kendall. You should know that."

"The task director promised, when I agreed to do all the shots with the cameras," Kendall said, her voice growing soft.

Ciddah frowned and shook her head. "I wasn't informed of this, Kendall. I'll have to check with his office."

Tears ran down Kendall's face, and soon she was outright sobbing.

Mason just stood there, shocked. "Why can't she see her baby?"

Ciddah narrowed her eyes at Mason, and in a harsh voice whispered, "It's not Kendall's baby. It belongs to all of us. And don't you say another thing that might encourage her to think otherwise." She tapped on her CompuChart again, and her tone returned to its former pleasantness. "I'll prescribe you some more meds, Kendall."

"I don't want more meds!" Kendall yelled. "I want my sorrow. I need it!"

Ciddah's face paled. "You *want* to hurt?"

"Better than numbing myself. And I don't want meds for the procedure. If I stay awake through the delivery, I'll get to see my baby before you take him away."

"Now, Kendall, many surrogates experience depression at some level. In fact, what I think would be best is for you to—"

"What *you* think is best?" Kendall sat up and swung her legs off the table. "You've never given birth, have you? Have you ever even been pregnant?"

Ciddah inched back a step, her eyes misty. "I— My body rejects the process."

"When I got here, they told me I would be happy, that pregnancy would be a wonderful experience. Well, they were wrong!" Kendall screamed. "I should get to *keep* my baby!"

Ciddah rubbed her eyes. "But it's not your baby, Kendall. He belongs to—"

"He's part me. He's half mine!"

Ciddah chuckled and tipped her head to the side. "You can't own a human being."

"He needs me!" Kendall's bottom lip trembled. "And I need him."

"That's ridiculous." Ciddah walked to Kendall's side and touched her shoulder. "What good would you do him? Your tasks have primarily been messaging. You've had no training in raising—"

"I could manage."

"If you have an interest in working with children, why not file a task interest form with the Registration Department and retest?"

"Just check with the task director, okay, Ciddah? He *promised* I could hold my baby."

Ciddah sighed, as if Kendall's request was a terrible inconvenience. "Okay, I'll check." She walked to the door, reached for the pad, missed, then turned and opened it. "I'll leave that prescription with Rimola." And she left, the door closing softly behind her.

Mason had stayed perfectly still throughout the outburst, and wasn't sure he dared move even now.

Kendall eased off the exam table, a hand pressed against her swollen belly. She glanced at Mason, her face streaked with tears. "What they do is wrong," she said, her voice a whisper.

Mason nodded. He could hardly believe what he'd just witnessed.

Ciddah had said, *Once Kendall delivers, they'll start in with Naomi*. The Safe Lands intended to remove Naomi's child too—a baby that was definitely not theirs to take. He had to find a way to help her—as well as the women of Glenrock, whether they were pregnant or not. Perhaps he was meant to be in this position. He might be the only chance any of them had.

When Ciddah dismissed Mason for the day, he followed the instructions he'd been given at registration and found his assigned apartment on the fifth floor of a building named Westwall. As much as he hated to admit, the place was incredibly nice, and the idea of living there even for a while excited him. The open room was divided by a partial wall that Mason could walk circles around. The front half held the entry, living, dining, and kitchen areas. A counter ran along the center wall and had a parallel island. The bedroom and bath were on the other side of the partial wall. A low, king-size bed sat against the other side of the kitchen.

The place had light blue walls, a white marble floor, and black cupboards, appliances, and trim. Pictures of black and white trees in black frames hung on the walls throughout the apartment, changing every few seconds like the flowers had in Ciddah's office. The tables and furniture were light sandy-colored wood. A wall of windows in the living room looked out into the city. Best of all, there were no security cameras.

As much as he wanted to linger inside his temporary home, he went back out and wandered the area the doorman of his building referred to as the Highlands. It didn't take him long to find the harem, which had been built in the center of town like some kind of fortress.

Mason stared at it for quite some time. It looked like getting out of the Safe Lands was going to be a lot harder than getting in.

Chapter 11

Omar found the Registration Department on the second floor of City Hall, but was told he first needed to visit the Men's Health and Wellness Department on the third floor. There, Omar received a humiliating physical examination and two SimTag implants, one on his right cheek and one on the back of his right fist, which were injected with a gun-like medical device. Both tags showed a number nine, and both itched fiercely. The medic also noticed Omar's sniffling and gave him an injection he said would clear it right up. Then the medic sent Omar to the Donation Center. Omar had known this part was coming—the requirement had been reiterated to him several times since he'd arrived.

That knowledge didn't mean it was something he'd been looking forward to. After an awkward fifteen minutes, he changed into his new enforcer uniform. He stood before the bathroom sink mirror and took in his new appearance. The navy blue fabric was so much softer than his Old clothes, and it had no odor. And the enforcer hat was better than his Colorado Patrol hat. He liked the way he looked in uniform, even though the number nine on his cheek seemed to whisper the word *traitor* in the back of his mind.

He returned to the Registration Department on the second floor, as he'd been instructed. A man named Dallin sat behind a counter. To the left was an open space filled with desks. Dallin's black and yellow hair was amazing, and Omar imagined drawing him with insect wings.

"Have a seat, and I'll work up your ID," Dallin said.

Omar sat at a desk and waited. He could now see Dallin from the neck up only. "How do they decide what number we get?"

"Our blood reveals to the Liberators which life we're in. A number one marks the first life. Nine marks the last. I'm a three, so I have six more lives before I reach *La Vie Dixième*. Most outsiders get low numbers. Your nine is shocking."

It was? "So I'm in my last life? What does *that* mean?"

"Just that you're nearly to the tenth life. So you should make this life count. Don't do anything foolish. Earn as much good fortune as you can. Also, according to the Liberators, pairing up with anyone from your own life number angers Fortune—so stay away from other nines so you don't mess up your future lives."

Oh-kay. "So the tenth life is heaven?"

"Some call it that." Dallin slid a handheld computer, like the one Kruse used, on the counter and twirled it in a half circle. A picture of Shaylinn's fat face filled the glass. "I need you to verify any romantic relationships between these women and men, including yourself." Dallin swiped his finger across the glass a few times, and the pages turned. "Keep flipping through until you get to the end. Tap each face and type in the relationship."

Omar picked up the device, which had the word *Wyndo* etched across the top. His mother's face now stared at him from the glass, looking tired and sad but hard as always. She'd had to be tough to survive marriage to Justin of Elias. Omar wondered where she was now, which made his eyes sting.

"Why must I look at these pictures?" he asked.

"We need to know if there are any pairings."

"This is my mother." Omar set his finger on his mother's picture, and a list of letters appeared over his mother's face. He touched each letter until he wrote *mother*, then pressed the word "Done." The letters vanished, and the word *mother* was now visible under her picture. He took a deep breath and flipped to the next page, which held Naomi's image. "Naomi is Jordan's wife. They're expecting a child sometime this fall." He wrote Jordan's name below Naomi's picture. "What will you do with the women?"

"Most will serve a term in the harem and, should Fortune bless them, bear children for the Safe Lands. Then they'll task and play like the rest of us."

Omar thought of his fifteen minutes in the Donation Center and nearly choked. "They'll be bearing *my* children? All of the women?"

"Not necessarily. All men donate—it's Safe Lands law."

Omar paged back to where he'd left off, but his hand had started to shake. Clenching it into a fist, he reminded himself he had to complete this last thing then he'd be free to find his new home and go with Skottie to the dance club. He forced himself to focus on the pictures on the screen. Nell was his cousin, as were Penelope and Lucy. Chipeta and Janie were his aunts. Mason was his brother. Jordan was Shanna's son, Jemma and Shaylinn's brother, Naomi's husband.

When Omar had completed marking the relationships, Dallin led him to stand by the wall and used the handheld computer to take his picture. "Now I just need your last name so I can finish your ID in the grid."

"I don't have a last name."

"Hold on." Dallin reached under the desk and pulled out a floppy book with thick white pages. "It really doesn't matter which name you choose. Take your time."

Omar leafed through the pages. They were organized by letter, but there were so many it was overwhelming. He flipped toward the end—startled by the number nine on the back on his hand—and stopped in the *S* section. His eyes fell on the perfect name. "Strong," he said.

"Omar Strong it is." Dallin tapped the name onto his glass screen.

Omar handed back the book. "Why do they mark the number in two places?"

"They put the number on your cheek so people can see it—your hair doesn't hide it. And they put the number on your hand in case you get too drunk to remember what's on your face." Dallin chuckled.

Omar laughed too, though he didn't understand why that was funny. "Alcohol was only used for sickness in our village." Yet he'd seen Levi drink when visiting Beshup in Jack's Peak.

"Yeah, well, you'll see plenty of it here. I wouldn't drink too much if I were you."

"Why not?"

"Just trust me, okay? You take it easy out there. I'd hate to see a healthy kid like you be liberated before his time. Especially a nine."

Omar bristled. "I look like a child?"

Dallin pulled up Omar's picture on his computer screen. "You look fine. Women have a thing for the uniform and for skin like yours. Just don't question everything. It makes you sound like a shell."

"Right."

"Your identification is in your hand tag. Use it to open doors, to buy things, to power on appliances in your home, to start vehicles—pretty much anything. Task credits are posted to your account every Friday morning. Be smart with your credits. If you run out, you'll be hungry until credit day. Got it?"

"Yes." It seemed easy enough, anyway.

"Your apartment is in the Snowcrest Building across the street. Any questions?"

A million, but Omar said, "No."

"Welcome to the Safe Lands, Mr. Strong. Find pleasure in life."

It was dark when Omar left City Hall. He walked over to the Snowcrest, taking in the spectrum of electric colors everywhere, admiring how these people had embraced all life had to offer and challenged themselves to create new and exciting things. He shoved down the memory of his father, not wanting to think about what getting access to this fantastic world had cost.

Omar pushed past the glass doors of the apartment building and entered a chilly lobby.

A man in a red uniform approached. "Good afternoon, sir. Are you meeting someone?"

"No, I live here now."

The man held out a Wyndo displaying image of a side fist print. "Identification, please."

Omar set his fist against the glass, and his picture appeared on the surface.

"Welcome to the Snowcrest, Mr. Strong. My name is Artie. You're in apartment number seven hundred sixteen. It'll be to your left when you exit the elevator. The even-numbered apartments have a spectacular view."

"I was told you could contact a friend for me," Omar said. "Can I give you his number?"

"Of course, sir."

Omar recited Skottie's number, and the doorman typed it into his Wyndo. "One moment, sir."

Footsteps clicked over the tile, accompanied by feminine murmurs and giggles.

"Good afternoon, Ms. Combs," the doorman said.

"Hay-o, Artie," a woman answered. "The girls are with me." Her low and raspy voice turned Omar's head.

Three curvaceous women approached the elevator, carrying with them a cloud of spicy scents. Omar suddenly realized he could breathe! No sniffles. And as far as first smells went, this one was amazing.

Omar had never seen anything like these women. All three wore short black skirts and spiky-heeled shoes, displaying nearly all of their legs. Their shirts were tight and strappy. No woman in Glenrock or Jack's Peak ever bared so much skin.

The women stopped an arm's length from where he stood. The nearest woman was a few inches shorter than him and bore the number seven on her cheek. Her hair was blood red, streaked with fluffy black feathers, and hung down in wide curls past her shoulders. Tiny SimArt flowers ran up the backs of her legs.

The other two women were blonde—both numbered five—one with shoulder-length hair that had been slicked back like she'd just taken a bath, the other a mess of tiny braids under a floppy black hat.

The redhead wore a purple top that was so tight her skin bulged out of the top. As if sensing that he was looking at her, the woman raised one eyebrow and fixed her eyes on Omar. How he wished for paint that deep sapphire color. The closest thing he'd ever made was from blackberries, and it was far too purple.

"Sir?"

Omar turned back to the doorman, who was holding out his Wydno. Skottie's face was moving on the glass as if he were trapped inside.

"Hey, shell!" Skottie said through the screen. "Listen, we're going to come get you in an hour or so, okay? Your doorman says you're in the Snowcrest. What's your apartment number?"

"Seven sixteen."

"Got it. See you later, peer." The screen went blank.

"Thank you," Omar said to Artie.

"You're very welcome, sir."

Omar stepped toward the elevators and the beautiful women. The elevator button was already lit up. All three women held several bags in each hand.

"Would you like help carrying those?" Omar asked the redhead, proud that he'd managed to speak at all to such a beauty.

Her dark, painted lips curved into a smile, and she glanced at her friends, who giggled again.

The elevator doors slid open with a low buzz.

"You going our way?" the redhead asked Omar. She stepped into the elevator, her friends right behind her.

Omar followed, mesmerized by their flowery scent, their movement, their legs. He reached for the button for the seventh floor at the same time as the redhead. Their fingers touched, hers icy and small and tipped with violet-painted fingernails. Omar jerked back his hand.

The redhead pressed seven with her thumb and studied Omar, her dark eyelashes long and thick, enhanced somehow like the rest of her body, which looked like a canvas to be painted. "Visiting someone?" she asked.

Her attention so flustered Omar that he had to force himself to answer. "I live here."

"Since when?"

"Since today."

"Promotion?" She tilted her head closer and parted her lips in a way that made Omar's heart quicken.

"Yes."

"What's your rank?"

"Captain."

The woman's finger slowly traced the seam on the front of his jacket. "Really. What area?"

"Uh..." He rubbed the scar on his nose. It had been going so well. A longer conversation than he'd had with a female in a long time. The elevator stopped on the seventh floor. Omar followed the women into a wide hallway and glanced at the nearest door: 705.

"You go ahead and keep your secrets, trigger," the redhead said, walking to the right.

"We should invite him over!" the blonde with the braids whispered. "He's a cutie."

"Tonight's girl's night, Venita," the redhead said.

"So? Girl's night is more fun with a guy, especially one with such great skin."

"He's barely out of boarding school," the second blonde said. "And it's got to be Roller Paint."

"That's *not* Roller Paint." Venita turned to Omar. "How old are you, cutie?"

"Eighteen," Omar lied, puffing out his chest and trying to look like it was a fact.

The second blonde giggled. "Sure you are, baby doll."

"No guys tonight," the redhead said. "We're watching *C Factor*."

"We can zip *C Factor* for later." Venita turned back to Omar, her braids and hat swaying with her movement. "What's your apartment number, sweetie?"

"Um, seven sixteen," he said.

"We'll come visit later, seven sixteen. Once I talk Bel into it." Venita winked.

Not knowing what to say, Omar followed the numbers to the left. He stopped at door 716 and looked back. The redhead, Bel, and her blonde friends entered a room on the opposite end of the hall. The door thumped shut behind them.

Omar couldn't believe those women were infected with anything. Their skin had been flawless. No sign of the flakiness or veins. Would they really visit?

He pressed his fist to the pad on the door. It took him a few tries to get the angle right, but he eventually got inside. He spent the next five minutes trying to figure out which panel turned on the lights.

Once he could see, he discovered that his new home was as rich as the task director's office, but he found the brown and cream palette more relaxing. There was a sitting area, a sheet of glass on the wall with the word *Wyndo* etched into the top, a little kitchen, a table, a bathroom, and a bedroom with a huge bed, a dresser, and a GlassTop desk.

He inspected everything, wondering if the girls would knock on his door. However, once he discovered the SimPad that turned on the Wyndo, which turned out to be a TV, he became captivated by the color and movement. He could touch the glass to change what was playing—not movies of Old, either. Each program displayed the title along the top of the screen.

One show depicted two men trying to kill each other on a stage surrounded by cheering onlookers. On a cooking show, a woman taught Omar how to make strawberry savarin, whatever that was. What Omar assumed was meant to be a beauty program showed fat people—bigger than Mary, Shay, and Megan combined—and how one woman wanted to go back in time and relive her third life to earn better fortune. On *C Factor*, a man with earrings was having relations with a woman. On TV! There had been a scene like that in the Old movie *Titanic*, but they hadn't shown it. A channel displaying things he could buy was selling something called a Personal Vaporizer that could be used to turn candy, alcohol, medications, and stimulants—whatever those were—into a breathable form.

On the TV, Omar found all he needed to learn how to fit in as a Safe Lands National. Two hours passed before Artie the doorman's voice came through a panel near the door announcing that someone named Dane Skott had arrived.

On the street outside the Snowcrest, Omar found Skottie waving from a sleek little red car that had bigger wheels in front than in back, which made the body of the car recline. One of the back doors slid over the top of the vehicle to open.

"Get in," Skottie said.

Omar barely fit in the back seat. A tall guy turned to face Omar from the passenger's seat, his head nearly brushing the roof. He had a thick neck and buck teeth.

"I'm Charlz," the guy said. "Skottie says you want more SimTags?"

Did he? Omar smiled. "Yeah, I think I would."

"Then let's do it!" Skottie steered the car out of the parking lot so fast, the momentum threw Omar across the seat.

The heaviness of the day drifted from Omar's mind. Everything was going to work out. Tonight, he could have fun and make friends. He leaned between the seats, trying to think of something flattering to say. "Thanks for taking me out. You seem to know everything about this place."

Charlz looked over his shoulder. "Skottie is decked. He says you're going to task with the enforcers. I task there too."

"That's great," Omar said. *Great?* Why not *decked*? He needed to learn the language so he didn't sound like a shell. Dallin had told him not to ask stupid questions, but he felt like he needed to keep up the conversation. "Do you have extra SimTags too?" Omar asked Charlz.

"Just a SimTalk. I got the others taken out. They aggravated my skin."

"Charlz is a little sensitive about his skin," Skottie said.

"It's already flaking more than most. I don't need a rash too."

"What time you coming in to the enforcer's office tomorrow?" Skottie asked Omar.

"They told me to arrive at ten," Omar said.

"Come in early, and I'll show you something decked."

"One of Skottie's femmes works in surveillance," Charlz said.

"And here we are." Skottie slowed the car and parked along the side of the street. "Surface is the best SimArt shop around."

Omar found the door panel and pressed his fist against it, feeling less shell-like as the door slid open. Smells from the street gusted into the car: popcorn and something meaty. He climbed out onto a bright street. People were everywhere, moving along the sidewalk like two herds pushing in opposite directions. Lights from the storefronts on both sides of the street lit the pavement with vivid reds and blues. Videos were playing on every glass surface, advertising whatever might be for sale inside.

Omar inched his way across the crowded sidewalk, feeling stupid for finding this so difficult. But he managed to arrive at the doorway in one piece.

Skottie smirked at him. "Let's tag you up!"

Inside, Surface was dark and loud. The place smelled strongly of incense, and Omar breathed in deeply. Glowing Wyndo screens covered every inch of the walls, flashing pictures of the types of SimArt a person could choose from: sleeve, fluorescent, cosmetic. Omar trailed after Skottie and Charlz, staring at the many designs.

"We need to get this one into a chair," Skottie yelled.

Omar turned his focus to Skottie, who was talking to a shapely woman so pierced and marked up that Omar couldn't guess how she'd originally looked.

The woman dragged Omar to a reclining chair covered in black leather and pushed him into it. "How many you want and where?"

Omar glanced at Skottie.

Skottie waved his hand. "Go on, peer, tell Suli what you want."

Omar swallowed and panned the Wyndo screens. What did he want? Everything looked mad good.

"It's not that big of deal," Suli said. "You don't like 'em? You can turn 'em off or come let me take 'em out."

Right. This wasn't like the tattoos of Old. These weren't permanent. "I want a sleeve."

"Right or left?"

"Right." He caught sight of one of the screens, which showed a hawk on a man's back with the wings trailing down both arms. He pointed. "I want that!"

Suli smirked. "Let's start with a sleeve. You like it, you come get more. If I give you that many tags in one sitting, you're gonna be real sorry when you try and sleep tonight."

"Okay," Omar said, feeling stupid for being so eager.

Together with Skottie and Charlz, Omar chose the perfect SimArt for his first sleeve. He landed on a black web that wound its way up his arm and reminded him of an Old comic book hero.

"Lose your jacket and shirt," Suli told him.

Omar did, wishing he were as muscular as the pictures of the men on the screens. Compared to them, Omar looked like a half-starved child.

Suli twisted Omar's chair and pulled up a flap on the right side. She set a thick roll of plastic on the flap and unrolled it. "Stretch out your arm."

Omar set his arm on the plastic, and Suli covered it with the material, then grabbed the sheet and walked away.

Skottie and Charlz stood on Omar's left.

"She's getting a simulation of your arm so she knows where to put the tags," Skottie said.

"I love watching the gun," Charlz said. "Wish I could buy one."

Suli returned with a thin plastic sleeve that she pulled over Omar's arm. It had circles and dots all over it.

"How many is he getting?" Skottie asked.

"Twenty-eight," Suli said.

Skottie threw back his head. "Aw, you long-armed ape. You beat me!"

Omar smiled, as if his having a longer arm that Skottie somehow made him worthy of friendship. He'd take every advantage he could get.

"Here we go," Suli said.

Omar looked back to his arm. Suli held a gun like the one the medic had used. She set it over one of the dots and fired. It made a soft clicking noise and stung. Only twenty-seven more.

Once they were all in, Suli programmed the tags and the design flicked on. Omar paid by touching his fist to a computer screen.

When they were done at Surface, Skottie drove them to a place called Main Event. It was dark inside, except for the pinwheels of orange and yellow light that spun on the ceiling. Omar's eyes slowly adjusted to the dim atmosphere. The room was filled with a maze of low counters and crowded with men.

"Is this a bar?" Omar asked, recalling the term from Old movies.

"That, and more," Skottie said.

Main Event turned out to be a bar where voluptuous waitresses walked on the counters to serve the drinks, and every time one of them was given extra credits, they all did a dance.

Omar liked watching them dance.

Omar had never drunk alcohol before, and he likely had too much. The night passed in a blur. The last thing he remembered was falling into bed in his apartment while his head and arm throbbed.

He didn't mind the pain. For too long, pain meant Omar didn't belong. Didn't fit in. Not so here. In the Safe Lands, Omar had finally found a place to call home.

Chapter 12

Levi woke with his face in the dirt, certain he'd heard a noise. He lay on the mound that was his father's grave. The realization brought back the heavy sorrow that sleep had numbed.

"Levi!" Someone grabbed his arm.

Levi pulled Sam's empty pistol from his waistband and rolled over, aiming the gun at... "Beshup?"

"I thought you were dead, my friend." Beshup was a tall man of twenty-six with white-blond hair, which he'd grown long and wore in two braids.

Levi let his head fall back to the dirt. "It seems like I'm the only one who's not." He always knew he'd be an elder someday. And here he was. But elder of what? Nothing was left.

"What time is it?" he asked Beshup.

Beshup looked into the sky. "The sun is nearing the west, but there are several hours before it will get dark."

Levi pushed to his feet and walked away from the graveyard, toward the square. Seeing the bodies he'd left in a line made him stumble. So many dead. He turned to Beshup. "What can I do with the dead? There are too many to bury."

"The coyote said that when men die, their friends should burn their bodies."

Burn them? "It's too dry," Levi said. "I'd be setting fire to the whole valley."

Beshup pointed to the square. "The stage can serve as a pyre."

Levi set his hands on his hips and studied the stage. It *was* in a clearing with no overhanging branches.

"It's too soon, though," Beshup said. "We should wait so your people can pay their respects."

"I'm all that's left, Beshup!"

His friend gestured to the bodies. "This is not all of Glenrock."

Levi scrubbed his hand over his face. "I think they took the women and children into the compound. But I need to deal with the dead before I go after them, or the wolves will get them."

Beshup stared at Levi, as if considering the dilemma. "I will help you. Then you must come home with me to Jack's Peak and speak with Chief Kimama."

Levi nodded. Maybe the chief would offer to help rescue Glenrock's people. This just as easily could have happened to their village, after all.

Levi followed Beshup's every instruction. They covered the stage in two more layers of wooden planks, alternating their direction. Then stacked firewood. Beshup insisted it be four feet high, so Levi used his ATV and cart to gather wood from every home until a massive pile covered the stage. They tried to keep the pyre as even as possible so the fire wouldn't burn lopsided.

As they worked, Levi distracted himself with a mental checklist. After this, he'd go with Beshup to Jack's Peak to ask Chief Kimama for help. Then he'd come back to gather supplies and check the cache to see if any ammo was left. Then... to the compound.

They poured ethanol over the wood. Levi worried he should have saved some, since he didn't know how to make more without Uncle Colton's or Penelope's help, but it was too late now.

Then they were ready to move the dead.

It was tricky getting all the bodies on the pyre. Twice, a chunk of firewood shifted under Levi's feet and fell off the side of the stage. Once all the bodies were on the pyre, Levi brought a couple of bedsheets from his house, and he and Beshup draped them over the top.

When Beshup sat on one of the benches in the square, Levi asked, "That's it, then?"

"You must say farewell."

Levi took a deep breath and looked up to the sky, thinking back to the funerals Papa Eli had given over the years. He spoke loudly, for all heaven and nature to hear. "'Let not your hearts be troubled... In my Father's house are many rooms.' He has prepared a place for you and now taken you there to be with him. 'O death, where is your victory? O death, where is your sting?'"

Levi's voice softened, emotion taking hold. "Take my people, Lord, into your heavenly home." Then he sang a verse from an old hymn.

So on I go not knowing, I would not if I might;
I'd rather walk in the dark with God than go alone in the light;
I'd rather walk in faith with Him than go alone by sight.

Levi and Beshup struck several matches and lit the pyre around its perimeter. It took a little while to get started, then the fire rose hot and fast, crackling, engulfing the stage in orange, yellow, and pink flames. Black smoke twisted into the sky like a tornado. The air became so hot that Beshup and Levi moved to the tree line, occasionally racing forward to douse a smoldering spark that leapt away from the pyre.

Even standing upwind, the village reeked of a sweet yet putrid smell, almost like tanned leather. Levi tried to ignore it, but the smell antagonized his stomach. These were his friends and family.

The entire pyre burned in less than an hour, but they waited longer for the coals to die down. Then Levi unhitched his cart from the back of his ATV, he and Beshup climbed on, and Levi pulled away, leaving behind the smoldering remains.

It was usually a two-and-a-half hour drive up to Jack's Peak, but without the cart—and in spite of all the potholes filled with rainwater—the ATV made it in two.

Jack's Peak sat on the edge of Mill Creek, which enabled the village to get clean water before the Safe Lands collected it into their dam and compound. For some reason, Safe Lands enforcers had not attacked here... yet.

Levi rolled to a stop near the village fire pit, and a crowd of children and young men clustered around his rig. The people of Jack's Peak wore leather, fur, or cattail clothing, mixing in nothing Old. Some tattooed their bodies with clay, charcoal, and plant juices.

"Beshup!" Tsana, Beshup's wife, threaded her way through the sea of onlookers. "What news of Glenrock? Our elders were worried when they saw the smoke."

Beshup and Levi got off the ATV, and Levi glanced over Beshup's shoulder to the valley below. "Glenrock is destroyed, our elders are dead, and our young men, women, and children are taken. I need to speak with your chief."

The group gasped and stepped back.

"Come on." Beshup led the way around a dozen cabins and teepees. Chief Kimama allowed her people to build cabins, but many lived in teepees made of animal skins and bark.

"*Behne*, Levi!" Kosowe waved from outside a teepee they passed. She stood over a washtub scrubbing a small red-headed child, the fringe of turquoise beads on her dress clicking against the tub as she moved.

The sight of her stiffened Levi's posture, and he looked away. Kosowe was the woman Father had foolishly tried to match with Omar.

Images from two years ago flashed in Levi's memory. Finding the alcohol. Hiding it in his cart to share with Beshup. Father making him take Omar along to Jack's Peak. Sneaking away with his friends. Drinking. Dancing. The buzz of the alcohol. Kissing Kosowe.

Omar finding them.

Omar... His little brother was somehow mixed up in this attack by the Safe Lands. If Levi had been a better example... if he would have destroyed the alcohol when he'd found it, then he wouldn't have messed up so badly that night, and maybe Omar wouldn't have either. A village elder couldn't afford to make such mistakes. He had to be an example for his people. He'd blown it that night, and he could never let that happen again.

Chief Kimama lived in the biggest teepee Levi had ever seen. He'd been inside it only once when he was a boy and had come to visit with Papa Eli.

"Wait here," Beshup said. "I'm sure she'll see you, but..." Beshup slipped inside the teepee. A moment later he held open the door flap. "Go on in."

Levi ducked inside. The sun shone through the animal skin walls, creating a golden glow. Two rectangular mats woven in fat red and tan stripes covered a ground of wood chips. Between the mats, a circle of stones held the smoldering embers of a fire. The smoke trailed out a flap in the apex of the roof.

Chief Kimama sat crosslegged on a mattress behind the fire pit. Kimama was a bit younger than Papa Eli, but she looked much older. Thick wrinkles creased her tanned skin from the corners of her wide nose to the sides of her mouth. Her white hair was parted down the middle and twisted into two long braids that hung to her waist. Her posture was so hunched she reminded Levi of a hen nestled down to rest.

"Levi of Elias," she said in a hoarse voice. "I smell death on the air. The shadow of the owl has been circling the valley for days. Has it fallen on Glenrock?"

Her voice chilled him, but he kept his posture straight and his voice strong. "Yes, ma'am. Safe Lands enforcers killed our men and took the women, young men, and children captive."

"How many were killed?"

"Eighteen, ma'am."

"And Elder Elias?"

"Dead, ma'am."

She worked her mouth as if she were chewing something. "You're certain he's gone?"

The image of Papa Eli closing his eyes flashed through Levi's mind. "I buried him myself."

Her eyes narrowed. "Your father was Justin?"

"That's right."

She rocked back and straightened her posture, revealing that she did in fact have a neck. "Then you are no direct relation to me."

"No, ma'am." Maybe he should sit or kneel. What if standing was disrespectful in Jack's Peak?

"You are welcome to join us, Levi of Elias. Several females in Jack's Peak are old enough to marry. I grant you leave to choose a wife from my tribe and build a life here."

Great, now he had to tell the woman no. He searched for the perfect words. "You're very generous, Chief Kimama, but I'm not looking for a wife or a place to live."

She grunted and settled back into her hen-like position. "What is it you seek from Jack's Peak, then, Levi of Elias?"

"Your help, ma'am. I intend to free my people and bring them back to Glenrock."

Chief Kimama laughed, changing the shape of her face so drastically that Levi took a step back. She had no teeth at all, and when she laughed, her eyes closed and her mouth curved like a U.

Her laugh wheezed to a close, and she focused her dark eyes back on him. "No one who enters the Safe Lands comes out."

"All the same, ma'am, would you consider taking the matter to your tribal council?"

Again she straightened, her eyes stormy and dark. "I would not. What you ask is impossible, as are your intentions."

Levi set his jaw. Nothing would keep him from trying to free his people—from freeing Jemma. But it would be easier if he had help. "Your village sits upriver from the Safe Lands. If we built our own dam, cut off their water supply—"

"I have no quarrel with the Safe Lands. Cutting off their water would be an act of war."

Levi stepped forward. "Destroying my village was an act of war."

"To Glenrock, yes." She slouched again. "But not to Jack's Peak."

Levi squeezed his hands into fists. "Ma'am, please. Have mercy. The women and children. With his last breath, Elder Eli bade me get them back. I believe my brothers and mother were taken. And my fiancée."

She chewed her gums. "You are betrothed?"

"Yes, ma'am. To Jemma of Zachary."

Her eyes flew wide. "Now that one is my blood. Did you know that?"

"Yes, ma'am. Jemma's grandmother was your daughter."

"That's right. Did you know that my dear Haiwee was named after my little sister, who perished in the Great Pandemic?"

"I did not."

She grunted, as if considering this new information. "This changes nothing. You've buried and burned your dead, and the shadow of the owl still circles. More will die, and soon."

Levi wouldn't give a bullet for her superstitions. "Likely the owl is circling those Safe Lands officials who'll die when I rescue my people."

Her lips curled and she chuckled. "You speak like a warrior, Levi of Elias. Are you one?"

"I'm whatever God asks of me."

She hummed long and soft. "I cannot involve my tribe in this mischief. We are few as it is."

What else could he say to convince her? "But Jemma is your blood, ma'am. And whatever the Safe Lands enforcers want with Glenrock, in time they'll come looking for it in Jack's Peak."

She shifted, ruffling her feathers again. "You cannot know that."

"Neither can you. Even if you refuse to help me, you should make use of my warning. Prepare against a raid such as the one that destroyed Glenrock."

"You are quite brazen for the last of your tribe, Levi of Elias, giving me advice." She pursed her lips, and her gaze traveled up and down his body. "I will allow such words. Honest words, spoken from grief. You may stay here for as long as you need."

Levi did all he could to keep his expression solemn. "Thank you, ma'am. I meant no offense."

She rumbled one last time. "You may leave now."

Gladly. Levi strode out of the teepee, right past Beshup, and headed for his ATV.

His friend's footsteps plodded after him. "What happened? What did she say?"

"She said I can stay, but she won't help me get my people back."

Beshup grabbed Levi's arm. "Slow down, my friend. Come and eat dinner. No sense wasting what little food you have."

Levi stopped. He might not eat again for a while. "Very well."

Beshup lived in a three-room cabin on the edge of the village pit. They sat at a plank table in front of a cold hearth. His wife, Tsana, served bowls of fish stew and flatbread. Before Levi could finish his food, someone knocked on the door.

Tsana let in Kosowe, who approached the table, holding a wad of plain linen. She bowed to Beshup.

"*Behne*, Kosowe," Beshup said, gesturing to Levi. "You know Levi of Elias."

Kosowe bowed to Levi and said softly, "*Behne*, Levi."

He kept his eyes on his bowl of soup. "*Behne*."

She thrust her ball of fabric into Levi's lap and bowed her head. "For you."

Levi put down his spoon and unwrapped the bundle. A warm round of white bread. He nodded to her. "*Aishen*. But I'm not trading today."

"No trade." She glanced at the floor then back to his eyes. "Gift." She smiled and backed away from the table until she reached the door, then spun around and left, her bare feet padding over the dirt. Tsana followed her out the door and, just before closing it behind her, shot her husband the wide-eyed look of a hint.

Levi looked from the door to Beshup to the bread. "Want some bread? Smells good."

Beshup chuckled and set down his spoon. "Want a wife? I think Tsana is plotting."

Levi winced and set the bread on the table. "Our fathers tried to marry Kosowe to Omar a few weeks ago, did you know that? Omar was there that night she and I... had our encounter."

"Kosowe's father keeps trying to make a match for her," Beshup said. "But she will marry no one but you. And you are fortunate her father never learned what happened."

Levi couldn't argue that. "I don't need a wife. I have a wife... Well, almost." And he wouldn't if Jemma ever found out about Kosowe. He pushed his bowl away. What was he doing here, wasting time? "You helped me with the pyre and fed me. Thank you, my friend. Now, I must get inside the Safe Lands."

Beshup grimaced as if the very idea gave him indigestion. "You're greatly respected here. A successful scavenger. A wise trader. Stay with us." He gestured at the bread Kosowe had brought. "You may like what we have to offer."

"Beshup—"

Beshup held up his hand. "At least stay for the night."

"I can't." Levi pushed his chair back and stood, leaving the round of bread on the table, lest he encourage Kosowe further. "I'm going to marry Jemma, Beshup. I will get her back."

Levi went outside into the early evening. Beshup followed him and walked him to his ATV.

"You aren't serious about going inside the Safe Lands, are you? There's no way out."

Levi was deadly serious. "If I can get in, I can get out."

"I've never heard of anyone who came out," Beshup said. "Something inside those walls changes people. And even if you did return, you'd probably carry the plague."

"There's a first time for everything, Beshup," Levi said. "I'm the patriarch of Glenrock at nineteen. It's *my* responsibility. I can't leave them in there. I won't. And I'm more than happy to die trying."

Beshup slapped him on the back. "May the wolf go with you, my friend."

Levi left Jack's Peak no closer to freeing his people. The trip had only served to increase the guilt of his mistake with Kosowe. He steered the ATV down the steep mountain trail and tried to come up with a plan.

He'd call Judson in Clean Creek, the only other village in the area. It was his last option. Papa Eli had said the rest of the world had perished in the Great Pandemic and that the water from Mount Crested Butte was the only safe drinking water on the planet. Levi's dad had doubted that claim, which was why he liked traveling to abandoned cities, hoping to find other villages or safe water sources. Not to mention, aircraft flew out from the Safe Lands every week, always headed north. They had to be going somewhere that had people and, presumably, good water. But Father's last trip north had uncovered neither.

Levi arrived home and called Judson on his dad's two-way radio. When Judson heard what had happened, he offered Levi a place to stay but refused to help beyond that. Too much risk for his own people, just as Chief Kimama had said.

Levi was on his own. And it was getting dark.

He went to the two aspen trees with trunks that twisted together at the base and located the strip of braided twine in the grass underneath them. He yanked a sod-covered lid loose, pulled it aside, and jumped down into the village's emergency cache.

Cool air enveloped him. He located the crank flashlight on the far end of the top shelf. The beam was nearly dead, so he took the time to wind up the battery. Once the light was bright enough, he shone it around the four-by-twelve-foot rectangular pit. Shelves lined both sides. Guns and ammo were stored on the left; shoes, dried food, and medicine were stocked on the right. Tubs of clothing sat on the floor under the right-side shelves.

Levi sat on the five-gallon bucket of jewels they'd scavenged from Denver City and dug through the clothing until he found some fresh packs of undershirts. He ripped open the package and traded a fresh one for his filthy red T-shirt then stuffed another clean one into his pack. He grabbed a bulletproof vest that Papa Eli had scavenged years before, and he changed into green camouflage pants and a long-sleeved matching shirt. The camo clothing smelled aged and would likely tear, but that didn't matter as long as it helped him stay invisible.

He placed the leather jacket Jemma had made him inside one of the tubs, snapped on the lid, then took stock of the ammunition. There was plenty for his rifle and the pistol. He strapped on a shoulder holster and put Elder Harvey's pistol into it. He tossed two packages of bullets for his rifle up onto the grass and all the ammo he could find for the pistol.

Strips of beef jerky and some dried apples went into a cloth bag. He gathered two more crank flashlights, a solar powered lantern, two wind-up two-way radios and a solar-powered one. He also grabbed a handful of jewels from the bucket in case he needed to buy something or bribe someone. He put his and Jemma's wedding rings on a chain around his neck, determined to put Jemma's on her finger at the first opportunity. Everything else he stuffed into a backpack and carried it toward his family home.

Night had fallen. Crickets sang, oblivious to the carnage that had taken place in the village of Glenrock that day. Levi wanted to go now, but he was exhausted. A few hours' sleep could only help.

As soon as he woke, he would set out for the Safe Lands' sewers and storm drains, which was the only way he could think of to get inside the Safe Lands undetected.

Chapter 13

The enforcer closed in, charging through the village square. The sting of a bullet entered Shaylinn's back, and she fell. Still, the enforcer came. With every ounce of strength she crawled across the dirt... trying to get away. Then someone helped her up, lifted her into his arms.

Omar.

But there was blood on his hands. Shaylinn's blood. He leaned down, and she thought he might kiss her, but he simply whispered in her ear, "I told them to come. And I told them to shoot you first, ugly crybaby."

Shaylinn's eyes shot open. Her heart sprinted in her chest, her stomach hollow with the horror of such words. It was just a dream. It had been years since Omar had said anything so cruel.

On the mirror above her dresser, the clock glowed 3:34 a.m. Too early to get up. But when she tried to go back to sleep, she couldn't. She crept into Jemma's room across the hall and climbed into her sister's bed. Jemimah didn't budge. The girl could have slept through the enforcers' raid on Glenrock.

The thought pulled Shaylinn's mind back to the raid and then to her nightmare. She studied Jemma's room, which was identical to hers, but navy blue instead of cobalt. Omar had taught Shaylinn about the color cobalt one day while she watched him paint. She'd decided then it was one of the most beautiful colors in the entire world.

In an attempt to distract herself, she imagined better times in Glenrock: weaving wildflower wreaths with her sister, playing tag with her cousins, dancing and singing after a ceremony in the Meeting Hall.

When Jemma's mirror clock read 5:48, Shaylinn went back to her room to shower. Hot water shot out from three sides. If her stomach hadn't started pinging with hunger, she might have stayed in there all morning. As it was, when she came out the mirror clock read 6:35.

There were no clothes in Shaylinn's dresser drawers, so she put on her deerskin dress and went out to the living room. Kendall was already up watching the wall of glass, which was a TV, her face aglow with the light of the screen.

"Good morning, Shaylinn," Kendall said. "Sona brought a tray. There's enough for everyone." She motioned to the table.

The tray held a platter of eggs and bacon, a bowl of berries and some sort of melon, and a plate of pancakes. Shaylinn put a little of each onto a smaller plate then sat beside Kendall. "Are you watching a movie?" she asked, nibbling a piece of bacon that was very salty.

"No. *Finley and Flynn.* I don't know why I watch. All they do is gossip."

On the TV, a man and a woman were sitting on a purple sofa. The woman was wearing a skin-tight yellow dress with a wide black belt. The man matched her with his yellow jacket over a black shirt and a black-and-yellow-striped tie. Both had black hair and pale white skin.

"Why do so many people wear yellow and black?" Shaylinn asked.

"Because of Finley and Flynn," Kendall said. "They set the trends, and people mimic them."

Shaylinn looked at Kendall, who was wearing a blue shirt and black pants. "But not you?"

"I don't care what Finley and Flynn wear. I've got bigger things to worry about."

"Being a mom?"

"I wish. It's the Safe Lands, remember? As my medic made clear yesterday, I don't get to keep him. He'll be sent away right after I give birth."

So sad. "It's a boy?"

Kendall nodded. "I'm naming him Elyot. That, at least, I get to do."

"Are you scared?"

"Sometimes." Kendall set her hand on her belly. "It's not painful or anything. I mean, I felt nauseous at first, but now mostly I just feel big."

"I feel big every day," Shaylinn said. "If I got pregnant, I'd be humungous."

Once everyone had gotten up and eaten, Kendall led them downstairs to the main sitting room. Jennifer, Aunt Mary, Eliza, and Chipeta were there, along with Matron, who was wearing an emerald green pantsuit with orange and yellow platform shoes. Shaylinn wanted to try on a pair and see what it felt like to walk in them.

"Why aren't you wearing black and yellow, Matron?" Shaylinn asked.

Surprisingly, the woman didn't seem offended. "Don't get me wrong," Matron said, "Luella Flynn is as precious as can be. But I mimic no one."

Matron gave Shaylinn a small piece of glass called a Wyndo. She'd given everyone else one yesterday before Shaylinn had arrived. Kendall said Wyndos worked like Old smart phones, but could also be used to change hair, skin, or nail color or designs; monitor health; record conversations for playback; or identify any national's face. Wyndos also had a SimPal, in which you could choose from over a hundred different people or animals to use as a personal assistant or simulated friend, who would speak to you through the glass.

Matron led the Glenrock women and girls to the Registration Department, where they each took a test to determine which jobs they would do after leaving the harem. Shaylinn's test resulted in all sewing-related tasks. Figured. In Glenrock, women mostly did the mending and cooking and cared for their families.

Shaylinn also learned from the man in Registration that the SimTag in her hand could be used to purchase things, and that she received one thousand credits a week for serving in the harem. The news left her feeling both curious and unsettled.

On the way back to their rooms, Matron showed them the wonders of the Highland Harem. They took the elevator to the top floor to see a view of the city, toured a spa, visited an indoor swimming pool, tried ice cream—which Shaylinn found delicious—and visited a movie theater, a game room, and a room filled with exercise machines.

"The Safe Lands is all about pleasure and comfort," Matron said. "And no place in the entire land offers more enjoyment and relaxation than the harem. So, sleep in and indulge in the comforts. Or if the idle life is not your fancy, you can begin task training. The choice is yours."

Wyndo screens hung everywhere. Big ones mounted in corners, little ones in elevators and hallways. Sometimes they were divided into four different images. Kendall pointed out dozens of little yellow cameras throughout the building which were run by the enforcers for surveillance.

Back in the dormitory, the huge picture windows that had once looked out on the grassy lawn were displaying the image of the the Safe Lands logo, a gold bell within a circle on a black background. "How did the windows become a movie screen?" Shaylinn asked.

"Most glass in the Safe Lands uses Wyndo technology," Kendall said. "If you ever want to know for sure, touch your fist to any glass surface and you'll find out."

Matron asked them to sit on the chairs and sofas that had been arranged to face the windows—W-y-n-d-o-s. So strange. Shaylinn sat between Kendall and Jemma.

A curvy woman in a pale yellow sleeveless blouse and flowing black pants stood in front of the screen. Her skin had a brownish orange tint and didn't look at all papery or veiny. Images of flowers and vines had been drawn down the ridges of her arms.

Shaylinn leaned close to Kendall. "Why does the plague affect some more than others?"

"It's not that," Kendall said. "People like Tyra are just better than others at hiding it."

"Tyra Grant, tasks as a beauty care specialist." Matron indicated the tanned woman, then tottered over to a chair near the stairs and sat. "If anyone can work a miracle, she can."

Tyra eyed the girls and beamed, her teeth whiter than the carpet. She held in one hand a small Wyndo like Shaylinn's. "My job is to help you become beautiful, okay? So we're going to talk makeovers, then we'll go shopping."

"We get new clothes?" Mia asked.

"Yes, and don't use your own credits. Clothing is on the harem."

Shaylinn grinned. Finally, something different than animal skins or faded Old dresses. But she reminded herself that they were prisoners. She wasn't supposed to enjoy it here.

"Now, I'm noticing a few things straight away," Tyra said. "Damaged hair... oily complexions... None of you shave or wax your legs?"

"Like candle wax?" Mia asked.

"Why would we?" Jemma asked.

Tyra wrinkled her nose. "Because hairy legs are ugly. And shaving your underarms decreases body odor."

Shaylinn twisted to smell her armpit. Smelled fine to her.

"Our goal today is to get you femmes beautified so you can meet the task director general on the Safe Lands ColorCast and attend the entertainment orientation," Tyra said.

"I don't want to meet the task director general," Naomi said. "He ruined our lives."

"This is mandatory," Tyra said, "so you may as well make the best of it."

"Fine," Naomi said. "When I meet him, I'll demand he take me to see Jordan."

"Where are the men being kept?" Shaylinn asked, wondering where Omar might be.

"*Please*, ladies," Tyra said. "The task director general is a wise man who deserves our respect. It's a privilege to meet him."

Naomi flubbed her lips. "None of you deserve my respect. You're clearly all insane."

"Let's get back on track, all right? Wyndo: slides." With Tyra's words the image on the windows changed from the Safe Lands' logo to three women captured mid-walk, laughing, dressed in clothing that hugged their curves and bared their arms and legs. They wore high-heeled shoes and clutched each other's arms as if they might fall over at any moment.

"Beauty," Tyra said. "It's every woman's birthright, if not duty. It makes us happy, desirable. But one mustn't judge beauty, for what's beautiful to me may not be to you."

Naomi coughed. "Hairy legs." Shaylinn snickered.

Tyra pursed her lips. "Wyndo: next." The screen flashed to a woman in a flowing red dress. "Wyndo: next." Three women wearing yellow and black. "Wyndo: next." A close-up of a woman's red lips exhaling black vapor. "Wyndo: next." An overweight woman dressed in a tight yellow dress that looked more like another layer of skin than clothing.

This time Mia giggled.

"Melana Georjan is the star of *Big is Beautiful*." Tyra pointed to Mia. "You. Come stand beside me."

"What did I do?" Mia asked as she approached Tyra.

"You volunteered to be our first project, okay?" Tyra said. "One of the best things about living in the Safe Lands is the availability of glamour. The freedom to be beautiful."

Shaylinn scooted to the edge of her seat.

"We *are* beautiful," Jemma said, tossing her hair over her shoulder.

"But you do nothing to display it." Tyra's gaze roamed over Mia's body. Shaylinn had always envied Mia's looks, but Mia looked plain next to Tyra, who was so sleek and vibrant in her black pants. "Mia, you have so much potential beauty just waiting to be enhanced. You're tall and have a great figure. Your skin is relatively clear, your is coloring nice. You don't even need Roller Paint. We'll get you some glossy clothes and lighten that drab hair, maybe give it some curl. Perhaps some blue contact lenses or... lavender?" She tapped notes on her handheld Wyndo. "What do you think, Matron?"

Matron exhaled a plume of green vapor. "She could use a posture class as well. She slouches."

Mia's eyes flashed. "I'm the prettiest girl in Glenrock. Why don't you pick on someone who needs help? Like Shay."

The impact of Mia's words made Shay jump.

"*Mia!*" Jennifer said.

Jemma took hold of Shaylinn's hand. Shaylinn looked down at her lap, noticing how tight her big legs made her dress and how chubby her fingers were compared to Jemma's.

"*Sor-ry*," Mia said.

"You'll *all* take a turn," Tyra said, "then we'll go to the salon and get started. Shaylinn, why don't you come up next?"

Shaylinn shook her head. "I don't want to." She wanted help—to be beautiful. But she didn't think she could take the humiliation.

"I'll go next," Jemma said, standing up.

"No, I want Shaylinn," Tyra said. "I want to use Mia's comment to make the point that everyone has something beautiful about themselves."

"May as well get it over with, honey," Kendall said, giving Shaylinn a side hug.

Jemma sat down, and Shaylinn made her way forward. She was taller than Tyra by a full head. Her girth and frizzy hair likely made Tyra look like a stick drawing.

"Let's see now." Tyra tapped her finger to her lips and examined Shaylinn. "You have a lovely complexion and lots of long, curly hair. Your features are nicely balanced. Threading that lip and those eyebrows will make a big difference right away." She made a quick note on her Wyndo. "Are you pleased with your weight? If so, you could work to gain more and audition for *Big is Beautiful*."

"I don't want to be on the TV," Shaylinn said. "And I hate being fat."

"Shay!" Jemma said. "You're *not* fat."

"I'll put you down for a cosmetic consultation, then." Tyra fiddled with her Wyndo. "And you might consider breast implants. I honestly don't know how you turned out so curvy with no breasts!"

"She's only fourteen," Jemma said.

"Oh. Tall for fourteen. Wait to get implants until your body is done growing." She fingered Shaylinn's hair. "Your hair is quite damaged. Do you brush it?"

Shaylinn shrugged. "Sometimes."

"You should *never* brush curls like yours. Or, if you hate the curl, you can have it straightened. Truthfully, with your round face, the volume of your hair isn't helping."

Tears welled up in Shaylinn's eyes, and she hung her head. These were all things she knew to be true. Ugly, ugly, ugly, just like Omar had said when they were little.

"Your skin is fantastic, but most of you girls could use an acne program." Tyra lifted Shaylinn's hand to look closer. "Is that dirt under your fingernails?"

"It's leather. I was working a hide when the enforcers came."

"A hide? But you've showered since, haven't you?"

"Yes, ma—" Shaylinn stopped herself before saying ma'am. "I like the showers here."

Tyra sighed and tapped on her Wyndo. "Manicures and pedicures for all." She then launched into a long discussion of the best types of clothing to wear depending on each girls' body type, using Shaylinn's shape to call out ways to slenderize a waist or create correct proportions. Each term Tyra used was like a key to unlocking a strange yet hypnotic new language.

When Tyra finally let Shaylinn sit down, Jemma moved beside her and whispered, "I think you're perfect already."

Shaylinn blushed and leaned against Jemma's side. Maybe, just maybe, if she let Tyra make her beautiful, Omar would ask to paint her.

The public humiliation continued. Naomi disputed each criticism Tyra dished out, but Shaylinn felt like Tyra made many good points. Shaylinn would love to know how to make her eyebrows look sculpted, and while the idea of different-colored eyes and breast implants scared her, she couldn't help wonder how a cosmetic consultation could help her be thinner.

They spent the rest of the morning in the spa, where they all received new hairstyles, waxings, manicures, and pedicures. Kendall talked Shaylinn into getting bright red paint on her fingernails and toenails. Shaylinn thought it looked ridiculous, but Kendall said it was *glossy*.

Shaylinn loved her hair now. The stylist left it long enough that a few tendrils still reached her waist, but it no longer frizzed; instead, it curled in wide ringlets. It was so pretty.

Tyra's assistants wheeled carts of clothing into the spa, and the girls tried different outfits. Some of the clothing was so ugly that the girls refused to try it, no matter how much Tyra begged. Shaylinn didn't care. She had a great time trying everything. The most ridiculous was a fiery pink dress covered in matching feathers that made her look like a fluffy bird. She strutted out of the dressing room and chirped until she had everyone laughing.

"Fortune, have mercy!" Tyra ran across the room. "Absolutely not! Take if off! I told you simple and streamlined for your body, Shaylinn."

"I was just playing." Shaylinn went back into the fitting room and made a nasty face at herself in the mirror, mocking Tyra.

Someone tossed a blue and white gown over the door. "Try this one, Shay," Jemma said.

Shaylinn lifted it down to take a look. The fabric was a beautiful floral print of navy, cobalt, periwinkle, and white. The dress had a V-neck—maybe too deep—an empire inset waistband, and a full pleated skirt that stopped just above her knees.

Shaylinn sighed at its beauty, knowing that something like this would never fit. She put it on anyway. She stepped out of the fitting room, smiling so wide that she covered her mouth with her hand.

"Oh, Shay! I love it!" Jemma said.

"Me too, honey," Naomi said. "You look mad gorgeous!"

"It's not my favorite on you," Tyra said. "I'd rather see you in black, even a pale yellow."

"I mimic no one," Shaylinn said, quoting Matron, "and I love this dress."

"But your skin is dark enough that pale yellow would be glossy with your dark hair."

"I'm not changing." Shaylinn ran her hands over the skirt, admiring soft fabric and the piping that edged the inset waist. It made her feel like one of Jemma's fairy tale princesses.

Shaylinn got to keep the dress. Jemma chose a lacy red dress with a black belt. Mia was wearing a slinky, floor-length black dress with bright yellow squiggly lines. Kendall picked a brown and orange floral chiffon dress. And Tyra talked Naomi into a royal blue satin dress.

Once everyone had shoes and jewelry to match, Tyra took the girls to a theater on the opposite end of the harem building. Shaylinn stumbled along in a pair of high-heeled white sandals. They'd seemed comfortable at first but were soon pinching her toes and were becoming hard to walk in.

"Sit somewhere in the middle ten seats of the first three rows," Tyra said. "We want the camera to make the theater look full, and we've only got about thirty people here tonight."

A handful of people were already sitting in the front of the theater, including the older women from Glenrock—Jennifer, Chipeta, Aunt Mary, and Eliza. Mia hugged her mother. Naomi and Jemma ran to talk to the other ladies. Shaylinn chose to stay beside Kendall in the middle of the third row. Seeing Mia and her mother together made Shaylinn miss her own mother, and Penelope and Nell too. Why weren't they here?

A bald man stood in the center of the stage, fussing over a microphone. He wore black gloves and had a funny black tattoo that covered half his head. "Testing, one, two, three, four..."

Shaylinn glanced over her shoulder. In back of the room, in a small black booth, two men were working, one standing behind a camera as big as he was. Both men wore headsets.

"Those gloves he wears make me think of the evil Count Rugen, the six-fingered man from *The Princess Bride*," Jemma said, sitting down on Shaylinn's left. Jemma was always referencing that film. She lowered her voice to a whisper and seemed to say to herself, "Maybe it's a sign Levi will come for me like Westley did for Buttercup."

"Ladies," Tyra said. "In a moment Luella Flynn is going to film an intro. It's thrilling, I know. So I need you all to be quiet while we're taping, but applaud when you'd like, okay?"

Shaylinn wondered how many of the girls would clap. Mia seemed to be enamored with everything around them, but Naomi and a few of the other Glenrock women were sitting with crossed arms, glaring at the stage. Shaylinn decided she would clap only if someone made her.

On the far right of the stage, Tyra greeted a familiar-looking woman who wore a blood-red sweater and a tight, black, knee-length skirt. Her brown hair was twisted into a mound on the top of her head and studded with what appeared to be diamond flowers. She held a microphone with the letters *SLC* displayed on a square box under the foam head.

"That's Luella Flynn from the Finley and Flynn show," Kendall whispered. "I guess we're done with yellow and black. Just wait—everyone will be wearing those diamond flowers. And black and red. Jemma, you match her!"

Jemma groaned. "Now I'll look like I mimicked her."

Shaylinn thought back to the TV show she'd seen that morning. "But Luella had black hair this morning."

Kendall smirked. "She changes her hair a lot. The brown is new. And so is the length. Probably a wig."

"Thirty seconds!" the cameraman yelled.

The women stopped whispering. Shaylinn continued to look back and forth between the stage and the men in the back, trying to understand what they were doing. Tyra ran onstage to retrieve one of Luella's diamond flowers off the floor.

"Ten seconds!"

"I keep losing those little beasties," Luella said, pushing at one of the flowers in her hair.

"In five, four, three, two..."

"Thanks, Finley," Luella said, her smile radiant. "Precious viewers, I'm live at the Champion Theater in the Highland Harem, juiced to meet the new conscripts. But first, the task director general is going to present a short greeting to the new nationals."

Luella went silent for a moment. "I haven't seen our newest queen. Yet. Rumor is she's *seven months pregnant*, which puts her delivery just two months behind Kendall Collin's. Now, I'm as stimmed as the rest of the Safe Lands about the prospect of two infant nationals, so I promise to get to the bottom of this to-*day* so we can see this miracle woman for ourselves."

The cameraman held up his hand. "We're clear."

Luella slouched and dropped the microphone to her side. "Just a little break for some product expos," she told the audience. "Did I lose any more clips?"

"No, you're fine," Tyra said from the side of the stage.

"Is the new pregnant girl out there?" Luella squinted into the audience.

"Right here!" Mia waved and pointed to Naomi.

"Thanks a lot, Mia," Naomi mumbled.

"Ug! I can't see you, femmy! The lights are too bright." Luella crouched and squinted at the audience.

"They aren't going to make me go up there, are they?" Naomi asked.

"Of course," Kendall said, "though they'll make me go up first."

"Why?" Shaylinn asked.

"Because I'm their spokesmodel. They want people to want to be like us."

"Pregnant?" Naomi said.

"Exactly."

"That's *so* weird," Shaylinn said. She hoped they escaped before that Ciddah woman summoned her, but *after* she got the magical cosmetic consultation.

"No, that's psychotic," Naomi said. "These people are nuts."

"Back in thirty!" the cameraman yelled.

"Kendall!" Tyra tottered up the aisle on her heels, waving. "I need you."

"Here we go." Kendall eased out of her chair and inched down the row, using the seat backs as a crutch. Tyra urged Kendall to hurry, but the girl had only one speed. Slow.

"In ten!"

Shaylinn watched Tyra help Kendall up the short flight of steps to the stage. A woman swooped in, fluffed Kendall's hair, and applied something to her face.

The cameraman spoke from the back of the room. "And five, four, three, two..."

On stage, Luella lifted the microphone in front of her chin. "I give you the task director general of the Safe Lands, Lawten Renzor."

Scattered applause broke out from the small crowd. Shaylinn wasn't about to clap for the leader of her captors. The man walked to the center of the stage. He was wearing a black suit with a black shirt and tie underneath. He didn't look very special.

"Greetings, conscripts. As Task Director General of the Safe Lands, I oversee all facets of our beloved city. As you now know, female nationals are summoned to serve a term in the Highland Harem every two years. Since you're new to our city, we've asked you to serve immediately. This provides you with a safe place to learn our ways and a chance at a successful surrogacy."

"Before we all catch the plague and die," Naomi whispered to Jemma.

Shaylinn frowned. The morbid thought seemed quite possible.

"I'm sure you've discovered that the harem is a wonderful place to live," the task director said. "Matron Dlorah informed me you've been through orientation, task testing, and have been ranked for surrogacy. Congratulations on making it this far."

Jemma folded her arms. "Why's he trying to turn being kidnapped into some kind of competition? It's not like we chose to be here."

"He's hoping we're as dumb as the people who live here," Naomi said.

Shaylinn didn't think that Tyra or Kendall were dumb. Tyra was blunt, but she knew her job and did it well. And Kendall was so nice.

"As you all know, Kendall Collin is our beloved queen," the task director said. "You've likely seen her gorgeous face smiling at you from DigiBoards and Wyndos all over our city. My receptionist even has Kendall's picture as the background on her GlassTop."

This got a chuckle from the people in the front row.

"Let's give a warm welcome to Luella Flynn and Kendall Collin," the task director said.

From the side of the stage, arm in arm, Luella and Kendall walked toward the task director. He stepped back from the microphone and applauded. The Safe Lands nationals seated with the harem stood, cheering. One whistled. Another yelled Kendall's name. Shaylinn wondered if she should stand. Mia had, but Jemma and Naomi were still sitting.

She stayed in her seat as Kendall and Luella reached center stage.

The task director hugged Kendall and kissed her cheeks. "How are you, Ms. Collin?"

Kendall peered at the audience and said in a thin voice, "I'm doing good."

"You're looking good!" Luella said into her microphone, and nationals in the audience cheered.

"Naomi!" a voice whispered. Tyra stood at the end of the row, waving.

"I'm not going up there!" Naomi said.

"Ignore her, then," Jemma said.

But Tyra slipped down the aisle. "Naomi, I need you."

"I don't really care what you need."

Something hard flashed in Tyra's eyes. "I don't like to do this, Ms. Jordan, but I'm told your lifer is being held in the Rehabilitation Center. Your cooperation will assure his good treatment."

Jordan in prison? Heat flashed through Shaylinn's chest. She hoped her brother would try to control his temper. It felt like a futile hope.

Naomi's lips parted; her jaw twitched. "Did you just threaten me?"

Tyra swallowed and looked at the stage. "I'm afraid so."

Naomi shook her head and stood, pushing past Tyra and knocking the tiny woman down into a seat. Jemma followed Naomi all the way to the side stage. Shaylinn didn't want to be left alone, so she got up and followed too. A lady with a brush approached Naomi.

"Don't touch me," Naomi said, and the woman skulked away.

Everything looked different from this position. Bright spotlights from the back of the room blinded Shaylinn and made the audience a white blur. She could see the stage perfectly, however, especially where the task director, Luella, and Kendall stood talking.

"Safe Landers," the task director said, "this baby is coming and soon! He's yours, and he's mine. Thank you, Kendall Collin, for your service to our great city."

Again the crowd applauded. Kendall walked off the stage, deflating a bit once she reached Shaylinn. "I *hate* being on the ColorCast," she said. "Especially with that man."

Luella spoke into her microphone. "Just yesterday, eight new women joined our nation. Like Kendall, they were once outsiders. And among them was their own queen."

Naomi crossed her arms on top of her belly. "I'm *not* going out there."

"A queen as lovely as our Kendall," Luella said, though Shaylinn swore she'd heard the woman admit to never having seen Naomi. "A queen that brought with her the promise of a future. People of the Safe Lands, I give you Naomi Jordan, who's carrying a precious baby boy!"

"Go!" Tyra pushed Naomi onto the stage.

"Boy?" Naomi staggered the first few steps after Tyra's shove, then slowed to a standstill. Shaylinn understood why Tyra had insisted Naomi wear this fitted blue gown over the flowy one Naomi had preferred. They were putting her pregnancy on display for all to see.

"Come now, Ms. Jordan. Don't be shy." The task director held out his arms as if Naomi was his long-lost daughter.

The pale shock on Naomi's face hardened. She straightened, tossed her head back, and marched to the center of the stage. "It's *Mrs.* Jordan," she said.

The task director embraced her and kissed both her cheeks, though Naomi may as well have been a tree.

"Oh, you darling creature!" Luella said, taking Naomi's hands and holding them out to the side. She let go of one and twirled Naomi under her arm. "Finley, isn't she stunning?"

The audience applauded. Finley's reply, wherever he was, wasn't heard in the theater.

"What a joy," the task director said to the audience, "to introduce Naomi Jordan, our new Safe Lands queen."

"I'm not your silly queen," Naomi said. "What have you done with my husband?"

Immediately, majestic music rose, drowning out Naomi's unamplified voice. The task director turned to the left side of the stage. Shaylinn followed his gaze and saw two men walk out from the curtains, shirtless! One carried a fat red pillow that held a crown and a long ribbon. The other carried a bouquet of flowers.

The men stopped beside the task director, who picked up the crown with both hands and settled it onto Naomi's head. Then he put the ribbon over her head, which turned out to be a sash that fell across her body. It bore the words *Safe Lands Queen* in gold glitter. He took the flowers from the second man and handed them to Naomi.

"Surrogacy," the task director said. "Giving life. This is true beauty. This is true patriotism. This is the highest glory to be had in our nation. Naomi Jordan, you are highly favored. We thank you for your service. You're a Safe Lands hero. May Fortune bless you."

"Finally," Kendall said to Shaylinn. "Maybe now they'll start leaving me alone."

Chapter 14

That evening Shaylinn and the other harem girls attended the entertainment orientation, which was held in several ballrooms on the second floor of the Highland Harem. There was a room for dancing, a room for singing, a room for playing musical instruments, and a room for learning how to act. Tyra informed them that they must try everything once as part of their task training.

Kendall had been given the night off for what Tyra had called "the upcoming momentous occasion of giving birth," so Shaylinn stayed close to Jemma and Naomi. They decided to get the acting out of the way, then do the dancing, and end with instruments and singing, which they thought would be more relaxing. Mia tagged along.

The acting room seemed twenty degrees hotter than the rest of the building because of all the bright lamps pointing at each of the stations. There were four stages set up in this room: a kitchen, a dance club, a living room, and a restaurant. Each had a row of seats for spectators.

"It's like a life-sized dollhouse!" Mia said.

Naomi found a food table. Shaylinn filled a plate with stuffed chicken rolls. Once they all had something to munch on, the group sat by the living room station and watched Eliza, Jennifer, and Chipeta read a scene about three friends in the Safe Lands Boarding School. Shaylinn found the process of filmmaking fascinating.

"There you are!" Tyra had found them. "I've been looking for you."

Naomi growled low, like a dog whose territory had been invaded.

Jemma flashed Tyra a hopeful smile. "You're going to let me take Naomi back to the dormitory because a pregnant woman needs her rest?"

"No," Tyra said, "but I'll make you a deal. The director wants to film some of the harem girls reading a scene for a thriller movie. He thinks it'll make great outtakes for today's 'behind the scenes with the new nationals' bit Luella's going to run on her show."

"They're filming us?" Shaylinn didn't want to be on TV.

"Of course!" Tyra said. "They film everything for the ColorCast."

"Good." Naomi shoved three chicken rolls into her mouth. "Whurs duh camma?"

Shaylinn cackled at how silly Naomi looked. The perfect woman for her brother.

"Be serious," Tyra said. "If you do this, and do it well, you can go back to the room."

"Done," Naomi said, gulping down her mouthful. "Where's my script?"

"Excellent!" Tyra handed them each a sheet of white paper. "I want Jemma and Naomi to read Mielle's parts, and Mia and Shaylinn will read the kidnapper. Then if you want, you can switch. It's being filmed on the kitchen set. Byran Kester is the director. He's waiting for you."

"I want to switch," Mia said. "I'd rather play the victim over the kidnapper."

Shaylinn rolled her eyes and settled back to read it over.

29 INT. APARTMENT - KITCHEN - DAY

A frightened Mielle is tied to a chair. Behind her, rebel propaganda posters cover the walls. Mielle struggles with the ropes that bind her hands.

KIDNAPPER 1 approaches Mielle, knife in hand. On his right, KIDNAPPER 2 is setting up a camera on a tripod. KIDNAPPER 3 sits on a chair behind them both, inhaling from a black vaporizer and breathing out black smoke.

KIDNAPPER 1

We're going to record a little footage to send to your Valentine in the Highlands so he knows you're alive. That way he'll be more willing when we—

MIELLE

I'm not doing anything you say!

KIDNAPPER 1

Don't you think your lover has a right to know where you are?

MIELLE

Kale and I do what we want. We're not lifers.

KIDNAPPER 1

That's not what I heard. I heard you've scheduled your liberation for the same day.

And you haven't been to
your apartment in six months.

MIELLE
You've been following me?

KIDNAPPER 1
(to Kidnapper 3)
I think she's catching on.
(to Mielle)
Now, unless you want a knife
shoved between Kale's ribs,
you're going to help us out,
you get me?

CUT TO:

30 INT. APARTMENT - KITCHEN - LATER

Mielle sits on her chair facing Kidnapper 2 and his camera. Kidnapper 2 leans in to record.

31 CLOSEUP - MIELLE

MIELLE
(tearfully)
Hay-o, Kale. I'm sorry I
got myself into this. I
shouldn't have believed
Tarme's lies about the
Liberation Department.
You were right about him.
About everything. I miss
you. The food is good, though.
(laughs)
Please do what they say. I'm
afraid of what will happen
if you don't. I love you.

Shaylinn looked at Jemma. "That's a scary story."

"Let's just do it so we can go, huh?" Jemma said.

They walked over to the kitchen set and found Byran. He was a small man, dark-haired, with a thin face covered in scruff. He wore a black shirt with all of the buttons undone so that his bright yellow tank top showed. A thick gold chain hung round his neck.

"I've got the script on the prompters," Byran said, "so you can just read it. We're still trying to get a feeling for which lines are the best for this scene. Think you can act this out?"

"It's not much of a stretch," Jemma said. "We are kidnapped people, after all."

Byran's laugh sounded forced. "Let's take you first, lovely. That's a pretty dress."

"Right on top of the trends." Naomi faked a smile.

"Let's have you sit on the stool, femme," Byran said. "We're going to come in close on your face, but try not to fidget, because we want you as still as possible. Willa's going to put a little makeup on you, pale that tanned face a bit, give you some fake tears."

"Let's see, you other two..." He looked to Shaylinn and Mia. "I'm just going to let you read how you want to. Try to sound mean."

Once Willa had finished applying makeup to Jemma's face, Byran said, "Both cameras are already rolling, so we can edit later."

"He's recording now?" Shaylinn asked, suddenly feeling awkward.

"Yep," Byran said. "I'm going to ask you all some questions to loosen you up a bit, help you get comfortable. Tell me, Jemma, how old are you?"

"Seventeen."

"And do you have a partner?" He looked at the script. "A uh... *boy* friend?"

"Yes."

"Of course you do, lovely little flame like yourself. And what's your trigger's name?"

"Um... Levi."

"Feeling a bit more comfortable?"

Jemma tittered and rocked in her seat. "No."

"How about you... Shaylinn, is it?"

Had Shaylinn made a mistake? "You didn't ask me anything!"

Naomi snickered, and then Jemma laughed for real.

"No worries," Byran said. "Jemma, go ahead and read the lines off the prompter screen. Shaylinn, you read the kidnapper, but stand back by this microphone, out of the way. We're just filming Mielle now."

It relieved Shaylinn to stand out of the way. She and Jemma spoke their lines. Shaylinn didn't like the kidnapper's part. His words embarrassed her.

When they finished, Byran said, "Okay, that's *reading* the lines. This time, I want you to act them out. I want to hear your fear. I want to see real tears in your eyes. But I want a real fake laugh, okay? Make it sound like you're trying to make light of this horror you're living through. Make your lover believe it. Make Kale scared for you. Pretend it's your Levi, if it helps."

And so they read the lines again. Shaylinn tried hard to pretend she was an evil man, but she just wanted it to be over.

"Great!" Byran smiled at Jemma. "That was great, really great. Can you repeat that last line for me? But this time say, 'You were right about him. About everything. You were right.'"

Jemma repeated the line the way he asked.

"You're a natural, Jemma. Naomi, you're up. Shaylinn, let Mia stand where you are to read the kidnapper."

When they finished with Byran and the acting station, Naomi insisted they leave. Once they were out in the cooler hallway, Naomi said, "Can we go back to the room now?"

"Tyra said we could," Jemma said.

"But we haven't done the singing room yet," Mia said, "or the instrument one. I know neither of you are very good at either of those things, but I happen to have some talent."

"Who cares?" Naomi said. "We're prisoners."

"So we shouldn't have any fun?" Mia asked.

"My father was killed, Mia," Naomi said. "Our mothers are missing. The children are probably terrified. You shouldn't treat this like a vacation."

"Are you trying to make me feel guilty because my mom is here and yours isn't? Fine! Go back to the room and cry. But I'm going to have some fun." Mia stomped away, her tiny steps reminding Shaylinn of the way Matron Dlorah walked.

"I want to stay," Shaylinn said. "I mean, you're right, we are prisoners. But all I can do in my bedroom is feel bad about what happened. Here at least I can forget it for a few more hours."

Jemma hugged Shaylinn. "Okay, Shay. You stay with Mia. And keep her out of trouble."

"I heard that!" Mia yelled.

Shaylinn and Mia went to the dancing room next. It had six stations, three on each side of the room. Instrumental music was playing at the station to the right of the entrance where a ballerina seemed to float across the floor on her toes, sweeping her arms from side to side. A small crowd had formed, and the girls stopped to watch. When the song ended, the crowds applauded and the ballerina curtsied.

"Anyone interested in learning the steps of ballet?" the ballerina asked.

Mia raised her hand, naturally, and the next thing Shaylinn knew, she and Mia were learning "ballet positions."

After the ballet station, they visited a station for a dance that required them to move very quickly to thumping music, one where they made noise using their feet, and one for what they called club dancing, which required them to roll and gyrate their bodies in a way that embarrassed Shaylinn. Mia picked up everything quickly, but Shaylinn's feet seemed too big and slow to do any of it right. Until they got to the one called ballroom dancing.

The flashing screen on the wall said their instructor, Maroz Zerrik, was a famous dancer. He had short blond hair, perfect posture, and broad shoulders. Every time he looked at Shaylinn, her cheeks tingled. He explained the waltz, the tango, the foxtrot, the jitterbug, performing each with a woman named Nelessa Kade, who looked almost naked in a light brown sequined dress.

"Now," Maroz said, "I will waltz with each of you."

Mia squealed and rushed up to Maroz as if he'd called her name. "Me first!"

Maroz chuckled. "As you wish, pearl."

Mia gasped at Shaylinn. "Did you hear that? He said 'As you wish.' I'll have to tell Jemma. Maybe I've found my own Westley."

By the look on Nelessa Kade's face, Shaylinn doubted that very much. As Maroz waltzed with Mia, however, she did just as good as Nelessa. The longer their dance lasted, the more Shaylinn worried about her own turn.

When Maroz's gaze fell on Shaylinn and he held out his hand, she nearly melted. Mia had to push Shaylinn onto the station floor. The man's touch made her stomach flutter. She couldn't remember if she was moving her feet or if Maroz had lifted her up for the entire dance, but somehow she glided along with him, both mortified and enthralled.

When the dance ended, Maroz looked at her with a wide smile. "With more practice, you could become quite good at this. You just have to—" But Shaylinn never learned what she would need to do, as Mia dragged Shaylinn to the singing room, which had one stage and a long line of people waiting to sing. Shaylinn had no desire to sing in front of people, so she sat and waited for Mia, who, when her turn came, crooned on the center stage.

Neither of them had much success in the musical instruments room, but making funny sounds out of a trumpet made Shaylinn laugh.

"I have my cosmetic consultation tomorrow morning," Mia said. "What time is yours?"

"Nine thirty."

"Mine's at nine. You want to come earlier with me? I'll wait for yours to be over."

"Okay." It would be nice to have someone there to talk to, and she was enjoying spending time with tonight's kinder Mia. "I think I want to do it."

Mia laughed. "Do you even know what 'it' is?"

Shaylinn smiled. "Making me thin, I think. Why are you going? You're beautiful."

"I know, but there's so much I'd like to improve, and if these people are willing to do it, I'm not going to fight it."

Shaylinn understood. Everything about this place seemed wonderful. The food, the buildings, the beds, the showers, the clothes... Granted, she was afraid of being pregnant and of catching the thin plague. But she was beginning to wonder if Papa Eli had been a bit mistaken about what happened inside these walls. She could get used to living here.

Chapter 15

The Safe Lands Rehabilitation Center, also called the RC, was located just north of City Hall. Omar arrived twenty minutes early for his meeting with General Otley, anxious to see what Skottie had wanted to show him. He checked in with the enforcer at the entrance, then waited in the lobby for Skottie. Portraits hung along the wall. Brass nameplates mounted under each displayed the person's name and task.

Daniel Miller: TRST founder
Born 1983—Final Liberation 2033

Taylor James: Founder of the enforcers
Born 1995—Final Liberation 2045

Poet Levon: Theater entertainer
Born 2016—Liberated to Seven 2066

Joie Champion: Communications anchor
Born 2021—Liberated to Three 2071

Bristol Cruz: Engineering
Born 2032—Liberated to Five 2072

Liberated. So strange. And too bad for Bristol Cruz. Skottie had said they'd changed the liberation date to forty back in seventy-two. Bad timing to lose ten years of your life, even if you were supposedly born into the next one.

When Skottie showed up, they took the elevator to the sixth floor. "You're going to love this," Skottie said. "One of my femmes tasks in Surveillance as a gatekeeper over the RC."

"What's a gatekeeper?"

"She's in charge of the locks. Nothing opens unless she says so. Now that, my peer, is a position of power."

The doors opened to the clamor of voices. Surveillance consisted of rows of narrow hallways lined with massive Wyndo monitors, three screens down and a dozen across, each screen divided into twelve images. People wearing headsets sat on rolling chairs facing the screens, one person to every six screens.

Skottie led him to the far left of the room where several offices sat behind glass walls. He walked straight ahead to the office in the left corner and tapped on the glass.

A curvy woman looked up from an L-shaped desk. She had lots of curly black hair that poofed out around her face. She grinned at Skottie and waved him in. Skottie opened the door and entered. Omar followed.

"Hey, Camella, how you doing?"

"Just working, trigger. Kind of quiet this morning. Who's your friend?"

"This is Omar. He's new to our world."

"New?" Camella's eyes shifted up and down Omar's body. "You look good, Omar. Where you from, baby face?"

Omar's chest filled with heat at her scrutiny. "Glenrock."

She laughed. "Yeah, I don't know where that is."

"Cammy, show Omar what you do," Skottie said.

Camella rolled her eyes. "Come on back, then."

Skottie grabbed Omar by the sleeve and dragged him behind Camella's desk. She had three screens. One huge one hung on the wall on the long side of desk. It had nine images up at once, but they were changing every few seconds. The other two screens were side by side, built into the GlassTop desk. One showed a close-up of a door, and the other showed a screen that said *SimTag Authorization System* and had a keyboard beneath it.

"What happens is, I get a tap when one of the enforcers needs a door opened," Camella said. "Then I pull up the location on my GlassTop. The enforcer has to verify who he is, and I check each name in the Authorization System. Once I've cleared them all, I code in the entry, and the door will open. Then I log it."

"No one can open a prison door without you?" Omar asked. "Not even Otley?"

She chuckled. "Much to General Otley's chagrin, no. Even he needs—" Camella touched her ear and turned away. "Please verify identification."

"Who's she talking to? I don't hear anything."

"SimTalk," Skottie said. "You should get one. They shoot it in your ear just like a SimTag, then you can talk without your Wyndo." He waved Omar to the office door. "Hey, wait outside for me, will you? I want to talk to Cammy alone for a minute."

"Yeah, sure." Omar slipped out of the office. He didn't want Skottie to think he was eavesdropping, so he wandered down one row of monitors, then another, looking at images of pedestrians, streets, offices, medical facilities, holding rooms, and stores.

This must be where enforcers monitored the feeds from all those yellow cameras.

A man tapped Omar's arm. "Sir? Harem women in the hallway." He glanced up from his screen long enough to realize Omar wasn't the "sir" he'd been looking for. "Sorry." He called out to an enforcer at the end of the hallway, "Sir, the harem women?"

Omar leaned in to study the image of a group of women walking down a wide hallway. He recognized Naomi, Jemma, Mia, and... was that Shay? His heart thudded inside his chest. It was his first look at anyone from home. They looked good, dressed in Safe Lands clothes. Omar felt a little lighter—clearly they were happier here than Glenrock. His bringing them here had made it possible.

"There should be four heading back to the dormitory from the spa," a nasal voice said. "Tyra Grant and Kendall Collin should be with them. Can I help you?" the enforcer asked Omar.

"I'm just looking," Omar said.

"On whose authority?"

"Uh... I'm meeting with General Otley in a few minutes."

"Then you should wait in the reception area on the first floor, Mr. Strong."

A rush of heat seized Omar. Was he in trouble? How'd this man know his name? "I'm sorry." He hurried to the elevator. Forget waiting for Skottie. He glanced back at the enforcer, wincing when he saw him talking to himself. Hopefully not speaking to Otley with one of those SimTalk implants.

Omar went straight to the first floor reception area, announced himself to the woman behind the desk, and sat down.

By the time the woman called him, he'd waited forty minutes.

Otley's office was plain and a tenth of the size of the task director general's. Bright lights glared down on a cracked GlassTop desk, three mismatched metal file cabinets, a set of black chairs, and Otley himself, sitting behind his desk, beefy arms folded across his massive chest.

Omar would sketch Otley as a giant boar ramming its tusks into the side of a house. The children would like that. But the children were in the academy now.

Otley grunted. "Sit, little rat."

Omar sank onto the black metal chair and studied the tusk in Otley's nose.

"Don't like traitors," Otley growled, "so I don't like you. Don't want you in my department. Don't want you owning a rank. It's not my choice, so here's what's going to happen: Report to training every day from eight a.m. 'til five at night. Take an hour off for lunch. Training is closed Friday, Saturday, and Sunday, so stay home those days. Don't want to see you. My people don't want to see you. Snoop around again, and you're cleaning streets. Get me?"

That enforcer in surveillance *had* tapped Otley. "Yes, sir."

"Good. Get out."

Omar stumbled over the legs of his chair but managed to make it out of Otley's office alive. He went straight to the elevators and up to the second floor.

Training turned out to be school, which had started three weeks ago. There were twenty guys in the classroom, all sitting at GlassTop desks. Omar saw Skottie and Charlz in the back.

Enforcer Stiller, a thick man with a flat nose and squinty eyes, was Omar's instructor. He asked the class to read up on tactics, then sat with Omar at the back of the room.

"So you got your captain's stripes without taking one minute of classes," Stiller said. "I bet you're proud of that, aren't you?"

Omar shrugged one shoulder and fought a smile.

"Yeah, that's what I thought. TeleFlash, shell. None of us are impressed that Renzor pulled rank to get you a promotion, got it? So watch your back, *Captain*. The guys like to hammer cheats. And I won't stop a good hammering every now and then, if you get me."

Omar wanted to run, but he sat very still and forced himself to maintain eye contact.

"First, shell, get some muscle on those arms. I'm going to teach you pretty much everything you need to know for your head, but I can't make you strong and neither can your last name. Most of these guys have been training for years. So run to the gym. Move in, if you have to. You're going to hurt for a while, but stick with it. How old are you?"

Omar lowered his voice. "Sixteen."

"Walls. You should be at the boarding school, kid. All right, sit in back with Charlz. He's too thick to know you're a shell. You make friends with him, you might survive training." He nodded to where Charlz was sitting. Skottie sat just in front of Charlz, reading from a Wyndo. "The manual is on the GlassTop."

"Yes, sir." Omar moved to a GlassTop desk in the back row beside Charlz.

Skottie turned and whispered, "What happened to you upstairs?"

"An enforcer kicked me out and tapped Otley."

"My fault there," Skottie said. "Shouldn't have abandoned you."

"*Mr. Skott*," Stiller said.

Skottie turned back to his Wyndo.

Omar tapped on the surface of his desk, opening little folders until he located the manual. He perused the table of contents. There were sections on arrest and booking procedures, investigation techniques, radio communications, report writing, weapons care and safety, marksmanship, stress management, community relations, hate crimes, missing persons, patrol procedures, building searches, vehicle stops, use of deadly force, and a firearms policy.

Overwhelmed, Omar closed his eyes. Levi used to leave him in charge of the lookout in Glenrock, which had always felt like a child's assignment. When Renzor had promised to make Omar an officer in the enforcers, Omar had imagined that someone would give him a gun and put him in charge of some men. His naiveté stung, as did the realization that he was again the youngest, that Otley hated him, and that some of his new classmates might resent him.

He wished he were standing in the lookout back home and that none of this had happened.

He shook the thoughts away. *This* was home now. And he had to prove to everyone that this place was better. Because if it wasn't... If he'd done all this for nothing...

Later, while Omar, Skottie, and Charlz were eating lunch in the cafeteria, Charlz started in on a whole apple pie, the flaky crust the same color as his skin.

"They got the best desserts in this caf." He pushed his tray toward Omar. "Try it."

The mere idea that a flake from Charlz's skin had fallen onto that pie made Omar queasy. "Thanks, I'm full."

Skottie inhaled a long breath on his vaporizer, then tipped his head back and blew a plume of black vapor above his head, leaving behind a spicy smell. "Tonight, we take you out. *We* show *you* the Safe Lands DarkScene."

Charlz howled like some kid pretending to be a wolf. "Ginger Oak, please, Skottie, please?"

Skottie nodded in slow motion, his frizzy brown curls swaying over his eyes. "Oh, yes. Ginger Oak for the outsider. *Precise*. It'll be a night to remember. I still can't believe you've never paired up. That's prude."

Omar's cheeks burned. He wished he'd never told them.

"We should pair him up with Diamoniqua," Charlz said. "Think she'll do it?"

"For enough credits, she'll do anything!"

The guys roared at their private joke, Charlz laughing so hard his neck turned pink.

Omar wasn't certain he could be one of the guys—especially without violating the rules the task director had set him to. But he was certainly going to try.

After classes, Skottie drove Omar to a store where he purchased his own Wyndo transmitter. He paid extra for the program that would allow him to design his own SimArt and couldn't wait to learn to use it. Then they went to Surface, and Omar got a SimTalk installed in his right ear.

After that, Skottie dropped Omar off at the Task of Art store because he had planned to meet Camella for dinner. "I'll pick you up around nine for Ginger Oak, okay?"

"Yeah, thanks," Omar said.

Omar entered the store. Charcoal, pencil shavings, and the chemical smell of oil paints lightened his steps. He was more intoxicated by the sight of art supplies than he'd been from the drinks he'd had at Main Event last night.

He grabbed pads of paper, several canvasses, two sets of oil paints, paintbrushes, some turpentine, an easel, a palette knife, some charcoal pencils, a package of pastels, a pack of colored pencils, and some art markers. He stopped himself from taking one of everything in the store—unlike in his raids of the abandoned stores around Glenrock, these items would remain just as numerous and varied the next time he came.

When the clerk saw all that Omar intended to purchase, he asked, "You sure you can afford all this?"

Was it a lot? Omar wished he'd paid more attention when Dallin had explained costs. "I think so."

"Most enforcers only make four hundred credits a week."

"Oh. Well, I've been saving up," Omar said.

The clerk raised one brow and added up Omar's purchases. "Okay, that comes to 1,349.29 credits."

All this stuff was worth three weeks' credits? He pressed his fist against the pad and waited. He had millions of credits. Didn't he? Maybe the task director had taken them back or hadn't given them out yet.

The clerk gave him a wide smile. "Thank you, Mr. Strong. Let me put all this in some bags for you."

Since Omar didn't really know where he was, he wasn't sure how to get home. He walked for several blocks, carrying his art bags, then, after seeing several people wave down a taxi, he tried it. The taxi cost him only twelve credits.

He carried his bags up to his Snowcrest apartment and set up his easel. He wanted to play with his new Wyndo, make a SimArt owl or tap someone to try his new SimTalk implant, but he wanted to paint more. He hadn't drawn or painted in days. Omar stood at his easel and used a piece of charcoal to sketch his neighbor Bel onto one of his new canvases. Once he was happy with the outline, he squeezed red, brown, orange, and white onto his pallete and started to paint her hair. He instantly noticed how soft the paint was, how smoothly it moved over the canvas. The colors came out exactly how they looked on the tubes, not like Old paints that were dull and thick and goopy or his homemade paints that were so thin.

When Artie tapped to tell Omar that Skottie was waiting downstairs, Omar almost didn't want to leave.

Almost.

Chapter 16

Levi parked his rig in a grove of aspen, swung his rifle over his arm, and crept to the edge of the trees. A rocky expanse with tufts of wild grass separated his location from the northern edge of the Safe Lands. The outer wall stood three stories high and was wide enough to support a two-way road on top. Beyond that wall was the canal, then the inner wall. A Jeep headed south along the outer wall at the moment, and Levi waited for it to pass out of sight. He'd be exposed as he approached the storm drain, but he couldn't risk waiting until nightfall to get inside. Who knew what had happened to Jemma and the others already.

Once the trill of the Jeep's motor had faded, Levi scrambled down the hill, keeping to the tall grass. He still wore the camouflage clothing he'd put on last night but had added the bulletproof vest, his backpack, a pair of gloves, and brown rubber chest waders he'd scavenged from a house in Denver City. They'd keep him dry from what he was about to wade through.

The sky was clear; no sign of rain. That, and his own adrenaline, had him in a full sweat. He'd never been inside the Safe Lands, no matter how many times he and Jordan had dared one another. Elder Eli had instilled a fear of this place that Levi knew not to toy with.

Blackberry bushes scratched his boots as he started up the hill to the wall. Overflow fed out of the bottom of the concrete wall in four large drains, evenly spaced around the bell-like perimeter. Each was a half circle, about six feet wide and four feet tall, covered with grates of crisscrossed iron. There was no way to swim through such small openings and no way to cut the iron that wouldn't call attention to his presence. The grates had hinges on one side, padlocks on the other. The hinges were Levi's way in. He repeatedly struck the concrete around them with a hammer, checking his surroundings after every five blows to make sure no one was approaching. After about an hour, his efforts had began to crush the concrete around the bolts into powder.

After that, it wasn't long before the bolts were loose enough for Levi to pull them out with his hammer, like nails. He pulled back the grate until he was able to slip past. His boots slushed in the water, and he tried not to think about what he was wading through.

Chest waders and gloves had been wonderful inventions of Old.

But it didn't smell like waste water. It even looked clean. With great care, Levi pulled the grate back into place and edged through the flow, careful to make as little noise as possible. The tunnel that passed under the outer wall looked to be about fifteen feet long, though he couldn't see where it let out from his position. All he could see was the inner concrete wall.

When he reached the opening, the sun warmed his face again. He stood in ankle-deep water in the mouth of the tunnel that branched off the main canal: a concrete gutter that cut a four-story gash around the Safe Lands compound, a manmade path for the river that was open to the sky. Levi's storm drain had let him in at water level, leaving three stories of walls towering overhead. Why were the walls so deep? The water would never reach such a depth. He supposed the real reason was to keep people from getting out, which made him very aware of how exposed he was to anyone who might be patrolling the wall above.

The water didn't look deep or fast. The dam likely held back much of the flow. Still, he lowered himself slowly off the storm drain's ledge, feet first, and was thankful to feel the bottom quickly. Standing in the canal put the water at waist level. The bottom was mucky under his boots. He swung his arms, slogging upriver toward the city for what felt like miles upon miles. It was hard to tell from his position, but he knew from having looked through his rifle scope up on the mountain that the Safe Lands had three areas separated by huge walls and gates. He should be in the middle area now and guessed that Jemma and the others would be in the upper city, the farthest away from escape.

He kept close to the outer wall, hoping such a position would make him invisible to patrols above. Every few yards, pipes opened into the canal from the inside wall, discharging trickles of brown waste water into the river. Most were about a foot in diameter, but there were a few bigger ones: some two feet in diameter, some about four. Levi hoped to find a six-footer, like the one he and his father had explored in Denver City. Large drains tended to lead right under city streets.

Levi reached another large grate—hinged on one side, padlocked on the other, just like the first one. This extended from the dividing wall that separated the middle area of the Safe Lands from the upper portion. Slowly, and with as little noise as possible, he worked the bolts over with his hammer until he was able to pass through and continue up river.

On the other side of the grate, the canal inclined some, greatly lowering the water level as it climbed the foothills of the mountain. The water flowed faster here, washing trash and leaves past Levi's ankles. In the distance, the canal turned slightly, obscuring itself as it curved around the top of the bell. Sounds from inside the city drifted to Levi's ears: engines, music, laughter.

For some reason the laughter stopped him. He leaned against the outer wall and closed his eyes, only to envision images of a destroyed Glenrock. His father's face. Papa Eli dying. His knees trembled. He sucked in a deep breath. He could mourn later.

He hiked up the curving incline, the sound of falling water music to his ears, but when the six-foot drainpipe came into view, it had no more discharge than a tiny creek. What, then, was that watery roar?

Levi passed by the drain, seeking the source of the noise. Another hundred yards around the curve of the canal and he caught sight of the dam, built into the wall at the crest of the bell. Water shot out into the canal from one of three spillways. A cement ladder ran through the water and up the right side of the dam. Above, a bridge connected the dam to a roadway. A generator rattled somewhere close by, perhaps the very one that got its power from this contraption.

"Hey!" A man in a gray jumpsuit looked down from the wall, standing above the dam. "You can't be in there, shell!"

Levi turned and ran. He made it three steps before he slipped and fell onto his side, sliding down the canal faster than he wanted to go. He turned his head away from the water and tried to stop himself. Something sharp snagged his hand through his glove, and he winced at the sting. He managed to slow himself to a stop before reaching the six-foot pipe. He pushed himself up, legs shaky. A blaring siren brought his attention to a flash of sunlight gleaming off the windshield of a Jeep cruising along the top of the outer wall, approaching from the west.

With a deep breath, Levi inched toward the six-foot pipe on the inner wall. About three yards before he reached the opening, bullets plopped into the water around him like stones skipping on the surface of a lake. His careful steps became lunges. Bullets cracked against the inside wall, blasting tiny dents into the concrete. Panicked, Levi dove into the pipe, twisting so that he landed on his side, lifting his head as he skidded through the water. The gunfire ceased.

He scrambled up, dripping, and started down the tunnel, slipping twice. His movement upset a swallow, which fluttered toward him. He crouched to let it pass.

The water was only inches deep, spanning a couple of feet at the bottom of the pipe. The only light in the tunnel was the sunlight from the entrance, now twenty yards behind him. He swung off his pack and fumbled for his solar lantern, only to discover the bulb had broken in his fall. Stifling a groan, he dug for a crank flashlight. The beam lit little of his surroundings, but the light was better than nothing. Squaring his shoulders, Levi headed deeper into the shaft.

The storm drain was concrete on the bottom half and rusted corrugated steel pipe on the top. He slipped again, catching himself just before he took another bath. Water that had leaked into his waders when he fell made his feet slosh against the inner soles.

Maybe the chest waders weren't as ingenious as he'd first thought.

He tried walking with his legs spread, one foot on each side of the pipe above the water where it was dry. This offered better footholds but burned his leg muscles. He moved carefully and shined his flashlight at the water. Now that he wasn't kicking it up, he could see it was cloudy brown with bits of trash and the occasional beetle. Stripes of rust on the pipe's sides marked higher past waterlines. Good thing he wasn't trying this after a heavy rainstorm.

After a while, Levi came to a square opening where three new pipes shot off in different directions. All were smaller than the one he stood in—two four-foot pipes and one two-footer. Thick chains draped across the openings of the larger pipes, and sheets of spider's webs filled the corners of the room and covered half the opening of the middle pipe. Graffiti above the smaller hole said "Black Army will prevail" over a drawing of bird's wings.

Levi chose the pipe on the far left, hoping to head toward the upper part of the city. He had to crouch to navigate this smaller drain. He kept his feet on either side of the water and his left hand on the wall to steady himself. This pipe was solid concrete, smooth but spotted with algae and the occasional graffiti. Every so often, he passed a rib where two concrete pipes butted together and thin, brown water dripped down.

He came to an indentation shooting off to the right and stopped to explore. A square chute ran straight up and looked to be two stories high. Rusty iron rungs jutted out from the wall, providing footholds. Levi tucked his flashlight into his mouth and started to climb. A third of the way up, a shell of rust crumbled off the rung, revealing a thin spindle of metal underneath that snapped under Levi's weight, causing him to drop to the previous foothold. He held tightly with his left hand and, once his heartbeat returned to normal, reached for the rung above the broken one. He tugged it first, and it snapped. Frustrated, he climbed back down.

The beam of his flashlight flickered over the walls. The tunnel curved, and he worried he'd come out back in the middle section of the Safe Lands with no way of getting through the second inner wall. An occasional foot-wide pipe emptied into the larger one, sending a stream of water down the chute. More pipes split off from the main one, but Levi stayed on the straight course. No sense in getting any more lost.

The next ladder he came to ran up the wall to a manhole. Light pulsed through a cluster of tiny openings in the lid, and thuds of tires and music echoed down the chute. Flashlight tucked between his teeth, Levi climbed slowly, checking each rung before putting weight on it. When he came to the top, the rhythmic *thump-thump, thump-thump* of tires lowered his spirits. He'd be a fool to exit in front of vehicles that might run him over or stop to capture him.

He climbed down and continued up the tunnel. Some of the connecting ribs rained steady streams of water over his head, cooling his sweaty body. The tunnel forked in two. Levi kept to the left, inching down a steep grade. The water rose quickly, and he noticed several cockroaches on the walls, moving in the opposite direction.

"If it's bad enough for roaches..." He marveled at the sound of his voice in the dark space. He turned back and took the right fork. This tunnel was cleaner and smooth. He passed some graffiti that said, "Lonn for Task Director General." The smell of fried food wafted down, and his stomach growled. He wondered how long he'd been in the drains and if he should stop and eat some beef jerky. Just ahead, red and blue electric light danced at the bottom of the tunnel. Another ladder up?

A shadow flashed long in the distance across the tunnel walls. A light shone behind him. He ducked down, then ran for the indentation in the concrete where the colored light had originated. Hidden in the nook, he peeked back down the tunnel. Two powerful lights shone his way, ten times brighter than his crank flashlight. A voice drifted down the tunnel. He couldn't understand what was said, but it didn't sound urgent. Perhaps, they hadn't seen him.

Levi started up the rungs, testing each quickly, and climbed to the top. Above, a rectangular grille blocked his exit. The sky was dark already. Levi could see the tops of lit-up buildings but little else. He didn't hear any vehicles, so he put one hand flat against the grille and pushed. Unexpected dirt and rust sprinkled into his eyes. He ducked and blinked, trying to clear his vision. Far below, the tunnel glowed bright and footsteps splashed. The men were almost beneath him.

Keeping his eyes down, he pushed again, pressing the back of his neck, head, and shoulders against the iron. It shifted. Dirt and rust tickled his neck and slid down the back of his shirt. He pushed harder and groaned under the strain. The iron popped free, upsetting a glass bottle that rolled on the ground above, clanking over what sounded like asphalt—maybe a road? He could barely slide the grille aside. It scraped over the ground.

"He's there!"

Light blinded him from below. He scrambled out of the hole and crawled onto asphalt. He lay between two buildings in a narrow ditch filled with bottles, broken glass, smashed paper cups, some kind of plastic, and crusts of half-eaten food. Music pulsed nearby, thumping in time with Levi's heartbeat. He pushed to his feet, covered in rust and dirt, which had practically turned to mud due to how wet and sweaty he was.

"See that? I must be vaping high, 'cause a man just climbed out of the trash."

"You ain't vaping, peer. I see him too."

Two grubby men sat on a curb across the street from the ditch, smoking.

"You the trash man, shell?" one asked, then said to his companion, "Them cleaning men get to go more places than enforcers."

Levi stood on the corner of an alley and a narrow road that divided a wall of buildings from a grassy expanse. Where to hide? He inched into the road, looked both ways, then sprinted around the two men and into the grassy area.

"There he goes!" a man called from the hole Levi had just exited.

Levi dodged around bushes and couples sitting on blankets on the grass. His feet were wet inside his boots, slipping on the rubber and making each step uncertain. A concrete wall loomed ahead, somewhat camouflaged in a thick array of foilage. He turned sharp, to run alongside the perimeter, but lost his balance and fell, sliding into some bushes near the wall. He lay still and peeked back, hoping they'd lost sight of him.

No such luck. Five Safe Lands enforcers approached, each with a gun aimed his way. Think! He wouldn't be a help to Jemma if he was dead. He crawled deep into the cover of the bushes, slipped his rifle over his head, then shrugged off his backpack.

"Come on out of there, shell! Nice and easy. We'll get you cleaned up."

"His SimTag isn't registering on my reader," another voice said.

"Mine either," said the first. "He must be a ghost." Then louder, "Pull your stunners!"

"Nothing to see here," a third voice said. "Go back to your pleasure."

Levi hid the rifle and backpack under a large, thick bush, then he pushed onto his hands and knees and crawled along the wall.

"He's moving!"

"Stun him, fool."

Something scuttled over the back of Levi's waders. He lay still, listening to a crackling sound. When the sound stopped, the enforcers moved in. Levi drew the pistol from the holster on his chest, flipped off the safety, and fired the gun.

They enforcers dove for cover, so Levi popped to his feet and carefully trained the pistol on the men. In turn they aimed their weapons his way.

"We don't want to hurt you, sir."

Levi wasn't certain they could. Their strange guns had had no effect on him, and if some shot actual bullets, he was wearing the bulletproof vest. He was safe... unless they shot for his head.

"Let me go on my way then," Levi said. "I don't want to hurt anyone either."

"Can't do that. Least not 'til we log this disturbance. It's illegal to to go without a SimTag. Now put that gun down, and we'll go talk this over at the RC."

Levi's gaze fell on a streetlamp behind the enforcers. After a moment of consideration, he aimed and shot. The lamp went out with a pop, and Levi sprinted between two of the enforcers, heading for the streets, hoping he could get lost in another drain or pile of trash.

"Aim for his shoulders!"

Another crackle lit the air. His body stiffened, and he fell. He hit the grass hard on his face and chest, sliding a few feet. His muscles cramped tighter and tighter until he thought he might explode. Then the crackling stopped. He grunted and tried to move. Someone knelt on his back, pulled his wrists behind him. His limbs were still tingling. He felt lightheaded.

"...violation of Safe Lands laws," a man said above him. "You'll appear before the Safe Lands Guild to plead your case. Anything you say or do can and will be held against you at trial. Do you understand?"

Levi grunted, unable to form actual words.

The enforcers put him in the back of a van with the quietest, smoothest engine he'd ever heard. They transported him to what they called the "RC," a three-story brick building with a sign over the entrance that read *Safe Lands Rehabilitation Center.*

The enforcers took Levi into an elevator, then to a white room that was barely larger in size. It was empty but for a small table with two chairs in the center of the room. Folded, light blue fabric lay in the center of the table.

"Change into the jumpsuit," one of the enforcers said before shutting the door.

"Why don't you make me?"

No one answered. Levi sat at the table and shuddered under a constant stream of cool air pouring through a vent above the table. He climbed onto the table, careful not to let his rubber boots slip on the shiny surface. He found no way to shut the vent. He pulled off his gloves and tried to pry the vent free, but only succeeded in ripping his thumbnail.

He gave the vent one last bang with his fist and fell back into the chair, shivering, sucking on his throbbing thumb. He noticed a gash on the top of his hand. That must have happened when he'd fallen in the canal. If Mason where here, he'd worry about infection.

Levi's hands were trembling, a sign that he was breaking down. He squeezed his fists. He was in their world now. At their mercy. The realization sent him into a rage. He stood, knocking back his chair, then grabbed the edge of the table and pushed it over, screaming as he did. He ran to the door and pounded and yelled for them to open it.

He sank to his knees and set his forehead against the door. He'd failed his people. His first day as elder, and he'd already failed. What could he do now?

No compromise, Papa Eli had said. Levi would *not* do what they asked. He would *not* put on their clothes or obey their commands. He would *not* compromise.

But then the gas came.

The next thing he knew, Levi awoke on a stiff mattress.

He sat up, queasy, and looked around. A small yellow camera peered down on him from above. When he stood, he realized he was wearing a light blue jumpsuit and a pair of sissy black slipper shoes. As far as he could tell, he was in a jail cell. Rows of cells ran along two walls and on both sides of him, separated by a narrow aisle.

The cut on his left hand was bandaged, but his other hand itched, as did his cheek. He caught sight of a faint white glow of *9X* on the back of his hand. "No!" They had *no right* to mark his body like he belonged to them.

He tugged at his hair and screamed until he lost his breath. Unable to stay still any longer, he ran to the bars of his cell. "Hey!" He gave the bars a good shake. "Hey! You people have no right to keep me here. Let me out!"

"You won't get out of here that way, shell," a man said from the cell diagonal from Levi's. He had a wide forehead; a short, graying beard; and shoulder-length wavy dark hair that hung in his face. "Name's Lonn. What's yours?"

Levi slowed his breathing slightly. "Levi."

"That X on your face new, Levi?" Lonn asked.

Levi touched his cheek again, nodded. "If it matches the one on my hand, it's as new as the number. What's it mean?"

The man's eyebrows rose. "Outsider, huh? Well, the X is a strike. It means you've been a bad boy. Three strikes are all you get in the Safe Lands before they put you away for good."

Lonn had three Xs on his cheek. Anyone with three strikes was all right by Levi. "So you're going away for good then?"

"Soon, yeah. But hopefully not without giving them one last expression of my distaste."

"So… I only have one X. Does that mean they'll let me out?"

Lonn swept the hair out of his eyes. "Maybe. Depends if you give them what they want."

Then he'd likely be in the cell forever. "They killed my people."

"That doesn't surprise me."

"Hey there, raven," a woman on Levi's left said, her voice a husky rumble. She stood against the bars that separated the side of his cell from hers. She was bone thin and wore a pale-blue jumper three sizes too big, which she'd unbuttoned to reveal impossible cleavage for someone so malnourished. Her face might have been pretty once, but her cheeks were gaunt and gouges circled her eyes.

Levi turned back to Lonn. "How often do the enforcers come down—"

"Don't look away, Valentine," the woman said. "Come on over here and let me trigger your stims."

Levi yelled as loudly as he could, "Anyone from Glenrock here?"

"Me!" a small voice cried from the cell on the other side of the crazy woman. Levi stepped closer and peered through his neighbor's cell. A dark-haired girl in a pale-blue jumpsuit. It couldn't be. "Penelope?"

"Levi? What are you doing here? You were supposed to free us," his cousin said.

Her words made him feel like he swallowed his heart. "I will, Pen, don't worry. Give me some time to figure this place out, will you? Is, uh, Jemma—?"

"She's okay, I think. She was with us in the transport. Your mom too. But Omar did this, Levi. Omar is a traitor."

A chill flashed over Levi, Omar's lies fresh in his mind. "You sure?"

"The enforcers gave him a gold envelope. Auntie Tamera said it was for a job."

No, no, no! Levi ran his hands through his tangled hair. Omar responsible for the death of their father? Of little Sophie? Sure, his brother had lied, but... "Anyone else from Glenrock in the jail, Pen?"

"Jordan. But he's unconscious. They put him down toward the front cells."

Yes! Hope surged in Levi's chest, and he craned in hopes he'd see his friend.

The gaunt woman stepped in front of Levi, blocking his view of Penelope. She reached past the bars and grabbed the sleeve of his jumpsuit. "Come on, Valentine. Let's you and me share a little love, huh?"

Levi stepped back, pulling his arm out of her grip. "I'm trying to talk to someone here."

"Natachah just wants a kiss," Lonn said. "And she won't shut up 'til you give in."

"I let her kiss my hand," Penelope said, her tone somewhat ashamed.

The people here were worse than Papa Eli had said. "Well, I guess I'll have to raise my voice, then," Levi yelled into the woman's face, "because I'm not touching you!"

Natachah screamed, threw herself on the floor, and began to shake as if having a seizure. She must have been faking it, but it sure looked real. Levi backed away from the bars and sat on his bed. Two guards ran down the corridor to the woman's cell.

"Give us a break, Natachah, will you?" one of them said as he opened the door. "You'll never get out of here if you keep this up."

The second guard secured Natachah's hands behind her back while the first held a white tube to her lips. Natachah pursed her lips around it and sucked in the longest breath Levi had ever seen. When the enforcer removed the tube, Natachah exhaled a plume of white smoke, blowing it out in a long stream, her face frozen like a skeleton's.

"Sleep it off, Natachah, huh?" the guard said, grabbing her by the arms.

The guards helped Natachah onto her bed, removed the handcuffs, and left her cell.

"You just think about giving her a little peck when she wakes up," one guard said to Levi. "Or she'll just start in with you again and none of you will get any sleep."

The guards left the cell and walked back the way they'd come.

Levi jumped up. "Hey!" he yelled after them. "I have some questions."

The guards ignored him.

"Levi!" Penelope still stood at the bars on the side of her cell.

Levi knelt at the bars that divided his cell from Natachah's. "Why you in here, Pen?" he asked, noticing they'd put the same number—9X—on Penelope's cheek.

"I got in trouble in science class. We went outside to collect leaves from one of the grassy areas, and while I was looking a boy asked to kiss me, since I was new. I told him no thank you, and he called me a proo dish."

Levi frowned and double-checked the word. "Do you mean prudish?"

"A prude dish," Lonn said. "That's an attractive person who won't play love games."

Levi didn't want to know what kind of love games were played in a school for thirteen-year-olds. It had better not be more than kissing in trees. "What happened, Pen?"

"He wouldn't leave me alone. And he tried to kiss me anyway. So I kicked him where you taught me and tied him to a tree with his belt."

"Ha!" Levi slapped his thigh and grinned. "That's my girl."

"The teacher saw, though. Said I was unloving and sent me to the assistant educator, who lectured me on hateful behavior, added an X to my number, and put me in here for the day."

If Levi ever saw that kid or the educator... "That's you and me, Pen. I guess 9X is the number to be, huh?"

"I don't want to go back to the school. I want to go home."

"Me too. And we will soon. Tell me about this boarding school."

"It's for all kids under fourteen. We have to live there. They said we can't see our moms again. Nell is in my dormitory. I hope she's okay without me. The boys were teasing her too, and I don't think she'll fight them off."

"Tell me everything that happened yesterday, Pen. In the village."

So Penelope did, starting with the attack on Glenrock: gathering in the meeting hall, the gunfire, the enforcers getting the women's names, Omar arriving with Jemma. "The enforcer gave Omar a gold envelope. Then they took us to this city and marked us with numbers. They took my mom somewhere—they have all our mothers. One of the men told me I won't see Mom until I'm fourteen or pregnant."

The word *pregnant* pulled Levi away from dwelling on his idiot brother. "*Excuse me*? Explain what you mean by pregnant."

"Exactly what I said, Levi. I'm not dumb. They took the older girls and moms to something they called the Highland Harem to take turns having babies. Nell said she was going to volunteer to get pregnant so she could see her mom sooner."

"No, Pen. You tell Nell to be smart. I'm going to get us out of here, okay? Don't let these people get to you. You fought today, Pen, and that was great. I'm proud of you. That was Papa Eli's blood in your veins. You keep on fighting, okay? But be careful too."

"I'm scared."

Penelope's words—*take turns having babies*—caused his stomach to lurch. "I know, Pen. I'm scared too."

"Dog-faced, manure-eating cockroach!"

Levi perked up at the familiar sound of Jordan's insults. He ran to the bars that separated his cell from Natachah's. Thankfully, the woman had been let out yesterday, the same day they'd released Penelope. Levi peered out and watched as enforcers dragged a somewhat limp Jordan through the door of a cell about six away from Levi's. The enforcers heaved his friend onto the bed and left.

When their footsteps faded, Levi called out. "Jordan!"

Jordan groaned and lifted his head off the mattress. "Levi?"

"Are you okay? What happened to you?"

Jordan blinked twice, squinted at Levi, and screamed "No!" so loudly that Levi crouched and covered his ears.

"What's the matter with you?" Levi asked. "You want them to come back and sting you again? Shut up!"

"*You're* supposed to rescue us, you droppings of a donkey... How'd you end up here?"

"They caught me sneaking into the city through the storm drains."

Jordan cursed another long, drawn-out, completely illogical phrase.

When he stopped, Levi asked, "What about you? What happened?"

Jordan pushed himself up so he was sitting with his legs dangling off the side of the bed. He rubbed his hands over his face. "They want me to join their people, so I tried to kick some enforcer's face in. But those electric guns! Hog's teeth, those things mess me over. By the way, they've got Mason up there somewhere. He decided to play along to see what he could learn."

"Why didn't *you*?"

"Are you mad? I'm not letting those maggots push me around. They already put their mark on me." He looked at the back of his right hand. "What does 4X mean?"

"Don't know about the number, but X means you're trouble," Levi said.

"Good. They'll cover me in Xs for what I'm going to do when I get my hands on that hairy, spike-nosed, vole-loving—"

"There's no way out of here," Levi said.

"Can we dig a hole like that Shawshank guy?"

"It's all cement."

"The drains then. Rip out that sink and follow the pipes."

"They're too small, Jordan."

"But we could get to the dirt that way and dig the hole."

"The cameras, Jordan. They're watching us."

"Shame what they do these days," Lonn said from his cell across the way. "They bring outsiders in here, make all kinds of promises, but most people end up dead before the guild even gets what they want."

"What do they want from us?" Levi asked.

"Babies. Uninfected ones if they can get 'em."

Levi stared at the older man, bewildered. Why did the Safe Landers want children? And if that was their goal, why were they keeping everyone separated? But before Levi could ask, Jordan jumped off his bed and walked to the bars of his cell. "The enforcer said the same. That our women would bear children for this place. Why?"

"Because our people can't," Lonn said.

"I don't give a pile of rotten robin's eggs about what your people can and can't do," Jordan said. "They took my wife. They will *not* keep her. Or my son."

"I like your fire, boy, but you've gotta be careful. Their so-called liberation ain't gonna get you what you want."

"So what will?" Levi asked. "They have my fiancée too."

"Patience and wit." Lonn grabbed a scrap of paper and scribbled something on it, then casually tossed the now-crumpled wad toward Levi. Being just as discreet, Levi leaned down and grabbed the missive, quickly reading the words:

If you boys get out of here, go to the Midlands and ask for Bender. When you find him, tell him I said, "Rose."

Levi looked at Lonn and nodded, then turned to Jordan and said in a low voice, "Looks like we have an ally."

"That's right," Lonn said.

"Why should we listen to you?" Jordan asked.

Lonn swept his hair over his head. "Trust me?"

Jordan laughed harshly. "I ain't trusting none of you maggots."

"The problem is, we won't get out of the city unless we find a way out of this cell," Levi said.

"Getting out might not be as hard as you think. They'll do something to convince you to comply and play nice," Lonn said. "It's how they operate."

Levi couldn't imagine anything convincing him to comply with these maniacs, unless it involved Jemma. He might be able to play the game for a little while, to keep Jemma safe. But if they hurt her in any way, they'd forever regret it.

Chapter 17

The redheaded guard, Ewan, escorted Shaylinn and Mia in a blue luxury car to their cosmetic consultations in a huge white building called the Plaza Medical Center. It was six levels high—bigger than the entire village of Glenrock.

Tyra Grant's office was on the third floor in the Beauty Care Department. As they entered the waiting room, Shaylinn couldn't stop staring at the walls covered with pictures of beautiful women. Could she possibly look like them?

While Mia went in for her appointment, Shaylinn sat on a cushy black sofa and tried to settle her nerves by looking on a GlassTop table at a variety of hairstyles and clothing choices that promised to "make the new you sparkle even more." She was just starting to relax when she heard Mia's voice.

"I can't wait to get everything done."

"I really think you'll do great," Tyra said. "Come on in, Shaylinn."

Shaylinn got up and followed Tyra. The light pink walls and Kelly green accents in Tyra's office took a moment to get used to as Shaylinn sat in a pink and green polka-dot chair.

"Shaylinn, you're going to love living here," Tyra said. "The Safe Lands has everything a girl could ever want."

Shaylinn wanted to believe her, but things were moving so quickly. "I'm not sure I want to have a surgery." She'd been caught up in the makeovers yesterday, but actually changing what she looked like...

"Oh, you're not here to talk about a surgery. Fortune, no!" Tyra chuckled and reached across her desk for a roll of white plastic. "Let's start with some simple InstaWraps. You have a slow metabolism, and these will burn away the extra fat, tone your muscles, and remove toxins. I'm also going to get you on a special diet so we can keep the weight off. I think you'll be very pleased with the results."

Shaylinn didn't like the sound of the word *burn*. "Will it hurt?"

"Not at all," Tyra said. "Stand up."

Shaylinn slowly pushed back the polka-dotted chair and stood. Tyra grabbed the hem of Shaylinn's shirt and rolled it up, baring her belly.

Shaylinn gasped. "What are you doing?"

"Showing you how to apply the wrap. Now, these are very advanced and quite expensive, but while you're in the harem, they're free." Tyra removed the top layer from the roll of plastic, which left her holding a rectangular sheet about the size of a pillowcase. "Once you get the backing off, all you have to do is press the moist side against your skin." Tyra peeled off a plastic layer. "Ready? It's going to be a little cold."

Shaylinn nodded and lifted her arms. As the wrap was pressed to her skin, she tensed against the coldness, but it was uncomfortable for only a moment.

"You can do more than one at a time if you have help," Tyra said. "The wraps need to stay smooth against your skin. No wrinkles or bubbles, okay?"

"What do they do?" Shaylinn asked.

"The formula on the wrap absorbs into your skin and speeds up the cells in body. The fat cells shrink as if you've been exercising for months. Now, I want you to do some other things daily. A half hour in the sauna to keep your metabolism going—but if you become pregnant, the saunas will have to stop." Tyra reached onto her desk and grabbed two thin cylinders. "These are SkinnySticks—use them to touch-up the places where you need a little more toning, or, Fortune forbid, in places where there was a bubble in the wrap and the fat didn't burn away completely. Also, drink lots and lots of water. Follow the diet I give you. Eat smaller meals, more frequently."

Tyra quickly wrapped Shaylinn's arms in the sticky paper then fetched what she called a compression jacket. "This will hold the wraps in place while you wear them. They only require twenty minutes, but you can wear them longer. Some women sleep in leg or neck wraps because it's more comfortable then wearing them during the day. I'm also going to give you some smaller masks so you can wrap your chin and neck."

Shaylinn had to remove her shirt to fit into the compression jacket, but she was able to put her shirt on over it, which was a small relief.

"You'll likely see a major difference in just a few days," Tyra said. "Especially if you start exercising and eating well."

Tyra sent Shaylinn home with enough wraps for the next two weeks. She showed them to Mia on the car ride back to the harem, whispering so Ewan couldn't hear.

But Mia practically screamed, "Shay, that's amazing! You're finally going to be skinny. Just think—if we'd never come here, you would have stayed chubby and plain forever. Now you're going to look gorgeous! I'm so jealous. I wish they could do implants and acne treatments as quickly as body wraps. We have to go out tonight and celebrate. Rand said he'd take me and my friends out anytime. What do you say?"

"Who's Rand?" Shaylinn asked.

"A piano player I met at the entertainment orientation. Do you remember that man who waltzed with us? Maroz Zerrik?"

"How could I forget?" Shaylinn had relived that dance over and over.

"Well, Rand plays for Maroz's show." Mia reached over the seat and grabbed Ewan's shoulder. "Didn't you say you could take me to meet Rand?"

Ewan looked at them in the rearview mirror. "I said I *could*."

Mia squealed. "I'm going to tap Rand right now." She slid her Wyndo from her jacket pocket. "I keep forgetting I can talk to anyone with this."

"I forgot mine at the harem," Shaylinn said, running her hands over her belly. Was she getting thinner right now? She couldn't tell.

"Someone there?" A man's picture was moving on Mia's Wyndo screen.

Mia lifted the Wyndo in front of her face. "Rand! It's Mia from the harem."

"Hay-o, pearly girl. What you doing right now?"

The leer in Rand's voice made Shaylinn shiver. Mia made plans to go out to a cab-array, whatever that meant. Shaylinn wasn't sure how she felt about this; but the look on Mia's face made her wonder if she was worrying over nothing.

By the time Ewan escorted Shaylinn and Mia back to the harem, Jemma, Naomi, and Kendall were eating lunch at the kitchen table in the Blue Diamond Suite.

"Just in time for food!" Naomi said.

Jemma pulled out the chair on her left. "Come sit down, Shay. How was your morning?"

"It was good," Shaylinn said. "Tyra gave me InstaWraps to help me lose weight."

"You're not fat, Shay," Jemma said. "You're perfect."

Sisters were supposed to say things like that. No *man* had ever told Shaylinn she was pretty, much less thin. In fact, several had told her the opposite, including her own father.

Shaylinn unfolded the approved food list Tyra had given her and scanned it. Fruit was the only match she could find on the kitchen table. With a deep breath, she took a wedge of melon and nibbled on it.

"My consultation was more than good," Mia said. "It was ah-mazing. They're going to get rid of my acne and a perform a breast enhancement."

Shaylinn's eyes bulged. Mia had mentioned implants but not the location.

"What on earth do you need implants for, Mia?" Naomi said. "You're bigger than me, and I'm pregnant!"

Mia rolled her eyes. "Look around you. If you want to get noticed, you need more than nice eyes and a decent figure." She ate a grape. "And I intend to get noticed. I even have a date tonight."

"Like in the Old movies where a boy comes by and gives you flowers?" Naomi asked.

"Sort of. But since boys can't come to the harem, I'm going out."

"With who?" Kendall asked.

"His name is Rand, and he plays piano for Maroz Zerrik."

"Maroz has a bad reputation," Kendall said.

"I don't like you spending time with a Safe Lander," Jemma said. "How well do you know this piano player?"

"That's what dates are for, Jemma," Mia said. "He's taking me to a musical show—I forgot the name—but he said I'd love it."

"What about Mason?" Jemma asked.

Mia ate another grape. "I could care less about Mason."

Jemma gasped. Mia grabbed another grape.

"How can you go out?" Naomi asked. "We're only allowed to leave the harem for doctor appointments. And then only with Ewan or some other enforcer glued to our sides."

"Ewan and Rand are friends," Mia said. "Ewan's going to take me to meet him."

"Then we all should leave!" Jemma said, suddenly excited. "If Ewan isn't guarding the door, we could get Kendall past the wall and back to Glenrock before she goes into labor and—"

"Like that would even work, Jemma," Mia said. "All this is going to be is a date—Rand's and *my* date. If you went, you'd get Ewan in trouble, and then Rand would be mad at me."

"Mad at *you*?" Jemma said. "They're going to take Kendall's baby, Mia. We've got to help her."

"*I* don't have to do anything." Mia stood up, grabbed a bunch of grapes, and walked to her bedroom.

Silence descended over the table.

Jemma jumped up and ran from the suite, headed toward Mia's mother's room.

Shaylinn watched the front door swing closed, torn. Jemma was right. They should do all they could to escape—to help Kendall. But Shaylinn wanted a little time for her InstaWraps and SkinnySticks to work. Plus, she was really looking forward to the cab-array.

Mia's mother forbade Mia to go out with Rand, so Mia dragged Shaylinn into her room and insisted they tried on their new clothes and model them for Jemma, Naomi, and Kendall. Shaylinn kept the InstaWraps on and was able to hide them under every outfit. Mia did Shaylinn's makeup and curled Shaylinn's hair into bobbing ringlets. When Shay looked in the mirror, she felt... pretty.

She desperately missed Penelope and Nell and hoped they were doing okay in the boarding school, but Shaylinn was actually having fun—with Mia. Maybe they'd become friends.

"That's the one," Mia said when Shaylinn had put on a short black strapless dress that flipped out in a full skirt. "Put this over your arm." She hung a thick purse over Shaylinn's head and shoulder so that its strap crossed her chest, then Mia made her put on a thick, floor-length bathrobe over the dress. "Say nothing."

Mia likewise put a bathrobe over her hot pink halter dress, then pulled Shaylinn into the living room. "We're going to get a snack from the kitchen. Anyone want anything?"

"We have snacks in our kitchen," Naomi said.

"I don't want those. Since my date was ruined"—she glared hard at Jemma—"I want something special from downstairs."

"I was just looking out for you, Mia," Jemma said. "You seem to forget we're prisoners here. I don't want you to get hurt."

Mia set her hand on her hip. "Do you want something or not? It's a simple question."

"No, thank you," Kendall said.

Jemma and Naomi shook their heads.

"Fine." Mia pulled Shaylinn toward the door. "We'll be back."

They walked down the stairs in their bare feet, crossed the harem sitting room, and entered the dark kitchen. A light above the stove and a green emergency exit sign barely lit the room. The chef was gone for the night.

Mia threw off her bathrobe and straightened her skirt. "Give me the purse," she said.

Shaylinn took off her robe and handed the bag to Mia, who dumped the contents. Two pair of shoes clattered onto the floor.

Mia stepped into the gold heels. "Put on the black ones, and hurry!"

"We're still going?" Shaylinn asked.

"What do you think? Come on."

Mia dragged Shaylinn through the emergency exit and into a cold stairwell. A man stood in the darkness, and Shaylinn screamed.

Mia clapped her hand over Shaylinn's mouth. "It's just Ewan. Walls!"

When had Mia started saying Safe Lands slang?

"There are no cameras this way," Ewan said.

He led them down the stairs. Shaylinn couldn't move very fast in the high heels and trotted after Mia and Ewan, down, down, down.

"Come on!" Mia whispered.

"I'm trying!"

The stairs let out into a large warehouse. They followed Ewan through it and out a door where a car was waiting. Mia climbed into the back, and Shaylinn got in beside her. Then Ewan jumped in beside Shaylinn and slammed the door shut.

"The Venetian Room," Ewan told the driver, then leaned back and put his arm over the back of the seat, behind Shaylinn's head. He leaned close to Shaylinn, and his hair tickled her face. "Hey, shimmer. You look pretty," he whispered.

Her eyes flew wide. "I do?"

He let his arm fall around Shaylinn and pulled her against his side. She stiffened and shot Mia a worried glance.

Mia raised her eyebrows as if to say, "Go along with it."

Shaylinn didn't really want to go along with it, though. She didn't know Ewan enough to be so close, and she didn't like the way his poufy red hair kept tickling the side of her face.

"Expect greatness tonight, femmes," Ewan said. "This show does something for the soul."

Well, that sounded nice, at least.

It didn't take long to reach the Venetian Room. Inside, the place looked like an Old concrete warehouse. It was dark, and red and blue lights rotated in bands across the walls and the high ceiling. The music was loud and thrummed through Shaylinn's body straight to her heart. Little round tables filled the space, and they all looked full.

Shaylinn followed Ewan and Mia to a table in the very front, where a handsome young man with slick yellow hair was waiting. He kissed Mia on both cheeks and they spoke. The music was too loud for Shaylinn to hear what they said, but Mia giggled and touched the man's arm, then pointed at Shaylinn. The man smiled and, before Shaylinn knew what was happening, he was kissing her cheeks as well. He smelled good, and Shaylinn enjoyed the way his scent lingered after he moved away.

He and Mia sat beside each other at the front of the table. Shaylinn sat in back beside Ewan. He scooted his chair close as if he might put his arm around her again. She leaned on the table in the opposite direction so he couldn't reach her.

A waitress took their drink orders. Shaylinn didn't know what to order, so she shook her head. Then the show began.

The music washed over her, the notes alternatively fading and coming in strong as the band played. The lights danced and swayed, changed colors, all perfectly timed with the music. Then suddenly, everyone was looking up.

A man hung from the ceiling, wearing only black underwear. And a woman! She wore a white bra and a flimsy white skirt. The man swung from a metal bar by the backs of his knees, then dropped to the tops of his feet, his arms and legs bulging with muscles. The woman tangled herself in yards of shiny red fabric, twisting and splitting and dropping right over the tables.

The music changed, and dancers ran out onto the stage, wild and stomping. Women wore black bras and fishnet stockings. Some had mustaches and some had clown noses. Men tumbled across the stage in their underwear, twisting their bodies and rolling together as if they were one person. More performers danced from ropes and strips of fabric, metal rings and squares, sometimes in pairs. Lightning flashed and flashed, white and red. The music thumped.

Shaylinn couldn't blink.

It seemed to go on forever, yet when it ended, Shaylinn felt like it had barely begun. It had been mesmerizing... and it made her feel wild and giddy inside.

The silence brought on by the end of the show shocked her ears. Shaylinn focused on those around her and was shocked to see Mia and Rand kissing more than each other's cheeks. Their faces seemed glued together. Shaylinn stared until she realized she was staring, then looked away only to find Ewan watching her with a hungry look in his eyes. She jumped and pulled her curls towards the front of her face so he couldn't see her.

She was suddenly cold and wanted to go back. She leaned across the table and poked her friend. "Mia," she said. "Mia!"

Mia and Rand's lips broke apart, and they both turned to look at Shaylinn.

"I'm ready to go," she said.

Mia scowled. "I'm not."

Shaylinn stood. "Well, I am, Mia. Let's go. Now!" Shaylinn couldn't explain the confusion she felt. She only knew she needed to leave. And she wasn't going to let Mia bully her into staying.

Mia's eyes sprang wide, and with that Shaylinn felt strong. "I'm sorry," Mia told Rand. "My friend isn't feeling well."

"Tap me when you get home?" he asked.

"Of course."

Shaylinn suffered through one more Mia and Rand face-sucking episode before she managed to drag Mia away. Ewan followed, but Shaylinn kept Mia between them as a buffer, even once they entered the car. She didn't like the look in his eyes.

They drove back in silence.

Ewan escorted them into the harem building through the regular entrance. They passed through the revolving door, walked across the orange and blue lobby, went up the elevator to five, and walked down the red and black carpet to the golden door engraved with the creepy cat-bird-woman. There they stopped. Shaylinn pressed her fist against the door. Nothing happened.

"Why didn't it open?" she asked Ewan.

"It only opens for staff," he said. "But touching it rings the bell, so someone will come."

"Well, thank you for bringing us back," Shaylinn said.

"You promised me a kiss," Ewan said to Mia.

Eww. Shaylinn looked from Mia to Ewan and back to Mia.

Mia clicked her tongue and prodded Shaylinn's arm. "Go on, Shaylinn."

"Me?" Shaylinn backed against the door. "I didn't promise to kiss anyone."

Mia sighed. "The only reason Ewan agreed to take us out tonight was because you'd give him a good-night kiss. Do it so we can go inside."

Shaylinn glared at Mia. "You had no right to promise that!"

Mia grabbed Shaylinn's arm and squeezed. "You already ruined my night," she said through gritted teeth. "Stop embarrassing me."

Shaylinn pulled away. "You're embarrassing yourself, Mia. Letting that Rand man kiss you in public like that. You hardly know anything about him."

Mia rolled her eyes. "That's why I'm getting to know him."

"The music was too loud for talking, so I doubt you learned anything except how well he kisses. You're going to get hurt. My mama says a girl should protect her heart."

"Like you with Omar?"

Shaylinn's chest smoldered. "You don't know anything about me."

Mia smirked. "I know you're always staring at Omar."

"I am not!"

"Shut up!" Ewan yelled.

Shaylinn jumped and turned to face him.

"I'll take my payment now." He grabbed Shaylinn's arms, pushed her against the wall, and forced his mouth onto hers.

He smelled stale and bitter at the same time, and he pressed so hard that Shaylinn's own teeth cut into her lip. She turned her head to the side and screamed as loud and long as she could.

Ewan let go and glared at her. "What's the matter with you?"

Shaylinn pulled off one of her shoes and threw it at Ewan's head. "You're a terrible—"

"Ow!" Ewan cowered under his arms.

"—rude, horrible, disgusting!" She yanked off the other shoe and hit him with it.

"Stop it, you crazy femme!" He tried and failed to dodge her blows.

"Shaylinn, stop." Mia grabbed Shaylinn's arm and pulled her back. "Matron's here."

Sure enough, Matron stood in the doorway, looking at Shaylinn like she was a disobedient child.

Oh dear.

Chapter 18

The clink of iron woke Levi. Before he could gather his wits, his hands were bound behind him and he was dragged to his feet. From down the hall, he could hear rustling and a few grunts.

"Get off me, you dung-wielding rot face!"

Apparently Jordan was being moved as well.

The enforcers took them to a cell on the third floor, where a huge TV hung on the wall opposite the entrance. A steel bench in the middle of the room faced the screen. They sat Levi and Jordan on the bench, side by side, and attached their restraints to metal loops on the bench. A quick yank of the chain confirmed the bench was bolted to the floor.

A third enforcer ducked through the doorway. He had dark, frizzy hair, parted down the middle, which tangled with his bushy mustache and beard. His eyes were a freakish yellow. Even weirder, two coils of gold metal curled out from each nostril like feelers on an insect. Medals and bars and fancy patches—including one that said *Otley*—covered his uniform. The number eight glowed on his cheek.

"Still like to get your cooperation voluntarily," Otley said to Jordan.

"You're not getting anything from us, you grizzly pukepile of a man." Jordan turned to Levi. "He's the maggot who killed your father, Levi. I saw him do it."

Levi turned his head slowly until he met Otley's gaze. He attempted to stand, but his restraints were so short that his body jerked back to his seat. He set his jaw, fighting to hold back his anger, then closed his eyes and tried to breathe calmly like Jemma had taught him. Recite his verse: *Refrain from anger. Turn from wrath.* His breaths came short and hard, but with them some clarity surfaced. He was the village elder. He had to help his people.

"Something you want to say to me, rat?" Otley asked.

Levi opened his eyes. Took a deep breath. *Refrain from anger. Turn from wrath.* "Not... yet."

Otley walked to the back of the room. "Wyndo: power. Play, pause." The TV powered on, black at first, but slowly colored to reveal Jemma from the shoulders up, wearing a red dress and sitting in a kitchen, frozen and slightly fuzzy. On pause.

"Jemma," Levi whispered.

"What are you doing with my sister?" Jordan yelled.

Otley's cheeks balled up in a smirk. "Wyndo: play."

Levi's chest heaved, his anger growing again, but the screen moved, and Jemma spoke.

"I'm sorry I got myself into this. You were right. Levi. About everything. I miss you. The food is good, though." She chuckled as if making a lame joke. "Please do what they say. I'm afraid of what will happen if you don't. I love you."

"Wyndo: pause," Otley said.

The screen stopped on Jemma's face, misty eyes wide, lips frowning slightly.

Levi could hardly breathe. "You threatened her?"

"Someone else would like a word. Wyndo: play."

The screen went black a moment before showing Naomi in the same kitchen. Levi didn't know if it was the angle of the recording, her tight blue dress, or the way she held her hands over her huge belly that made her look like she might burst.

"No!" Jordan stood, arching his body backward and pulling at his bonds. His face reddened, veins popped out on his neck.

"Jordan? Baby? I'm so sorry this has happened."

Jordan wilted at Naomi's voice and fell back to his seat. "No, baby, no."

"They're treating me well. But I don't want to be here anymore. Some of them scare me. I'm scared for our baby." Naomi started crying.

Jordan moaned, and it slowly morphed into another scream of rage.

"Wyndo: stop," Otley said. The TV went black.

"Put her back!" Jordan yelled. "Please!"

"Naomi is correct," Otley said. "We're currently treating them all very well. But that ends if you continue to cause problems. You both must become Safe Lands nationals, obey our laws, or your women will be killed." Otley looked to Jordan. "We'll wait until your baby is born before killing her, of course. But this is nonnegotiable. You have three minutes to decide."

With that, Otley and the enforcers left the room.

"We have to do what they say." Jordan's voice was small.

Levi felt like his brain was going to explode. *Refrain from anger. Refrain from anger.*

"Levi! Say something."

"I'm thinking!" What Jemma had said didn't make sense. "What was I right about? And why would she apologize? This wasn't her fault."

"You think they faked those movies?"

"I don't know. But being stuck in this prison isn't getting us anywhere." Levi leaned close to Jordan. "So let's play along, like Mason. Then we make a plan to get out of this place. Good?"

Jordan sniffled. "Mad good."

Levi and Jordan were taken for a medical examination, after which enforcers escorted them to the Donation Center, which, from Levi's perspective, was wishful thinking on Otley's end. Jordan lost control again, broke a door, and ended up restrained, but for some reason the enforcers released him when they reached the Registration Department. They had their pictures taken, chose last names—Levi Justin and Jordan Harvey, after their fathers—and were instructed to sit at glass desks and task test.

"What's a task test for?" Levi asked Dallin, who worked in Registration.

"And why's your hair look like a bumblebee's butt?" Jordan asked.

"Testing determines what task you will perform in the Safe Lands," Dallin said. "And I'm updating my hairstyle tomorrow—the yellow and black is *so* yesterday. I should really get HairTags."

Tapping one letter at a time, Levi entered his name into the glass computer. Dallin walked back to his desk.

"Hey," Levi whispered, "just don't forget how much we both like to clean things."

Jordan looked his way, eyebrows raised. "Clean fish?"

"Clean up messes. I saw a guy in the park. Said that cleaning people get to go more places than enforcers."

"I got you," Jordan said. "Cleaning is my favorite."

"No talking!" Dallin said, then muttered something about crazy outsiders.

Levi answered the questions carefully, trying to guess which selections might result in a cleaning placement. He wondered how Jordan was faring. His friend wasn't very methodical.

Nearly an hour had passed when Jordan pushed back from his desk. "Ha! Beat you!"

Levi leaned over and read the words off Jordan's desk: *Task test complete. Please report to your test director.*

"All done?" Dallin asked.

"Yeah." Jordan got up and swaggered to Dallin's desk.

Levi continued to answer questions, watching Jordan and Dallin, wanting to be done too. Thankfully, it wasn't long before his test ended.

Levi walked over to Dallin's desk and found the man talking to himself. "Yes, sir... I haven't run the other one yet... I understand. Thank you, sir." He turned to face Jordan. "Okay, Mr. Harvey. You'll serve your first six months in maintenance for the Grand Lodge. The task director general says this will allow you to visit your lifer, uh, I mean, your... wife."

Jordan gripped the end of the counter. "Can I see her now?"

"After you're fully processed, we'll set up an appointment."

"An appointment to see my own wife?" Jordan yelled.

Levi elbowed him. "That's good, Jordan. You'll get to see Naomi."

Jordan frowned, but reined in his temper and released the counter.

"You'll be housed in the Grand Lodge," Dallin said. "Your room number is 345. First thing tomorrow, report to the maintenance room in the Grand Lodge to meet your task director."

"What about me?" Levi asked.

"If you'll be patient..." Dallin fiddled with his glass computer screen in what seemed like slow motion. "Mr. Justin, your first run is street cleaning in the Highlands. Your task director is Dayle Mardon at Highlands Public Tasks. Go see him today, and he'll get you a schedule. You'll reside in the Larkspur Building in the Midlands. Has a great fight club called The Hunter. I spent a lot of time there as a graduate. They put little arrows in all their drinks."

"When can I see Jemma and my mother?"

"Surrogates are not permitted visitors."

"What? How come Jordan gets to see Naomi?"

"Mr. Harvey's lifer is already pregnant, so she cannot complete surrogacy duty."

"What does that matter? I want to see Jemma and my mother."

Jordan elbowed him. "Naomi can tell me how they're doing."

Levi bit his tongue so hard he tasted blood. "Fine. But why does Jordan get to live in the Grand Lodge, and I have to live in the... whatever you called it?"

"The Larkspur." Dallin shrugged. "I'm not a programmer, Mr. Justin. I just do as the computer says."

Levi gritted his teeth. "Of course you do."

Dallin handed Levi a sheet of paper with his task test results. "Use the SimTag in your hand to open doors and to make purchases, including meals."

Levi held up his fist. "How many things can I buy with this?"

"You're given four hundred credits to start. Nationals are paid every Friday. You won't get more until credit day, so be smart about what you purchase."

Levi and Jordan left City Hall and stood on the sidewalk in front of the building. In the light of day, people filled the sidewalks, the majority wearing red or black and sucking on metal cigarettes. The streets were clean—no sign of trash here. And the cars...

"What kind of rides are those?" Jordan asked.

Levi watched the vehicles. Strange and sleek, shaped like bullets, the roofs and doors tinted glass, the carriages shiny. Taillights and headlights rimmed in glowing tubes of red, blue, or green light. Fat tires spun like pinwheels. "They don't make any sound. How?"

"Let's get one and drive it," Jordan said.

"Focus, Jordan. See that place?" Levi nodded toward the grassy expanse adjacent to the City Hall building. "Let's meet there tomorrow, just after dark. I'm going to see if I can find my rifle and pack. I had some two-way radios in there. Wouldn't mind scavenging up some of those electric guns either."

A yellow car that had *Safe Lands Taxi* written on the door stopped at the curb in front of them. A video of a half-naked woman dancing over the words *Ginger Oak Gentleman's Club* showed on the car's windows, turning the side of the vehicle into a TV screen. A man got out of the taxi and yelled at Levi over the front hood his car, "Hey, you need a ride, or what?"

"Suppose I do." Levi slapped Jordan's shoulder. "Say hi to Naomi for me. And don't get into any fights." Levi walked to the passenger's door of the taxi. No door handle.

"The back, shell!" the driver yelled. "Get in the back!"

The back door had slid up onto the roof, so Levi obeyed, though he felt ridiculous sitting in the back seat when the front was empty. Once the door shut, Levi marveled that he could see through the windows—no dancing woman on this side of the glass. The car was so silent that the fuzzy static of a radio caught his attention. He looked between the front seats at the dashboard, which appeared to be a giant computer.

"ID?" The driver tapped a black square on the console between the two front seats.

Levi stared at it a moment, then set the side of his hand on the pad. Something beeped, and Levi's picture appeared in a little square on the windshield.

"Where to, Mr. Justin?" the driver asked.

"Uh..." Levi fumbled for his task test results and read from the sheet of paper. "I need to go see Dayle Mardon at the Department of Public Tasks."

"You got it."

Looking over his shoulder and out the back window, Levi watched Jordan and City Hall shrink away. He was glad Jordan would get to see Naomi, but the idea of him not seeing Jemma was unacceptable. And he certainly couldn't allow her to become a baby machine.

"Dispatch to all cars. I've got a man at the Whetstone looking for a ride to the Midlands."

"Taxi 248, I can get him."

"Thanks, 248."

"Is that a two-way radio?" Levi asked the driver.

"It's the cab company's private frequency," the taxi driver said.

"You can talk to other drivers?"

"Yeah, but it's not a Wyndo, shell. Dispatch can hear everything we say."

Of course it wasn't a window, but before Levi could clarify, the taxi dropped him off in front of a gray building. Inside, Levi found Dayle Mardon in a huge garage filled with a half dozen bullet trucks with *Department of Public Tasks* written on the doors. Dayle was a short man with cropped black hair and muscular arms that were painted in black, red, and blue tattoos.

Dale gave a gruff speech about basic cleaning protocol and took Levi before a wall map of the Safe Lands. "I'm gonna assign you Mornin' Glory Way, Sunflower Drive, and Buttercup Lane." He pointed at a section of streets. "You got four days to clean it each week. Three days off, then back on for four and so on."

"I clean streets?"

"Sure, shell. You get down on your hands and knees and scrub 'em real nice like."

"With what?"

"Fortune, save me. Look kid, I was jokin', right? You sweep leaves off the streets, pick up trash, mop up spills, paint over graffiti, blow leaves off the sidewalks in the fall, shovel snow off the sidewalks in the winter, knock icicles off street signs, stuff like that. Stay out of the buildings. I don't care if some dandy pearl asks you to carry in her shoppin' bags. You on duty, you stay out of the buildings. Got it?"

"Can I clean the streets by the Grand Lodge?"

"Rewl cleans them streets already. I need you on Mornin' Glory, Sunflower, and Buttercup." He walked to a metal cabinet filled with gray jumpsuits and work boots. "When you work, wear your uniform and boots. Check out two in your size and take the extra home, got it?"

More flimsy Safe Lands clothes. The boots looked nice, though. "Yeah, Mr. Task Director, I got it."

"Don't call me mister, and don't call me task director. It's Dayle."

"Got it, Dayle."

"You can drive, right?"

"Sure." Though Levi had only driven an actual car a couple times. He mostly drove his ATV.

"I'll assign you a truck. Use it as your private vehicle if you want. Just call in when you arrive and when you're ready to go home for the day. If I find out you aren't fulfilling your task, I report you. And you don't want to be reported. It's a trust thing. Can I trust you?"

"Yeah..." Until he couldn't, of course.

"They always be sending me Xs. What you get yours for, kid?"

Levi stared at Dayle. The guy was crotchety, but there was something real in his eyes. "They've got my girl over in the harem."

"What's your problem, then? She's having the time of her life up in that party house. Don't you worry 'bout her. And don't you go snooping around the harem, neither. They don't like uninvited guests."

Great. Levi checked out two uniforms—gray jumpsuits with the letters *DPT* embroidered on the front pocket—and put one on. He loved the feel of a pair of sturdy boots on his feet and tossed the sissy slipper shoes in the trash.

Dayle took him to the parking lot and assigned him a shiny white bullet truck, then showed him how to start it with the SimTag in his hand and how to tap an address into the dashboard computer to get directions to wherever he needed to go.

Levi left his clothes and second uniform on the passenger's seat while Dayle showed him the supplies in the back of the truck—trash bags, cleaning sprays, brooms, a leaf blower. Then he showed him the dumpsters in the parking lot where Levi would dump the trash, and the supply closets in the garage where he'd get new supplies when he ran out.

The truck had a radio that allowed Levi to talk to what Dayle referred to as the dispatcher for the Highlands Public Tasks system, or talk to other Highlands DPT taskers. "You can tap channel two and talk to Midlands Public Tasks, though you got no business doing that unless I tell you to. Dispatch will let you know if there's a problem in your area."

"What kind of a problem?"

"I don't know. Accidents, fire, flood, some rebel with a gun. It's rare, but stuff happens."

Once Levi found his pack, he'd have to be careful to find an unused channel.

He entered his assigned street names into the GPS and started the truck. It felt big and smooth beneath him. He steered it out the driveway, waited for a break in the line of moving vehicles, then pressed the gas—make that electric—pedal. The truck shot out into the lane and over the yellow stripes in the center, headed straight for another vehicle. Levi wrenched the wheel to get back into his lane, narrowly missing the other car, which honked its horn.

His arms shook, and he gripped the steering wheel with both hands. He recalled his father explaining the freeways in Denver City and how there had been rules to driving in the Old Days. Levi should've listened better. Road rules made sense with so many cars around.

The words *Highland Harem* captured his attention. A beige building with a brown roof peeked up over a wall of thick bushes. Levi could barely see curls of barbed wire between gaps in the thick green foliage. A car horn jerked his attention back to the road. How'd he get in the other lane again? He steered back to the right. The harem was behind him now. He saw City Hall ahead on his right, then the Grand Lodge, and just past it, the Rehabilitation Center.

Well, this was all good to know. Jemma and the others weren't far. He just needed to locate the boarding school Penelope had told him about. And find a way to keep in steady connection with Jordan. He suspected Otley had intentionally separated the two of them so they couldn't plan an escape. As strange as Otley looked, the man clearly wasn't a fool. Levi supposed he'd better do his job if he wanted to stay out of the RC long enough to make a plan.

The GPS told him to take Marcellina Road west. He obeyed and quickly located his route. It was a residential neighborhood, but instead of little homes like the Old ones near Mt. Crested Butte, these looked like metal shoeboxes standing on their ends. Some lawns were green and colorful like the field of wildflowers outside Glenrock. And some were... odd. One had pink grass and black flowers. Another was a checkerboard of grass and dirt.

Levi started on the east side of Morning Glory Way and drove his way down one side of the road until he reached a dead end, then circled around the other side until he came to Sunflower Drive. He picked up litter and swept leaves off storm drains, tempted to climb down into one and escape. It wouldn't do him any good to be free without the others, though.

He came across some graffiti on the sidewalk that said *FFF.* He found a can of gray paint in his truck and sprayed himself in the chest while trying to figure out how to open the thing. He eventually managed to cover the graffiti and set out a "wet paint" sign.

People were everywhere, walking, driving, riding bicycles, but Levi could rarely guess where they were going by how they were dressed or what they carried with them. Weird that so many people wore red and black. Were they uniforms of some kind? He didn't see any other DPT uniforms.

Sunflower Drive took him to Buttercup, which made him think of Jemma. Buttercup brought him back to Sunflower, which turned out to be a long road. He worked his way down one side, around the dead end, and all the way up the other side until he arrived back on the opposite side of Morning Glory Way.

The sun was now low in the sky, and he figured that meant he was done for the day. Plus, he was aching for food. He picked up his "wet paint" sign and drove out onto Marcellina Lane. A few blocks down he pulled into a parking lot, drawn by the words *Marcellina Steakhouse*.

The one-level log structure with a red slate roof was dwarfed by all the tall buildings around it. Inside, the aroma weakened his knees. Most of the red-clothed tables were occupied, and Levi stood feeling helpless until a woman, whose nametag said Londie, greeted him and sat him at a table by a window. Londie looked normal compared to most the women he'd seen today, except that she had orange eyes. Levi tried not to stare, but he couldn't help it.

"How do you make your eyes look like that?" he asked her.

"They're contact lenses, dim."

That didn't bring Levi any closer to understanding.

"Did you order in advance?" Londie asked.

"How would I do that?"

"On your Wyndo." Londie pulled a leather book out of her apron pocket and handed it to him. Inside it was a glass screen with pictures of different food options. "Our special today is a bacon-wrapped sirloin for ten credits."

She'd won him at bacon. "Can I have that, please?"

"Sure thing. You want salad with that?"

"Okay."

"What kind of dressing?"

"What's good?"

"I like the ranch."

"Uh... that sounds fine." He closed the leather book and handed it back to her.

She reached out for it but hesitated. "And what can I get you to drink?"

"Water?"

"Sure thing." She took the leather book and slid it into her pocket. "Be right back."

Levi examined those around him. Red or black clothes dominated the wardrobes here as well, and many had tattoos and odd-colored eyes, skin, or hair. Perhaps it was common here to paint yourself in as many ways as possible. Levi certainly felt plain with gray overalls, brown hair, and skin-colored skin.

Londie returned with a glass of water. She also set down a plate of lettuce, tomatoes, carrot shavings, and purple cabbage drenched in white sauce. "There you go. Your steak will be out in a few minutes."

"Thank you." Levi picked up the fork from the red cloth napkin and ate a bite of the salad. It was almost icy on his teeth. The milky sauce was cold too—and delicious. Salt and pepper and herbs flavored it, greatly improving the taste of lettuce. By the time Londie returned with his steak, Levi was wiping the extra sauce off his plate with his finger.

"Careful," Londie said as she set a platter in front of him. "The plate is hot."

One look at the steak and the word *beautiful* came to mind. Dark grill lines had been seared across the meat that was wrapped in three strips of crisp bacon.

"Would you like a side of ranch for your steak?" Londie asked him.

"Yes," he said, elated to get more of the sauce.

"I'll get that for you. Anything else?"

Levi shook his head, waiting for her to leave. When she did, he cut a bite off one end of the steak and ate it. Never before had meat melted in his mouth like butter.

Londie brought him a tiny dish of the sauce. "You need anything else?"

"This is delicious," Levi said. "What does it take to cook steak like this? Refrigeration?"

Londie laughed a short, high trill. "I'm glad you like it. But if I told you the secret, we wouldn't have a very successful restaurant, now, would we?"

Levi scarfed down his steak then used his spoon to finish eating the bowl of ranch dressing. A woman at the table next to him stared. He wondered what he was doing to earn such a look from a woman with six gold rings pierced around her bottom lip.

"I need to get some real clothes. I can't keep wearing this uniform everywhere," a young man said from behind him.

Something about the voice was familiar. Levi looked up. There, standing just inside the doorway with two men, was Omar. All three were dressed in enforcer uniforms.

Levi's mouth went dry. He stood and strode to the entrance. "Omar."

When Omar's eyes met Levi's, his neck flushed pink. "Brother! I was hoping you'd decide to come inside." His eyes shifted to the floor, and he rubbed the scar between his eyes, revealing a black tattoo that crisscrossed from his wrist and up his arm until it disappeared into the sleeve of his uniform. He had the number nine on his cheek. No Xs. Not surprising; Omar had always been a follower. The name on his uniform said *Strong*. Levi couldn't suppress a smirk.

Omar's enforcer friends studied him, their eyes questioning.

"It's okay," Omar said. "Why don't you get us a table?"

The enforcers glared at Levi and walked to Londie's counter.

"So, I guess you know that Beshup never showed at the cabin," Levi said.

Omar rubbed his scar and stepped toward the enforcers. "I don't have a really long lunch break, Levi, so I should get going."

"You're an enforcer, huh? What's 'strong' mean?"

"My last name."

"Omar Strong? So it's a play on words, huh? An oxymoron?"

Omar scowled. "You're the moron."

The enforcers came back to stand beside Omar.

"Marcellina's a little out of a cleaner's credit range, isn't it?" This enforcer had a sissy mustache and the name *Skott* on his uniform. "How much they give you to start?"

"Four hundred credits," Levi said.

Skott laughed. "Better stop eating at steakhouses, shell."

"He just means that those credits have to last you until you get paid again," Omar said.

"What about you?" Levi asked. "You're eating here."

The other enforcer snorted. His name badge read *Charlz.* "Enforcer *captains* make a great deal more credits than street cleaners."

"Hey, Skottie." Londie walked toward an empty booth. "Got your table ready."

"Thanks," Skott said, trailing after Londie. "You free tonight, femme?"

Omar waited until the enforcers were across the room. "Look, Levi. It's not a good idea for us to spend time together. People will think we're up to something. I'll see you later."

Omar started to follow his friends, but Levi grabbed his collar and pulled him close. Despite the intimidating uniform, Omar was still scrawny.

"Why'd you do it?" Levi whispered.

Omar tried to pull away. "Get your hands off me, Levi. You can't touch an enforcer and get away with it. It's my job to maintain order."

Levi held tightly. As much as he wanted to beat his brother into mud, Omar was right. Levi would likely end up back in the prison with a second X on his face. "Our elders are dead because of you. Our father's dead because of—"

"It wasn't supposed to happen that way!" Omar blinked back tears.

Refrain from anger. Turn from wrath. Levi pushed Omar back and released him. Omar stumbled against a table where a man and woman were eating, knocking over a pitcher of water. "I didn't mean for things to happen the way they did," Omar said. "I'm sorry. Truly I am. But... life is so much better here. You'll see."

"You're a fool, Omar. A pathetic, sissy—"

"Don't call me that!" Omar drew a gun from his belt and pointed it at Levi. "I'm sorry so many died, but I fit in here. And we all know that was never going to happen in Glenrock."

Destroying an entire village to fit in? "Just make sure that the thing you're living for is worth dying for, Omar. How many had to die so you could *fit in*? Everything has a cost, and you had better be ready to pay up."

"You know what I'm ready for, *brother?*" Omar said with a new edge to his voice. "I'm ready to hammer you for the first time in my life." He waved his arm at his lapdogs. "Take him out back."

As the enforcers hauled Levi from the steakhouse, Skott told Londie, "Hold our table, femme. We'll only be a minute."

Chapter 19

"We need to up the dosage on her fertility stims," Ciddah said. "Change it to 150 milligrams."

Mason made a note on the CompuChart. "But isn't that a lot of hormones? Won't that affect her body in other ways?"

"I'm the senior medic here, Mason. Let me worry about that."

"But—"

Rimola leaned around the doorframe. "Enforcers just dropped off a patient in exam two." She'd been Roller Painting her skin dark pink ever since Luella Flynn started wearing red and black. Her spiky black hair hadn't changed. "He's been arrested for assaulting an officer."

Ciddah looked away from the CompuChart. Mason watched her profile, studying a strand of wispy blonde hair that had fallen from her hair clip. "What'd they do to him?" Ciddah asked.

"Don't know," Rimola said. "His face is pretty bloody. They said to keep it quiet."

"Wonderful." Ciddah patted Mason's back, her hand lingering there longer than necessary. "Why don't you assist me, Mason?"

"Sure." Mason followed her out of the office. So far, he'd done little but enter data into CompuCharts, weigh patients, and take blood pressure measurements, all of which constituted a multi-stepped process Ciddah called *taking the vitals*. Ciddah allowed him to do some *saliva tests*, but no *blood draws* until she had time to teach him. All of it was fascinating.

Yet Mason had never met a more bewildering woman. Or more beautiful. Her wisdom and care with patients impressed him greatly. But with him, her words were all business, though her hands touched him more than was necessary. So many contradictions.

None of it mattered, of course. Mason needed to focus on his goal of getting his people back to Glenrock, not how long Ciddah's eyelashes were, how tightly she wore her scrubs, or how her hair swayed against her waist as she moved down the hallway.

Having seen her medical history, Mason knew she was Levi's age, that she had the thin plague, and that she'd had four miscarriages. *Four.* After having learned about embryonic transfer from Ciddah on his first day, he knew that four miscarriages didn't necessarily mean she'd been intimate with a man, but Mason wondered. He also wondered about the psychological impact of such losses.

He followed Ciddah inside exam room two. A man in a gray uniform had been secured to an exam table. His face was purpled and bloody, the bridge of his nose cut open.

Levi.

"Looks like the enforcers paid him back double," Ciddah said. "Dumb shell. Why don't you get him cleaned up, then I'll check him over?" Ciddah left Mason alone to deal with the patient.

Mason looked his brother over, wondering what had happened. He must have snuck into the city compound, trying to free them, and, like Jordan, discovered that fists wouldn't work against these people. They were too strong to defeat that way. The numbers on Levi's face and hand already had two Xs behind them. From what Mason had learned through ColorCast reports about some guy named Lonn, that wasn't good.

Mason put on a pair of rubber gloves and located the bottle of sterile water. He poured the water over Levi's face and wiped it with fresh gauze. Levi jerked his head to the side, which startled Mason. He'd thought his brother was unconscious.

"My name is Mason Elias," he said in a voice louder than necessary.

Levi's eyes, somewhat hidden behind his swollen face, shifted until they met his brother's. "Mason." His voice croaked, and he panted in a few short breaths before speaking again. "It was Omar. He did this."

"Omar? He beat you up?"

"No. Well, yes. But... it's his fault we're here. All of us."

"What? How could any of this be Omar's fault?"

"The little maggot sold out our village..." Deep breath. "For a job with the enforcers. To *fit in here*, he told me."

Mason groaned, remembering Levi and Jemma's engagement party, when Father had mocked Omar. "I knew he was unhappy. But... you're sure?"

Levi coughed and worked to clear his throat. "He all but confessed... wearing his enforcer... uniform... with his enforcer buddies... smiling before he stomped on... my face."

Mason squeezed the bottle in his hand, and sterile water overflowed, slapping onto the floor. *Keep it together.* "Hold still. I've got to clean you up before the medic comes back." Mason grabbed some fresh gauze and some paper towels, tossed the paper towels onto the floor and stepped on them, then mopped up his mess on the exam table.

Levi's eyes found Mason's again. "Aren't you the medic?"

"Just a lowly assistant." Mason wiped under Levi's nose.

"Was I really that bad to him?" Levi gasped in a breath. "Mother and Jemma both said I needed to be nicer, but they're girls, and I figured... what do they know about men, you know? About brothers." Another large breath. "Did he ever say anything to you?"

"He said he wanted to be included. With you and Father. He wanted to go along."

"Even if he hated us... Even if that hatred was justified... why betray the entire village?" A tear ran down the side of Levi's face, pooling in his ear. "I found eighteen dead, Mase... Papa Eli died in front of me. I buried him myself."

Mason inhaled slowly, fighting back his emotions. He'd failed to save Papa.

Stop. He needed to stay focused. This wasn't his fault.

Levi seemed to be pleading with Mason through his eyes. "If I would've been nicer... Do you think Omar would've...? Is it my fault that...?"

Stage two of the grieving process: they were both blaming themselves. "This is not our fault, Levi. The Safe Lands is the enemy. Not Omar. He's just their pawn. General Otley killed Father and Papa Eli, and Lawten Renzor sent Otley and the enforcers. And they'll likely still kill us if we aren't more careful."

"Mase, I can't breathe too good."

Mason stopped swabbing and gave Levi a chance to breathe. "Your nose might be broken."

Levi's shoulders shook. Tears pooled in the hollow between his eyes and the ridge of his nose, mixing with the blood.

"Try to stay calm." Mason tossed the bloody gauze then started on the other side of Levi's nose.

"Have you seen Mother?" Levi asked.

"I haven't seen anyone but you since they took Jordan away."

"They brought him down to the RC." Levi paused to gasp in a breath. "That's where I was... They showed us movies of Jemma and Naomi... We had no choice but to—"

"How's it coming?" Ciddah asked, appearing at Mason's elbow.

Mason jumped, wondering how much she'd overheard. "Almost done."

"It's fine." She stepped in front of him so that her body brushed against his, filling his senses with the smell of vanilla and cinnamon. "I can work with that."

Mason stepped out of her way and set the bottle of sterile water on the counter.

"Here." She handed him the CompuChart. "See if you can fill in more of that."

Mason looked over the chart. Levi had chosen the last name Justin. Not surprising—Levi and their father had been close.

"My name is Ciddah." She smiled down on Levi, gloved hands held out to the side, no unnecessary touching. "I'm going to take a look at your nose, okay?"

"I can't breathe through my nose," Levi said.

"That could be due to swelling." Ciddah slid one of her gloved hands behind Levi's neck and tilted his head back to examine him. Mason watched, intrigued by everything Ciddah did, especially her gentleness with patients. As much as Mason didn't want to be in the Safe Lands, he longed for Ciddah's medical knowledge. She was a level nine medic. From what she'd told him, the highest medic ranking was a twenty.

Mason wanted enough medical wisdom to rank a twenty.

"Looks like it's broken, Levi." Ciddah released her hold on his neck. "I don't like to set cartilage until the swelling has gone down. Come back in a few days if you'd like to have it reset. Later on, if your nose looks crooked and you're interested in reconstruction, we can set up an appointment with the Cosmetic Center."

"I don't care," Levi rasped.

"Maybe later, then. Mason, finish cleaning him up." She left the room, blonde hair swaying. All business again.

Mason pushed away his confusion with Ciddah, got some fresh gauze, and resumed cleaning the blood from Levi's cheeks and neck. Levi needed a shave. "They have stores here. G.I.N., which Ciddah says stands for Get It Now. You can use your ID to buy razors and soap. They have special cream to shave with too. Keeps away the rash."

"Penelope said the women are in a place called the Highland Harem." Levi fixed his bloodshot eyes on Mason. "Jordan says they're going to make them have babies. Explain *that*, Dr. Mason."

Mason grunted, still somewhat confused at the process. "They call it surrogacy. With the thin plague, most Safe Lands nationals are sterile, so they reproduce by using a medical procedure, selecting those who are still healthy enough. Ciddah explained it to me. They harvest seed from the males—"

"The Donation Center?"

Mason shuddered. "Yes. Did you?"

Levi choked on a breath. "No!" Another cough. "Did *you*?"

"Not *yet*." Mason thought of those all-knowing eyes on the top floor of City Hall. "I had to get clever. But the task director general is watching me. It's important to the survival of their people that they get us to comply. They need uninfected nationals to repopulate their city with uninfected people. Without us, they'll die."

Levi groaned and shifted his head on the exam table. "Wish they'd die quicker."

Ciddah came to mind then. Mason didn't want someone so smart and beautiful to meet that fate. "Well, despite the reason they're doing it, the whole process is pretty amazing." He wiped away a bit of crusty blood on Levi's cheek.

"Amazing?" Levi's eyes flashed. He grunted, pulling against the restraints until his face and neck were flushed purple. "They're going to make Jemma pregnant, and you're amazed?"

Mason hated this side of Levi, the part that reacted in anger like their father. He stepped back and tossed the bloodied gauze toward a trash can. "I'm just saying the technology is amazing. I don't want anything to happen to Jemma or anyone else."

Levi closed his eyes, breathed in and out, silent for several calming breaths—a trick Jemma had taught him to calm down. Mason sent up a silent thank you for her wisdom. Levi opened his eyes and asked, "So if *you* visit the Donation Center, Jemma could carry *your* child?"

"I..." The question knotted Mason's thoughts. "I don't know. I suppose it's possible."

Levi lifted his head off the exam table as if trying to sit up, but the restraints caught him again and his head slapped back against the table. "You'd like that, wouldn't you?"

"Of course not!" Mason glanced over his shoulder, saw the empty doorway, then whispered to Levi, "I'm trying to learn so I can help the women. I have a... plan... to deal with the donation issue, should it arise again. You and I need a way to communicate. And you've got to be careful. You've got two Xs already."

Levi choked out a cough. "Two? I only had one this morning. How'd they change it?"

"It's a computer chip. They just change it. Three Xs and you'll be liberated."

"What does that mean?"

"I don't know. But liberated people go away and don't come back."

Levi panted in a breath. "I've got some radios in my backpack. I've just got to find it."

"What building did they put you in?"

"Larkspur. It's in the Midlands, I guess. Haven't gone there yet."

Leave it to his brother to get in a fight before even spending one night inside the compound. "I'm in the Highlands, at the Westwall. I'll send you a message. I'm pretty sure all messages are read, so I won't say much. But send one back, okay? Don't write anything you don't want the enforcers to see. If we can message each other, we can communicate. Maybe we can use a code or something."

"And I can tell you if I get the radios—"

"Mason?" Rimola knocked on the doorframe. "Ciddah needs you in exam four."

"I'll be right there." He turned back to Levi. "Keep in touch."

Mason found Ciddah in the exam room standing over a girl who was crying.

"What took you so long?" she asked.

"Sorry." Mason stopped on the other side of the exam table and glanced at Ciddah, whose wide blue eyes were focused on the patient.

"This is my third miscarriage." The girl couldn't have been more than eighteen.

"Your best bet is to keep trying," Ciddah said. "And next time you conceive, come to the harem right away. I can't promise we could have done anything to save the baby, but we do have methods to assist with delicate pregnancies."

The girl's words came out in a mournful sob. "I promise."

Ciddah swept a strand of hair from the girl's face. "I'm going to give you a med that will help your body recover, and might even help prepare you to carry a child again." She motioned Mason to follow her to the counter against the wall.

In a very soft whisper, she said, "Mason, what I'm about to give her is going to hurt her—a lot. I'm going to need you to grab her and keep her as still as you can once she inhales." Ciddah reached into a drawer and removed a small disposable vaporizer.

They returned to the patient's bedside, and Ciddah administered the drug. As Mason held the girl's arms, he saw tears welling in Ciddah's eyes.

As soon as the girl was still and breathing steadier, Ciddah left the exam room. Mason jogged after her.

"You interested in Rimola?" Ciddah asked without turning around. "I hear she's gratifiable."

Mason stopped in the hallway. "What? No. I barely know her."

Ciddah glanced over her shoulder, eyebrows raised. "What's *that* matter? She's attractive, you're attractive..." She continued down the hallway.

I'm attractive? Mason started after her again, killing this bizarre line of questioning with a question of his own. "Do you know why that girl miscarried?"

"They all miscarry these days," Ciddah said as she turned into her office. Mason stopped in the doorway. Ciddah settled behind her desk and tossed her hair over her shoulder. "The plague weakens the body so much that women can't carry a pregnancy to term. I've been asked to explain this to you. I think now is a good time. Have a seat."

Mason moved a stack of papers off one of the chairs in front of Ciddah's desk and sat down. Ciddah didn't speak, simply stared at him, and a Bible verse came to mind: "Who is this that appears like the dawn, fair as the moon, bright as the sun, majestic as the stars in procession?"

The thought embarrassed him. Why wax poetic over a woman he'd just met? A confusing woman. He stared at his hands, unable to look at her again until she finally spoke.

"The thin plague ravages the immune system," Ciddah said, "which in turn affects the reproductive systems in both men and women. What you told your outsider *friend* about Safe Landers being sterile is not completely true."

A rush of heat seized Mason. "You heard that?"

"Some nationals are sterile. Some are not, but their donations are too weak to survive fertilization, which amounts to the same thing. And some women just don't have the strength to carry a child to term, even with the help of fertility stims. You were also mistaken about pregnancy. Many women become pregnant in the Safe Lands, but they always miscarry. There hasn't been a child born to a Safe Lands national in over three years."

"But Kendall Collin—" Mason said.

"Kendall is an outsider. Like your women, she came to the harem uninfected. But the male donor was infected, so her child will be too." Ciddah's eyes were suddenly hard and angry. "I'm not a member of the Safe Lands Guild, but I do know that outsiders are brought here to save our people. We're dying. And if you and your outsider friends refuse donation, we have no chance of survival."

Mason sat up tall in his chair. "Your government holds our people against our wills. We don't owe you anything. We've survived, uninfected, all these years by having a wiser way of life."

Ciddah huffed and shook her head. "So *you* say. But you can't imagine what it's like for a woman to lose a child."

Mason *could* imagine, actually, more than most men. But he didn't see her point. "What does that have to do with us? *You* can't imagine what it's like to have your freedom taken away."

"There's freedom in the Safe Lands," Ciddah said simply. "If you comply."

Mason scooted to the edge of his chair. "Forced compliance is the opposite of freedom."

She raised her eyebrows and looked down her nose. "Not if you choose it."

"Choosing compliance over death is not freedom," Mason said, grabbing the edge of her desk and leaning against the smooth glass. "It's blackmail."

Her tone became heated. "You're a healthy male. It's your duty to donate!"

Mason didn't know what to say. Clearly Ciddah was upset. He realized he'd practically climbed onto the end of her desk, so he leaned back in his chair, wanting to understand. "You resent me because I won't donate?"

"Because you're selfish and narrow-minded." The words felt like a slap, and Mason didn't know why. "Thousands of women desperately want to bear a child, yet since it's not your *belief* to donate, you refuse. And you leave hundreds brokenhearted."

Mason took a few short breaths. "I'm sorry women have to experience that kind of pain. But it's not my wish to mate with hundreds of women."

Ciddah growled. "You don't have to! Don't you get it? The Surrogacy Center does it for you."

Couldn't she see how awkward *that* statement was? "Yes, but it's still my child. My children."

"No," Ciddah said, softening her voice. "Children belong to the nation, are raised in the nursery and boarding schools until they're fourteen."

Wait, this was what Kendall Collin had been talking about. She'd said that she wanted to hold her child, and Ciddah had said that the child belonged to all of them, but Mason hadn't understood fully until now. "What of their mothers?"

"Surrogates are given six weeks of rest, then they return to their lives."

Questions tumbled in Mason's mind. "What about bonding? What about breastfeeding?"

Ciddah wrinkled her nose. "Bonding is a myth. And breastfeeding isn't sanitary. Plus, the plague passes through a surrogate's milk. All infants are given formula. There's no reason for the mother to stay with the child. The true reward of giving birth is knowing you helped your community survive."

"The mothers never see their babies again?"

"Surrogates can apply for a revealing. And when a child comes of age, if the child also applies for a revealing, they can meet. Male donors may also apply for a revealing. But both surrogate and child, or donor and child, must apply before a revealing is granted."

To never know family? To have no parents or siblings? How horrible. The Safe Lands had many good things—excellent medical care, the technology to do things Mason had never imagined—but they were misguided about so many more important things.

Mason looked directly into Ciddah's eyes. "So you've grown up all alone? Never saw your parents together?"

"Like I said, no one does. It's not how things are supposed to work."

"In my village," Mason said, "a man and woman grow fond of one another, spend time with one another, and if they decide they'd make a good match, they appeal to the elders for marriage. If the elders grant their request, a three-month waiting period begins. Then the man, if he hasn't already, must choose a trade and build a home. And the woman, if she hasn't already, learns a trade as well. Both are mentored by an elder as to how to be a good husband or wife. At the end of the three months, the man stands before the entire village and announces his intention to marry." Unless, of course, no one wanted him, and his parents arrange the marriage.

Mason went on. "If no one objects, the wedding is scheduled. Then the mentoring elder joins the couple in marriage and they are declared man and wife. Should they have children, those children live with them in their home until they're old enough to choose a spouse of their own. That's the way of my people."

Ciddah's cheeks pinked, and she folded her arms. "Some of that sounds comforting, but isn't it a lot of work to have to have two tasks? Raising a child *and* working a trade?"

"My mother never complained. And she was a doctor *and* taught school."

Ciddah shook out her hair, something Mason now realized she did when nervous. "You're of age. Did you appeal to your elders to marry?"

Mason didn't want to mention Mia to Ciddah. It hadn't been his idea, anyway. "No."

Again she tossed her hair, this time with a flutter of eyelashes. "Why not?"

Now that Mason *could* answer. "I didn't feel... I hadn't found the right woman yet."

Ciddah transformed before him then. Gone was her honest anger and vulnerability and personal questions. Her eyes became distant, her posture stiff. "You must think my people cold and lazy to only work one task."

"Some of them, yes. But not all of them. Not you."

She came back to him then, instantly softening at his compliment. "Have you witnessed a birth? A natural birth?"

"Hundreds—of animals." He chuckled. "But only one human birth."

This time Ciddah leaned over her desk. "Tell me about it. Please?"

Was she serious? She'd never seen one? Heat crept up the back of Mason's neck. "It's... difficult to describe."

She slapped her palm on the top of her desk. "Mason Elias, you exasperate me with your modesty. Just tell me what you saw!"

Now she was mad again. Ciddah's moods were like the weather: sunny days, wind, thunderstorms, lightning, and if he waited long enough, the sun would come out again. "Okay," he said. "And I hope it'll help you understand why I'm here in the Surrogacy Center."

Chapter 20

When Mason came to work Monday afternoon, Ciddah sent him up to the task director general's office. "Lawten wants to see you," she said.

Lawten? As Mason rode the elevator to the eighth floor, he pondered the reasons Ciddah might be on a first name basis with the task director general. Nothing he came up with pleased him.

Kruse led him inside the office. "It's the intellectual one, Mr. Renzor."

See? Even Kruse called the man *Mr. Renzor*. Without waiting to be asked, Mason sat in the red leather chair in front of the task director's desk. The man looked... weathered. Mason didn't really know what made men handsome to women. Muscles seemed to matter. And that sort of rugged, courageous hunter thing Levi and Jordan had going on. Lawten Renzor had neither. Surely Ciddah wasn't romantically involved with this man.

"We've taken the time to show you why donation is important to our survival," the task director said. "Now, will you comply?"

Not going to happen, *Lawten*. "I understand why you ask me to donate. But not why I should help. You killed my father, all the elders of my village. You claim to value life, yet you willingly destroyed it. And to clean up the mess you've made of your city, you ask me to reproduce with my friends and family. It's completely unacceptable."

The task director looked at Mason, his eyes dark, unnerving. "What *will* make it acceptable?"

"Nothing. Let my people go back to our village to rebuild our lives as best we can."

"We can't do that, Mr. Elias. If we let you go free, we die."

"You have yet to show me why that's my problem."

Those eyes stripped Mason, making him feel exposed. "If you refuse, we'll be forced to use infected donations on your women. Then their children will be born infected and the process will likely infect the surrogates as well."

Anger shot through Mason, but it was short-lived. The man was bluffing. "Then you gain nothing. You need uninfected donors if you're to survive."

"Yes... You know, we are receiving regular donations from Omar Strong."

Omar! That foolish, careless... "Sounds like you got what you want, then."

"I cannot excuse you from donating simply because you have a brother," the taskdirector said. "You must do as every other national does."

Mason clenched his teeth. This man was cruel. Insane. Depraved. "Your actions... Your procedures... You don't need donations—you need to find a cure."

"You're our cure, trigger," Kruse said, flashing a glowing smile.

Mason stood up and leaned on the task director's desk. "If *I* find a cure, will you release me and my people?"

The task director laughed. "What makes you think you can find a cure?"

Mason had no idea how to cure anything, but he said, "What makes you think I can't?" *God, I hope you plan to help me with this one.*

"Uh, let's see now, shellie..." Kruse said. "Our scientists have been looking for a cure since the end of the Great Pandemic and keep failing. Yeah... that's pretty much it."

"We do healing differently where I come from," Mason said, as if his head were filled with secret knowledge. "At least let me try."

The task director leaned back in his chair and folded his arms. "Very well, Mr. Elias. I'll allow you to see our history and research. But unless you offer something constructive in one month's time, this experiment will end and Kruse will take you to the Donation Center himself."

"I don't understand," Ciddah said when Mason returned to the Surrogacy Center and found her sitting at her desk in her office. "Contributing to the population is our responsibility as citizens of the Safe Lands. Every male national *must* donate. Every female *must* be a surrogate. Why would Lawten excuse you?"

Lawten again. "Because I'm going to find a cure," Mason said as he sat in the chair in front of her desk.

Her eyes flew wide, baring every bit of the whites. "For the thin plague?"

When Mason nodded, Ciddah burst into deep laughter, a sound that should've annoyed him since she was mocking his plan, but somehow endeared her to him instead.

She stopped laughing. "There *is* no cure, Mason. Everyone knows that. Most people don't even want one."

Not want a cure? So people really were insane here. "Ciddah, if I find a cure, the task director promised to free me and my people."

Ciddah frowned, her eyes growing distant. "Why do you want to leave so badly? How can you stand living in the dirt?"

Man, she got mean when she was angry. "How can you stand living in a gilded cage?"

Her eyelashes fluttered. "A *what* cage?"

"Gilded. It means covered in gold."

She shook her head, tossing her hair over one shoulder.

"It's a metaphor, Ciddah. I'm saying the Safe Lands is a beautiful cage, but it is a cage nonetheless."

Her brow scrunched up, wrinkling her forehead as she tried to think of a retort. Mason liked arguing with her just to see her facial expressions.

She finally said, "We stay inside the bell to be safe from the dangers outside."

"What dangers? Do I look dangerous?" Mason clapped his hand against his chest. "I'm not even infected! The plague only exists inside your walls. The only serious dangers outside these walls are your enforcers murdering or abducting innocent people and bringing them here. You can't even leave. It's a cage."

She lifted her chin. "Some have left, but they always come back and say it's dangerous."

"Probably because they don't know how to survive without all the gilding. The way everything is handed to you here... Who does your hunting? Butchering? Who plants your food? Who makes your clothing? Even I could kill an animal if I had to, though I'd probably live off tubers and vegetation instead."

Again with the forehead wrinkle. "Must every word from your lips be a riddle?"

Mason grinned. As fun as it was to debate with her, he had work to do. "No more than the words from yours. If you don't need me for anything else today, I'd like to leave. *Lawten* said I could work on a cure, but only on my free time." He stood up and walked toward the door.

"Wait. You're not going to the HC, are you?"

"If the HC is the History Center, then yes. *Lawten* gave me permission to read the information on the computers there. Don't worry. They'll be monitoring me. I can't ruin anything."

She crossed the room and stopped inches from him, bathing him in the smell of vanilla and cinnamon, but she looked down, not to the floor but sort of into nothing, mumbling to herself. "*So* unfair! Months away from HC access. Stupid Lawten." She looked up at Mason, forehead crinkled. "You've been here two weeks!"

He couldn't help but smile. "I'll tell you what I learn, if it means that much to you."

"How will you even know what you're looking for?"

Mason shrugged. It was a good point. "I don't know. But I have to try."

She grabbed his arm in both hands and tugged. "Take me with you."

He wanted to. "I don't have permission to take anyone along. I don't want to abuse *Lawten's* trust."

Ciddah released his arm. "Why are you calling him that?"

"You do." Mason waited to see her reaction.

She just stared. Her left eye twitched. "Fine." Ciddah shoved past Mason and strode down the hall toward the front desk. "I'll work harder," she said without looking back. "I'll reach level ten by the end of the year. Then I'll have access to the computers too, but *I'll* be able to work there during the day. And *I'll* have an HC task director to mentor me." She glanced back, her hair a golden cape swirling with her movement. "You won't."

He chased after her. "Ciddah, I'm not trying to compete with you."

She waved her hand over her head. "I know. You're just trying to rescue your people from us *caged* barbarians." She started to walk away. "Well, I'm sorry that you hate us so much. That you hate me so much!"

Her reaction bewildered Mason. Had he insulted her somehow? Insulted her people? Taken the Lawten comment too far? She was clearly jealous that he could visit the History Center. But calling her jealous wouldn't temper the situation. He could think of nothing to say that would help, so he simply remained silent and followed her to Rimola's desk.

When he reached her side, she folded her arms and scowled. "You have nothing to say?"

"I don't hate you."

Ciddah slouched, shifted her weight to her other foot, her expression softening.

How long did he have to stand here? "Um... Do I have your permission to leave?"

"Sure, Mason. Have a fun time." She flashed an ugly smile and patted his arm.

"Oh. Okay. Thanks." He headed for the elevators.

Behind him Ciddah growled, walked back down the hall, and slammed her office door.

Mason glanced at Rimola, who seemed to be fighting a smile. Embarrassed for reasons he couldn't define, he pushed the button to call the elevator.

Women made no sense whatsoever.

Chapter 21

The fight with Omar had earned Levi a broken nose, a second X, three nights in a solitary jail cell, and now a meeting with the man who'd killed his father. Levi sat shackled to a chair in a holding cell across a metal table from General Otley.

"Behavior like yours is only permitted in fight clubs, little rat."

Levi imagined breaking free from his restraints and strangling Otley. But he couldn't do that even if he had the strength. He was village elder, and so far, he'd done a pathetic job of upholding that rank. His business with General Otley would have to wait until his people were back in Glenrock. For now, it was time to buck up and do what he had to do to get back on the streets.

"Got two Xs already," Otley said. "One last chance to get it right. Got more rage to let out, join a fight club. But no attacking enforcers, whether they deserve it or not."

Levi stared at a dent in the shiny tabletop, wondering if a captive with a temper like Jordan's had put it there. "I won't hit Omar again." There was no point. The kid was drunk on his own ignorance.

"Want to go back and task?"

"More than anything."

"Sarcasm does not assure me of your compliance."

"I guess you'll just have to be surprised, then."

"Let him go," Otley told the enforcers. "Return to your tasks and play, rat. I see you again in this room, you'll be liberated."

"I look forward to it."

The enforcers led Levi downstairs and uncuffed him in the lobby.

"Good fortune, shell," one of them said.

Outside, it was pouring rain. It was Monday. Levi had missed his meeting with Jordan in the park. Now what? He wanted to go look for his pack, but with two Xs, it would be better to wait for dark.

He took a taxi to the steakhouse, but his truck was gone, so he took another taxi to the Highlands Public Tasks building and went inside. Maybe Dayle would tell him to leave and he'd be free to find his backpack and look for Jordan.

But when he found Dayle in his office, the man winced and set his hands on his hips. "Two Xs, huh. What'd you do?"

"Got in a fight with an enforcer."

"Yeah, that'll do it. Look, kid, I don't want to make trouble for you, but I need people to show up to task, otherwise I look bad. And I don't want no Xs on me."

"Yeah, I'm sorry. It won't happen again."

"That's good to hear. Now, I got a flood down at the end of Morning Glory Way. Need you to go check it out."

"What am I supposed to do about a flood?"

"Check the manhole. Sounds like the one in the cul-de-sac isn't letting water into the storm drain. Could be plugged up with leaves or trash. I'll get you a hook. Come on."

Dayle got Levi a manhole hook and showed him the pressure washer feature on his truck. "You only need to use the pressure washer if you can't get it open with the hook."

Once Levi had restocked his truck, he set out. His route was cleaner than it had been last Thursday, though he did find three little diamond flower-shaped hair clips Jemma would like. Who would throw something like that away?

He discovered that the flood at the end of Morning Glory Way had been caused by a plastic sack covering the drain slots on the manhole's cover. Levi removed it within seconds, and the water started to trickle through. At that rate, the flood would take all day to drain. He tried to remove the cover with the manhole hook but couldn't get it to budge, so he drove his truck next to the manhole and tried the pressure washer. The lid came free, and the water poured through.

When he finished his route, it was just after four. He was hungry but figured it was about time he saw his new home. He needed a base of operations. He typed his apartment address into the GPS and drove where it told him to. He found himself nearing the wall that separated the Highlands from the Midlands. Great. Another wall between him and Jemma.

The road widened before the wall to the Midlands, splitting into four lanes with a tiny booth and gate at each. Levi took the lane on the far left, still a little shaky steering around so many moving vehicles. He stopped before the gate and punched three squares on the dash before he found the one that rolled down his window.

The man in the booth stared. Levi stared back.

"ID?" The man pointed to a black pad sticking out from his booth. "You're not vaping and driving, are you?"

"No." Levi reached out the window and fisted the pad. "I don't even own a vaper."

The man chuckled as the gate started to rise. "Find pleasure in life, shell."

"Yeah, you too." Levi steered through the gate. A black car honked as it raced by on his left, nearly crashing into him. Levi took a deep breath, looked over his shoulder for other vehicles, waited for two more to pass by, then steered back into the single lane that tunneled through the wall to the Midlands.

In going from the Highlands into the Midlands, Levi left behind the wonder and color of the magical city and returned to stark black-and-white reality. The buildings were clean, but shorter and shabby. Rows of houses, shops, and apartment buildings. Where the buildings in the Highlands were crammed together, there was more land out here. Open space. There also seemed to be more billboards. Levi tried to read one of the signs but ended up swerving out of his lane.

He passed a graffiti-covered wall and managed to make out the words, *Virus, FFF*, and what looked like *Black Arm*, though some street cleaners were painting over it.

The GPS led him nearly to the next wall. The Lowlands, perhaps? Or outside? Before he reached the gate, the GPS had him turn right, which sent him parallel along the wall.

The Larkspur was a log building, four stories high. He found a slot to park in and got out of the truck. There was a spinning door in the front, but Levi found a regular one on the side and went in. The lobby looked straight out of an Old Western movie: roughhewn furniture and wagon wheel chandeliers. The place smelled like woodchips.

A doorman met him inside and checked his ID on a handheld computer. "Welcome home, Mr. Justin. My name is Colter. If you need anything, please use the help on your Wyndo."

Whatever that meant. "How do I find my room?"

"You're in 206. You can take the elevator or stairs to the second floor. Your apartment will be to the right. If you'd like lunch, The Hunter serves a great hamburger. There are also two restaurants down the block: Wingers and Café Eat, if you don't mind InstaFood."

"What's InstaFood?"

"It's frozen. Already been cooked, then they heat it up. No waiting."

Bizarre. Levi took the stairs to the second floor. His new home was a hotel room of Old: narrow and clean. It had a bed, one of those glass wall TVs, a separate indoor bathroom, a sink, and a small refrigerator.

Seeing no reason to hang around, he decided to find lunch. He took the stairs back to the lobby, and as he descended, his gaze caught sight of the words *Black Army* that someone had written in dark ink on the back of the steps above his head. He'd eat, and afterwards he'd see if he could find out what some of this graffiti stood for. And maybe he could find Bender, like Lonn from the RC had suggested. He had to be careful, though. He couldn't afford another X.

"Is everything okay, Mr. Justin?" Colter asked when he entered the lobby.

"Just looking to get some food," Levi said. "How do I find that instant café?"

"Café Eat is to the left. It's on the corner before the next light."

Levi started for the door. "Hey, how do I send a letter to a friend in the Highlands?"

"I can call a messenger for you, sir. They do charge a fee."

"Will they read it?"

"Certainly not, sir."

"Where can I get some writing materials?"

"There's a G.I.N. store just before Café Eat."

"Thanks. Hey, one more question. How can I look up someone, to see where they live?"

"You could use your Wyndo to access to the grid, or you could leave the individual's name with me and I'd be happy to try and locate them."

"Yeah, okay, well, his name is Bender. I don't know if that's his first or last name."

Colter's eyes widened. "For the record, Mr. Justin, residents of the Larkspur are law-abiding nationals. I hope you aren't involved with the Black Army."

"Bender is connected to the Black Army?"

"Oh, yes. He's one of their leaders. But I must warn you..." He glanced at Levi's cheek where the two Xs were bared for all to see. "Associating with people connected with the Black Army will only get you liberated before your time."

Levi definitely needed to find this Bender fellow. "Look, I'm an outsider who just moved here. Some guy told me to see if I could find Bender. I didn't know he was trouble, and I certainly don't need any more. Sorry if I upset you. And thanks for setting me straight."

"Not at all, Mr. Justin. Enjoy your lunch. And find pleasure in life."

"Yeah, I'll do that." Levi walked to the truck but could see the Café Eat sign from where he stood, so he decided to walk. A wall of cement followed the sidewalk. Thick gray paint had recently covered large sections of it. Levi strained to make out the covered-up words but couldn't tell what had been written underneath. Street cleaners in the Midlands did good work.

He waited at the intersection for the light to change. The G.I.N. store sat kitty-corner from where he stood. He'd stop in there on his way back to his apartment.

Café Eat had a vastly different atmosphere from the Marcellina Steakhouse. No fancy tablecloths. Everything was red and white plastic. The patrons were loud, laughing and yelling across the room at people on the other side.

Levi waited inside the door, but when no waitress approached, he wandered to one of two vacant seats at a counter where waitresses and cooks worked on the other side. A waitress wearing a short red dress with a white apron set a plate of food in front of a man, then stopped before Levi.

"Know what you'll have?"

"Beef with ranch sauce?" he asked.

"How about a bacon ranch burger?"

"Sure."

"You'll have it in three, or it's free." She walked away.

Three what? Minutes? Could that be safe? Levi inspected the man sitting on his left. He was tall and bony, and his arms were covered in tattoos. He had two Xs on his cheek.

"How'd you get *your* Xs?" Levi asked.

The man glanced Levi's way and grunted.

"What can I get you?" The waitress had stopped in front of Levi again, but she wasn't looking at him.

A kid had claimed the stool on Levi's right. He looked about Omar's age. He wore black gloves, had brown hair like a trimmed porcupine, three tiny gold hoops on one side of his nostrils, and was missing his left ear. Bummer. A five was inked onto his face. The only thing he lacked was an X.

"Chicken sandwich with honey mustard and some onion rings," the kid said.

"Back in three, or it's free." The waitress wandered off.

Levi tried not to look at the kid's ear when he asked, "Know where I might find Bender?"

The kid laughed. "Seriously? Look, peer, you're going to have that third X by the end of the day if you go around saying that name."

"Bender?"

"No, bacon ranch burger," the kid said, still chuckling.

"Well, how am I supposed to find the guy?"

"Don't know why you'd want to, you dim shell, but unless you want to end up in this month's liberation ceremony, you'd better think of a plan B."

All right. "Live here all your life?"

"Yep."

"How did you manage to lose an ear and not get at least one X?"

The kid's jaw twitched. "You really have to burn someone to get one X, let alone three."

"Yeah, but I'd guess you'd really have to burn someone to lose an ear too."

Levi's burger came then, as did the kid's chicken sandwich and onion rings. Levi figured he'd done enough damage with his mouth and stuffed his face.

The food satisfied but didn't compare to the steak from Marcillina's. The tall man finished and left without saying a word. Levi was only half done eating when the earless porcupine got up to go. He'd eaten barely half his food.

"Another time, shell," the kid said. "If you last that long."

Levi finished eating and headed for the G.I.N store. The place resembled Old stores he'd scavenged over the years, but this one was bright, clean, cobweb free, and filled with fresh products. Levi found a rack of greeting cards and grabbed a few different ones, including one for Jemma with kissing birds that looked like hearts. Would a messenger really deliver it to her?

By the time Levi left G.I.N., it was dark. From the sidewalk, he could see the tops of some Highlands buildings over the distant wall. He hated that Jemma was so close but he couldn't get to her. He prayed she was safe—that all the Glenrock people were. He needed to learn how things were done here. He needed a friend who could explain. The earless porcupine had been nice enough but obviously didn't want to associate with Xed people.

Levi went back to his apartment and wrote cards to Jordan, Mason, and Jemma. Then he took them down to Colter for delivery.

Patience and wit was what Lonn had told him he needed. Perhaps he'd go out and watch for graffiti artists, follow them to see if they led him to Bender. If he didn't see anyone, he'd take his truck back to the Highlands and find his backpack.

It felt mad good to have a plan.

Levi forced himself out into the night. He walked the opposite direction from Café Eat, came to an alley, and decided to explore it, but without streetlamps it too dark to see anything. As he started back for the main road, bright headlights startled him. He moved to the right. The vehicle passed by, and he saw it was a taxi.

Just as he stepped back into the road, tires skidded over gravel behind him. Car doors creaked open, and two masked men ran toward him.

No way was he going back to the RC. Levi sprinted for the main road, but another vehicle turned down the alley, lights blinding him. He paused only for a moment, trying to decide what to do, but it was all his pursuers needed. Stun wires bit into his back, and he hit the ground.

Masked men taped Levi's hands and ankles and put a fabric sack over his head. He felt his body lift off the ground and plunk on a somewhat soft surface. A door slammed. Apparently, he was inside the car, which quickly sped away. He lay across the seat on his stomach trembling and trying to think of how he'd get free before they inked his third X.

The car turned once and stopped. Car doors opened. Someone climbed on Levi's back and several sets of hands grabbed him, pushed him down against the seat. Someone cut the tape on his hands and squeezed his right wrist.

"Get off me you filthy, depraved maggots!" Levi tried to wiggle free, but he may as well have been buried alive.

"Don't move, and this won't hurt as bad," a man said.

A scratch tickled Levi's hand, then throbbed like a bee sting.

"What are you doing?" Levi yelled. "Get off me!"

The same man said, "Here, go have a drink at the Hunter. And don't lose that."

"You got it," a younger voice said.

"One drink, Rewl," the man said.

"Yeah, yeah."

The man on top of Levi pressed something over the sting on his hand, then wound tape around Levi's wrists again. The weight left his back. Both car doors slammed. And the car lurched forward. Several minutes passed this time. Levi tried to calm down. To think. Enforcers wouldn't do whatever this was. He just needed to stay calm and be smart.

The car turned at least five times before stopping again. Levi allowed himself to be pulled out and dragged between two people, his boots scraping over a smooth surface until one of his abductors said, "Sit." A different man's voice this time. Older.

Levi squatted carefully until he felt the edge of a chair press against the backs of his legs. He lowered himself onto the surface. "Bender?" It had to be.

A man chuckled. "What makes you ask?"

Levi's breath made the fabric stick to his face. He blew it away and said, "I've been a guest in the RC twice now. This isn't how they do things."

"Right you are, boy. Sorry we had to cut you, but they track SimTags these days. Take off the bag, Zane."

The sack came off Levi's head. He sat on a metal folding chair in front of a desk in a dark office with Old wood paneling. The place looked as ancient as the man sitting behind the desk—far older than was allowed in the Safe Lands. A few days' growth of a gray beard shaded his wrinkled face. A burn scar pinched his left eyebrow down over his eye so he looked as if he were winking. Levi glanced over his shoulder and saw a kid standing in the corner, arms crossed.

The earless porcupine.

"You following me, chicken sandwich?" Levi said.

Zane nodded once at Levi. "How's it going, bacon ranch burger?"

"I hear you're looking for me," Bender said, pulling Levi's attention back.

"Lonn told me to. I met him in the RC."

Bender took a deep breath. "I don't suppose he sent a message?"

A message? Who was Lonn anyway? "He said you'd help me if I told you 'Rose.' I thought it was a code or something."

"That's it?"

"Yeah."

Bender sighed and rubbed his eye. "We can do that for Lonn, but since he's not here to tell us why, we're going to ask a favor. See, we've been watching you. Got our own surveillance tapped into the grid. Saw you came in carrying a rifle. Lost you in the park, but we know the rifle didn't come out. You didn't have it, the enforcers didn't have it, so where is it?"

"I hid it."

"That's what we figured. But even with my excellent trackers, we haven't found it."

"That's what this is all about? You want my rifle?"

"Not exactly," Bender said. "Very few enforcers are trained as snipers in the Safe Lands. And with Lonn in the RC, I don't have a sniper. So I want to know if you can shoot."

Levi huffed a laugh. "Can I shoot my own rifle? Yeah."

"How do I know you're not lying?" Bender asked.

"Why would I?"

Bender stared at Levi for a moment, then opened a desk drawer and pulled out a pistol with a silencer attached. "Zane?"

Zane pulled a knife and cut through the tape on Levi's wrists and ankles.

Bender handed Levi the gun. "Why don't you tell me if this is loaded?"

Levi gripped the gun in his right hand, which triggered the laser sights on the wood-paneled wall. He popped out the clip, saw that it was empty, shoved it back in, and pulled back the action, pretending to chamber a round. "It's empty." He flipped the safety on and off, aimed it at the wall to check the sights. "Can I have this?"

Bender looked at Levi, impressed. "No, you can't have it. But you can help us."

Levi handed the gun back to Bender. "I'm not killing anyone."

Bender returned the gun to the drawer. "Not even Otley? We heard he executed your caretaker. People tend to have strong attachments for their caretakers."

"I miss my caretaker every day," Zane said.

A chance to take out Otley? "I'll think about it."

Bender sat back down. "Think fast. We've only got a few days to make our move."

"But you're going to help me, right?" Levi asked.

"This about a femme?"

Femme meant girl, didn't it? "What makes you think that?"

Bender grinned, flashing a few rotten teeth. "Lonn is a, uh... What's the Old word for softies, Zane?"

"Romantic." Zane fluttered his eyelashes.

"Right. Lonn had a lifter named Martana Kirst. But he called her Rose."

Thank you, Lonn. Maybe these were the friends Levi needed. "Enforcers attacked my village and brought us here. Our women are in the harem. I need to get them out."

"I could maybe get one or two out," Bender said. "How many are up there?"

"I'm not sure. Ten, maybe? Twelve? And our children are somewhere too, but I don't know where. There's about a dozen kids." Levi really needed to make a list. If he did manage to pull off a rescue, he didn't want to leave anyone behind.

"Hold the flavor. I don't do kids," Bender said. "They got high security up in that school—spies too. Listen, this is going to take time."

Levi wanted to scream. "I don't know how much time I have."

"I get that. I'll be thinking how I can help you out. And you let me know what you decide about being our sniper." Bender leaned back in his chair and knocked on the wall.

A woman walked in. She had short, spiky red hair that curved around her face instead of sticking up like Zane's. She was holding a pair of black gloves.

"This one goes by Red." Bender gestured to the woman. "Come here, femme."

The woman bounced up to the desk and handed the gloves to Bender. She was pretty, despite her ashen skin and how her body was all sharp angles where it should be soft.

"The right-hand glove has a pocket for your SimTag," Bender said. "The one we cut out of your hand."

Levi looked at his hand. A sticky bandage clung to the side. "And the one in my face?"

Bender shook his head. "You can get a hundred SimTags in your body. They all answer to the one in your hand. And once they're more than twenty feet apart from the host tag, they lose their connection. You see any numbers on my face?"

"No."

"But when you saw Zane in the café, you saw his numbers, right? He was wearing his gloves. Be smart about this. Going out in public? You wear your gloves, even to eat. Don't want enforcers knowing where you are? Leave the gloves someplace you spend a lot of time. Where the gloves are is where the enforcers think you are. Right now your SimTag is having a drink in The Hunter." He tossed the gloves to Levi. "So when you get back and my guy gives you your tag, put the tag in the pocket. Get me?"

"Yeah. Can you do that for a couple of my people?"

"If I can get to them, I can do that for all your people. Zane, get him a Wyndo."

"You didn't say he was such a raven, Zane," Red said, staring at Levi like he was steak.

Zane walked to a shelf across the room. "You didn't ask."

Red touched Levi's cheek with her index finger. "How can he be so soft?"

"'Cause he's not infected," Bender said. "And don't you be changing that."

A slow smile spread across Red's face as she studied Levi. "I've never seen eyelashes like those on a guy. Most *femmes* can't even pull off eyelashes like that without three coats of mascara. That your real hair too?" She combed her hand through his hair.

"Stop touching me." Levi didn't want any woman touching him but Jemma—especially not someone with a plague.

"Walls, you're so blessed," she said. "Mine's half plugs."

Levi watched Zane digging for something on a shelf across the room. "I don't know what that means."

Red twirled her finger around a lock of Levi's hair. "It means half my hair fell out, and I got it replaced with fake hair."

Levi grabbed her wrist and pushed her hand away from his hair. "I have a fiancée."

She laughed. "Now *I* don't know what you mean. What's a fiancée?"

"A lifer," Bender said.

"Lifer?" Red pouted. "She must be some lover."

"Her name's Jemma." Levi tugged the cord with their rings out of his shirt and held it where they could see. "I scavenged these rings from Denver City. We were supposed to get married last Friday."

"That's sugar sweet." Zane handed Levi what looked like an Old cell phone. The letters *CB* were engraved at the top and designed in a way that created two people's profiles, talking.

Levi touched the screen, and it lit up. "A phone?"

"A Wyndo is way better than a phone," Zane said. "Phones are ancient. Play with it tonight. Learn how to use it. It's already got Red's and my numbers in it. You can use it to talk to us, but if you use it to talk to others, be careful. Don't tap in your SimTag. The Guild monitors all transmitters, and since ours are off the grid, putting your SimTag in or talking to someone whose transmitter is on grid will only call attention to your big bad illegalness."

"What if I need to talk to Bender?"

Bender glanced up. Levi had forgotten his scar and thought he was winking. "You tap Zane or Red, and I'll tap you. That's all the time I've got for you tonight, shell."

Zane held up the fabric sack. "Sorry. Gotta put this on again."

Zane left Levi's arms and legs free for the drive to the Larkspur but made him lie in the back seat to avoid being seen.

"Be careful with Red," Zane said.

Levi lay on his back this time, with his knees up. "Careful how?"

"She wants you."

"Wants me to what? Wait... aren't you and she... together?"

Zane snorted a laugh. "No way. I mean, we traded paint a few times when I first started working for Bender, but... she's a lot to maintain."

Sometimes Levi could barely understand what these people said. "What's that mean?"

"She gets gummy, you know? Wants you to be with her all the time. It's intense."

"Well, I'll be careful." The last thing Levi needed was more guilt.

"Don't drink anything she gives you," Zane said. "She stimmed me a few times to get what she wanted. She's one crazy flame."

It was almost ten at night by the time Levi got back to his apartment. He climbed in his truck and drove toward the Highlands, hoping his backpack and rifle were still in the park. But when he got to the gate, they wouldn't let him through.

"Sorry, Mr. Justin. You have a work ID only. Unless you enter the Highlands with a Highland resident, you're only permitted to enter between seven a.m. and five p.m."

Oh, come on! This place had more rules that the book of Leviticus. "Fine."

Levi turned around and drove back to the Larkspur. He'd just have to look for his backpack tomorrow after his shift. Once he got the radios, he'd get Mason and Jordan a meeting with Bender so they could lose their SimTags.

Then he could rescue Jemma.

Chapter 22

Shaylinn was sitting with Jemma, Kendall, Naomi, and Mia in the Blue Diamond living room, watching the Safe Lands ColorCast program *C Factor*. Jemma had barely spoken to her since the night she and Mia had snuck out. Shaylinn kept looking for an opportunity to talk about it, but her sister was always with Naomi, as usual.

Shaylinn was torn. She liked looking pretty. And the clothes. But she hadn't liked Ewan's behavior at all. Her first kiss. Stolen by a bully.

"Why's Page kissing Bolton?" Jemma asked. "Doesn't she love the earring man?"

"That's Fivel," Kendall said. "She only paired up with Fivel to make Bolton jealous. But Bolton is using her to get horn implants."

"What are horn implants?" Shaylinn asked.

"They're silicone horns," Kendall said.

Shaylinn wrinkled her nose. If the Lord had wanted her to have horns, she'd have been born with them. She frowned. Wasn't the same true of her body? If the Lord had wanted her to be thin, he'd have made her thin?

On the screen, Bolton pulled Page's shirt over her head, leaving her in just her bra.

Jemma shrieked and covered her eyes. "Don't want to see!"

Shaylinn leaned closer to the screen, staring at two lines of gold rings on Page's back. "What are those things on her back?"

"That's a surface corset," Kendall said. "You should've seen her in the gown she wore two weeks ago. It was backless, and her corset looked so glossy with satin laces."

"Laced up rings in her back?" Shaylinn asked. "Doesn't that hurt?"

"Naw. They put a silicone layer under the skin and numb the pierced areas. I saw an edudrama about it. *Cosmetic Confessions*."

"Someone should make an edudrama about the Safe Lands called *Psychotic Confessions*," Naomi said.

There was a knock at the door. Jemma jumped up. "I'll get it."

She opened the door to a young man dressed in green shorts and a white T-shirt with the letters *SLMS* on the upper right. "Messenger service," he said.

Kendall shrieked and reached toward him. "Hay-o, Chord!"

Chord jogged around the sofa and leaned down to give Kendall a hug and kiss both cheeks. "How are you, femme? Walls, you're famous now. Your face is everywhere."

Kendall groaned and patted her belly. "I know. Almost done, though."

"You're huge!" He laughed.

"Thanks," Kendall said. "Chord, this is Jemma and Naomi and Shaylinn and Mia. Girls, this is Chord. We were messengers together in the Midlands before I came here."

"Nice to meet you." He stared at Naomi, his gaze shifting from her face to her belly. "You're famous too."

Naomi pursed her lips and looked back to the ColorCast.

"Can't stay," Chord said. "Lots of messages to deliver. Oh my fortune! You guys are watching *C Factor*. I can't stand that show. Hey, which one of you is Shaylinn Zachary or Jemma Harvey?"

Jemma gasped.

"I'm Shaylinn."

Chord handed Shaylinn a gold envelope, then held out a black touchpad that was attached to his belt. "ID?"

Shaylinn pressed her fist against the pad.

"Got it." Chord tapped on his Wyndo. Looked up. "And Jemma?"

"Right here!" Jemma stood, waving both hands. "It's from Levi. I know it is!"

"How?" Naomi asked.

"Because here my last name here is Levi. But Levi wouldn't know that. He might assume I chose my father's name instead."

"So might your mother," Naomi said.

Jemma's grin faltered as she gave Chord her ID. "True. A letter from my mother would be good too."

Shaylinn slowly opened the gold envelope as Jemma tore into her own mail. Jemma squealed and grinned and cried over a colorful card. Chord and Kendall were talking, but Shaylinn wasn't listening. Her heart fluttered like a flag in the wind.

The Safe Lands Guild Surrogacy Center
OFFICIAL SUMMONS

To: Shaylinn Zachary

It is your responsibility to be in the Surrogacy Center on Wednesday, June 23, 2088 at 11:00 a.m. Failure to appear will result in the issuance of a warrant for your arrest.

Being ranked first in line, she'd known it was coming, but she'd shoved aside the reality and indulged in all the fun things this place had to offer. Now, here was the price. They were going to make her pregnant.

Chord hugged Kendall again and left. Shaylinn tucked her summons between her knees and tried to pay attention to the others.

Naomi slid to the edge of the couch. "Stop screeching, and tell me who it's from."

"Levi sent me a card!" Jemma hopped up and down and giggled, but it morphed into a confused cry. "That means he's okay. Right?"

"I'd say so." Naomi patted the couch beside her. "Come, sit. I want to hug you, but I'm not getting up."

"'I wish I had no heart, it aches so...'" Jemma sat beside Naomi, who gave her a side hug. "I'm going to write him back."

"Can I see it?" Shaylinn asked.

"Sure." Jemma thrust the card to Shaylinn.

The front said *Love* and had two red birds flying toward each other. Inside, the birds were kissing and their touching bodies formed the shape of a heart. The pre-printed words said, "I'm glad we're in this together," but underneath, in black pen, "I miss you, Buttercup. Write me back. Your Westley. Larkspur, Room 206, Midlands."

A tear ran down Shaylinn's cheek. She gasped and quickly wiped it away. She never cried. *How annoying!*

"Shay, what's the matter?" Jemma asked.

Shaylinn returned the card. "I always wanted to be a mother. Someday though, you know? Not now. I know none of the boys like me. But I don't want to have a baby like this!" Her bottom lip trembled in a terrible frown, and she turned her head in case her eyes betrayed her and spilled more tears.

Jemma got up and knelt on the floor at Shaylinn's feet, put her hands on Shaylinn's knees. "Shay, what's wrong?"

"Was it your letter?" Kendall asked. "Was it the summons?"

Shaylinn pulled out the envelope, now slightly crumpled, and handed it to her sister.

Jemma read it. Her expression hardened. "No! Honey, this is *not* okay. We have to do something." She passed the paper to Naomi.

"Oh, Shaylinn," Naomi said. "I'm *so* sorry. We'll think of something."

"We can try and sneak out!" Jemma said. "Make that Ewan guy help. He owes Shay."

"Sometimes the procedure doesn't work," Kendall said.

"Yes!" Jemma said. "Way to think positive. The procedure might not work."

Shaylinn looked to Kendall. "It worked on you."

"Yeah, but you never know," Jemma said.

"Easy for you to say, Jemma. Everyone has always loved you. Levi, Mason, Omar—they all would have chosen you. I don't have anyone. And now I'll have a baby, and no boy will like a girl with a baby."

Tears filled Jemma's eyes. "I'm sorry, honey. I don't know what to do or say to make this better."

"You guys are looking at this all wrong," Mia said. "It's not a big deal, Shaylinn. You're forgetting that it's the Safe Lands' baby, not yours. You won't be a single mother. Once you have it and they take it, you'll be free and have a ton of credits and fame."

"I don't want fame or credits. I want what Jemma has."

"You like Levi?" Jemma asked, her voice a high squeak.

"No. I just want someone to love me. To think I'm beautiful." Even though he'd turned in the entire village, her heart still wanted Omar, but she'd likely never see him again.

"Ewan thought you were beautiful," Mia said. "And you were. You *are*. I don't know why you don't think so. I'm kind of tired of hearing about it, frankly."

"Shaylinn, you have us. And we're all getting out of this place long before you'd deliver this baby." Jemma glared at Mia. "That's a long time from now, and Kendall's right. You're not pregnant yet. Let's pray about this, okay?"

"But what about Kendall's baby?"

"My baby will go to the nursery, and I'll go back to the Midlands Messaging Office." Kendall smiled and blinked so rapidly that Shaylinn knew she was trying to be strong. "I've gained a ton of weight. Trust me. I need the exercise."

"You said you were a messenger before coming here," Jemma said. "Don't you have to change jobs every six months?"

"You can apply for an extension if you like your task, and I did. When I first got here, I tasked as a runner for City Hall. I think they like to keep new outsiders close at first."

"Then why did the task director make Levi live in the Midlands?" Jemma asked.

"He probably got a strike," Kendall said. "And maybe to separate him from his friend and from you. The enforcers have enough trouble with the rebel groups."

"There's a rebellion in the Safe Lands?" Shaylinn asked.

"Think Levi has already found them?" Jemma asked Naomi.

"Knowing Levi, I wouldn't doubt it," Naomi said.

"Tell us about them," Jemma said to Kendall.

"There are some groups that protest the government. They're pretty violent. I found out about them when I worked for City Hall, and once I moved to the Midlands, I saw their graffiti everywhere. They set bombs and kidnap people. Sometimes they kill. They want to change things. I guess they figure if they can kill off the Safe Lands Guild, maybe they can take over."

"We should start our own rebellion," Jemma said. "A more peaceful one. Plot a way to get out of here before Shaylinn's appointment and Kendall has her baby."

"Careful, Jem," Naomi said. "You're starting to sound like me."

"It's too dangerous," Kendall said.

"No it's not," Jemma said. "They need us. We're too valuable to kill. And what's the worst that can happen? Kendall still loses her baby? Shay and the rest of us get pregnant? We've got to try."

"What do you have in mind?" Naomi asked.

"We start by sending Levi a message," Jemma said. "I need some paper and a pen."

Shaylinn tuned out the conversation. Jemma's letter to Levi wouldn't reach him before her appointment in the morning. She read her summons again and closed her eyes.

God? Is this what you want for me? Why?

Someone sat beside her on the couch. Shaylinn opened her eyes. Mia.

"I think you're lucky," Mia said.

Shaylinn scowled. "You're such a liar."

"You're going to be famous. Everyone is going to worship you. And I'm *not* lying."

"Then trade places with me," Shaylinn asked.

"I already asked. They said our numbers are based on our biology or something like that. Nothing can be done. But they said we'll all be pregnant within the next six weeks, so it won't be long."

Shaylinn stared at the summons again. Tomorrow. No, it wouldn't be long at all.

Shaylinn sat on her front porch, knitting a hat for her baby. Her belly was huge, the perfect table for her project. It wouldn't be long now, and they would be a family of four.

The children ran past the porch, giggling, holding fistfuls of dandelion clocks, loose seeds drifting behind them.

She watched them run, her heart light and free and very full. They ran straight to their father, jumping up and down at his feet and begging him to blow, blow.

He did, and the seeds danced in the air to the laughter of the children, bringing a wide smile to Shaylinn's lips.

She woke as if someone had gently nudged her shoulder. It had been only a faceless dream, yet she felt calm and peaceful.

Is everything really going to be okay, God? Could the dream be true? Did Shaylinn have a real family in her future?

Chapter 23

Omar pressed the down arrow and stepped back from the elevator, staring at his scabbed knuckles as he pulled his hand away. It had felt good to hurt Levi—to dominate him for the first time ever. But it hadn't taken long for the thrill to turn to guilt. Skottie and Charlz had taken Levi to the medical center and said Levi had gotten a second X for assaulting an enforcer.

They were trying to comfort him. But Levi's anger was justified. Omar scratched the scab on his middle knuckle. If only no one had died. If only the enforcers had come to Glenrock peacefully. If only...

No matter how Omar tried to shift blame, it always rebounded. *He* was responsible for all the deaths. His father and uncle... nine men, two women, a child, and possibly more.

"What are you doing?" a velvety voice asked.

Omar whirled around and saw Bel, his red-headed neighbor, standing behind him. She was wearing a short gold dress that draped off the edges of her shoulders, clinging to her body like it was trying not to slide off. Square nets of gold and black metal dangled from her ears. Black boots stretched up past her knees. There were no feathers in her hair today; she'd straightened it into a silky red curtain.

Bel never seemed to mimic the styles. Skottie had talked Omar into buying a lot of black clothes because he could mix them with the color trends yet still fit in. Today, he was wearing shiny black pants and a stiff red shirt that buttoned only halfway up.

"Could I paint you?" Omar asked, bolder after several nights out with Skottie and Charlz. "Your portrait, I mean."

She blinked her thick, dark lashes. "Walls! You move kind of fast, don't you?"

"I'm an artist," Omar said. "And you're beautiful. It would be wrong not to paint you."

The elevator dinged, making Omar jump. Bel laughed, her shoulders trembling with the movement. Omar wasn't sure if she was laughing because he'd asked to paint her or because the elevator had startled him. He stepped toward the open doors, but Bel caught his hand and pulled him back. The elevator closed.

Her lips curved in a slow smile. Still holding his hand, she lifted it toward her face and examined his knuckles. "You got into a fight." She kissed each scrape, then released his hand. "I hope she was worth it."

Omar couldn't breathe. His hand tingled, which *had* to be his imagination.

"You meeting a femme tonight?" She withdrew a purple metal vaporizer from her purse, put the end to her lips, and breathed in.

"No."

"You're an outsider, aren't you?" she asked, her voice hoarse as she held her breath.

"I'm a Safe Lands national."

She turned her head, blew out a stream of bright green vapor, and fixed her gaze back to his. "But you *were* an outsider, right?"

"I'm that obvious?"

She laughed again. "Yes."

"What am I doing wrong?"

"I wouldn't say *wrong*. You just look so healthy. And lost and lonely and… intense. I'm Belbeline, or Bel, by the way. I guess you heard my friends call me that already. What's your name?"

"Omar Strong." He pressed the down button again.

"Where you headed right now, Omar Strong?"

"To a club."

"I'm going to need a little more than that. Which club?"

He was meeting Skottie and Charlz at Ginger Oak again, but a girl might not like that. He shrugged. "First one I come to."

She clicked her tongue. "Oh, that'll never do. Come with me tonight, trigger. I'll be your guide. What's your stim?"

Omar glanced at the purple vaporizer delicately balanced between her long, pale fingers. "I like beer."

She rolled her eyes. "Do you have a vaporizer?"

"No." Skottie kept telling Omar he should get one, but he wasn't sure he was ready for whatever they held.

"You'll need a good one." Belbeline squeezed his arm. "Are you *really* of age?"

No. But Omar said, "Yeah."

"You look so young, you blessed thing."

"You look young too."

"Flattery will get you… exactly what you want, I imagine," she said, giggling.

He grinned, not sure if he was supposed to reply.

"For a guy who asked to paint me, you're a bit of a neo."

He stiffened, not understanding her criticism.

"*My*, you have a quick temper. Don't be so serious. I'm teasing you. Stick with me, and I'll take good care of you tonight, Valentine."

The elevator arrived then. In the lobby, Belbeline called a taxi, which carried them to a dance club called Blue Heaven. Omar tapped Skottie and told them not to wait for him.

As the taxi slowed to a stop outside the club's entrance, Omar could hear the thump of bass inside the car. "It must be really loud inside," he said, watching the way the blue lights pulsed in the night sky.

"It is." Belbeline slid across the seat and opened the door. She said something to him and winked, but Omar couldn't make out her words.

He followed her into the dark interior, where the sound intensified until the beat was like a physical force, almost pushing him back toward the street. At first he couldn't see, but his eyes slowly adjusted.

Shards of colored light slashed from the ceiling across the dance floor. Squares of light dotted the dance floor. Those dancing on them seemed on fire, while the rest of the crowd appeared as fragmented limbs and faces, their bodies lost in the darkness until the colored light cut across them.

Belbeline took his hand and pulled him through the bouncing mob, past bare skin, long legs, black leather, red dresses, a cloud of perfume and vapor, and couples whose bodies were tangled together. Some girl's hair slapped his face. A guy brushed up against his side. It wasn't possible for Omar to not touch someone. Skottie and Charlz had never taken him anywhere so... fast.

Belbeline released his hand and spun around. Blue light slashed across her face, highlighting her features. She smiled slowly, swayed, moved her feet, grabbed the sides of her skirt and swished it around. Omar's stomach seemed to slide down one leg of his pants and onto the floor as she lifted her arms over her head, shaking out her curtain of hair. This was *not* how people danced in Glenrock.

She moved closer and put her hands on Omar's waist. He hugged her close, liking how she felt in his arms. They danced through several songs, moving in time with the mob. Omar felt connected, included. This was all he'd really wanted: a beautiful woman to choose him.

She leaned close and yelled in his ear, "I know something that will really make your night wild." She tugged him by the hand through the crowd.

Omar would have followed her anywhere.

They left the dance floor and walked down a narrow corridor, up a flight of stairs, and down a wider hallway. The walls were painted black, lit by twinkling lights that zigzagged along the ceiling.

"Where are we going?" he called.

"Somewhere more quiet," she said.

Halfway down the hall, Bel stopped at a door, knocked twice, paused, then knocked five more times. The door swung in, revealing an imposing man in jeans, a black jacket, and dark sunglasses. He stood beside a black podium that held a SimTag pad.

Belbeline set the side of her hand against it, her other hand still clasping Omar's. "How are you tonight, Dag?"

"Decent." The man glanced from Omar to the pad, then up again. Omar swiped his fist as well. The man gave him a nod. "Enjoy."

Belbeline led Omar into a dark room clouded with vapors that smelled sweet, minty, and of something else that tickled his nose. Small tables and chairs, couches, oversized pillows, and recliners in black and silver were arranged on either side of a low, two-sided glass bar that stretched down the center of the room and glowed brightly with blue light—the only light in the room. The barkeep stood on a floor that was lower than the one Omar was walking on. Dozens of people sat vaping, talking, kissing.

Belbeline set her vaporizer on the counter. The purple metal tube rolled a little over the glass. "Give me my usual, and vape me with a five," she said to the barkeep. "Pink, strawberry, grass. And my man here, I'm going to buy him a PV. You have a silver bullet?"

"Yeah."

"Okay, fill it with grass… a two. Black. No flavor. And get him a—" She looked at Omar. "A black velvet to start."

"You got it." The barkeep held out a pad, and Bel pressed her hand against it.

"We'll be in the corner." Belbeline took Omar's arm and led him to the far side of the room, where they claimed a black leather sofa and a tiny square table. "Girls where you live probably don't dress like us or dance like us, huh?"

"Uh, no." He laughed, trying to picture Shay in Bel's dress.

"You and I, Omar… We're going to have so much fun together."

Omar ran his fingers over the scabs on his knuckles, wondering what kind of fun Belbeline had in mind. It didn't seem fair that so many were dead because of him, yet here he was with this beautiful, friendly bomshell. He'd expected God to punish him for what he'd done, but his life here seemed like a reward.

That bothered him more than he cared to admit.

The barkeep arrived with a tray. He set two glasses on the table before them. One was a goblet-like glass filled with clear liquid and several olives. The other glass was tall and thick, filled with two stripes of dark liquid and froth on top. The barkeep also set a silver plate between the glasses with the vaporizers propped on little indentations, Belbeline's purple vaporizer and a thick silver one. "You guys behave, now."

"Oh, we will." Belbeline reached for the glass with olives. She took a sip, then set the glass back on the tray. She pushed the other glass toward him. "Find pleasure in life."

Omar picked up the glass, which was cold in his hand, and took a sip. His top lip sank into the froth, and the liquid below was cold, fizzy, beer with a bitter, creamy taste. It also tasted smoky, a bit like unsweetened chocolate. He started to put down the glass, but Belbeline set her hand on his arm.

"Don't give up. Give yourself a chance to get used to the taste."

He took another sip, liking the way the drink seemed alive and whispering.

Belbeline picked up her vaporizer and took a long breath. "Since you're so sweet, I bought you one," she said on an exhale, her words hoarser than normal as a pink cloud of vapor seeped from her lips. "It's a personal vaporizer. Most people call them PVs."

"Thanks." Omar still wasn't certain he wanted one, but the guys had wanted him to try it. He wasn't sure what was holding him back. "What are they for?" Omar had watched an entire show about it and still didn't know.

"Whatever you need. Or want. You can vape anything. People take their meds this way. Some like to vape stimulants." One side of her mouth quirked up. "There are all kinds of juices from plain flavors, which is like candy, to harder stuff. You order a hit level, which is how powerful the vape will be. And if you want, you can also ask for color, which will color your fog."

"Fog?"

"Your breath when you blow out."

Omar stared at the silver tube. "What's in mine?"

"I got you grass at a hit level two. You ever tried marijuana?"

"No." Some people in Jack's Peak smoked marijuana. Omar had heard stories of Jordan's grandpa smoking it. "It wasn't allowed in our village."

"Well, *everything* is allowed here. And grass will help you relax, so we can go downstairs and really dance."

Omar swallowed, embarrassed by his hesitation. He'd much rather go back to the dance floor now. "Don't you smoke marijuana, though? I guess I don't understand how a vaporizer is different."

"Smoking is against Safe Lands law. It's unhealthy, and it gives you bad breath. Plus it can start fires. Vaporizers don't even have a smell, unless you get flavor."

Was that why marijuana was bad? The smoking? Papa Eli had never specified. Perhaps the Safe Lands had found a way to eliminate the danger. Doubts nagged Omar, but he supposed it wouldn't hurt to try it once.

He picked up the silver tube, wanting to please Bel. "How do you do it?"

Belbeline snatched the vaporizer from his fingers. "I'll get it started for you. New PVs don't work quite right at first." She put her lips around the end and took a few quick breaths. The tip lit up bright blue with each draw. With almost no emotion on her face, she blew out a quick puff of black vapor, sucked longer, then blew out a long stream of black vapor that felt cool as it hit Omar's face. "That's better." She handed it to him, a ring of red lipstick around the end of the silver tube. "Now you try."

He put the end into his mouth and sucked. Nothing happened.

"Push the button," Belbeline said.

He tried again, this time pushing the small circle on one side. Hot air filled his mouth and burned the back of his throat. He opened his mouth and croaked, "It's hot."

"Take shorter breaths until you're used to it. They have cold PVs too, you know. They're kind of fun if you want chilled vape."

Omar took a short breath, and the hot moisture filled his mouth like breathing in steam from the sauna. He held it there, not sure what to do. He swallowed and choked.

"Don't swallow it, dim. Breathe it all the way into your lungs."

Omar tried again. The hot air passed into his mouth, down his throat, and filled his chest with a slight burning.

"Now blow it out," Bel said, her sapphire eyes like black diamonds in the low light.

The stream of vapor came out in a black plume, like a curl of smoke from a dirty chimney. Omar smiled and tried it again.

Belbeline inhaled on her own vaporizer, and exhaled a bright pink stream into Omar's black one. He laughed, and for a while they simply sat and blew vapor at each other.

The nerves in Omar's body began to tingle, even behind his eyes. He could feel his heart thudding in his chest, faster, it seemed, as if he'd been running. "Did they turn up the music?" he asked Belbeline, who was fishing an olive out of her drink.

"That girl is waving at you." Belbeline put the olive in her mouth and tucked it into her check. She nodded over Omar's shoulder. "Do you know her?"

Omar squinted across the dark room. Mia sat at a little round table with two men and a woman. Mia smiled, spoke to one of the men, then stood and walked toward him.

Lights seemed to flash as Mia came over. Omar squinted against the brightness and leaned back against the sofa, feeling like he could melt into it. His arms prickled like static was in the air.

Mia stopped before their couch, her posture straight as a lamppost. "I just wanted to say that even though the way you did this was wrong—that people shouldn't have had to die—I agree with you. Life here is better than it was in Glenrock." She glanced at Belbeline. "Who's your friend?"

Omar glanced at Belbeline and remembered that she'd wanted to dance.

"I'm Belbeline Combs."

"Are you a dancer?" Mia asked.

The sound of Belbeline's laugh warbled in pitch from high to low and back to high. Omar winced and shook his head to get rid of the sound.

"Right now I task as a masseuse at the Highland Grove Spa. I've also tasked as a barista. I love to dance, but just for fun."

The olives in Belbeline's glass reminded Omar of tiny frogs sticking out their tongues. He snorted, trying not to laugh.

"Well, you're pretty enough to be a stage dancer," Mia said.

"Thank you...?"

"Mia. I'm from Omar's village. I'm here with Rand MacCormon. He's a piano player for Maroz Zerrik and Nelessa Kade."

"I've seen their show. They're amazing. And Rand is quite the Valentine." Belbeline ate another olive. "He and I go way back."

"Oh." Mia's smile faltered. "He took me to a steakhouse. The food was so good!"

Omar fought back another desire to laugh but failed, chuckling deeply.

Mia turned her gaze to where Omar sat, which made him laugh harder for some reason. "What's the matter with him?"

"First time trying a vaporizer."

"Oh."

Was that it? The vaporizer was the reason he felt giddy?

"Well... enjoy your night," Mia said. "Bye, Omar."

Omar watched her go, snickering at how she wobbled on a pair of very high-heeled shoes.

"I think you've had enough." Belbeline snatched the vaporizer from Omar's fingers.

"Hey!"

"I'm glad I only got you a two." She tucked his vaporizer into her purse and took a long drink from her frog-filled glass. "Let's go dance." She bounced up and pulled Omar by his hand.

He stumbled after her, out of the dark room and down the stairs.

"These stairs are steep. I wonder if people ever fall down them." He concentrated on the last two, feeling proud to have made it. "How do you walk in those shoes?"

"Carefully. But it's worth it—I feel gorgeous in high heels."

"You're mad gorgeous."

Belbeline laughed. The thumping music grew louder as they neared the dance floor. Then, as if he jumped over a few minutes of his life, suddenlyn Omar and Belbeline were back in the mass of writhing bodies, dancing.

The night went by in erratic time. Some moments lingered in Omar's mind: dancing with Belbeline and eating something called an orange. Others were a rush of images: meeting up with Belbeline's friends, swimming in an indoor pool with his clothes on, kissing someone—not Belbeline—more dancing, drinking, and vaping. Like a child, Omar felt like he could do whatever he wanted forever and ever and ever and ever and ever.

Omar awoke on the floor of a strange apartment, clutching his vaporizer to his chest and shivering violently. His sleeves were rolled up to his elbows, his clothing was damp, and his socks and shoes were gone. He pushed up to his feet and almost puked. Breathing through his nose to keep the nausea at bay, he brought the vaporizer to his mouth, then thought better of it, worried it might make him feel worse.

Where was he? Soft music played nearby. Across the room, a man danced alone in front of a mirror. A soft snore lowered Omar's gaze to where a couple lay in each other's arms, sleeping on the length of the sofa. The rest of the apartment looked empty.

Through an opening in a wall of fluttering curtains, a swimming pool glowed, the lights beneath its surface making it look electric. Omar walked outside, but the slightest movement made his head throb. A cool breeze gripped him, his moist clothing making the chill worse than it likely was. The pool was on the roof of a building. How did they keep it from flooding the rooms below?

The stars were dim overhead, muted by the city lights. Two rooftops away, a vehicle passed through the sky. A second, more careful look proved that it was actually driving along the top of the wall that divided the Highlands from the Midlands. On the Midlands side, an image of two dancers hung on the side of a building, their sweaty bodies knotted together, caught in an intimate moment that looked vaguely familiar.

Why would people allow themselves to be photographed while they were doing that? They'd probably had too many stimulants and couldn't remember what they'd done.

The thought sent a shock through Omar. Had he done anything like that last night? He recalled the task director's warning. Surely he'd remember being held that way. And he hadn't vaped anything really strong, right?

He spotted one of his shoes on the edge of the pool and picked it up. It was full of water, which he dumped out onto the deck. It took him much longer to locate his other shoe, eventually finding it on a chair with his balled-up socks. He tucked his socks into the dry shoe and looked for Bel. He couldn't find her and figured it was time he left.

It was even colder in the hallway and elevator. The air-conditioning must run constantly. Omar shuddered, goose bumps appearing on his forearms. He tried to use his vaporizer, but it tasted like ashes. The cylinder was warm, though, and he pressed it against his cheek.

The elevator stopped in the lobby. He walked toward the exit, and a doorman opened the door for him. "Good evening, sir."

"Can you call me a taxi?" Omar asked, trembling.

"Of course, sir."

"Thanks." Omar started toward a bench, then turned back and asked the doorman, "Is there somewhere to get this checked?" He held up his vaporizer.

"The bar is through that doorway, sir."

Omar wove his way into the bar and collapsed onto one of the stools.

A somewhat kind-looking man walked over and leaned his elbows on the counter. "How can I help you?"

"I, uh, was wondering if my vaporizer is broken. Nothing's coming out."

"Your first time, eh? It's just empty. Want me to fill it?"

The marijuana had been fun at first, but Omar didn't like not remembering where he'd been or what he'd been doing. Maybe he could vape something else. "Yeah."

"What's your juice?"

Juice? Was that the same as stim? "Can I have beer?"

The barkeep sighed. "I can get you a beer to drink or alcohol to vape."

"Oh. I want to vape it."

"Alcohol then. What level?"

"How many are there?"

The barkeep laughed. "Ten, shell."

"Let's go with a five, then," Omar said, feeling mature.

"Any flavor? Color?"

"Sapphire. No flavor."

"I got blue." The barkeep slid a SimTag pad toward Omar.

Omar tapped his fist against it, and a few minutes later was sitting on a bench outside what turned out to be the Django Building, waiting for his cab, eager to see if his vaporizer could help him get a little warmer on the inside.

The first puff burned the back of his throat and made him cough. His second breath was more careful. The stream of hot vapor hit his tongue, and he held it in his mouth a moment before breathing it into his lungs. At least it didn't burn the back of his throat this time, and it definitely warmed his insides.

The taxi arrived and carried him to the Snowcrest Building. Not too long after, he entered his apartment. The carpet was inviting under his bare feet. He'd barely closed the door when his doorbell rang. He opened the door, and Belbeline pushed inside.

"Magnificent Fortune!" She grabbed him in a hug. "You're freezing! What happened to you?"

He took a quick puff and blew a cloud of blue vapor into her face, then chuckled at her surprised expression.

She snatched the PV from his hand. "You refilled this. When?"

"It was empty. Give it back." He pried it out of her fingers.

"You have to be careful, Omar. You can make yourself sick vaping too much grass. Too much anything. No more tonight, okay? I don't want you getting liberated before your time."

"I'll be careful." He felt clever to have filled his PV with alcohol. "How'd you know I was back?"

"I asked Artie to tap me when you came in. I thought you left me!" She slapped his arm.

"I woke up in some strange apartment, on the floor behind the couch."

Belbeline started to laugh, but it trailed off as her eyes went wide, looking past his arm. "Is that me?" She pointed to where his easel was set up in the kitchen.

Omar's cheeks burned. "Uh... yeah. I couldn't stop thinking about your hair."

She walked into the kitchen and stared at the canvas. "You really *are* an artist."

Omar joined her. "It's not done." He suddenly felt heavy and exposed and wanted to cover the canvas. "I'm sorry. I should have asked first. Are you mad?"

She turned those gorgeous eyes back to him. "I'm not mad, and you *did* ask. I want you to paint me again."

The heaviness fell away. "Really?"

She ran into his living room and crawled onto his couch. She twisted and turned and settled onto her side, shaking back her hair and making his breath catch. "How's this?"

A thrill bounced through Omar. She wanted him to paint her now? "Okay." He lifted his painting of Bel's face off the easel and leaned it against the wall, then put up a fresh canvas. "Just let me grab my paints."

Chapter 24

Mason woke up at five thirty and showered. He didn't have to go to the SC until ten thirty, which gave him several hours of free time. Perhaps this morning would be a good time to explore a little. Take another look at the harem before Levi made contact and wanted to plan a rescue.

He again read the card Levi had sent him. Despite the silly message, which featured a cartoon of a pile of body parts—"I'm falling apart without you"—Levi had written only, "Write me back. L," and his address in the Midlands. Mason would have to pick up some cards at the G.I.N. after his shift. Not much was open at this hour.

He took a taxi to the Snowcrest and crossed the street. The harem took up several blocks in the center of the Highlands and was surrounded by a fence topped with coils of barbed wire. Were the fences meant to keep people out or the women in? Mason walked the perimeter, taking note of the entrances and the locations of each yellow camera.

The drop-off zone in front was in public view, but the loading docks in back might be a possibility. They all let out onto Snowmass Road, but an alley that cut between the Axtel and the Whetstone buildings connected the harem's loading docks to Emmons Road. If the women were somehow able to get to the loading dock, they could easily be picked up. Still, a bright yellow camera looked down on the loading dock.

The cameras were a problem.

Mason headed toward City Hall, just people-watching at this point. The skin colors and piercings, the bizarre hairstyles, the clothing, the extremely well-endowed women... So much rested on personal appearance here. He passed a group of women who were sitting on a bench and blowing different color vapors into the air and giggling.

He stopped and turned back. "Excuse me," he said. "I'm conducting an experiment. I wondered if you ladies would mind telling me what substance each of you are vaping."

"Grass," they said together.

"Thank you." Mason continued along his path to City Hall, asking the same question of anyone using a vaporizer. The majority answered that they were vaping a combination of caffeine and alcohol or grass, which Mason figured out was marijuana. A few visits to Jack's Peak, and Mason would recognize that smell anywhere. He thought several were vaping sugar, until he asked some follow-up questions. It turned out that in most cases, *candy* just meant *flavor.* The other fluffy-sounding answers were much more daring substances: brown sugar was heroin, golden ice was methamphetamine, and white cocoa was cocaine.

Mason knew a bit about narcotics from the book *Addiction Medicine* his mother had on her shelf in the sick house. It had intrigued him because of the thick layer of dust covering it. He'd asked his mother why she kept an obsolete book that she never read. "Knowledge is never obsolete," she had answered.

So Mason understood the damage that the habitual use of stimulants could impose upon the organs of the body that were already burdened by the thin plague. Surely Ciddah would know that such substances were harmful to a pregnancy.

But what if she didn't?

Perhaps he could use this observation to his advantage. He had visited the History Center once and been unable to find much medical knowledge at all. Perhaps a medic with a higher rank would be permitted to access more. He would simply have to take Ciddah with him.

He sighed. Time to see *Lawten* again.

"I have some theories I want to talk to you about. I think it might prevent miscarriages."

Ciddah looked up from the CompuChart on her desk. "Don't you knock anymore?"

Her snide tone deflated Mason's confidence. "When I knock, you don't let me in."

She swept three little black plastic rectangles into her top drawer and slammed it shut. "Fine." She shook out her hair, fluttered her eyelashes, and—finally—made eye contact. "What are your theories, O brilliant outsider?"

Mason flushed at her insult but stuck to his plan. He needed her help. "Only if you come to the History Center and read the files with me. The task director said you could join me."

Ciddah swelled with a deep breath, smiling wider than Mason had seen yet. "When did you ask him?"

"I just came from his office. I had to wait an hour to get in to see him."

Ciddah snorted, and it turned into a silent laugh. "An hour is *amazing*. Some people wait months to see Lawten. Some never get in."

"Oh. Well, he didn't mind about you coming with me to the HC. Said it was fine. See?" He handed her the letter the task director's receptionist had given him.

The paper trembled in Ciddah's hand. "Why would he agree to this?"

"Because I can be very convincing." Mason bared his cheesiest smile. "He thinks I might be able to help. I have a theory I wanted to—"

"Well, I don't." She crumpled the paper and threw it toward the trash. It bounced off the rim and onto the floor. "How could you possibly know more than Safe Lands medics?

You were raised in the woods by rabbits or something." She twisted a strand of her hair. "There's no way..."

There she went, being cruel again. Something had upset her, but what? "That's pretty narrow-minded for someone who calls *me* narrow-minded."

She softened a little. "Fine. I can do it on Friday, but then you have to give me your theory. And it had better be amazing, Mason. Because if it's not... I won't waste more time explaining things to you."

He grinned, electrified by the idea of seeing her outside the SC. "Thank you, Ciddah."

"You can leave my office now," she said without casting even a glance his way.

Not wanting to push his luck, Mason stepped out into the hallway and shut the door. He didn't understand Ciddah's rolling hills of emotions—he was just glad she'd agreed to come along. With her help, he should be able to find the medical data in the History Center.

"Here's the information for the one in the waiting room," Rimola said, jerking Mason out of his thoughts. She handed him a CompuChart and walked back out to her desk.

Mason read the patient's name. "Shaylinn Zachary?"

"Mason?" Shaylinn's voice.

Mason walked out past Rimola's desk and, sure enough, there sat Shaylinn in the waiting room. She looked different, older. They'd done something to her hair. Or maybe it was the clothes.

"Mason!" Shaylinn squealed and jumped up, waving both hands.

"Does she know why she's here?" Mason asked Rimola.

"Said she was here because of her summons."

Mason's stomach twisted into a knot. "Why was she summoned?" He found the answer on the chart the moment Rimola answered, "ETP."

Embryo Transfer Procedure. "No!" The task director general had promised.

"Something wrong?" Rimola asked.

"Everything." Mason strode to the elevator and hit the button.

"Mason?" Shaylinn asked. "Are you okay?"

He squeezed his hands into fists and hit them against the sides of his legs. Where was the elevator? "I'll be right back." He opened the door to the stairwell and ran all the way to the tenth floor.

The task director general's receptionist was talking to someone on her GlassTop. Mason walked right past her.

"Excuse me!" she yelled, then said to her GlassTop, "Can you hold, please?"

Mason pushed open the door to the task director's office and went inside.

"Sir!" The receptionist chased him inside. "You can't come in here without an appointment."

"Clearly that is a false statement," Mason said.

The task director sat at his desk across from a man in an enforcer's uniform.

"We had a deal," Mason said, ignoring the enforcer and hoping the man wasn't armed. "You said the Glenrock women wouldn't be made into surrogates until I had a chance to look for a cure. You said a month."

The task director's flaking face became animated, fixing into a smile that revealed a row of shiny, small teeth further dwarfed by his massive nose. He looked at the enforcer. "My apologies for the interruption, Colonel Stimel."

"Would you like me to remove him?" the colonel asked.

"This will only take a moment. Then, depending upon his reaction, perhaps I will require your assistance." The task director fixed his eyes on Mason. "Mr. Elias, I allowed you to postpone *your* donations for a month while you searched for a cure. But I don't need your donation to start procedures on the women. As we discussed, I have an uninfected donor in Omar Strong."

Once again, Omar had sabotaged things. But was this arrangement really what they'd agreed on? Mason tried to recall the exact wording of their conversation, certain he'd bought everyone some time. "You intend to make all the women carry Omar's children?" Not that he could even call Shaylinn a woman. The girl was only fourteen.

"Omar's donations will provide us with as many children as I deem prudent. But if you are concerned about the similar DNA, never fear. I've recently located another uninfected male donor."

"From where?" Mason asked.

"Wyoming, where Kendall Collin came from. He has been tested and has already made donations. Now all the females from Glenrock can be scheduled for surrogacy without delay, and you are free to conduct your research. You are also free to leave my office."

Mason suddenly felt unable to move.

"Mr. Elias, that wasn't a suggestion."

Chapter 25

Shaylinn sat on the exam table, swinging her legs. She wore another thin white gown. This room looked just like the one she had first awakened in. The door, the cupboard, the strange screen were all in the same place. Behind the exam table was a counter and sink with a mirror above it.

Shaylinn slid off the table and stood before the mirror. She studied the mirror clock, leaning close to see how it worked. No use. It was simply magical, like all glass in this place.

She drew her hair in front of her shoulders and twisted the curls together to form a fat ringlet on each side. She ran her hands over her waist, admiring how thin it seemed after so many InstaWraps and tiny meals. With so many major changes, why didn't she feel pretty? She could tell she was pretty. Prettier anyway. Not like Jemma or Mia, of course. But she wasn't ugly.

Then why did she still feel ugly?

Maybe because she was going to get pregnant? But that didn't make sense. Both Kendall and Naomi were beautiful even with their bulging bellies.

Shaylinn sat back on the exam table. Eighteen minutes passed by on the mirror clock before someone knocked twice and cracked open the door.

"You ready, Shaylinn?" Mason's voice.

She smiled, eager to see someone else from their village. "Yes, come in."

Mason pushed in the door and closed it before meeting Shaylinn's gaze. His eyes were fierce and moist and ringed in deep circles.

"What's wrong?" she asked.

He scratched the back of his neck and looked just about every place in the exam room he could but at her.

"Mason, look at me."

So he did, drumming his fists against the sides of his legs. "I can't stop it, Shaylinn. I tried. I mean..." He stepped up to the exam table and lowered his voice. "We could run. But they can track our SimTags, so they'd catch us and just do the procedure anyway."

"It's okay, Mason." Shaylinn lifted her chin. "I'm ready."

"What?" His eyebrows sank low. "How can you be so calm?"

Shaylinn shrugged. "You're going to laugh."

"No, I won't."

"I... I had a dream. A beautiful dream. And... I think God is going to do something big. This place needs hope. I mean, there's so much wonder in this city, and it looks good at first, but it's empty. I can't explain it very well, I guess. But I just wonder, what's the point of looking beautiful on the outside if you're dead on the inside?"

Mason's posture wilted. "Shaylinn, do you feel dead inside?"

Did she? "Sometimes. There are things that poison me, I think. Words I tell myself. But I was thinking, if I didn't know that God loved me the way I am, if I didn't believe he made me who I am for a reason, I'd feel dead all the time. Every little thing would poison me, and I'd do anything to try and make it better."

"Shaylinn, you're not broken."

"I know. I do. It's hard to remember sometimes. But I think God is going to turn death into new life. It's what he does, right?"

Mason's face softened. "I didn't expect you to behave so calmly, Shaylinn. Your maturity is quite impressive."

For some reason the word *maturity* embarrassed Shaylinn, and she looked at the floor.

"Okay," Mason said, "let's get you weighed." He helped her lay back then extended the table to its full length. "Put your feet up, please."

Shaylinn swung her legs up onto the table. "Mason?"

"Hmm?" His gaze shifted between the scale's readout on the edge of the bed and his CompuChart.

"Do you think I'm pretty?"

He looked at her and swallowed.

She pursed her lips. "Don't worry. I'm not in love with you."

He fought a smile. "Thank you?"

"I ask because it's one of my poisons—thinking I'm hideous and fat," Shaylinn said. "And I thought if a man told me how pretty I was, everything would be okay. But the other night a man did say I was pretty, but it didn't change anything. Maybe because I didn't want *that* man to say it. What's wrong with me?"

"There's nothing wrong with you, Shaylinn. You're human." He tapped on his CompuChart and helped her sit up. "We all believe lies about ourselves. Something likely happened to make you believe you were hideous and fat—which I don't think you are, by the way." He paused. "I hope my father's words didn't make you think you were ugly. You never were. You aren't."

She remembered when Elder Justin had called her fat. But there had been many such things before then. And none had ever bothered her as much as when Omar had called her an ugly crybaby. "Do *you* believe a lie, Mason?"

Mason moaned out a laugh. "Shaylinn..."

She shook her head. "I won't tell a soul."

"All right." Mason took a deep breath. "I believe that I'm... backward somehow. Girls don't like the smart guy. They like muscles and whoever can kill the biggest bear. So... when we were in Glenrock I used to always think, who would ever love me? No one."

Shaylinn's eyes glossed with tears. "That's not true, Mason."

He grinned and lowered his gaze. "Yes, I know. And your lie isn't true either. Shaylinn, you're a beautiful young woman. Believe anything else, and you're believing a lie."

"Thank you, Mason."

"Glad to help."

The door opened, and Ciddah entered. "Are we ready to proceed?"

"Uh... no," Mason said, his cheeks flushing. "I'm not quite finished."

Ciddah folded her arms. "What's taking you so long to get her vitals?"

"We were—"

"Mason was counseling me on a personal matter," Shaylinn said. "He's very wise. And handsome. And loveable."

Mason glared at Shaylinn.

Ciddah raised her eyebrows. "Yes, well. We all love Mason." She glanced at him and flipped out her hair. "Please come get me when you're ready."

"I will," Mason said.

Ciddah left and closed the door behind her.

Shaylinn gasped. "You like her!"

Mason edged away and tapped on his CompuChart. "Another lie you believe, I think."

"*No...* I saw the look on your face when she walked in. You blushed."

Mason set down his CompuChart and picked up the blood pressure cuff. He took Shaylinn's hand and slid the cuff up her arm. "I *don't* blush."

She laughed and kicked her feet. "No boy blushes more than you, Mason of Elias. So? What are you going to do? Are you going to kiss that pretty doctor?"

Mason squeezed the bulb again and again, and the cuff got tighter and tighter. "If you don't stop talking, I'm going to sphygmomanometer you to death."

"What?"

"Sphygmomanometer." He tapped the blood pressure cuff. "It's what this is called."

"That's a crazy long name. Say it again."

A smile grew on Mason's face. "Sphygmomanometer."

Shaylinn giggled. Mason took off the cuff and turned to set it against his CompuChart.

"Will I get the thin plague like Kendall?" Shaylinn asked.

"That's doubtful," he answered, his back still facing her.

"Why?"

"The thin plague is passed through blood. Or bodily fluids," Mason explained. "And supposedly the donor..." He paled, and his eyes lost focus.

Shaylinn thought of Mia and Rand sucking each other's faces. "You mean kissing?" She gasped. "Is *that* why you won't kiss the doctor?"

Mason snapped out of his daze and rubbed his temple. "No, Shaylinn, I don't mean kissing. Mostly, uh... relations. As long as you aren't intimate with an infected person, you can't contract the thin plague."

Shaylinn pondered that. "Strange that I can have a baby but never have...you know."

"Yes," Mason said, nodding at the floor. "It is strange." He picked up his CompuChart and faced her. "Um... I'm finished, Shaylinn. So I'm going to leave now. Ciddah will be in momentarily, I'm sure. I'll be praying for you. I'm glad God gave you peace about this, but, well, I'm still nervous on your behalf."

"Thank you, Mason. When will I know if it worked or not?"

"Ciddah says you're to come back on Monday to find out."

"Monday," Shaylinn said.

"That's right."

Shaylinn swung her legs from side to side. "Until Monday, then."

Shaylinn didn't feel all that different after the procedure. It had been awkward and cold, but it hadn't hurt. And now she was tucked into bed, being spoiled by Jemma, Naomi, and Kendall. She even ate a bowl of ice cream Jemma had brought her, despite it not being on Tyra's list of approved foods.

Mason had said that the thought *Shaylinn is hideous and fat* was a lie. And Shaylinn refused to believe any more of those. Something big was going to happen soon, and Shaylinn was holding on to that dream of a calm and peaceful future.

Chapter 26

Dayle called Levi on his truck radio while he was working his route. "Rewl needs some help with a big graffiti job over in front of City Hall. They want it covered fast. Go help."

"Yes, sir." Levi drove over to City Hall and parked along the street. The graffiti was hard to miss. The words *Free Lonn* had been painted across the second-floor windows.

A Highlands Public Tasks truck had been parked up on the sidewalk right in front of the doors. A man wearing a gray jumpsuit was shooting water at the graffiti with a hose that was attached to the truck. He had wide-set brown eyes, big lips, and very little brown hair.

Levi walked over to Rewl. "Dayle said you need some help."

The man lowered the hose and stopped the water flow. "Nah, I got this, shell." He spoke like he was pinching his nose. "I just painted it a few hours ago, so it's coming down nice and easy."

Levi looked around them, but there was no one. "You did that? How'd you get up there?"

"That's my secret." Rewl grinned, baring teeth that were etched with black stripes. "Listen, I'm the guy who held your SimTag last night." Rewl lifted his fist. He was wearing gloves too. It had been so dark in The Hunter last night, Levi hadn't gotten a good look at the guy. "Bender says to tell you, 'Where's your transmitter, shell?' Says he can't help you if he can't reach you."

Levi had left the piece of glass at the Larkspur. "Sorry. I mean, tell him I said sorry."

"Tell him yourself, shell." Rewl raised the hose and turned it back on. Water shot out at the graffiti and sprinkled on Levi's head.

A distant chorus of voices captured Levi's attention. He strained to make out the sound, but the water from Rewl's hose was too loud.

"Do you hear singing?" Levi asked.

Rewl shut off the hose again and tilted his head. "It's coming from the Harem Gardens."

Levi blinked at Rewl and sprinted toward the harem.

"Hey, shell! Where you going?"

Levi darted down the sidewalk and over a grassy lawn that led up to a wall of bushy green trees. When he got closer, he found that the spaces between the foliage were filled with chainlink fence. Through the links Levi could see nothing but a wall of trees on the other side. The coil of barbed wire on top of the fence ended the brief thought that he might climb over. He could hear the singing more clearly now.

Let not your heart be troubled,
His tender words I hear;
And resting on His goodness,
I lose my doubt and fear.

Tho' by the path He leadeth,
But one step I may see,
His eye is on the sparrow,
And I know He watches me.

"Jemma!" Levi slipped between two bushes and edged along the fence looking for a break in the wall of green, any place that would allow him to see inside.

Someone grabbed his arm from behind. "Hey, *softie*," Rewl said. "It's illegal to talk to the harem girls. You're going to earn that third X in a hurry."

Levi's heart was beating so fast his hands were trembling. "I can hear my fiancée!" At Rewl's blank expression, he grasped for the word Bender had used. "My lifer."

Rewl's gaze flickered between the fence and the street. "I'll keep watch, but if I see anyone coming, you've got to run, hear me?"

Levi pressed deeper into the tangle of trees. The singing had stopped, but the bubbling sound of women's voices reminded him of passing the meeting hall on a tanning day. A lot of talking and giggling, and little he could pick out of the conversations. A gap in two trees revealed the women sitting in a circle on the grass. There was Jennifer! And Chipeta and Mia and... Jemma sat between Mia and Naomi. She was wearing a light blue dress.

"Jemma!"

Her head twitched, turned to the back fence.

"On the other side of the fence!" Levi yelled. "In the trees!"

The other women's heads turned; the entire circle focused on the back fence. Jemma stood and helped Naomi stand. Levi couldn't help staring at Naomi's belly. She looked like she'd swallowed a small boulder.

The women began to sing again, all but Jemma and Naomi, who slowly made their way toward the fence, stopping to pick a flower here and there. Their pace was maddening.

Finally, they were close enough that he heard Jemma ask, "Who's there?"

"It's Levi, Jem."

"Oh!" She ran into the trees then leaving Naomi behind. He lost sight of her a few yards to his left. "Where are you?" Her voice sounded panicked.

He scraped through the tangle of branches, trying to reach her more quickly. "Here."

She stepped into view between two bushy trees. Her beauty stole his breath, and he threaded his fingers through the chain links and squeezed, wanting to rip away the metal barrier.

She slid her fingers over his and pressed her face against the fence. He kissed what he could of her lips and face, tasting the bitter metal between them.

She finally pulled back, and her brown eyes flit over his face. "Oh, Levi! Your nose. What happened?"

Levi scowled and rested his forehead against the chainlink. "Omar."

"Oh, love. Thank you for the card." She reached her finger through the bars and rubbed his prickly cheek. "Two Xs? You look... scary."

Not exactly the words he was hoping to hear. "Yes, I'm a regular Dread Pirate Roberts."

She jerked on the fence and pursed her lips. "I meant scary because you only have one more chance."

"Don't give up on me, Jem. I'm going to get you out of here.

Her chin quivered. "I'm afraid for you. I'm afraid you'll do something foolish."

"I've been good, Jem. I've been doing your breathing trick to keep my temper in check. I need you to trust me. Remember when we were out looking for berries and we saw that black bear?"

"He wanted to eat us."

"He wanted the berries, Jem, and you didn't believe me, but you trusted me. And you were so brave. Now I need you to keep being brave, okay? Here." Levi reached into the neckline of his shirt and pulled the chain over his head. "You take these. Keep them safe. As soon as I get you out of there, we'll get married, okay?"

She pulled the chain through the fence and started to cry.

"No, no. I didn't give them to you to make you sad."

"They're just so beautiful, Levi." She fingered the diamond on the woman's ring. "It's cut like a teardrop."

"You hold all my tears."

"I won't let them fall." She gripped his fingers. "I want you to hold me."

"Soon, Buttercup. Listen, if I hide some two-way radios in these trees, can you get them?"

"I think so. Which ones?"

"I'll mark the spot somehow. With a ribbon or something colorful."

"Won't that draw attention?"

"How about I stash them in the branches of the tree to the right of the one I mark?"

Jemma nodded. "When?"

"I don't know. I'll try to come back tonight or tomorrow. Don't talk until I test it. Can you get one to Mason?"

"I think so. Shaylinn said he's working in the doctor's office."

"He is. Tell him the same. And keep them on channel four."

"Okay." She sniffled. "They did something to Shaylinn today." Several tears fell down Jemma's cheek. "They're trying to make her pregnant. I'm so scared for her."

Not Shaylinn. Levi fought back his rage with a growl. “What about you?”

She shook her head. “I don’t have to go in for another two weeks.”

“I’ll get you out before then.” He kissed her again. What else did he have to say? “Oh, I met some people.”

“The rebels?” She smiled—so beautiful. “When Naomi and I heard about them, we knew you’d find them.”

“Well, they want me to kill Otley.”

“What!” Her eyes flew wide. “Levi, you can’t kill anyone. You mustn’t!”

He wasn’t sure he had a choice. “It might be the only way to get the rebels to help us.”

“No.” Jemma shook her head.

“Otley is the one who killed my dad and Papa Eli.”

“Oh...” She sniffed back tears. “Still, Levi, that doesn’t make it right. Revenge? That’s not what Papa Eli would have wanted. You can find another way. I believe in—”

“Time to go!” Rewl said.

He kissed her again. “Be careful, Jemma. Remember, I’ll always come for you.”

She grinned past her tears and played along. “But how can you be sure?”

“Because this is true love. You think this happens every day?” Levi kissed her fingertips, her lips, then forced himself to turn, to claw his way out of the trees. He saw Rewl running down the street with an enforcer on his heels. Levi turned and sprinted toward his truck.

Levi lingered in the Highlands until after dark. He parked his truck by a dumpster at the edge of Champion Park and walked inside, carrying a trash bag and a can of spray paint in case anyone spotted him. His biggest concern was hiding his rifle as he walked back to his truck, assuming the rifle was still there.

Please let it be there!

The park was about a half a mile wide and consisted of a forested area, a lake, and paved walking trails. One side of the park ran alongside the Highlands-Midlands wall. Levi realized he had originally come up through the grille at the northeastern corner of the park, only a block from Marcellina Steakhouse.

He kept to the shadow of the wall and quickly found the area where they’d caught him. Crickets were singing. He could hear the distant murmur of voices but saw no people. He kicked every bush he came to, peeked underneath trees, and had almost given up when he tripped over the barrel of his rifle.

He shoved the pack and rifle in the trash bag and carried it to his truck. Then he drove to the Snowcrest and parked in the lot that faced the harem. The garden fence was well lit. He considered using his rifle to shoot out some streetlamps but couldn’t risk anyone coming to investigate the noise while he was hiding the radios. Better to just come at the gardens from the other side.

The darkest location seemed to be on the far end where the fence met the back of a building called the Whetstone. Levi drove to the Whetstone lot and looked in his pack. He'd give the windups to Jemma and Mason; Jordan could have a solar one. He shoved two windups and a pair of wire cutters into a trash bag and darted along the back of the building.

When he reached the fence, he was on the far right of where he'd talked to Jemma. It would be easy to hide the radios in the bushes here, but he couldn't risk her missing them. So he threaded his way through the trees that hid the fence, slowly making his way to the other side.

When he reached the general location of where he'd spoken to Jemma, he cut through enough links in the chain fence so he could push the radios through and tuck them into the lower branches of a bush on the other side. Then he cut some wires by the next bush over and tied the length of trash bags to a branch. The black plastic draped all the way to the grass, then blew in the gentle breeze. Not exactly colorful, but less obvious was better.

By the time he'd mended the fence and drove back to the Midlands, it was almost ten o'clock. Apparently, Midlanders could leave the Highlands at any hour, just not enter. He parked his truck and started across the parking lot toward the front doors of the Larkspur, carrying his trash bag–covered rifle and backpack.

A car pulled in front of him. The window slid down and Red said, "Get in."

Levi desperately wanted to take his stuff into his apartment, but he couldn't afford to ignore Bender. He got in the passenger's side, holding the trash bag with his backpack and rifle on his lap. Red pulled out onto the street.

"Where are we going?" he asked.

"Nowhere." Red turned left out of the lot. "Heard you saw your lifer today."

"Yeah." Levi smiled at his fresh memory of Jemma.

"Still floating for her, then?"

Levi didn't know what "floating" meant but wasn't about to let Red know that. "I've known Jemma all my life. She and I, we… I don't really know how to explain. We're two parts of a whole. We help each other be better people."

Red drove past the G.I.N. and turned left before Café Eat. "Better than who?"

"Better than how we are alone."

Red grunted. "Sounds boring. Like you let a computer match you up or something."

"There are no computers where we're from."

"Well, being with the same person forever doesn't sound fun to me."

Why was he talking about this with Red? Why was she so nosy? "Where I'm from, if a man marries a woman, he stays with her his entire life. No matter what. They're a team. And they never give up on each other. Even when it's hard."

"Sounds like unnecessary trouble." She drove into a left turn lane and stopped to wait for the light. "But it's your life, shell. I just think you'd be wise to shop around."

"That would only destroy what we have." The guilt from his night with Kosowe was heavy enough. He didn't need any more of that.

Red turned at the light and turned right again at the next one. She was circling back to the Larkspur. Good. "Listen, Bender says to tell you that hanging around the harem and talking to surrogates is against the law. He says you do that again, he isn't going to help you."

"It won't happen again because we're going to get her out."

Red rolled her eyes. "You're so strange. Bender also said to tell you that he's going to rescue your boys on Saturday—that medic and your angry friend. That's the earliest he could coordinate it with their task schedules."

"Saturday will be fine." Saturday was well before Jemma was scheduled for her procedure.

Red pulled the car into the Larkspur's parking lot. She powered off the vehicle and scooted to the middle of the seat, roughly pushing Levi's trash bag aside before placing her hand on his knee. The smell of her perfume pulled his gaze to her lips.

"What do you want to do now?" she asked.

Red's hand was sliding higher up his thigh. He looked down and seized her wrist. He wasn't going to make a mistake like this again.

He tapped his fist against the doorplate, and the door glided open. Second later he'd grabbed his stuff and slid out of the car.

"I'm going to go to bed. Alone."

Chapter 27

A knock woke Omar. His head throbbed between his ears, and he grabbed a pillow to muffle the noise.

The knock sounded again, sharper. He should sit up. Go deal with whoever that was.

"Just a minute!" a woman's voice said. Belbeline.

He opened one eye. He was at Bel's place. In her bedroom. The reality of his weakness brought on a sudden panic, and he searched the ceiling for bright yellow cameras, wondering if the task director knew he was here. Again. Or that he'd failed. Again.

He didn't care. He was going to marry Belbeline anyway. And she couldn't possibly have the thin plague. She was too pretty. Too soft.

Muted voices carried from the far side of the apartment. He squinted at the bedside table. *Yes.* His vaporizer was there. He reached for it, but his arm didn't obey. It felt like it was encased in steel.

What time was it, anyway?

Must. Move. He propped himself up onto one elbow and peered at the open bedroom door. The voices became clearer.

"Left you five messages, Bel-bel, and— Who painted that?" A man's voice. Deep.

"You're not my task director, Ollie," Belbeline said. "I don't have to report to you."

"And those! Whose shoes are those?"

Belbeline clicked her tongue. "I don't know. People come over a lot. I can't keep track of who leaves their stuff here."

"You're not alone."

It's wasn't a question. It was a realization. And it didn't sound happy. Omar raised his eyebrows and looked around the dark room, wondering where he might hide.

Wait. Why should *he* hide? Belbeline was his girlfriend. And he was an enforcer. He should storm out there and confront this jerk who was hassling her. He threw off the covers, but the cold air clapped around him, and the throbbing in his head intensified. He grabbed his vaporizer and burrowed back under the covers. One deep breath later, his head cleared.

Until the lights flashed on. Omar shut his eyes and pulled the covers over his head.

"That who I think it is?" the man's voice said.

The blankets were pulled away, leaving Omar cold and half naked on the bed. He strained to see the large, hairy man who loomed above the bed.

General Otley! *What?*

Omar could only stare, his PV pinched between his thumb and two fingers. Soon the cylinder was at his mouth, and he took another long drag. The stims were helping him wake, but his brain felt foggy, loose. Or maybe his brain was fine, and this was more of a communication problem between his brain and limbs.

Otley grabbed Omar's ankle and pulled him off the end of the bed. Omar's back hit the floor first, then his head. Otley held his ankle in the air and shook it, glaring down. "Those are *my* pajamas, little rat."

Omar looked himself over. He was shirtless, wearing the black satin pajama pants Bel had given him. No wonder they were so big. He looked to Bel, and his voice came out raspy, the blood rushing to his head. "You said these were a present."

Otley threw Omar's leg down and kicked him, his heavy boot like a hammer to Omar's ribs. The blow flipped him onto his stomach. "This ends now, *rat*. Don't even look at Bel-bel again."

Omar crawled around the side of the bed, wanting only to get away from that boot.

"Don't be a prude, Ollie," Bel said. "I can see who I want."

"And I can task who I want."

"I'm *not* going back to that club."

"Keep away from the shell, and you won't have to." Otley strode out of the bedroom.

Bel followed. "You don't own me, Ollie. Why do you have to be such a fun-downer?"

"I'm the enforcer general. All part of my image. And I'm taking this painting."

The front door slammed, shaking the windows. Omar's stomach throbbed. He still clutched his PV in his fist, so he took another long drag and pulled the blanket off the bed and over himself, curling into a ball on the floor. Some of the pain ebbed away, but the ache still held him in a fist. *This can't be real. It just can't.*

Bel's footsteps pounded into the bedroom. "He's *so* controlling. You'd think an enforcer would know all about a person's rights, but *no*... Omar?"

"Here," Omar said from the floor.

Bel's steps pattered toward him. She knelt at his side and pushed her hand back over his hair. "Oh, trigger, I'm sorry. Are you hurt?"

Just his pride. "These are really my task director's pajamas?"

Bel rolled her eyes. "What's it matter? They fit, don't they?"

"Not really." Omar took another drag, desperate to float again. "Are you and my boss...? Did you...? With him?"

Belbeline sat back on her heels. "Did I *what*? Spit it out, Omar."

He took a quick puff on his vaporizer for courage and sat up. "If I'd known you were involved with Otley—my *task director*—I never would've pursued you."

She raised her eyebrows and laughed. "*You* pursued *me*, did you?"

"Looking for a wife. I've got to be a better choice than Otley."

She cackled now, the expression of amusement on her face like a knife to Omar's bruised torso. "I see now why you never paired up in your outsider village."

His chest tightened. "What does *that* mean?"

"You're delusional, Omar. *I* picked *you* up. *I* showed *you* how to have a good time. If it wasn't for me, you'd still be standing at the elevator staring at your knuckles."

That wasn't how it happened. "I had a good time before I met you."

"With who?"

"Charlz and Skottie. We went to the Paradise Saloon and the Ginger Oak Club."

Belbeline stood up and sat on the edge of her bed. "Those are tasked clubs, Omar. Those girls are credited to play with men."

Omar shook his head. "No, they're not."

"Look, Omar. It's been a party, okay? But we need to take a break."

Omar's head became light, but not in the way he'd hoped. "I thought you liked me."

"I do like you. But it's been two days, and you're already way too gummy."

He felt insignificant lying on the floor while she was on the bed. Though it hurt his head and the growing ache in his side, he forced himself to sit up, to stand. "You like Otley better?"

She pulled her curls back from her face and twisted them. "It's not like that. Ollie does me favors, I do him favors. People say he's going to be the next task director general, and I can't afford to cut that tie."

She wanted Otley for his position of power. He guessed things here weren't that much different from Glenrock after all. "Then how could you have betrayed him?"

Bel stood up and paced to the door. "Omar, you're so caught up in the Old ways. Relationships aren't exclusive here. We have fun. We pair up. We see someone else we like the looks of, we play with them. Ollie gets that. He does the same. He'll get over his little jealous phase, and then maybe you and I can pair up again."

"You're really leaving me?" Omar hated the sound of his voice. The hint of a whine. He gritted his teeth. *Be strong*, he reminded himself. *You are Omar Strong now, not some sniffing little kid.*

Bel sighed. "Why are you making this into a big deal?"

"Because it *is* a big deal! I want to marry you." At her blank look, he said, "Be a lifer."

Her laughter came so fierce and fast that she snorted. She held her hand in front of her mouth until she stopped, and her hair untwisted and fell loose around her face again. "I'm not going to fight over this. If you can't accept it, I won't tap you again."

How could she dismiss him so easily? "Just like that?"

"Just like that," she said, walking out the door. "Go home, Omar, but leave the pajamas."

After his shift, Omar went straight to the Regal Lounge, which was a theater club in the Highlands. A woman holding a tray of shots greeted him. He took two of the little glasses and made his way to a table in front. He shrugged out of his enforcer's jacket. Time to relax.

A man and woman were in the middle of the stage, singing about some kind of disagreement. The man had wanted the woman to dance exclusively for his cabaret, but the woman liked to work many clubs. Sounded familiar.

The song shifted into a big dance number, and a half-dozen dancers filed out onto the stage wearing skimpy, sequined outfits and doing high kicks. Omar swallowed his first shot and studied the women. One caught his eye.

Mia.

Elbows on the table, he held his face in his hands, watching her through his fingers. From the look on her face, she was enjoying herself. See? The people of Glenrock liked living here. But watching Mia made him feel ill. The way they had dressed her...

Relationships aren't exclusive here, Bel had said. Is that what Mia would discover? Would she fall for some entertainer, then be cast aside when he became interested in someone else? Is that what Omar was supposed to do? Look for someone else?

He didn't want anyone else. He wanted Belbeline.

The Regal Lounge had a hitroom, so Omar went upstairs and set his PV on the counter. The barkeep was speaking with a blonde woman at the far end of the bar. She had skin that glittered like gold.

"Brown sugar four, plain," the woman said.

The barkeep took her PV and paused in front of Omar. "Know what you want?"

"I'll have the same," Omar said, tossing his jacket on the stool on his left. "And a black velvet."

The barkeep set a SimTag pad on the counter, and Omar tapped his fist.

The woman got up and moved to the stool on Omar's right. "You a sweet tooth for brown sugar too, baby face?"

"Naw," Omar said, clueless as to what she was referring to. "But it turns out I need to try some new things."

The woman traced her sparkling gold finger up along the lines of his SimArt tattoo. "What kinds of things?"

He glanced at her and met a set of eyes that were golden brown. "All kinds."

Omar and the woman, whose name turned out to be Lexanna, relocated to a set of pillowy chairs, reclining on either side of a small table where the barkeep set their PVs.

When Lexanna leaned over and kissed him, he wanted to scream. He didn't know this woman, and he didn't want to know her. He pretended she was Bel for a few minutes, but that just made him feel pathetic. Plus, she was getting gold glitter all over his uniform.

He broke away and inhaled a long drag on his PV. Nausea gripped him. He held his breath and let his head fall back on the chair. What in all the lands was brown sugar, anyway? And why would anyone want to feel sick like—

A sudden rush of velvety euphoria sent tingles swirling over Omar's body, a powerful, yet completely peaceful feeling. He was sitting on the top of a hill in a white haze. He could see the silhouettes of people around him, and while they were unrecognizable, he knew it was Levi, Belbeline, and his father. They swam through the haze on the top of that hill, trying to reach one another but not really caring if they ever did. In fact, nothing mattered at all now. This was a safe place. Like being inside one of his paintings.

Lexanna spoke, but Omar didn't comprehend her words. Or maybe he did but forgot what she'd said. All he wanted to do was be on that hill.

The feeling faded a bit, so Omar took another long breath through his vaporizer. His stomach clenched against the nausea, but this time he waited for it to pass, waiting for...

Euphoria drenched him again. He closed his eyes, doubting he could have kept them open even if he'd wanted to. He was standing on the roof of a building, the wind blowing hard against him. He leaned into it until he was parallel to the ground, the wind so strong it held him there.

Strong.

But he wasn't on a roof. He was in the hitroom of the Regal Lounge with Lexanna. His body felt hot, melting from the inside out. His head drooped until his chin nearly touched his chest. He must look asleep. Maybe he was, nodding in and out of sleep. It was a nice feeling. No guilt. No loneliness.

Until Lexanna started talking again, pulling on his arms, slapping him. He kept his eyes closed, wishing she'd go away, wanting to tell her to leave him alone.

There was a man's voice and the sensation of standing. Someone shook his arms. Bright lights. Movement. More people he didn't recognize, looking at him, talking to him.

Mason?

Omar awoke in a white room under glaring lights, wearing a dress. Something beeped. His arm itched. A small needle was taped just below the inside of his elbow. It had a hose attached to it that ran up to a bag of liquid hanging on a stand.

Was this the medical center?

His mouth was dry; his lips felt cracked; his body hurt all over, a dull, heavy ache in his nerves. He scanned the room for his vaporizer but didn't see it. A quick taste would ease his discomfort. Who had taken it? He needed it.

Someone passed down the hallway outside the open door to his room.

"Hey!" He reached out and noticed that his hands were coated in gold glitter.

An angel stepped through the doorway, white and glowing with sapphire eyes. Eyes like Belbeline's. "Good!" She leaned against the doorframe. "You're awake."

Not Belbeline. A blonde. A medic. "Why am I here?"

"You OD'd," the angel said. "And since you were in uniform, they brought you to me."

Omar frowned. "OD?"

"Overdose. Too much. Your body couldn't handle what you put in it."

Omar bristled at the insinuation he was weak. "Really? It felt good."

The medic gave him a one-sided grin. "It usually does the first time or two. If I were you, I'd quit while I was still alive. There are much safer poisons." She glanced out the door. "Someone wants to see you." She pushed off the doorway and left.

Let it be Belbeline, sick with worry and begging his forgiveness.

But Mason appeared, looking clean in a turquoise medic outfit, hair neatly combed. "Hey, brother," he said. "Glad to see you up. You've been trying the vaporizers?"

Mason tasking as a medic—figured. "Yeah, I have." *And you can't control me, Mason, so don't try.*

Mason walked up and examined the bag of fluid. "Which stims? Do you even know?"

Mason's tone filled Omar with a rush of anger. "Do *you*? I'm not stupid, Mason."

Mason tipped back his head and smiled. "Right. I forgot how you planned all this and got half our village killed. Good one, Omar. Brilliant, really. My favorite part was when you almost killed yourself too."

"Are you just going to stand here and lecture me?"

"A little, yes. So you're trying the PVs and drinking. And what about women, Omar? Have you been intimate with women too?"

"Why's any of this your business?"

"You have the thin plague, Omar. You're infected."

Nausea rolled in Omar's stomach. He fought to keep his features even, calm. "So give me the cure."

Mason coughed out a half laugh. "You know very well there's no cure, brother. That's why we're all here. Thanks to you. But it's a slow death, if that makes you feel better."

"Why are you being so mean?"

Mason winced, as if thinking it through. "Papa Eli used to say, 'A person becomes wise by watching what happens to himself when he's a fool.' I love you Omar, but you've made some very bad choices. Now you have the chance to become wise—*if* you learn from your experiences." He patted Omar's leg and left.

Omar lay back on the bed, exhausted, longing for the peace he'd felt last night in a breath of brown sugar. Especially now that he knew he contracted a death sentence. He cursed and wondered if the task director general knew his girl had the plague. Belbeline was so beautiful, and she used those body paints that made her skin smooth. But of course, she was infected. They all were. Their dying nation was the main reason they'd talked Omar into helping them. Well, as the task director had predicted, he wasn't very useful to the Safe Lands anymore, was he?

He never *had* been very useful.

Omar wanted his PV. Now. Would Mason return it when he left the medical center? If not, he'd just buy a new one. He was dying anyway. No reason to suffer more than necessary, right? In fact, the sooner he could numb himself, the better.

Chapter 28

Mason slipped the CompuChart into the slot beside the door of exam room two and peeked into Ciddah's office. "Exam two is ready."

"Thanks," she said.

Mason walked toward reception to see if Rimola had any new arrivals for him to check in. He stopped when he heard her talking with someone at the front desk.

"You're one of the new outsiders?" Rimola asked.

"Yes," a female voice said.

"Good. None of us know what to do with the male conscript they sent us, Mason Elias. He's so raven we can't breathe, but he won't flirt with anyone. He's the prudest dish I've ever met."

Mason slowed his steps. He was prudish?

"The things he says!" Rimola went on. "It's like he's speaking another language."

"Yes," the mystery woman said. "I know exactly what you mean."

Jemma! Suddenly Mason's feet couldn't move fast enough.

Jemma was standing on the other side of Rimola's desk when Mason entered the lobby. A smile stretched across her face. "Mason!" She ran around the desk and wrapped him in a hug.

He stiffened, not used to such physical affection. "How is Shaylinn?"

Jemma released him. "Better than I would be. She said you two had a nice talk. Thank you for being so kind to her."

Mason's cheeks warmed, and he looked at the floor. "I wish I could have done something to—"

"Is there somewhere private we can talk?" Jemma asked.

Mason glanced at the enforcer sitting in the waiting room. Why had Jemma come? She had no appointment. Rimola was tapping on her GlassTop, eyebrows lifted as a sign of her intention to eavesdrop. Mason took Jemma's sleeve and pulled her down the hallway.

"Where are you going?" Rimola called after them.

"We'll be right back," Mason said.

He led Jemma to the end of the hall. When he was sure no one had seen them, he opened the supply closet door and flipped on the light. Jemma followed him inside and pushed the door shut behind her, bumping Mason so that he almost fell backward over the mop bucket. He grabbed the shelf to catch himself.

"Here." Jemma pulled a wadded-up trash bag out of her purse and thrust it into his arms. "It's from Levi. A radio. I have one too. He said to keep it on channel four but wait until he calls you."

Mason's heart leapt at the thought of speaking with Levi. He wrapped the excess bag around the radio until it was a small roll and tucked it under the supply shelf so that it was completely invisible. No one should find it there. "Where'd you put yours?"

"Under my mattress."

"Take care, Jemma. There are cameras everywhere."

"Not in my bedroom. But if Levi doesn't get us out soon, I'm going to have to plan an escape. Kendall and Naomi don't have much time."

"It's too dangerous," Mason said. "And what about the others? How will—"

The door flew open. Jemma screamed.

Ciddah stood in the doorway and stared at them. "What are you doing in here?"

Mason started talking without thinking. "Exam room two needs a fresh gown, but Jemma came and needed, uh..." He lost his train of thought.

"Mason was just showing me where he works," Jemma said. "Then he was going to refill my prescription. I broke one of the vials."

"Mason doesn't fill prescriptions," Ciddah said. "I do."

"That's what I was telling her." Mason grabbed Jemma's sleeve and pulled her out the door, cursing his stupidity and hoping Ciddah didn't decide to search the supply closet.

Mason didn't dare look back as they walked down the cooridor, Ciddah's footsteps clicking behind them. They made it halfway back to the reception desk when Ciddah spoke.

"I'd like to speak with you and your femme in my office, Mason. Now."

He took a deep breath and led Jemma into Ciddah's office.

"Messy in here," Jemma whispered.

Ciddah brushed past them to stand behind her desk. Mason couldn't look at her, for fear of the expression clouding her face. Granted, it *had* looked bad.

"The Safe Lands Guild does not oppose pair-ups during breaks, but only when approved by the office task director. And I *never* approve of physical displays of affection in this office. People who come here... many have miscarried. They don't need to feel worse about their situations because of your carelessness."

"Doctor, Mason and I are not... romantic," Jemma said as if the idea was ridiculous, which, he supposed, it was. "We grew up together. I'm engaged to marry Mason's brother Levi. I'm sorry we didn't ask permission before he gave me a tour."

"I see." Ciddah's posture relaxed. "Thank you for your honesty. It may interest you to know that the man called Levi was brought here a few days ago for a broken nose. He was taken to the RC for assaulting an enforcer, and he received a second X. Forgive me if my words are harsh, but if he were my lifer, I'd want to know."

If Jemma had seen Levi, she must have known all this. Still, tears pooled in her eyes and she said, "'I am not afraid of storms, for I am learning how to sail my ship.'"

Ciddah frowned. "Yes, well, if you'll excuse me, I have a patient waiting." She circled her desk and held open the office door. Mason and Jemma walked out, and Ciddah followed, closing the door behind them. "If you leave your information with the receptionist, I can have your new prescription delivered to the harem this afternoon."

"Thank you," Jemma said.

Ciddah glanced at Mason then stepped across the hall and entered exam room two.

"Wow." Jemma elbowed Mason. "She must *really* like you."

Jemma's statement set off fireworks in Mason's head.

"No access?" Ciddah tapped on the GlassTop, her fingernails clicking with each stroke. "That's so strange. Why would they hide them from people? Are you even listening?"

She was annoyed now. Ever since Jemma had confirmed Ciddah's affection for Mason, he had been overanalyzing everything she said and did.

"I'm listening," Mason said.

They were alone in the History Center, which took up the entire third floor of the Treasury Building. It brought to mind the libraries in Old movies. There were rows of shelves filled with real books that were not allowed to leave the room. Mason and Ciddah sat at one of a dozen GlassTop desks around the perimeter wall. The glow from their screens was brighter than any bulb on the ceiling.

"I have questions of my own that I want answers to," Ciddah said. "It's clear I can't trust Lawten. I can't trust anyone. I should never have agreed to any of this. I knew better!"

She was mumbling now, talking to herself. Mason watched her. The attraction he felt toward her was making him irrational. He'd never shared such stimulating conversations with anyone. But if she were to declare her affection, what would he do? She was a Safe Lander. There could be nothing romantic between them. He hoped they could remain friends, but if he did have to reject her, she would simply start avoiding him.

He didn't think he could reject her.

His heart started up again. What would he do if she said something? How would he respond? There was far too much risk in all of this. Risk of rejection and loss. Risk of infection like Omar.

Ciddah looked at him. Their eyes met, and Mason felt awkward.

"Why are you staring at me?" she asked.

Why indeed? He looked away. *Completely irrational.*

"What's the matter with you?"

He was a logical prude, right? Well, he could provide her with a logical answer. "I was thinking about the women," he said. "The task director found an uninfected donor from another location."

Ciddah laid her hand on his thigh. "I'm sorry this is so difficult."

Her touch and sympathetic words confused and thrilled him. He fought to keep focus. "I wonder why he complied. Was he blackmailed in some way?"

"Maybe he hates his life in Wyoming. Maybe he's simply more open-minded about saving lives."

That statement fell like cold water on his mood. They'd had this discussion before. And while it would be enjoyable to debate again, here was the perfect opportunity to discourage her affection. Mason picked up the notebook he'd been compiling his theories in and stood.

Ciddah stood with him. "Where are you going?"

"Home." Mason started across the darkened room toward the elevator. As much as he loved being in her presence, it would be a relief to put distance between them tonight.

"Why are you being like this?" Ciddah asked.

He turned back and found her right behind him. "Like what?"

"You owe me your theories." She poked his chest. "It's not my fault I don't have access to the files. I kept my side of the bargain by coming tonight."

"A valid point."

She took his hand and tugged him back to his chair. "Why did you decide to study medicine?"

"I thought you wanted to hear my theories. Why are you changing the subject?"

Ciddah pushed out her bottom lip. "I want to understand you better. Please?"

Her expression made him chuckle. Why did she have to be so alluring? He sat back down. He should return to his apartment, turn on the radio, and listen for Levi, not linger here with Ciddah Rourke.

"I never liked killing, but I was born into the Elias tribe, and the Elias tribe are hunters. My friend Joel, he wanted to be a hunter more than anything and often tagged along on hunting trips. One day, the men set out to track a bear. Joel wanted to go. Wanted me to come too. I refused. But I loaned him my gun because it was a better weapon."

Mason's pulse was too high. Why was he telling her this in so much detail?

"Something happened?" Ciddah asked.

Indeed. "Yes. An accident. Joel's gun—my gun—backfired." Irrational. He was out of control around this girl. The logical thing to do would be to protect his own mental state and pride by fleeing.

"I'm sorry." Ciddah squeezed his hand.

He made himself pull away. "People who lose a loved one, Ciddah... it's hard to get over. Feelings run deep. I don't want Shaylinn to have that pain." Which reminded him of his theories. Omar must be Shaylinn's donor. Unless it was the man from Wyoming. "Why do they take babies away from their mothers? Have they always done this?"

"As far as I know."

Perhaps this is why Ciddah was so moody and insecure. "One of the first textbooks I read was on child psychology. Did you know that when a child is born, it needs to bond with its mother, and the sooner the better? Studies of Old showed that babies who bonded with their mothers were more secure in life and had better relationships with others as adults."

"Our children seem to get along together just fine."

More facts poured into his brain. "Infected women should avoid narcotics and alcohol. They burden an already weak immune system. Everyone I see seems to be vaping. They're only killing themselves faster."

Ciddah rubbed her eyes. "Thank you, O wizened one."

"Wait—you know this? Then why don't you do something about it?"

"It's not that easy, Mason," Ciddah said. "Our way of life... people like it."

"You could at least let the women know that drugs and alcohol are bad for them."

"I do. They know. And I've reminded many. Some women do avoid stimulants. But it's never made any difference. People are just trying to enjoy this life and get to the next one with as much good fortune as they can earn."

Fortune indeed. "'For it is by grace you have been saved, through faith.'"

Ciddah fought a smile. "That's, um, lovely. What's it mean?"

"That you can't earn your way to heaven—or Bliss. It's what I believe."

She leaned back in her chair and folded her arms. "Now wait a minute. You just said you became a doctor out of guilt for the death of your friend. It sounds like you're trying to earn fortune, just like the rest of us."

Her comment rocked Mason to his bones. *Was* he obsessed with works? He'd never meant to be. He thought of the lies Shaylinn believed. Was he punishing himself for Joel's death? Serving a life of penance? "Sometimes it's not easy to live out your faith."

"Then why bother?"

"Because I believe there's only one life before eternity. Not ten."

"Nine," Ciddah said. "The tenth life is eternity in Bliss."

Ah, the tenth life. "I'm sorry, but that begs the question, how do you explain transmigration along with your population decrease?"

"Excuse me?"

"When your people die and those souls are transferred to new bodies for new lives, wouldn't there be a shortage of bodies with no new babies being born? Where do all the souls stay while they wait?"

"I don't..." Ciddah scowled at him. "Why are you always arguing with me?"

She was upset again. "*Argue* is the wrong word choice, Ciddah. There is no anger or frustration involved. I'm simply trying to help by pointing out where your logic is flawed."

"You're trying to help me by criticizing me?"

This was futile. His goal in coming here tonight had been to get Ciddah's assistance in accessing the medical history of the Safe Lands. If she couldn't help him, Lawten had never intended to allow Mason to learn anything here. Though why the task director had made the offer at all, he still didn't understand. "I'll see you tomorrow."

"Wait. Do you want to share a taxi? I live in the Westwall too."

She did? And how did she know where he lived? He'd never said. "Not tonight, no."

But as Mason sat alone in the taxi, riding back to the Westwall—Ciddah's face and smell and touch heavy on his mind—all he could think of was, "Come back, come back, so that I may gaze upon your beauty!"

She was the wrong woman for him in so many ways, but the words still rang in his head. *Come back.*

Once Mason was home, he turned the two-way radio to channel four and set it on his kitchen counter. He watched TV for a bit and had nodded off when he heard Levi's voice.

"This is Jackrabbit with a call out to Eagle Eyes. Do you copy?"

Mason scrambled to get up from the couch and grabbed the two-way radio off the counter. "This is Eagle Eyes. I copy. Over."

"Eagle Eyes, you beautiful bird, you. Where you been?"

"Tasking mostly. The experience has been both fascinating and discouraging."

"I hear you, brother. This place is like that. Look, I want you to take a walk tomorrow morning at nine. There's a place where you and Jem and Mother would have spent a lot of time. A big place. Behind that place is a cactus. Wait for a ride out front."

"Can you confirm that, Jackrabbit? A cactus? Over."

"Affirmative. Don't worry, you won't get pricked. Well, yes, you will, actually."

A cactus? Levi's riddles were never that difficult to solve. Mason tapped his forehead. A place he and Jemma and their mother would have spent a lot of time? The hospital, of course. Ah yes. There was a restaurant behind the hospital called the Green Cactus Grill. "Understood, Jackrabbit," Mason said. "I'll visit the cactus at nine tomorrow morning."

"Mad good. Oh, and Eagle Eyes? Stay calm. It'll only hurt for a moment."

Hurt? Mason hoped he wasn't going to get stunned. "Copy that, Jackrabbit. Over and out."

Chapter 29

Levi parked his truck at the Department of Public Tasks and went into the garage to get more bags. He'd been looking over his shoulder since he left the Larkspur, anxious about seeing Jordan and Mason. When were Bender's people going to show?

Levi had talked to Jemma for hours on the radio the past two nights. Being able to hear her voice on a regular basis made things seem almost normal. He opened the cupboard that held the trash bags and pulled one out.

"Hey, Levi!" Dayle called from his office. "Come on in here a minute, will you?"

Levi wrapped a half-dozen trash bags around his arm to keep them from slipping all over the place and walked into Dayle's office, which was a closet-like room at the end of the garage.

Dayle waved him around to his side of the desk. Once Levi was standing beside Dayle's chair, Dayle tapped his finger against his computer screen. It showed a picture of the empty garage. Dayle hit a key—on an antique keyboard Levi hadn't noticed before. The screen blinked but kept the same image... until Levi saw himself leave Dayle's office and walk out the garage doors and into the light of day.

Whoa! "How'd you do that?"

"Bender thought it best if we do your meeting here. All my guys are out on jobs, so we've got at least two hours."

A chill ran up Levi's arms. "You work for Bender?"

"For Bender... *with* Bender... Bender tasks for me. There's really no boss now that Lonn is in the RC. We all just keep doing our part."

Levi looked Dayle over. Could this be a trap? "You're not wearing gloves."

"I still have my SimTag in place. Not all of us can live underground."

"How do I know you're telling me the truth? You could be an enforcer."

Dayle folded his arms behind his head and leaned back in his chair, displaying his brightly colored arm tattoos. "Why don't you go ask *him*?" He nodded at the open doorway.

Levi peeked out. A black car had pulled into the garage. Levi ran out of Dayle's office just as Bender climbed out of the driver's seat and smoothed out his jacket. He was dressed like some fancy businessman, but the scar over his eye made him look like an Old mobster. What did Levi know? Maybe Bender was a new kind of mobster.

"You got Jordan and Mason with you?" Levi asked, looking toward the car.

"They're coming in a different vehicle."

"So what's the plan?" Why had Bender come out of hiding for Levi's meeting?

"That's what I need to decide, outsider. And it all depends on you."

The sniper thing. "I can't kill anyone," Levi said. "At least not premeditated."

Bender sighed and leaned against the back of the car. "I'm sorry to hear that."

Levi didn't like the guy's tone. He also didn't trust Bender not to call off bringing Jordan and Mason to see him. "But I've been thinking," Levi said. "I can cut the power to the Highlands. Then you and your people can swoop in to rescue Lonn while the cameras are off."

Bender looked skeptical. "How you going to cut the power?"

"With my rifle. Shoot out the transformers."

"You can do that?"

"Yep. That's my diversion plan for when I get the Glenrock women out of the harem. But I'm not particular on when I do it, so long as it's soon. I could time it with Lonn's liberation ceremony."

Bender pushed off the car and approached Levi. "Take Zane with you when you enact your plan, and you've got a deal."

"Fine by me."

Bender clapped his hands and laughed. "Lonn is coming home!"

Levi sat on the hood of a DPT truck, alone in the garage, and watched a black torpedo car pull inside. Dayle and Bender were in Dayle's office, talking business Levi hadn't been invited to hear. Fine with him. With Dayle's pre-recorded footage being fed into the system, the enforcer's surveillance cameras could see nothing of what was really transpiring at the Department of Public Tasks today.

Once the garage door had shut all the way, the driver got out. Rewl. He was wearing his Highlands Public Tasks jumpsuit. He smirked Levi's way and opened the back door.

"—sagging piece of cow liver!"

The sound of Jordan's voice made Levi chuckle. Zane got out of the passenger's seat, and together he and Rewl dragged Jordan out.

Rewl then helped Mason out of the car as well. The sight of Jordan and Mason with sacks over their heads amused Levi almost as much as the contrast in their behavior. Mason wore a bluish-green outfit that looked like Old pajamas, and stood like a statue just where Rewl had left him. Jordan wore a black and red uniform from the Grand Lodge. They'd taped his wrists together. He knocked his elbow into Rewl's gut and tried to pull away. Rewl pushed him, and Jordan stumbled to a stop in the middle of the garage.

"Pulling a knife on *me*? You maggot-kissing, beetle! Cutting *me*?"

"He's wrapped tighter than a cabaret corset," Rewl said. "I'm done." He walked into Dayle's office and, apparently, was allowed inside.

Zane came to stand beside the front of the truck. He handed Levi two sets of gloves: a black pair like Levi's and a brown pair. "Brown for the medic. But he's going to have to do something else when he tasks. Wrap his hand in a bandage or something. He can't wear these in the SC."

Levi set the gloves on the hood and jumped down. "Jordan!" He walked up to Jordan and patted his back. "I'm going to take this sack off."

"*Levi!* Argh!" Jordan kneed Levi's thigh and tried to head butt him.

Levi just laughed and backed out of the way. "I'll leave it on if you don't play nice."

Jordan fell onto his knees, his head sagging down to his chest. "Come on, Levi! Some guy put a bag on my head and cut up my hand. What would you do?"

"He cut out your SimTag so the enforcers can't know where you are. Sorry they didn't explain first." Levi took Mason's pillowcase off first. "How are you feeling, brother?"

"Fine." Mason narrowed his eyes. "You look terrible. You never had anyone fix your nose?"

Levi shrugged and grinned. "Haven't had time."

"*Levi!*" Jordan's tone oozed with frustration.

"*All right.*" Levi darted behind Jordan, pulled off his pillowcase, and snapped it at Jordan's back.

Jordan twisted around still on his knees. "How come Mason isn't taped up?"

"Because Mason isn't an angry mule. Calm down. We don't have much time."

Jordan hopped to his feet, hands still taped behind his back. He sucked in a deep breath that made his shoulders look huge, then blew it out in a growl. "I'm calm."

"Zane, can you cut his bindings?" Levi asked.

"If you're sure. If he lashes out, it's on you." Zane pulled a knife from his pocket and walked slowly toward Jordan, creeping as if approaching a bear. "Easy now, shell boy, I'm not going to hurt you."

Jordan shot Zane a dirty look. "Shut up, maggot."

Zane straightened then cut through the tape on Jordan's wrists.

Jordan jumped on Levi, tucked Levi's head under his arm and squeezed. Levi tried to pull back, but Jordan had him. Of all the immature...

"You want to go back to rehab, brother? Lose your visits with Naomi? Time to be serious. Let go!"

Jordan obeyed, but his voice came out mopey. "Those rat-eating maggots make me talk to her through a window. I can't even touch my own wife."

"At least you're both still living," Mason said. "And healthy."

Levi straightened his jumpsuit and brushed a hand through his hair. "We're going to get her out, Jordan. We're going to free the women on July first, during Lonn's liberation."

"Really?" Zane said. "How you going to do that?"

"I'm going to kill the power in the city. You're coming with me, Zane."

Zane grinned and the rings on his bottom lip spread apart. "Sounds like a stimming adventure."

"What about Kendall?" Mason said. "She's scheduled to deliver on Monday."

This Kendall girl wasn't Levi's concern. "Nothing I can do about that. So here's how it's going to work: Zane and I will take the storm drains to shoot out the transformer. Mason, when the power goes out, I need you to pick up the women. Bender's people will get you a van or something. You'll drive them to the back of the Bradbury, which is between the Gamble House and that BabyKakes bakery. Take a walk over there to check it out so you know what you're doing. Get some cupcakes. They're good."

"What do *I* do?" Jordan asked.

"You're going to meet Mason and lead the women through the storm drains to some underground bunker Bender's setting up. That way Mason can take back the van and keep his cover."

"If we're escaping, why do I need a cover?" Mason asked.

"We have no way to get the kids yet. So you need to stay where you are. Look like a proper Safe Lands national."

"If our women escape, they'll know I had something to do with it."

"They'll suspect you did—that's why you need an alibi. Think you can get one? Maybe the doctor? Jemma says she likes you."

"A girl likes Mason?" Jordan cackled.

Mason's face paled. He looked like he might puke. "I'll think of something."

"Good. Call me on the radio. They monitor the Wyndos," Levi said. "My only concern is that once the women are free, they might put the children in the RC."

"Not the RC, but they'll be guarding them for sure," Mason said. "Still, I don't see another option. We won't know the results of Shaylinn's procedure for a few more days, but we can't risk waiting for—"

"What procedure?" Jordan asked. "What happened to my sister?"

Mason shook his head. "If we don't do this now, it'll be too late for the other women."

"Too late is not an option," Levi said.

"I'm still not sure how we'll get out," Jemma said over the radio. "Even without the power, there will still be enforcers in the hallways."

"You have to think of a way," Levi told her. He was lying on his bed in the Larkspur, staring at the ceiling. It was late Saturday night. Levi had spent the early evening with Jordan, Zane, and Rewl, slogging through storm drains between the Highlands and the Midlands, so that Jordan could learn how to get the women to Bender's underground bunker.

"I'll try," Jemma said.

Levi's Wyndo started singing a techno beat. He sat up and grabbed it from his bedside table. Red's picture covered the screen. He tapped it. "Hello?"

"I'm out in front of the Larkspur," Red said, as if she was stuck inside the glass. "Bender needs you. Come on out."

Levi checked the time on his mirror clock—1:34 a.m. "Now?"

"Yes, now. And wear something normal, shell." She disconnected.

Static fuzzed on the radio. "Levi? Are you there?"

He pressed the talk button. "Yeah, but I've got to go, Buttercup. Bender needs me."

"Be careful. 'All my heart is yours, it belongs to you.'"

He smiled. "I'll take good care of your heart. I promise."

Levi put on his Old jeans and one of the fresh white tank tops from his backpack. He doubted that was what Red had meant by normal, but it was normal for him. It was a little chilly when he got outside, and he wished he had his leather jacket.

He found Red sitting on the hood of a black car in the parking lot. She was wearing what looked like a black towel, lacy fingerless gloves that likely held her SimTag, and clunky shoes with heels as long as Levi's hand.

"Aren't you cold?" he asked.

"Aren't you?" She slid off the hood and opened the driver's door. "Get in."

Levi climbed into the passenger seat. "So where are we going?"

Red started the car and drove out of the lot. "A club called the Savoy. Our mission tonight is to be seen together. One of my contacts, Nash, who tasks on the ColorCast gets jealous. Bender needs a few more details about Lonn's liberation and thinks I can get them from Nash."

"I don't like it," Levi said. "What if the guy jumps me? I can't afford another X."

"Nash won't hit you. He'll just buy me a drink and ask me to ditch you."

"Then how do I get home?"

"Take a cab."

Great. "Why didn't Bender mention this earlier?"

"He won't always tell you everything, shell."

Levi wanted to tell Red to eat dirt and Bender to feed it to her. He didn't appreciate such beckon-and-call moments. And he didn't trust Red. But until his people were freed, what choice did he have?

Red drove them into the Highlands and parked the car. While they waited to get into the Savoy, Red fluffed her hair, pulled some kind of purple makeup crayon out of her cleavage, and drew it on her lips. She handed it to Levi. "Hold this for me?"

"What's wrong with putting it back in your...?" He motioned to her chest.

"It'll fall out when we're dancing. You've got baggy pockets."

"Fine." Levi pocketed the crayon.

When they finally got inside, it was like some kind of torture chamber. Dark and hazy with blinding bluish-white lights flickering from the ceiling. Bodies everywhere, packed in and wiggling like they all had to pee. Deafening noise with a steady thumping rhythm and a wailing voice that needed to be put out of its misery. Madness. Give him a grassy clearing and the Glenrock women singing any day over this.

Red took Levi's hand and dragged him through the wriggling bodies. She stopped in the center of the mob and slid her arms around his waist, tucking her hands into his back pockets. He grabbed her arms and pulled them out.

She yelled into his ear. "We have to look like we're together."

"We are together." He couldn't believe he had to scream just to be heard.

"Like we're pairing up." She moved in close and ran her hands over his chest. "Like you want me."

With Red this close, Levi's could see way too much. "I'm not comfortable with—"

"There he is! Dance with me." Red pressed close, rocking her body against his.

Levi grabbed his hair, anything to keep his hands off this crazy woman. He squinted at the flickering faces around him, looking for a man who might be watching them.

"You have to *dance*, shell!" Red pulled Levi's arms down and around her waist.

Levi felt exposed and embarrassed standing in this crowd with a half-naked woman rubbing against him like a bear scratching on a tree. She was both repulsive and alluring.

Too long, they danced. Too much, Red touched him. And when she pressed up onto her toes to try and kiss him, he turned and left the dance floor to get far away. He made it all the way outside before she caught up with him.

"What was that about?" she yelled.

"I'm done. I don't care about your mission. Call Zane to be your scratching post."

Red's eyes glinted, her face sallow under the lights of the Savoy sign. "I can't. Nash knows Zane."

"If Nash isn't jealous by now, he never will be."

She shot him a nasty glare. "What do you know?"

"I know I'm going to take my cab now."

"Bender will hear about this, shell."

Levi considered that. But Bender had understood about Jemma and had told Red to leave Levi alone. "Fine. I'll explain the situation." It was worth a lecture from Bender to get away from the temptation Red's roaming hands had awakened in him. He took a cab back to his apartment in the Midlands, but it was hours before he managed to fall asleep.

Chapter 30

"Jemma?"

Shaylinn opened her eyes. She lay in her bed in the harem, and when she looked over to the clock, it read 2:12 a.m.

"Jemma?" Kendall's voice out in the hall. "I think the baby is coming."

Shaylinn sat up, slid off her bed, and searched her floor for something to wear.

"Did your water break?" Jemma asked.

"I don't think so. How will I know?"

"You'd know."

Shaylinn pulled on a pair of stretchy pants under her nightgown and ran across the hall to Jemma's room. Kendall was sitting on the edge of Jemma's bed, her face pinched, gripping her belly with both hands.

Jemma held the radio to her mouth. "Buttercup to Jackrabbit. Come in." She looked to Shaylinn. "Go fetch Naomi and Mia and tell them to come here."

"But what are we going to—?"

"Shh. Go, quickly." Jemma tried the radio again. "Jackrabbit, are you there?"

Shaylinn slipped out the door and woke Naomi, but Mia's room was empty. She was likely out with Rand again. Shaylinn had no idea how Mia had managed to talk Ewan into helping her. She was just thankful not to be a part of it.

Naomi was already in Jemma's room when Shaylinn got back. "Mia isn't here."

Jemma closed her eyes and sighed. "Fine."

"Mason then?" Shaylinn suggested.

Jemma nodded and spoke into the radio. "Buttercup to Eagle Eyes, come in." She clutched the radio to her chest. The four of them remained frozen: Jemma sitting up in bed, Shaylinn standing just inside the doorway, Kendall sitting on the foot of Jemma's bed, Naomi standing beside her, rubbing her shoulders.

Kendall suddenly moaned and rolled forward, clutching her belly. The sound scared Shaylinn, and she hugged her own stomach, wondering if life was growing inside her.

"What are we going to do?" Naomi whispered.

"I don't know," Jemma said. "Shay, go fetch Aunt Chipeta. She'll be able to help."

"Just tap them," Kendall said.

Shaylinn ran back to her room, happy to get away from Kendall's pain. She found her Wyndo on the floor beside her bed and brought up Jemma's aunt's picture. It rang and rang and rang before a sleepy Chipeta answered.

"Shaylinn? Is something wrong?"

"Kendall is in labor. Jemma wants you all to come to our suite."

"Oh, dear. We'll be right there."

Shaylinn sat for a moment to catch her breath. She set her hand against her abdomen; something told her there was life inside even though she didn't feel any different. The peace she'd had the day of the surgery fled, and fear gripped her like the bite of an electric gun. She didn't want to have a baby, and she didn't want any pain. But if she was going to have a baby, she really didn't want anyone to take it away.

Her Wyndo vibrated in her hand. She tapped Chipeta's image. "Hello?"

"Come let us in!" Chipeta said.

Shaylinn ran to the front door and opened it. The women filed inside and went to Jemma's bedroom. Aunt Mary gave Shaylinn a hug.

"No one is answering my calls!" Jemma said.

"Then we need to leave on our own," Chipeta said.

"Where's Mia?" Jennifer asked.

"She snuck out again," Shaylinn said.

"Please," Kendall said. "I don't want any of you to get into trouble. Let's call Ciddah."

"No." Jemma threw back her covers and got out of bed. "We'll just have to deal with this ourselves. There is no way I'm letting them take Kendall to the hospital, not when they'll steal her child." She squared her shoulders. "I know Levi had a plan, but I think we should try to leave the harem tonight. Even if it's only to hide somewhere until Kendall's baby is born."

"We'll get caught if we try to escape," Naomi said. "The cameras are everywhere."

"We could try and go out through the kitchen," Shaylinn said.

Jemma stepped into a pair of shoes. "What do you mean?"

"The night Mia and I snuck out, we went through the kitchen," Shaylinn said. "Stairs back there lead to a big garage in the back of the harem."

"Are there cameras?" Naomi asked.

"Ewan said there weren't."

"If you're determined to do this, we'll need to split up," Chipeta said. "You young girls will go Shaylinn's way. Us older women will go out the front, create a diversion just in case Ewan was wrong about the cameras."

Jennifer folded her arms. "I'm not leaving without Mia."

"We won't actually get away, Jennifer," Chipeta said. "They'll catch us."

"But what if they don't? What if we get away and Mia comes back and we've left her?" She shook her head. "I'm not leaving my daughter."

"I'll stay with Jennifer," Aunt Mary said.

"We should leave the radio with you, in case we do get away," Jemma said.

"No!" Aunt Mary said. "How will you reach Levi or Mason without it? Besides, it will be my turn to visit the Surrogacy Center soon enough. We can speak with Mason there."

Another painful moan from Kendall silenced any further discussion. Chipeta planned to give the girls a five-minute head start in case there was an enforcer outside the harem's front door. Everyone exchanged hugs and kisses, then Shaylinn, Kendall, Jemma, and Naomi each filled a pillowcase with belongings and crept downstairs. Shaylinn had packed her favorite new dresses, though if she were pregnant, she doubted they would fit much longer.

Shaylinn guided them across the main sitting room, hoping and praying this would work. When she reached the kitchen door, she pushed it open just a crack. It was dark inside. Jemma entered and held the door for Kendall and Naomi. The light above the stove and the green emergency exit sign gave them enough light to see. Shaylinn led the way through the exit door and into the stairwell.

When the door closed behind them, their surroundings became pitch black. Shaylinn fumbled in her pillowcase until she located the Wyndo. She tapped the glass and it illuminated the stairwell in a dull gray glow.

Shaylinn took the stairs slowly, trying to be quiet, but the scuffing of their shoes over the concrete steps seemed terribly loud and convinced her that an enforcer would catch them any moment.

Kendall stopped and cried out, and the sound seemed twice as loud in the confined space.

Jemma ran to her side. "Another contraction?"

Kendall nodded. Several strands of her tangled brown hair were sticking to her flushed cheeks. "I don't like it."

Jemma sucked in a wincing breath. "Shaylinn, what time is it?"

Shaylinn glanced at the time on her Wyndo. "Two thirty-three."

"Be sure and tell me when the next one happens, Kendall," Jemma said.

"I'm sure you'll know." Kendall limped a few steps, stopped and whimpered.

Jemma hooked Kendall's arm with hers. "We'll wait until you're ready."

Kendall's lips pressed into a thin line. "I'm ready."

They continued slowly down the stairs. Shaylinn braced herself for another outburst from Kendall, but it didn't happen. They reached the bottom without meeting anyone. Maybe this would be simple. Maybe there was truly no one up at this hour. Maybe the enforcers had never thought of guarding this door or putting cameras in this place.

She peeked through the door at the bottom of the stairwell, saw no one, and led the girls into the warehouse, keeping close to the wall. Only a few lights were on, making the room appear to be lit by a full moon. The air smelled oddly of cardboard boxes. Shaylinn put the Wyndo into her pillowcase and moved along the edge of the wall while trying to keep in the shadows. The door was here somewhere.

She walked until they came to a corner, then followed the next wall. The bright glow of an exit sign quickened her breath. She could see it clearly at the end of the row. Though she wanted to run, she forced herself to move slowly.

The exit door let out into a narrow street between the harem and another building. It was dark to the left. To the right, Shaylinn could see the Harem Gardens, beyond them, a busy street and the huge Medical Center. Shaylinn walked to the left, hoping that staying in the shadows would be wisest.

They reached the end of the alley. An expanse came into view on their right. The Noble Gardens. Beyond them, City Hall stood like a watchful eye. They needed some place quiet where Jemma could try to call Levi on the radio again.

They walked along the sidewalk edging the gardens. Shaylinn's gaze fell onto a truck idling at the curb. The driver's door was open, and the seat was empty.

"The truck?" she whispered to Jemma. "I think I could drive it. It looks empty."

"The truck, go!" Jemma ushered Kendall and Naomi toward the vehicle, but a maintenance man stepped out from around the front of the truck, ducked in the driver's door, then moved back to the front hood, which Shaylinn now saw was opened. A tool box sat open on the driver's seat.

Jemma backed away from the vehicle, grabbing hold of Kendall and Naomi as she moved. "That's not going to work, Shay."

"Evening, femmys."

Shaylinn whirled around. An enforcer was making his way across the grass, coming at them from behind.

"Any fortune?" he asked the maintenance man.

"Not yet. It just won't hold a charge."

"Well, a tow is on its way." The enforcer stopped beside the truck and turned back to the girls. "You femmes lost?"

"No. Just taking a walk." Shaylinn turned her back to the enforcer and mouthed the word "Go" to Jemma, Naomi, and Kendall. They turned, and Jemma helped them hobble over the wet grass.

"Wait, are you femmes *pregnant*?"

The question sent fire through Shaylinn's veins. "I'll catch up with you." She turned back to the enforcer, who was walking toward her, his brows furrowed. She smiled and tried to sound calm and confident while holding her pillowcase behind her back. "I'm sure you've seen ColorCasts of Kendall Collin and Naomi Jordan, the two women about to deliver babies to the Safe Lands. They get stressed being caged in the harem all the time. It's bad for their pregnancies, so I bring them out for a walk each night when it's not so crowded and people won't mob them."

The enforcer's brow furrowed. "But that's not allowed."

"Not officially, no. But you know how the harem is. Anything for our queens. As long as we're back before sunrise, Matron looks the other way."

His face relaxed into a smile. "Oh, well... I guess I will too, then."

Shaylinn offered her biggest smile, trying to bat her eyes the way Mia did. "I appreciate that."

"Sure thing. Hey, is Matron Dlorah your task director?"

"Yeah." She'd have to be if Shaylinn were out walking the surrogates.

"I've heard she's tough," the enforcer said.

"Oh, she's not so bad once you get to know her."

"What are your off days?"

"Um... they're different every week. You know, surrogates and their medical appointments and such. This task doesn't really allow consistent free time."

The enforcer pushed up his sleeve, revealing a Wyndo watch. "Well, maybe next time you're free you could tap me? It seems every woman I've met this year is a two. But you're a four. Maybe we could pair up sometime."

Shaylinn's cheeks burned, but she forced a smile. "Oh, thanks." She touched the screen of his Wyndo watch and read his name. "Reglan Brown."

"That's me."

"Well, I should catch up to them. Don't want them getting lost."

"You didn't tap."

She swallowed. "Oh. Sorry." She set her fist against the screen of his watch. It clicked, and Shaylinn's picture filled the glass. All it said was her name, ID number, and Highland Harem. Maybe he wouldn't—

The radio clipped to Reglan's shoulder crackled and a female voice said, "Calling all units. We've got a 10–98 at the harem. Be advised, suspects are four women in their late teens, all dark-haired, two pregnant."

Shaylinn turned and ran.

"Hey!" Reglan called after her. "Stop!"

Shaylinn quickly caught up to Jemma, Kendall, and Naomi. "They're coming. We've got to hurry."

"I can't go any faster," Kendall cried.

Jemma slowed some. They reached the other side of the Noble Gardens and jogged across the street. It was mostly deserted, though one car was forced to slow because of Jemma and Kendall in the road. The driver honked and yelled as he cruised past.

"Here!" Jemma handed Shaylinn the radio. "Call Levi. See if he answers."

Shaylinn took the radio and started for the Snowcrest apartments, but an enforcer's car pulled into the parking lot. Shaylinn reversed their direction, but before they reached the next building, another enforcer's car pulled off the road right in front of them, emergency lights flashing. The officer climbed out and started toward them.

Shaylinn fumbled to press the button on the radio. "Levi? Are you there?" She turned back to the Snowcrest and yelped at the nearness of two enforcers coming their way. She tugged Jemma and Kendall off the sidewalk and through a circular flower bed. Before they reached the other side, one of the officers cut them off. The three officers were closing in. Shaylinn didn't know what to do.

"Levi," she said into the radio. "Levi, we need help."

"Get away from us, you creeps!" Naomi yelled.

"Don't be upset, girls," Kendall said. "I love that you tried to help."

Shaylinn shoved the radio into her pillowcase and hugged Kendall. "I'm so sorry we failed."

Jemma hugged Kendall next. "I love you, sweet girl. I'll be praying for you."

"I love you too, femmy," Kendall said.

An enforcer pointed his gun at Shaylinn. "Don't move! Put your hands behind your neck."

Shaylinn obeyed, and the enforcers arrested them all.

Chapter 31

"Kendall's in labor!" Ciddah's yell carried all the way to exam room three, where Mason was cleaning the Wyndo screen. It was very early in the morning, and the place was dead. "I'll contact Luella at her private number and let her know to meet me over there."

Mason ran to Rimola's desk in time to see Ciddah call the elevator. "Can I come?"

Ciddah turned and frowned. "I'm sorry, Mason. Outsiders are prohibited from the procedure."

"Why?"

The elevator dinged and slid open. Ciddah stepped inside and set her palm against the door. "Since an outsider tried to kidnap our babies tonight."

Outsider? Levi? Jemma? Mason ran around the desk. "Tell me what happened? Was anyone hurt?"

"Jemma, Naomi, Shaylinn, and Kendall tried to run," Ciddah said. "Don't worry. They're all fine. They took Kendall to the Medical Center and the others to the RC."

"Rehabilitation Center?" Mason stopped in front of the elevator.

Ciddah lowered her hand, and the door slid closed.

Mason mumbled to the closed elevator, "Kendall and Naomi's babies are *not* yours."

He ran to the stairwell and pulled open the door, completely abandoning the SC. He took the stairs down the five levels and hailed a taxi to his apartment in the Westwall. By the time he held the radio, he had to catch his breath before he could speak.

"This is Eagle Eyes calling Jackrabbit, come in." There was no answer, so he repeated his call. He glanced at the clock. It was 5:49 a.m. Levi had to be home. "Jackrabbit, you copy?"

The radio crackled, and a weak voice spoke. "Jackrabbit here. What's your tidings?"

"Uh..." Mason scrambled to come up with some kind of code. "Buttercup and her little sister and Stampede's other half and uh... Buttercup's friend, uh, Springing Heifer... They made a run for it because Springing Heifer was about to... uh... spring. Now Buttercup is in the fishtrap. Over." Mason rubbed his eyes and hoped Levi could translate that ridiculous message.

"Did you say Buttercup is in the fishtrap? *My* Buttercup?"

"That's a 10–4, Jackrabbit. Buttercup, her little sister, and Stampede's other half are all *in* the fishtrap. Over."

A stretch of silence passed. Mason pictured Levi either destroying his apartment or sitting up in his bed with his forehead wrinkled as he tried to figure out what Mason was talking about in the middle of the night.

"That's a 10–4." Levi said finally. "We stick with the plan and hope they get out. Cut some Zs, Eagle Eyes. But let me know if you hear anything else. Copy?"

"Copy. Over and out."

Mason made his way back to the SC and finished his shift, then went home.

He slept until his doorbell buzzed at almost eleven thirty in the morning. Who would ever visit his place? Levi?

He rolled out of bed and opened the front door, eyes half closed.

Ciddah stood outside his doorway holding two bags. The smell of eggs mingled with Ciddah's everyday scent of vanilla and cinnamon knocked him back a step.

She took advantage of his surprise and swept past him into his kitchen. She looked tired, but he'd never seen her smiling so wide. He liked it.

"Good morning," she said as she reached into her bag. "I hope you're hungry."

He awoke quickly then. "I... well..." He surveyed his apartment. Not too bad, actually. The shirt he'd worn last night lay on the floor in the doorway to his bedroom. He swiped it up, then realized he was wearing only his scrubs bottoms. He clutched the dirty shirt over his bare chest. "Uh... be right back."

He darted into his bedroom, tossed the shirt into his laundry pile, and pulled a fresh one over his head. Green shirt, navy blue pants. It would have to do.

When he returned to the living room, Ciddah was setting out omelets and toast.

"You brought me breakfast," he said.

"You're welcome. I felt bad about the way I left you alone in the SC."

"How's Kendall?"

"Good. Very good. I'm sorry you weren't able to witness the birth. It was incredible. The surgeons said she was too far along to stop labor, so they let her deliver naturally. They were as nervous as I was. There hasn't been a natural birth in the Safe Lands in ten years."

"The baby's okay?"

She squealed and clapped her hands. "He's absolutely precious! He's in the nursery already getting comfortable."

Mason closed his eyes. He wanted to yell, but this wasn't Ciddah's fault. It was so much bigger. *How can I possibly do any good in this place?* Were his people and other outsiders like Kendall doomed to a life here, slowly killing themselves and being bred like cattle?

A sniffle caused him to open his eyes. Ciddah stood in his kitchen, one hand on the counter, the other covering her mouth. She was crying.

Without thinking, Mason was at her side. "Hey, what's wrong?"

"I lied." Ciddah sniffled. "It was awful." Another sniffle. "Kendall was completely out of control. The birth went fine, but not what happened afterward. Lawten had promised she could hold the child, but in light of her attempted escape, he said there was no way he could allow that to happen. But she was awake when the baby came and—" She broke into another long sob.

Mason stared at her face as it transformed before him. Her tears washed a stream of black from her eyes, down her cheeks. He handed her a wet cloth to clean her face, and the eye makeup smeared with cream-colored liquid, becoming gray goo. All this time, the smoothness of her skin had been painted on. In the clean streaks on her cheeks, Mason could see her real skin, cracked, transparent. He'd always known—in his head, at least—that she was infected, but her perfect appearance had made it seem possible that she really was just a healthy young woman.

To see hints of her true face... He wanted to hold her. But he also wanted to push her out into the hall and shut the door. No, he wanted to wash away the paint and see what she really looked like.

He didn't know what he wanted.

Ciddah went on, oblivious to her exposure. "Kendall... I've never seen anyone fight off sedation." She sniffled. "We had to give her three doses before she calmed down."

"It's a terrible crime," Mason said, thinking of the thin plague that made Ciddah hide behind so much paint, thinking of Kendall mourning the loss of her child.

"I know!" Ciddah choked in a few calming breaths. "Jemma and Shaylinn and Naomi. Their twisted priorities robbed Kendall of her chance to hold the child."

Mason set his jaw. "I wasn't talking about that, Ciddah." He walked into the living room to put some space between them. "A woman's child was taken. It's the worst crime I can imagine—the greatest evil."

Ciddah stomped toward him, her face a glistening mess. "Don't you *dare* call me evil, Mason Elias." She shoved his chest with both hands. "I did my job." She shoved him again. "I can't help that you don't understand."

When she came at him again, he caught her wrists and held them. "I understand. You're only doing what you've been taught is right. But, Ciddah." He pulled her hands against his chest. "What if you were taught wrong? Ignorance is no excuse for evil."

Her bottom lip trembled. "*Again* you call me evil."

"Not *you*, Ciddah."

She tried to pull away, but Mason held tightly.

"I thought you were starting to understand," she said. "I thought tasking in the SC was helping you see that our ways aren't *so* bad." But then she moaned, a soft sound like a distant wasp that slowly grew into jagged sobs. It reminded him of his aunt last spring, who'd wailed after her child came stillborn. He wrapped his arms around Ciddah and held her close, wondering what she was mourning the loss of.

Chapter 32

"A messenger brought me this," Omar said, holding up a gold envelope so the task director general's receptionist could see it. "It said to come at nine this morning."

"Have a seat. I'll let him know you're here."

Omar sat and patted his chest pocket, comforted by the feel of his new vaporizer. He'd vaped in the elevator, but he was so nervous he wanted another puff. Why had he been summoned? He bet the woman doctor Mason tasked for had told Renzor that Omar had gotten infected. Some angel.

Twenty minutes passed before the receptionist sent him in. He knocked on the door out of respect. Or maybe it was guilt. Trying to suck up to the big task man.

"Enter." Kruse's voice.

Omar took a deep breath and entered the office, stopping before the task director's desk. Kruse stood in his usual place by the task director's side.

Omar sat, annoyed at how soft the chairs were, as if comforting his backside was going to make this any less painful. "You wanted to see me, sir?"

"Mr. Strong, General Otley is unhappy with your recent behavior, as am I."

Omar swallowed. "It was an accident, sir. I didn't know brown sugar could kill me."

"A captain should possess more common sense than to ingest high doses of stimulants, especially when in uniform and committed to weekly donations."

"I'm sorry. It won't happen again."

"It's too late for apologies, Mr. Strong. You disobeyed my orders and have contracted the plague. You're useless to us now. General Otley wants you out of the enforcers, and I have no reason to disagree."

Tears wouldn't help matters, so Omar clenched his teeth to fight them off. "You're demoting me?"

"Discharging, actually. Report to the Registration Department to turn in your enforcer badge and personal ID for reassignment."

"That's not fair!" Omar yelled, the pitch of his voice that of a swindled child. "Otley's just mad at me because of Belbeline."

"You failed us. That's all that matters."

"But you still have all the women in the harem. Because of me."

"You were compensated for those women. It is not my fault that you threw it all away. Good day, Omar Strong."

While sitting in the Registration Department, Omar looked over his task list:

Construction: Painter
Enhancement: SimArt designer
Entertainment: Makeup artist
Communication: Graphic illustrator
Entertainment: Set designer

The only task Omar knew was SimArt designer. "What's a makeup artist do?"

"Makeup for programs on the ColorCast," Dallin said from behind his desk. He'd changed his hair from the black and yellow stripes to dark red. "But you aren't there yet. Painting in construction is hard physical labor. You paint walls inside and out. If I were you, I'd do your six there, then try to get into enhancement. Or do six in entertainment and try to get an extension. I wish I could work in entertainment."

"Couldn't you just retest and cheat? Say you're interested in entertainment?"

"You have to be careful cheating. It can anger Fortune and the task directors. Some get away with it, but if you fail your task, you can get discharged. And if you get discharged three times, you get an X." Dallin looked Omar directly in the eye. "I also suggest you don't pair up with any more of Otley's flames."

Omar was convinced his new task was the worst possible assignment one could draw. His task director, Radcliff, a short, wiry man with brown skin, put him on a paint crew. Omar had worked six hours straight, painting the walls of some apartment blue over green. Omar wanted to ask, *Why?* But he'd had his fill of disciplinary action. Besides, it was all he could do not to beat in the wall with his fist.

When he made himself stop thinking about Radcliff, Belbeline's face kept appearing before him. He'd painted her eyes on the wall then painted over them three times now. Why didn't she want him anymore? What was wrong with him, anyway?

"Hey, Strong!" Radcliff yelled. "I think you got that spot, all right? Keep moving."

Omar kicked his paint tray down a few feet and started on the next section.

Belbeline.

When Omar got off for the day, he met Charlz and Skottie in the hitroom of a Highlands club called the Savoy. Once they settled in at a table on a balcony overlooking the dark dance floor below, he told the guys about the brown sugar, his discharge, and Belbeline.

"Forget that prude!" Skottie said as he stroked his mustache. "Why do you want to make a fashion of her? Get you some stims, and we'll find you a new flame."

"There's Yedra," Charlz said. "She's gratifiable. And Janique. One of my favorites who's always willing. Know what? Forget you. Janique's mine tonight." Charlz got up from the table and headed for the stairs.

Omar watched Charlz approach the tangle of swaying bodies that were mostly wearing red and black. Mimics. Not unique like Belbeline.

"Janique *does* fill the need," Skottie said. "Wish I'd seen her first."

"You've paired up with her too?" Omar asked, a little surprised at that coincidence.

"We've all pretty much paired up at least once, except with our same numbers. There are a few femmes I haven't been with. Highbrows. Entertainers." He slapped the table, and the beer in Omar's glass swelled over the side of his glass. "I paired up with Luella Flynn back in boarding school. She won't even look at me today, the prude."

Omar pointed at a blonde woman with spiky hair. Venita, Belbeline's friend. "Her?"

"Venita, sure. She's deluxo. Great legs."

Omar pointed to another woman, short and round with curly black hair.

"That's Camella. You've met her. Tasked in massage? Now she tasks in surveillance? Covers the RC? I took you up where she works, remember? She's a favorite of mine."

"Belbeline tasks in massage," Omar said.

"Enough!" Skottie called the barkeep and handed him Omar's PV. "Fill it with brown sugar—"

"No!" Omar said. "I can't—"

"A *one*. Plain," Skottie said as he raised one eyebrow at Omar. "A one won't hurt nobody, and you need a hit of something."

Omar's heart felt heavy, like it contained the weight of all his poor decisions. All the dead in Glenrock, everything he'd done living here. He *did* want that feeling again. That free, happy, light feeling that nothing mattered. He pressed his fist against the barkeep's SimPad and watched him walk away, knowing this was a mistake. Not really caring.

His gaze flitted down to the dance floor where Charlz was dancing with Janique and Venita. Did pairing up with different women bring pleasure in life? Was Omar a prude for wanting only one? Would this heaviness in his heart double and triple and quadruple until he needed a hit of brown sugar at level ten to make it go away?

Skottie and Charlz lived that way, but they didn't look depressed. And Omar already had the thin plague, thanks to Belbeline. He may as well see if he could find this elusive pleasure everyone else seemed to already have. When the barkeep returned, Omar took a long drag from his PV and headed for the dance floor.

Chapter 33

An enforcer opened the door to Shaylinn's cell. "Let's go, femme."

Shaylinn stepped out into the narrow hallway that separated the two rows of jail cells from one another. Naomi already stood beside a second enforcer, the X after her number a sobering reminder that they were property of the Safe Lands. Shaylinn's X had been there when she'd awakened that morning.

"What about my sister?" Shaylinn asked.

The enforcer motioned for Shaylinn to walk toward the exit. "Just you two today."

Shaylinn turned and looked past the enforcer to Jemma's cell, which was at the very end of the row. "Jemma!"

"It's okay, Shay," Jemma said. "Go with them. Don't worry about me."

Shaylinn's heart squeezed within her chest. "I don't want to leave you here."

"And I don't want to stun you, but I will if you don't move along," the enforcer said.

Shaylinn inched toward the exit. "I love you, Jemma!"

"I love you too, Shay!"

The enforcer pushed Shaylinn's shoulder, and she barely caught her balance. "Let's go, femme. Today!"

The enforcers took Shaylinn and Naomi to the lobby where Matron was waiting. Her black pantsuit with a bright green scarf almost made her look more severe than normal. "I'm very disappointed in you girls," she said.

"What about Jemma?" Shaylinn asked. "Why does she have to stay?"

"Jemma can sit there until summoned to the Surrogacy Center," Matron said. "You two are far too precious to breathe the same air as the vermin who inhabit the RC."

Shaylinn glanced at Naomi, who shrugged. *What makes me so special all of a sudden?* The thought sent a chill over Shaylinn. "I'm pregnant, aren't I?"

Matron smiled. "Get your things from the enforcer, girls, and let's go. Luella Flynn is meeting us at the SC, and I don't want to keep her waiting."

For Shaylinn, the day passed by in a blur, starting with a trip to the SC for confirmation and prenatal prescriptions, three interviews with Luella Flynn, a shopping trip with Tyra, and ending with a coaching session on the proper foods to eat each day.

By the time Matron dismissed her, Shaylinn was exhausted. She entered the Blue Diamond Suite and found Mia watching TV in the living room. "Where's Naomi?"

"In her room," Mia said. "Congratulations, by the way."

The word made Shaylinn queasy. Nothing would be the same without Jemma and Kendall here. She realized suddenly that this place had never even been close to being a real home. All the comforts had been a distraction. She started down the hallway toward her room, wanting nothing more than the peace of sleep.

"I saw Levi," Mia said.

Shaylinn turned back. "Where?"

"At a club Saturday night while you guys were sneaking out."

Shaylinn narrowed her eyes.

"He wasn't alone, either. He was dancing with someone. It was pretty wild."

Night after night, Shaylinn had tolerated Mia's stories of all the dancing and the many fancy drinks she'd tried at the places Rand had taken her around the Highlands. She had believed Mia's story of seeing Omar, though it had nearly broken her heart, but Mia had to be lying about Levi.

"You just think you saw him," Shaylinn said. "Levi would never go to such a place. He's not like that."

"*Such a place?* The Savoy is a wonderful, glorious nightclub, Shay. Stop judging these people because they live differently than we used to. And I know what I saw. I saw Levi dancing *badly* with some gorgeous Safe Lands national."

"Mia, we're prisoners here. And there's nothing more dangerous than an enemy claiming to be your friend. These people mean to use us and throw us away!"

Mia tipped back her head and moaned. "*Shaylinn...*"

"Ever since we got here, you've loved everything they've placed in front of you. But your turn is coming. And I know you think being pregnant will be amazing, and you might be stronger than me, but no one is strong enough to survive this place."

Mia looked back to the TV. "You try and help a person..."

"My thoughts exactly," Shaylinn said as she went to her room.

Shaylinn cried, and it felt good. She lay in bed, burrowed under her covers. Forget stupid Omar calling her an ugly crybaby. Forget Mia and her obsession with Rand. Omar and Mia could just stay here forever with these horrible people.

"Jack... it to... uttercup, come in."

Levi? Shaylinn sat up and wiped her eyes. She looked around her room, and leapt out of bed once she spotted her pillowcase by the door. She dumped the pillowcase out. Her Wyndo snapped into three pieces, but the wind-up radio bounced over by the dresser.

She picked up the radio and pressed the talk button. "This is Shaylinn."

A bit of static, then, "You need... it."

She held the speaker to her lips. "What?"

"Wind, wind... ind!"

Oh, wind it. Shaylinn grabbed the handle and cranked it in circles until her arm was sore. Then she tried again. "Levi? Is that you?"

"Copy, yes. Hello, Shaylinn. Is Jemma there?"

"No. She's in the prison."

"I was afraid of that. How long you think they'll keep her there?"

"Matron said until her appointment."

Everything seemed terribly quiet while Shaylinn waited for Levi to reply. He was probably upset. Jemma's appointment was scheduled days after his planned rescue.

Static hissed over the radio, then Levi finally responded. "Ten-four, Shaylinn. I'm going to need someone to help get our people out of there. Think you can you help me?"

"Yes." Shaylinn would do anything to get away from this place.

"Good girl."

Chapter 34

Announcements for the Lonn Liberation were playing more frequently on the ColorCast. Mason spent almost every spare moment talking with Levi, Jordan, and Shaylinn on the radio, and soon a detailed plan was formed, all the way down to a secret knock.

But Mason still had to work out some sort of alibi that would keep the enforcers from suspecting his involvement in the escape. Ciddah was his only hope. They hadn't spoken much since her visit to his apartment last Sunday morning. Perhaps she was embarrassed about having literally fallen apart in his presence, or perhaps he'd finally driven her too far away with his beliefs. He didn't know. But he waited all day for an opportunity to broach the subject.

It came that afternoon. He finished cleaning exam room four, and when he walked into the hallway, Ciddah was standing outside her office reading a CompuChart.

"You going to watch the liberation?" he asked.

She looked up from the CompuChart, met his gaze, and smiled. "Of course."

"I've never seen one," Mason said, hoping his voice sounded casual.

Her smile faded, and her eyes grew distant and cold. But she said, "Would you like to watch it at my apartment?"

There it was, the moment he'd been hoping for. Yet something felt wrong: the look in Ciddah's eyes. The coldness. Could she somehow know what he and Levi were planning? She'd invited him awfully fast. Mason pushed away his paranoia and tried to keep his smile small, not wanting to appear eager. "Sure. If you don't mind explaining every little thing to an outsider."

"I'd be honored." Her expression faltered, and for the briefest moment an authentic, shy smile appeared. But it vanished just as quickly. Perhaps he'd imagined it.

He wished he hadn't. He wished for a world without disease and prisoners and lies and theft. A world where he could spend each day trying to coax such a smile from this lovely girl. A world where she wasn't the enemy and he wasn't the captive.

On the day of the liberation, Mason arrived early to Ciddah's apartment. She answered the door in a short peach-colored dress that had one sleeve and a crooked hem. Mason had never seen her wear anything but scrubs. He couldn't stop staring.

Since they lived in the same building, their apartments were almost identical. Ciddah's walls were brown rather than blue, and she'd decorated with a food theme, specifically baked goods: cookie-shaped pillows on the sofa, framed pictures of cakes and pies, curtains over the windows with tiny cinnamon rolls on them, and decorative bowls filled with wax pastries.

The place even smelled like vanilla and cinnamon—of course—and of sautéed onions and something else sweet.

"Sit wherever you like," Ciddah said as she went back to the kitchen. She turned on the faucet and scrubbed a dish. "I was just cleaning up. I hope you're hungry, because I made us a feast."

He glanced at a steaming pan on the stovetop as he sat down on her sofa. "You did?"

"I did." She gave him a real smile then. It distracted him a moment before reality caused him to sink back against the cookie pillows. If Ciddah made dinner, he couldn't volunteer to fetch it from the Blue Bell Diner—which had been his plan to slip away just long enough to free the women. Dessert maybe? That cupcake place?

Ciddah banged around in the kitchen, opening and closing cupboards, checking whatever was cooking in the oven. "I hope you'll extend a little mercy my way, Mason. I'm not a bad cook, but I'd never tried to roast beets before. I think I should've peeled them after they were cooked." She held up her hands, the palms of which were stained dark pink.

So preoccupied with the crisis in his agenda, Mason's laugh came out forced. "Shanna was the dye expert in Glenrock. I think she had us all help her with red and purple at some point."

Ciddah crouched out of sight behind the island counter. "Did you all help each other with tasks?"

"Whenever someone needed help, they'd ask."

Ciddah carried two plates into the living room and set them on the table before the couch. There was a thick steak, a sautéed red and green vegetable dish that Mason guessed was part beets, and a thick slice of brown bread topped with a hunk of melting butter. She sank beside him on the sofa, so close their arms rubbed together.

How could he tell her that he didn't eat meat? "This... looks amazing, Ciddah. Thank you. Did you bake the bread yourself?"

She touched her finger to the butter on her slice of bread and swirled the lump over the surface. "Baking is my favorite, especially anything that's kneaded. It's relaxing." She picked up her bread and bit into it.

Mason did the same. It was excellent. "Do people live in the lowlands, where the animals are?"

"I've never heard of anyone living there. I think it's just farmland."

"People must be tasked there, right?"

"I suppose." She shrugged one shoulder. "But everyone I know is a medic."

"Except Lawten," Mason said.

She stiffened beside him. "He was a level twenty medic in the SC when I did my first internship. He got me into the program."

"Oh." Ciddah and Lawten had known each other for years then.

"It's starting! Wyndo: increase volume: twenty-three." The volume came on.

Mason hadn't known he could set voice commands for his Wyndo. He tried a bite of the roasted beet salad and found it quite good. "Mmm, this is—"

"Shh!"

On screen, Finley Gray and Luella Flynn were standing in the center of a packed auditorium. They were dressed to match, as always: Finley in a white suite with a silver vest and Luella in a silver gown that glistened like it was made of glitter. Tomorrow the Highlands would be coated in white and silver mimics.

"So many celebrity nationals have shown up for this historic event," Luella said. "I'm simply thrilled."

"I'm still in awe over Lawten Renzor's suit!" Finley whistled.

An image of Lawten in a satin blue-and-black-printed suit flashed on the screen.

"He looks amazing," Luella said. "He'll be inspiring his own mimics with that look."

"Walls! I hope so." Finley chuckled. "You know, I might even be one of them."

"Well, we're almost there, Safe Landers," Luella said, gazing into the camera so that it seemed like she was looking right at Mason. "Only five minutes until show time. Stay tuned."

The Colorcast went to a bit about silver glitter Roller Paint. Apparently the trends weren't so random after all.

"You're not eating your steak," Ciddah said.

Mason glanced at her and winced. "I'm a vegetarian."

Her eyes widened. "Oh."

They stared at each other a moment, then Mason said, "The beets and bread are really good."

Ciddah's cheeks turned pink. "Well, there's more, so have as much as you want."

The program started again. The screen displayed pictures of the dozen or so Safe Lands nationals who Finley claimed were going to be liberated today.

"Wait," Mason said, "I thought this was just for Lonn. Who are these other—" His words fell away as he recognized some of the portraits. Five were older women from Glenrock, including his own mother, Tamera.

Mason stood up so fast he knocked his plate to the floor. He stepped forward. Stopped. Walked to the door. Turned back.

Ciddah set her plate on the sofa and stood. "Mason, what's wrong?"

What could he do? He'd left the radio in the van. Even if he ran down there, Levi probably had no way of contacting Bender at the moment.

"Mason?"

Could he just sit here and watch them kill his mother? Maybe Bender would free everyone who was being liberated tonight. But what if he didn't? "Liberation is death?"

"I don't know; I think so."

"Ciddah, please! Tell me what exactly is going to happen to these people. It's important."

She wrung her hands. "Liberation is a mystery. That's part of its splendor. We don't know what happens, only that it's wonderful."

"Basing your death on hearsay is illogical. Who says it's wonderful? Has someone been liberated and returned to tell the tale?"

"No, but—"

"Then how do any of you know it's wonderful?"

"Mason, please sit down. You're frightening me."

He glanced back to the screen. His mother's picture was displayed alone. She'd been a number nine at thirty-nine years old, so Luella led a chanting prayer to Fortune to have mercy on her as she entered the tenth life.

"That's so sad," Ciddah said. "Entering Bliss before age forty. Did you know her?"

"Yeah." Mason prayed he could expose liberation for whatever it truly was, that his mother was still alive, and that he could hold himself together in front of Ciddah. The other women were counting on him. He knelt and started to pick up his food that now covered the floor. His hands were shaking.

"Let me help you." Ciddah ran into the kitchen and returned with some napkins. When the mess was cleaned up, Mason sat back down on the couch.

The last national highlighted was Richark Lonn. Majestic music played as pictures of Lonn flashed and text listed facts about his life. Born in 2037, he excelled in mathematics and science. After graduation, he'd entered medic training and was the fastest national to reach a level twenty at age twenty-three. He'd maintained a steady relationship with Martana Kirst that had started in boarding school. She and Lonn had gifted the Safe Lands with eight children. Most of the pictures had both she and Lonn in them.

Luella Flynn's voice spoke over the montage of images. "Martana was liberated suddenly in 2068 in a complication with her tenth pregnancy."

"That's not exactly true," Ciddah said.

"How do you know?" Mason asked.

"It's kind of an urban legend amongst medics. They say that Martana did miscarry the tenth child, but she didn't die from it. She killed herself afterward."

"That's terrible!"

"She and Lonn made seven babies together in a span of twelve years. She wanted to be done, but the Guild said no. She was still strong, and they wanted to keep her as part of the harem. She completed one surrogacy term—baby number eight—then had a ninth child by Lonn. At that point, she was on meds for depression. When she didn't conceive again on her own, she was conscripted for surrogacy, but when she lost that tenth baby, it was too much. She took her own life. And that's why Lonn started the Black Army—so they say."

"Because really, the Safe Lands killed her," Mason said.

Ciddah leaned back against the couch. "That's a strange way to put it."

"If I were the man who loved her, I'd see it that way. She wanted the pain to stop, and the Safe Lands refused. What you saw Kendall go through, Martana suffered that nine times. I told you, Ciddah, a mother and her child have a bond. To be kept apart from your child nine times… I can't imagine how she must have suffered. Lonn too."

"You think a donor suffers as well?"

"Lonn was more than a donor in a closet in City Hall. He loved Martana. And he knew those babies were his. Of course he suffered."

Applause brought Mason's attention back to the ColorCast. The history montage had ended. Lonn stepped out onto the stage to a thunderous reception, but he was not smiling. He walked to the center of the stage, where Luella Flynn sat on a sofa, and sat down beside her.

"You have a special message you want to share tonight, don't you, Richark?"

"I do." He looked into the camera. "A revealing is a wonderful experience. If you've ever wondered who your donors were, fill out a revealing waiver today. And if you learn that I'm your donor, I love you very much."

"Love is so special, Lonn," Luella said. "Isn't liberation a wonderful time to communicate peacefully with all the Safe Lands?"

Lonn chuckled, and they cut away without letting his reply be heard.

Mason glanced at Ciddah. Tears streaked down her cheeks from eyes so suddenly bloodshot they looked more red than white. "You think Lonn and Martana are your parents?" Mason asked.

She laughed. "No!" She tried to laugh again, but it came out more like a gasp. "You're so dim."

"How can you be so sure? The ages fit."

"Because my donors live in the Midlands. In the Prospector."

Mason swallowed. She'd never mentioned anything so personal before. "How long have you known?"

"I applied for a revealing on my fourteenth birthday. Found out who my donors were that same day. Met them the day after that."

"They had both filled out waivers?"

"The day I was born."

"And they were together? Lifers?"

She nodded and smiled. "They're a lot like Lonn and Martana were. According to my donors, I have three siblings out there. But none of them have come looking."

"That's exciting, isn't it? Knowing your parents. Knowing you have family."

"Some days. Some days it's only depressing." She used her fork to move her beets around her plate, then jumped up suddenly and walked to her Wyndo screen. She picked up a small black object from the top of the screen then put it back. Her shoulders rose and fell in a deep breath, and she returned to the couch, eyes glossy with tears.

Mason wanted to ask what that was all about, but the look on her face made him wait.

"I have to admit," Ciddah finally said, "when I found out my donors knew each other, that I was a product of love, not donations and schedules, I was so overcome with joy. Does that sound stupid?"

"Not at all. It's natural to love one person, to create life together, to help it mature to the point when it's ready to love and produce its own life. Family is a good thing." Most of the time.

"I believe you."

Knowing how difficult it must have been for Ciddah to admit that, Mason's heart cracked. He could feel her nesting inside. He refocused his gaze so he could see their reflection in the Wyndo screen, sitting side by side on the sofa.

He pictured himself standing at a crossroad. One way, the road ran smooth and straight. Mason discovered the cure for the thin plague, cured the entire Safe Lands population, and changed the confining laws of this place. He married Ciddah, started a family, and they grew old together.

The other road was rocky with steep twists and turns. Mason found no cure and was forced to make donations. He filled out revealing waivers each time in hopes of meeting any children who might result. The Safe Lands remained a controlling place, stealing women for surrogacy from all corners of the world and wresting babies from their mothers' arms. Mason continued to work as a medic and after ten years reached level twenty. He pledged his life to Ciddah, and he contracted the thin plague. She continued to miscarry, and that hardship haunted their relationship until they were liberated together when Ciddah turned forty.

"My father knew Lonn," Ciddah said, jerking Mason from his daydream. "The first time my mother was conscripted for surrogacy, my father got involved with the Black Army. It was pretty new back then, so no one really thought of it as a rebellion against the Safe Lands."

"Your father's a rebel, and he told you?"

"He's not a rebel anymore. He told me to warn me that fighting back isn't worth it. That the Safe Lands will always win."

Lawten clearly was good at controlling the people through fear—he could even weaken a father's resolve. "That's a pretty negative outlook."

"Not when you've seen what he has. My father was there when Arris died."

Mason looked at Ciddah, unable to remember that name. "Who?"

"I forget sometimes you don't know all our history. Arris and Lonn started the Black Army together. Arris had a memoriam liberation because he was killed. They all were—around twenty of them. My father was the only one left alive. The enforcers told him to make sure the rebels knew what happened to traitors, and if any of them told a word of the deaths, they'd all die with bad fortune."

"But I don't understand. I've never seen any reports of death on Finley and Flynn's show. In fact, I've never seen any reports of crime."

"People do die here. And there are bar fights, overdoses, heart attacks, and murder. When death happens, there's a memoriam liberation. But only the positive parts of life are shown on the ColorCast. You won't hear any mention of Lonn's three Xs or the Black Army in this liberation ceremony, unless Lonn says something. But violators never do. It's strange. I wonder what stops them."

Lonn's voice came loud and clear through the Wyndo screen. He stood at a podium before a huge crowd and spoke into a mounted microphone. "I lived my life as best I could. I learned, I loved, I played, but I also questioned. If we accept everything in life without question, we forfeit the chance to reach our potential. The Safe Lands can be a better place if you insist on it."

The camera focused on Luella Flynn. "Some ways you can make a difference, Safe Landers? Retest in tasking to see if you're serving in the right area. Adopt a pet from Pet Squad. Or join Safe Watch, an organization committed to keeping our city secure."

It seemed to Mason that Luella had turned what Lonn had said into something else. "Sounds like Lonn still thinks people should fight back."

Ciddah grunted a response, staring at the screen, her arms folded.

"You still think I should make a donation?" Mason asked.

She didn't move. "Yes."

"Why?"

"Because the Safe Lands could only be benefitted by having more nationals like you."

He felt himself blush. "Well, uh, thank you, Ciddah. But I'm going to keep on questioning, like Lonn said. Find a cure instead. Won't that be better for every—"

A shrill siren rang out. Mason clapped his hands over his ears. What was that?

"Oh no!" Ciddah ran to the kitchen and opened the oven. Smoke billowed up to the ceiling. She screeched and jumped back.

Mason grabbed a potholder, pulled a pan from the oven, and dumped it into the sink. Ciddah flipped on the faucet, then turned back to the oven and switched it off. She stared at him with wide eyes as she used a towel to fan the air until the noise stopped.

"Oh!" Ciddah frowned and the pan in the sink.

"What was it?" Mason asked.

"A cake."

He chuckled. "I think it's done."

She swung at his chest, but he caught her fist in his hand. She tried to pull free, but he held tight. Something about her smile and the way her eyes sparkled made him glance at her lips. He could kiss her. See what it was like. Or he could be smart.

He released her hand and glanced at the clock. It was ten minutes before he needed to leave. *Close enough.* "How about I run get some cupcakes from BabyKakes?"

"You'll miss the rest of the speech!"

"I'm kind of missing it already."

"I'm sorry."

"Don't apologize. I'll be quick, okay?" He glanced in the sink. "You like chocolate?"

She swatted him again. "It was a spice cake."

He raised his eyebrows at the black lump. "If you say so. Be right back." He darted out the door before she could say another word.

Mason had parked the minibus in the Westwall's uncovered lot. He started it and shakily steered onto Gothic Road. It had been years since he'd driven a vehicle, and he'd certainly never handled something this large. A horn honked, and a car sped around him. He pressed the accelerator harder to try to keep up with the rest of traffic. To make matters worse, the roads were wet from the rain.

He eventually parked in the alley between the Highland Harem and the Noble Gardens. Once the power went out, he'd circle around to the alley that led to the loading dock where the women were supposed to meet him—if Shaylinn managed to get them out. He should've driven slower. Hopefully, no one would ask why he'd parked here. Everyone was likely watching Lonn's liberation anyway.

He reached back to the first passenger's seat, grabbed his two-way radio, and pressed the talk button. "Eagle Eyes to Jackrabbit, you got your ears on?"

The answer came instantly. "This is Jackrabbit, go ahead."

"The ark is in position," Mason said.

"Glad to hear it, Eagle Eyes."

"Saw Mother and four other Glenrock women on the liberation program. Think we can get them out too?" *Please say yes. Please.*

"I'll look into it right now. Jackrabbit over and out."

Mason dropped the radio on his lap and leaned back against the seat, hoping it wasn't too late for Levi to help their mother. He had never been so thankful for a burned cake. Not only had it given him the opportunity to fulfill his part in the escape and possibly help Mother, but it also had gotten him out of Ciddah's apartment before he'd done something he would've regretted. His feelings for Ciddah were only getting stronger, but she had the thin plague. To love her would mean his own death. He could just hear his father mocking such a choice.

His father wasn't here anymore, but Mason was leaving the Safe Lands soon. He also had a list of logical reasons against pursuing Ciddah, so despite his overactive imagination about the future, there really wasn't anything to decide.

Chapter 35

"I don't like it," Zane said.

"It's not your problem," Levi said as he carried the manhole hook toward the hole.

"There's no exit." Zane gestured down the dark alley to the drive that circled the Mountaineer. Grass and a fence of trees met them on one side, the building on the other. "We come back up out of here and someone sees us—enforcers see us—we're dead."

Levi leaned on the manhole hook like it was a cane. "Dead? Not liberated?"

"Hey, not everyone goes in for that tenth life juice. I'm a rebel, aren't I?"

"Yeah, yeah." Between Jemma being in the RC and his mother and the other women in the liberation ceremony, Levi found it almost impossible to stay focused on Zane's words.

"Look, I picked this alley because no one will see us," Levi said. "And it's closest to the dam. Stop criticizing and help me open this."

Levi inserted the hook into one of the slots in the manhole cover and lifted the edge. He'd made a point to clean it yesterday, so it came up easily. He pulled it toward him while Zane squatted on the other side and pushed, and together they slid the cover across the pavement and onto the grass. Levi traded the manhole hook for a road construction sign he'd nabbed from the Highlands Public Tasks. He set it up beside the manhole, and once they had both climbed through the opening, Levi pulled the sign over the hole.

The stagnant odor of algae and mud brought him back to the day he'd come into the compound. It hadn't been that long ago. As his feet lowered into the water, icy liquid soaked through his pants legs and onto his skin. He slowed until his foot felt the ground, then he let go of the rungs.

The water at the bottom of the storm drain reached his knees. Almost twice as much as there had been on the day he'd tested the route. He readjusted his rifle that he'd slung over his back, then dug his flashlight and Red's makeup crayon out of his pants pocket and darkened the X on the tunnel wall before the exit chute split. He'd marked the exits on his test run but figured they could stand to be more visible.

"What are you doing?" Zane's face, barely illuminated by Levi's flashlight, appeared to Levi's right. Dressed in a gray maintenance uniform, Zane's head looked like it was floating in the darkness.

"Marking the way." Levi waded past Zane. The water was too high to walk on the sides of the pipe and avoid getting wet. Yesterday, it had taken him twenty-two minutes from the road to the canal. They were already moving slower. At least it had stopped raining.

Their footsteps sloshed through water as Levi led the way down the storm drain. He stopped to darken his hash marks at each exit shaft but tried to move as quickly as possible.

"I'd like to have a look at that gun later," Zane said. "It looks like you made it out of wood."

"I didn't make it—it was my great grandfather's. But parts of it are wood. It came from a place called Arizona, which is pretty far south of here."

Thinking of Papa Eli reminded him of home, which made him think of Jemma. Shaylinn had told him how they'd tried to reach him on the radio the night Kendall went into labor. If it hadn't been for Red's dance mission, Levi would've heard their call for help.

"Do you know if Red managed to get the information she needed from Nash?" Levi asked. "She said it was important to Bender for tonight."

"Nash?" Zane started to laugh. "Oh, you're so dim. What'd she talk you into?"

Levi turned and pointed his flashlight at Zane. "She took me to some dance place and said we had to make Nash jealous so he'd pick her up. That was the night Jemma got arrested."

Zane's laugh dwindled. "Walls, I'm sorry. I *told* you to be careful."

Heat burned into Levi's cheeks and chest. "She made it up?"

"That flame is tricksy," Zane said.

Of all the insane... Levi spun around and splashed through the water. He breathed hard and fast and could almost taste rusty dirt on the air. *Refrain from anger. Turn from wrath. Refrain from anger...*

They passed some graffiti that said *Arris & Lonn: For all lives*. The closer they got to the exit, the shallower the water became. By the time the tunnel's opening appeared in the distance—a circle of night that swallowed his flashlight's beam—the water was only a foot deep, gushing toward the main canal.

Levi looked back at Zane. "How much time do we have?"

Zane pulled out his Wyndo and glanced at the screen. "About twelve minutes 'til Bender makes his move."

"Then we'd better make ours." Levi waded the rest of the way out of the storm drain and up the canal. The moon was fuller than he'd have liked. Thankfully, numerous clouds in the sky dampened its glow. They reached the dam and the fish ladder that ran up the powerhouse wall. Levi stepped carefully on the sides of each pool, hoping his footing stayed sure.

At the DPT office, Levi had discovered that unlike in Old cities, the Safe Lands electrical substations weren't located in the center of town. Aesthetics mattered more than convenience to Safe Landers, so the substations were on the top of the wall, on appendages that shot off the roadway like Old scenic lookouts. There were eight substations for the Safe Lands: two for the Highlands, two for the Midlands, and four for the Lowlands. Levi had guessed that the eastern one fed power to the ColorCast studio, since it was closer, but he didn't know for certain. He prayed his guess was right.

Halfway up the fishtrap, they climbed over the railing to a concrete ledge that separated the fish ladder and powerhouse from the roadway. The trill of the generators buzzed through the powerhouse walls, vibrating the ledge under Levi's boots. They jogged along the ledge until it met the wall that surrounded the roadway. There they stopped to look out.

Streetlamps lit the roadway, spaced about one hundred feet apart and alternating on each side of the road. Inside the walls, the city glittered. Outside, the land was pitch black, disrupted momentarily by a set of receeding taillights out near the western wall. Levi could see no other vehicles.

The distant substation was a tangle of gray metal on a field of black maybe three hundred yards out. The four gleaming spotlights that towered over the station didn't cast their glow far.

"Nowhere to hide," Zane said.

"We won't be here long enough to need to hide." Levi jumped down onto the roadway and crossed to the inner wall that came up to his waist. He lifted the strap of his rifle over his head, set the rifle on the wall, and crouched to look through the scope, turning the zoom until the substation glowed in the lens. After locating the row of transformers, he tried to figure out which way they ran. If he could hit the first transformer in the series, everything else would go out.

Levi pulled back the bolt and loaded a round into the chamber. "Keep an eye on the studio's location, and let me know if it goes dark." He flipped off the safety and took aim at the transformer on the far left. One deep breath, and he pulled the trigger.

The shot cracked around them, echoing off the concrete walls of the dam. Through the scope, Levi saw no sparks or evidence that he'd hit anything. He glanced up at Zane.

"Prospector apartments went dark," Zane said. "All the way to... Wow, that's weird. The power went out in the Highlands all along the edge of the Highland–Midland wall."

"It's an arch." The first one must be the other end then. Levi chambered another round and aimed for the transformer on the right end. Just as he pulled the trigger, Zane spoke.

"Someone's coming."

The shot rang out, but Levi knew he'd missed. He cocked the gun and straightened, looking where Zane was pointing. Two sets of headlights were approaching from the other side of the inner wall. They'd just passed the other Highland substation.

Levi crouched and aimed for the transformer again. "Don't talk." He took a deep breath and held it, then fired. He straightened to glance toward the city below.

Zane yelled, "You got it!"

Levi tucked the rifle strap over his head. "Let's go."

As they sprinted across the road, the headlights from the approaching enforcer vehicle lit their way. Levi boosted Zane up onto the roadway wall, then Zane pulled up Levi.

"Stop!" an enforcer yelled.

Levi followed Zane along the wall to the ledge that separated the powerhouse. Over the railing they went and into the fish ladder. Zane flipped on a flashlight, and they splashed down through the fish ladder as carefully as they could. A door on the powerhouse above opened, but Levi didn't look back.

"They went downriver!" a man yelled.

Zane tripped on the last step of the fish ladder and fell into the canal. Levi jumped over the last two steps and pulled Zane to his feet. They splashed downstream, staying against the inner wall. Above, enforcers' flashlights roamed the canal.

Gunfire pelted water around them, urging them to move faster. Zane stopped in front of the storm drain and shone the light into the tunnel, waving at Levi to hurry.

"Don't wait for me!" he yelled.

Zane hoisted himself into the tunnel and soon cried out and dropped his flashlight, which slid out of the pipe and plopped into the canal, dimly illuminating the brown water from below.

Levi lunged up into the tunnel, took hold of Zane's waist, and pulled him into the drain.

Zane's voice was a whisper. "I think I cut my leg."

"Hold on." Levi helped Zane sit, then skidded back out the drain. He squatted down for the glowing beam of the submerged flashlight, grabbed it, and crawled back into the pipe. Zane was slumped along the curve of the tunnel, his waist submerged in the flow of water, his legs elevated on the other side. Levi shone the light on Zane's face, turned the beam to his legs, and then to the water, which ran red from Zane's legs and past Levi's boots.

Levi looked up to Zane's welling eyes. "It's no cut. They shot you."

Chapter 36

"Only lights I see are headlights." Charlz's voice came from the darkness across the room, his form a black shadow before the pale outline of the window. "Power's out everywhere."

Omar shifted on Charlz's couch. Before the power had gone out, they'd been watching Lonn's liberation and listening to Charlz's enforcer scanner.

The scanner crackled and a male voice said, "B46, 11–99. Highland Substation Beta, 11–99. Shots fired."

"Rebels, I bet," Skottie said from Omar's right. "They're all worked up about this Lonn thing."

"That makes sense," Omar said. "Think they're trying to free him from liberation?"

"Nah, the guy's old," Skottie said. "It's the way of things."

Mad lot of sense that made. "Lonn's a rebel. What if he doesn't agree with liberation?"

"Why would anyone disagree?" Skottie asked. "Liberation is the highest honor."

The radio buzzed again, and this time a woman spoke. "B46, 11–99. Highland Substation Beta, 11–99. Shots fired. All wall units respond. Code 3."

"Too bad I'm not out there," Charlz said. "I'd pop those prudes with my stunner and watch them twitch." Charlz drew an imaginary gun and pretended to shoot it.

"You'd miss," Skottie said. "And Otley would use you for the next target practice."

"Shut it," Charlz said, shooting Skottie with his nonexistent stunner.

A fizzle of static. The female voice again. "Units responding to wall, suspects are two white males, wearing gray Department of Public Tasks uniforms, last seen near the powerhouse."

Omar slid to the edge of the couch.

"It *would* be the cleaners," Charlz said. "Hey, Omar, maybe it's your outsider brother. He's mad 'cause you broke his nose, and he wants payback."

"Why wouldn't he come shoot up Omar's apartment, then?" Skottie asked.

The radio crackled, and Omar yelled, "Quiet!"

The female voice. "Units responding to wall, suspects entered a storm drain, pursue with caution."

Omar's thoughts tumbled together, recalling Levi's two Xs, his promise to free their people, and how he'd entered the Safe Lands through the storm drains. He stood up. "We need to find a DPT radio. Now."

"Why?" Charlz asked.

"Because I'd bet you my PV that my brother is using them to make trouble. And I think I know how to locate him."

It took longer than Omar had liked to find a maintenance worker. None seemed to be working at this hour. Thankfully Skottie remembered that his friend Nash tasked for the DPT, so they went to Nash's Mountaineer apartment and borrowed his radio. Not that they moved much faster once they got to Nash; Charlz kept complaining they were missing the rest of the liberation.

"It's not on anyway. The power is still out," Omar said.

"Still, we could be doing something better than chasing after your hunch. You're not even in enforcement anymore, remember?"

"At least I'm doing something."

When they were back inside the car, Skottie asked, "Where to?"

"Just wait a minute." In the back seat, Omar flipped through the channels on the radio, listening. One: nothing. Two: some guy at a malfunctioning fire hydrant. Three: nothing. Then he hit station four.

"—to stop the blood flow. Then get moving. Over."

"10–4, Eagle Eyes," Levi said. "Meet in the dead-end alley behind the Mountaineer."

"Negative," the other voice said. "I've got to fill the ark and deliver the cargo. You're on your own, Jackrabbit, so hurry. Over and out."

"Copy, Eagle Eyes," Levi said. "Over and out."

Channel four went dead. *Sweet mercy.* "They're coming here," Omar said.

"Who's coming here?" Charlz asked from the passenger's seat. "And what's a Jackrabbit?"

"A code name for my brother. We've got to stop them." This was it: Omar's chance to get back in with the task director general and Otley.

"What's that mean, *cargo*?" Charlz asked.

"It means they're stealing something," Omar said. "You guys got your weapons? They took mine."

"I've got stunners at home," Charlz said. "Been collecting them a while."

"Not enough time for a trip to your place," Omar said.

Skottie reached across the car and opened the glove compartment. "We've got one," he said, removing a stunner.

"One will have to do," Omar said. "Now let's find that alley."

Chapter 37

Shaylinn kept everyone in the downstairs sitting room watching Lonn's liberation so that when the power went out, they'd be close to the kitchen and the stairs to the garage. Seeing her mother's face on the screen with the other women of Glenrock almost made Shaylinn too frightened to lead the escape. But by the time the lights blacked out, her fear had turned to anger.

They were getting out of here tonight. No more of this friendly prison.

They reached the garage without incident. Shaylinn saw a transport parked in the alley where Mason was supposed to be. She just needed to make sure. She lifted the two-way radio to her mouth. "Eagle Eyes, give me your signal. Over."

The lights on the transport flashed on and off.

Shaylinn waved Naomi forward. "Go, go!"

The transport had steps. Mason came down to help Naomi up the first one.

Naomi hugged him. "Thank you, Mason."

Eliza hugged Mason as well. Aunt Mary pinched his cheeks. Chipeta, his aunt, wrung his hands and kissed his cheeks.

And then there was Shaylinn.

"Only five of you?" Mason asked.

"Jemma is still in the RC. Mia went to watch the liberation with Rand at some fancy party. She said we were *dim* for trying to escape again and that she didn't want an X. And Jennifer refused to leave without Mia." Shaylinn still couldn't believe she'd considered Mia a friend, even for a brief time.

"Get in," Mason said. "We have to keep moving."

Shaylinn climbed the steps and sat in the first row of seats across from Aunt Mary. Mason got into the driver's seat and started the transport.

"Mia wants to stay here?" Mason said. "Really?"

"Oh!" Shaylinn clapped her hand over her mouth. She'd forgotten Mia and Mason were engaged to be married.

"I'm sorry, Mason," Chipeta said. "We couldn't keep hold of her. The draw of so much glamour... She never looked back."

"Mia chooses the gilded cage," Mason mumbled. "Fascinating." He steered out onto the main road, and the transport started to pick up speed. Shaylinn looked out the window and could barely see the harem shrinking away in the moonlight. Good riddance.

"What about the children?" Eliza asked.

"We can't leave the children here," Aunt Mary said.

"What happened to Kendall?" Shaylinn asked. "Where is the RC? Are we going to rescue Jemma?"

"I'm taking you to meet Jordan, who'll lead you to a safe location," Mason said. "Levi will meet us there, and you'll all make plans to free the children." He swerved over the yellow line and back. "Sorry. I'm not the best driver."

"What about you?" Naomi asked. "You're not coming with us?"

"I'm going to stay in the Highlands, so I can have access to the children."

Shaylinn looked at Mason with a new appreciation; she hoped his bravery wouldn't be a mistake. "Won't they know you helped us?"

"Not as long as we hurry so I can get back," Mason said.

"Bless you, Mason," Chipeta said. "You're a good boy."

Mason drove over to the Grand Lodge and parked beside a large truck. "I've got to do a little surgery on each of you before we go farther." He got up, turned on a flashlight, and removed a first aid kit from under the dashboard.

"Surgery for what?" Eliza said.

"SimTags. The computer chips they put in your hands. Scoot over, Shaylinn."

Shaylinn obeyed, and Mason sat beside her on her seat.

"I won't lie to you. It's going to hurt. I'll be as careful as I can, but I also need to be quick. We don't know how long the power will be out." He held up his flashlight. "Can someone hold this?"

"I will." Chipeta grabbed the light and held it aloft.

Mason took Shaylinn's right hand and set it on his lap. He tore open a little package and rubbed something cool over the side of her hand. Her heart skipped a little as he removed the lid from what looked like a pen but turned out to be a little knife. He wiped the blade off and looked into Shaylinn's eyes.

"Ready?" he asked.

She nodded. Mason twisted her arm so that the side of her hand faced up, which felt awkward. He squeezed and pressed the knife into her flesh. Shaylinn gasped at the sting and jerked her hand, but Mason held tight while she looked away and gritted her teeth.

"Got it," Mason said. "Can you hold this?"

Shaylinn looked back. Mason held up his finger, and on the top sat a tiny metal tube, covered in blood. Shaylinn pinched it off his finger, then Mason bandaged her hand.

"Don't lose that," he said. "Who's next?"

Mason worked fast, and soon had removed the SimTags from each of them.

"Don't tell Jordan I cut you," he said to Naomi, and she smiled.

Mason collected all five SimTags in his hand and took them out of the transport. Then they were off again, moving through the dark city. He had to slow at intersections, as the cars that were out were having trouble deciding who should go first. In some places, enforcers waved traffic through, and each time their vehicle passed, Shaylinn found it hard to breathe.

Finally, Mason stopped again and got up. "Wait here." He opened the door and descended the steps. "I thought I saw a pair of eagle eyes," he said to the bushes.

"Just a stampede," Jordan's voice answered.

Naomi squealed and moved to the front of the bus.

Mason lunged back up the bus steps. "Okay, quickly now. Let's go!"

Naomi ran off the bus, the other women close behind.

"Naomi!" Jordan jumped out of the bush. He looked his wife up and down and set his hands on her belly. "You're both okay?"

"We're fine," she said, though tears coated her cheeks.

Jordan clutched handfuls of Naomi's hair, kissed her, and said, "Omi, omi, omi," between kisses. Naomi laughed and cried at the same time.

Shaylinn looked away, embarrassed. Finally, Jordan and Mason led them around the bushes to an open manhole in a paved clearing at the back of the building. Jordan climbed down first, then Mason helped Chipeta onto the ladder.

Once Chipeta was down, Naomi peered down the dark hole. "I don't think I can bend over far enough to even get my feet on those rungs."

Jordan called up to her. "I'll help you down, baby."

While Naomi descended, Mason held her hand as he had for his aunt. "I doubt he'll ever let you out of his sight again," he said.

"Give him time," Naomi said, wincing as she slid her protruding belly past the lip of the hole. "He'll be desperate for a hunt."

"Not much to hunt in the Safe Lands," Mason said.

"True, but we won't be here much longer."

Mason waved Eliza forward, then Aunt Mary.

Shaylinn was the last to go. She sat down and put her feet through the hole.

Mason crouched beside her. "Shaylinn," he said, "thank you for your help and your courage. Is there anything I can do for you?"

There was only one question Mason might be able to answer, and while it embarrassed her to voice it, she forced out the words. "I'd like to know who the father is."

Mason's face paled a bit, then he nodded. "Fair enough. I'll find out."

Chapter 38

Once the women had cleared the storm drain, Mason pulled the cover over the opening, which proved to be nearly impossible for one man. Or maybe he was simply a weakling. He finally managed to push it into place, then ran around to the front of the bakery.

The door was unlocked, but when he went in, someone yelled, "We're closed!"

"I need a couple cupcakes," Mason said, inching through the darkness toward a glowing handheld Wyndo. He reached the counter, and his eyes adjusted to the low light.

A tiny man sat on a stool behind the glass case, Wyndo in hand. "Power's out. Can't process your ID."

"I'm a medic. My credit's good," Mason said. "Take down my number and process it when the power comes back on. Please? I've got a girl with a sweet tooth who I don't want to cross."

"What if I run your ID and it's empty?"

"Then you can turn me into the enforcers."

The man grunted. "I suppose. How many cupcakes you want?"

Mason set his hands on the glass case. "A half-dozen okay? You have spice cake?"

"Yeah, I've got spice cake."

"How about three spice cake and three chocolate?"

"What kind of frosting?"

"Surprise me."

The clerk boxed the cupcakes and wrote down Mason's ID number.

"Thanks!" Mason ran back to the transport and called Levi from the road. "Jackrabbit, this is Eagle Eyes. Come in."

"Got good news, Eagle Eyes? Over."

"The cargo had reached the promised land. Over."

"Any sign of Buttercup?"

"Sorry, Jackrabbit. No sign." Mason dropped the radio into his lap and used both hands to turn the transport onto Gothic Road. He picked up the radio and said, "You copy?"

"Yeah, I got that, Eagle Eyes."

"How's the leg?" Mason wished there was a way for him to be of more help. "Over."

"He's still breathing, Eagle Eyes. Over and out."

Mason said a prayer for Levi's friend and for Jemma, and for Levi not to lose his mind wondering where Jemma was. The lights were still out when he got back to the Westwall. He parked the transport and walked inside the building, carefully making his way up the stairs to Ciddah's floor. He raised his fist to knock on her door, but before he could, the door swung in.

Ciddah stood in the doorway, white-faced and red-eyed. She grabbed him in a hug that froze his breath. "Thank Fortune! I thought something had happened to you!"

"The power is out," he said, inhaling the vanilla-cinnamon smell of her hair to get his lungs working again.

"I know that!" She pulled him inside and tugged him past the kitchen where a bright beam momentarily blinded him.

"What is that?" Mason asked.

"A flashlight I set on the counter. What took you so long?"

"It's kind of hard to order cupcakes when the power is out. I had to convince the clerk it was an emergency." A clerk who would hopefully be Mason's alibi should anyone ask.

Standing in his shadow, Ciddah looked up into his face, her eyes like two crystals. "A cupcake emergency? Did she believe you?"

"He. And yes." Mason held up the box.

Ciddah grinned. She took the box and sat on the sofa. He sank beside her and closed his eyes, thankful the women were free—or at least in hiding.

They'd actually done it.

A gasp from Ciddah caused his eyes to flash open. "You got spice cake."

"You said you liked it."

"And you listened."

He grinned. "Is that so foreign?"

"A man who listens?" Her expression darkened. "You'd be surprised."

Mason stretched his left arm along the back of the sofa and turned his body a bit, so he could see her face. "Okay, surprise me."

She cast her gaze to the box of cupcakes. "Mason, most men who live here... they're not like you."

"They're women, then?"

"No." She chuckled. "They're... selfish."

"Not your father."

"In a way, he is. When I told him I was going to be a medic, he worried they'd use me."

"Worrying about your daughter isn't selfish. It's a father's duty."

"Fine. I said *most* men."

He wanted to ask about Lawten, but something held him back. "You knew many men who bought you the wrong kind of cupcakes?"

"One did. He always ordered my food. And when I said, 'I don't like my steak rare,' he'd say, 'Yes you do, shimmer.'"

"He called you 'shimmer'?"

"That's a word men use for beautiful. He called me shimmer all the time, but he never made me feel beautiful. He'd say things like, 'You're going to wear that?' or 'Shimmer, you should probably skip dessert. Walls, skip breakfast tomorrow too. I like my women slim.'"

"He sounds like a jerk."

"He was. But I..." She ran her finger through the frosting on one of the spiced cupcakes and licked the end of her finger.

Mason didn't know how to respond. He wanted to ask why she spent time with a cruel man, but he could tell from her pinched brow that it hadn't been that simple. And he'd been set up to marry Mia, so clearly he wasn't one to judge the inner workings of relationships.

"Omar betrayed my people," Mason said. "He's responsible for my father's death and the death of countless others. But he's still my brother. I hate what he did and the choices he's making now, but... I love that kid. I always will. Sometimes relationships are complicated."

Ciddah turned those crystal orbs on Mason. The low lighting made her skin, and even her hair, appear bone white. She blinked, and when her eyes reopened, she was looking at his lips.

Heat crept over him. He wanted to kiss her. Instead, he removed his arm from the back of the couch and gestured to the box on her lap. "Are you going to share?"

She jolted a bit, as if coming back from someplace far away. She glanced into the box. "You like chocolate, I see."

"Doesn't everyone?" Mason said.

"I prefer spice cake." She handed Mason a chocolate cupcake with rainbow sprinkles. "Thanks for being my friend, Mason."

He let his gaze travel her face. The part in her hair... her tiny nose... those thick, impossible eyelashes... the soft fuzz of her pale eyebrows... the curve of her lips. "I like being your friend."

"But nothing more?"

Her words made him study the sprinkles on the top of his cupcake. Here was the moment he'd been dreading. And how should he answer? Win her love? Lose her friendship?

Ciddah's voice came cold and detached. "Forget I said that, okay?"

"Ciddah..." *Do something! Don't let her think you don't care.*

"Mason, I didn't mean it. I mean, I did, but..." Ciddah lowered her voice. "I just didn't mean to say it."

He stood and set the cupcake back in the box. And now he was Omar, running away. "I should probably go." *No! Stay, you fool!* What was the matter with him?

She popped up beside him. "Can't you wait until the lights come back on?"

"It might be hours—or days."

She stepped close, gaze focused on his shirt. "You could sleep on my couch." She touched one of the buttons on the front of his shirt. "Please?"

He *could*. But he didn't think she meant sleep. "Ciddah... It wouldn't be right."

She looked up, brow pinched. "Your prudishness drives me crazy, do you know that?"

If she only knew what he was thinking. "It's not prudishness so much as propriety."

She reached up and touched his cheek, then brushed her thumb over his lips. "Your innocence is so stimming attractive."

He frowned at her flawed logic. "So you want to take it? Then that which attracts you to me would be gone. And I would be at a disadvantage."

"Mason, what you hold as conventional standards of behavior are foreign in this place. Safe Lands propriety would dictate that you stay the night, because you want to spend more time with me and would find it enjoyable. That is, if you would... like to, I mean."

"I would." He closed his eyes, not at all comfortable with the impulses welling up within him, trying to take control. "I do."

"Then stay!"

He shook his head then opened his eyes. "What has Safe Lands propriety gained you, Ciddah? You said it yourself. Your men are mean. They lack self-control. They play, but they suffer no consequences for their actions. All in good fun, no matter who gets infected or hurt or heartbroken, correct? And that's what you want from me? Just another good time?"

She looked deep into his eyes and whispered, "I want someone who cares and won't leave."

Oh, how her words tempted him. But he dug down deep. "Believe it or not, Ciddah, my leaving right now is proof that I care for you a great deal."

Chapter 39

Levi shined his light over the ridged pipe until he spotted the purple number two he'd written with the makeup crayon. "One more." He shone the flashlight at his feet and took careful steps, holding Zane's waist with his other arm, half carrying him. They were almost back.

"Lonn will help you go after your girl," Zane said. "Now that he's free."

Maybe, but it wouldn't be easy. "If Bender knew how to break someone out of the RC, he'd have gotten Lonn out long ago." Levi moved the light away from the dirty water and over the pipe until he saw his number one. "This is it." He helped Zane stand beside the ladder. "Think you can climb up?"

"If I use my right leg and drag my left."

"I'll go up and move the sign. If you need help, I'll come back down." Levi put the end of the flashlight into his mouth and climbed. When he reached the top, he slid away the sign, hoping no one was near enough to hear it scrape over the concrete. Once the space above him was free, he climbed another rung and peeked out. The dead-end alley was vacant.

"How you doing?" he called down to Zane.

"I got this," Zane said.

Good. Levi climbed out and carried the sign toward the grass where they'd left the manhole cover. The wind blew his wet clothes against his skin, chilling him through.

When Zane's head appeared above the roadline, Levi pulled him up and helped him sit in the grass. Then Levi inserted the manhole hook into the cover to pull it.

"Need some help with that?" a voice from behind him said.

Levi spun around. Three men in civilian clothes blocked the alley's exit. Omar with his two enforcer friends.

"Hay-o, brother." Omar pointed a gun at Levi. "Guess this will be three marks for you."

"If you say so," Levi said as he reached for his rifle.

"Don't bother." To Levi's shock, Omar shot first.

For the third time, enforcers led Levi into the Rehabilitation Center and down the narrow pathway between the cells. People shouted at him, but the enforcers dragged him all the way to the end and put him in a cell on the right.

"Looks like you're here for your last visit," the enforcer said and closed Levi's door.

Levi fell onto his mattress, face first, and lay there exhausted, trying not to think. So many thoughts filled his mind. Omar had betrayed him again. Would they liberate Levi immediately? Would it be on the ColorCast? At least he'd freed the Glenrock women. All but Jemma.

He could hear her voice calling for help. He closed his eyes, overwhelmed at how he'd failed her. What if Levi never saw his love again? What if she were forced to live here forever? The thought made him sick.

"Levi of Elias."

He sat up and looked into the adjacent cell. A toothless man pointed away, across the corridor. Levi followed his direction to the cell directly opposite from his.

Kneeling at the door, face pressed between the two bars that she clutched with her fists, was Jemma. She smiled. "I thought maybe they'd given you a sedative."

"Jem!"

He practically flew across his cell to the door and reached out. Jemma reached as well, stretching until their fingertips brushed. Levi twisted so that his shoulder slipped between the bars. Jemma mirrored him, and their palms pressed together.

Levi bent his fingers around her hand and squeezed. She had an X by the number four on her cheek. "Are you okay? Did they hurt you?"

"I'm fine. But I don't know what happened to Shaylinn and Naomi and Kendall."

"Kendall had her baby, and they took it from her. Shaylinn and the others..." He paused, not convinced the walls didn't have ears. "They're safe."

Jemma started to cry. "What about the children?"

"Still working on that."

"But what about you? You have three Xs. Are they going to execute you?"

The look on her face, as if he were dying in her arms, was too much. He couldn't let her worry. "Maybe. But don't worry, Buttercup. Death cannot stop true love. All it can do is delay it for a while."

Jemma's face lit up. "I will never doubt again."

"There will never be a need."

Chapter 40

Omar sat on the soft red chair in the task director general's office, giddy with the knowledge that Renzor again owed him. As usual, Kruse stood beside the desk, holding his Wyndo and looking too busy to bother with Omar. Wait until the task director issued the reward—then Kruse would pay attention.

The task director leaned back in his chair. "Mr. Strong, what *shall* I do with you? You must know I'm not a fool."

"Of course not, sir," Omar said, distressed by the tone of the man's voice. A tone void of gratitude.

"How do I know you didn't help them? You never turned in your enforcer uniform."

Because he'd forgotten. And he'd been holding out hope. "I *didn't* help them. I stopped them."

Those vulture eyes watched him. "How did you know to listen to the radios?"

"I told you. I know my brother. And when I heard that someone in a DPT uniform was shooting, I figured it was Levi, since he tasks in maintenance and is still a scavenger at heart. He would've stolen radios from someplace. Why not from where he tasks?"

"But where did he get the gun? And how did he know where and when to shoot? These are things an enforcer has the resources to learn."

Cold despair threatened to bring tears. Anything but tears. Omar composed himself, fought to control his emotions. "But I caught him. I brought him to you."

"And I grow tired of seeing your face. You'll report to the Registration Department—"

"I don't believe this!" How could the task director think he'd helped Levi?

"—for task reassignment—"

"That's not fair! I helped you!"

"—and receive new lodgings in the Midlands."

Omar breathed slowly through his nose, glanced at Kruse, who stood like a tree shading the task director. A tree oblivious that Omar was even there. "That's my only option?"

"Unless you'd rather join your brother in the Rehabilitation Center."

"Gee, let me think it over, will you?"

"Your attitude does not bode well for your future here."

"So sorry, *sir*. If you ever got up out of that chair, maybe I'd do a better job at kissing your—"

"Good day, Mr. Strong."

Omar pushed off his chair, set both hands on the edge of the task director's desk, and leaned forward. "May you be liberated soon, you flaking zombie." That was finally enough to get Kruse's attention. The pink-painted assistant threw Omar out of the office.

Omar took the stairwell to the Registration Department, trembling so badly he had to sit on a step and vape just to calm down. This was *all* his brother's fault. Levi, who just had to be a hero. And now Levi was going to be liberated. Another death for Omar to feel responsible for.

Because liberation had to be death, and Bliss some twisted idea of heaven. Right? But Omar couldn't imagine people looking forward to death, even with the belief of returning as someone else. He also didn't put it past the guild to lie.

Where else would the people go, though? Helicopters and planes came and went from the area every so often. Maybe they took the liberated to some city called Bliss? No, that was just desperate thinking.

Why didn't the Safe Lands nationals question any of it? They all longed for liberation as if it were a puff of brown sugar. Couldn't these people think for themselves? Why did they scarf down everything the ColorCast fed them?

After a quick visit with Dallin, Omar walked across the street to the Snowcrest, stewing over his situation. Living in the Midlands would make visiting the clubs in the Highlands more difficult. He hoped Skottie would come get him. The only positive thing to come out of this situation was that his reassignment meant he would be tasking as a SimArt designer. Dallin told him to report to a place called Sim Slingers.

Omar pushed up his sleeve and studied the black lines that wrapped around his arm. Maybe now he could do his owl.

Back in his apartment, he packed up his clothes, his art supplies, a few paintings, and several vials of juice. He was up to a brown sugar three now and a ten with grass. In the back of his mind, he wanted to cut back, but every time he went to buy more, his willpower betrayed him.

He went into his bathroom to grab his shaving tools and studied his reflection in his bathroom mirror. He didn't look sick. How long until his skin started to flake? How long until his veins started to show?

Belbeline.

Her name made him ache. Memories of her laugh, her touch, her eyes. Why couldn't he forget her? Brush her off like Skottie did with women? It was pathetic that he couldn't.

What if he simply filled his PV with a brown sugar ten? That would end this for good. Then he'd know if liberation was a load of dung.

Whatever remained of the old Omar insisted he leave before he did any more damage to himself. Get out of the city. Go to Jack's Peak or Wyoming.

Jemma's face came to mind suddenly, surprising him at the powerful emotions she stirred within him. He'd heard on Charlz's scanner that she was in the RC. Jemma was one of the few people who'd always been nice to him, treated him kindly, and stuck up for him when his Father treated him like a cowardly animal.

Omar hated her. The thought made him laugh. Okay, so he *wanted* to hate her. But who could hate such light and beauty? Such goodness. No one. Especially not Omar.

Perhaps, if he was careful, he could find a way to help her.

The buzz of his doorbell made him jump. *Belbeline?* His heart swelled within him. Maybe she'd changed her mind. Wanted him back. He ran to the door and pulled it open.

Instead, Skottie stood on his doorstep, Charlz leaning beside him. "It's about time, peer," Skottie said. "Don't you answer your transmitter?"

As Skottie brushed past on his way into the apartment, Omar gazed down the hallway hoping for a glimpse of a red-haired beauty. But the hallway was vacant, filled only with memories. He closed the door.

"You listening to me, Omar?" Skottie said. "Look at him!"

Omar turned then and saw that Skottie was supporting Charlz's weight, that Charlz was bloody and dazed. "What happened?"

"*Now* you're home," Skottie said. "You been vaping the sweet stuff today?"

"A little."

"Well, help me get him to the couch. He weighs a ton."

Omar moved to Charlz's right, and together he and Skottie hefted their friend to the couch. "Who did this?"

"Otley," Skottie said. "Turns out Janique is one of Otley's claims. When she heard Charlz was in the RC, she came to find out what happened. Otley didn't like that. Had Charlz worked over. They interrogated me too, asked a lot of questions about you and your outsider brother, like we know anything about that prude. But they didn't hit me. Just Charlz."

For the first time, Omar noticed that Skottie and Charlz both had an X by the numbers on their faces. "They Xed you guys?"

"Yeah, and kicked us out of the enforcers. Guess where I get to task now? Stimming taxi driver. And I've got to move to the Midlands. I've never been so fried in all my life."

Charlz spoke, slurred and soft. "I gotta clean poop."

"Sewage cleaner," Skottie said. "They made us both retake the test. Charlz was too out of it to really read the questions. He botched it bad."

Omar sank onto the couch beside Charlz. "This is my fault. I shouldn't have tried to catch Levi. And I definitely shouldn't have dragged you guys with me. Maybe my father was right, maybe—"

"Stim down," Skottie said. "Charlz and I aren't minors, you know. We make our own choices. Frankly, I don't blame those rebels for trying to get their peers away from Otley.

Wish I had some way to burn that overgrown, hairy downer. Make him regret he ever saw me."

"Wait. You think my brother was right to shoot out the power?"

"I don't know. Maybe. Now that I'm banned from enforcement, the law just doesn't matter. Not like it used to."

"Wish I could liberate Otley," Charlz said.

Omar's mind felt like it was working clearly for the first time since he'd arrived in the Safe Lands. Skottie knew that Camella woman in Surveillance. They'd all done their tour of the RC in class. And Charlz had a collection of stunners. "I have an idea that could make the enforcers wish they'd never demoted us. But you need to help me get my brother and his girl out of the RC."

"Serious? Now you want to help him?" Skottie said.

"I'll help you do anything that'll make Otley mad," Charlz mumbled.

Omar raised his eyebrows at Skottie.

"Fine," Skottie said. "But you better have a plan, 'cause I don't want a premie lib."

"Did you guys turn in your enforcer IDs yet?" Omar asked.

Skottie shook his head.

Charlz said, "No."

"Me either. Skottie, tap that girl up in Surveillance and see if you can stop by. Charlz, I'll need you to help me get past the front desk and take out the enforcers at the RC, then keep watch. How are you feeling?"

"I'll be fine. Just need to clean up."

"Good." A rebellious thrill surged over Omar, making him feel powerful, strong.

"How we know Skottie's up there?" Charlz asked as they walked up to the front doors of the RC sometime after three in the morning. The sky was like a canvas coated in midnight paint flicked with glitter and illuminated by an oblong half moon.

"We don't," Omar said, bringing his gaze back to earth. "We just have to hope he is."

"And you're sure she can override the Authorization System once we get to the cells?"

"According to Skottie, she can log us in as anyone she wants."

Thanks to Charlz's connections with several female receptionists, they faced minimum questioning as they entered the RC, passed the front desk, and called the elevator. When the door finally slid open, Omar was relieved to find it empty inside.

He'd been smart to come at night. Fewer enforcers tasking at this hour. Fewer witnesses and possible fights. Omar wasn't looking forward to having to punch someone.

As soon as the elevator doors opened, Charlz slid in and covered the yellow camera lens as Omar put on a creepy Luella Flynn mask Charlz had grabbed from his apartment on the way over. It smelled like chemicals. Omar had wanted to wear the Finley one, but

Charlz had insisted on first pick. Omar would never get why anyone would pay credits for stupid masks like these, though he was glad Charlz had them. His friend's odd quirks were finally coming in handy.

The elevator opened. Charlz stuck his boot against the door and peeked into the guards' chamber. "I see one. He's mine." He drew his stunner and ran out of the elevator.

Omar drew his own stunner and followed, but by the time he reached Charlz's back, the clicking of Charlz's weapon had stopped and an enforcer lay on his side, moaning. Omar took the man's weapons and handcuffs, which he used to secure the enforcer's arms behind his back. He dragged the man into the bathroom and ripped off his shoulder radio. Omar attached the radio to his own shoulder and returned to the guards' chamber.

Charlz was sitting at the front desk still wearing his Finley mask. "I'm Finley Gray, coming to you live from the RC. Find pleasure in life."

Omar glanced up at the camera and hoped Skottie had it covered. "Only one guard?"

"It's three in the morning, peer."

Omar looked at the computer screen, though the information meant little to him. "You find them?"

"Cell thirty-nine and forty. Should be all the way to the end."

A man's yell drew their attention to the bathroom. The guard.

"I'll take care of him." Charlz said. "Get your people."

Omar held his stunner ready in case there were guards inside, and, with a long breath, he opened the door.

The cell block was dark but for three lights evenly spaced along the ceiling. Omar knew from his training tour that they shut down most of the lights at ten o'clock each night. No sign of enforcers. He strode down the aisle, his breath a steady hiss against the rubber mask.

His gaze darted back and forth across the aisle, checking the cell numbers. *Ten, eleven... sixteen, seventeen... Halfway there.* He glanced up at a yellow surveillance camera and really hoped Skottie had been able to get his girl to help.

When he reached the end, he nearly stepped on Levi and Jemma's arms, which were stretched out into the corridor, fingers intertwined. The way they were both lying on the floor against the bars, he couldn't open either cell without waking them.

He stood there, frustrated, trying to decide which to open first. An image of Levi choking him to death popped into his mind. He spoke into the enforcer's shoulder radio. "E112 to Highland Gatekeeper, requesting entry to prison cell forty."

"Please verify identification," a woman's voice replied.

Omar set his fist against the black pad on the cell door and held his breath. Come on, Skottie. His girl better come through.

"Identification verified," the woman said.

Omar blew out his relief and nudged the door open. Jemma sighed dreamily, released Levi's hand, and rolled over enough that Omar was able to squeeze inside. He crouched, reached for Jemma's shoulder and—

"What are you doing?" Levi's voice made Omar jump. "Get away from her!"

Omar turned to see Levi standing at the door of his cell, gripping the bars and glaring.

"It's me, brother," Omar said, remembering his mask. He spoke into the radio again. "E112 to Highland Gatekeeper, requesting entry to prison cell thirty-nine."

"Please verify identification."

Omar slipped out of Jemma's cell and set his fist against the pad on Levi's door. "Keep your voice down, or you'll wake everyone," he said to Levi.

"You betrayed me again, Omar. What's your angle this time?" Levi asked.

"Identification verified," the woman said.

Omar pushed in the door. "To get you and Jemma out of here."

Levi glanced at the stunner in Omar's hand. "You going to shoot me with that?"

"No! Look, I'm sorry about before. I'm trying to make it right. But we don't have much time, so come on!" Omar ran back into Jemma's cell and grabbed her arm. "Jemma! Wake up!"

Levi tackled him from behind, and Omar felt all air leave his body. Levi smashed Omar's face against the concrete, and though Omar tucked his chin to protect his nose, his right temple slammed into the ground. The mask was little cushion as blinding pain shot all the way down his neck.

"Stop it!" Jemma said. "Levi, don't!"

The weight vanished from Omar's back. It took a moment to straighten the mask, and when his eyes looked out through the holes, the cell was empty. He pushed up to his feet and saw Levi and Jemma halfway down the aisle, standing at another cell. Levi shook the door.

"Who's in there?" Omar asked, jogging to catch up. "One of ours?"

"None of your business," Levi said.

"E112 to Highland Gatekeeper requesting entry to prison cell..." Omar glanced up. "Eighteen."

"Please verify identification."

Omar pressed his fist to the pad on the door just as Levi slammed his shoulder into Omar, knocking him out of the way. Omar stumbled to the side and barely caught himself on the bars.

"Levi, stop!" Jemma said.

But Levi pushed past her and grabbed Omar's shirtfront. "Stay away from me." He slammed Omar against the cell grate. The back of Omar's head struck—

"... now, Omar? Huh?"

Omar blinked. Two bars pressed into his back. He squinted. What had Levi asked? "Uh... I'm trying to..." Omar struggled to breathe over the pain throbbing in his temple and the back of his head, straining to remember. "Make it right. That's all. Know I can't, but..." He choked back a sob. "Just trying, okay? Should... hurry."

"Identification verified." The woman's voice came through the speaker on his arm.

The door clicked open. Levi elbowed past, knocking Omar to the ground again. A wave of dizziness swept over him. He stumbled into bars on his right and took a deep breath, watching as Levi and Jemma helped a man with a bandaged leg out of cell eighteen. Omar grabbed the nearest bars and stepped toward them, but his leg gave out. He fell, nausea gripped him, and he threw up. The vomit pooled between his face and the mask, making him gag further.

"Omar!" Jemma yelled. Someone grabbed his hand. "Levi, help!"

"I'm helping Zane!"

The mask was pulled off his head, and Jemma's face swam above Omar's, a haze of beauty and concern. She wiped his face with the rubber mask.

Omar opened his mouth to tell her how pretty she was, how he missed looking at his drawing that hung above his bed in Glenrock, but her face went away, and Levi was there, scowling like always.

"You never... smile," Omar said. "Why you... hate me, brother?"

The scowl faded to a look of shock. Levi grabbed Omar and heaved him up to a standing position, but Omar's legs still weren't working, and he slumped in Levi's arms.

"Wasn't supposed to happen," Omar whispered. "Forgive me."

Levi crouched and bent Omar's body over his shoulder.

The rest was a blur. Omar floated. Charlz spoke. Stairs. Screaming. Clicking stunners. Levi's voice. A yelling woman—not Jemma. Cool night air on his face. Sleep...

When Omar opened his eyes, his head was in Jemma's lap, her fingertips brushing through his hair. He wanted to stay in this place forever. But then the pain came, swelling from within, crushing his skull.

"He tried to set things right, Levi, and you could have killed him," Jemma said. "He asked forgiveness. You should respect that."

"Are you hearing yourself, Jem? He may as well have killed eighteen people with his own hand. Not to mention whatever happened to your mother and mine. How can I respect that?"

"And are you hearing yourself? He asked forgiveness. End of story."

"Jem—"

"Anyone who knows the good he ought to do and doesn't do it, sins." Jemma looked down on Omar then, met his gaze, and said softly, "I forgive you, Omar."

Chapter 41

Levi was tired. Omar's friend Charlz drove them all to the back of the Bradbury—the place Jordan had taken the women underground the night of Lonn's liberation. Zane cut out Omar and Jemma's SimTags. He put Omar's in a pair of gloves, but destroyed Jemma's.

Zane didn't think he could handle another trek through the storm drains on his leg, so he asked Charlz to drive him to the Highlands Public Task department, likely to see Dayle. Zane took Omar's gloves with him, promising to lead the enforcers on a pointless chase until Omar decided what to do next.

Levi, Jemma, and Omar traveled the storm drains until morning, making their way to the underground bunker. Evidently, Jordan had removed all Levi's purple crayon marks—smart thinking—to erase their trail, but it made it difficult for Levi to find the way.

When he finally located their destination, he made Omar stand back in the darkness of the tunnel. "Until I can talk to Jordan," Levi said. He stepped into the alcove that held the bunker door, took hold of Jemma's hand, and gave the secret knock.

The door swung in and revealed Jordan's smiling face. "What took you so long? I've been waiting all—*Jemma!*" He hugged her, kissed the top of her head, and rocked back on his heels, lifting her feet off the ground. "So glad to see you, sister."

"Everyone's here?" Jemma asked. "Everyone's okay? Shaylinn? Mama?"

Jordan's brows drew together. "We've got the women from the harem, all but Mia and Jennifer, who wouldn't come. But the liberation thing... It didn't work out."

Levi stiffened. "What do you mean?"

"When Bender got there, no one was there. Turns out the liberations are recorded in advance."

"Why would that be?" Levi asked.

"We learned about this when we were in the harem," Jemma said. "It's so they can edit them. "If they film in advance, they can make sure the people see only what the directors want them to see."

"Yeah"—Jordan shrugged—"that's pretty much what that Bender guy said too."

So... Levi's mother was already dead? Or was liberation something else? He couldn't have lost his mother too. "What about the children? You come up with a plan to rescue them?"

Jordan snorted. "You kidding? Most of the women are paranoid because Mason didn't cut the SimTags out of their faces, and every mother here has a different plan for how to get her kids back. I'm not cut out to be Elder of dung. I'm so glad you're here to take over."

Levi doubted he could handle the tension any better. First things first: He had to fix this mess with Omar. "I need a favor, Jordan. And you must promise not to hurt him."

Jordan's brow wrinkled low over his eyes. "Who?"

"Promise me."

"Yeah, if you say so. I promise."

Levi stepped back, reached around the corner, and pulled Omar out by the arm.

Jordan eyes flashed. He tried to push past Levi, but Levi held him back. Before Levi could react further, Jordan spun the other way, knocked past Jemma, and slid to his knees in the storm drain, splashing into the shallow water. He grabbed Omar by the legs and yanked him onto his rear. "You rabid, dung-licking..." Jordan pushed Omar's head into the water.

"Jordan, no!" Jemma yelled.

Omar squeezed his eyes shut and pressed his lips together, though the water only reached his ears. He tried to squirm free. "I'm sorry! Don't hurt me!"

"Yeah, beg, you poor excuse for a maggot." Jordan scooped water over Omar's face.

Levi grabbed Jordan's waist and pulled him back. "You promised me!"

"Get off, Levi. This needs to be done."

"You want me to be the elder? You've got to respect my word. And I say stop it, now!"

Jordan elbowed Levi and crawled to standing. "Yeah, okay, *Elder Levi*. But you've got to convince me why I can't kill him. Can you do that, huh?"

"Yes. But I need you to keep him safe until I can prepare the women for his arrival. Can you hide him somewhere without anyone seeing him?"

Jordan growled. "Yeah, I can do that."

"Without hurting him?"

"I said yeah."

"Do it then." Levi helped Omar stand, and they all followed Jordan inside. Jordan secured the door and led them down a short tunnel. It smelled stale, as if it had been ignored for years.

"The big room with the kitchen and TV is to the right," Jordan said. "The bedrooms and bathroom are to the left. I'm gonna take your swine-stinking brother to my room."

"Actually," Levi said, "now that I've seen the layout, just hold him right here. I'll only need a minute. I'll call you in."

"You're the elder, *Elder*."

Levi ignored Jordan's snark, knowing how hard it must be for Jordan not to pound Omar into flatbread. A few yards ahead, the hallway ended in a rotted wooden door. Levi and Jemma pushed it open. The "big room" wasn't all that big. It had a one-wall kitchen on the end, three round tables with chairs in the center, some ratty couches, and an Old TV.

"Jemma!" Shaylinn ran to the door and hugged her sister. "They found you."

The next half hour was a mix of mourning and celebration in the bunker under the Midlands. Levi didn't know which to feel, as he still had Omar to deal with. He finally brought his fingers to his mouth and whistled. "Listen up, everyone. We should make a plan to get you all out of here. I'd like to take you to Jack's Peak, where you'll have some protection until I can figure out how to get to the kids."

"What about the children?" Eliza asked. "We need to get them out of here."

"They're all alone..." Mary's words disintegrated into sobs.

Aunt Chipeta smiled at Levi. "We appreciate your wanting to protect us, but none of us could live with ourselves if we simply left. That you got us out of the harem has given everyone hope we will see our children again."

Perhaps there was some way they could all help. "I don't know what they do with liberated people. I hope they're not... Well, we need to find out. But Mason says the kids are in the boarding school or the caretaking facilities. The enforcers are going to be watching both closely for a while. So we need to be patient. And forgiving. I know this is really stressful on everyone, but we need to stand together. Love each other. Do you trust me?"

"Of course," Aunt Chipeta said.

"What's your plan, Levi?" Eliza asked.

Here goes. "First... I ask you all to hold your tongues and open your minds and hearts at what you're about to see. Jordan?"

The door opened, and Omar stepped into the room with Jordan behind him, broad-shouldered and menacing.

"Oh!" Shaylinn clapped her hand over her mouth.

"What's *he* doing here?" Mary asked.

"Did you capture him?" Eliza asked.

Levi smiled at Omar, hoping it didn't look forced. "He freed me and Jemma from the RC."

"Omar rescued us," Jemma said.

Eliza narrowed her eyes. "Why?"

"Let's see what Omar has to say?" Levi sat down so that Omar would have the floor. His little brother, at only sixteen, looked hunched and frail. His skin was pale, his eyes bloodshot and creased with heavy circles, and the black tattoo that peeked out from his sleeve made him look wild. A true "shell" if Levi had ever seen one.

"I didn't mean for anyone to die," Omar blurted out. "I just wanted to do something my father would be proud of. Show I was good enough." He rubbed the scar between his eyes. "But I'm not. And the task director lied to me." Omar heaved in a deep breath. "I don't know if I can ever make up for what I did, but—"

"You can't," Jordan said.

Omar looked at his hands and threaded his fingers together. "You're right." He glanced up, eyes bloodshot, then back at his hands, then up again. "I know you're right."

"What do you want?" Eliza's voice was low.

"To say I'm sorry."

"Sorry doesn't undo anything, Omar," Eliza said. "It doesn't bring Mark back."

"Why did you do it, really?" Jordan asked. "Your father wouldn't have been proud to see you in an enforcer's uniform."

Levi didn't understand Omar's logic either.

"So he could prove his dad was wrong about him," Shaylinn said. "That he had worth. Elder Justin was so mean to him. He was mean to me too."

"My father was honest," Levi said. "He never meant to hurt anyone."

"But he did." Shaylinn folded her arms. "And he never apologized. I don't mean to speak ill of your father, it's just... We've all hurt people without meaning to. Isn't that right, Omar?"

Omar nodded at Shaylinn. "I never wanted any of these horrible things to happen."

"Fine," Eliza said. "Then why didn't you move to the Safe Lands and leave us be?"

Omar's forehead wrinkled. "Do any of you remember when Papa Eli told my father to take me hunting with him and Elsu? And how my father reacted?"

Levi hung his head in memory of that awkward moment. Father *had* been cruel.

"The next day I took a rig to Crested Butte," Omar said, "hoping to scavenge something that would prove to my father that I wasn't a useless mouth to feed. Instead, I ran into some enforcers. They asked if I wanted to see the city and took me to meet the task director general. The city was amazing, and I wondered what it might be like to live there. The task director said I could, that he'd send some men to Glenrock to see if you all wanted to give the city a try as well."

Omar had walked right into the lions' den. If only Levi had reached out to him sooner.

"I told them to come while Father was in Denver City," Omar said. "I figured that when he returned and found me gone, he'd be relieved to finally be free of me."

"Omar..." Aunt Chipeta said.

Omar's words were a fist to Levi's gut. He'd truly believed their father hated him.

"It's true, and you all know it," Omar said, matter of fact. "I didn't really understand what they wanted. I was stupid, like always. But no one was supposed to get hurt." He heaved a deep sigh. "Anyway, I just wanted to explain and say I'm sorry. Because I am. And now I'll leave, and none of you will ever have to see me again." He walked toward the exit.

What? He's just going to leave? Levi started across the room to stop him.

But Jordan was already blocking the exit.

"One of the things that drove Elder Justin nuts about you was how you always run," Jordan said. "So prove your father wrong, Omar. Saying sorry isn't good enough. You need to stay and work to help put things right."

"I got Levi and Jemma out of the RC," Omar said.

"That's a start," Jordan said. "But this ain't over 'til were home. All of us. And this place ain't home."

Omar rubbed the scar on the bridge of his nose. "What else do you want me to do?"

"Sit down, and let Elder Levi talk." Jordan pushed Omar into a chair and went to sit beside Naomi.

A swell of pride filled Levi at Jordan's words. He looked around the room and said, "I'm not the elder unless that's what everyone wants."

"You're next in line," Naomi said.

"That may be, but Aunt Chipeta is the eldest." Levi nodded to where his aunt sat beside Jemma. "Then Mary, then Eliza, then Jordan, *then* me."

"Age doesn't matter," Aunt Chipeta said. "You're Elder Elias's heir. You're meant to be patriarch."

Levi agreed, but he didn't want to do this alone. "Papa Eli had an elder council to help him. I'd like one too."

So they formed a council: Mary, Aunt Chipeta, Eliza, Jordan, Levi, and Mason once he escaped as well. The five present council members crowded around one table to have their first official meeting. Jemma, Shaylinn, and Naomi went into the kitchen to make lunch. Omar sat alone on the sofa.

The council's first decree was that no one would leave the Safe Lands until every possible member of Glenrock had been rescued. They also discussed whether they should send a message to Jennifer and Mia and if they could be trusted, and ways they might try to free the children. Levi said that their efforts largely depended on Mason and Bender now.

Jemma approached the table and circled to stand behind Levi. She put her hands on his shoulders and squeezed. "The food is ready."

Levi turned to look up at her. He caught sight of the gold chain disappearing into the neckline of her dress and jumped up. "Elder Jordan!" He took Jemma by the hand and pulled her to Jordan's side of the table. "Will you marry us?"

Jemma gasped. Naomi hurried toward them from the kitchen.

"Oh, yes! Please do, Jordan," Aunt Chipeta said. "They should've been married days ago."

Jordan pushed up from his chair. "Really? Can I do that?"

Levi's heart raced. This was finally going to happen. His wedding to this beautiful woman. He removed the necklace from over Jemma's head and handed it to Jordan. "Only an elder can. And we are elders now."

"I'll do my best then." Jordan raised his voice. "Gather round, witnesses. We need your eyes. This man and woman wish—"

With a shout of protest, Aunt Chipeta, Mary, and Eliza all stood at once.

"Not right this moment, Jordan," Aunt Chipeta said.

"While this is far from the ideal circumstance, a bride deserves some time to prepare, both physically and spiritually," Eliza said.

Then the women whisked Jemma away to one of the bedrooms, leaving Levi speechless.

"But what about lunch?" Jordan called after them.

"Eat it," Naomi yelled. "We'll get some later."

And the boys were left alone.

Jordan walked toward the kitchen. "Guess I'll help myself then."

Omar's laugh pulled Levi's gaze to where his brother sat on the couch.

Levi went and sat beside him. "What's so funny?"

"Did you really think the women were going to let Jordan say, 'I declare you married' and be done with it?"

Levi fell back against the stale couch cushions. "That would have been nice."

They sat together. Omar was watching a show called *Easy Bake*, in which a woman was teaching how to make something called boule bread, which reminded Levi of Kosowe, a woman he didn't want to be thinking about just before his wedding.

Maybe this was the time to do something hard. To try and dismantle this unspoken wall between him and his youngest brother. "Omar," Levi took a deep breath. "Do you remember a couple years ago? When we stayed the night in Jack's Peak?"

Omar raised one eyebrow and smirked. "I remember."

Levi wished he hadn't. He forced himself to speak. "I'm hoping you'll... I don't think Jemma needs to, you know, know. I thought of telling her but... I was wrong even to—"

"You weren't engaged to Jemma then," Omar said. "And you didn't really do anything to be ashamed of."

Levi sat up straight. "I didn't?"

"You don't remember?"

"Only waking up in Kosowe's teepee." And seeing Omar's face.

"You kissed her. A lot. But that was it. All five of us slept in there. Beshup and Tsana got up at a decent hour, but you and Kosowe were dead to the world. I got bored and woke you up so we could go home."

Levi's face tingled at the realization that he had wrongly jumped to the worst possible conclusion. And Kosowe had let him. All this time the guilt had been for nothing. He looked at his brother in a new light. "Thank you, Omar."

Omar shrugged and looked back to the TV. "Glad to help clear your conscience."

Levi took a deep breath. Suddenly, he was trembling. "Omar... would you... That is, will you stand up with me? For the wedding?"

Omar turned his bloodshot eyes back to Levi and broke into a smile. "Sure."

The women bustled about all afternoon, making food and decorating the underground home with all manner of oddities. When Levi discreetly asked Aunt Chipeta about the fuss, she looked at him more seriously than he was prepared for. "I want to make sure Jemma has a wedding she deserves." She nodded toward Eliza and Naomi, who were making a bouquet out of pink and white tissues. "I think even the trivial things have a greater meaning right now. Plus, doing this for Jemma is a welcome distraction."

"I guess I didn't think about it that way," Levi said. "I just wanted to marry Jemma this minute."

Aunt Chipeta laughed. "As soon as Shaylinn and Mary finish putting together Jemma's dress, we should be ready. But while you're waiting, I suggest you take a shower. You look like you've been wearing the same thing for three days. I saw a shirt and a pair of pants in one of the bedrooms—don't come back until you've changed."

Levi did as he was told, though he discovered both the dark green long-sleeved button-up shirt and the dark blue pleated pants were way too big. When he returned to the main room and Mary saw him fisting the waistband, she threaded a black silk scarf through the belt loops.

Jordan and Omar laughed at Levi's outfit, so Mary put them to work moving the tables and setting up the chairs, which made an aisle that faced the shower curtain backdrop Aunt Chipeta had put up on the wall.

Then it was time.

Jemma stepped into the doorway, a princess in white. The other ladies stood and started to sing.

Here comes the bride dressed all in light,Radiant and lovely she shines in his sight.G ently she glides graceful as a dove,Meeting her bridegroom her eyes full of love.

Jemma walked toward Levi. She wore a sleeveless white dress with a short flowing skirt that showed off her legs. Her hair was long and loose, clipped back above one ear by a single tissue flower. A layer of sheer white fabric poofed over her hair, barely covering her face. The world's shortest veil.

Levi took hold of her hand, thinking he'd never let go.

"Witnesses," Jordan said. "This man and woman wish to become one. Let us hear their pledge and hold them to it." He looked at Levi. "Levi of Elias, you bring a request to the elders of Glenrock?"

"I want to marry Jemma of Zachary," Levi said.

Jordan turned to Jemma. "Jemma of Zachary, your favor has been petitioned. What's your response?"

"I accept the offer."

Jordan leaned close to his sister. "Even though he snores?"

She grinned and tugged on Levi's hand. "Yes."

Jordan straightened and looked at the other faces in the room. "Does anyone have reason to speak against this union?" When no one spoke, he asked, "What elder will speak for this couple's commitment to one another?"

Aunt Chipeta stood up. "I will."

"People of Glenrock, you have witnessed an offer of marriage, an acceptance, and an endorsement by a village elder." Jordan's face blanked, as if he'd forgotten what came next.

Levi held up the rings.

"Right." Jordan took the rings from Levi and held them on his palm. "Exchange these rings as a token of your promise to one another."

Levi and Jemma took a ring and slid it onto each other's fingers.

"All right then," Jordan said. "She's yours! Take her in your arms and—"

"Don't forget the Father!" Naomi said.

"Of course!" Jordan clapped his hands. "My wife is wiser than me. Will you both serve our Father, the God in heaven, better together than you could on your own?"

"We will," Levi and Jemma said together.

"Then I declare you married! Be fruitful and multiply, and stay true to the ways of our elders. Kiss her, Levi, and keep her 'til God takes you home."

The little remnant from Glenrock cheered.

Levi wrapped his arms around Jemma's waist and looked down into her eyes. "You know, since the invention of the kiss, there have only been *six* kisses that were rated the most passionate, the most pure. *This one* will leave them all behind."

And it did.

Chapter 42

The Safe Lands Guild had summoned Mason to appear before them in regard to the escape of the harem women. He'd heard rumors they'd summoned Omar as well, after Jemma and Levi disappeared from the RC, but so far no one had been able to locate him. He hoped his brother was somewhere safe.

An hour and a half before the scheduled meeting, Mason dressed in the new outfit he'd bought, thinking it better not to appear before the Guild in scrubs. He came into his kitchen and glanced at the clock in the glass of the oven door. Time to go.

As he walked toward the door, he noticed the framed picture that hung over his couch was crooked. He crossed the room—stalling, he knew—and pushed up one corner of the picture until it was even.

Something fell off the top of the frame and landed with a soft *thwup* on the back of the couch. Mason picked up a small black rectangle and stared at the tiny words *MiniComm* that were engraved just over an on-off switch. The device was turned on.

He'd seen these before. On Ciddah's desk at the SC and on top of her Wyndo screen the night of Lonn's liberation. She had to have put it there. Ciddah was helping Lawten spy on him.

Mason's throat swelled, making it hard to swallow. He blew out a shaky breath and sat down on the couch. She'd no doubt left this device in his home the night Kendall had given birth, which meant that whoever was listening should have heard all his radio conversations with Levi. And now Mason had been summoned. No excuse he could give would stand against his own voice making subversive plans. Should he ignore the summons and try to find his brothers?

But if the Guild knew what he'd been doing, why hadn't he experienced opposition when he'd helped the women escape?

He thought back to when Ciddah had gotten up and gone over to the Wyndo the night of Lonn's liberation. Had she turned off the device? Changed her mind about helping Lawten? Or maybe she wasn't working for Lawten, but gathering information instead. But for what or whom?

Still feeling like his heart was lodged in his throat, he placed the MiniComm in the exact location where Ciddah had left it on top of the picture.

He'd been nervous about the summons before, but now... Lord, help him. Suddenly, he felt very alone in this city. He should've left with the others.

But the children...

Without recordings of him and Levi plotting, he didn't believe they could prove he'd had anything to do with the escapes. There'd been no cameras that night, not with the power out, so there should be no images of him driving the women across the Safe Lands. And he had the clerk from BabyKakes as a witness—and supposedly Ciddah.

She'd become the one person he'd thought he could trust in this place.

Clearly, he couldn't trust anyone.

BOOK TWO

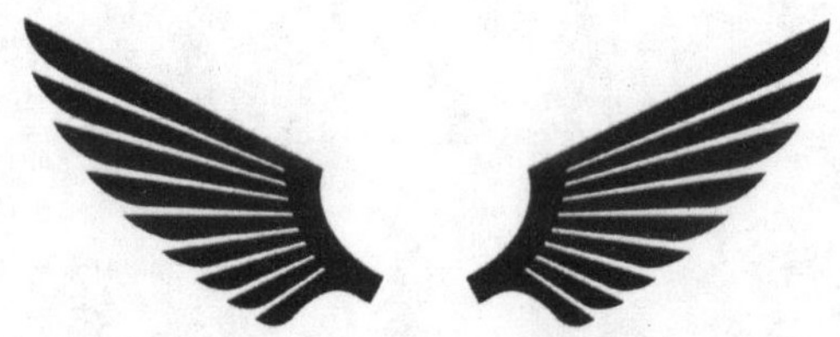

OUTCASTS

To my sister Beth Britton, for wanting to read book two so desperately.
Thanks for your enthusiasm and support.

PROLOGUE

JULY 2088

"Very truly I tell you, no servant is greater than his master, nor is a messenger greater than the one who sent him."
—John 13:16, NIV

John 13:16, NIV

Almost there.

Kendall strode around the curve of Belleview Drive and fixed her gaze on the messenger sign at the end of the block. The flying white envelope on a red circle flickered in the night.

She wanted to run—to at least jog—but held back, forcing her legs into long strides. She swung her arms and breathed in the scents of dryer sheets and waffle cones from the Belleview Laundry and Cinnamonster ice cream shop.

Barely four weeks had passed since she'd given birth in the Surgery Center, and only two since she'd moved out of the harem and back to the Midlands. Kendall's medic had told her to wait at least six weeks before doing serious exercise. So, Kendall walked everywhere, determined to firm up her abdomen, look normal again. Determined to forget.

She wasn't supposed to work for six weeks, either. But staying home with no baby to hold... Add to that her depressing thoughts, worry over the girls from Glenrock, and the task director general's summons—it had been too much. She'd begged Tayo to let her come back to the messenger office early.

Kendall picked up her pace. What could the task director want now? He'd taken everything from her. She'd served her term in the harem, had given the ultimate sacrifice. This couldn't be a surrogacy request. Safe Lands customs said she deserved a two-year reprieve for her service to the nation.

This summons had to be personal.

A taxi turned down Belleview and sped toward Kendall, its headlights blinding. She lowered her gaze. The vehicle passed—and the product expo on its side caught her eye.

The face of her son. The words "Welcome, Baby Promise" scrolled underneath.

Kendall stopped. Watched her son's face shrink away until the taxi vanished. Fortune was mocking her pain.

What kind of a name was Promise, especially for a boy? More Safe Lands strangeness. Her baby would always be Elyot to her.

Kendall choked back her sorrow and trudged the rest of the way to the messenger office. She pressed her fist against the pad, using her SimTag to let herself inside, and set her messenger bag on the front counter in the lobby.

A single bulb cast yellow light and hard shadows over the messenger workstations and rows of nearly empty package shelves. Kendall slipped behind the counter, her running shoes scuffing over the concrete floor. She continued down the first aisle of shelves, her shadow creeping along beside her.

This place had always been ghoulie at night.

The task clock hung outside Tayo's office door, located at the back. Kendall tapped her fist on it, officially tasking out for the night, and started back toward the lobby.

A low moan rose from the dark. She jerked her head around, spine tingling. Cocked her ears.

Silence.

Kendall swallowed, peered through the shelves on her right. "Hay-o? Who's here?"

A gargled breath. "Help me."

The words squeezed her throat. For a moment Kendall couldn't move. Pushing down her fear, she forced herself around the end of the shelves. Peeked down the next row.

Empty.

She inched toward the third one.

Nothing.

Kendall glanced at her messenger bag. Her portable Wyndo was inside. She could tap Enforcer 10 for help.

She bit her lip and eased around the fourth row. Halfway down, a man in a messenger uniform lay on the floor, one hand on his stomach, the other under his back. White-blond hair. Big feet.

"Chord?" Kendall ran to him.

Red everywhere, like a bottle of spilled Shower Paint. It had soaked Chord's white T-shirt and the top of his green shorts, puddling under him. Still spreading.

She swallowed the bitter burning of nausea. "What happened?"

Chord lifted his hand. Kendall reached for his bloody fingers, but he pointed upward, to a large box high on the shelves.

"You want the box?" she asked.

He nodded and choked out the word, "Hurry."

Kendall had to climb on the lowest shelf to reach the box. She held a shelf with her left hand and slapped the cardboard with her right, careful to use her arms and not put strain on her stomach. The box finally slid over the edge. She stepped down with it, keeping her hand underneath to catch it as it fell. It was light and open at the top. She set it on the floor and pulled out a messenger bag. Chord's? She met his gaze.

"Deliver," he rasped.

"You want me to deliver your messages?"

"To the... addressees. No one else. Secret."

She found four messages in his bag. Messages with no codes. In the Safe Lands, it was illegal to deliver mail off the grid. Enforcers monitored everything. She read the addresses. Chord worked the Sopris route, but these addresses were mostly in Old Town, which was her route.

"Chord, why do you...?" Kendall looked up to find him staring past her knees. Unblinking. Unseeing. His eyes dull, mouth half open, face slack.

A breath rattled past her lips. She spun around, slipping in the blood. She ran to the counter, withdrew her Wyndo from her own messenger bag, and tapped one zero. Her thumb—shaking over the glass screen—produced a one-eight-eight. She deleted the numbers and carefully tapped one zero again.

One ring, and a silver-haired female face appeared on the glass. Mimicking Luella Flynn, no doubt. "Enforcer 10. Where are you located?"

"Midlands-east-messenger-office." Kendall gasped in a deep breath. "A man's been hurt. He's bleeding. I think he's... dead. Oh, walls! Don't let him be dead!"

"Try to stay calm," the woman said. "Can you tell me what happened?"

Kendall's thoughts clouded, tears lacing every word. "I don't know. I didn't see. I came in and found him here."

"You found him dead?"

She stared at the woman on her Wyndo screen and set her messenger bag back on the counter. "No. He was just talking to me, but now he's only staring." She looked back down the aisle to where Chord lay. No change.

"Okay, I'm dispatching Enforcer 10," the woman said. "I see two SimTags at the address you gave me. ID#5–71–36, Chord Prezden and ID#1-W1, Kendall Collin. Is this Kendall?"

"Yes. And Chord is hurt."

"Kendall, do you see any weapons?"

A new wave of horror seized her. "I didn't." Had Chord been shot or stabbed? "Should I go back and look?"

"No, stay where you are," the woman said. "I need you to preserve the scene until Enforcer 10 arrives. Do you know the victim?"

"Yes! Chord tasks here." Tears were flowing down Kendall's cheeks now. She paced the length of the counter. How could this be happening? Who would kill Chord?

The front door whooshed open, bringing the smell of dryer sheets and waffle cones inside the lobby. Kendall spun around. A man stood on the other side of the counter. She screamed and dropped her Wyndo, which broke open on the concrete floor.

"Hey, sorry," he said. "Didn't mean to scare you."

The man looked familiar. He was wearing a messenger uniform, but he wasn't stationed here. Where had she seen him before? He had a 9X on his face. Was this Chord's murderer?

Trapped, Kendall crouched behind the counter to pick up her Wyndo. She was still holding Chord's messages in her hand and shoved them into the waistband of her shorts. She pulled the hem of her T-shirt over the messages and collected her Wyndo and the solar pack. Where was the back? She never understood how these things looked like transparent glass until they came apart. Technological magic was the worst kind. It made her feel ignorant for not comprehending how it worked.

Calm down! Look for it. She scanned the floor for any reflection.

The man stepped around the end of the counter, his messenger sneakers, bare legs, and green shorts a blur outside her focus. There! She spotted a rectangle of clear plastic across the floor, by the man's foot. She blinked and looked up to his face.

Alone with a strange Xed man who was blocking her way to the exit and might be a murderer. No Wyndo. Not good. If she survived this night, she vowed to reconsider a SimTalk implant.

The man's dark eyebrows rose, causing his forehead to wrinkle. "You okay?"

He was young, his voice soft and a little hoarse, like he had a cold. Cute. Boyish, though his jaw and upper lip were shaded in the soft scruff of a first attempt at a beard. He was likely harmless. Not every man was like Lawten. But this one looked *so* familiar.

The answer came a second later. Omar. The new rover. Tayo had introduced him at Monday's staff meeting. See? It was okay. He had a right to be here. So... probably not a murderer, then. Right?

"Hey." Omar crouched and picked up the back of her Wyndo from the floor beside his foot. He held it out, baring thick black SimArt lines that swirled and knotted their way up his left arm. A chain. "Don't worry. It's probably not broken. For bits of plastic and glass, they're pretty sturdy."

She snatched the back from him and fumbled with the pieces, trying to put the contraption together. She had the solar pack upside down, so she flipped it over and clicked it into place.

Enforcer 10 was coming. She'd be okay.

"Aren't you that Kendall girl from the ColorCast?" Omar asked. "The queen? The one who just had the, uh...?" His gaze flicked down to her belly.

"No," Kendall said, hating that she'd lied. Lawten had made her afraid of everyone. Her legs shook from squatting so long, yet she felt safer crouched against the counter.

She snapped on the back of the Wyndo, but when she tried to power it up, the glass remained dark. *No!*

"So, what's your name, femme?" Omar asked.

She met his gaze then. A risk. But perhaps conversation would distract him until Enforcer 10 arrived. His eyes were slate blue, rimmed in thick, dark lashes. Natural eyes that made her think he might have once been an outsider too. His skin looked healthy—she could see actual pores. No Roller Paint. But he was marked 9X. Weird. Outsiders weren't usually nines, but they did tend to get an X or two before they figured out how to live here. Especially the men. Maybe he hadn't been in the Safe Lands long. Maybe he wasn't like the others.

Maybe he was.

"Why do you want to know my name?" she asked, tempted to look at Chord's body, wanting to help him in case it wasn't too late, but wanting to get away even more.

Omar's lips spread into a slow grin that completely lit up his face. "Okay, never mind. Um..." He ran his fingers through his hair, creating three thick waves that swooped back over his head. "Have you seen Chord? I was supposed to meet him."

His words threw the fear back in her face. "You were supposed to meet him?"

"That's what I said." His eyes narrowed. "Are you sure you're okay?"

Shards of ice slid down her back. If Omar had hurt Chord, would he hurt her too? Kendall couldn't help it. Her body betrayed her, and she glanced down the aisle to where Chord lay.

Omar followed her gaze and gasped. "Wait, what?" His voice rose in pitch, panicked. "Is that Chord?" He ran down the aisle. "No! Why?" He picked up Chord's messenger bag, reached inside it. "His messages are gone." He turned back to Kendall. "What happened? What'd you do?"

He wanted Chord's messages. The ones Chord said were secret. "*Me?*" Kendall stood, fumbled for her bag, and backed toward the end of the counter. "I didn't do anything. I just came in to task out for the night and found him there. He said—"

"He spoke?" Omar walked toward her, his eyes bearing down, intense.

Kendall turned and ran around the end of the counter.

"Whoa! Hold on!" Chord's bag clutched in hand, Omar jumped against the counter, slid his legs up over the top, and landed on the other side, cutting off Kendall's exit. He was standing so close she could smell the hint of metallic mint on his breath. He was a user.

She wanted to scream but had no lungs or legs or breath at all.

"What did he say?" Omar asked. "Did he say anything about his messages?"

Kendall shook her head, almost a tremble, back and forth, back and forth. Chord had said to tell no one about the messages. And if Omar had killed Chord, he would kill her too. She tried to walk around him, but he stepped to the side, blocking her way.

Where was Enforcer 10? *Hurry!*

"Please." Omar dropped Chord's bag on the floor and grabbed her shoulders. "It's important."

Beastly hands squeezing... Kendall screamed.

Omar quickly let go, swallowed, and held up his hands, palms facing her. "I'm not going to hurt you. I just need to know what he said."

Lies. Lies. Her voice came in a rush, sounding like someone else. "All he said was, 'Help me,' so I tapped Enforcer 10." *Can I go now? Please let me go. Need to walk. Need to run.*

Omar closed his eyes and exhaled a breath that took four inches off his height. That stopped Kendall, confused her. He wasn't exactly acting like a killer. And the mention of

Enforcer 10 being on the way didn't seem to alarm him. But why had he been going to meet Chord here? And why did he seem to be looking for the messages?

The sound of a siren grew in the distance—finally!—giving strength to her legs. Kendall darted past Omar, but he caught hold of her messenger bag and looked inside it, deflating again when he found it empty.

Kendall snatched it back and walked toward the door, holding her wrist against her hip to keep Chord's messages from sliding past her waistband. She stepped outside just as Enforcer 10 arrived.

The enforcers questioned Kendall and Omar, scanned their bodies for blood residue—finding it only on their shoes—then released them. The process took so long that Kendall had mostly calmed down by the end, though she kept Omar in sight. He hadn't hurt her, but he still could.

She tried to slip away, but a familiar voice called her name. "Kendall! Come say hay-o, you sweet femmy."

It was Luella Flynn, the ColorCast co-host and most famous face in the Safe Lands, waving her signature handheld microphone like a flag, her silver hair shining brightly under the streetlamps. Kendall groaned but knew if she ignored Luella now, the woman would simply invite herself to Kendall's apartment later. Might as well get it over with.

Kendall walked up to Luella and Alb, the cameraman who was Luella's shadow. Luella looked stellar, as always. Tonight she wore a purple-and-yellow houndstooth jumper over a silver bodysuit. She'd been wearing the tinsel weave in her hair for a few weeks now. Silver: a trend that had lingered longer than the celebrity usually allowed. Half the Safe Lands had been dressed in silver since Lonn's liberation four weeks ago. Maybe the purple and yellow was a sign that the fashions were about to get brighter.

Luella kissed both Kendall's cheeks, then spoke into her microphone. "Kendall Collin, our former queen, can you tell us what happened here tonight?"

"I don't know if I'm allowed. The enforcers didn't say."

"You can tell me, femmy. Lawten okays everything I record before it's broadcasted, so no need to worry."

Lawten. The man was on a first-name basis with far too many women.

"I understand a man was murdered tonight?" Luella said, eyes shining as if death was thrilling. "Chord Prezden? And you called Enforcer 10."

"Well, I don't know if he was murdered. But he is dead." Though if Luella knew that Chord was dead, she knew all that Kendall knew—except for the messages tucked into the waistband of Kendall's shorts.

"Did you witness the murder?" Luella asked.

"No," Kendall said. "I had just finished my shift and found him when I went to task out. There was no sign of any attacker."

"Can you describe how he looked for the Safe Lands viewers? How was he killed? Did he suffer?"

"I..." Chord's dying body flashed back to her mind, helpless, bleeding.

"We really didn't see much of anything, Miss Flynn," a soft voice said.

Kendall looked just behind her. Omar stood there, his attention focused wholly on Luella Flynn. Where had he come from? And what did he want? Did he suspect she had the messages?

Luella's eyes narrowed. "And you are...?"

"Omar Strong. I'm the new rover. I came by just after Kendall called Enforcer 10. Chord and I had plans for tonight. We were supposed to meet here and then go to Dreamland. Have you ever been?"

Luella pressed her hand over her chest, displaying her purple-and-silver-striped fingernails. "I adore Dreamland Disco. Most turbulent music in the Midlands." She smiled and set her hand on her hip. "And you're a clever raven to change the subject. How'd you get your X, Mr. Strong? Don't bother lying, either. I can look it up."

"Look it up then," Omar said. "Pleasure meeting you, Miss Flynn. Sorry we couldn't be more helpful. Kendall? Are you ready to go?"

His question took Kendall off guard, as did the way he held out his hand like they were together. Pairing up was all Safe Lands men ever wanted. "Um..." She *did* want to get away from the microphone and the woman holding it, but she didn't want to give Omar the wrong idea. She stepped beside him and glanced at Luella, who watched them with raised brows.

Omar took hold of her hand anyway. His palm was rough, like he tasked outdoors. She wanted to let go, embarrassed to touch a stranger in such a familiar way, but she didn't want Luella to ask any more questions.

"Good night," Omar said, pulling Kendall away from the camera.

"Maybe I'll see the two of you at Dreamland," Luella called after them.

"Maybe," Omar said, without looking back.

But Kendall looked back at Luella three times as they walked away, worried that the woman would follow them, see they weren't really together, ask more questions. Then she changed fears and hoped Luella would come so Kendall wouldn't be alone with Omar. But Luella finally waved her microphone at one of the enforcers and stepped into the crowd, Alb on her heels. Gone.

Kendall pulled her hand from Omar's grip, and they continued walking side by side, though Kendall's senses were on alert. It was only another few yards to the corner where she could wave a cab and get away. "You're asking for trouble, playing games with Luella Flynn."

Omar shrugged one shoulder. "You looked like you wanted to escape. I was trying to help."

She *had* wanted to get away from Luella. "But the way you cut her off and didn't answer her question about your X... You don't want her as an enemy."

He shoved his hands into the front pockets of his shorts. "Aw, she doesn't scare me."

Fool of a man. "She should. Luella Flynn is the most powerful woman in the Safe Lands."

Those bright eyes of his met hers again. "Why'd you say you weren't Kendall Collin?"

She didn't owe him any explanations. "How *did* you get your X?" Murdering someone, perhaps?

His smile lit up his face and eyes, making him look even younger. She wanted to ask how old he was but doubted she'd get the truth.

Omar stopped walking and turned to face her, hands still stuffed into his pockets. "Can I walk you home, Kendall?"

It could have been a line from one of the Old movies Kendall had seen as a child. Men didn't say such things in the Safe Lands. "No, thank you."

Omar pulled his hands from his pockets and stepped toward the curb. "Let me wave you a cab, then. I don't like the idea of you walking alone with a murderer on the loose."

Again with the chivalry. How could she know whether or not it was an act? He had a macho way about him, though he wasn't much taller than she was. He had a little muscle on his arms, but if she wasn't recovering from childbirth, she'd bet she could run faster than he could. "I like walking. It's why I task for the messenger office."

"Okay." He pocketed his hands again. "Well, good night, Kendall. Be careful." He flashed one last wide smile and walked off down the sidewalk.

What a weird man. Boy. Person. She forced herself to stop watching him and waved a cab. Sure, she preferred to walk, but Omar had made a good point. No need to tempt a murderer.

Not until she was safe in her apartment with the door locked did she remove the messages from the waistband of her shorts. She carried them to her kitchen table and spread them on the glass surface.

Four white envelopes addressed to four different people: Dane Skott, Ruston Neil, Domini Bentz, and Charlz Sims. None had a grid code or return address. Three were private residences, and the fourth was an MO Box from her own branch.

She didn't recognize any of the names. But Kendall had lived in the Safe Lands only a few months before she'd gotten pregnant and been sent to the harem, so she'd never met many people outside the messenger office. Chord had always been kind, had never tried to pair up. He'd been a real friend. Kind and authentic. And if delivering these messages was his dying wish, Kendall would make it happen, murderer or not.

Chapter 1

Defying any government was a dangerous game. And while Safe Lands enforcers considered rebellion an X-able offense, the acts that inspired rebellion were far greater crimes, in Mason's opinion. Crimes against humanity and liberty. Crimes of manipulation and terror.

Ciddah would likely disagree.

Mason pushed the beautiful woman from his thoughts and entered the train station. Zane had told him to find locker 127. The lockers were located outside the gate. He found number 127 easily and tapped onto the pad the code Zane had given him.

The locker clicked open. Inside, Mason found a small metal box. He opened the lid and removed a pair of black gloves that supposedly held a generic SimTag in the right hand. The metal box had somehow concealed the SimTag's location, which would now appear on the grid.

Ever since rebels had cut the official SimTag from Mason's hand, he had to choose whether or not to carry it with him. Today he'd left it in his apartment, hoping those monitoring him might think he was watching the ColorCast or sleeping. But he couldn't pass through the gate from the Highlands to the Midlands without a SimTag of some kind, hence these gloves.

He pulled them on, shut the locker, then walked to the Midlands turnstile and tapped his right fist—his right *glove*—on the SimPad. The red turnstile light flashed green, and Mason walked through.

Of all the remnant of Glenrock, only he, Mia, and Mia's mother, Jennifer, still resided in the Highlands. The others were now in hiding in the Midlands under the protection of the Black Army rebels. Except Omar, who had a Midlands apartment.

Mason took the train to the Belleview station and got off. He found locker 127 in that train station and deposited the gloves into the metal box inside. Now, without a SimTag on his person, he should be invisible to enforcers monitoring the grid. But that didn't mean he wasn't being followed.

He thought back to his trial before the Safe Lands Guild, and their accusations. Though they hadn't been able to prove he'd been involved in the harem escape, Lawten Renzor, the task director general of the Safe Lands, had said they were watching him.

So as Mason made his way down Belleview Drive, he scanned the street and sidewalks for suspicious persons. This was his first time in the Midlands, and its dullness surprised him. The structures and fake vegetation were the same strange colors—he passed a building of turquoise bricks with pale pink shrubs out front—but the place lacked the cleanliness and polished luxuriousness of the Highlands.

There were plenty of Wyndo screens flashing the latest mimic styles and product expositions to the public, but they were caked with dust and grime and the occasional cobweb. The streets were cracked and dirty. The buildings were flaking with patches of paint that covered graffiti. Some had graffiti still, doubtlessly put there by rebels. Mason passed by some that said, "The Black Army wants you" and "Enforcers are evil."

It wasn't only the scenery that was more rundown than the Highlands: Even the Midlands people didn't seem as extravagant. Sure, silver was everywhere as people mimicked Finley Gray and Luella Flynn, but there was less Roller Paint here. And Mason couldn't be certain, but it seemed like less cosmetic surgery as well.

A plane flew overhead and Mason stopped to watch it. All his life he'd seen them and wondered. Now he knew the Safe Lands sent planes to Wyoming to trade and to other places to scavenge. Since there were people here in Colorado and in Wyoming as well, there were likely other civilizations in the world too. Perhaps the Safe Lands Guild knew of more.

Mason took a deep breath and continued on, recalling Levi's directions to the rebel meeting place. His older brother had never been great with details, but so far Mason had encountered no obstacles or confusion. He walked past the G.I.N. store, past the charge station, and stopped in front of the Sim Slingers SimArt shop where Omar officially tasked, though his little brother also did various jobs for Bender that the Safe Lands Registration Department didn't know about. Besides Mason, Mia, and Jennifer, Omar was the only other outsider who was still officially registered as a Safe Lands national.

A steady beat throbbed from within the shop. The windows were Wyndo viewing glass, and Mason found himself watching the image of a technician altering SimArt on a computer while a SimArt flower on her client's shoulder changed colors. The technology reminded Mason of painting. No wonder Omar liked it.

Sim Slingers stood beside the Cinetopia Theater on Whetstone Road, separated by an alley. That was where Mason needed to go. He slipped down the narrow street, then poured on the speed, hoping to reach the corridor before anyone passed by on the street behind. He scanned the alley for the break in the wall that supposedly led to the back of theater nine, which was where Bender's rebels met.

Mason looked over his shoulder more often than he should, which caused him to almost miss the narrow opening in the cement wall of the theater. He darted into the corridor. Ahead, two men stood beside a door, looking like pillars.

Mason walked up to them and stopped, unsure what to say.

"Name?" Pillar One asked.

"Eagle," Mason said, which was short for his radio call sign, Eagle Eyes, and the code name Levi had told him to use for meetings.

Pillar Two pulled out a SimScanner and ran it over Mason's body, the dull buzz seeming to prolong the awkwardness of the moment. "He's clean."

Pillar One stepped aside. "Go on in."

"Thanks." Mason entered the building and passed down a dark hallway that let out in the left front corner of a small movie theater. The low rumble of Bender's voice signaled that the meeting had already begun.

The theater held maybe a hundred seats, all covered in thick red fabric. According to Levi, Jakk, the man who operated the theater, was one of Bender's rebels. Years ago, he'd built a wall over the interior entrance to theater nine to offer a secure meeting location for Safe Lands rebels. The only entrances now were through the back alley or a chute in the floor that led to an underground storm drain. The rest of the theater was open for business and showed the latest Safe Lands feature films to the public.

There were maybe two dozen people scattered in the seats in the front three rows of the theater, all eyes on the rebel called Bender, who stood in front of the darkened movie screen.

Bender looked to be in his fifties—too old to exist legally in the Safe Lands. His forehead was a mass of soft wrinkles, and a short gray beard covered his cheeks and chin. A scar had melted the skin over his left eye so that he always appeared to be squinting. He wore all black. Fitting for a man of the shadows.

Mason spotted Levi in the second row and made his way toward him as Bender continued his speech. Levi still had a small scab on the bridge of his nose, which was now slightly crooked since he'd never had it fixed after Omar had broken it.

"...learned a valuable lesson in all this. Liberations are a sham. They're not filmed live. We should've known, really. It's always been obvious that they edited things out. Just never suspected... I take full responsibility for failing Lonn."

Mason slid past the knees of those sitting in the second row: Shaylinn, Jordan, Levi. Jemma, Levi's wife, scooted down, leaving the seat between her and Levi open for Mason.

He sat down, thankful to have finally arrived. "Thanks, Jemma."

"You're late," Levi whispered.

"Sorry. My rebel skills are not as proficient as yours, brother." Mason truly didn't want to be here. The news he was carrying would only depress everyone further.

Zane sat in the row ahead of Mason. The rebel teen had been shot in the leg trying to help them free the women from the harem and still walked with a limp. He had short, spiky brown hair, was missing one ear, and had three spirals of gold metal looped through one nostril. He raised his hand and leaned back in his seat, which cracked under his weight. "You think Lonn is dead, then?" he asked Bender. "You think that's what liberation truly is?"

"Don't know what to think," Bender said. "I don't feel like he's dead. Either way, his liberation has people scared, and rightly so. We've lost eleven that I know of in the past year. We need to assure our followers that the Black Army is strong. That we have purpose and safety. And we need more members."

"Maybe you should stop using the messenger offices." Omar's soft voice came from the back of the room.

Mason looked over his shoulder and saw that his little brother was sitting alone in the very top row of the theater. The light on the end of the personal vaporizer he was holding to his lips glowed blue, which meant he was inhaling.

"Someone knew Chord was up to something," Omar said, his voice hoarse from the vapor.

"You were on watch, Omar," Bender said. "Why didn't you see anything?"

Omar didn't answer. He simply blew out a plume of black vapor.

Mason winced at his little brother's attitude. He understood it, but Omar was in a dangerous place right now, and picking fights with the head of the rebels was ignorant.

"We can't stop using the messenger office," Bender said. "It's vital to communication between rebels and potential recruits. Levi, since Chord was killed when one of yours was on watch, you provide a replacement."

"I don't think so," Levi said, and his tone made Mason flinch. "It's one thing to ask us to man your lookout posts, but making your deliveries is too much. We don't want to get involved in your little war."

"I'm not asking," Bender said. "Find me a replacement for Chord, and I want your people helping us scout for new members."

Levi made to stand, but his best friend, Jordan, held him back. "Why should we help the Black Army?" Jordan asked. "We just want to get to our kids and get out of this dung pile."

"Levi and I made a deal." Bender scowled, which made his scarred eye close as if he were winking angrily. "I let you and your people stay in my bunker and keep you fed. In exchange, you do what I say. Once you're gone, you're gone. Until then, you work for me."

"You want my pregnant wife to walk up to people and say, 'Hey, you want to help take over the government?'" Jordan asked. "Are you nuts?"

"None of you will recruit," Bender said. "Just be on the lookout. I want the names of people who've been Xed, complainers, people who've lost a lifer. Ask questions. Listen. You get the feeling someone might join, tell me and we'll make contact. But be careful. Some of these people might be spies. Otley's not a shell. He didn't like that you outsiders got your women out of the harem and made him look incompetent."

"I'd like to volunteer," Shaylinn said. "To work in Chord's position."

"Um, no she wouldn't," Jordan said, glaring at his baby sister.

"*Yes*, I would," Shaylinn said. "I'm tired of staying indoors."

Jemma leaned past Mason's knees to look down to where Shaylinn sat at the end of the row. "It's not safe, Shay. Your face is plastered all over the Safe Lands."

"Then we can dye my hair or something." Shaylinn was tall for fourteen, but it would be foolish for her to go outdoors with Safe Lands enforcers looking for her. They'd impregnated her in the Surrogacy Center just before the women had escaped the harem, and the task director general wanted her back.

"We could certainly create a convincing disguise," Bender said. "Did you make a connection to Kendall Collin when you were in the harem, Miss Shaylinn?"

"Yes." Shaylinn leaned forward on her chair and bounced, as if Bender's attention were a special gift. "She was my mentor."

"Stop talking, Shay," Jordan said.

"You'll be perfect," Bender said. "I'll have Red come by this evening to work on a dis—"

"No." Jordan stood up and strangled the back of the chair in front of his. "She's not doing this."

Levi stood as well. "Omar will take Chord's place."

"But *Levi*." Shaylinn leaned past Jordan and fixed her gaze on Levi, big brown eyes blinking, lips turned in a frown. "I want to help. Please?"

"Omar already knows the messenger office, Shay, so he's the logical choice."

How very diplomatic of Levi to make it sound like Omar was merely the best candidate for the job when Mason knew his brother would never send a fourteen-year-old girl to be a spy. Omar was only sixteen, but Levi didn't have a lot of options.

"I'm just a part-time rover," Omar whined from the back. "I can't guarantee I'll get the right shifts."

"The shifts don't matter," Bender said. "New messages will show up in your sorter."

"Then that's settled," Levi said, sitting back down.

"Good." Jordan fell back to his seat as well.

Shaylinn slouched and scowled at her lap. She might not look pregnant, but that didn't change the fact that there was a child growing inside her. Perhaps once she began to show she would stop volunteering for risky positions.

"That's all I have for today," Bender said. "Levi, feel free to use the theater as long as you have need." Bender walked toward the exit.

Over half the people stood to leave. Levi climbed over the front row seats and chased Bender. He caught up with him just before the exit. Jordan got up and squeezed past Shaylinn, then met Levi down front.

With the movement of so many people leaving, Mason couldn't hear what Levi and Bender were talking about. Shaylinn got up from her seat at the end of the row and scooted down until she sat beside Mason.

Jemma, still sitting on Mason's left, leaned over his lap. "Shay, why do you insist on antagonizing him?"

"I just want to do something important," Shaylinn said. "Soon I'll have a kid and my adventuring days will be over."

"I'm no expert on the subject," Mason said, "but my mother always claimed that raising her boys was her greatest adventure."

"Well said, Mason." Jemma patted his arm. "See, Shay? Adventure is coming! Oh, Levi is waving me over. Excuse me."

Mason twisted his knees to the side to let Jemma pass. Once she was down the stairs, Shaylinn lowered her voice to a whisper. "Were you able to find an answer to my question?" She winced, like she wasn't quite sure she wanted to know.

Mason could relate. "I'm sorry, Shay. I've been distracted lately with the trial." And there was the fact that Mason wasn't eager to learn the answer. This mystery donor from Wyoming, who was supposedly the genetic father of the baby Shaylinn was carrying, troubled him. But the alternative was to hope she was carrying Omar's child, which was an equally disturbing idea. "I should be able to find out this week." A promise he would have to keep this time.

"Thank you," Shaylinn said. "I mostly just want to make sure I wasn't infected during the procedure. I heard Levi and Jem talking, and, well... Levi thinks I am."

Mason's older brother was paranoid. "The goal of the Surrogacy Center is to produce healthy children, Shay, don't forget."

"But Kendall got infected."

"Yes, but my understanding is that Kendall's donor was infected."

Shaylinn wrinkled her nose. "And you think mine wasn't?"

Oh, he hoped not. "That's my theory."

She smiled the same smile her siblings, Jemma and Jordan, had. One that bared full lips and perfect teeth. "Is it frightening living up there all alone?"

"The trial was a difficult time," Mason said. "But since they acquitted me, I've been treated like any other Safe Lands national. And when I'm working, I'm too busy to worry." Worrying wasn't logical, anyway.

"If you'll all quiet down, we need to discuss some things," Levi said, facing those who remained: the remnant from Glenrock and Levi's Safe Lander friend Zane. Levi stood in front of the movie screen, in the same place Bender had spoken from. Jemma and Jordan now sat in the front row. "First, I want to hear from Mason."

Wonderful. May as well get the worst over with. Mason scooted to the edge of his seat. "I'll start with some news from the harem. Jennifer and Mia are both pregnant."

The other women gasped and murmured around him. He wondered how their reactions might differ if they knew Mia had gotten pregnant on her own just days before she was scheduled for her ETP procedure. It was a fact he'd decided to keep to himself. But that now made two people from Glenrock who had contracted the thin plague. Omar and Mia.

Mason needed to find a cure.

"That's regrettable," Levi said. "But remember, we've already voted that we're not going after Mia and her mother. It's too risky to try to rescue those who will likely refuse to come. So, this is no surprise. They made their choice."

"Thank you for telling us, though," Aunt Chipeta said to Mason.

Indeed. Better to find out from him than from Luella Flynn on the Safe Lands Color-Cast. A sob from Mary spurred Mason to change the subject. "How am I to communicate with you without the radios?" Mason asked. Omar had destroyed that communication line before his change of heart. "Are we strictly sending paper messages now?"

"I'm getting you an untraceable Wyndo," Zane said. "I'll have it soon. Levi, Jordan, and Omar already have them. You'll be able to tap them on that. Just know that everything deletes after it's sent or read. That way, if you lose it or someone tries to take a look, everyone is safe."

"What did you find out about the kids?" Levi asked.

Mason took a deep breath. "The nursery is on the sixth floor of the Medical Center. I haven't been able to get over there yet. The older kids are in the boarding school. I've studied the school from the outside, but it's as much of a fortress as the Safe Lands itself. Penelope's class walks to the park every Tuesday. I'm going to attempt to make contact with her next time."

"Tell her I love her," Aunt Chipeta—Penelope's mother—said.

"What's taking you so long?" Jordan asked. "It's been a month since we got the women out of the harem. You should have talked to Penny by now."

"I'm being cautious," Mason said. "My concern is that one of the teachers will see us speaking and perhaps not allow her to leave the school anymore."

"Still, you could have tried," Jordan said.

"With tasking in the SC and the trial, I haven't had time," Mason said. "And even though they acquitted me, I'm afraid I'm being watched."

"Of course you're being watched," Jordan said. "Figure out who it is and ditch them."

"It's not as easy as someone following me everywhere," Mason said. "I'm not even sure what to look for. I mean, I found a MiniComm in my apartment."

"What's a MiniComm?" Jemma asked.

"Exactly," Mason said. "I've since learned that it's some sort of recording device."

"They transmit," Zane said. "I'll come sweep your apartment."

"Thank you," Mason said, thankful that Zane was their friend. "But don't disturb anything you find. I don't want them to know I know they're listening. If something disappears, I'll look suspicious. Like I have something to hide."

"You do," Jordan said.

"No, he's right," Zane said. "Leaving things be will keep them off his back."

"Another thing," Mason said. "When I first spoke to the task director general, he mentioned that I could task in Research. I might ask him for a reassignment."

"Why?" Jemma asked. "You're in a good place in the Surrogacy Center."

Mason looked at his hands clasped together between his knees. "Ciddah put the MiniComm in my apartment."

"You're sure?" Jemma asked. "Why would your boss do that?"

"And what was she doing in your apartment?" Jordan asked.

Mason didn't want to lift that boulder, so he kept talking. "I think she's assisting Lawten—the task director general. I can't imagine I'll be able to learn much under her... observation."

"But you need to be at the Surrogacy Center for Mia and Jennifer," Aunt Chipeta said.

"It's too late to help Mia and Jennifer," Mason said. "But if I left the SC and tasked in Research, I'd have better access to learning about the disease. A better chance at finding a cure."

"Hang finding a cure, Mason," Levi said. "A cure is not our goal. Stop wasting your time and get to the kids."

"The Tasker G is not going to let you learn anything, anyway, you know," Omar said from the back of the theater. "All the man does is lie."

"And if you go to a new task, you'll have to start over," Jemma said, her soft voice a soothing change from Levi and Omar's sharp criticism. "You need Ciddah."

He *wanted* to spend time with Ciddah, but he didn't need anyone. Mason had always been fine on his own. "I don't trust her."

"Mason," Jemma said, "you can't trust the task director general either."

Point taken. "I simply think it would be good to put distance between myself and Ciddah." Why couldn't he be stronger? Tell Levi no. Or be strong enough to smash his feelings for that infernal woman.

"It doesn't matter if you trust her," Levi said. "You can't trust anyone in the Safe Lands. Stop thinking of her as a person. She's the enemy, Mase. Use her to get what you need so we can all get out of here."

Use her. Mason had already abused his relationship with Ciddah a great deal, and he didn't like the heaviness his actions had brought to his heart. Ciddah had abused their relationship too, planting that MiniComm. But somehow Levi's suggestion seemed worse. More cutthroat. Sinister. Evil for evil.

Though why should Mason care? Ciddah had been toying with him from the start. None of her words could be trusted. Levi was right. Mason needed to forget his feelings for Ciddah and do his job, find out how to free the children so they could get their people out of the Safe Lands before any more became infected.

But he couldn't give up his search for a cure, either. Especially not now that both Omar and Mia were infected.

Yes, the children needed to come first. But Mason would continue his research, no matter what Levi said. There was simply too much at stake.

Chapter 2

"You. Have a. SimTalk tap. From... Red."

The electronic voice of Omar's SimTalk implant roused him from his stim nap. The remnant from Glenrock was still here, so he hadn't been nodding long. "Answer," he said.

"Hey, trigger, where are you?" Red's voice came tinny in his ear.

"Theater."

"Be there in five. Wait for me?"

"Sure." Omar sucked in a long breath on his personal vaporizer. He watched his brother Levi ascend the theater steps to where Omar had claimed a seat in the back. His PV was filled with a combination of meds, grass, and brown sugar—low doses of the stims to keep Levi from strangling him. Though that looked like it might be about to happen anyway.

Omar closed his eyes and held the vapor in his lungs, savoring the way the stims eased the ache in his soul.

Levi's footsteps scuffed in the row in front of Omar. "How could you mess this up?"

Omar blew out a stream of vapor and opened his eyes. He still hadn't gotten used to the way Levi's nose looked. His brother hadn't gotten it fixed—on purpose, as a reminder to Omar of his betrayal. "Don't yell at me."

"You were late, weren't you? You were late meeting Chord."

Omar paused to think how to answer, hesitating enough that Levi kept talking.

"Why were you late, Omar?"

"Between Sim Slingers and the messenger office, I'm tasking two locations. Give me a break." But he didn't deserve one. Chord was dead. It should have been him.

"You told me you were done at Sim Slingers at five. You were supposed to meet Chord at eight. Was three hours not enough time for you to get from Sim Slingers to the messenger office? What is it... three blocks?"

Levi's interrogations only made Omar feel worse. "I went to dinner."

"Where?"

"Does it matter?" What was done was done. The dead didn't come back.

Levi's expression actually softened a bit. "Look, Bender put me in charge of certain things. I don't like it any more than you, but I'm in his debt right now. So where were you?"

"Just because you're elder—"

"*Where*, Omar?"

"At the Paradise, okay? Eating dinner—"

"With Red."

It wasn't a question. Levi had been on Omar's case for spending time with Bender's errand girl—a crazy, wild, and physically friendly femme. Omar narrowed his eyes. "What makes you think I was with Red?"

Levi barked out his disgust. "Omar, I'm not stupid. I know she lives in the Paradise."

"I'm not stupid, either." *I'm not.*

"Could have fooled me, brother. All you had to do was show up at eight at the messenger office and bring the messages back to Bender. Simple. Now Chord is dead. The messages are missing, and Bender is all worked up over it."

"See, I don't get that," Omar said. "They've never been *Bender's* messages before. And if Bender wanted them, why not ask Chord for them himself?"

"Zane thinks Chord was murdered because he discovered something important. My guess is that Bender knew Chord had information to bring him and wanted your help throwing Otley off track. But Otley's men got to Chord before he delivered his messages. So, thanks to you, we'll never know what they said."

Great. Just what Omar needed: more guilt. "I didn't kill him, Levi."

"No, but you're so consumed with this place, with that... vapo stick, that you can't even think straight."

"Do you hear me sniffing, brother? No, because I'm vaping my allergy meds. And the ACT treatment." And a little added sweetness to take the edge off Levi's lectures.

Levi paled a bit at Omar's mention of the ACT treatment. *Elder Levi* hated that Omar was infected with the thin plague. So, Omar did his best to bring it up as often as he could.

"I wish you'd get your act together," Levi said.

That was all the lecture Omar could take for today. "No one respects me. I'm sick of it." At sixteen, Omar was too young to rally older men to the rebels' cause, and those who knew him knew he'd betrayed their village to Safe Lands enforcers. Even after he'd helped Levi, Jemma, and Zane escape the prison and apologized to everyone, people still treated him badly.

"It's going to take time, Omar. It hasn't even been two months since Glenrock was destroyed."

"But working two jobs isn't fair. And now I've got to worry about Otley's men watching me too."

"Contrary to what these flakers in the Safe Lands believe, life is not fair, Omar. Sometimes you get dealt a bad hand. Sometimes you earn it. But you can deal with it or drown. I'm not going to coddle you. I need you to do your share."

"I'm fine doing my share. But why should I do more than everyone else?"

"You have a lot to make up for. You want people to respect you? Show them you've changed. Stop whining. Stop sucking on those poison sticks. Start acting like you want out of here someday."

Did Omar want out of here? "I don't know what I want."

"Figure it out, Omar. Or it's going to be more of the same. And stop hanging around with those flakers. Red, especially."

"They're people, Levi. Like you and me."

"They're the enemy. Stop pretending they're not."

"I'm a flaker too. It won't be long until my skin looks like theirs. So does that mean I'm the enemy?"

"This is about us and them. Catching their sickness doesn't make you one of them. Don't be stupid. And stop treating your body like a canvas."

"Stop telling me what to do."

"I'm elder, Omar. Telling you what to do is my job. And for now, I want you following that Kendall woman. Bender thinks she might have the messages."

"You just said Bender thought Otley had the messages."

"No, I said Otley got to Chord before he delivered the messages. But Otley didn't get them. If he had, Bender said this place and our bunker would be compromised and they would've already raided us. Either Chord hid them or he gave them to someone. Bender thinks it's Kendall Collin. Find out." Levi walked away, not giving Omar a chance to argue.

Not that he wanted to.

Kendall Collin, the girl with the sweet face and the silky brown hair... that wasn't a bad assignment. Omar would very much like to get to know her better. He sucked in another hit from his vaporizer, closed his eyes, and enjoyed the thrill, letting the fog seep from his lips. He could never tell how much time passed when he vaped the hard stuff. He nodded off again, thinking of Kendall Collin.

"Hey, trigger."

Omar opened his eyes. Red stood before him, looking glossy in a short silver dress with black boots that went up over her knees. She sometimes mimicked the clothing, but never messed with her hair, which was vermillion red, not carrot orange like Belbeline's had been.

Walls, he missed Bel.

Omar looked past Red to the bottom of the theater. Levi, Jordan, and Zane were still there, standing in a huddle by the entrance, but everyone else had gone.

"I thought you were sleeping," Red said.

"Not sleeping." He held up his PV.

"Ooh, gimme." She snatched his PV and took a long drag.

Red reminded him of a warrior. There was a hardness to her. An inner metal. He'd met her three weeks ago when he'd started up with Bender and the rebels. Omar and Red were both angry deep down, their souls ravaged by this city. They understood each other's pain.

Red sat crosswise on Omar's lap and put her arms around his neck. She smelled nice, softer than the spicy smells Belbeline wore.

"Want to go dancing tonight?" she asked him.

"Can't."

She ran her fingers through his hair at the nape of his neck. "Why not?"

"Levi's mad at me for missing my meeting with Chord."

"Yeah, that's a bummer about Chord. He was a valentine."

Her words pricked Omar's nerves. He hated how Safe Landers shared each other. He wanted a girl who wanted him and no one else. He wanted what Jordan and Naomi had. What Levi and Jemma had.

But Red thought like Belbeline. The word *commitment* didn't exist in their vocabulary. They just wanted to play.

Red seemed to sense she'd upset him, because she fisted the front of his shirt and tugged. "Hey, he's not as valentine as you, though."

"Really." He didn't believe her. Not even a little. But he liked her aggressive ways.

She set her forehead against his and stared into his eyes. "You have gorgeous eyes."

When she set her mind to it, Red had a way of saying just the right thing. *Her* eyes were pink today. It was weird, how she changed her eye color like Omar changed his shirt. She kissed him then. She was a good kisser. Almost as good as Belbeline.

"Get a room, Omar!" Jordan's voice carried from below.

Omar ignored him.

But Red pulled away and grinned. "That's a good idea." She hopped off Omar's lap and stood. "Let's go, trig." She pulled him out of the seat and down the steps toward the exit. They passed Levi, Jordan, and Zane at the door.

"You dirt bunnies make me sick," Jordan said.

"We try, shell," Red said, blowing Jordan an air kiss.

A few more steps through the darkness of the corridor, and he and Red left the theater. Red stopped to give one of the guards at the door a lingering kiss. On the lips. One of her old conquests, Omar assumed. Mad annoying. But if he said anything, they'd fight. Omar just needed to get used to how things worked here.

Or maybe find a girl who wasn't from here. A girl like Kendall. She was an outsider too. Maybe they'd make a better match.

Finally, they reached the sidewalk, passed Sim Slingers, and headed toward his apartment. Red walked with her arms around him, one hand fisting the front of his shirt, the other tucked into his back pants pocket. It made him uncomfortable, like he didn't know her well enough for such a public display of affection despite the intimate things they'd done in private. The thought gave him pause, didn't make sense.

Omar took another drag of his PV, and the stims relaxed him. Red's hands did too. Kissing while walking wasn't the easiest of tasks, so they made several stops on their walk to his place to enjoy each other. Red made him feel alive, like the brown sugar. He wanted to feel alive. He needed to.

Find pleasure in life, right? That's what they always said in the Safe Lands.

It was during one such stop in the park that the sound of an owl drew Omar's attention.

"What's wrong?" Red asked.

Omar stepped back from Red, his gaze flitting over the branches above. "I heard an owl."

"So?"

He kept looking, every rustling leaf a potential perch. "I didn't know they came into the Safe Lands."

"Who cares?"

Omar did. And when the curved shadow of the bird panned across the lamp-lit street that edged the park, Omar chased it.

"Where are you going?" Red called.

Omar sprinted down the sidewalk after the receding shadow. He ran for three blocks and lost the bird somewhere over the Outrunner building. He stopped to catch his breath, consumed with the image of the wingspan stretched across the center of the street. He needed to draw.

"You. Have a. SimTalk tap. From... Red."

"SimTalk off," Omar said.

He ran all the way to his apartment in the Alexandria. He walked inside and tripped over the dumbbells he'd left on the floor by the door before he remembered to turn on the lights. Once he could see, he grabbed a fresh sheet of paper and nub of charcoal and fell onto the tile floor in the middle of his kitchen, which was really more of an art studio now. He quickly sketched the shape of the owl's wings. He blended the shadow with the side of his fist, caressing the paper, creating the look of freedom. Wings that could carry him away from this place. Away from the chains that bound him so tightly.

Oh, how he wanted to be free.

Five sheets of paper later, Omar sat back on his heels and studied his work. He'd drawn the face of an owl on the body of a man. A flowing cape framed the figure.

It was the Owl—Omar's favorite superhero from the comic books of Old that his Grandpa Seth had given him years before he died.

Levi was right; life wasn't fair. But that was okay. Because if everything was fair in the world, nobody would win. And Omar was sick of losing.

He was also sick of numbing his pain with temporary pleasures. There had to be another way to deal with his grief and guilt. A way that would prove to Levi that Omar wasn't a worthless flaker. That he could be a hero too.

He could become the Owl, a superhero for the Safe Lands.

He grabbed a fresh canvas and propped it on the easel, then began to paint the Owl.

"Omar?"

He jumped at the sound of Red's voice in his apartment. *Maggots.* He didn't want her here, but he'd added her ID to his door lock a week ago, and now she could come and go as she pleased.

He kept his back to her, hoping if he ignored her, she'd leave. But her footsteps crossed the room. She crouched just behind him, blocking some of his light, and reached up the back of his shirt. Her long fingernails scratched lightly up his spine and caused goose bumps to stand out along his arms.

He didn't want to want this girl. He wanted to paint. He wished she would go away. Why couldn't he just tell her that? *Go away, Red. Leave me alone.*

Instead, he allowed her to take the brush and palette from his hands. She set them on the paint-splattered floor, then turned him to face her, slid her fingernails up the backs of his hands and over his wrists and forearms, slowly moving her hands up his arms, up, up, until her fingers locked behind his neck.

He let out a happy moan and thought, *Go away, Red.*

But she kissed him. And he kissed her back, weakling that he was. How could someone so weak become any kind of superhero?

He couldn't.

Women were nothing but trouble for superheroes. As soon as she left, Omar would reprogram his door lock so she couldn't get inside next time.

Next time. It would be easier to resist her next time.

Chapter 3

Mason paced in front of the G.I.N. vending machine that sat across the street from the Safe Lands Boarding School. It was Tuesday morning, and the older students should be walking to the park soon. The boarding school housed kids from age three to thirteen. He'd seen Penelope and Nell, who were both thirteen, in the group before, and he was determined to speak with one of them today.

The clamor of children's voices rising up from behind the red brick wall surrounding the school antagonized him. Somewhere inside, children from Glenrock were playing. Were they afraid? Lonely? Or were they enjoying themselves? Mason had found much of the Safe Lands fascinating, and he could only imagine what Safe Lands novelties might distract children. What if the children refused to leave when he and others from Glenrock finally tried to rescue them? What if they preferred this eternal playground to home.

Surely a longing for their mothers would trump fancy innovations.

On his left, an iron gate yawned open, and a line of students departed the school, single file, down the sidewalk toward where he stood. Excellent. He faced the vending machine, but instead of examining the contents for purchase, he used the glass's reflection to monitor the passing students.

"Get the flakes," a boy told him.

Mason turned and met the boy's cheeky grin as he walked by.

"Flakes are the best," the boy called after him.

A dark-haired girl grabbed Mason's arm. "Buy me a fizzy?" She had long fake eyelashes and a familiar face. Penelope. "Pen— Please?" Mason glanced wildly for the teacher, hoping he hadn't been overheard. "Um... Don't forget your manners."

"Please!" a dozen children sang.

"Leave the gentleman to his shopping," a teacher said from the end of the line, her tone stern yet bored. "Keep moving."

Penelope slipped something into Mason's hand and stepped back into line.

Mason watched her go, then thought better of it, and again regarded the vending machine. He had planned to simply follow the class today, but perhaps Penelope's idea was the better one. He purchased a package of chocolate chews from the vending machine and followed the students, keeping a dozen yards behind. Up ahead, the street ended, forcing traffic to the left or right along the road that edged the park. The students trailed across the street, blocking traffic. Mason went into a Lift on the corner, which was an establishment that sold hot and cold beverages with the option of adding "lifts" or supplements, be they vitamin, adaptogen, or stimulant.

He sat at a table at the window and watched the students enter the park. When they'd all gone in, he unfolded Penelope's paper.

Kids sneak out of the school two ways.

1. A storm drain off the southeast corner of the basement in the boys' dorm. Kids have been using it for years and getting caught, so right now it's boarded up. I'm trying to talk this girl into showing me, because she's always bragging about all the places she's been. But she could be lying.

2. The girls' dorm roof is five stories high, the same level as the roof of the Nordic Apartments. Kids sometimes go up on the roof to vape and drink alcohol. There's a wooden plank up there that is long enough to stretch between the two roofs. I went over with a few kids last week. We didn't leave the Nordic. But we were able to go and get back without getting caught. That's our best plan. It will be hard to get all the kids together without being seen, but if you tell me the date and time, I think I can do it.

Love you!
Penny

The tension left Mason's shoulders. There was hope here. And Penelope still wanted out, which probably meant most of the others did too. Good.

He exited the Lift and walked back past the school. He scanned the skyline and considered the placement of the Nordic Apartments, the roads, and the yellow cameras that were everywhere in the Safe Lands. Zane had promised he could take care of the cameras.

The Nordic was located on the three-way corner of where Emmons Road crossed one end of Treasury Road. To the east, Treasury dead-ended at the Midlands wall. Mason likely wouldn't be able to get the kids through the Midlands gate. Perhaps there was a way to take the storm drains, which would make the basement exit ideal... But if they couldn't get to the drains through the boys' dorm and had to use the roof of the girls' dorm, they'd still need to come out of the Nordic, then find a way underground.

He'd have to ask Levi to explore the drains underneath the school.

If they were going to get out via the roof, it would be nice to speak with someone who once attended the school, especially a female. Unfortunately, the only female in the rebel group was Red, and Levi had forbidden Mason from involving her in their plans.

There was Ciddah, of course. But ever since Mason had found the MiniComm in his apartment, he'd been avoiding Ciddah, working beside her in near silence.

Levi's words came to mind: *"Stop thinking of her as a person. She's the enemy, Mase. Use her to get what you need so we can all get out of here."*

Was Ciddah Rourke Mason's enemy? Despite the MiniComm, he simply couldn't accept that—at least not as harshly as Levi had put it. No one who treated patients with such gentle care could be all bad.

Ciddah had gone to the boarding school. She had the information he needed. She'd never help him. Not with this. He couldn't even risk asking her about the school because she might report his suspicious questions to enforcers. Was it worth the risk to try?

Mason didn't know. He liked Ciddah too much to play the games Levi had asked of him. He had no other options; though the woman made him an irrational mess.

Enough of these pathetic emotions. Getting out of the Safe Lands and finding a cure for Omar and Mia was all that mattered. Mason could lament his poor choice in women once all of Glenrock was safely outside this diseased fortress.

He took a deep breath and headed back to his apartment. Tomorrow he would engage Ciddah in a conversation that would, hopefully, lead to some answers. Time to "use her," as Levi had said, the way she'd been using him from the start.

Chapter 4

Twenty-six days had passed since the women had escaped the Highland Harem. That was exactly how long Shaylinn and Naomi had been banished to the underground bunker in the Midlands. In that time, Shaylinn had been allowed to leave only twice, both times to attend Bender's rebel meetings with her brother.

Naomi hadn't been allowed to leave at all. She was far too pregnant now. And she took more naps than a cat.

When Shaylinn wasn't in the bathroom on her knees dealing with tedious amounts of morning sickness, she entertained herself by cleaning the bunker. It was hard work, but the place was gross, and she didn't like the idea of her soon-to-arrive nephew crawling around in such filth—though hopefully they'd all be long gone before the child learned to crawl.

Shaylinn filled a bucket with soapy water. Jemma wanted her to use bleach, but Shaylinn couldn't tolerate the smell. She carried the bucket out of the main living area and into the corridor. The space was concrete and cold and stretched out like a very long and wide hallway. It smelled of moss and metal. Burnt sienna stains painted stripes down the walls where rusty water had run and dried. Omar had taught Shaylinn the color burnt sienna, and the rusty stains reminded her of the boy she loved.

Maybe she was too young to love a boy. She hadn't meant to. If she had, she would have had the sense to love someone else, someone who might love her back, someone who wasn't so... lost. And stupid.

Tears flooded her eyes, thinking about Omar being infected with the thin plague. Why had he done everything Elder Eli had warned them not to do?

She wished her mother were here so she could talk to her about all this. Mother had always been a good listener. Jemma was too intent on fixing everything, but some things just couldn't be fixed.

Shaylinn reached into the warm water, squeezed out her sponge, and scrubbed at the stain on the wall. The bright color smeared, coming off easily. Drops of burnt sienna water rolled down the wall, leaving clean stripes of gray behind.

A while back she'd had a dream that had hinted at a happy future. Shaylinn and a man in a home with several children. The dream had helped her when she'd needed confidence to get through the embryo transfer procedure in the Surrogacy Center. But that had been almost a month ago, and her confidence had waned since then.

It wasn't fair. Pregnant without ever having kissed a boy. Unless she was to count kisses from her father or the time Ewan, one of the harem enforcers, had kissed her without asking. But Shaylinn didn't count those kisses.

She thought of Omar and that day at the kissing trees when he'd—

The seal on the iron door that separated the bunker from the underground storm drains cranked open, echoing slightly in the concrete corridor. Shaylinn took a step back to stay in the shadows. She wasn't expecting anyone for another hour.

Two men and a woman stepped through the door. One of the men had wide shoulders and was as tall as Jordan. The other was shorter. They were not from Glenrock. Shaylinn's stomach turned, and she pressed against the wall, straining to get a good look at their faces.

She recognized the shorter man first. It was Rewl, who reminded Shaylinn of a grown toddler... until he smiled. He'd gotten SimArt implants in his teeth, which gave them diagonal black pinstripes. So gross.

Next came Red, the woman who was always with Omar. Red hadn't been the one to infect Omar, according to Mason, but Shaylinn hated her anyway, even if it was wrong to hate. Red looked like a skeleton wearing a skin jumpsuit, but her chest was so large Shaylinn wondered how she could walk and not fall over. She had electric pink eyes and wispy, chin-length, maroon-colored hair that looked fake. That's what she was: 100 percent fake.

Red stepped deep into the corridor, holding a fat bag. Rewl and the other man pulled the door closed until the clamp clicked into place, sealing off the bunker again, which would keep the water out if it rained. The men turned toward the entrance to the main room, and Shaylinn recognized the second man.

"Mr. Bender." She relaxed and stepped into the light.

The leader of the Black Army reminded Shaylinn of Grandpa James. He had wrinkled skin and short gray hair. A strange scar over his left eye made him squint, like he was always thinking about winking but never made up his mind whether or not to do so.

All three wore black gloves. Shaylinn had never seen a Black Army member without gloves.

"Miss Shaylinn," Bender said, his voice low and kind. "Exactly the femme I'm looking for."

Shaylinn squeezed the sponge. A trickle of water splashed on the floor, which made her step back and lighten her grip. "You want to talk to *me*?"

"Why don't we go in and sit?" Bender said. "It'll be more comfortable."

"Okay." Shaylinn dropped her sponge into the water and picked up the bucket. She went to open the door to the main room, but her hand slipped on the knob, still wet from the wash water.

Rewl darted forward. "Let me help, Miss Shaylinn." He opened the door and held it there, baring his striped teeth in a smile.

Shaylinn slipped past him and into the main room. It was warmer in here than the corridor. The room had a one-wall kitchen on one end, a TV and sofas on the other end, and three round tables in the middle. Shaylinn set her bucket in the kitchen sink and dried her hands on a towel, staining the white terrycloth a peachy orange color from the rusty water on her hands.

Bender made his way to the sofas and sat on the brown one, which was the one with the least holes. Red perched beside him. Rewl closed the front door and stood in front of it like he was guarding the place. Something about his posture made Shaylinn's neck tickle. She decided then that she didn't like Rewl either. She wondered if he were carrying a gun.

"Yesterday at the meeting, you volunteered to work in Chord's position," Bender said.

Shaylinn walked to the other end of the room and stood beside the Old TV set. "Omar is going to do it," she said with a glance at Red. But Bender knew that already.

"I have a proposition for you, Miss Shaylinn," Bender said. "I need to find out if Kendall Collin has the messages Chord was supposed to bring to me. You think you could find out?"

"Oh." Why was he asking her? "I'd like to help, but it would be wrong to go behind Levi's back. Or my brother's." Plus, Jordan would yell and scream.

"I understand. And I admire your loyalty to your people." Bender sighed and stretched his arms up on the back of the sofa, tucked one behind Red. "It's a shame about Kendall, though. She seems like an honest femme."

Red gasped and pressed her hand against her gigantic chest. "You're not going to kill her, are you, Bender?"

"Not me," Bender said. "I'll have Rewl do it."

"What?" Shaylinn couldn't have heard that right. "Kill Kendall?"

"I wish I didn't have to," Bender said, "but without knowing for certain if she's got those messages and what she's going to do with them, I don't have a choice."

Of course he had a choice. No one was putting a gun in his hands.

"You can't take the risk," Red said, patting Bender's knee. She looked at Shaylinn, and those pink eyes seemed electrified, like Red was a robot. "It puts the entire Black Army in jeopardy. And the outsider shells too."

Did it? Either way, Shaylinn couldn't allow them to kill Kendall. "I guess I can try to find out if she has them, but you're wrong to mistrust her. She hates the Safe Lands government. They took her baby."

"You get burned enough, femme, you don't trust anyone anymore," Bender said.

"And why would she care about them taking the kid?" Red said. "It's what they do. It's not *her* baby."

Shaylinn folded her arms. "Of course it's her b— Wait, aren't you a rebel? Don't you think the Safe Lands is wrong to take babies?"

Red snorted and flicked her hair over her shoulder. "I don't like the government telling me what to do. But babies aren't my interest."

Shaylinn pursed her lips. "Men are your interest, right?"

"That's right." Red giggled, low and secretive as if she knew something Shaylinn didn't.

"You'd better not hurt Omar," Shaylinn said.

This comment seemed to make Red's pink eyes glow as she glared at Shaylinn. "Omar knows what he wants. And he wants me."

A rush of anger welled up inside Shaylinn. "No, he doesn't. He's sad and confused because of everything that's happened. And you're taking advantage of him."

Red cackled like an evil witch in an Old movie. "Omar can wipe his own nose, femme. He doesn't need you sticking your—"

"Focus," Bender said. "Kendall Collin?"

Shaylinn scowled at Red once more before giving Bender her full attention. "Can you bring her here?"

"Nooo. She can't know about this place," Bender said. "You're going to have to be a spy, Miss Shaylinn. Spend time with her. Get her to tell you about the messages without mentioning me *or* the Black Army."

"But how can I go outside when I'm supposed to be hiding?" Shaylinn asked.

"I've got a couple ideas," Bender said. "I can get you hired at the messenger office as a janitor during Kendall's shifts. Or Rewl can drive you around, follow Kendall, and you can bump into her when she goes to the G.I.N. or wherever. Or we can get you moved into the apartment beside hers."

The idea of having her own place thrilled her. "I'd like the apartment, please. But... Jordan. When he finds me gone, he'll come and get me and lock me up." And yell and scream. And probably hit something. But if he didn't know about the apartment, she could always sneak out again.

"Then you'd better act fast, femme," Red said.

Shaylinn didn't like the way Red looked at her and bossed her, so she kept her side of the conversation between her and Bender. "My picture is on the ColorCast all the time. And Jordan said he saw it on the train too. What if someone recognizes me?"

"Red is going to give you a little makeover," Bender said. "No one will recognize you when she's done."

As a last-ditch effort to get them to leave her alone, she said, "But I'm pregnant!"

"You're not even showing yet," Bender said. "You'll be fine."

Shaylinn looked back at Red then, met those electric-pink eyes. "As long as she doesn't make me look like her."

Red smiled, and it was an ugly, fake smile. "Why would I do that? One of me is all the Safe Lands can handle."

Shaylinn hummed as if considering her comment. "It's all I can handle too."

A few hours later, Shaylinn was standing alone in her new apartment that was located next door to Kendall's in the Belleview Building. A kitchen, sofa, and bed filled one small room. The only other room was a tiny bathroom. The whole place was decorated pink and green and reminded Shaylinn of the polka dot chair in Tyra Grant's office.

Thoughts of the harem's beauty care specialist sent Shaylinn walking toward the mirror for the fifth time since Bender, Red, and Rewl had dropped her off downstairs. She'd been worried that being underground with no access to InstaWraps and SkinnySticks would have made her get fat again, but it hadn't.

Silver was still the hot trend, set by Finley Gray and Luella Flynn, the hosts of the Safe Lands ColorCast. Shaylinn had refused to allow Red to cut her hair, so the woman had straightened it and given her a tinsel weave, which mixed in strands of metallic silver hair with her natural brown hue. Shaylinn's hair now reached her elbows in a flat, shaggy mop. Red had also given Shaylinn a pair of contact lenses that made her eyes look a natural green, and black lace gloves with no fingers that held a SimTag so she could enter buildings and pay for taxis or whatever she might need.

That had been more than enough to transform Shaylinn into a completely different person from the poster of the frightened girl that had been plastered all over the Safe Lands. Red had also given her several sets of clothes, enough to last the week. They were sexy clothes that clung to Shaylinn's body and showed off her growing chest.

She hadn't needed breast implants after all. The pregnancy had taken care of that.

Shaylinn had always wanted to be beautiful, but she wasn't certain she liked what Red had done. She looked like someone from *C Factor*. And even though Red had promised this new look would help her blend in with other Safe Lands women, Shaylinn was sure it would only call attention to herself.

A bell chimed. Rewl had rigged up the device to signal whenever Kendall's apartment door opened. Shaylinn ran over to the peephole on the wall and looked in.

Kendall was home. She walked to the kitchen table and set her messenger bag on one of the chairs and a box of chicken from Leghorns on the table.

Shaylinn drew back. Bender wanted her to wait until she and Kendall bumped into each other on the stairs or outside. To create a coincidental meeting. But Shaylinn had no intention of doing things Bender's way. The moment Jordan realized she was gone, he would come looking. If Shaylinn was going to help Kendall, she needed to do it now.

She left her apartment and knocked on Kendall's front door. She heard footsteps, saw movement in the peephole. The door opened, the chain keeping it from going farther than a few inches.

"Yes?" Kendall said.

"Hi, Kendall." Shaylinn leaned close and whispered, "It's Shaylinn. From the harem."

Kendall's eyes narrowed and studied Shaylinn from head to toe. The door pushed closed, the chain rattled, and the door opened again. "Come in."

Shaylinn slipped inside, awkward in the high-heeled shoes Red had given her. The smell of fried chicken made her stomach flutter. *Oh no.*

Kendall closed the door behind her and came to stand by the kitchen table, arms folded. "You escaped the harem. I've seen your picture on the ColorCast. What do you want?"

Shaylinn pressed up against the front door and fought to hold back the sickness, but the smell of the chicken… She looked around the apartment and spotted the bathroom door in the same place it was located in her new apartment. She ran for it. "Need to use your bathroom."

Shaylinn fell to her knees at the toilet and wanted to cry. She had no control over how smells affected her anymore. How was she supposed to keep from throwing up all the time? When she finished, she washed her hands and rinsed out her mouth, then tottered back into Kendall's kitchen/living room/bedroom.

"I put the chicken in the oven and opened the windows," Kendall said. "My morning sickness only ever came in the mornings. But they say if you get it really bad, it means you're having a girl."

"Maybe," Shaylinn said, tickled at the idea of a cute little daughter to take care of.

"What about Jemma and Mia and the others?" Kendall asked.

"We got out in time. I'm the only one who was made pregnant."

"And Naomi?"

"She's safe too. And she's huge! That baby is coming any day, Jemma says. What about you? Have you seen your baby?"

"Once." Kendall's jaw hardened. "They don't allow that, really, but Lawten had promised I'd be able to hold Elyot whenever I wanted. But after the first time I went to the nursery, they wouldn't let me back in." Tears pooled at the corners of her eyes. She blinked rapidly. "So, who glossed you up? You look like a dancer."

"You're a shell!" a strange voice said. "Tch tch tch."

Shaylinn jumped and looked toward the window where a rounded cage sat on a narrow table. Something moved inside the cage, flying from corner to corner. A little bird. It was yellow and blue with black-and-white wings. "What's that?"

Kendall waved her hand as if the topic bored her. "Oh, that's just Basil."

"He talks?"

"Give me a kiss," the bird said in a dull, almost electronic voice. "What time is it?"

"I'm sorry, but… why are you here, Shaylinn?"

"I have something important to tell you, but I need you to let me finish before you interrupt me or get angry. Do you promise to listen until I'm done?"

"Okay."

Shaylinn took a deep breath. "Well, since we escaped the harem—"

"Budgie. Basil's a budgie. Tch tch tch. Give us a kiss."

Shaylinn grinned at the bird.

"Just a minute." Kendall walked to the cage and pulled a drape over it. "Good night, Basil."

"Good night, Basil. Tch tch tch."

"Will he go to sleep?" Shaylinn asked.

"Yeah. He's funny that way. You were saying?"

"Right. Um, the Black Army has been hiding my people. Levi befriended their leader, Bender. Well, I mean that Bender is their new leader now that Lonn has been liberated."

"Go on."

Shaylinn hoped she was explaining things correctly. "Bender thinks you have messages Chord Prezden was meant to deliver. He said if he couldn't figure out whether or not you were trustworthy, he was going to have you killed. So, I volunteered to spy on you so I could warn you."

Kendall paled. "Kill me?"

"I know you're not a murderer, Kendall. So, if you have Chord's messages, I figure you have a good reason."

"I have them," Kendall said, her eyes glossy with tears.

Shaylinn breathed out a sigh, hoping Bender would leave Kendall alone once he had the messages in his possession. "Can I have them? To give to Bender?"

Kendall's bottom lip trembled. "When I found Chord, he'd been attacked. With his dying words he asked me to deliver the messages to the addressees and no one else. I think Chord knew someone else would come looking."

"Maybe Bender is worried the addressees will be exposed to enforcers," Shaylinn said. "Maybe he's just trying to protect his rebels."

"Maybe Bender killed Chord."

What a terrible thought. "Why would he do that? He's a good guy."

"Anyone who threatens to kill someone is not a good guy."

Yeah. That made sense.

"I've had the messages for three days," Kendall said, "trying to decide if I should deliver them or destroy them. Let's read them."

"That seems a little nosy," Shaylinn said.

"It's the only way we'll find out the truth." Kendall walked to her refrigerator and opened the freezer. She removed the ice bin and dumped its contents into the sink. Then she peeled a plastic bag off the bottom of the bin and left the bin in the sink.

She carried the bag to the kitchen table and sat down. Shaylinn sat in the chair beside hers. It felt good to get off her feet. The high-heeled shoes were painful after wearing them too long.

Kendall opened the plastic bag and arranged the four messages on the glass tabletop. "Three are private residences. But this one"—she tapped the message addressed to a Ruston Neil—"is an MO Box from my branch."

"What's the difference?" Shaylinn asked.

"This Ruston person doesn't get mail at a residence. He picks it up at the messenger office."

Shaylinn read the names on the envelopes: Ruston Neil, Dane Skott, Domini Bentz, and Charlz Sims. "I know Charlz's name. He helped Omar get Levi and Jemma out of the RC." And it had earned him an X after his number, same as Omar.

"Let's open that one first, then." Kendall ripped open the envelope and removed a single white card. There were only three lines of text.

Want freedom?
We have answers.
Cinetopia, Theater 9.

"Sounds subversive," Kendall said. "If Chord was involved in some rebel cause... that might explain his death. People who rebel in the Safe Lands don't rebel for long. As Luella Flynn would say, 'Rebels are a blemish that must be painted over.'"

"Chord was a rebel," Shaylinn said, feeling as though that supported Kendall's theory. "And theater nine is where we meet—the rebels, I mean. To talk about our plans. This must be an invitation for Charlz to join the rebels."

"So, this Bender man wants to kill me in case I might expose his potential recruits?" Kendall asked. "That doesn't seem like adequate motive."

"Let's open the others," Shaylinn said, curious if they were all the same.

The messages to Dane Skott and Domini Bentz were identical to the one addressed to Charlz Sims, but the message to Ruston Neil was totally different.

Mr. Neil,

Zane told me to contact you if I ever needed someone to trust and he wasn't around. Since Zane didn't answer my tap today, and I didn't think it was safe to leave a voicemail, I'm writing to you.

I left my messenger bag at the warehouse yesterday, and when I went back to retrieve it, I overheard Bender take a tap from General Otley. I couldn't hear what Otley said, but Bender asked how Otley's plans were coming along. He also said that once Otley was the task director general, Bender would be the enforcer general.

Nothing else notable was said, but before Bender ended the call, he said he'd take care of it, whatever that means.

While I can't imagine that I misheard, I felt the best plan was to bring this to your attention. Bender summoned me to the warehouse today. I'm afraid he somehow found out I'd overheard his tap, so I decided to write this letter in case something happened to me.

Thanks for your time,
Chord Prezden

"Bender must have killed Chord," Kendall said. "What are we going to do?"

Shaylinn's head tingled. So did her arms. Hot and cold all at once. Bender kill Chord? She jumped up and trotted toward the door. "I have to go! I have to tell Jordan and Levi."

"Wait!"

Shaylinn reached the door and slammed her glove to the SimPad. It swung inward, but Kendall arrived and pushed it shut.

"What are you doing?" Shaylinn pounded her fist against the SimPad again, tears blurring her vision. "Let me out! If Bender killed Chord, he could kill any of us. Whenever he wants! I have to warn them!"

But Kendall closed the door again and this time took hold of Shaylinn's shoulders. "Just think for a minute, Shaylinn. Please. We have to be very careful and very smart. If Bender sent you here, he could be outside, watching. If you go running out of here, upset like you are... It will look bad, okay?"

"Okay." Shaylinn scanned the room, wishing there were another exit, but Kendall's words slowly sank in. She took a deep breath. "Okay."

"Come back and sit at the table so we can decide what to do."

Shaylinn obeyed, rubbing her eyes as she clomped across the kitchen. She fell onto the chair and took another huge breath. "What if we delivered these but kept copies? We'd need new envelopes, and we'd have to make them look as dirty and rumpled as these. But I could take the copies to Bender, and you could mail the real ones."

"I don't know." Kendall paced between the fridge and the table. "What if we get caught? If Bender never delivers any of the messages, then these people show up at your theater meeting with the original letters..."

Good point. "Then we'll make new envelopes and give these originals to Bender." Shay gathered the recruitment cards. "But we need to deliver the original letter to Mr. Neil and give Bender a copy. That's the only way to make Bender leave you alone and still honor what Chord risked his life for."

Kendall stared at the letter to Ruston. "I suppose. But won't Ruston's letter expose Bender? If Bender gets proof that Chord saw him and wrote a letter telling someone, he might assume that Chord told others as well. And if he thinks any rebels know about his deal with Otley, he might—"

"Tell Otley where my people are hiding!" Or worse, kill them. That left only one option that Shaylinn could see. "So, we give Bender the three recruitment letters and that's it. But we also have to go to Levi right away and hope he can come up with a plan before Bender betrays us all.

Chapter 5

"You sent her where?" Levi fought back the energy threatening to magnify his voice—*Refrain from anger. Turn from wrath*—but the careless look on Bender's face almost put him over the edge. They were sitting in the main room of the underground bunker. Levi had brought Bender and Rewl in for a quick discussion about recruiting Omar's friends Charlz Sims and Dane Skott, but instead had found Jemma in hysterics over her missing sister.

Bender had confessed straight away, as if his forcing Shaylinn to work for him was no big deal. "You worry too much." Bender leaned back on the sofa and stretched his arms along the top. "The girl is stronger than you think."

"That's not the point." Levi tapped his chest. "Where my people are concerned, *I say*, not you."

"Where did you send her?" Jemma asked, her voice quavering.

"We set her up in her own apartment next door to Kendall Collin's place," Bender said. "I need someone Kendall trusts to spy on her."

Levi motioned to his brother, who sat at the table, vapo stick hanging from his lips. "I sent Omar to spy on her."

"She's got a bird," Omar said. "It sits in her window and sings."

"Omar won't get the answers we need," Rewl said. "My sources tell me Kendall doesn't trust men."

"Go to Kendall's place and bring back Shay," Levi said to Omar.

Omar nodded and stood, exhaling a cloud of black vapor. "On my way."

"There's no need." The soft voice drew Levi's gaze to the door. A woman stood there, wearing a glimmering silver tank top, black half-gloves, tight black pants, and silver shoes with spiky heels. Her hair hung to her waist, long and straight like a horse's tail and streaked with strands of silver.

Who in all the lands was this? And how had she gotten in?

"Shay!" Jemma set her hand over her heart.

Omar's eyes widened. "Walls..."

Shaylinn? *Really?* Levi squinted at her as she thumped across the room, unsteady on those ridiculous shoes. Her eyes were green and she'd changed her hair. And he could hardly even look at what she was wearing, but, yes, her face was there. Little Shaylinn, looking far too grown up.

"Red cleaned her up nicely, don't you think?" Rewl smirked, his eyes locked onto Shaylinn's body in a way that made Levi want to throw him out into the storm drain.

"Red did this?" Omar said, still staring at Shaylinn.

Shaylinn stopped before Bender and tossed three messages onto his lap. "Kendall didn't deliver them. Chord asked her to, but she was too scared. She was keeping them in her freezer. When I asked about Chord, she gave me the letters. Will you leave her alone now?"

"Of course." Bender shuffled through the stack. "This was it?"

"Yes. I hope they were worth it. You scared me and Kendall practically to death."

"Oh, they were worth it, femme." Bender smiled up at Levi. "I told you this one has talent. We could use her to—"

Levi grabbed the front of Bender's shirt and pulled him to the edge of the sofa. "You talk to my people again behind my back, and we're done. You get me?"

The click of a gun cocking stiffened Levi's spine.

"No!" Jemma yelled.

Rewl had pulled a handgun—what looked like a real one, not a stunner—and had aimed it at Levi. "Let him go."

Levi shoved Bender back against the sofa cushions and glared at Rewl, wondering if the kid could shoot. "Omar, show Bender and Rewl to the door, will you? It's time for dinner."

"You know what? I'm ready to go, anyway." Bender stood and walked toward the door. "Thanks, Miss Shaylinn."

Shaylinn glared at Bender, and Jemma wrapped her in a hug.

Omar got up and followed Bender, yet he stared at Shaylinn until he nearly walked into one of the tables. Rewl kept his gun trained on Levi as he waited for his boss.

Levi pretended he wasn't looking and sat on the couch, but he watched out of the corner of his eye until they were gone. Then he tore into Shaylinn. "What were you thinking?"

Shaylinn folded her arms. "He threatened to kill Kendall if I didn't help him."

"I don't care who he threatened or—"

"She's my friend, Levi," Shaylinn said. "I knew he was tricking me." She glanced at the door as Omar returned and locked it. "Bender and Red both tricked me. But I didn't see any other way. And you should know something about Bender. He—"

Levi jumped up from the couch and clapped his hand over Shaylinn's mouth. "Not here," he whispered. Their gazes locked, and Levi raised his eyebrows until Shaylinn nodded. He released her and turned to face the table. "Omar, we're going out. Shaylinn, go change. You're coming with us but not dressed like that. Is there a SimTag in those gloves?"

Her face paled. "Yes. But Bender said it wouldn't show up underground."

"Probably a ghoulie tag," Omar said.

Levi sighed. Bender said a lot of things. "Give me the gloves." He walked over to Shaylinn and waited for her to take them off. "Naomi? Tap Jordan, please. Tell him we've got Shaylinn and to meet us at Café Eat."

"What about dinner?" Jemma asked.

"Eat without us, Buttercup. We'll be awhile."

Levi, Omar, and Shaylinn all put on pairs of gloves that held ghoulie tags, which were SimTags Zane made that reflected numbers on their cheeks and hands but were off-grid. And just in case, Levi tossed the lace gloves Bender had given Shay into a dumpster.

When they arrived at the café, Jordan and Zane were already eating at a table in the back corner. Levi, Omar, and Shaylinn joined them, and within seconds, the waitress appeared.

"Where were you?" Jordan asked Shaylinn. "And what happened to your hair?"

"In a minute," Levi said, nodding at the waitress. "First, let us order."

Jordan fell back in his chair and shoved a handful of fries into his mouth, while Levi and Omar ordered burgers and fries, and Shaylinn ordered a salad.

"Back in three or it's free," the waitress said, walking away.

"Jordan, you can talk with Shaylinn later about what she did," Levi said, knowing Jordan would want to discipline his sister. "Right now, we need to address how it happened and what she found out. Bender came into the bunker when he knew Shaylinn was alone, and he tricked her into helping him spy on Kendall Collin."

"That cud-chewing maggot." Jordan glared at Shaylinn. "How'd he trick you?"

Shaylinn cowered a little under her brother's glare. "He said he thought Kendall had Chord's messages and that he was going to have Rewl kill her in case she was working with Otley. I knew he was talking down to me, but I didn't see any other way to save her. So, I volunteered to see what she knew."

"He tried to scare you," Zane said. "Fear is one of Bender's favorite methods."

"And the rest of the story?" Levi said, eager to know himself. "Tell us what you found."

Shaylinn glanced at Zane. "Are you sure?"

"I trust Zane." There was really around 1 percent doubt in Levi's mind as to Zane's loyalties, but he had to trust someone in this place, and Zane had yet to let him down. "We're here to ask his advice on all this. Tell us what happened."

"Kendall and I couldn't figure out why Bender wanted the messages. So, we decided to open them." Shaylinn reached into her back pocket and pulled out a folded piece of paper. "There were actually four messages. Three of them were rebel recruitment cards. But the other one was a letter from Chord. We put the recruitment messages into new envelopes, and I gave them to Bender. But not this one." She held up the folded paper.

Zane frowned at Shaylinn. "He didn't suspect?"

"He didn't seem to," Levi said. "But he did act like there was something missing."

"What does the message say?" Zane asked. "The fourth one."

Shaylinn unfolded the paper, but before she could speak, the waitress arrived with their food.

She set it all on the table and asked, "Can I get you anything else?"

"Just some privacy, please," Levi said. "Thanks."

"Right, well, thanks for visiting Café Eat. Find pleasure tonight."

Levi watched her walk away, and only when he was sure she was out of earshot did he say, "Go ahead, Shaylinn."

Shaylinn handed the message to Levi. "It basically says Bender is working with Otley."

"What!" Jordan slapped his hands on the table and stood. Levi and Omar's sodas sloshed over the side of their cups.

"*Jordan*." Shaylinn grabbed a napkin and mopped up the spilled soda.

"I'm not surprised," Omar said. "Bender is a maggot."

The mere notion sent fire through Levi's chest. But people were staring. Levi raised his eyebrows at Jordan. "Have a seat, Jordan."

Jordan plopped back to his chair and folded his arms.

Shocked and confused, Levi read the message, then passed it to Zane.

"Is it bad, brother?" Omar asked.

"Yeah." But why would Bender partner with Otley? A month ago, he'd wanted Levi to shoot Otley. Was this a recent alliance? Or had Bender been talking with Otley even back during Lonn's days? Maybe that was how Lonn had gotten caught, which painted a terrible theory of the botched Lonn rescue in his mind. Well, if Bender had killed Chord and turned on Lonn, he wouldn't hesitate to betray Levi's people. They had to move. Now.

Zane sighed and passed the letter to Omar, but Jordan snatched it away before Omar managed to touch it.

"Hey!" Omar said.

This conversation might be too scary for Shaylinn. "Omar, you and Shaylinn go sit at the counter, will you?"

"I don't get to know?" Omar scowled and gestured at the letter in Jordan's hands. "I don't even get to read it?"

"Not you, brother." Levi nodded to Shaylinn, who was picking at her salad.

"Fine." Omar sighed. "Let's go, Shay." He whisked her plate out from under her hands and carried it to the counter.

"Hey!" Shaylinn got up and followed him.

Once they were both seated at the counter, Levi asked Zane, "Is Shaylinn safe? What she did with Kendall... defying Bender like that. What if he knows? What if he put one of those MiniComms in Kendall's apartment or put one on Shaylinn somehow? I mean, look at that hair. There could be anything in that mess."

"I don't think he'd put an ear on her," Zane said. "But he's been watching Kendall since Chord was killed. Rewl and I followed her a few times."

"You think Bender had Chord killed?" Levi asked.

"He must have. My guess is Rewl did it."

Rewl. Maybe that kid *could* shoot. "Who's Ruston Neil?"

"How much rebel history do you know?" Zane asked. "Have you heard of the FFF?"

"I've seen graffiti in the storm drains," Levi said.

"The FFF was the first resistance movement in the Safe Lands. Where the Black Army is mostly made up of disgruntled Safe Landers, the FFF is the real underground made up of Naturals. Been around almost since the beginning. Stands for Freedom for Families."

"Wait. Families? Here?" Levi asked.

"This place didn't start out the way it is now, peer," Zane said. "Things happened. Over time. And in the beginning, there were people who didn't like what was happening. Anyway... Ruston Neil is the current leader of the FFF. Ruston and Lonn were friends, worked together on a lot of things."

"So, Chord figured Ruston needed to know about Bender and Otley," Levi said.

"We all needed to know," Jordan said. "We need to take down that maggot."

Zane shook his head. "Don't do anything yet—at least not to Bender."

Levi couldn't just sit around and wait to be arrested or killed by Otley. "What if I went to Dayle up in the Department of Public Tasks?"

"Dayle would just go to Ruston too," Zane said.

"Does Bender know Ruston?" It seemed like all these rebels knew each other.

"Yes, but he doesn't know where he lives. Ruston keeps off the grid as much as possible. He's only got a few guys who run for him. Bender can't find him. No one can."

"Can you?" Levi asked.

Zane smiled and ate one of Levi's fries. "I can find anyone."

"That's what we want," Levi said. "We have to leave the bunker. I can't keep my people vulnerable to Bender. Plus, I'm sick of him telling me what to do."

"I've got a place," Zane said. "No one knows about it. Not even Rewl or Bender. It will be a tight squeeze. But you could bring your women there. At least until I can talk to Ruston about someplace bigger."

"Oh, no," Jordan said. "I'm not getting separated from my wife again."

Levi didn't like the idea of dividing their flock either. "Can we all go there?"

"Yeah, sorry," Zane said. "I meant all of you. You'll fit." But he didn't look so sure. "We'd have to move you at night or really early in the morning, go through the storm drains, at least until we're on the outskirts of the city."

"Our leaving would tip off Bender that we don't trust him, though," Levi said.

"It won't be a problem if he can't find us," Jordan said.

"What about Omar?" Zane asked. "You want him to stay on grid and task?"

"No," Levi said at the same time as Jordan said, "Yes."

"It's too dangerous," Levi said.

"If Omar goes into hiding, Otley will know," Jordan said. "Bender said the enforcers were still watching him."

Right. "But *Bender* said, Jordan. He could have been lying."

"What if he wasn't?"

"What if Omar runs into Bender?" Levi said. "What if he asks Omar about me or where all our people went to?"

"Omar tells him you got the women out one night, and that they're back in Glenrock," Jordan said.

Levi didn't like that plan. "It puts Omar in a vulnerable place."

"Look, I'm going to take this letter to Ruston and get the new place ready," Zane said. "I'll tap you with the plan. Until then, play like you know nothing about Bender and Otley."

"Who?" Levi said.

Zane smirked and stood. "I'll tap you. Oh, here." He removed a Wyndo from his pocket. "This is for Mason. Remind him that messages automatically delete once they're read. I'll start on the ones for the femmes when I can get the parts."

"Thanks, Zane," Levi said.

"Part of my pleasure." Zane limped out of the café.

"I don't like this, Levi," Jordan said. "I want out of here yesterday."

"Me too. Hopefully Mason will have a plan come Saturday. Once I get him this Wyndo and we can talk without having to send paper messages, things will move faster." At least he hoped it would. He had no idea what was taking Mason so long up there.

"Mad good." Jordan slapped the table. "Then talk to Omar about staying away from Shaylinn, will you?"

"Since when?" Levi turned on his chair. Omar and Shay were sitting at the counter. They were both laughing, using plastic forks to smash Omar's french fries into mush. It was the first time in weeks that Levi had seen his little brother acting his age. "What's he doing wrong?"

"Nothing yet," Jordan mumbled. "But he will."

Levi wished Jordan would let up on Omar. But saying so would only start a fight. "Shaylinn isn't stupid. You're going to have to trust her at some point."

"Like you trusted Omar? Look where that got all of us."

Levi gritted his teeth through that insult. "Omar and Shaylinn are different people."

"Not as different as you'd like to think. They're both youngest kids, family misfits, insecure, and looking for meaning in the world. Omar thinks he's found it. And I don't want him showing his version of 'meaning' to my sister."

"He knows right from wrong," Levi said. "He might be trying to justify his actions now, but he'll grow out of it."

"Until he does, keep him away from her."

Levi didn't think Omar would dare touch Shaylinn, but he didn't really know Omar that well. Probably never would. "He's going to die slowly before our eyes."

"It's what he deserves," Jordan said, as if Omar's impending death was no big deal.

Levi couldn't let that comment slide. "You forgave him. Don't act like you didn't."

"I know. But… I loved my father. I loved yours. And every time I look at his face, I…"

"They would have forgiven him," Levi said.

Jordan stared at Levi, his eyebrows high. "Elder Eli would have. Our fathers? I don't think so."

Levi checked himself. He had the tendency to glorify his father's memory, but Jordan was right: Levi's father would never have let Omar live this down. "But you agree forgiveness is right?"

"Some days, yeah. But not when I see him living like an animal and loving every minute of it. He was repentant before. And I could tell he was sorry then. But lately… he's been acting like a maggot again."

"I don't think he's loving it," Levi said. "I think he's miserable."

Levi climbed into bed and snuggled against Jemma's back, pulling her close. It was selfish to wake her, but he wanted to talk. The elder of Glenrock was responsible for much. No one helped him with the pressure like Jemma. He played with her hair and tickled the back of her neck until she stirred.

She moaned in a deep breath and turned in his arms. Her eyes fluttered open and met his. "Hello, my Westley," she mumbled.

He smiled. "Did you sleep well?"

She blinked sleepy eyes. "Until you woke me up."

He pulled her on top of him for a long kiss. When he released her, he combed his fingers into her hair. "Bender is working with Otley. We're all moving in a few days."

Her eyes widened, and she pushed off him and sat up. "You're certain?"

He nodded, feeling slightly guilty for ruining her night. "You know, I never really trusted Bender. There's always been something off about the man."

"What are you going to do?" Jemma asked. "When are we moving? And where?"

"Zane has a place. We'll probably go tomorrow night or the next."

"And you're sure you can trust Zane?"

"Yes, Buttercup. I'm sure." He was 99 percent sure, anyway.

Tears flooded her eyes. "I want to go home."

"I know. Me too. I need to talk to Mason. We have to get the kids out before more get hurt." Or infected or impregnated or brainwashed…

Jemma ran her finger over the wrinkles on Levi's forehead, then down to the scab on his nose. "I hope nothing bad has happened to any of the kids."

He caught her hand and pulled her down beside him, cradling her in one arm. "They're tough kids, Jem. They're smart."

"Did Jordan behave with Shaylinn? Did he make her cry?"

"He reined his temper enough. But he hates Omar, and I can't change his mind."

"Jordan has always held grudges too long. Omar *is* trying. I see it."

"But he's so caught up in the ways of this place... I feel responsible. Yelling at him has done no good. I've thought about beating him up or letting Jordan—"

Jemma smacked his arm. "Don't you dare. What good will that do? You can't force his mind. God has given us all freedom to choose our own path. Violence will only push Omar away."

"I don't like him spending time with Red. Can I forbid that?"

"I wish you could, but she treats him like a man. That is why he likes her. Omar has only ever wanted to be one of the men. To be a part of *your* life. So, set an example: Respect his freedom. Praise his good work, and he'll find his way back."

"I'm afraid for him. That Red will break him when she decides she's bored. That the plague will make him waste away in front of me. That he'll suck down so much vapor it will kill him. The way these flakers live, indulging every craving of the flesh with no regard for the consequences? It's madness."

"They're bored," Jemma said. "And spoiled and lazy. They have no serious responsibilities to give them purpose in life. It leaves them aching for meaning. So, they fill themselves with pleasure. It won't ever satisfy in the long run. They need the Lord."

The Lord. Levi had always assumed he'd have time to read the Bible when he was older. As village elder, it was his responsibility to train the next generation in their faith. How was he supposed to do that when he barely understood it himself?

"I'm worried about Naomi's baby," Jemma said. "I can help her through a regular birth, but what if something goes wrong? I'll need Mason's help."

Not this again. "Jordan won't allow it. End of discussion."

Jemma sat up and shot him that look, like he was wrong, wrong, wrong. "And if Naomi's life is at stake?"

"Are you certain Mason truly knows more than you?" Because Levi didn't think so. Mason had witnessed one human birth before their village was attacked. One. Jemma had helped in at least a half dozen.

"I don't know. But I'd feel better if I wasn't alone. Ciddah's help would be ideal."

"Well, you can't have Ciddah's help. Mason's either. Start training Eliza and Aunt Chipeta to help you. They've had plenty of babies. They must know something." Suddenly Levi was tired. He'd woken Jemma for sympathy and support, but she'd stolen the conversation and added to his long list of burdens.

"I'm worried about Mason too," Jemma said. "The look on his face when you told him to use Ciddah... I think he loves her."

"Mason in love with the medic?" Levi couldn't imagine Mason in love with anything but a book. "I'll believe it when I see it with my own eyes."

"He blushes when she's around," Jemma said. "She's a nice person, you know."

"She's a Safe Lander. They're all harlots."

"Levi!" Jemma folded her arms. "What a horrible thing to say."

He rolled onto his side and propped his head on his hand. "It's true. You've seen how they live. The men too."

"They're people, Levi. People who don't know any other way."

"I can't spare sympathy for them, Jem. As elder of Glenrock, it's my duty to get our people out of here before they're destroyed like Omar."

"Omar is not destroyed," Jemma said. "He's mending."

"Not if he keeps sleeping at the Paradise with Red."

"I know." She sighed as if Omar were her responsibility and she were failing. "Levi, I'm tired. Will we ever get our 'happily ever after'?"

"Of course, Buttercup."

"But there is so much pain around us. And we're all still grieving the loss of our elders. I miss my parents so much. How can I help Shaylinn? She's going to be a mother with no husband and no prospect of one. Mother would know what to do, but I don't."

"I'll tell you what to do: Sleep. There will be plenty of time to worry about Shaylinn once we are free from this place."

She hummed and smiled. "I'm proud of you, Elder Levi."

That stoppered his anger. "What for?"

"You take on so many burdens. You're a good man."

Hmm... He wasn't so sure about that. "Well, if I'm good, it's only because I married a good woman."

Chapter 6

When Mason arrived in the SC Wednesday morning, Rimola said, "Ciddah wants to see you in her office."

Mason circled Rimola's desk and started down the hall. "Good morning to you too."

"Sorry," Rimola called after him. "Just... be nice to her."

Mason stopped and turned around, taken aback by such a plea. "When have I ever been otherwise?"

Rimola rolled her eyes and turned back to her desk.

Odd.

At the door to Ciddah's office, Mason knocked, still puzzled over Rimola's words. Had he said something to offend Ciddah? He had in the past, but he'd barely spoken to her since he'd discovered the MiniComm. Perhaps his silence had been offensive. Who could understand women, anyway?

"Come in," Ciddah said.

Mason set his fist on the SimPad beside the door, and the entry swung open. Ciddah was sitting behind her desk, her posture rigid, but beautiful as always, with golden hair, a perfect body, and electric-blue eyes. He entered, and the door closed behind him.

"Have a seat," she said.

As usual, Ciddah's office was messy. He gathered a stack of files off the chair in front of her desk.

"You're been avoiding me," she said before he'd even managed to sit. "Have I done something to offend you?"

Wait. She thought *he* was offended? Mason set the files on the end of Ciddah's desk, waiting to make sure they were balanced before letting go. Then he sat down and met her icy gaze. "Silence from a man is not evidence of vexation." Though in this case...

"Were the beets *that* awful?" she asked.

Mason thought back to the night he'd gone to Ciddah's apartment and she'd cooked dinner. That had been a good night, despite the tension of his role in breaking the women out from the harem and the horror of seeing his mother's face on the liberation broadcast. "On the contrary, the beets were quite good."

"It's because I asked you to stay, then, isn't it? I scared you away."

She hadn't scared him. She simply hadn't been able to wrap her mind around his morality. What Ciddah and Mason deemed moral were polar opposites. He didn't like this conversation. It felt like an attack, like she wanted to fight. He was not suited for romantic missions. Levi or Omar had no difficulty speaking with females, but Mason never knew what to say.

"The beets were quite good," he said softly, hoping she would think him funny.

But Ciddah sighed and looked away.

See? He'd already said the wrong thing. How could he fix it? Was she seeking some kind of reassurance? "I do not disdain you for your advances, nor do I fear them."

Her head turned slowly, and the cold look on her face made Mason shiver. "You're being temporarily reassigned to the pharmacy in the lobby," Ciddah said, her voice aloof and businesslike. "One of the pharmacy techs is taking two weeks off, and you're going to fill in."

The pharmacy? "Why me?"

"Because there's no one else who's trained, and I think you can handle it."

But... "This is not a punishment for my poor communication skills?"

Ciddah began to sort through the mess on her desk, as if suddenly too busy to give him her full attention. "No. Though I would dock your credits if I could."

He blinked, trying to ascertain which words he'd said that had been bad enough to penalize his earnings. "By how much?"

"It was a joke, Mason." But Ciddah wouldn't meet his eyes. "The head pharmacist downstairs is named Philo Brock. He's expecting you."

"I'm to go right now?"

She picked up a stack of papers and scanned the top page. "Yes."

How was he to get Ciddah's help if they were apart? And how was he to find a cure for the thin plague? "Will I be back?"

She flipped to the second page. "In about two weeks—on the thirteenth of August, actually."

Well, this would never do. "Can I... um—?"

The speaker on Ciddah's desk beeped. "I just put a patient in exam two for you," Rimola said.

Ciddah pushed a button on the speaker. "I'm on my way." She set down the papers and stood. "See you in two weeks, Mr. Elias."

The pharmacy in the lobby was a Pharmco, which was the only type of pharmacy Mason had seen in the Safe Lands besides those located inside G.I.N. stores. This one was a single black counter in the corner of the City Hall lobby. Mason announced himself to the girl behind the counter, whose name badge read Saska, and she called Philo Brock out to the front.

Where Saska was dark and round, with black hair and bronze skin, Philo was light and thin with skin the color of milk and hair like a baby chick. The Old rhyme *Jack Sprat* came to mind as Saska and Mr. Brock spoke to each other just out of Mason's hearing, though it wasn't likely these two were a couple.

"Mr. Elias. Excellent!" Mr. Brock opened a half-door on the end of the counter. "Come on back."

Mr. Elias... Mason expected such formality from strangers like Mr. Brock, but not from Ciddah. Her coldness upstairs had shaken him. It had been a grave error to ignore her for so long. Had he lost everything he'd worked so hard to build? There must be some way to salvage it.

Mason followed Mr. Brock behind the counter, where rows of shelves were stocked with bottles of medications. Mr. Brock passed them all and turned down the last row where a long desk was covered in equipment.

"First of all, you touch none of this. I work back here. You assist. Got it?" Mr. Brock looked at Mason, his eyebrows raised over a pair of bulging eyes in a gaunt face. He must have been nearing the liberation age of forty.

"Yes, sir," Mason said.

"You'll start each task shift by checking in with me. This branch is only open during business hours, so I'm always here. I eat my lunch here. I take my breaks here. Ciddah told me you're bright, but I'll judge that for myself. This is *not* a task that tolerates errors. With every prescription passed over that counter, someone's life is at stake. Got it?"

An extreme view of pharmaceutics, but technically accurate. "Yes, sir."

"You deal with the customers. You answer the phones. You check the order report. You process prescriptions. Can't read the prescription? Don't ask me. Call the medic and find out. *My* time is valuable. *Your* job is to let me do mine. Got it?"

So... never speak to Mr. Brock again. "Yes, sir."

"Well, at least you're polite," Mr. Brock mumbled.

Saska showed Mason how to check the order report and process prescriptions. Then she showed him how to work the credit register. "If you think you've got it, I can get caught up, and then have more time to show you things."

"I believe I can handle the register." But a line soon formed, made up of people with crossed arms, tapping feet, or glaring eyes.

Saska came back to help Mason, and together they worked faster. She handed Mason a prescription for the next man at the counter, then left to find it.

Mason scanned the prescription over the register and read from the screen. "Ten credits."

"It's always been five," the man said.

Mason met the man's narrowed eyes, then turned to look for Saska, who had gone halfway down the first row of medications. He went over to her. "The customer says his prescription always costs five credits."

everyone but Mason will take a different storm drain into the Midlands. We checked it today, and the enforcers still haven't found it."

"Then Dayle will drive Mason to the Medical Center and pick up Omar's team," Ruston said. "Everyone piles in back, and Mason gets to work on the babies. Dayle will drive back to the drain, and when you get the babies on the other side, we'll have another truck waiting. Omar can drive it up to the cabin for the night. We'll move your women and babies to the basements on Sunday night."

"If we had Ciddah with us, she could do half the SimTags," Mason said.

Again with the medic? "No," Levi said. "We need you with us tonight, brother."

Mason eyed Levi a moment, lips pressed into a thin line. "Perhaps I should teach someone how to remove SimTags. It's not that difficult. One of Bender's people removed mine."

"You'll be fine," Zane said. "You'll have lots of time. I'm going to broadcast one of the Owl videos we prerecorded at the same time you enter the school. And one of my peers is going to put on the costume and create a disturbance in Champion Park. That should keep the enforcers distracted a bit."

"It wasn't you in Omar's costume last night?" Levi asked Zane.

"With *my* limp?" Zane said. "Naw, peer. Just someone who owes me a favor."

"He better not mess it up," Omar said. "Do you have any plan for the nursery?"

Hadn't Levi already said? Was Omar not listening?

"Just to the doors," Zane said to Omar. "We're going to have to talk to Kendall tomorrow about what to do once we get in. But here's what I know. The nursery is on the sixth floor of the Medical Center. The nursery team will follow you through the tunnels to an alley off Gothic. Then you're going to walk to the MC. I'll figure out which cameras to tap, so I'll be your eyes. It's going to be tricksy, though. I've never tried to swipe babies from the MC."

"Skottie had a femme who's gatekeeper for the RC," Omar said. "So that's you, Zane. You're our gatekeeper. We couldn't do this without you."

Levi conceded that much. Without Ruston and Zane, they'd be lost. He hated having to rely on them, but there was nothing he could do about it. The Safe Lands were like a foreign world. It would be a miracle it they ever got out alive.

Chapter 24

It was still dark. But at 5:00 a.m., the moment the clerk opened the Lift on the corner of Anthracite and Winterset, Omar went inside with Mason and sat at a table to wait for Kendall to arrive. Omar used the ghoulie tag ring Mason had given him to purchase a smoothie drink with five lifts of grass, hoping it would stop the itch for his PV. Now that he was off-grid, he didn't have any credits to buy a new one since ghoulie tags never had many credits on them.

"You'd be wise to avoid stimulants, brother," Mason said. "It only complicates your condition."

Ice shot up Omar's spine. "Why does everyone feel the need to tell me what to do? Wait—" He tapped his Wyndo watch to the memo screen. "I forgot that you were an expert on my life. Let me take notes."

"I'm sorry, Omar," Mason said. "I didn't mean to criticize."

Another chill ran over him, one that reminded him that Mason was right. "Look, Mase, five lifts of grass is like vaping a two in a PV. It's not doing much, trust me." But he hoped it would.

Omar took a long drink through the straw. Only two nights had passed since Otley had shown up at his apartment. He'd been itching something fierce since he woke up in the RC. He'd tried going to his apartment last night, but enforcers had been camped outside. Apparently, Otley didn't like that Omar had cut out his SimTag the same day he'd been warned not to.

Surprise, surprise.

Two nights felt like two hundred. Omar was still mad at Zane for not helping him get a new PV. Zane said Omar was better off without it, but Omar needed it—was sick without it. He was so tired, but he couldn't sleep, couldn't even get comfortable. Plus, it was seventy degrees out, and he was freezing. Shivering and shaking like a kitten in a toddler's hands.

Maybe that was the lynchpin: destroy wherever stimulants were created. Without juice to vape, Safe Landers would go insane, government officials included. Then Levi and the rebels could sweep in and take over. It actually wasn't a bad idea. Maybe the Owl could do it. Omar the Owl, though, not Zane's copycat impostor.

"She's here," Mason said. "What in all the lands?"

Kendall trudged into the Lift parking lot holding a suitcase in one hand and her birdcage in the other.

"Could she be any more obvious?" Mason asked. "The whole point of doing this when it's still dark is so no one will see us. But a girl carrying a birdcage is pretty unforgettable."

Pretty stupid. If Kendall had wanted to bring the bird, she should have tapped Omar about it. "I'll wave us a cab."

"Where are we going to put the bird until I'm done?" Mason asked.

"I don't know." Omar hoped this was one of those things they'd laugh about someday. Right now, he wanted to wring Kendall's neck. He took another drink, still not feeling the effects of the grass. What if the clerk had forgotten it?

"How about you sit with it while I take her into the bathroom?" Mason suggested.

"Just make it quick," Omar said. "This bird talks."

Mason walked down the hall to the bathrooms seconds before Kendall opened the front door. Omar got up and took the cage so she could drag her suitcase inside. He carried the bird back to the table and sat down.

Seconds later, Kendall dropped her suitcase beside the birdcage. "What happened to your eye?"

"Meet Mason in the bathroom," he said.

Kendall blinked at him, so he repositioned his chair in front of the cage, hiding the bird as best he could. Now, if the critter would just stay silent.

When Omar looked up, he saw that Kendall had walked away. She knocked on the bathroom door, then slipped inside.

"Give me a kiss. Tch tch tch."

Omar jumped. Why hadn't she at least covered the cage? He opened her suitcase to see if she had brought the cover. Clothes blossomed out and spilled onto the floor. Great. No sign of a cover, either. Omar did his best to pack it back nicely.

"Basil's a budgie, budgie."

"What do you have there?" the clerk asked from behind the counter.

See? That bird was guaranteed to cause trouble. "Oh, it's just a dumb bird."

"Juice off, Lawten. You're a shell!"

The clerk eyes widened, and he walked over to Omar's table. "You teach it to say that?"

"Naw. My friend's idea of a joke." Omar took a drink of his smoothie. Why couldn't he taste the grass? He wasn't feeling a thing.

"Doesn't sound like much of a friend," the clerk said. "An enforcer hears that, they'll arrest you for slander."

They'd arrest him for more than that. "Yeah, well, that's why I'm trying to get rid of the dumb thing."

The clerk eyes widened. "You selling it?"

"Tch tch tch. Omar's the Owl."

Omar blanched. She'd taught the bird to say *that*? What was Kendall's problem, anyway? "Hey." He kicked the cage. "People are trying to enjoy their drinks." He wished he was enjoying his, but the grass lift must have been defective.

"Did he just say Omar's the Owl?" the clerk asked.

Omar did his best to think fast and make it sound legit. "The bird's name is Omar. He saw all that stuff on the ColorCast about that Owl fellow. Now he thinks he's the Owl."

The clerk laughed. "Walls! That's funny."

"Tell me about it." Omar glanced down the hallway to the bathrooms. *Today*, Mason. His muscles ached—his very bones ached. He sucked down the rest of the smoothie, desperate for the grass to provide some relief.

The clerk squatted beside the cage and looked at Basil. "Well, if you're selling him, I'm interested."

Of course he was. "Yeah? Well, I'm headed over to the Prospector now to meet a potential buyer, but if it doesn't work out..." Omar pushed up his sleeve and held out his Wyndo watch to the clerk.

"Oh, sure." The clerk tapped his fist against the Wyndo screen, which displayed the clerk's face with his name and ID number underneath.

"Thanks, Keny," Omar said, reading the screen.

"What time is it?" Basil said. "Tch tch tch. Owl. Omar's the Owl."

Omar rolled his eyes at Keny. "I'm warning you. He never shuts up."

"I think he's stimming decked," Keny said. "Well, I should get back. Hope to hear from you."

"Yeah, we'll see."

The clerk returned to the counter just as Mason and Kendall approached the table.

"I'm going to wave a cab." Omar got up and walked to the door, anxious to get out of there. "Come out as soon as you see I got one." He didn't wait for their answer. *Omar's the Owl?* What had that crazy femme been thinking?

Soon they were all riding in the cab, headed toward Zane's house, but Basil's chatter drew them into another awkward conversation with the driver. Omar had to interrupt Kendall's explanations to give the same story he'd given Keny. Consistency was key in a situation like this. Otley wouldn't have any trouble tracking them if he thought to ask about the bird.

When they were all safely inside Zane's house, Omar let Kendall have it. "What were you thinking, bringing that dumb bird? And why did you teach him to say Omar's the Owl?"

Kendall frowned and looked at Basil's cage on the living room floor in the middle of the circle of chairs. "He copies me sometimes, and I didn't want to leave him behind."

Copies her? "So, who did you say 'Omar's the Owl' to?"

Her cheeks flushed and she glanced at Omar, bottom lip pouting like he should feel sorry for her. "No one. Just... myself."

Kendall had already proved how big her mouth was. She'd told Jemma about the scene Red had made at the train station and that Omar was the Owl. The bird wouldn't have been there for that conversation. "You sure you haven't accidentally told anyone else anything about me or the rebels or the Owl or where you're going tonight?" Omar asked. "Any friends?"

"I don't have any friends." Now her eyes were all teary, which made Omar feel like a jerk.

"You do now," Mason said, ever the peacemaker.

Omar picked up Basil's cage and headed for the garage. They needed to get to the cabin unseen, so they were taking the van. Omar carried the "tch tch tch-ing" bird, Mason the suitcase, and Kendall followed. Nash drove them to the cabin, the bird yakking the whole way. Omar had never been more thrilled to get to a place where everyone thought he was a traitor.

The three of them created quite a stir when they entered the cabin. Jordan came running, gun in hand. Omar wondered if he had any ammo for it yet. Aunt Chipeta ushered Mason up to the attic with Kendall's suitcase. Shay and Jemma came next. Shay looked pale, and Omar wished he'd thought to get her a pastry from the Lift. Or maybe she was just unhappy to see him. Either way, he owed her an apology. He dropped the cage in the hallway and took her hand, pulling her toward the bathroom.

"Is that Basil?" she asked, plodding alongside him.

"I want to talk to you," he said.

"Tch tch tch. Omar's the Owl."

Shaylinn gasped and looked over her shoulder. "Did he just say—?"

"Yes, and I wish he'd stop." Omar pulled her inside the bathroom. He shut the door and locked it, then lowered the lid on the toilet seat. "Will you sit down?"

Shay sat.

Omar sat on the side of the tub and took her hand. "I'm sorry, Shay. I was a jerk. Kendall told Jemma that I was the Owl. In case you missed his announcement, she even told the bird. And who knows who else. I should have believed you when you said you kept my secret, but I was too busy being angry. I said cruel things that I didn't mean. Your messages are so special to people. To me. Will you forgive me?"

She grinned, though her eyes were teary. "Of course I forgive you."

Really? "That's it?"

She tugged on his hands. "Did you want me to yell and make you feel guilty?"

"I guess not." The smile on her face filled him with a rush of joy, and for a few seconds he almost felt better. He wanted to ask to paint her, then wondered how long his paint supplies would be in his apartment before the Registration Department assigned the place to someone else.

"I don't like fighting, Omar."

"I'm sorry." Those words had become his mantra. He really needed to quit screwing up all the time.

"You already said that. No need to say it again." Shay set her hand on the top of his head, and her touch made his heart race. "What happened to your eye?"

"Otley punched me."

"Oh, Omar. Please be more careful." She let her hand fall back to her lap. He wanted to hold it again, but didn't feel like he had any reason to. The tub had started to hurt his backside, so he moved to the floor and leaned against the wall. It was cold and he shivered, his arm hair standing on end. "How do you know what to write in your messages?"

She fidgeted with her skirt. "I pray and take my best guess."

"'Temptation,' you wrote in mine."

Her cheeks flushed a brilliant magenta. Not many people turned so dark when they blushed. Shay and Jordan did, but not Jemma.

"Your PV always seems to be attached to your hand," she said, "though I don't see it right now."

Oh. Her messages had been referencing his temptations to stims, not women. She was spot on with both, though. What was he doing here with someone as good as Shay?

"Do you believe a lie about yourself, Omar?" she asked.

He admired the way her hair curled over each shoulder and into her lap. "If I did, I suppose I wouldn't know it was a lie, since I believed it."

She chuckled, and the sound was light and fun and made him grin. "I never thought of it that way."

But Omar suddenly knew his answer. "I believe I'm worthless."

Shay tilted her head and stared at him, her eyes sad but accepting.

"Nobody ever wanted me around," he said. "But it's not a lie."

"You're wrong." She leaned over and squeezed his shoulder. "I've always wanted you around."

How did she do that? Make him feel so worthy? "Why?"

"Because you're funny and talented and handsome. I loved watching you sit in the square and paint, and you'd always tell us about your dreams, that you were going to do great things. It made me want dreams of my own."

She'd been listening. Always. He wanted to kiss her, but he stayed put on the floor. Shay was too special to move so fast. He needed to wait for her, to be patient. He needed to make himself worthy. Do something to earn her respect. "I'm sorry I was mean to you," he said. "Ever."

She blushed again, this time putting her hands on her cheeks like she had felt it happen. "Thank you, Omar. But I'll not accept any more apologies from you today."

He winced, overplaying it. "That might not be wise. I mess up a lot."

She leaned over and kissed his cheek. She smelled sweet, like honey, and her hair tickled his neck. "I will always forgive you. Now, go away so I can be sick." She set her hand over her stomach and suddenly looked much paler than she had before.

Omar slipped out of the bathroom and closed the door. Standing felt good—for three seconds. Then he wanted to lie down and weep at the intensity of the itch.

It struck him as ironic that his father had always threatened to marry him to Shay, a fate Omar had dreaded. How stupid could he have been?

After Kendall had helped them plan out the nursery rescue, the day was filled with agonizing boredom. Everyone sat around, waiting for night to come. Basil was the only entertainment. Some took naps. Omar went down to the basement for a while and lay down on one of the beds, where he tossed and turned, drenched in a cold sweat. But when he couldn't sleep, he decided to go check on Shay. He went upstairs and found Kendall sitting alone on one of the couches in the living room. It was late now—11:33 p.m. Almost time.

"Will you sit with me awhile?" Kendall asked. "I'm worried about tonight."

Omar sat beside her on the couch. "Worrying won't do you any good."

"Once I get Elyot, where will I go?" Kendall asked.

"Into the basements with us until we can get out of this place," Omar said, wondering how he'd get stims from now on. Perhaps the Owl would need to visit a hit room and help himself. If he didn't get something real soon, he had a feeling he'd die.

"I'll have no way to earn credits," Kendall said. "How will I provide for my son?"

Like he knew how life would be underground. "I don't think they use credits in the basements. I'm sure some of the Natural women can help you figure all that out. Everyone will have the same problems. The Naturals wouldn't bother helping us if they didn't care about how we'd all live."

"Will you help me?"

What did *that* mean? He turned to look at her. "What could I do?"

She bumped her shoulder against his. "Keep me company. Maybe help me raise my son."

His cheeks tingled as the blood drained away. "Kendall... I don't know anything about raising a kid."

"But you're going to be a father. You'll learn."

Which still terrified him. "Sure, but—"

She leaned in and kissed him. He turned his head to stop her. "Kendall, I can't. Shay..." He should have made himself clear before. "If I'm going to help anyone, it's her."

Kendall rolled her eyes. "She's not like us, Omar. You and me, we have the thin plague. How could you expect to be with her and not infect her? You'd kill her."

Kill Shay? Omar's chest tightened. "I don't know." He hadn't thought about all that—the future. Once they freed the kids, there'd be time to figure everything out. To talk to Shay. See what she wanted. He was only sixteen, for crying out loud. All his life he'd wanted to be treated like an adult, now he just wanted the simplicity of being a kid again.

But his childhood was gone forever.

"I think we could work, Omar," Kendall said, taking hold of his hand. "You and me. Lifers."

Lifers...?

She kissed him again, and this time he let her, trying to decide if she was right. He didn't want Shay to be infected. But if Mason could find a cure, then—

"Really?"

Shay's voice broke him away from Kendall. She stood in the archway to the kitchen, Jordan's pistol in her hand. Was she going to shoot them?

"You're not a very nice friend," she said to Kendall, her voice cracked, broken. Then she turned her betrayed expression on Omar. "Either of you."

Omar got up from the couch and walked toward her, slowly, as if trying not to frighten a bird into flight. Her eyes widened and she inched back, shaking her head slightly. "Either of you, Omar."

He reached for Shay's arm, but she backed out of his reach. "Shay, wait." He grabbed her wrist that held the gun and pulled the weapon away, still holding on to her wrist. "It's not what you think."

"Let go." She pulled until her hand squeezed through his grip, then jogged toward her bedroom, so he ran past her and blocked the door. She spun away and slipped into the bathroom. He just managed to get his foot in the opening before she shut the door. It struck his shoe.

"Shay, let me explain."

One of her eyes glared out the opening. "I don't need an explanation." Her voice was a hard whisper. "When in the Safe Lands, do as the nationals do, right? Pair up? Trade paint? Find pleasure in life?"

"Please, it's not like that. I'm different now that—well, I'm trying to be."

Shay rolled her eyes. "Let me know when you grow up." She kicked at his foot, to no avail.

"Shay, please listen. I told her to stop, that I couldn't do it."

"But you did." Shay looked at him through the crack, her eyes teary now. "You made your choice. Just... Take Jordan's gun. I was bringing it to you. He got ammo for it, but Levi won't let him take it tonight, so he hid it under his bed. I want you to bring back Penny and Nell, okay? I'm going to need someone to help with the babies, and they're my real friends." She reached out and shoved him. He stumbled back a step, and she slammed the door. The lock clicked.

Gun in one hand, Omar used his other to knock on the door and shake the knob. "Shay? Open the door."

Instead, a door opened behind him. Omar turned to see which one. Jordan stepped into the hall, eyes sleepy. "What's going on?"

Omar hid the gun behind his back, tucked it into the back of his pants. "Nothing."

"Who's in there?" Jordan motioned to the bathroom.

"Shay."

Jordan pushed in front of Omar. "Go downstairs. I'll take care of her."

"Right." Jordan likely thought Shay was sick again. Omar couldn't risk being here when Jordan found out the truth. He turned and strode toward the front door. Kendall said something as he passed the living room. He darted back and found her sitting on the couch. She smiled as if nothing was wrong.

"You and me aren't going to happen, Kendall. Get that straight." He left the cabin and started walking. That girl had ruined everything. Why was he always so stupid?

He checked the gun and found that it was indeed loaded. Panic shot through him. Shay could have hurt herself. But he'd hurt her first. Why did he keep hurting her?

Maybe Kendall was right. Maybe Omar was all wrong for Shay. He was infected and she wasn't. He was dying and she was very much alive.

But she was the only person who made him feel like he could ever be good again. He was pretty sure he'd die a lot faster without her in his life.

He was shivering badly by the time he reached Kokanee Lane. He needed a hit now. Maybe Skottie or Charlz would help him. He hadn't spoken to either in almost a month, but he knew they'd understand the itch. If nothing else, maybe they'd buy him a beer.

He kept walking. It never hurt to ask.

Chapter 25

"Come on, Shay," Jordan said through the locked door. "Open up."

"I'm fine." She yawned over her tears. She was so tired. She should have stayed in bed. Then she'd still be dreaming of her nice moments with Omar before he'd ruined everything. Again.

It wasn't fair. Her parents had been killed. The Safe Lands had made her pregnant. And just when it seemed like Omar had noticed her, just when she thought he might actually care about her, Kendall had come along. How could she compete against a beautiful, mature woman like that?

They'd had such a nice talk today. He'd really seemed to care about her. Why was she so blind about boys? And why were boys so dumb?

A wave of queasiness seized her, and she went to her knees before the toilet. Naomi had promised the morning sickness wouldn't last. But Shaylinn was still sick no matter the time of day. It seemed a terrible joke. If she'd been married and had a husband who loved her, the sickness would be bearable.

But to be so alone...

When she finally exited the bathroom, she found Jordan sitting on the floor against the wall, sleeping. Sweet, stubborn brother. She nudged him. "Jordan, it's almost midnight."

He gasped and coughed. "What's for breakfast?"

"Why don't you go downstairs and make sure the other men are awake?"

He rubbed his eyes. "You okay?"

"Just tired." Though she didn't think she'd be able to sleep until she knew everyone had been rescued.

Jordan pushed up to his feet. "Love you, sis." He hugged her and kissed her hair.

The act brought tears to her eyes. "Be careful tonight, okay?"

He pulled back so he could see her face and gave her that wide, crooked grin of his. "Tomorrow you can see Penny and Nell. My gift to you."

"Thank you. Be safe."

"Always."

Once the men—and Kendall—had set off, Shay found Jemma in the room she and Levi had been using. Her sister lay in bed, staring at the ceiling.

"Chipeta is leading prayers in the living room, but I need a break," Shaylinn said. "Mind if I join you?"

"I'd love it," Jemma said, throwing back the covers.

Shaylinn climbed into bed with her sister, and they nestled close. Jemma began to braid strands of Shay's hair. It almost felt like they were kids again in the cabin bedroom they'd shared in Glenrock.

"How are you feeling?" Jemma asked.

"Sick." And brokenhearted.

"I'm sorry, love. Did you and Omar talk? Did you make up?"

Tears flooded her eyes. "He apologized for what he said before."

"That's good, right?"

It had been good. A lovely moment. She was thankful for that, even if it hadn't lasted long. "Later I saw him kissing Kendall."

"What!" Jemma sat up and looked down on Shay's face. "Oh, honey. I'm so sorry."

Her reaction brought Shay's tears to the surface. She hated crying but hadn't been able to control it lately. "Maybe it's just that he's a lot more experienced than me. I don't think he wants to be with a girl so... prude?"

"Ugh. If that's the case, he doesn't deserve you. But I know Omar. I knew him, anyway. I can't believe he'd leave you alone."

"I don't want him out of his guilt, Jem. I want him to love me."

Jemma finger-combed out the braid she'd started in Shaylinn's hair. "Omar should have to earn your love, Shay. If he's not willing, then he's not worth it. Don't risk your heart on a lazy man. He'll take what he wants from you and not give back. And that's not love, honey. That's just not."

Jemma acted like there were a lot of men to choose from in the world. But there weren't. "You never doubted Levi's love for you."

Jemma expression softened into a smile. "No. My heart is, and always will be, his."

Shaylinn sighed, knowing she'd never have anything like her sister had with Levi. "Why can't I have that certainty? Why do I have so much doubt?"

"Because you are you and I am me. And because Omar hasn't exactly been an unchanging rock of a guy. If we all had the same life, there'd be no surprise. I'm angry that Omar hurt you. He's a stupid boy, and if he were here right now, I'd tell him so and whack his head. I hope you did."

"I didn't." As if Shaylinn could ever strike anyone like that. "I told him to bring back Penny and Nell because I'd need help raising the babies."

"Oh, you're a clever girl. Guilting him."

Had she? "I didn't mean to. I'm just tired of feeling so alone." She really did want Penny and Nell back in her life. She missed them desperately.

"You're not alone, dearest. You have me."

Only when Levi and Naomi were busy. "I'm so angry at them both."

"You have a right to be. Sit up and let me finish braiding your hair."

Shaylinn pushed herself up and turned her back to Jemma. "But if I'm angry... if I judge him, I'm not loving him."

Jemma again combed her fingers through Shaylinn's hair and started a new braid. "How can you love him if he's loving someone else?"

"I don't think he loves Kendall. He's addicted to doing whatever makes him feel good. And there are too many things that make him feel good in this place."

"Don't make excuses for him. Men become men by making sacrifices and doing what's hard. He's going to have to decide if he wants to grow up or not. Marriage means something to Omar—I know it does. Despite how he's been acting since we came here, he's *not* a Safe Lander. He's from Glenrock. And his mother raised him to know what's right."

"I don't think he cares about how his mother raised him. Not anymore." Tamera would have cuffed Omar upside the head ten times by now.

"I don't believe that," Jemma said. "The way he paints? As moody as he is? All he's ever wanted was to find the right girl to spoil with all his romantic ideas."

Yeah. "Maybe I'm the wrong girl."

Jemma tugged on Shay's braid. "That's not possible."

But why? Just because Shay wanted something didn't mean God would give it to her. He might have another plan. "I so believed that God was going to do something big in my life with these babies. I thought part of it was to finally bring me and Omar together. But I'm just a dreamer, really. Making things up in my head. I wanted what you and Naomi have with Levi and Jordan. I wanted something real. But I don't know how to have a real relationship with anyone." She might only fourteen, but she knew that not every person got married. Some stayed single forever.

"There's nothing to know, Shay. You just do your best. You talk. Become friends. See if your life goals are a match."

"I don't even know what Omar's life goals are—or mine, for that matter, apart from loving Omar. And I don't think Omar knows his goals, either. So, how could we possibly know if they matched?"

"By talking to each other."

"Every time we talk, someone ruins it. Me, or Omar, or someone else. Now Kendall. I thought she was my friend. I told her I loved Omar. Why would she do this?"

"If she gets Elyot back tonight, she'll be raising him alone. Maybe she wants something real too. But I'm sorry that she felt like her own happiness was more important than her friendship with you."

"I miss Penny and Nell. But they won't know what to say to any of this, either. These are grown-up problems, and none of us are grown-ups."

"There are no grown-ups, really," Jemma said. "Just old kids who still feel young inside despite the fact that their face no longer looks it."

Shaylinn smiled at Jemma's words. "Is that from a book or a movie?"

"Papa Eli." Jemma tucked the end of the braid into the neckline of Shaylinn's tank top.

"I miss him. He was such a kind man and a wise elder." Shaylinn fell back on the bed. "Everything was so much easier when I believed I was ugly and Omar would never, ever want me."

Jemma brushed a loose wisp of hair off Shay's forehead and looked down on her face. "Longing is good for a season. And while living in that wanting place might feel safe, it's hiding from real life. Live your life, Shay. And seek out—"

A knock on the door made both girls sit up. Chipeta burst in. "Come quick—Naomi's in labor."

Chapter 26

The sound of nine pairs of feet sloshing through ankle-deep water set Levi's nerves on edge. He wished they'd all take more care and walk on the sides of the pipe—at least try not to announce their presence to enforcers who might be on patrol.

Despite what Levi wanted, he wasn't fully in charge of this mission. Getting Ruston and Zane's help tonight meant he had to trust them, like it or not.

He and Ruston had done a run-through that morning, so Levi, at least, knew what to expect. They'd already removed the storm drain cover in the alley and covered it with a maintenance sign, so there'd be little delay getting above ground. The bridge board was waiting there too, behind a dumpster. Levi was most concerned about Yivan, who'd tripped three times since they'd started out. He wished they'd left the fifteen-year-old klutz behind.

Soon they were climbing to the surface. Levi waited with Ruston until all nine of the men had climbed out. Jordan retrieved the bridge board and tucked it under one arm. They all carried stunners on gun belts Ruston had provided. Even Mason had taken one. But they were SimScanners, not regular stunners. SimScanners read a target's SimTag, then stunned them, without the wires even coming out. The best part was that the guards' SimScanners wouldn't work on the rebels since they had removed their SimTags. Levi greatly appreciated what that added to their odds of success tonight.

The alley stretched between an auto repair shop and the back of the Nordic apartment building. Treasury Road wasn't much wider than the alley. There were no streetlamps. The west side of the road butted up against a fence that was the back of the ColorCast lot where they filmed much of what appeared on TV. The east side of the road was the back end of the auto repair shop. From where the road dead-ended at the Midlands wall, it stretched about 100 yards to where it met Eammons, which edged the north side of the Rehabilitation Center.

Levi didn't like their proximity to the RC. He removed his SimScanner from his belt and held it by his side.

"Okay." Ruston stopped behind the Nordic, where the smell of clean laundry blew strong. "Farran, Nash, Levi, Mason, and Jordan—with me. The rest of you, wait here. We shouldn't be long."

Ruston led Levi and the others down the road, which had no sidewalk until they reached Eammons. They circled the building and stopped outside the front entrance.

"We're at the Nordic," Ruston said. "You ready, Zane?"

Zane's answer came as a soft gurgle from Ruston's SimTalk implant. "Ready. I own the cameras."

Ruston pushed through the front entrance and walked toward the elevators. Levi followed, nerves on high alert, scanning the tiny lobby for the doorman.

No sign.

Ruston reached the elevator and turned. "No doorman, Zane."

"He was there a minute ago," came Zane's muffled reply.

"Should we go?" Mason asked.

Levi was just as anxious to get out of sight. "Not if we don't want to happen upon him on the way back down."

Ruston took a deep breath and panned his gaze across the lobby. "He can't have gone far, and we need to take him out."

"Maybe he went up to one of the residents' apartments to deliver something," Mason said.

Levi started around the perimeter of the lobby. It was small, about the size of a living room, with glass windows facing the street. In the far corner opposite the elevator, Levi passed a door to the stairwell. Three more steps, and he came to another door. This one said "Restroom." A stripe of yellow light lit a crack at the bottom of the door.

Levi snapped his fingers three times. The men's gazes locked on his, and he pointed to the bathroom door.

Ruston and Farran came running, clutching their SimScanners. A quick look and Ruston said, "Farran, come with me. Levi, stand watch."

Ruston pulled open the bathroom door and entered, Farran on his heels. Mason joined Levi next, then Jordan, who set down the board and made to follow the men into the bathroom, but Levi stopped him.

"They got it, Jordan."

A loud bang preceded a man's shout. "What are you doing? Get out of here!"

Jordan chuckled, delighted with the situation. "They got the maggot on the pot."

Levi rolled his eyes at his friend's boorish sense of humor.

A minute later, the bathroom door opened, and Farran stuck out his head. "Nash. We need you."

Nash slipped past Levi and Jordan and went inside.

"I'm stronger than that weed," Jordan said.

Jordan was simply anxious to be put to good use. "You'll get your chance to be a hero," Levi said. "For now, we trust Ruston." No matter how hard that might be.

Another minute passed, and the three men exited, Nash wearing an extremely tight doorman's shirt.

"Go fetch the others," Ruston told Farran, who headed for the exit.

"What's this?" Jordan asked Nash.

"My dim brother neglected to warn us that the doorman was a child," Nash said.

"Shortest man I've ever seen," Ruston said. "Skinny too. No way Farran could fit into his uniform."

"I couldn't get his pants past my knees," Nash said.

Jordan busted up laughing.

Farran returned with Beshup and the three Jack's Peak teens. Ruston, who was wearing gloves, pressed the Up button on the elevator, and the door slid open immediately.

They piled inside. Ruston hit the button for five, and the elevator sailed up. From the fifth floor, Zane worked his grid magic and unlocked the door to the stairs that led to the roof.

A cool breeze hit Levi when he stepped out onto the roof. It didn't take long to locate Penelope's plank. It was no more than twelve inches wide and stretched four feet across the narrow space between the Nordic and the school. Five stories down there was nothing more than a dead-end alley with a dumpster. Anyone who fell would hit the ground hard.

Jordan walked up beside Levi and stopped, the bridge board under his arm. "I could jump that."

He probably could. "But you won't," Levi said.

"I won't. But I could. And my board is bigger." Jordan hefted it out until it crossed the gap, then he moved it until it was right next to Penny's board. Jordan's was twice as wide.

"Levi," a voice called out from the other roof. "Mason?"

Levi scanned the roof of the school and spotted Penny and Nell standing by a shed that looked like the access to the stairs. Nell squealed and jumped up and down. Levi waved and set his finger against his lips.

"*Girls*," Jordan mumbled. "If we make it out of here with everyone, it will be a miracle."

"Then pray for a miracle," Mason said.

Indeed. Jemma had promised to have the women praying all night, but Levi tossed up a quick prayer of his own.

"What am I supposed to do?" Farran asked. He'd been planning to act as the doorman downstairs and Nash as the lookout, but the tiny uniform had changed their plans.

"Cross over with us and perch on the edge of the roof overlooking the courtyard," Ruston said. "You see trouble, talk to Zane, who'll talk to me."

While Ruston was coaching Farran, Levi holstered his SimScanner and crossed the board. Penny ran to him and gave him a tight hug.

"I'm so glad to see you," she said.

Nell joined their hug, making it a threesome. Until Jordan and Mason crossed over, then they each got double hugs as well.

"What's the plan, Pen?" Levi asked.

"Nell and I are the only two girl thirteens. The thirteens and the twelves have their dorm on the fifth floor. The tens and elevens share, and the sevens, eights, and nines share—both those dorms are on the fourth floor. Then the threes, fours, fives, and sixes are together on the third floor."

Should Levi have memorized that?

"Is that the same for the boys?" Mason asked.

"Yeah," Penny said. "Dakav and Etu, and Trevon, Jake, and Sakima are going to sneak out on their own and meet us in the courtyard, but you'll have to go back for Joey and Brian and the Jack's Peak boys. There are six boys in the littles."

"That's what we call the three-to-six-year-olds," Nell said.

"And the girls?" Levi asked. "You were able to warn them all?"

"Yep," Penny said. "They should be waiting, if they didn't accidentally fall asleep."

"Are the dorm rooms locked?" Mason asked.

"Not the rooms, but the buildings are. That's why I wanted the bigger boys to help, so they could prop open the door to the boys' building."

"What about guards?" Ruston asked.

"There are two, but they only guard the front entrance to the school."

"They play Wyndo games all night," Nell said.

Good. Levi would take any distraction he could get. "So, my team needs to get Meghan from the fifth floor—"

"No, we got Meghan. She's guarding in the stairwell."

Penny would make a smart elder one day. Levi clarified, "So, my team needs to stop on four and three?"

"Two stops on four and one on three," Pen said.

"And I only need to meet the boys in the courtyard, then go back up to three?" Mason asked.

"Right."

Fantastic. "Pen, lead the way," Levi said.

Penny took them into the stairwell, where they met Meghan. Another quick hug exchange, and they followed Penny down two flights of stairs to the fourth floor.

"Ruth and Lucy's room is on the left-hand side of the hallway," she said. "The Hs are on the right: Hailey, Heather, and Haiwee. You guys should wait in the stairwell. Nell will go and get Ruth and Lucy, and Meghan will get the Hs. Once the girls are in the hall, get them upstairs. Then you should spit up. Levi and whoever can come back down with Nell to get the littles, while Jordan and whoever helps the girls cross the board. I'm going to take Mason and his team to the boys."

"Pen, you're so organized you could have gotten out weeks ago," Levi said.

"Sure. But I didn't know where to go once we got out. Come on, Mase."

Mason grabbed Levi's shoulder. "Good luck, brother."

"And to you," Levi said.

Ruston spoke as he passed by Levi. "If you can free more children, we'll provide for them."

"I'll try," Levi said, though he didn't see how to manage it when there was no time to try to explain who they were. Children would be terrified of strangers in the night trying to steal them from their beds.

Penny continued down the stairs with Mason, Beshup, and Ruston. Levi took out his SimScanner and followed Nell into the dark hallway, but Nell waved him back.

"Just wait in the stairs," she said. "If one of the caretakers comes out and sees girls, she'll get mad at us. But if she sees a man, she'll call the guards."

"Okay." Levi backed into the stairwell. Bossy things, these girls.

Jordan had his SimScanner in hand too. "At least there's a window in the door."

"I hate leaving this up to them," Levi said, "but I guess they know this place better than we do."

Levi watched through the window, his heartbeat thudding in his ears. Finally, Nell came out. But she had five girls with her, instead of two.

"How many was she supposed to bring?" Jordan asked.

"Two," Levi said, cracking the door open.

Ruth came through first. She met Levi's gaze and beamed. Again, he set his finger over his lips. Girls were a bundle of squeals, weren't they?

Next came the three strangers, then Lucy and Nell.

"What's this?" Levi asked.

"This is Chetta, Ren, and Leebelle," Lucy said. "They want out."

"I hate it here," one of the girls said. "The others are mean to me, and I love Lucy."

Lucy hugged her and the girl hugged her back.

"Our caretaker makes me do more chores than anyone else," another girl said.

"The boys are always picking on me," said the third. "I hate boys. But not you, because you're our heroes, like the Owl."

"Do you know the Owl?" the second girl asked Levi.

"I do, actually," Levi said. "He's my brother."

Nell squealed and clapped her hands. "I knew it was Omar! He's obsessed with owls and—"

Levi clamped a hand over Nell's mouth. "Enough of this. Yes, you can all come, but only if you stop talking." He turned to Jordan. "Run them upstairs. Start getting them across to the other roof. I'll send Nodin up with the next bunch, then Yivan and I will follow with the third group."

Jordan holstered his SimScanner and saluted him. "You got it, Elder Levi." Then he started up the stairs with the girls.

Nell ran back into the corridor. Levi watched through the window until the returned with two of the Hs—the girls from Jack's Peak. Levi opened the door and the girls ran into the stairwell.

"Where is Hailey?" he asked Nell.

"She and her friend are trying to talk another girl into coming. The girl wants to come, but she's scared. I'm afraid they're going to wake the others."

Levi looked to Nodin, then Yivan. "Stay here with the girls. We need silence." Then he said to Nell, "Show me."

Nell pattered down the hallway and into the dorm room. Levi followed and peeked in. It was dark, but he could hear the harsh whispers of girls to his left. His eyes adjusted, and he recognized Hailey. A quick scan of the room showed that the other girls were asleep.

He crept inside. Nell, Hailey, and a third girl stood beside the bed of a fourth, who was sitting cross-legged, tears running down her face.

"Levi!" Hailey whispered. "She's scared to come."

"Hailey, you and your friend stay with Nell. You're going to follow me, okay?"

Hailey nodded and cast one last longing look at the crying girl.

"I'm here to help you, okay?" Levi said to the girl. Then he scooped her up and ran toward the door. The girl squealed. Levi had to toss her over his shoulder to get the door open. Once he was in the hall, he clamped his hand over her mouth and ran for the stairs. Nodin opened the door, and Levi ran into the stairwell and up a flight of stairs. He didn't dare take his hand off the girl's mouth. He couldn't believe he'd taken her. It was such a stupid risk. Not to mention that he felt like he'd just abducted a little girl against her will. What had become of them all?

Ruston's bleeding heart, anyway.

Levi ran all the way to the roof. Jordan was carrying Lucy across the plank, so he waited for Jordan to return. He looked down to the girl. "I'm not going to hurt you, okay? The scary part is over. We're on the roof, and now we're going to go across and then you'll be safe with your friends. Can I let go of your mouth? Will you be quiet for me?"

She nodded, eyes wide.

Hailey arrived beside him as he set the girl on her feet and released his hand from her mouth. The girl's bottom lip started to tremble.

"What's her name?" Levi asked.

"Kittie," Hailey said.

"Kittie, watch this big guy walk across that plank."

The little heads turned to look. Jordan stepped on the plank only twice as he came back.

"Jordan, this is Kittie," Levi said. "She's a little scared, so why don't you take her first. She's promised to be very quiet. Right, Kittie?"

Kittie stared at Levi, her eyes as wide as chicken eggs.

Levi grabbed Nell's arm and pulled her back toward the stairs. Nodin and Yivan were watching from the open stairwell door.

Levi waved them ahead. "Down to the third floor."

Nell clomped down the stairs louder than Levi liked, but he kept up with her, and they both passed Nodin and Yivan on the way. On the third floor, Levi stopped to watch through the window as Nell ran down the hallway. Yivan arrived and plowed into Levi's back, slaming him against the door.

Levi turned and glared at the boy.

Yivan shrank back. "Sorry."

Levi forced his attention back to the window. The first child to appear was Sarajawea, a little girl from Jack's Peak. She wandered aimlessly down the hall, dragging a pillow behind her.

Then Nell stepped out and waved Levi to come.

"Get Sarajawea into the stairwell," Levi told Nodin, then ran to meet Nell.

"I think we need the other men to help too," she said when he reached her. "They're all sleeping, and I don't know who's who. I think I just woke up the wrong girl."

Levi went back and told Yivan to sit with Sarajawea, then he brought Nodin with him into the girl's dorm. Beds lined both long walls, but some of them were only bare mattresses on wire frames.

"They're on this end," Nell said, leading the way.

Of the five girls left, he was supposed to take two, but Levi could hardly see, and even if he could, he wasn't sure he'd recognize Kaylee and Rosalie, anyway.

"We'll take them all," he said. "Pick up a girl and carry her to the stairwell. Then come back for the last two. We've got to be quick and quiet, though. Can you do it, Nell?"

"I think so."

"Good. You get this one closest to the door."

Nell reached for a sleeping child, Nodin went for another, and Levi walked to the last bed in the row. He scooped up the little girl and held her close, hoping she'd sleep until he was in the stairwell.

They made it there safely, though Nell looked like she might drop her girl. Yivan and Sarajawea were sitting on the steps looking bored. Nodin passed them, taking his girl up to the roof.

"Yivan, help Nell," Levi said, wishing his crew had a little more common sense.

Yivan jumped up and grabbed the little girl, but he got Nell's shirt too and pulled her so hard that she fell onto her knees.

"Let go," Nell cried.

Yivan put down the little girl, who started crying.

"That's Rosalie." Nell crouched beside the crying girl and rubbed her back. "Hey, Rosalie, don't cry. We're going to take you to your momma now."

Levi winced. Rosalie's mother, Susan, had died in the raid. Apparently, Nell didn't know that, but at least her words had calmed the child for the moment.

The child in Levi's arms shifted and opened her eyes, staring at him. He was pretty sure she wasn't Kaylee.

"Yivan, take Rosalie upstairs. Sarajawea, can you walk? Go with Yivan and Rosalie?"

Sarajawea stood up, holding her pillow, and stared at Yivan. The boy picked up Rosalie and started up the stairs. Sarajawea followed.

"That's three. And, Nell, if you take this one, that will be four." Levi handed off the child in his arms. "I'll go get the last two, but send someone down to help me, okay?"

"Okay, Levi." Nell started up the stairs.

Levi opened the door and crept back to the dorm. He bent down and examined the first girl, then the second. They both had dark hair. He had no idea which was Kaylee.

He picked up one and set her on the edge of her bed. Her body slumped back over onto her side and she pulled for her blankets. Levi picked up the second girl and sat her on the edge of the first girl's bed. This one stayed upright. He propped the first girl up again so that the girls were sitting side by side. He squatted before them, wrapped an arm around each, and stood. They were light, but the one on the left was slipping. He hefted them up and headed for the door.

He should have propped it open.

He pressed himself against the door, bending his knees until the backs on his fingers felt the knob. He strained to turn and pull at the same time, and only managed to rattle the door. He thought about putting down the girls, opening the door, and picking them back up, but he kept at the knob until it finally bounced open far enough that he was able to jab his foot into the crack. He had to lean back to keep hold of the girls, but he managed to wedge his other knee into the crack and knock open the door enough to dart out.

He ran to the stairwell door, which was closed, and set the girls on their feet. One of them started to cry. Levi opened the door and waved them through.

"Go to the stairs," he whispered.

Okay, Mr. Strange Man. Sure. He couldn't blame the girl for being scared out of her mind.

The second girl stared up at him. "Are you Levi?"

Well, now he knew which one was Kaylee. "Yes. I've come to help you and your friend. Go on out through the—"

"You there! What are you doing with those girls?"

A woman stood at the opposite end of the hallway.

Levi shoved Kaylee and the crying girl into the stairwell. "Sit there, Kaylee. I'll be right back."

Levi shut the door and walked toward the woman. "Sorry, I'm a guard, and I heard a noise up here." Yeah, that made a lot of sense. When he was close enough to know he couldn't miss, he drew the SimScanner and fired. The woman grunted, her face distorted into an ugly grimace, and fell.

Levi holstered his weapon and carried the woman into the girls' dorm. He laid her on one of the mattresses, then ripped the sheets off a nearby bed. He whipped the sheet into a long snake and used it to tie the woman's hands to the wire headboard. He repeated the process with another sheet, tying her feet to the footboard. By then she was coming to, moaning. He found a tiny stuffed cat and shoved its head into her mouth.

It would have to do.

He ran back into the hallway and sprinted to the stairwell. When he opened the door, the crying girl screamed.

"You hurt her! You hurt her!"

Perfect. Levi grabbed the girl and covered her mouth with his hand. "She's not hurt, just sleeping. She'll be fine."

The girl jerked away and bit his finger. Levi growled and reapplied his hand in a way he hoped would keep her from opening her mouth. "Kaylee, come on. We have to run fast up these stairs."

"Okay," Kaylee said.

Levi ran up to the fourth floor, but when he turned back, Kaylee was taking her time, one hand on the rail.

"One step, stop." She stepped up with her right foot, then brought her left foot to join it. "Two steps, stop." Then she stepped with her left foot and brought her right to join it. "Three steps, stop."

Oh, come on, little one. "Faster, Kaylee. Can you go faster?"

"Four steps, stop. Five steps, stop." She increased her speed, but not her rhythm.

Levi would just have to come back for her. He ran up. Around the bend of the fourth floor, he met Nodin coming from above.

"Here," Levi said. "She screams and bites, so be careful." He handed off the girl, and she managed a quick screech before Nodin got a good grip on her mouth.

Levi ran back down until he found Kaylee.

"Seventeen steps, stop. Eighteen—"

Levi tossed her over his shoulder and headed back up the stairs. Just as he passed the door to level five, it swung open.

"Who is out of bed?" a woman asked.

Her eyes met Levi's. He fumbled for his SimScanner, but he was holding Kaylee on his right shoulder and couldn't grab it. The woman darted back inside.

"Intruders," she yelled. "In the girls' dorms. Come quickly to the fifth floor."

If she had SimTalk, which she likely did, there was no point in chasing her down and stunning her. So, Levi continued on, hoping Mason wasn't far behind.

Chapter 27

Mason followed Penelope down the stairs, Ruston behind him, then Beshup. The SimScanner on his hip felt heavy and foreign, despite not being a killing weapon. He hoped he wouldn't have to use it. This whole event had him terrified, not that he'd admit it aloud, especially within Levi's hearing, but all he could think of was that day the enforcers had come to Glenrock and killed so many. Seeing his father and uncle die. Trying to save Papa Eli.

At the bottom of the stairwell, Penelope stopped at the exit door and turned to face them. "When we leave the building, whoever's last, make sure you don't kick out the stick that's keeping the door propped open. Okay?" She looked from face to face, then pushed open the stairwell door and headed into the dark hallway.

They passed by classrooms filled with GlassTop desks and Wyndo wall screens. The wall screens in the hallway flashed images of artwork and assignments. Penelope led them to the front door where a thin aspen branch lay against the doorframe, keeping it open.

Penelope held the door, motioning them to come outside and get behind a hedge of bushes beside the entrance. When the three men were behind the bushes, she carefully closed the door, making sure the branch kept it from shutting fully.

She joined them in the bushes and peeked over the top of one. Mason followed her gaze. A courtyard edged in shrubs separated the girls' dorm building from the boys'. Concrete paths wove through the courtyard, curling to different destinations: a garden of flowers, an area with stone tables, a fountain, a strange sculpture of a horse woman. It reminded Mason of Champion Park and the picnic he'd had with Ciddah. He wondered where she was at the moment and hoped she was safe.

"I don't see them," Penelope said, "but they have to be in there. Let's run!"

She crouched low and jogged into the courtyard, head turning as she scanned the area. Mason stayed on her heels. His adrenaline was so high his hands were shaking.

"Pen," someone said. The voice was low, and if Mason hadn't been straining to hear, he might have missed it.

Penelope took off again, running toward a brightly colored playground.

As they approached, a figure came down the slide, twisting with the spiral until he slid off the edge and stood. Trevon.

Movement in the structure brought several more figures into the dim light of the streetlamp above. Mason recognized Jake and two faces from Jack's Peak, but there were some new children here—children that had to be from the Safe Lands.

"Levi and Jordan are getting the girls out now," Penelope said. "We have to hurry."

"Who are your friends?" Mason asked Trevon.

"Grayn is with me," Trevon said. "And Dakav and Etu brought Holt."

"I didn't dare ask any of the boys in my dorm," Jake said.

"Why not?" Ruston asked.

"Most boys here are filled with the coyote's mischief," Dakav said.

"And Jake's room is the worst," Trevon said. "I wouldn't trust those maggots with my shirt."

Jake grimaced. "They play a lot of pranks on me."

"The rest of you are certain there are no other boys who'd come with us?" Ruston asked.

"None," Dakav said. "Holt and Grayn are different."

"Maybe the littles, though," Trevon said.

"Yeah, they don't cause much trouble," Etu said.

"And that's where we're going now," Mason said. "Though I don't see any reason for us all to go. How many boys are there in the littles?"

"Nine," Dakav said.

They could get all nine. "Okay, then. Penelope, why don't you take Trevon, Jake, Sakima, and...?" He pointed to Trevon's friend.

"Grayn."

"Grayn," Mason said. "Take them to the roof. The rest of us will go for the little boys. Seven of us should be enough to fetch nine."

"Surely some of the boys will be able to walk on their own," Ruston said.

"That's my hope," Mason said.

"Are you sure you can find your way back to the roof without me?" Penelope asked. "The boys don't know the girls' building."

"You just brought me through it," Mason said. "I didn't forget the way."

"Okay." Though Penelope didn't look happy to be leaving. "Please be careful, Mason."

"We have weapons to use, if need be," Ruston said.

Mason tried not to think about the gun on his hip. Hopefully it wouldn't "need be."

"Can I have a weapon?" Dakav asked.

"No," Mason said, "but you can lead the way to the boys' dorm."

Penelope gave Mason one last look, like she didn't like this plan at all, then grabbed Trevon's hand and dragged him toward the girls' dorm. Grayn, Jake, and Sakima trailed after them.

Mason followed Dakav farther into the courtyard, passing the fountain and the flower garden. Dakav paused at the edge of the courtyard, looked both ways, then jogged to a brown building that was identical to the girls' building, only reversed.

A rock had been used to prop open the entrance. Again, Mason thought of Ciddah. What must it have been like to grow up in this place? They trooped up two flights of stairs and out into the hallway on the third floor.

Dakav pointed to a door on the right side of the hall, then pulled it open and slipped inside. Mason caught the door and peeked inside. The dim light of a streetlamp filtered through the windows, revealing two rows of beds, one on each wall.

"See if you can find yours," Dakav said to Mason. "Explaining things before we leave will make everyone calmer." He sat on the edge of a bed and shook the shoulder of the boy sleeping there. "Yas, time to wake."

Beshup pushed past Mason and walked down the row of beds, examining the face of each boy as he went. Mason followed, but he didn't see Joey or Brian.

"Chua." Beshup knelt beside a bed at the end of the first row and stroked the boy's hair. "Chua, my son, your father has come for you."

Mason hadn't realized Beshup was a father. He knew so little of those who lived in Jack's Peak. Levi and Omar had visited there often, but Mason had been there only once.

The men had roused several boys now, and Mason searched the second row for familiar faces. He found Brian first. The boy was already awake, clutching his blankets to his chin, eyes wide. When he saw Mason, his face lit up in a smile. "We're going home?"

"Yes," Mason said, though it wasn't the whole truth. "Can you put on your shoes? We need you to be able to run fast and silent."

"Like Owl Man?"

"Just like the Owl Man, yes," Mason said, amused that so many had heard of Omar's antics. His brother had become a legend in only a few weeks. These people must be hungry for a hero.

Mason found Joey next and told the boy to put on his shoes.

"Where we going?" an unfamiliar boy asked Mason. He had the roundest eyes Mason had ever seen.

"You're not going with us," Brian said. "You gotta stay here."

"That's Weiss," Joey said. "He's not from Glenrock *or* Jack's Peak."

"That's okay," Ruston said. "We're taking all the boys with us. It's not safe for them here."

Weiss's eyes actually seemed to get larger. "The school's in trouble?"

"Yes," Mason said. "And we must get you all out quickly."

"Before Mr. Hemoth comes." Joey looked to Mason. "Mr. Hemoth is mean."

"Is Mr. Hemoth coming with us?" Weiss asked.

"No," Mason said. "He has to stay here."

Weiss raised his hands above his head and jumped. "Hooray!"

"Shh," Mason said. "We must be silent, like the Owl Man, or Mr. Hemoth will catch us."

"He already has," a man said.

Mason spun around. A man stood in the doorway, hands on hips.

"Just who are you people, anyway?" Mr. Hemoth asked.

Before Mason could construct a response, Ruston shot Mr. Hemoth with his SimScanner. Mr. Hemoth went rigid before he fell like a pine tree and hit the floor with a terrible smack. Mason twitched at the sound. The boys stared. Weiss screamed and covered his head.

Mason lifted the boy in his arms and started for the door. "Let's go, boys. Quickly." As he stepped over Mr. Hemoth, Weiss wrapped his arms around Mason's neck and nestled his head onto his shoulder. The boy's arms were so short and chubby, Mason felt smothered.

The patter of feet filled the hall behind him as he carried Weiss toward the stairwell. Mason opened the door and held it. The boy trembled in his arms. Mason gripped him tightly and counted those who passed by. Beshup, carrying his son and holding another boy by the hand. Dakav and Etu, each carrying a boy. Joey and Brian, walking side by side. No Ruston or Holt or their boys. Where were they? Mason peeked down the hall and saw them coming.

Six adults, nine children. They had everyone. Time to get out of this place.

When Ruston passed into the stairwell, he said, "I thought I should restrain Mr. Hemoth."

"Oh." Mason should have thought of that. "Good idea. Thank you."

They quickly caught up to the others. Though Joey and Brian looked to be moving as fast as their little legs could go, they were holding up the back half of the line.

Finally, the boys reached the bottom level, where Beshup held open the stairwell door. It relieved Mason to have everyone in his sights again. How Levi and Jordan and Omar thrived on such exciting adventures, Mason could not comprehend. Give him an injury to mend over this any day.

They made it out of the building and across the courtyard without incident. As Mason approached the girls' building, the front entrance door came into view. It looked to be closed, but surely that was only the angle. Holt reached it first and turned back. He set his boy on the ground and pulled at the door.

"It won't open," he said.

"Penelope wouldn't have let it close," Mason said. The girl had been extremely cautious.

"I'll be right back," Holt said.

"Wait," Mason said. "Where are you going?" He didn't want to let anyone out of his sight.

"The girls usually leave the bathroom window open so boys can sneak in," he said, walking backward. Then he turned, sprinted along the side of the building, and darted around the end.

"We should get behind those bushes again," Mason said, "where Penelope hid us before. At least until we figure out if Holt can get inside."

"Agreed." Ruston brushed by Mason and stepped behind the bushes on the right of the entrance door. "Come on, boys."

They had barely assembled in the tight space when a horrible siren split the night.

"It's the alarm," Dakav said.

Mason's hopes sank. If they were caught here tonight, all was lost. And what would become of Ciddah? Was Lawten holding her captive? Or was he merely keeping her away until Mason could be apprehended?

"Stay put," Ruston said. "All of you get down."

The little boys squatted into balls. Beshup put down his son and drew his SimScanner. Though the idea of Mason touching his own gun, SimScanner or not, repulsed him, he set Weiss on his feet. "Squat down." He made himself draw his SimScanner and peeked over the bushes.

Lights in the boys' building flicked on, but Mason saw no sign of guards or enforcers.

The front door to the girls' dorm banged open and Holt appeared, a wide grin on his face.

"Go," Ruston said. "Go, go!"

All at once, the boys jumped up and mobbed the entrance.

"Stay with them, Beshup," Ruston said.

Mason squeezed the grip of his gun and kept his finger far from the trigger. He tried to count as each boy went inside, but there was too much confusion.

"Hey, stop!" A guard was running toward them, gun in hand. "G12 to base. Intruders at SLBS. Request backup."

Ruston took off, sprinting toward the guard. He couldn't know whether the guard had a stunner or a real gun. That was true courage: doing what was necessary in spite of the possible consequences.

The guard seemed taken aback by Ruston's actions. "Stop!" He aimed his gun at Ruston. "Put your hands on your head and turn around."

Ruston kept running. The guard fired. Nothing happened, which meant he must be using a SimScanner.

The guard looked down at his weapon and slapped it with his palm, fired it at Ruston again. "G12 to base. We've got ghosts!" Eyes wide, he dropped the SimScanner and drew a second gun. "SimScanners won't work. Copy? Use—"

But it was too late. Ruston fired his SimScanner at the guard first, and the guard went down the same as Mr. Hemoth.

Mason shooed Holt and Weiss inside and held the door open. Ruston picked up the guard's guns and ran toward Mason. He passed by in a gust of wind, and Mason chased after him. The siren was wailing indoors too.

At the end of the hall, Beshup stood, holding the stairwell door as the boys filed through. Panic overwhelmed Mason suddenly. The hallway seemed to stretch out an infinite distance before him. Everything morphed into slow motion. Beshup at the door. The boys going through. Nearly there, Etu and Dakav, each carrying a child. Joey and Brian trotting behind them. Ruston sprinting past Holt, who was waving Weiss to hurry. Weiss, halfway between Holt and Mason, plodding along.

Was Mason in shock? Or was fear taking over his mind?

A ding on his left drew his gaze. An elevator. Its doors slid open and two women stepped out, entering the hallway between Ruston and Holt. Before Mason could think of what to do, Ruston turned back and stunned one. She collapsed.

The second woman screamed and ran three steps toward Holt, but when she saw Ruston, she doubled back to the elevator and pushed the button. The doors slid open, but Ruston shot her with the SimScanner before she could get inside, and she fell in the open doorway. The elevator closed against her legs, then slid open again.

"Hey!" Beshup yelled from the stairwell door, Joey and Brian standing beside him. "I need help carrying these boys up the stairs. They're too slow."

Ruston reached Beshup first and swept Joey into his arms. Holt looked back at Weiss, then turned around and headed for him.

"Stop!" a voice yelled from behind Mason.

Mason turned. A second guard had entered the building and was headed toward them, gun in hand. SimScanner or stunner? That was the question.

He should shoot him, but instead, Mason ran toward Holt and grabbed Weiss on his way, tucking the boy on his hip. "I've got him. Into the elevator!"

But Holt didn't follow. He screamed, clenched his right hand into a fist, and fell to his knees. The guard must have gotten him with the SimScanner.

Mason stepped over the woman and set the boy in the elevator. "Wait right there, Weiss." He holstered his gun and ran back out, grabbed Holt under the arms, and dragged him past the woman, who was now moaning, and into the elevator. The guard pointed his weapon at Mason, but since he had no SimTag, the gun had no effect.

Mason managed to push the woman's body out of the way so that the doors finally slid closed. He pushed the button for five, and only when it started to rise did he breathe. He crouched over Holt and slapped his cheek. He didn't know how long SimScanner stuns lasted. If it was as long as a manual stun, he wouldn't be able to get the boy up to the roof and over the plank.

"Is Mr. Hemoth going to catch us?" Weiss asked.

"Nope. Mr. Hemoth should still be tied up."

The elevator stopped and the doors opened. Mason shooed Weiss into the hall, then dragged Holt out. It wasn't until he'd pulled Holt away from the elevator that he noticed the floor number on the frame of the elevator.

Three.

He lowered Holt to the floor, then leapt over his body to try to catch the elevator. The doors shut and he hit the Up button. Too late. It was already up on five. Should he hit the down button? He watched the elevator numbers count down: four, three, two. There is stopped. Which meant that someone else had called it and it would soon come back to three.

What was he going to do? There was no time. The battle in Glenrock came back to him again, when he'd tried to carry Shaylinn.

He hoisted Holt over his shoulder, but he only made it three steps before his knees buckled. The boy was too heavy. Weightlifting must've been a required course for boys in the boarding school, because Holt's arms were twice as wide as Mason's. He would never make it up two flights of stairs. For the first time ever, Mason wished he'd spent more time trying to build muscle strength.

He glanced at the elevator. It was now on level one. He crouched at Holt's side. "Can you hear me?"

Holt moaned.

Mason had no choice but to hope that was a yes. "We have to leave you, Holt. I'm so sorry. You're a hero for getting that door open, for wanting to leave with us. When they ask you what happened, tell them you heard a noise and went to investigate, and that some strangers were taking the boys and you tried to stop them." Mason took a deep breath. The elevator was on two. "If at some point you can get out into the city, go to the Highlands Department of Public Tasks and ask for Dayle. Tell him Mason sent you. He'll get you to us. Okay?"

The elevator dinged. Mason grabbed Weiss and ran for the stairwell.

"Found some!" a man yelled.

Mason reached the stairwell and yanked open the door. He ran inside and started up the stairs. The door banged shut behind him, then open again. The man was coming, which meant Mason was going to have to shoot him. It was only a SimScanner. And if he did it in the stairwell, he'd have the advantage of being above his pursuer.

He rounded the fourth-floor door and ran up the first half toward five. He could hear the man thundering up the steps below him. Mason set Weiss down.

"Keep going up, Weiss." Mason drew his gun. "Up to the top."

The boy scampered away. Mason looked down the stairs, aiming his gun. He clicked off the safety.

The footsteps grew nearer. A drop of sweat rolled down Mason's temple. The man's head appeared, then his torso. Mason aimed, set his finger on the trigger.

The man saw him and stopped, lifted his arm, gun in hand. "Don't shoot."

Mason winced and fired.

The man grunted, as if fighting the electrical disruption of his nervous system. He toppled backward, fell on his back, and slid down the half flight of stairs until he came to rest on the landing below.

Mason's arms were trembling. He eyed his attacker's motionless body. Falling down concrete stairs could be injurious, to say the least. He hoped the man hadn't broken any bones or received a concussion in the fall. He should check on him, at least make sure he was still breathing, but the sound of a helicopter pulled him back to his goal.

Ciddah was waiting. If he failed here, she might be waiting forever.

He holstered his gun and ran up the last level to the roof. The first thing he saw was Ruston carrying Weiss across the board.

Then he saw the bright lights of the helicopter in the dark sky, headed toward them.

Mason ran, hoping the pilot hadn't seen them yet. He crossed the board in two steps and sprinted after Ruston, reaching the door before the helicopter neared the school.

Ruston was taking the stairs, so Mason followed. What if some had taken the elevator? How could he be certain they had everyone? But the elevator would likely beat Ruston and Mason downstairs. It would be okay.

As Mason rounded the landing on the second floor, he drew his gun. He didn't want to use it again, but there might be enforcers in the lobby.

Only Nash was waiting, holding open the front door. Mason stayed right behind Ruston, like a shadow. His breath was heavy, and his side ached from so much running.

"That's all of us," Mason managed to pant out as he passed Nash at the door.

Ruston glanced over his shoulder. "What about Holt?"

Mason shook his head. "He got stunned."

Enforcer sirens wailed in the distance, melding with the drone of the school siren.

Mason thought of Ciddah, wondering if she were at Lawten's home and if Levi would really help him rescue her once they got the children to safety.

He hoped so.

Chapter 28

Shaylinn stood behind Jemma, who was crouched at Naomi's bedside. "You were hiding your labor, weren't you?" Jemma asked after another contraction had passed.

"What was I supposed to do?" Naomi lay in bed, sweat matting her hair to her forehead, her cheeks flushed. "If I'd said one word, uttered one groan of pain, Jordan wouldn't have left. And Levi needs him tonight."

"Oh, honey." Jemma took hold of Naomi's hand. "You're so brave."

Naomi rolled her eyes at Shaylinn. "If your sister is going to be like this through my labor, I want her out."

That brought a smile to Shaylinn's lips. "Jemma, stop being dramatic. Naomi needs you, and she can't tolerate such sweetness. Did you forget that she's married to my brother?"

All three girls burst into laughter.

"Jordan is very sweet," Naomi said in an offended tone. Then she winked at Shaylinn. "Just not when any of you are watching."

"Good," Shaylinn said. "I don't think I could stomach seeing him be sweet."

"You can't stomach anything right now," Naomi said.

They all laughed again. It felt good, but Shaylinn was afraid for Naomi. Her sister-in-law was the toughest woman Shaylinn knew, but she'd had suffered two contractions since Shaylinn had entered the room and the pain had been obvious. Jemma said it would only get worse.

"Mason sent a box of pain meds if you want to try them," Jemma said.

A small shake of the head. "I don't need any of that stuff."

An hour later, Naomi changed her mind. It took Shaylinn and Jemma a bit to figure out how to load the vaporizer, but once they did, Naomi sucked down the meds like they were water. Soon after she seemed to relax.

"She's very close," Jemma said. "Go get Chipeta and Aunt Mary."

Shaylinn probably didn't need to run, but the whole experience had her terrified. She hurried into the living room, where she found the three women still praying. Eliza was in tears.

"How is she?" Chipeta asked.

"Jemma thinks she's close. She said for you and Aunt Mary to come."

Aunt Mary pushed up from the sofa and trotted out of the room. Chipeta followed.

Shaylinn sat down on the sofa across from Eliza, feeling strange to be sitting with a woman who was crying. She didn't know if she should try to comfort her or not, so she just sat there, feeling useless.

"Did you hear that?" Eliza sniffled. "Listen."

Shaylinn held her breath. A heavy silence descended, then three knocks sounded on the front door. She jumped so high it felt like her heart had stopped. She met Eliza's gaze.

"I thought I heard someone. Maybe they're back already." She got up and ran out of the living room.

"It's too early, Eliza." Shaylinn got up and followed her. "Wait. Don't open the door yet."

But it was too late. Eliza had already cracked opened the door. "Oh, hello."

"Sorry to bother you," a familiar voice said, "but I have an urgent message from Levi."

Eliza gasped and opened the door wider. "What happened? Is it the children? Come in."

Rewl entered and stopped just inside the door. He looked past Eliza to where Shaylinn stood. "Hello, shimmer."

Shaylinn tensed at the sound of his oily voice. Why would Rewl have an urgent message from Levi when Levi didn't trust him? How did he even find the cabin?

"What's the message?" Eliza asked. "Is everything okay?"

"It will be." Rewl reached behind his back and pulled out a gun.

Eliza's eyes flew wide and he shot her.

Shaylinn screamed. Eliza slumped to the floor. A black cartridge clung to Eliza's chest and *click, click, clicked*, bringing a hint of relief to Shaylinn—it had only been a stunner. But Shaylinn's eyes filled with tears as she stared at Eliza's motionless body and the way her eyes were still open and moving. She stepped toward Eliza.

"None of that now, femme," Rewl said, training his gun on Shaylinn.

"Shaylinn?" Aunt Mary ran out from the back and stopped when she saw Eliza's body. "Oh!"

Chipeta appeared second. "What's this?"

"Back off," Rewl yelled, pointing the weapon at Aunt Mary, then Chipeta. "I've got a job to do, and you femmes are going to let me do it or I'll stun every one of you."

"What do you need to do?" Chipeta asked.

"I'm taking Shaylinn on a little ride."

Shaylinn's heart fluttered. She didn't want to leave the cabin, especially with Rewl.

Aunt Mary started to cry. "Please don't hurt Shaylinn."

"I don't want to hurt anyone, but if you cause me any grief, I will." He waved the gun at Shaylinn. "Let's go, shimmer. We've got somewhere to be."

Shaylinn glanced at the ladies, then moved slowly toward the door. She didn't know what else to do. She didn't trust Rewl, especially since she was almost certain he'd been the one who had killed Chord.

Rewl slapped his hand against his leg. "Faster—let's go. Open the door."

Shaylinn had to step over Eliza's body to get to the door. She hoped Eliza wouldn't be stunned long.

"You two get back!" He waved the gun at Chipeta and Aunt Mary, and they retreated down the hallway.

Shaylinn opened the door. A black car was parked in front of the cabin.

"Down the steps and into the trunk of that car."

Shaylinn whipped her head around to look back at him. "A trunk!"

"Not your interest, shimmer. You won't be in it long."

Shaylinn walked out into the cool night. A breeze pressed her clothing tightly against her, and she shivered. The trunk was already open. Shaylinn walked to it and looked back again.

Aunt Mary and Chipeta had come to the door and stood watching, looks of horror on their faces. Behind them, Shaylinn could see Jemma kneeling beside Eliza. Rewl backed down the stairs, his steps crunching over the gravel as he neared, still pointing his gun inside the open door of the house. He glanced at Shaylinn. "What are you waiting for? Get in!"

"You're a bad man," Shaylinn said.

"I'm a stimming hero, which you'll see soon enough. Lawten Renzor messed up a lot of stuff. But Bender is going to set it straight. Now, get in!"

Shaylinn climbed into the trunk. It looked like it would be cramped once the top slid shut.

"Lie down on your side."

Shaylinn obeyed. The carpet on the floor of the trunk was scratchy and smelled like metal.

Rewl looked down on her. "You don't have to worry, femme. I'm going to keep you safe. And once you have those babies, you and I can talk paint."

The innuendo made her breath hitch, though she barely understood it. "I will never talk paint with you."

He flashed his striped teeth in a wide grin. "We'll see, neo. We'll see."

The trunk slid closed, engulfing Shaylinn in darkness. She could hear Rewl's footsteps crunch over the gravel, the car door slide open and closed, the engine purr to life. Then the vehicle rocked back and lurched away.

What could Rewl possibly want with her? How did it involve Bender? Maybe he was turning her over to General Otley as a favor. If so, would Otley take her back to the harem?

She sang songs to comfort herself on the drive, but the journey didn't last long. No more than ten minutes had passed when the car stopped.

Shaylinn tensed, waiting for the trunk to open and Rewl to order her to get out. But he didn't come. After a while she pounded her fists against the lid above. "Hello? Is anyone there?"

"Just me, femme," Rewl's voice came from the front seat.

"Why are you keeping me in here?" Shaylinn asked.

"We're waiting for someone. It won't be long."

Waiting for who? Shaylinn sang to herself some more and prayed. Moments later a vehicle approached and stopped behind Rewl's car. Someone got out and walked over what sounded like concrete.

"You got her?" It was Bender's voice.

"She's in the trunk," Rewl said. "Are you sure we can trust him?"

"No, but I don't see another way."

"He makes me nervous," Rewl said.

"It's our best option," Bender said. "We can't keep doing things the soft way. We need to change if we're ever going to make a difference. This is the best chance we've got right now."

"I hope you're right."

"Come sit in my car with me," Bender said. "She isn't going anywhere."

Shaylinn listened to the shuffling of steps and the sound of power doors rising and falling. Then there was silence.

Chapter 29

Omar tapped Charlz. His friend had been about to go out but promised to wait until Omar stopped by. Ten minutes later, Omar knocked on door 322 of the Twister, where Charlz lived.

Charlz opened the door, and Omar was struck by how bad his friend's flaking skin looked. "Long time, peer," Charlz said. "Where you been?"

"Keeping busy." Omar followed Charlz into the kitchen. The table was cluttered with stunners. Charlz didn't sit and didn't ask Omar to.

"Why don't you come out with Scottie and me tonight? We're going to Melman's."

Ah, the Safe Lands DarkScene. "I can't. I need your help." Omar explained about what had happened with Otley, cutting out his SimTag again, and losing his apartment and access to stims. "I've got something important to do tonight, but the itch is so bad, I'm nearly sick. I need something to get me through the night."

"You know I can't get involved in that, peer." Charlz touched his ear as if to say someone was listening. "Otley almost killed me last time I got roped into your plans."

Omar, Charlz, and Skottie used to be enforcers, until Omar had talked them into helping him and they all got reassigned. Was Charlz saying no for real or only because someone might hear? "I just need a hit of something. Anything."

"I can give you a beer," Charlz said, walking to his fridge. "I know how the ache feels, peer, and I'm sorry. But if you vape too much right now, you'll be wasted when you're supposed to be doing whatever tonight." He got a beer from the fridge and handed it to Omar. "And while you can mix stims—vape your downers now then vape some uppers before you head out—I wouldn't risk it when you've got someplace to be. Plus, that's a great way to end up in the MC or premie libbed."

So, Omar sipped his beer like it was the most precious substance on earth, then went with Charlz to Melman's, hoping Skottie would have more mercy.

When they found Skottie outside the dance club, he wasn't nearly so prude. "You've been off the vape how long?"

"Two days," Omar said, rubbing the scar on the bridge of his nose. "But I have to be someplace in a couple hours. It's really important that I don't mess it up."

"It's too risky," Charlz said, but Skottie waved him off.

"I think he can take it."

"I can," Omar said. "Thanks, Scottie. Anything you can do, I really appreciate it." He felt pathetic and desperate, but he would keep begging until someone helped him.

They went to the hit room at Melman's and claimed a table in a back corner. But before Skottie would place an order, he taught Omar a few things about the stims he favored. It turned out that Omar liked downers, which helped him relax, took him to a blissful, euphoric oblivion where nothing mattered in the world. Uppers wound him up and made him jittery and anxious but helped him think fast. Grass, brown sugar, and alcohol were downers. Golden ice, white cocoa, and the cocktail mixes were uppers.

"Can I just have some grass and brown sugar? Low doses are fine."

Skottie shot him a dirty look. "Were you even listening to me?"

"He's practically a husk," Charlz said. "I'm telling you, be careful."

Skottie removed two PVs from his pocket and set them on the table. "Charlz?"

Charlz sighed and set his own PV on the table. "I still think this is a mistake."

When the barkeep came again, Skottie gave very specific instructions. "Empty all three of these. Fill one with a four of brown sugar, one with a two of white cocoa, and the third with a five of grass."

Omar got jittery just hearing that order. "Thanks, Skottie. Seriously. I really appreciate this."

"Not a problem, peer." And when the barkeep returned, Skottie handed Omar the brown sugar first. "Now sit here and take your sugar very, very slowly."

Omar did, and all the pain went away. So did his worries. Relief.

Sweet relief.

Omar probably would have stayed in the chair at the hit room for a week, but Skottie woke him after an hour and made him vape the white cocoa.

He woke up fast. The euphoria was fast too, came and went in a few minutes. After two days of aching pain, it felt good to feel strong again. Energized. Indestructible.

Then Skottie let him take the PV that had grass in it. "Save this until you need it, you hear me? And come visit me later if you need more of the sweetness."

Omar didn't doubt for a minute that he'd see Skottie the next night.

He left his friends at Melman's and met Kendall and the two Jack's Peak men, Mukwiv and Tupi, at Zane's house. Zane gave Omar a gun belt with a SimScanner. Once they left the house, Omar put Jordan's gun on the other side of the belt. He didn't think Zane would have approved of a real weapon, but Omar knew from his time with the enforcers that many of them carried the dual-action pistols.

They walked through the storm drains and into the Highlands. Omar felt good. Alive and awake and whole. The trip passed by in a blur, and soon they were above ground again, approaching the Medical Center from the back parking lot.

"SimTalk: tap: Zane," Omar said.

"You there yet?" Zane asked.

"Yeah. We're in the back parking lot. What do you see?"

"The stairwell is empty. Go for it."

Omar waved the others to follow and walked toward the stairwell as if he had every right to be there. It was a trick he'd learned in his time spent being a rebel. If you looked suspicious, people thought you were. But if you looked like you belonged, people didn't question why you were there.

They climbed the stairs to the sixth floor, and by then Mukwiv was panting pretty heavily. The guy had to be under forty or he would've been liberated like Omar's mother, but Mukwiv had almost as many wrinkles on his face as Papa Eli once had. Tupi was much younger, maybe Jordan's age. They were all wearing black, which had camouflaged them in the tunnels and outside, but would make them really obvious in the MC.

"We're on six, Zane," Omar said. "What do you see?"

"Not a good time. There's a janitor."

"Are you kidding?" Omar wanted to get this done, not hover in the stairwell, waiting to get caught while a janitor mopped the floor. "What do we do?"

"Hang tight. Or you could jump him. I've got the cameras off."

"Zane says there's a janitor out there and that we could jump him," Omar said.

"No," Kendall said. "It's better if fewer people see us."

"He could be cleaning for hours," Omar said.

"I don't think so," Zane said. "He just emptied a trash can and is pushing his cart toward the elevator."

Omar glanced at his team. They were all wearing harnesses to carry the kids. Mary and Shay had made them out of strips of fabric.

Shay.

Hopefully, once they all moved into the basements, Ruston would put Kendall and her kid far away from wherever he put Shay. Maybe Omar could suggest that to Ruston. But no matter where Kendall wound up, he had to apologize to Shay. He wondered if she really would always forgive him. Kissing Kendall had been a major screw-up.

"Janitor just got into the elevator," Zane said. "Go now."

"Janitor's gone," Omar told the others. "Let's move." He pushed open the door and walked down the bright hallway. "Where am I going, Kendall?"

"There's a big entrance on the left, about halfway down," Kendall said. "Wooden doors. A plaque that says Safe Lands Nursery. You should be able to go right in, but stop just inside the front doors. And be quiet."

The doors came into view. Omar opened one and held it for everyone. "Wait right inside," he whispered.

Once they'd all gone in, Omar followed and held the door as it closed behind him, careful not to let it slam. "We're in," he said to Zane.

"All right. Let me find you. The cameras here aren't labeled."

Omar leaned against the wall just inside the door and took a breath from Skottie's PV. It felt good to be back to normal.

They were in a waiting room with rows of chairs and a counter that was dark. A short hall on the other side of the waiting area stretched out for a few yards before turning a corner. Light illuminated the back end of it.

"Got you," Zane said. "You guys were hard to spot. What's your plan?"

"Hold on." Omar waved Mukwiv and Tupi over and stepped close to Kendall. "Zane wants to hear the plan. Talk close to my ear so he can hear you."

When they were all huddled together, Kendall explained. "First, we need to stun the femmes at the caretakers' station. It's straight ahead and to the right. Once they're down, we can find the kids. The hallways are a big U, and there are rooms all along it. That's where they keep the babies."

"I see the station," Zane said. "The caretakers are just sitting there talking. Two of them. Have your SimScanners ready."

"I'll take them out," Omar said. "Stay close behind me." He drew his SimScanner and walked forward, trying not to let his shoes make noise on the tile floor. As he passed through the waiting area and down the hallway, the light got brighter and he squinted. He reached the corner and could hear voices.

"He didn't even listen to me," a woman said. "So, I told him to take me home. Then he got angry, started treating me like I was the one being ridiculous. I mean, I can understand if he has another femme, but to try to pick one up while he's out with me... I'm sorry, but that's not acceptable."

Omar stepped around the corner. The caretakers' station wasn't as close as he'd expected. He could see both women's heads, just above the top of the high counter that circled them, but they hadn't seen him yet.

He flipped off the safety on the SimScanner, keeping the weapon ready at his side. He strode toward them and reached the counter before either woman looked up.

"You did right," a second woman said. "Did I ever tell you about the time I had dinner with—"

She stopped, and Omar realized the first woman had turned slightly and was now staring right at him. "What do you need, trigger?" she asked. "We're closed."

Omar lifted the SimScanner and shot her, then aimed at the second woman and shot her too before the first had even hit the floor.

"SimTalk: Enforcer 10." A woman's voice, coming from a little office in back of the caretakers' station. "I've got a man with a gun in the nursery. Two caretakers have been stunned."

Maggots! "Someone called Enforcer 10, Zane." Omar heaved himself up against the counter and slid over the top to the other side. He leaped over one of the stunned caretakers and charged into the office. The third woman was cowered behind a desk. "Please don't shoot me!"

"It's just a stunner." Omar fired, wincing at the look of horror on the woman's face as she collapsed. "Zane? Anything you can do about Enforcer 10?"

"I'll try. But you'd better move fast, just in case."

"Spread out," Omar said to the others. "Bring the kids here, and we'll help each other strap them on. Be quick about it. Enforcers are on the way."

Kendall took off for the nearest door. Mukwiv and Tupi ran to the rooms on the left. Omar banged out a swinging half-door and walked to the right. The room on the far right was empty. So were the next three. Then he found a sleeping boy— Eliza's Ben. Omar grabbed him and ran him to the caretakers' station, where Mukwiv was setting down another toddler. Tupi stood cradling a smaller baby in his arms.

"My boy, my boy," Tupi said, nuzzling the kid's neck.

"Love on him later." Omar laid Ben on the floor. The boy's eyes were still closed, and his legs curled up to his chest as he rolled to his side. "We've got five more to find."

"Four more," Kendall said, pushing through the half door and setting little Carrie down on her feet. The toddler's cheeks were red and she was sucking her thumb.

"Find them." Omar ran to the next room. Inside he discovered his cousin Hazel, Aunt Chipeta's youngest. He carried her back to the station and saw that both Mukwiv and Tupi had found another child each. One of them was crying.

Kendall ran out of a room and into another. She came back out. "You guys checked all those?"

"Yes," Tupi said, helping Mukwiv strap a kid to his back.

"And I checked the rooms on this side," Omar said. "Who we missing?"

Kendall's voice came out in a whimper. "Elyot."

Figured. "I'll see if I can wake one of the caretakers." Omar ran behind the counter and slapped the cheek of the first femme he'd stunned. "Where's Elyot?"

She groaned.

Kendall crouched beside Omar. "Baby Promise. Where is he?"

The caretaker's eyes widened, and her voice came out a raspy whisper. "He doesn't live here."

Sure, he didn't. "Where else would he live?"

"She's lying. I saw him here before." Kendall grabbed the gun from Omar's waistband and pointed it at the woman. Jordan's gun. "Where is he?"

"Walls, don't, Kendall!" Omar said. "That's not a stunner."

"Good." She prodded the barrel against the woman's chest, then set it against her forehead and held it there. "This is an Old gun. Loaded with bullets that send you to the next life. So, tell me where my baby is, now!"

Omar could only stare at Kendall, horrified. Two of the kids were crying now. He stepped to the side to try to block the view through the doorway.

"I can't," the caretaker said. "If I do, I'll be liberated."

Kendall used her thumb to pull back the hammer. "If you don't tell, you'll die right here."

Omar stared at Kendall in total shock. She could use a gun? "How do you even know how to use that? To pull back the hammer?"

Kendall glowered at the caretaker. "I know all about guns, Omar, and drugs and liars too. My uncle was the biggest liar of all." She jabbed the gun at the woman's forehead again. "Tell me!" she screamed.

The woman shuddered. "He lives at Champion House. The task director general has a live-in caretaker who's responsible for him."

"Why?" Kendall asked.

"An experiment, I was told. His assistant said the task director general wants to see how an infant is raised."

"He took my baby," Kendall said to Omar, her tone wistful yet filled with understanding. "It's all he ever wanted from me."

Omar didn't know what she was talking about, but he didn't like the look in her eyes. The screaming babies probably weren't helping. He reached out his hand. "We'll get him, I promise. Can I have the gun back?"

Her eyes shifted to his, then down at the gun that was still pointed at the woman. She lowered it a little and released the hammer.

Good. He reached for it and—

The caretaker jumped up and knocked into Kendall, stealing the gun. She ran to the corner of the room and pointed it at Kendall, then Omar. She frowned at the gun and used her other hand to pull back the hammer.

Omar froze. He couldn't be certain she'd correctly cocked the gun, but it sure looked that way. "Kendall, get down!" He slowly reached for his SimScanner.

"Don't you touch that!" the caretaker screamed, and Omar lifted his hands where they could be seen.

"What's going on?" Zane asked in Omar's ear. "I can't see in that office."

"The caretaker has my gun."

"I won't let you take our future," the caretaker said. "The children stay here." And she fired the gun at Kendall, the recoil deafening in the tiny space.

Omar quickly pulled his SimScanner and shot the woman. She collapsed. He ran to her and ripped away the gun. Then he looked back to where Kendall had been standing, but she was on the floor. "Kendall? You okay?" He couldn't see any blood, but she was wearing all black.

"Omar?" Zane asked. "Speak to me, peer. That didn't sound like a stunner."

Mukwiv stood in the doorway to the room, staring wide-eyed at Kendall. A kid was strapped to his front.

Omar ran to her side and saw the wetness seeping through her shirt. "Kendall's been shot in the chest. One of the caretakers got my gun." Had the bullet missed her heart? Did it even matter?

"Where did you get a real gun?" Zane asked.

"It was Jordan's," was all Omar could say.

Zane muttered a string of curses. "No one was supposed to bring that."

Omar grabbed hold of Kendall's body, pulled her onto his lap, which left a smear of blood on the white tile floor. *Oh no no.* "We need a medic," he said to Mukwiv. "Zane, we need a medic."

"No, Omar. You need to get out, now. Enforcers are in the building and there are all kinds of medics in the hallways, looking around. Someone will find her."

"You have to go," Kendall whispered.

"We can't leave you like this. We should have brought Mason." Mason would have known what to do.

"The gunfire will have drawn the interest of other people," Mukwiv said.

"Omar, you have to get out of there, now!" Zane yelled. "Enforcers are coming."

"I'm so sorry, Kendall," he said. "I'll get your baby, I will."

"Take care of him?"

"Yes, of course. We all will."

"Wait," she whispered. "I told Otley you were the Owl. Because... the summons. I went. And Lawten let me see Elyot. My baby was here then. He's so beautiful, my Elyot."

Seriously? Did everyone have a price in this world that they'd betray anyone for? Did Omar have a price too? Shay, perhaps? If someone threatened Shay, what would he to do keep her safe? Could he even—

"There's something else." Kendall fumbled for his shirt and pulled him toward her. For half a second he thought she would kiss him. But she pulled his head past her face, putting her lips by his ear. "When I first got here. Lawten... He bought me from my uncle, said I was his wife. But when I got pregnant, he sent me to the harem. And when I asked why I couldn't be his lifer, he said he already had one. Ciddah, the medic. Tell your brother for me? Mason has always been..."

Her hand fell away from her shirt, and her eyes were frozen, staring at the ceiling.

"Kendall?" Omar grabbed her shoulder and shook it. "Kendall!"

"We must go," Mukwiv said.

Omar screamed out his frustration and pushed Kendall's body off his lap. But he couldn't look away from her face, the way her eyes stared open at the ceiling. His hands shook as he reached out and closed her eyes, something he wished he would have done for his father.

Then he jumped up and ran back out into the caretakers' station. At least half of the kids were crying now. There was so much noise, and they'd just seen adults shooting each other and falling to the floor. And all the blood. Omar wanted to scream for everyone to shut up. Instead, he grabbed Hazel and tried to put her leg through the harness.

Mukwiv and Tupi had already harnessed the Jack's Peak children to their fronts and backs.

"Help me," Omar said to Mukwiv.

The older man helped Omar strap Ben to his front, while Tupi strapped Hazel to his back.

All that was left was Carrie, who was crying around the thumb in her mouth. Omar squatted and picked up the girl and settled her on his hip. Three kids weighed a lot more than he'd expected. "Let's go."

Omar pushed out past the half door and walked toward the entrance, shushed Carrie and tried to bounce her. His heart was racing. His limbs shaking. He could feel Skottie's PV pressing against his hip and wanted a vape, but he had no free hands. "Zane? How about those enforcers?"

"Two getting off the elevators now. You're going to have to stun them to get out."

"We've got two enforcers coming." Omar shushed Carrie again. "Can you guys stun them?" He changed the tone of his voice, trying to sound soothing. "It's okay, Carrie." The other babies had quieted, but Carrie's cry was going to give them away.

Tupi drew his gun. Mukwiv already had his in hand. "Should we wait for them to come in?"

"No," Zane said. "Those doors have an alcove that will be good cover. Go, go."

Omar relayed Zane's message. Tupi held the door for Mukwiv, and the two men slipped out. The door started to close, and Omar caught it with his foot. He heard a man yell, shoes squeak on tile. He heaved Carrie up on his hip and crept forward.

"They've got them down," Zane said. "Get out of there. To the stairwell."

Omar pushed all the way out the double doors and into the hallway. Tupi and Mukwiv were waiting. "To the stairs." He tried to run, but the kids bounced so much that Ben's head smacked into his chin, and the boy started to cry. Great, now two were crying. At least Hazel was happy on Omar's back.

"Hold him while you run," Mukwiv said.

Omar pulled his arms tight around Ben and Carrie and jogged toward the stairwell. Awkward, but much better. Ben instantly quieted.

"You've got two more coming up the stairs," Zane said.

Omar warned Mukwiv, who took the lead into the stairwell. "Be careful to keep out of their line of sight," Omar said. "The babies have SimTags and could get stunned."

But Mukwiv and Tupi had the advantage of height as they came down, and easily stunned the ascending enforcers. They made it to the ground floor. Omar paused at the door to the back parking lot. "Zane? Can we come out?"

"Yeah, yeah. More enforcers are coming in the front, but the back is clear. They still don't know I've hacked the grid and taken over their cameras. Dim shells, anyway."

Omar pushed out the door and walked across the empty, dark parking lot. Carrie had mostly quieted and hopefully would stay that way until they were safely in the truck. In the distance, headlights flashed twice, and Omar changed direction, headed for Dayle's truck.

Just before they reached the vehicle, the back doors opened and Mason looked out. He took Carrie from Omar and set her inside, then pulled Omar up into the back. "You did it, brother."

"Yeah." But not without loss. Another person dead. Omar's fault. Omar's gun. And nothing but bad news about Mason's medic. He dug in his pocket for Skottie's PV, and once he had it in hand, he fell on his knees on a pile of blankets that covered the floor of the truck and took a long drag.

"Where's Kendall?" Mason inched over to help Omar remove Hazel from the back harness and laid her on a pile of blankets.

"May." Hazel crawled over Carrie's body back toward Mason.

"Hey, Hazel." Mason swept her up in a hug and touched her nose. "How are you?"

"Wuv May."

"I love you too," Mason said, setting her back on the blankets. "Though you won't like me very much in a minute." He looked around the interior of the truck. "I thought Kendall went with you. And where'd you get that PV? I thought yours was gone." He moved over and started to unhook the baby from Tupi's back harness.

Omar leaned back against the wall of the truck, keeping one hand on Ben's back. He held the vapor in his chest, shaking, wishing it were brown sugar. Some of the kids were crying and he shut his eyes, wanting this to be over, fighting back tears of his own.

Once everyone was in and the truck was moving, Mukwiv answered Mason's question. "The one called Kendall was killed."

"What? How?"

"It's my fault." Omar opened his eyes and met his brother's. "Shay gave me Jordan's gun. We weren't supposed to take anything more than the stunners, but she was worried and..." Omar squeezed Ben and rocked back and forth, more comfort for him than for the little boy. "One of the caretakers said Kendall's baby is with Renzor."

"Talk about this later," Zane said in Omar's ear. "Get the SimTags out."

Never a moment to rest. "Zane says we have to get out the SimTags."

"Right." Mason shook the shock from his face and picked up a black backpack. "I'm going to need some help holding the kids."

"I'll help." Glad for something to do, Omar scooted across the back of the truck until he was beside Mason.

"It would be best if you held her." Mason picked up Hazel and handed her to Omar, but the little girl clung to Mason's neck.

"May. Wuv May."

Mason had to pry her hands free. "I'm not looking forward to this. It's pretty rough."

"How many you do tonight?" Omar asked, suddenly realizing he hadn't even asked how things had gone at the boarding school. "Did you get the others out?"

"We did." Mason pulled a backpack onto his lap and removed a bottle of rubbing alcohol. "Thirty-four. The kids brought friends, and we only lost one, a Safe Lander. He got stunned, not killed." Mason swabbed Hazel's hand with the alcohol. "Hazel, I have to make an owie on your hand, okay? Omar is going to give you hugs."

Easier said than done.

Mason used his scalpel to slice the side of Hazel's hand. She shrieked, a high-pitched sound louder than any siren. Her tears were contagious. Carrie and one of the Jack's Peak kids instantly started to cry.

The next fifteen minutes were horrible. Babies screaming, tongues curled, faces red, blood and more blood. But Mason worked quickly and kept calm and soon had a collection of seven SimTags in a little plastic container.

"Knock on the wall, will you?" Mason asked Mukwiv, who was closest to the inner cab wall.

He did and the truck slowed to a stop.

"I'm just going to toss this," Mason said, "then we'll be good to go."

Mason slipped outside and returned in seconds. He closed the door, motioned to Mukwiv to pound on the wall again, and the truck sped away.

"What did you do with it?" Omar asked.

"Threw it in a dumpster."

Omar did his best to hold Carrie and Ben on his lap as Dayle drove toward the storm drain. The kids were still whimpering. At least they didn't have much farther to travel. It was dark enough in the back that Omar let himself cry for Kendall.

Once Dayle stopped, Mason helped Omar get the kids back in the harnesses. Then they carefully descended into a storm drain that would take them to the Midlands.

They had to go very slowly so they wouldn't slip and hurt the kids, whose cries were so loud Omar was certain they'd be caught any minute. He almost didn't care. What was the point, really? Death would win in the end. It would take them all.

Zane had left a truck for them in the Midlands, and once everyone was loaded up, Omar drove it to the cabin. He came upon the building slowly, making sure there were no other vehicles out front. The place looked deserted. He checked his SimTag detector just to be sure, then turned the truck around and backed up to the porch. Then he shut off the truck and got out to open the back doors. By the time he reached them, Mason was already out and knocking on the front door of the cabin, Hazel and Ben in his arms.

Aunt Chipeta opened the door. "They're here! Oh, Hazel, my sweet baby!" She took her child and started bawling.

Mary pushed out onto the porch, her girth filling the doorway. "Any word from Levi?" Mary's kids were older, and she was the only mother here without a child to hold.

"When we were in the tunnels, Zane told me they were back," Omar said. "Hailey and Meghan are fine."

Mary hugged Aunt Chipeta and squealed. Eliza came running next and claimed Ben. Mukwiv and Tupi carried the Jack's Peak children into the cabin, and Mason went back to the truck to pick up Carrie, whose mother had been liberated with the other women over forty a few months ago. He handed her to Mary. Omar shut the truck doors.

"Mason." Aunt Chipeta waved him inside while still holding Hazel. "Come and check on Naomi. She had her baby. It's a boy!"

Another baby. Mason hurried inside, and the women followed, leaving Omar alone outside. He could hear the tearful reunion from where he stood outside by the truck. He imagined the mothers embracing their children, crying but happy. Such a scene would make a nice painting. He should go and watch. After all, he had helped bring about this great reunion. See? Not everything he did turned into a disaster.

But Kendall was dead. So, he stayed outside, vaping and wishing he hadn't taken Jordan's gun. He should go inside, find Shay, apologize. And he needed to tell Mason what Kendall had said about the medic woman, but he was tired of doing hard things. For now, he just wanted to stand here in peace and grieve and—

The door flung open and Jemma ran out. "Omar!" She ran down the porch steps. At first, he thought she must be glad to see him, but then he noticed her bloodshot eyes. "Rewl took Shaylinn."

Ice slid through Omar. "Took her where?" How did Rewl even know about the cabin? And what did that mean for the rest of them? Were they safe here?

"He stunned Eliza, then threatened to shoot Aunt Mary and Chipeta if Shaylinn didn't go with him."

This was very bad. What did Rewl want with Shay? Or had he done this for Bender? "Did he say where they were going?"

"No. He made her get into the trunk of his car. It was a big black car."

The ice in Omar's chest melted into heat. "When was this?"

"About an hour ago."

Omar needed help and fast. "SimTalk: Zane."

"Hay-o, peer," Zane said. "Make it to the cabin yet?"

Omar relayed what Jemma had said about Rewl kidnapping Shay. "Can you track his car?"

"Give me a minute," Zane said, then he mumbled to someone. "First let me do this for—" A sigh. "Fine. Omar, Levi wants you to drive the women and kids to my place. He's very... concerned about everyone's safety in the cabin. Now let me check on the car. I'll tap you back." And the implant went silent.

Move everyone right now? Omar took a deep breath and glanced at Jemma, who had tears in her eyes. "Zane's trying to track Rewl's car." Jemma blurred before him, and Omar realized tears had filled his eyes as well. Would the madness never end?

Jemma's lips pursed into a scowl, and she slapped the side of his head.

"Ow! What was that for?" Did mothers teach that to their daughters? Because that was exactly how his mother always struck him, right down to the stinging ear.

"For kissing Kendall. What's the matter with you?"

Oh. "I..." What was the point of trying to explain? "Kendall's dead."

Jemma's anger melded into shock. "What do you... why would you say that?"

"Because it's true. She got shot with Jordan's gun that Shaylinn took from under his bed to give me so I'd be safe in case enforcers showed up with real guns." He screamed into his hands then. "It's my fault. I'm so stupid."

Tears rolled down Jemma's cheeks. "I didn't even realize she hadn't come back with you. Where's her baby?"

"He wasn't there. I have to find him, though. I promised."

The door opened and Aunt Chipeta stood there wearing Hazel on her back. She must have taken one of the harnesses from Mukwiv or Tupi. "Omar, Jem, would you like something to eat? I'm warming up a casserole."

So, they went inside, silent, both of them dazed. Omar nearly stepped on Carrie, who was toddling around the kitchen with her thumb in her mouth. Eliza and Mary and several of the babies were missing, likely in one of the rooms. No sign of Mason either, so he must still be talking with Naomi. The Jack's Peak men were sitting in the living room, Mukwiv on Jordan's chair, Tupi on the couch, still holding his son. Omar sat beside him. This was where he and Shay had talked together. Where Shay had kissed his cheek when he'd given her the painting.

Where Kendall had kissed him.

Mason walked into the kitchen then, and Jemma greeted him. Omar should tell him about the medic and Renzor, but his SimTalk implant spoke first. "You. Have a. SimTalk tap. From... Zane."

"Answer."

"Omar," Zane said. "I found Rewl's car. But, peer, he's parked at Renzor's place. Champion House."

Why had he taken her there? Omar cursed. How could they possibly—

"Omar, language!" Aunt Chipeta crouched to cover Carrie's ears. They were all staring at him: Mason, Jemma, Mukwiv, Tupi...

"Rewl took Shay to Champion House," Omar said.

"What's that?" Jemma asked.

"Then let's go," Mason said, hands on his hips like this was nothing more difficult than sweeping the carpet. "He's got Kendall's baby, and Ciddah's there too."

"Wait. What's that mean?" Jemma asked.

Ciddah the medic. His brother might not be so eager to rescue the woman if he knew she didn't want to be rescued. "It's not that easy, Mase. Zane said that place is a fortress."

"There must be a way," Mason said.

"Yeah, you're going to have to give me some time on that," Zane said in Omar's ear. "You'd have to be invisible to break into there."

Omar thought on that word: *invisible*. "I could create a SimArt design," he said. "I'd have to get body implants for it to work, but I could make my skin all black or something. Sneak inside. Hide in the shadows?"

"Walls, that's clever, peer," Zane said. "I don't think we have time for you to get that made. But let me check a few things. I'll also see if I can pick up any enforcer chatter for that location. Maybe I can find out if something is going on there."

"Get back to me as soon as you can." The connection died. Omar let his head fall back against the couch.

Jemma walked over to where he sat and looked down on him. "What is Champion House? Where's my sister?"

"It's where Lawten Renzor lives," Omar said. "It has very high security."

This set off Jemma's tears again, and she walked over and hugged Mason.

"Could we not save this rescue until after we free our women from the harem?" Mukwiv said. "That would give you all more time to make a plan."

"The harem women are safe for now," Mason said. "We don't know what Rewl wants with Shaylinn or what Renzor wants with Ciddah or Kendall's baby."

"Why would he have Kendall's baby there?" Jemma asked, then turned to Omar. "And why would he take Shaylinn?"

"I don't know." Omar didn't know anything. He just wanted to make sure Shay was okay. Then he wanted to visit Skottie and vape the sweet stuff. But there was no point holding back what he did know. "Okay, listen. Levi wants you guys to get in the truck and drive to Zane's. He doesn't like Rewl, and therefore Bender, know where we are. You may as well pack up and go while it's still dark."

Aunt Chipeta stepped into the archway and handed Mason a bowl of something steamy. "Move tonight?"

"Do you want to lose Hazel again? Yes, move tonight." Omar felt like a jerk, but there was no point trying to be nice if everyone wanted to argue. "Mason, before she died, Kendall said Ciddah and Renzor were lifers. I'm sorry. I'd still like your help going after Shaylinn, but if you'd rather drive the truck to Zane's, that would be fine."

Mason eyes widened and he frowned slightly. "I–I don't..."

"But Naomi just gave birth," Aunt Chipeta said.

"She'll be okay as long as she doesn't have to walk," Jemma said. "Did you tell Levi about the baby, Omar? Now that they're back, Jordan should know."

"Would anyone else like something to eat?" Aunt Chipeta asked. "Omar? You other men? Forgive me, I don't know your names."

"Sorry," Omar said. "This is Mukwiv and Tupi from Jack's Peak."

"Nice to meet you," Aunt Chipeta said. "Would you like something to eat?"

"Yes, thank you," Mukwiv said. Tupi nodded.

"Omar?" Aunt Chipeta said.

"No, thanks." Omar didn't think he could keep anything down.

Aunt Chipeta passed out bowls of noodles and beef. Jemma told them about Naomi's labor and more about Shaylinn's kidnapping, then she asked Mason to tell which kids he saw at the boarding school.

The question seemed to surprise Mason, like he hadn't been listening. Omar felt bad for upsetting him with what Kendall had said.

"Um... I saw all the boys. And quite a few mentioned the Owl," Mason said with a glance at Omar. "You're a legend with the kids, brother."

"Really?" The fact that the kids liked the Owl made him smile despite his pain.

"You. Have a. SimTalk tap. From... Zane."

Omar stood and walked out of the room toward the front door so he could hear Zane better. "Answer."

"Okay, peer. We've got the makings of a plan here. Why don't you put me on speaker, if you still have your Wyndo watch, that is."

"Oh, yeah, hold on." Omar walked back into the living room and tapped "speaker" on the watch. "Listen up, everyone. Zane wants to talk." When the room quieted, Omar said, "You're on speaker, Zane."

"First, I'm supposed to say that everyone not going after Shaylinn needs to pack up and move down here. Also, Levi says Jemma is not to go after Shaylinn."

Jemma scoffed and folded her arms. "Tell Levi that I said—"

"That Naomi had the baby," Omar said, hoping to prevent a fight. "It's a boy, and they're both fine." Right? He looked to Jemma, who nodded, though she was still scowling.

"I'll do that," Zane said. "Now, here's what I learned. There's a big enforcer bust scheduled for six this morning at Champion House. Several teams have already been deployed. They're armed with dual-action pistols."

Omar looked at Mason. They both knew what that meant: guns that could both stun and kill.

"You think they're going to bust Lawten for something?" Omar asked. "Can they do that? Isn't that like the sheriff arresting the president?"

"The enforcer general runs the enforcers but also heads investigations to protect the Safe Lands. If he found the right dirt on Renzor, he could arrest him," Zane said. "It's pretty intriguing. As I see it, you have two options: Go in now, or wait until it's over and see where they take Shaylinn, then plan to get her from there. My guess is they'll take her back to the harem, and that's our next target anyway."

"Yes," Mukwiv said. "Do not risk exposure and capture when we could take more time and make a safe rescue of all the women."

"But they're going in with real guns," Mason said. "Anyone can get killed in the crossfire. I saw it happen in Glenrock. And I don't trust Otley not to shoot Shaylinn just to make us mad."

"Otley's a psychotic maggot," Omar said. "I'm not leaving her there, knowing he's involved."

"I agree," Jemma said.

"Do you have any way of helping us, Zane?" Omar asked.

"I had nothing until you suggested the SimArt and my dad reminded me of TRO."

"What's that?" Omar asked.

"Hold on," Zane said. "Ruston is tapping in."

"Omar, you hear me?" Ruston asked.

"Yeah, we hear you. Go ahead."

"The Technology Research Organization was originally called Technology Research Teams. It was founded just after the Great Pandemic. Its job was to go out into the world and rescue technology. If the Safe Lands were to keep moving forward, they needed to learn how to create things. Teams were sent out on assignment to bring back the knowledge of creating everything from industrial machines to pharmaceuticals."

"That's how the Safe Lands were able to keep so much technology from the Old world?" Mason asked.

"Yes. And to keep creating new technologies. Over time, there was no more need to rescue Old technology, and the Safe Lands changed TRT to TRO. Now they work on new inventions."

"And this will help us rescue Shay?" Omar asked.

"I know a guy," Ruston said.

Omar smiled at Mason. Zane and his father were a lot alike.

"He owes me," Ruston went on, "and a while back he showed me what he was working on. You've seen WyndoFlex screen, yeah?"

"Like my watch?" Omar said.

"Exactly. Well, my contact, he's got a couple full suits of it."

"Why would anyone want their body to look like a TV?" Jemma asked.

"That's not the goal," Ruston said. "If you have a screen on fabric, it can reflect whatever you want it to reflect."

"It can reflect its surroundings," Mason said, eyes wide.

"Exactly," Ruston said. "These suits use cameras to record what's behind them and project that onto their fronts."

"You think he'll let us borrow them?" Omar asked.

"No. But like I said, he owes me a favor. How many in your rescue team?"

Omar took a deep breath and met Mason's gaze.

"Two," Mason said.

"Two. Fine. Nash will pick you up in twenty minutes."

"We'll be ready." Omar disconnected from Zane, eager to do something more than sit around feeling useless and sad and guilty. "Finish eating, brother. We're going to visit Champion House."

Chapter 30

"I need to be there," Jordan said. "Hogs teeth, I should have been there already!"

Levi and Jordan were in the nest with Ruston and Zane. "Just wait, Jordan. Until I figure out what I'm doing. Please." Levi looked back to Ruston, who'd forbidden anyone to leave until the enforcer chatter on the boarding school escape had died down. "I'm elder of Glenrock. I'm their brother. And I know more about this sort of thing than they do. I should be going with them."

Ruston stood and stepped into the tunnel. "Come with me."

Levi sighed and followed the man out into Zane's basement.

Ruston gestured at the ratty old couch. "Have a seat."

Levi didn't like feeling as though he was about to be manipulated. He sat down.

"A good leader has sense enough to pick good men to do what needs done and enough self-restraint not to meddle," Ruston said. "Trust your men."

"And if Mason and Omar were skilled at breaking into fortresses—if I'd assigned them to such a chore—I might even trust them with it. But Mason's a doctor, and Omar is... Omar."

"Omar has shown himself to be clever and persistent. With Zane's eyes and my connections, I don't see why they can't succeed."

Maybe. "At least let me and Jordan go help move the women and babies over here."

"Again, there are two men to help, and the women are also quite capable. There is no reason for you to leave."

Levi rubbed his eyes. He didn't like how Ruston was treating him like a prisoner, even if he made sense. "I can't just sit here and wait."

"Then don't. You and I need to make plans on how to divide the children. I can't do this without you. Only you know your people."

"I gave you Jemma's list." What else did the man want?

"A list of children's names. I need to know the families so I can place them together. Haven't they been separated long enough?"

"More than," Levi said.

"Make a new list while I'm gone."

Levi stood up. "Wait, where are *you* going?"

"I can't get your brothers the help they need without going out. I'll be back long before they start their mission. Then I'll want to see your list."

"Take Jordan, then. Drop him at the cabin when you pick up Mason and Omar. He's going to drive us all crazy if you don't."

"Agreed. I will have him go with Nash."

"And what will I do while my brothers risk their lives?"

"You could sleep. It *is* the middle of the night. Or you can sit with Zane and watch your brothers. We'll be able to see most everything on the cameras."

That was some consolation. "Then that's where I want to be."

Ruston nodded once, as if Levi had passed some sort of test. "When I return, we'll figure out where to place the families. After that, I want to talk to you about something... special."

Levi narrowed his eyes. "Are you going to start asking favors of me like Bender did?" Because Levi didn't think he could take much more of that. He was elder of Glenrock. That might be only two dozen people, but they were his responsibility. No one else's. And he didn't want them made into slaves, himself included.

"No, nothing like that," Ruston said. "See, I have a theory, though my son thinks I'm dimmer than a dead Wyndo screen. But I think that you and I are kin."

Chapter 31

Ciddah couldn't possibly be Lawten Renzor's lifer. Mason told himself this for what must have been the one hundredth time since Omar had passed on Kendall's message. The mere idea made him sick. Kendall had had the tendency to exaggerate. She must have misunderstood. She must have.

Aunt Chipeta and Jemma were well into directing the packing up of the cabin when Nash dropped off Jordan, then drove Omar and Mason to the TRO, which was a warehouse ten blocks away that said "Safe Lands Industries" on a sign out front. It was still dark out. According to the display on the windshield, it was 4:07 a.m.

"What's Safe Lands Industries?" Mason asked Nash as they made their way to the building's entrance.

"Nothing," Nash said. "The TRO has always kept a secret location for their research facility. Trying to keep the technology away from thieves and rebels and Luella Flynn."

Omar laughed. "I understand the need. That woman's persistent."

His little brother was still wearing one of the baby harnesses. It looked funny on him, but Omar had left it on, saying he might need it if they found Kendall's baby. Mason had wrapped a scalpel, three alcohol swabs, and three bandages in a strip of denim and shoved them into his pocket. If they were going to rescue Ciddah and the baby, he'd need to remove their SimTags. And he didn't want to risk not having supplies in case Shaylinn had been re-tagged.

Nash opened the door at the front corner of the warehouse, and they stepped inside a small reception area. Two hallways stretched out on each exterior wall, white walls and thin gray carpeting. The place was dark and appeared to be deserted. Nash paused, looking both ways as if he wasn't certain where to go.

"Ever been here before?" Mason asked.

"Nope. SimTalk: tap: Zane." Nash peeked down the hallway on the left. "Hay-o, bro. We're at the TRO. Where am I going?... Gotcha, thanks. SimTalk: end tap." He walked down the right hallway. "We go this way."

They followed Nash down the hall until they came to an open area. A two-story wall ran perpendicular, enclosing the office portion of the building on the front end of the warehouse. The rest of the warehouse spread out before them. Only a quarter of the ceiling lights were lit up. On the right perimeter wall, shelves stuck out like the teeth of a comb, holding small objects Mason couldn't identify. The rest of the space contained strange vehicles and machinery, each in its own squared-off section of floor.

"I'd love to walk around here sometime," Mason said.

"Dream it," Nash said. "If they find out we were here, they'll probably move the place."

Nash led them along the office wall toward a long gash of light that spilled across the dark cement floor. An open doorway. As they approached, Mason heard voices.

"B–But... but why the suits?" a man asked. "Anything else, I... I wouldn't flinch to let you b–borrow."

"We need to be invisible." Ruston's voice. "This is the fastest way."

"Do you have a... a slower way of b–being invisible?"

"Maybe," Ruston said. "I'll tell you that when we return the suits."

They reached the doorway and entered a laboratory. Not a medical one, though. This one was filled with GlassTop computers and Wyndo screens, tables covered in stacks of fabric, and racks of white jumpsuits. Ruston stood beside a man sitting at a GlassTop computer console that had six screens.

The man turned his attention to where they walked through the doorway. He was in his mid-thirties, with flaking white skin, a cropped brown beard, and a thatch of messy hair. His eyes were wild, like a cornered animal.

"This is Mason and Omar, and you know Nash. Boys, this is Lhogan Rayscott," Ruston said. "He's a TRO engineer."

"I'm not comfortable with... with this, Ruston," Lhogan said. "If anything hap–happens to these suits, you'll see me p–premie lib–libbed."

Mason and Omar stopped just inside the door, but Nash walked over to the computer where Ruston stood. "We could set it up as a break-in," Nash suggested.

"No one is sup–posed to know where TRO research takes p–place," Lhogan said. "If it b–became known that the facility had b–been compromised, they'd likely liberate us and train new... new researchers."

Mason saw no logic in such fears. "Surely they wouldn't kill the people who know the technology."

"No one is above lib–liberation in the Safe Lands. Do you know... know what TRO founders went through to rescue technology from the Old world? P–People of Old were selfish, hiding technology from each other to make a p–profit. They didn't share. And they didn't take p–precautions. And when the world ended and no one was left who knew how to do anything, it wasn't easy to figure it out. TRO made sure it won't hap–happen again. If the Guild needs to get rid of us, they b–bring in new p–people. The tutorials train them."

The idea of tutorials intrigued Mason, as did the man's stutter. "Are these tutorials only for the TRO or for other tasks as well, like medical procedures?"

"There are tutorials for every... everything. B–But they're only shown to p–people in task training. Ruston, the suits are going to be too b–big."

Ruston walked over to one of the racks and fingered a white sleeve. "Better too big than too small."

"I sup–suppose." Lhogan got up and produced a plastic bin from a shelf on the corner, from which he removed three tiny plastic boxes. "B–Before you ask, Mr. Mason, without getting overly tech–technical, these are simp–ply contact lenses that have MicroTag resisters emb–bedded into the p–polymer. P–Put them into your eyes, and once I activate the SimSuits, you'll b–be able to... to see one another."

The idea of trying contact lenses thrilled Mason. "Are they sanitary?"

"I always clean them b–before put–putting them away," Lhogan said. "B–But you should all wash your hands at the sink." He gestured to an industrial sink in the corner.

"What about my SimSight lenses?" Omar asked.

"Take them out," Lhogan said. "You can't wear b–both."

"Do you have something I can put them in? They were really expensive and I don't have any more credits."

Seriously? Was Omar really worried about something so trivial at a time like this?

"I sup–suppose I can find something." Lhogan went back to the shelf.

Mason washed his hands and returned to Lhogan's desk. "How do you get them in?"

"Ah, yes. Well, p–put one on the tip of your finger, cup... cup side up. Make sure there's no dust. If there is, I've got some solution here somewhere." He wandered over to the shelf again. "Ah, here we are." He carried a little white bottle back to his desk. "Use your other hand to p–pull your skin away from your eye and p–put in the contact. Go... go slowly. And try not to b–blink or move your head. Oh, and b–before you let go of the contact, make sure to center it on your... your eye. Move it around if necessary."

"It's easy, Mase," Omar said, removing one of his SimSight lenses to the tip of his finger.

"When you think... think it's in and you let go of your eye, b–blink slowly. It might hurt as you b–blink out any air bub–bubbles."

"It doesn't hurt," Omar said. "But I don't see anything yet."

Omar had them in already? Mason was still holding his first on his finger.

"That's b–because I haven't turned you on," Lhogan said. "And you're not wearing the... the suits."

Mason managed to get in both his contacts. They made it feel as if he were going to cry. He blinked, and a tear rolled down his cheek.

"Now the suits." Lhogan walked to the rack and looked through the suits. He lifted one. "This is the smaller of the two pro–prototypes." He handed it to Omar, then gave Mason a second suit. "Not to offend you, b–but these were designed to... to fit some of our undercover enforcers."

Mason wasn't offended. "Strength alone does not make a man."

Lhogan flashed Mason a rare smile. "I like that. Very... very good."

The suit weighed as much as chest waders and was just as stiff, though the fabric was thinner, bright white on the outside, and black inside.

"P–Put them on over your clothes. You'll need the extra p–padding."

Mason moved his surgical kit to a front pocket on the suit and made sure it didn't show. Then he slipped off his shoes and stepped into the suit. His feet prickled against a built-in rubber tread on the inside of the boots. "Should I have kept my shoes on?" he asked.

"Yes, sorry. There are snaps inside the... the feet to fasten over your shoes and keep them tight."

Mason stepped out of the suit and carried it and his shoes to the nearest chair. He sat down and put his shoes back on, then slid his feet into the legs. He found the snaps, which were attached to a pouch in the lining that covered his shoes. He fastened them, then pulled the legs up, threaded his arms through the sleeves, and pushed his hands into the gloves. The suit zipped up from waist to chin and sagged around his middle, clearly designed for someone built like Jordan. At least Mason was a few inches taller than Omar.

"How do these work, anyway?" Mason asked.

"It's SimTech illusion technology ap–plied to a different surface," Lhogan said.

Fine, but that didn't explain anything. "But what's SimTech illusion technology?"

"It's the technology of creating illusions on different surfaces. In a p–person's b–body, that's done b–by imp–planting a SimTag for ID numbers and SimArt. For Wyndos that's done with... with MicroTags."

"So, the suit is filled with MicroTags?" Mason asked.

"Sort of. Think p–polymer light-emitting diodes. We emb–bed them into 140 Denier p–polyurethane p–polyester, ap–apply a film of p–poly methylmethacrylate, followed by a layer of p–poly muslin. That makes the... the fabric."

It sounded fascinating, but Mason didn't understand most of what Lhogan had said. "There must be a lead tag, right? Like the hand tag that speaks to additional SimTags in the body?" Mason thought of Omar's SimArt tattoos that came and went when he wore his gloves.

"P–Precisely. We cut out the suits from the... the fa–bric and sew them up. A CamTag is sewn into each suit in the... the front right shoulder. After that we pro–program the micros to the lead and test them. The MicroTags in the fa–bric simp–ply rep–plicate the... the feed. Just like the lead SimTag controls the others in the b–body, the CamTag controls the other MicroTags in a suit. They've never b–been used for any real tactical situation b–before. I'm not p–positive they'll work in all environments and... and temp–peratures."

"Why wouldn't they?" Omar asked.

"I... I don't know. That's just it: we would never send an enforcer into danger wearing a... a suit that we haven't fully tested. We're several months away from completing the testing on... on the SimSuits."

"They're the only chance we've got." Mason appreciated Lhogan's taking the risk when he was clearly uncomfortable about it. "Thank you for letting us use them."

Lhogan blinked, eyes still wide and paranoid. "Yes, well, let me get you the... the hoods, and I'll make sure you're all showing up on my... my GlassTop."

The white hood seemed to be made from the same fabric as the suits. It had no eye holes or mouth opening, yet when Mason put his on, he could see through it and breathe. "How does this work?"

Lhogan's rare smile returned. "You ask that a lot, Mr. Mason. The hoods are made invisible by adhering a... a light-emitting p–polymer skin to the b–back of the fabric."

"This is amazing," Mason said. Omar looked like a human-shaped snowman. "When will it make us invisible?"

"Once I turn you on." Lhogan sat at a GlassTop computer and started working. Mason walked behind him and watched over his shoulder. Lhogan opened a program that brought up an animated version of a man wearing a suit. "This is for suit one, which is the... the small suit." Lhogan's fingers made dull thuds against the GlassTop as he typed. Mason watched Omar, who was standing by a rack of belts.

Omar disappeared.

Fascinating. "Omar! You've vanished," Mason said.

"Whoa." Nash walked out into the middle of the room. "I can't see you at all!"

Mason strained to see his brother and caught the faint, bulky outline of his suited form moving around, like a ripple in the surface of a lake. The cameras didn't quite work perfectly. The line was off a bit, but he really had to be looking to see it. "That's incredible."

"Thank you." On the screen, as Lhogan tapped away, the image of the man in the suit changed to another. "This one is yours," he said.

Mason stepped back and waited for it, his nerves tingling. He held his hand in front of his face and glanced at Lhogan's GlassTop, and when he looked back to his hand, it was gone. A thrill shot through him. His brain knew his hand was still there, yet part of him still reacted to the fact that it could not be seen.

Mason waved his hand and caught a slight vibration in the air. These were extraordinary inventions. Who would ever know to look for them? With these, the rebels could do almost anything in the Safe Lands. But if the enforcers began using them...

Mason tried to locate Omar in the room and found he couldn't. "How will we not run into each other?" he asked. "Or see each other if we need to? I thought the contacts—"

"I need to activate the... the contacts, and then you'll see," Lhogan said, tapping away.

"I see Mason!" Omar shouted. "You're a blue blob."

Mason's lenses suddenly activated as well, illuminating a blue form across the room.

"There is a... a number on the chest and b–back of each suit. Number one is the small suit, um... Omar. Mr. Mason is number two."

Mason could barely see the white outline of the number two on his chest. The number one on the back of Omar's suit was much larger.

"What about weapons?" Omar asked. "Won't they see them if we're carrying?"

"The suits have a... a flap at the waist that covers where a b–belt can be worn. I don't have any weapons, though."

"I've got some in my truck," Ruston said. "Lhogan, do you have the link for Zane to run these?"

"Ah, no. I'm running them."

"Are you sure you want to be involved?" Ruston asked.

"I have to b–be. What are you using them for, anyway?"

"We need to pay a little visit to Champion House," Omar said, punching his palm.

Lhogan's eyelids fluttered. "Did I... I mention if anything happens to... to these suits...? Or if you're caught...?"

"Yeah, you did," Ruston said.

"Just let Zane run them and you won't have to worry," Nash said.

"The–the suits are my responsibility. If I give the... the eyes to Zane, I've got nothing b–but your word that you'll return them. I... I trust you, Ruston. But I... I don't know these b–boys, I don't know where Zane's GlassTop is, and I certainly don't trust whatever crazy ad–adventure you're planning at Champion House. My eyes only. F–Final offer."

Mason walked around the room, playing with the suit. He didn't quite understand what Ruston and Lhogan were talking about, but he felt badly that Lhogan was feeling pressured.

"Can Zane at least watch the feed?" Ruston asked. "If he can't see..."

"Yes, I... I can do that. But if he tries to... to hack me, I'll move the feed and... and he's out."

"He won't hack you," Nash said. "He's a good boy."

"What's his–his message ID?" Lhogan asked.

"Techwiz dot sl," Ruston said.

Lhogan tapped it in. "I... I still don't like this. I'm risking every–everything. The p–price is much higher than what I owe you."

"Then I owe you now," Ruston said. "Can you record the lens feeds?"

"I can."

"Do it. My guess is that these two will see something tonight that will be useful for blackmail. If anyone comes after you, show it to them and promise that the Owl will release it to everyone in the Safe Lands if anything happens to you."

"The Owl?" Lhogan asked. "You think Task Director Renzor is involved in... in something sinister?"

As far as Mason was concerned, Lawten Renzor was always involved in something sinister.

"If not him, someone who wants to frame him," Ruston said. "Either way, we should know soon enough."

Lhogan sighed. "I'll re–record it. B–But if they don't see anything that can b–be used as b–blackmail, I won't have anything to pro–protect myself from accusations."

"If nothing happens, you won't need to protect yourself," Ruston said. "And, like I said, I'll owe you."

"Everything is ready," Lhogan said, pushing back from the GlassTop. "Take good care of–of them."

The suits, of course, not Mason and Omar's lives.

"They won't get a scratch," Omar said.

Mason hoped it was true.

Chapter 32

Omar was glad to have the loaded gun on his hip, even if it had betrayed him once tonight. He wouldn't have felt safe going up against Otley and those dual-action pistols with only a stunner. He needed the same heat that overgrown boar would be packing.

Nash drove the DPT truck down a winding road filled with massive homes, headed for Champion House. The three of them sat side by side in the cab—a tight squeeze, with Omar in the middle.

The suits gave them an advantage. Tonight, Omar was the Invisible Owl, embarking on his most daring mission yet. The suits were sweltering, though. He was glad he'd removed the hood for the drive, but every time he looked down and his body came into view, glowing blue, he jumped. Three times in the space of five minutes, he completely forgot the contacts in his eyes. He needed sleep—and Skottie's PV, which he couldn't get to with the suit on.

Omar burned at the idea of Shaylinn in a car trunk; sweet Shaylinn who never said a mean word to anyone, who prayed for people and wrote kind messages, who'd been forced to produce *two* babies, who loved him in spite of the wretched person he was...

Who'd seen him kiss Kendall.

Omar was sick. Sick with it all. The Owl was supposed to make a difference. But he needed more time to plot Operation Lynchpin. And this... complication with Shaylinn, and now Kendall's death... None of it was helping him keep his focus.

Why was he so stupid? He could have stopped Kendall's kiss. Stood up. Moved away. Then Shaylinn wouldn't have gotten upset, and Omar would have had more time to think about the gun. Might have decided to leave it behind. Then Kendall would be—

"SimTalk: tap: Zane." Nash pulled into a driveway in front of a massive green house and killed the headlights. "Yeah, what's going on just above, uh..." He squinted to see the house number above the door... "Fifty-three Summit Road?"

Omar glanced out Nash's driver's side window. In the distance, where the road curved around a bend and up the hill, a dozen taillights glowed.

Shay was up there. He wanted her out, and he wanted Rewl and Otley and Renzor to pay. Maybe it would all end tonight with three bullets from Omar's gun. Bang, bang, bang. And they lived happily ever after.

The crack of the gun flashed in his memory. Kendall falling. Nothing happy about that.

"Let me put you on speaker," Nash said, tapping his Wyndo watch, which looked identical to Omar's. The time was 5:06 a.m. "Go ahead, Zane."

"Enforcer troops have been deployed to Champion House." Zane's voice came out tinny through the watch speaker. "You've got a collection of eight enforcer vehicles up there. Chatter tells me they're not going in until six."

"Why wait?" Omar asked.

"No idea," Zane said. "The way I see it, you can either wait until they move in, then follow. Or you can sneak past them now."

"Can we do that?" Mason asked.

"With those suits you should be able to walk right up the middle of the road, but if there are enforcers on foot, I wouldn't risk it. Walk in the ditch or something. And I'd avoid walking in front of headlights. Might make shadows. The real problem is the gate. It's shut. And it has to open for you guys to get through."

"You can't hack it?" Omar asked.

"Nooo. Their security is too good. I can get in and watch, but if I so much as turn a camera a millimeter, they'll see me and lock everything down. You're going to have to walk up there and wait for it to open, then walk in along with the vehicles. There's no other way."

"Can't we climb over?" Omar asked. "Are the fences electrified?"

"Not that I know of," Zane said, "but they're ten feet high and topped with some nasty barbed wire. I don't think you have time for that. And if you mess up those suits, my dad will kill us all."

Not to mention they'd be visible again.

"Is there a back gate?" Mason asked. "One that's easier to get through?"

"It's identical," Zane said, "and you'd have to hike around the perimeter or drive back out Summit and go all the way around to Forest Lane to get to it."

"That's too far," Nash said.

"No storm drains here?" Omar asked.

"They're closed off. Have been for years. And none of us have ever had a premie lib wish to risk exploring them. Stop arguing with me. I've checked this. Trust me. Walking in with the cars is your only option. There will be guards at the guardhouse, too, so keep an eye out for them."

"We've got the advantage of being invisible," Mason said. "That greatly decreases our odds of encountering danger."

Yes, and Zane would be looking through the cameras. And didn't that engineer say Zane would be able to see through the contacts too? "Can you see what we see, Zane?" Omar asked.

"Only one at a time. I'm looking through your eyes right now, peer," Zane said. "Your eyelids keep drooping. Need a nap?"

Desperately. And another breath of brown sugar wouldn't hurt. "I'm fine."

Zane chuckled. "I've got no control over what I see, though. Lhogan's running the vids. If I need to switch to Mason's eyes, all I can do is message Lhogan and ask nicely."

"What about Rewl's car?" Omar asked. "Where is it?"

"Let me look." The soft tap of fingers on glass came through the speaker. "His is the first car outside the gate. Go ahead and get closer. You might be able to see if he still has Shaylinn."

Omar sure hoped so. "All right. We're going."

Omar and Mason got out and said good-bye to Nash, who promised to wait with the truck. They walked down the center of the street, headed for the hill. Their suits swished like snow pants. The rubber soles under Omar's feet scuffed against the concrete.

"Think we should get off the road?" Mason asked.

"Not 'til the corner," Omar said. "The houses and sidewalk should end there, then we can walk in the ditch."

They eventually came to the last driveway, about a stone's throw from the nearest enforcer car. Omar had been such a fool to believe that being an enforcer would make him happy. To think he'd given up a peaceful life in Glenrock with Shay to lick Otley's and Renzor's boots.

And now he'd lost everything.

He wished he could get at his PV right now. He could really use a vape.

He caught himself being negative again and shook it off. What would the Owl do? Something good, not mope about everything. He was going to rescue Shay and get her to Ruston's basements. She was going to have a peaceful life, even if he couldn't.

Omar led Mason down into the ditch, trying to walk carefully in the fake green grass. He couldn't hear as well with the hood on. He kept his gaze bouncing from his feet to the road, inspecting the parked cars they walked past. So far, the enforcers were just sitting inside the vehicles, two to a car, from what he could see, talking with each other as if this was merely a routine bust.

They had to be wondering, didn't they? What kind of bust goes down at Champion House? Whatever Otley had planned, it was going to be big news. He was surprised Luella Flynn wasn't here with her cameraman.

Four cars in, Omar could clearly see the front gate and the guardhouse behind it, the windows lit up with bright yellow light. Rewl's black sedan was parked right up against the gate with its driver's door up, open to the night air. Omar walked through the ditch until he stood across from the door. No one was inside. He stared at the trunk, tempted to walk over and look inside. "No Rewl in the car," Omar whispered to Mason.

"He's in the one behind," Mason said.

Sure enough, when Omar looked through the windshield of the second car in line, he saw Bender in the driver's seat and Rewl sitting beside him.

"It's so weird to see them like this. When I first met them, I thought they were heroes," Omar said. "Yet here they are with Otley. Maggots, anyway."

"Do you think Shay's still in the trunk?" Mason asked.

The lights on Bender's car were off. "I'm going to find out."

"They'll hear you," Mason hissed.

But Omar was already halfway up the shoulder of the road. His boots backslid a few steps on the incline, but he moved faster and reached the top.

At the edge of the road, he stayed put a moment, making sure no one had heard him. When nothing happened, he started across the road. Bender's headlights were off, so he walked between the two cars. There was about ten feet between them. He stared through the windshield of Bender's car to where Bender and Rewl were talking, laughing, like this was all part of some game. But their windows had to be up, because Omar couldn't hear their voices at all. Good.

He squatted by the trunk, made a fist, and knocked on the back. The gloves muted the sound. "Shay?" He kept his eyes on Bender and Rewl and tried to measure his voice. Loud enough for her to hear, but soft enough so that no one else could. They hadn't seemed to hear him, so he tried again. "If you're in there, answer quietly. It's me, Omar."

"Omar? Help!" Shay's voice bordered on hysteria. "Get me out of here."

Bender and Rewl's heads both twitched in the direction of Rewl's trunk. Omar held his breath until he saw them relax and start talking again. "Quietly, Shay. Calm down. Listen, I can't get you out just yet. People are watching."

"Please, Omar. Please get me out." She had quieted her voice, at least, but her tone bordered on hysteria.

Omar was no good at saying the right thing. What would Shay say if their situations were reversed? He struggled to remember one of the hundreds of Bible verses his mother had made him learn as a child. "The Lord's your shepherd, Shay. Don't be afraid. What can these maggots do to you?" Close enough. He wished he could just jump in the front of this car and drive it away, which he couldn't do without taking off the suit to reach the ghoulie tag. Plus, there were two dozen enforcer vehicles blocking him in. But at least he'd found her. When she didn't answer, he asked, "Shay, did Rewl say anything about what his plans are?"

"He said Lawten Renzor did bad things and that Bender was going to make everything right."

Cryptic. "Did he say why he needed you? What he planned to do with you?"

"No. Well, he did say that he was going to keep me safe until I had the babies, then we could, um, 'talk about painting.'"

Painting? Omar pictured his easel and the picture of Shay that Otley had ruined. Rewl didn't paint. Not that Omar knew what Rewl did in his spare— "Wait. Shay, you mean trade paint? Does Rewl like you?"

"He wanted to take me dancing once. He said Bender is his father and that he wasn't infected. That he's a Natural."

Both had grown up in the basements, yet both had turned their back on that life. Rewl might be a Natural, but the only reason he wasn't infected was because he was a creepy shell who probably scared the femmes away. No, that was unfair. Omar didn't really know Rewl, except that the maggot had put Shay in a trunk. And for that, he would pay.

"Shay, listen. I have to go."

"No! Don't leave me."

"I won't be far away. But I can't get into the trunk, so I have to wait until they take you out, okay? I'll be close by."

"Please don't go." Her voice was laced with tears again. "Omar? Omar, are you there?"

The electric hum of a vehicle door opening split the silence. "I'll grab it." Rewl's voice. Outside the car.

Still crouched on his toes, Omar spun around. Rewl was on top of him, headed back to his car, going to cross between the two vehicles from the passenger's side of Bender's car to the driver's side of his. Omar shrank as close to the bumper as possible, but Rewl slammed into him and tripped.

Omar didn't wait to see what happened. He scrambled around the back of the car and up the passenger's side.

Another door slid open. "What happened?" Bender's voice.

"I tripped over something. Someone was there."

"Where? You saw someone?"

"No, but I—"

"Get in the car," Bender said. "Otley's coming."

Otley. Rewl's headlights were off too, so Omar crossed in front of the car and looked down the road. Headlights were approaching on the wrong side of the road, headed his way. Omar crouched in front of Rewl's car, waiting.

An enforcer's Jeep stopped beside Rewl, who was still standing at the back of his car. The passenger window on the Jeep slid up onto the roof. "What are you doing out here, little rat?" Otley said.

"Talking to Bender."

"Get in and follow me." Otley's Jeep sped by Omar's hiding place and pulled up to the front gate.

Omar ran after it, then to the left side of the road to stay out of the way of Rewl's car. He turned back and located the blue figure that was Mason in the ditch beside the guardhouse and waved his brother to follow.

When Mason caught up, he asked, "What's our plan?"

"We follow them in. Shay's still in Rewl's trunk, so I'm going to stay with his car and try to get her out. You stick with Otley and look for your medic and Kendall's baby. If we don't see each other inside, once you get the medic and the kid, get out of the house. We'll meet behind the guardhouse, inside the fence. We'll probably have to wait for the gate to open before we can get out, but I guess we can figure that out later."

"Sounds good," Mason said.

Mad good. They walked through the open gate just as Otley spoke to the man at the guardhouse.

"Safe Lands Enforcers. We have a warrant to search these premises."

Chapter 33

The iron gate rattled as it slid open on wheels. Mason walked behind Omar, who was shadowing Rewl's car. He didn't know what to think of his little brother becoming a father, but Omar had certainly grown protective of Shaylinn. Mason was glad of it. Maybe it would give him some focus in life.

The mansion was made of gray stone and was so massive that its roof looked like three mountain peaks. Bright yellow light shone out narrow windows. A grassy lawn—real grass—surrounded the building. The drive split ahead. To the left it went straight around the back of the house. To the right it circled the yard and ran back to the front gate. A fountain and a rose garden decorated the center of the circle. The smell of flowers made the early morning air sweet. The sky was growing pink. Almost dawn.

General Otley drove to the right. Rewl continued on toward the back of the house. Mason waved to Omar and ran to keep up with Otley.

The man stopped his Jeep in front of the house and got out. Mason looked back and saw that the other vehicles had followed Otley. Bender got out of the second vehicle in line, while enforcers exited the others. They all wore gun belts laden with weapons. From what Mason could figure, they each had a SimScanner, a stunner, a dual-action pistol, and some kind of stick.

Four men in black suits met Otley at the bottom of the steps.

"I'll see that warrant now," one of the men said.

Otley pulled a piece of paper out of his inner jacket pocket and handed it over. "Signed by the Guild. It's good."

The man glanced over the document and sighed. "There is no pregnant girl here, but search if you must." He led the way up the wide steps and rang the bell. Otley followed, Bender at his side. Mason stayed with them, keeping on the far edge of the steps so as not to touch anyone. The enforcers followed.

The front door opened, revealing a young man dressed in a black suit. "Yes?"

"General Otley has a warrant, Mr. Berg. His men will be conducting a search. And my men will be accompanying them."

"Of course. Well, come right in, General Otley. I'm Mr. Berg, the butler. The task director general was not yet awake at this early hour as he *is* on vacation. He'll be with us shortly. He's asked me to see you to the small parlor."

Otley grunted. "Bender, Nicol, Leech, Robb—with me. The rest of you, wait here."

Mason slipped into the house after Otley. The foyer was wide and square, with cream-colored walls, and floored and trimmed in dark wood. Long rugs in red, navy blue, and cream patterns covered much of the floor. A dark wood staircase wrapped up the left-hand side of the foyer, carpeted in the same colorful rug. The ceilings were higher than what Mason knew to be normal. Fancy iron furniture and tables lined each wall amid vases and statues. Directly in front of Mason stood a life-size bronze-and-iron statue of a woman and three large dogs, each on its own leash. Where the railing curved at the foot of the stairs, a vase filled with fresh, long-stemmed roses stretched as high as Mason stood tall.

Once all the enforcers had entered the house, Mr. Berg closed the front door and crossed the foyer to an open walkway at the bottom of the stairs. "Right this way."

Otley stomped after the butler, his boots clumping over the shiny wood floor and thin rugs. Mason followed closely and carefully, making sure to keep his distance from everyone else. Would Ciddah be with Lawten? Or somewhere else? At this hour, she'd likely be sleeping. Where might the bedrooms be in such a house?

The "small parlor" was as big as Mason's Glenrock house. The walls were also cream, which made the room look bright. There were eight sofas—four cream and four red—and at least a dozen wing chairs, all arranged to face the middle of the room. Tables and lamps and mirrors and vases and pillows... The place was cluttered yet looked immaculate. A brown piano as big as a car sat in one corner of the room. A fire in a marble hearth crackled on the opposite wall. Two archways led out the back of the room, one on either side of the fireplace. To the bedrooms, perhaps?

Otley approached a mirror hanging above the fireplace. He bared his teeth and picked them with his thumbnail. The men in black suits filed inside the room, followed by Bender and the three enforcers. They stood in a line behind one of the red sofas.

Lawten's assistant, Kruse, entered then, still pink-skinned and bald, and still wearing the same black SimArt hand on the side of his head. He led the way for his boss, who seemed extra frail today and hobbled like an old man. Mason had never seen the task director general walking, and now he saw why. No one should have that much trouble walking at thirty-nine years old. Why was his condition so accelerated? Ciddah had said she'd loved him once. Did love go away like a stomachache? Mason didn't think so. It must hurt to see someone you love waste away from illness. She couldn't really be his lifer, right? He'd betrayed her.

The head of Lawten's security carried the warrant to Kruse, who started to read it.

"General Otley," Lawten said, "what right have you to barge into my home at this hour?"

Otley turned away from the mirror and stood with his hands behind his back. "I have a warrant for your arrest and to search your house."

Lawten lowered himself onto one of the red chairs. "And what am I being arrested for?"

Kruse stepped up behind the couch, just to Lawten's right. "Kidnapping and conspiracy against the Safe Lands, according to this." He handed it to Lawten, who waved it away.

Lawten crossed one leg over the other. "Preposterous. Who have I supposedly kidnapped?"

"Baby Promise," Otley said.

Mason edged toward the far wall and peeked out the doors there. A formal dining room. Perhaps the bedrooms were upstairs.

"Baby Promise is here as part of an experiment, General Otley," Kruse said. "I can produce the paperwork, if necessary."

"Now that we've cleared that up, what conspiracy do you accuse me of?" Lawten asked.

Mason started back toward the door he'd come in, intent on reaching the stairs.

"We have reason to believe you helped several outsider women escape the harem," Otley said. "That you bring them here to receive medical check-ups from Ciddah Rourke."

"Miss Rourke is my lifer," Lawten said. "And I've never brought any harem women to my home."

Even though Mason had been prepared for it, the statement that Ciddah was Lawten's lifer shook him. And Otley's accusation of medical check-ups compounded the doubt in his mind. He reminded himself that Otley was trying to frame Lawten. The Glenrock women had never come here for check-ups. So, Ciddah was here for a different reason, but what?

"We'll see, Mr. Task Director," Otley said. "My enforcers are going to search your home."

Lawten narrowed his eyes at Otley. "And who will your men find, General Otley?"

"How could I know?" Otley said, innocently.

"Oh, I think you know. This isn't the first time you've tried to frame me. All of the dead in Glenrock. I know you ordered your men to kill."

"I warned you it might be necessary. The outsiders were armed."

"But you fired first. And it made me look bad. That's what you wanted, wasn't it? To make me look incompetent?"

"You've served the Safe Lands well for many years, Mr. Task Director," Otley said. "Because of that, I'm willing to negotiate."

"I'm listening," Lawten said in a low voice.

"Resign as task director general, and I'll dismiss the charges. No X. No record."

"No task?" Kruse said.

"Oh, he'll task," Otley said, "just not as the TDG. And not in the Highlands. Or the Midlands."

Mason had heard enough. It wouldn't be long before the remaining enforcers were let inside to do their search. He wanted to find Ciddah first. He slipped out of the parlor and climbed the stairs.

Chapter 34

When Ruston returned from helping Mason and Omar, he and Levi and Beshup went over the list of Glenrock and Jack's Peak families until Ruston had found a basement location for each to move into. Then Levi sat beside Zane and watched on the video screens as Mason and Omar walked through the gates surrounding Champion House, invisible to the enforcers they were walking beside.

So strange.

"I can't believe I'm seeing this," Zane said. "I mean, I knew Bender and Rewl were doing their own thing, but seeing them walk beside Otley..."

Ruston, who was standing behind Zane, squeezed Zane's shoulder. "I know, son."

"But what are we going to do? Bender and Rewl, they know the basements as well as anyone."

"We keep doing what we do and trust God will continue to protect us. He has from the beginning, you know."

Zane sighed heavily, like he didn't like that plan. Levi wanted to ask Ruston what he meant by "God," but his brothers were approaching the gate. Levi was thankful that Jemma and the others were already on their way here. But if Ruston's basements weren't any safer than the cabin, what was the point?

"I wish we could hear what they're saying," Zane said. "I don't know the cameras so well inside, so bear with me." He switched the view on one of his six screens to a camera on the front porch, looking out at the approaching vehicles. No sign of Levi's brothers, though on another one of Zane's screens, Levi could see through Omar's eyes as the second car branched off and Omar followed it.

Seeing his brothers walk into danger and having no ability to help them was strange. Levi didn't like feeling so helpless. There was nothing to do but watch and pray.

He glanced at Ruston, who stood beside him, arms folded as he watched the screens. Could the two of them possibly be related? It seemed insane, but Levi hadn't been able to stop thinking about it the entire time Ruston had been gone. "That was quite a statement you left me with," Levi said.

Ruston grinned without removing his gaze from the monitors. "Got you thinking, did I?

Thinking you're mad. "I'd like to hear why you believe we're related."

"Good," Ruston said, "because I'm happy to explain."

Zane groaned and turned on his chair. "He's always telling it. The *Tale of the Outsiders* has been a legend to basement kids since before I was born."

"Because my father told me stories of *the* Elias McShane," Ruston said, "the smart young man who got away from the Safe Lands and took his family into the woods to live off berries and rabbits."

Zane spun back to the monitors. "As if people would eat a rabbit."

The back of Levi's neck prickled. "Elias McShane was my great-grandfather."

Zane's twisted his chair around again, eyes narrowed. "Hold the flavor."

"Didn't I say so, Dathan? Didn't I?" Ruston broke out a wide smile and grabbed Zane's shoulder. "The stories are true!"

"Dathan?" Levi asked.

"My real name," Zane said. "We all have fake ones to use above ground. I was born Dathan McShane."

"And I'm Seth McShane," Ruston said, "named after my—"

"Papa Eli's father?" This was too weird. McShanes in the Safe Lands? How?

"You called Elias McShane 'Papa Eli'?" Ruston asked, as if the mere idea was ridiculous.

But Levi wasn't jumping ahead to that until he got more answers. "How can you be related to Papa Eli's father?" No one from Glenrock had ever moved into the Safe Lands. Papa Eli would have said, wouldn't he?

"First, let me show you this." Ruston went to the ammo shelves and pulled down a rifle from the very top.

Levi's heart fluttered at the familiar weapon. "That's my gun! How did you get it?"

"Dathan told me about it after he went with you to shoot out those transformers. He said it looked a lot like mine and that you claimed it came from Arizona."

"For the record, I thought it was merely interesting," Zane said. "I did not believe my dad's crazy stories were true."

Ruston pulled down a second rifle from the top shelf. "This is my gun. It belonged to *my* grandfather, Seth McShane." He handed the rifle to Levi.

It didn't have the engraving Levi's had, but they were almost identical.

"I've got a guy loyal to me in the enforcer's evidence warehouse," Ruston said. "After you got thrown in the RC, I had my guy steal the gun. When I saw the engraving, I knew."

Levi turned his rifle over, baring the engraving on the bottom of the stock. He already knew what it said: *Elias McShane—March 22, 1996.* "It's Papa Eli's birth date."

"That's right. When Dathan told me so many of you were nines, I pieced things together. See, our family are all nines too."

Levi looked at Zane, but he wasn't wearing his gloves right now. "But Zane, er, Dathan... He's a five." Levi hadn't forgotten that.

"It's fake," Zane said. "I can program SimTags to bear any number. Nines get too much attention from Safe Lands medics, so we always use lower numbers. I've got Mason's eyes on the screen now, by the way. Lhogan switched suit two to the main feed. I wish he'd give me access to his GlassTop so I could see all his screens."

Levi eyed the second screen. Mason was standing in a fancy room with General Otley, Bender, Lawten Renzor, and Renzor's weird assistant. "No sound?"

"Nope. All we can do is watch," Zane said. "Unless Omar taps us."

"What do you know about Seth McShane?" Ruston asked.

"Uh..." Jemma would know the story better. "Papa Eli's father sacrificed himself so that Papa and his friends could get out of the Safe Lands. He made a deal with the singer woman—took the blame for something Papa did and went to jail. Papa Eli said they'd never have gotten out otherwise. As far as we know, no one else ever got out."

"So, Seth McShane is a legend to your people, and Elias McShane is a legend to mine." Ruston smiled. "Isn't that something?"

Bewildering was a better word. Levi didn't think it had ever occurred to Papa Eli that his father might start a new family in the Safe Lands. "Papa Eli always made his father look like a, uh..." What was the name of those men of Old who didn't marry? "A missionary priest?"

That seemed to tickle Ruston, and he hooted in laughter. "Once those gates closed him in, Seth McShane had seven more children."

"Seven!" Levi couldn't believe it. "Papa Eli only had four, and he was a lot younger."

"I still can't believe Elias McShane was a real person," Zane said. "All this time I thought it was just a story."

Levi had greatly respected and admired his great-grandfather, but it was weird to hear people talk about Papa Eli like he was some kind of legend. "Otley shot him," Levi said. "In the raid. But he died later when I found him." Died right in front of him.

Ruston's eyes bulged. "He was still alive? After all this time?" He walked across the nest and sat on the chair in front of the green wall. "How?"

"He was ninety-two," Levi said, smiling, "and he could still keep up with me on hunting trips."

"Ninety-two? That's stimming ancient," Zane said.

Ruston just stared at Levi, his expression awestruck. "I can't believe you knew him."

"Lived in the same house as him," Levi said. "You must have old people in the basements, right?"

"Old people, yeah," Zane said, "but none *that* old."

"We don't have great access to medical care," Ruston said. "If our elderly get sick, we can't take them to the MC."

"Because they'd be liberated," Levi said. This place was nuts. "Do you have the thin plague?" Levi asked Ruston.

"Not me. Some Naturals do, most don't."

"I'm a flaker, Levi," Zane said. "Go ahead and hate me."

"I don't hate you." But Levi doubted that was enough to convince Zane, whose words brought a rush of shame over Levi. No one had helped him more than Zane. "Liberation," he said, thinking of his mother. "What is it?"

"Ah, that I can't tell you," Ruston said. "We've tried to figure it out for years. And we have some men in very high positions within the Safe Lands government too. But the Guild is very careful with the truth about liberation."

"Could it be death?" Because that's the only thing that made sense to Levi.

"Could be," Ruston said. "Killing Xed people would be one thing, but I can't imagine it would help the Guild's cause to kill the innocent."

"We have to find out what it is," Levi said. "There's got to be a way."

"Then we need to take down the government," Ruston said.

"Operation Lynchpin," Zane said.

"What is that, anyway?" Levi asked.

"Omar's idea for taking down the government," Zane said. "He thinks we need to do something that will cut off the food or water supply to the people, which would force everyone to leave the Safe Lands. It *could* work, but enforcers have a lot of supplies stocked up. And they can always take flights to Wyoming to get more."

"So, find a way to cut off access to flights," Levi suggested.

Ruston shook his head. "Only a few helicopters are kept inside the walls. The rest are out at the Old Crested Butte airport."

"Are any of your people pilots?" Levi asked.

"I wish," Ruston said. "Flight is a heavily guarded task in the Safe Lands. They have the test programmed to select only two new pilot candidates each year. And even though we have a man in registration, the pilot positions are always assigned by the task director general."

"And the tutorials for pilots are kept in some vault," Zane said. "Not really, but it sure seems that way when I've tried to— Mason's leaving the room."

The comment drew Levi's attention back to screen two, which showed Mason walking up a fancy staircase.

Be careful, brother, Levi thought, wishing he could see Omar too, wishing he was there to keep them both from getting killed.

Chapter 35

Shaylinn forced herself to calm down as the car rolled forward. Omar would come back. He had to avoid being caught or he couldn't help her. He'd be back. He'd promised.

But she didn't know what to make of Omar's promises. Loving him was easy, but trusting him was hard. At least he'd come for her. *Omar* had come. Not Levi or Mason or even Jordan. That had to mean something, didn't it? She repeated the verse Omar shared—or at least tried to: I trust in God and won't be scared. What can man do to me?"

Man could kill her. But then she'd be in heaven with her mother and father and grandparents and her brother Joel, and she'd be happy. That wouldn't be so bad, right? She recalled a quote Jemma loved. "If we find ourselves with a desire that nothing in this world can satisfy, the most probable explanation is that we were made for another world."

The car left the smooth road and rocked over jagged terrain before coming to a stop on an incline. Shaylinn slid forward and pressed her hands against the back of the trunk to protect her head.

She struggled to turn until she had her back to the wall, which was a bit more comfortable. If she thought too much about where she was—that she was trapped and couldn't extend her legs—panic fluttered in her chest. She wanted to get out, yet staying in the trunk might be safer. At least the trunk was a barrier between her and Rewl and his icky teeth.

But then the trunk slid open. Shaylinn covered her face with her hands, hoping that whoever it was would think she was sleeping.

"Get out," Rewl said. "Don't make me drag you."

Shaylinn blew out an angry breath and pushed herself to a sitting position. "You don't have to be mean."

Rewl stepped back from the car, his gun trained on Shaylinn. She looked beyond where he stood and gasped. Rewl had parked on a grassy hill beside a castle made of smooth gray rocks. Lights lit up the doorways and balconies like yellow stars glowing in the dim light of dawn. The sky was pink with purple-gray clouds, and the pine trees that loomed beside the house were black silhouettes against it.

"It's beautiful." Who might live in such a place? She wished Jemma could see it.

"Hurry up." Rewl lunged forward and grabbed her arm. He pulled so hard that she scrambled to get her feet underneath herself so she wouldn't fall onto the ground.

They walked up to the house, and once she was level with the back patio, she saw the pool. "Oh!" Like a mirror of glass, it stretched out from the back of the house, surrounded by the patio made from slabs of gray rock that matched the castle. Fat stone bowls edged the pool and were filled to overflowing with dark pink and purple flowers. Shaylinn breathed deeply, enjoying the mixed scent of the spicy sweet flowers and pine.

Rewl grabbed her arm again and pulled her along the patio onto a porch of wood slats. Just ahead, an enforcer was holding a door open for them, and they entered an oval-shaped room with a stone floor. The walls were paneled in light pine. Ugly blue-and-peach-flowered chairs sat around the perimeter except where three long closets broke the space. The closets had no doors and were filled with outdoor clothing and skis and helmets.

"Where am I taking her?" Rewl asked the enforcer.

"I'll show you."

The enforcer led them down a hallway that was covered in paintings of landscapes. She wondered if Omar would like them. They took a narrow, wooden stairway up to the second floor and walked down another hallway. This one was twice as wide as the one downstairs and covered in soft beige carpet that reminded her of the harem.

The enforcer opened a door and held it. Rewl nudged Shaylinn inside and remained right behind her.

"Wow." Shaylinn stopped inside a bedroom. Almost everything was white. The bed was fat with white pillows and a fluffy blanket. Curtains ran floor to ceiling over the balcony windows. The carpet was green covered in white flowers and dark leaves. Here and there accents of jade and gold complemented the room.

A baby's gurgling pulled her gaze to one of two green wingback chairs sitting before a golden hearth. A blonde woman sat in one of them, holding an infant. Ciddah, the medic Mason loved.

"Oh," Shaylinn said, wondering if Ciddah was helping Rewl or not.

"Talkative one, isn't she?" the enforcer said.

"Wait here to be discovered," Rewl said. "And don't try to escape." He walked out of the room and the enforcer closed the door, leaving Shaylinn alone with Ciddah and the baby. What did that mean, *Wait here to be discovered*?

"You *can't* escape," Ciddah said. "I've tried and failed three times since I got here."

Ciddah was a prisoner too? Shaylinn was glad, for Mason's sake. "Is that your baby?"

Ciddah rocked the baby in her arms. "It's Kendall Collin's baby."

Oh, dear. Kendall must have been very upset when she didn't find her child in the nursery. Omar probably had consoled her. Shaylinn scowled at the idea.

Stop it, she told herself. Jealous thoughts could change nothing. They would only make her angry.

"Why did he bring you here?" Ciddah asked.

"Something to do with getting the task director general in trouble." Shaylinn sat on the second wingback chair. It was soft. "Omar is here. He's going to rescue me. Us, if you want to come."

"Omar?" Ciddah raised her eyebrows. "Isn't he the one who got your people into trouble in the first place? The one who OD'd?"

"Yes, but he's changing. Or starting to, anyway." He just needed people to believe in him, like Shaylinn did—or tried to.

"Have you seen Mason lately?" Ciddah asked, and, for some reason, the worry in the medic's eyes made Shaylinn blush.

"I saw him tonight—last night, before they left."

"Who's they?"

Should she tell Ciddah about freeing the children? It might not be wise. Mason had said once that he didn't trust this woman. Shaylinn suddenly realized just how he felt—to love someone you couldn't trust. It was awful.

"Just some people from my village," Shaylinn said. "Why are *you* here?"

"Because Lawten Renzor is insane. He thinks I am his lifer. And whether or not I like it, whether or not it's true, he has claimed me as such."

Chapter 36

Omar didn't dare attack Rewl when he had the stunner pointed at Shay, so he waited and followed them into the house. What a place! Omar's senses were on overload as he took in the ornate decor. He tried not to look, and instead focus on Shay and Rewl and where they were going. But a painting on the wall in the hallway stopped him cold.

He'd seen this painting in one of his Old art books. It was called *Starry Night*, and it had been painted by Vincent van Gogh in 1889, one hundred and ninety-nine years ago.

How could it be here? How could it even exist still? The frame looked new, so it must be a copy, perhaps a giclee. Omar leaned close to study the strokes, but footsteps on the wooden stairs pulled him away. Shay.

He found the staircase and walked up as softly as he could, coming out into a plush hallway, marveling at yet another painting on the wall.

Just ahead, the enforcer opened the door. Shay and Rewl went inside. Omar could hear low voices but couldn't make out what they were saying.

Should he go in or wait? He didn't know. The enforcer was standing in the doorway, so until the man moved, Omar had no way around him.

Then Rewl came out and closed the door behind him. "Stand guard here until I come back."

Rewl walked back toward Omar, so Omar turned and darted into the stairwell to wait for Rewl to pass by. But when he turned back, Rewl was coming down this staircase. Idiot! Why hadn't he stayed up in the hallway?

He turned and crept down ahead of Rewl, as quickly and as quietly as he could manage. He crouched under the van Gogh, fighting the urge to look at it. He drew his stunner, and when Rewl appeared, he fired. Rewl collapsed in the hallway. Omar ran to his side and dragged him to the nearest open door. A small bathroom. Perfect.

He pulled Rewl inside and shut the door. Rewl's eyes were squeezed shut, so Omar slapped his face and used one finger to push up his left eyelid.

"Hey," Omar said. "You stole the wrong girl, you know that?"

Rewl frowned. His eyes flickered around the room, unable to find Omar's face.

"That's right. I'm haunting you, you traitorous maggot. So, Bender is your dad, huh? Did he kill Chord or did you do it for him?"

Rewl moaned, as if trying to speak but unable.

"You're both pathetic. Trusting Otley for anything is insanity. He *will* betray you. It's what he does."

Omar looked for something to tie Rewl up with, but he couldn't find a thing. So, he stunned him again and darted back out into the hall.

At the van Gogh, he leaned close and inspected the individual brushstrokes and the thickness and texture of the paint. The swirling strokes directed his gaze around the peaceful scene. The church steeple and the tree both pointed to the heavens. Man and creation worshiping their Creator, perhaps?

Or maybe pointing upstairs to Shay.

Omar crept up the stairs, knowing that the painting had been no copy. Someone must have sought out the treasure to hang it here, in a random hallway off a kitchen. That such paintings still existed had never occurred to Omar. To think he might scavenge the world in search of masterpieces of Old.

A thrill grew in his chest at the very idea.

Four steps before he reached the top of the stairs, a blur of blue light walked by on the hallway above.

Mason.

Omar lunged up the last few steps to join his brother.

Chapter 37

Mason stopped in the hallway, staring at the enforcer who was leaning against the wall outside a door, looking bored. Could that be where Ciddah was? Or Kendall's baby? So far, every other bedroom door had been open and no one had been in any of them.

Mason reached for his stunner, yet hesitated. What if that was a bathroom, and the enforcer was merely waiting for his partner? Mason might be making more trouble for himself. He would wait. Though he didn't have much time to spare. He wished that Omar was—

Something shot past his left arm. A crackle. The enforcer seized up and slid down the wall into a heap on the floor, a stunner cartridge stuck to his chest. Mason spun toward the glowing blue form of his brother.

"Got him," Omar said. "Why don't you go say hello to your medic?"

"She might not be in there."

"Well, that's where Rewl took Shay," Omar said.

Mason ran inside. A bedroom. White and bright and totally empty.

Behind him, a voice whispered. "I don't see anyone."

Mason turned around. Ciddah stood, pressed against an indentation in the wall beside the closet, holding a jade vase as if to slam it over the head of whoever might enter.

Behind him, Omar pulled the guard inside the room, which to Ciddah likely looked like a man sliding across the floor by himself on his back with his feet in the air. She screamed.

Mason darted forward and pressed his hand over her mouth. "Ciddah, it's me, Mason."

She dropped the vase and her eyes bulged, rolling in their sockets as she looked for him.

"We're wearing suits that make us invisible," he said.

Her eyebrows sank. Her fingers felt Mason's hand on her mouth, then up his arm. He released her. "Mason?" she whispered.

"When Omar closes the door, I'll take off my hood."

"Guess I'll close the door, then, brother. Let me get that for you." Omar dropped the guard's feet and stepped over him. The door clicked shut. "Where is Shay? I saw her come in here."

"Here." Shaylinn's voice came from the closet.

Omar darted past Mason toward the closet. Mason removed his hood.

A breath tremored past Ciddah's lips as her eyes grew wide again and looked him up and down.

"What? You don't like my outfit?" Mason asked.

A smile chased the fear from Ciddah's face. "I thought I'd never see you again."

"Not see me? We're you afraid you'd go blind?"

She laughed, a breathy laugh, then grabbed his ears and kissed him.

Mason let the moment take him, lost in the feelings she stirred within him. If this was not real love, then Mason would never understand it.

Omar cleared his throat and Mason pulled away, though Ciddah's fingers slid down his arm and took hold of his gloved hand. Shaylinn was holding a baby, standing beside Omar, who looked to be nothing more than a severed head, floating slightly higher than Shaylinn's.

They were both staring at them.

"Kendall Collin said you were Lawten Renzor's lifer." Omar raised one eyebrow as if daring Ciddah to deny it.

Omar... Now was not the time.

"He's obsessed with the idea of creating an Old family. And he mentioned moving away." Ciddah looked up into Mason's eyes and squeezed his hand. "You don't believe I still care for him, do you? I don't want to go with him." Her eyes flicked back and forth from one of Mason's eyes to the other. "You do. Mason, no. I love *you*. I want to stay with *you*. I want my donors to come too and—"

"Explain later." Omar flashed Ciddah a fake smile. "Right now, we need to get out of here."

Mason wanted to shake Omar for his "help" in regard to Ciddah. He only felt more flustered and confused now.

"Do you invisible boys have a plan of escape?" Shaylinn asked.

"I think we should put the girls in the SimSuits," Omar said, already zipping down the front of his. "That way we'll be sure they get out safely."

"Excellent suggestion." Mason unzipped his suit as well.

"I'm going to wear that?" Shaylinn shifted the baby to her other arm and reached for Omar's invisible middle, patting it with her fingertips.

"What about Baby Promise?" Ciddah said.

"I'm wearing a harness," Omar said, shrugging off the sleeves of his suit. "The same one I used to carry Ben. One of you will have to put it on."

"I will," Ciddah said.

"You saved Ben?" Shaylinn said, beaming.

Omar stepped out of one leg of his suit. "We saved all the children, except..."

"Except what?" Shaylinn asked. "Is it Jemma?"

Omar struggled to get his other foot out of the suit. "Nothing. Never mind."

"Jemma is fine." Mason didn't think now was the time to bring up Kendall's death. He could imagine the effect the news would have on Ciddah and Shaylinn. It would not expedite their escape. Mason left his SimSuit on the floor and removed his surgical kit from the pocket. He unrolled it on the bed.

Omar took off the harness he was wearing. "We can give you our suits, but not the contact lenses. So, you'll have no way of seeing each other. Hold hands or something, so you don't get separated."

Mason took the harness from Omar and helped Ciddah put it on. "I need to remove your SimTag next, Ciddah, or they'll be able to track you. Did they give you a new one, Shaylinn?"

"No," Shaylinn said. "I just got here."

"Mason, what about my donors?" Ciddah asked. "We need to find them first."

He met her eyes. "Your *parents* are in hiding. Omar and I got them to safety on Friday."

"Oh, Mason!" She threw her arms around him and hugged him so tightly he could feel her heart beat.

He wanted to linger in her arms, but he made her sit on the bed. "Hold still so I can do this."

Omar took the baby so Shaylinn could get into his SimSuit. While Mason removed Ciddah's SimTag, he shared what he'd overheard from General Otley. "It seems like it won't be long until he's the task director general. Though I don't know why he wouldn't just wait a few more months until Lawten is liberated."

"Because then the Guild takes a vote," Ciddah said. "And if Otley can make himself look like a hero before then, he stands a better chance of getting the job."

"That's madness," Omar said. "It will be worse for everyone then. Do you think he'd really let Bender be enforcer general?"

"Bender has no enforcer experience," Mason said. "I believe Otley is manipulating him." He taped a bandage over the incision on Ciddah's hand. "Sorry I can't do better than that right now."

"It's fine," she said. "You were right about our land: It's anything but safe. In fact, the only place I've ever felt protected has been in your presence."

Mason took hold of her hand. "Then I will never leave you."

"Wow," Omar said. "Keep that up and you two are going to make me sick." Omar pulled Shaylinn to the bed. She was now the one with a floating head. "Sit and hold the baby for Mason. And you"—he nodded to Ciddah—"put on Mason's suit, will you?"

Ciddah got up from the bed and Shaylinn took her place. She hugged the child to her chest, which looked so strange with her body being invisible. "You're going to cut him?"

"I have to. They'll track his SimTag otherwise."

Omar stood guard at the door, stunner in hand, while Ciddah got dressed in Mason's SimSuit and Baby Promise screamed. Mason worked fast, though, and once Kendall's child was bandaged up, he quickly fastened the boy into the harness Ciddah wore, then zipped her up until she was only a floating head too.

"How will we get out?" Shaylinn asked. "I don't know where to go."

"You'll stay with us unless something happens," Omar said. "And if it does, get out of the house and walk to the black truck that's parked at a green house around the corner. Nash will drive you to Zane's place."

"Can't we just go to the cabin?" Shaylinn asked.

"Not now that Rewl knows where it is," Mason said. "Everyone will be at Zane's now."

"Just get out of the gates," Omar said. "Zane says they can find you wherever you are as long as you keep the suits on. So, get out and look for Nash. If you can't find him, sit somewhere and wait. He'll find you."

Ciddah grabbed Mason's hand, and the thick suit glove felt strange against his skin. "I don't want to be apart from you ever again," she said.

He looked down into her eyes. He wanted to say that his love didn't change when they were apart, but Omar would mock him, and he still didn't know with absolute certainty that she was being honest. "Stay alive, please. That's your only task now."

"I will, if only to see you again." She kissed him, and Mason couldn't believe how happy he was capable of feeling.

"I think it's time for the hoods," Omar said, a little louder than necessary. Then he mumbled, "Walls, you two are worse than Jemma and Levi." He laughed, then added, "Levi agrees."

Mason and Ciddah broke apart, and Mason's cheeks burned. He'd forgotten that people were watching through his eyes. He lowered the hood over Ciddah's head and she vanished from sight. It was difficult to find the snaps with the suit already activated. He found the first two, but the third must have been twisted under the hem somehow because—

The door burst open. "Don't move!"

Rewl walked into the room, gun trained on Mason, then Omar, then Mason again.

"You can't shoot us both at the same time," Omar said.

Mason was glad to see that his brother had gotten Shay's hood on in time. Perhaps if he were able to stall Rewl, Omar could get the girls out. He looked for his stunner, then realized it was still strapped to his belt, which was coiled on the floor at his feet.

"Where are they?" Rewl asked. "Where's the baby? I can hear it."

The baby cooed from somewhere near the closet. He hoped Ciddah hadn't gone inside, but then he saw her blue form inching along the wall toward the door.

Rewl stepped forward and motioned Mason to walk to the foot of the bed, where Omar was standing. Mason backed up slowly as Rewl moved toward the closet. Rewl turned quickly, so that his back was to the closet and his gun aimed at Mason. He pulled the closet door aside.

Empty.

Rewl frowned and looked at Mason. "I don't understand."

His aim drooped enough that Mason took his chance. He tackled Rewl, knocking him into the open closet. Mason's hand and temple scraped the wall as they fell. His elbow struck the metal runner for the closet doors, and pain coursed up his arm.

"Go, Omar! Go!" Mason yelled, both hands on Rewl's gun hand, pushing it away from him. No matter what, he had to hold on long enough for them to get out of the room.

Somehow Rewl got on top and jammed his knee against Mason's abdomen. Mason froze, as if paralyzed. His diaphragm was stuck in the inhale position. Too much air with no place to go. His spine instinctively curled. Rewl untangled himself and stood, then he shot Mason with the stunner.

The electricity from the stun cartridge was stronger than Mason would have imagined. His muscles seized and felt like they were being stretched beyond their limits. The pain surprised him as did the fact that he had no voice, no motor control at all. Yet he was completely cognizant of his surroundings. Rewl was searching the room. Mason saw him look under the bed and behind the chairs and curtains, out on the balcony.

Yet Mason couldn't move. It was the strangest sensation he'd ever experienced.

Then the cartridge ran out of current. Mason's body relaxed, though every nerve still felt like it was vibrating.

"He's there," Rewl said to someone. "Pick him up and follow me."

Two enforcers appeared over Mason. Hands descended upon him, and he was dragged out of the closet and from the room. The enforcers carried him after Rewl, through the house and down the stairs. While Mason's body no longer hurt, his muscles had yet to resume taking instructions from his brain.

It truly was a fascinating experience.

Suddenly the enforcers stopped. They were in the small parlor again. Lawten was still here, sitting on the same red chair. Kruse sat beside him now. Two enforcers stood behind Lawten and Kruse, guns in hand. Two of the bodyguards in black suits lay on the floor. Stunned. Dead? Mason couldn't tell. The others weren't present. Bender sat on one of the beige sofas across from them. General Otley stood before the fireplace.

"Well, surprise me," Kruse said. "It's the handsome medic. I did not expect *that*."

Otley turned and looked at Mason, then at Rewl, who walked farther into the room.

"What's this?" Otley asked.

"The girls are gone, sir," Rewl said. "All I found in the room was him and his brother."

"Gone?" Otley roared. "How? Where? What about the baby?"

"I don't know," Rewl said, his voice so low it was barely audible.

Otley narrowed his eyes. "*Which* brother did you see? He has two."

"Omar," Rewl said.

Otley walked up to Rewl. "Where is Omar now?"

"He got away, probably with the girls and the baby."

Otley drew his gun and shot Rewl. The gun let off an airy pop.

Mason's arms flinched, fear bringing his muscles back into action. He knew that sound. It was the same sound he'd heard when they killed his father.

Rewl collapsed. Bender jumped up from the sofa and stared at his son. "You— What did you do?"

"What was necessary," Otley said. "Clearly Mr. Renzor is working with those outsider rats. But without the girl and the child, we have no proof of kidnapping charges. So, find Omar Strong, find the girl, and find the child. Now!"

The two enforcers holding Mason dropped him on a chair and ran out of the parlor. Mason sat there, legs still shaky, staring at Rewl's body, wondering if there was anything he could do. He tried to move his hands and only one finger curled.

Bender crossed the room and knelt at Rewl's side. He pulled his son onto his knees, leaving a circle of red stained onto the rug. A breath released from Mason. Too much blood loss. Too late.

He could only stare and pray that Omar and the girls had gotten out.

Chapter 38

Shaylinn clutched tightly to Ciddah's arm as they followed Omar down the hallway. He turned a sharp corner, and when the girls caught up, Shaylinn saw him standing three steps down a half-flight of narrow, wooden steps, looking back up, waving them to come.

Omar turned, but before he took another step, footsteps clattered up the steps from below. Shadows jostled on the wall of the landing. Omar spun back to them. Shaylinn reached out and took his hand, and he ran up the steps and darted ahead, pulling Shay along. She had to run to keep up, and she squeezed Ciddah's arm even tighter.

Omar ran past the room the girls had been kept in and followed the hall until it turned a corner. Here the passage stretched out the length of one room before it turned yet again and ended in a grand staircase. Shaylinn thought she saw the front door at the bottom of the stairs. They were almost free.

Omar went down the steps quickly and silently. Shaylinn tried to be silent as well. She could hear little Elyot fussing and hoped no one else would.

Just as Omar stepped off the stairs, General Otley swept out from a doorway on the right.

"You!" Otley grabbed the front of Omar's shirt and swung him around, jerking Omar's hand from Shaylinn's and knocking over a vase of roses with Omar's feet. The vase fell with a crash, spilling water and porcelain and flowers across the floor.

Shaylinn bit back a scream. Footsteps on the stairs behind them signaled the approach of two enforcers.

"Did you find the girls?" Otley asked the enforcers, still holding Omar's shirt as Omar struggled to get away. His words were heavy and mean, like punches.

"No sign of them in the rooms, sir."

Shaylinn clutched Ciddah's arm and watched Omar reach for a shard of the broken vase.

"Look again," Otley snapped.

"Yes, sir." The enforcers turned and scurried back up to the hallway.

Omar stabbed the broken shard into General Otley's leg, which made the beastly man growl. With a flick of his arm, he threw Omar through the archway and stomped after him, disappearing from sight.

A tug from Ciddah, and Shaylinn followed her down the stairs. When they reached the bottom, Shaylinn could see into the room where General Otley had gone. Omar lay on the floor on his back, General Otley's foot on his chest. *Don't hurt him!*

"Where's the girl, little rat?" General Otley leaned on Omar, pressing down with his foot. "Where's the infant?"

Omar grabbed the general's boot and twisted out from under it. He rolled up into a sitting position and pushed back on the floor, panting slightly. "I don't know anything about a girl or an infant." Omar took a breath. "Or a rat, for that matter. Me and my brother were looking for a new house, and we liked the looks of this one."

Otley kicked Omar's stomach, and Omar slid over the wooden floor, rolled onto his chest, and moaned.

"Leave him alone." Mason's voice. Somewhere deeper in the room. Shaylinn saw the back of his head above a fancy red chair. Why was he just sitting there?

Someone hitched in a muffled sob, which drew Shaylinn's gaze to Bender, kneeling on the bloodstained floor, cradling Rewl's head in his lap.

Shaylinn lost her breath.

They should do something to help. But what? If only Shaylinn had a stunner. She would shoot Otley and end all this.

The baby let out a long gurgling coo. Ciddah pulled on Shaylinn's arm, and, reluctantly, Shaylinn followed Ciddah, but her eyes stayed on Omar until she could no longer see him.

She heard him moan again and gasp for breath, so she increased her grip on Ciddah's sleeve until her fingers ached.

Ciddah turned the knob on the front door, and it swung it open. An enforcer on the porch turned to look, a gun in his hand. Ciddah pulled Shaylinn back as the enforcer walked through the open doorway. He looked up the stairs, then into the room where that horrible man was hurting Omar.

Ciddah towed Shaylinn behind the enforcer, out the door, and down the steps. Shaylinn looked back to see the enforcer step outside again and close the door, shaking his head. She stumbled over a rock and almost fell.

"Sorry," Ciddah said. "I just really wanted to get out of there before they caught us."

But the tears lacing Ciddah's voice were obvious, and Shaylinn started to cry too. She didn't want to leave Omar and Mason behind, but there was nothing they could do, not without help and not with a baby in their care.

She prayed for a miracle. That General Otley would let Mason and Omar live.

Chapter 39

Omar could barely see the foyer from where he lay on the floor. But he'd seen the blue suits walk to the door, open it, saw the enforcer come inside and look around, and watched the blue suits go out. The girls had gotten away. They were safe. And Omar was done being a kicking bag.

He scrambled to his feet and picked up a lamp from a table by one of the sofas. He ripped off the shade and threw it at Otley. The enforcer general batted it away, so Omar bashed the lamp over Otley's head.

Otley growled. It started low and rose to a scream that turned his face a mottled shade of magenta. Omar grabbed a vase and threw that next, but it only bounced off Otley's chest and landed near the chair Mason was sitting on. Omar didn't know what had happened to his brother, but he didn't look so good.

Otley went for his gun, so Omar dove behind a sofa. Great plan, *Owl*. Now what? He'd only needed to stall long enough for the girls to get away. Now that they had, he needed to get Mason and get out.

Footsteps over the floor had him momentarily paralyzed.

"He's come 'round the piano side," Mason said, his voice slurred.

Omar crawled along the back of the couch and around the corner just as a bullet pierced the floorboards. He bit back a curse and crawled faster. Real bullets from an enforcer-issue dual-action pistol. Omar reached for his own gun, but it was gone. It had likely fallen out of his waistband when Otley had been using him as a kickball.

"Gunfire is our cue to leave, Mr. Task Director," Kruse said.

"You're not going anywhere," Otley said.

Omar looked around for a place to hide, for anything he could use as a weapon. He was almost to the fireplace, which had a rack of tools beside it. The poker hanging by the little broom and shovel looked sturdy. He crawled toward it.

"You're going to shoot me, General Otley?" Lawten asked. "The bullets would match your gun, and you would be caught."

"Maybe you got hit by a stray. I was shooting at one of your rebels when he attacked me. Unfortunate accident."

"You'd still be liberated for my death," the task director general said. "And you know what that means."

"I will *never* be liberated."

"It's that or the Ancients," Lawten said. "I didn't think you liked them. And I doubt they'd accept you, treasonous as you are."

"Enough of this. Hay-o, rat! How do you like this?" The gun fired again, a pop of exploding air. Mason gasped, and released a hissing groan.

Mason! Fire shot through Omar. He grabbed the poker and crawled to the end of the couch.

"You want me to shoot him again, rat? I kind of like making holes in him."

Unbelievable maggot of a human being. Omar peeked at the scene. Mason was doubled over in the chair, pressing his hands to his thigh. Omar couldn't see his face. Otley stood only a few paces ahead of Mason, gun still pointed at him, his back to Omar's side of the room. To Otley's right, Bender sat on the floor cradling Rewl's body. And Renzor and Kruse were standing across the room, near the exit to the foyer.

What now? Even if he managed to strike Otley, with Mason's leg injured, they wouldn't be able to move fast enough to get out of—

"Tell me something, Mr. Elias," Lawten said. "Who shot first when the enforcers came to your village?"

"General Otley shot first," Mason said in a tight voice. "I'll never forget. He said, 'One kill each. Sleep the rest of the village.'"

"Witnesses, general," Lawten said. "And I bet he's not the only one."

Fire filled Omar. That overgrown boar had killed his father on purpose? Why hadn't Mason ever said so?

Omar sprinted out from behind the couch and bashed the poker against the back of Otley's head.

Otley roared and wheeled around, gun still in hand. Omar hammered the poker down over Otley's forearm. Once. Twice. The gun clattered to the floor and Omar kicked it away.

Otley punched Omar, who dropped the poker and fell against a wing chair so hard he knocked it over. Omar hit the floor but flipped himself onto his stomach and scanned the rug for the gun. He saw it on the floor by Mason's foot. Mason must have seen it too because he moved his foot and carefully pushed the gun under his chair.

Otley stalked over the carpet, looking for his gun and growling under his breath. When he didn't find it, he walked back toward Mason. As he passed, Omar grabbed his boot and yanked with all his strength.

Otley tripped and fell on his knees. Omar tried to slip past him to get to Mason, but Otley snagged the back of Omar's shirt. Omar snapped backwards and landed on his rear in front of Otley, who wrapped his arm around Omar's neck.

Omar's breathing ended right there. He struggled against Otley's hold, but there was simply no way he could get free. His head started to tingle. He rolled his eyes up to focus on Otley's face and reached for the tusk in the man's nose.

"Don't you dare," Otley said.

But he did. Omar took hold of the metal, winced, and yanked hard. A scream burst out of Otley that sounded like a boar stuck in barbed wire. Blood dripped hot and wet on Omar's neck, but Otley's grip lessened enough that Omar slipped away and crawled to his brother's chair. He reached between Mason's legs for the gun, but his fingers knocked against the weapon, which slid to the other side of the chair.

Omar got up to go around for it, but an enforcer picked it up. Two other enforcers stood behind the first, guns in hand. *Maggots.* Omar put up his hands.

"I'm going to break your neck, rat," Otley said, stepping toward him. Blood had painted a glossy red, three-inch stripe down his lips and beard and onto his uniform, and it looked like he had only one nostril. "And once your brother sees you die, then I'll break his."

A gunshot rang out. Loud. Old.

Omar jumped. Mason yelled. But neither brother fell.

Otley's body tipped like a felled tree and smashed onto the floor, rattling the nearest lampshade. Behind him, Bender was pointing Jordan's gun in the direction of where the enforcer general had been standing.

Omar stayed put, waiting to see what Bender would do next. But the man dropped the gun and looked down at Rewl's face.

"Thanks," Omar said to Bender. He grabbed Mason's sleeve and pulled it. "Let's go, brother. Can you walk?"

Mason looked almost green and his eyes were closed. "Ciddah?"

Good grief. "Come on, Mason. I need you to stand up, brother."

"Oh no. You're not going anywhere," Renzor said.

Omar had almost forgotten the creep was there, now standing over by the walkway to the front door. "We saved you," Omar said. "You'd be dead if it wasn't for us."

Renzor waved a few enforcers into the room. "He wouldn't have killed me."

"Yes, he would have!" Omar said. Renzor was a fool to think otherwise. "Wait. Is this because my brother stole your medic woman?"

"I'll find her," Renzor said, narrowing his eyes. "Ciddah belongs to me."

Omar snorted. "Really? Because I don't know if you've seen them together but, uh... I just don't think she likes you anymore."

"Arrest them," Renzor said.

"Down on the floor," one of the enforcers said. "Hands on the back of your head."

Omar sighed. There was nothing to do but comply.

Chapter 40

After two days in the Medical Center, Mason joined Omar in the RC. Two more nights there and Mason and Omar were transported to Champion Hall to appear before the Safe Lands Guild. That seemed a bit rushed to Mason.

Their arms were bound behind their backs from the moment they left their cell, and they remained bound as they were led down the wide hallway toward the auditorium.

Luella Flynn stood beside the auditorium doors, armed with her signature microphone and accompanied by her cameraman. "Mr. Elias," she said, "do you know the whereabouts of Ciddah Rourke and Baby Promise?"

Mason smiled at her. "That's one story you'll never get." He hoped. He prayed again that Shaylinn and Ciddah had made it to safety. They must have if Luella Flynn was looking for the story. Since Otley had killed Rewl, perhaps Bender wouldn't be so eager to betray the location of Ruston's basements. Bender had been in the RC too, but he'd been taken out yesterday and hadn't come back.

The guards pushed Mason through the front doors. Every step hurt. His leg was still sore from being shot, though he knew he was doing remarkably well, considering. If he had doctored his own gunshot wound, he would still be in bed.

The auditorium was icy cold, and the sweat on his body made him shiver. The place seemed small compared to how large it had looked on the ColorCast. The paint job was hideous: purple floor, orange theater seats, and lime-green walls. Omar probably thought it was artistic, but Mason didn't dare ask his brother anything with the guards and their stunners so close.

Mason did *not* want to be stunned again. Or shot, for that matter.

Omar didn't look so good. The RC had given him a mercy vape, but he was suffering from a pretty bad withdrawal.

The auditorium seats were filled with people. Tables edged the front and side walls and sat up on platforms, like a dais. People in black robes with pointed hoods that hid their faces sat behind the tables. There were six people on the left, six on the right, four in front, and Lawten Renzor, right in the middle of the front table, the only person on the platform not wearing a robe.

"What's with the creepy death hoods?" Omar whispered to Mason.

"Silence!" the guard on Omar's right yelled.

The guards led Mason and Omar down the center aisle and up into a raised box with half walls. It reminded Mason of the witness boxes people sat in during trials of Old, though rather than facing the audience, this box faced the front—faced Lawten.

The guards instructed Mason and Omar to stand at the front of the box, then they stood behind them. On the dais, Lawten was talking with a hooded person, their heads cocked toward one another as if Lawten were having a conversation with Death.

Mason was glad they'd freed everyone, truly, but the only thing that really mattered to him right now was that Ciddah had chosen Mason over Lawten. She loved Mason and no one else. Knowing that gave him the strength to stand before the Task Director General one last time.

An enforcer dressed in a formal black uniform walked to the front of the room and faced the audience. He stood directly under the place where Lawten sat. "All rise."

The audience stood, but Lawten and the hooded people remained seated.

"The distinguished court of the Safe Lands Guild is now in session. Task Director General Lawten Renzor presiding. Please be seated."

Rustles and murmurs filled the auditorium as the audience sat.

Lawten spoke next, his voice amplified through speakers. "Good morning, Ancients of the Safe Lands and ladies and gentlemen of the audience. Calling the case of the Safe Lands versus Mason Elias and Omar Strong. Be advised that national status has been revoked from these two outsiders. The safety of this land and its people make it necessary for this Guild to invoke Ancient authority over these men. We allowed them into our fair city on Fortune's faith, and they have not measured up. Therefore, they will not be permitted legal counsel or a right to testify on their own behalf."

Mason glanced at Omar, who raised his eyebrows. This shouldn't be surprising, but it made Mason's gut churn. They were going to be liberated, he was certain.

"Colonel Stimel," Lawten said. "Are you ready with the facts?"

A man seated in the front row stood and approached the enforcer, who was still standing at the front of the room. Colonel Stimel was the enforcer Mason had seen the day he'd barged into Lawten's office.

"Ready for the Safe Lands, Mr. Task Director General," Colonel Stimel said.

"You may proceed," Lawten said.

"Mr. Task Director General, Ancients of the Safe Lands, ladies and gentlemen of the audience, the defendants have been charged, and their charges read thusly: removal of SimTag identifiers from their bodies, theft of government property, trespassing, kidnapping of Safe Lands nationals, possession of illegal firearms, assault on Safe Lands officers, and war crimes against the Safe Lands. You, the Ancients, have read the evidence against them. I encourage you to see that they are guilty as charged."

"Thank you, Colonel Stimel. Does the Guild have any questions at this time?" Lawten asked.

"Are the accused infected with the thin plague?" a scratchy voice asked from the right-hand side of the room. One of the hooded people.

"Yes." Lawten looked down his nose at Mason, and his beady eyes seemed to rake Mason's courage into shreds. "Both outsiders ignored my warnings and contracted the virus from Safe Lands nationals."

"He's lying!" Mason yelled. "I don't have it!"

The enforcer behind him pulled his stunner and pressed it against Mason's back. "None of that, now."

"Another outburst and you are to stun him, officer," Lawten told the enforcer.

"Yes, sir," the enforcer said.

Mason shot a quick look at Omar. He had supposed these hooded people wouldn't liberate someone clean, that they'd rather lock him in the donation room until he turned forty. But Lawten wanted payback for Mason's rescuing Ciddah. That was what this whole trial must be about, that and it was Omar's third X.

So, Mason smiled at Lawten, imagining Ciddah and her parents sitting with Levi and Jemma over a nice meal, caring for Baby Promise, Lawten's son.

Lawten looked away from Mason around the room at the hooded people. "Any other questions?"

No one spoke.

"Very well. The evidence has been presented," Lawten said. "This Guild will vote. All in favor of liberation?"

A chorus of "Aye" made Mason jump.

"All opposed?"

Silence.

"The Safe Lands Guild finds the defendants guilty of all charges. It is the judgment of this Guild that both men be liberated without delay."

"Well, this should be fun," Omar said.

Fun wasn't the word Mason would have chosen, but at least, for them, the mystery of liberation would finally be solved.

BOOK THREE

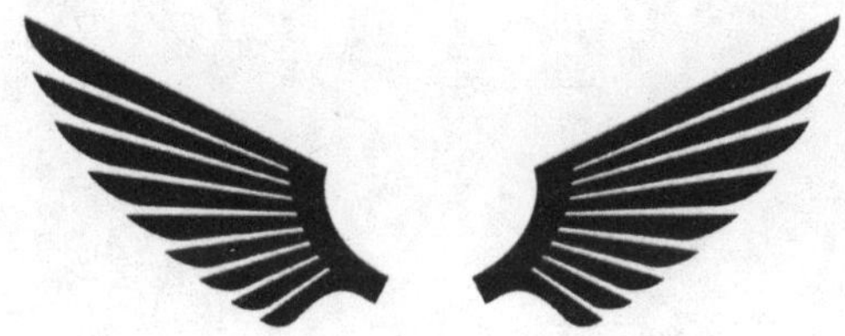

REBELS

To Larry Nielsen and Michael Vernor for your brainstorming genius.
Thank you.

Chapter 1

"The purpose of life is not to be happy. It is to be useful, to be honorable, to be compassionate, to have it make some difference that you have lived and lived well."
—— Ralph Waldo Emerson

Levi woke to the sounds of chaos. Footsteps thumping through the house. Giggling toddlers. Screeching children. Women unsuccessfully shushing.

He rolled over. Gazed at the vacant place his wife slept. No sign of her. She must be up already and keeping the children out of the room.

It all came back then: Mason and Omar had been captured. General Otley had shot Mason in the leg. Beat up Omar.

At least Otley was dead now. But what would become of his brothers?

Outside the room, someone banged against the door, followed by an ear-piercing squeal. This was no way to remain inconspicuous to neighbors.

Levi wondered what time it was, but this room had no clock.

When he'd finally laid in the wee hours of the morning—after having seen his brothers captured and after Nash had brought Shaylinn, the medic named Ciddah, and Kendall's baby boy to Zane's house—there had been over fifty bodies crammed into the small dwelling in the Midlands. They'd covered the floor, sleeping side by side and head to toe.

Now all of them seemed to be wide awake and filled with energy.

Levi slid out of bed and opened the door. Three little girls ran past, nearly knocking him over, filled with shrieking giggles. They all met at the end of the hallway, colliding like cornered chicks.

"Give it back!" one yelled. "I found it!"

Then they ran back toward him.

He reached out and caught the first by her arm. It was Eliza's Kaylee, a rhinestone butterfly pinched between her fingers. The other two girls stopped behind her, and she pulled her hand close to keep her treasure away from her pursuers.

"No running in the house," Levi said. "And you must keep your voices down."

One of the other girls darted toward Kaylee, snatched the butterfly, and ran off.

Kaylee's eyes flashed wide and she tried to pull away from Levi. "It's mine!" she yelled. "Give it back!"

"Shh!" Levi turned Kaylee to face him. "We have to be quiet. Do you want the enforcers to come here and take you away?"

"No!" Kaylee jerked away from Levi's grasp, and he barely kept hold of her. "Don't send me back there, Uncle Levi, please!" Her bottom lip trembled.

Maggots. He was no good with children. Where was Jemma? He scanned the house and caught sight of her brown hair in the kitchen. He looked back to the little girl. "No one will take you away, Kaylee, but you must try and be quiet. Quieter, at least." He released her, and she ran after the other two girls—silently, for now.

Levi closed the bedroom door and walked into the kitchen where Jemma and Shaylinn were putting together sandwiches. Peanut butter and jam, by the looks of things.

"Hi, Levi," Shaylinn said.

Jemma spun around, a smile on her face. "Levi! Sleep well, my love?" She set down a knife and embraced him.

He held her close, breathing her in, suddenly overwhelmed by the stress of their situation. He wished the first few months of their marriage had gone differently, that they might have lived in the cabin he'd built in Glenrock. "What time is it?"

"Five thirty."

"At night?"

"You slept all day." She kissed his cheek and pulled away from him.

He released her reluctantly. "Why didn't you wake me?" He couldn't believe he'd lost an entire day. There was much to be done.

She picked up the knife and continued making sandwiches. "It was a stressful night for all of us. You needed rest."

Other things came to his mind then. The move from the cabin. The birth of Jordan's son. "How is Naomi?"

"Doing fine. The baby too. 'Harvey,' Jordan called him this morning."

After Jordan's father. "Nice. Where is Jordan?" He scanned the house. "Where are the others?"

"Ruston tried waiting for you, but there were just so many people in here he had to start taking them below. The other women, plus Jordan and Beshup and the Jack's Peak men, went down with him and Nash to see the new homes. He also took two of the little Safe Lands boys to his wife."

"How long have they been gone?"

"They left after lunch. Ruston said that when they got back, the adults would know the way to the new homes and could guide the rest of us. Said it was better than all of us going down at once and frightening the people who live there."

"The Kindred." That's what Ruston had called them. It was still hard to believe that Ruston and his sons, Zane and Nash, were Levi's distant relations.

"I'm excited to meet them." Jemma smiled. "I don't know why, but hearing about them made me think of some Old books I've read." She set down the knife and sighed. "I miss my books. I miss reading."

He rubbed her shoulders. He wanted to promise that they'd get out soon and she could read all the books she wanted, but he was tired of showering his wife with empty promises. They were going into hiding again. That almost seemed further away from freedom.

Another shriek turned his head to the living room. "These kids are being too loud."

"We're doing the best we can. Lunch kept them quiet, so hopefully dinner will too." She handed Levi two plates, then took two herself.

Levi helped Jemma pass out plates with sandwiches. The kids sat cross-legged on the floor, which left room for Levi, Jemma, and Shaylinn to eat at the table.

"Did Zane go with Ruston?" Levi asked.

"I believe he's down in the nest, monitoring enforcer radios or something," Jemma said. "I'll have Shaylinn take him a plate when we're done."

"No need."

Levi turned in his chair at the sound of Zane's voice. His friend wasn't alone. Ruston, Nash, Jordan, Beshup—everyone had returned. Ciddah and her parents too.

"Is there enough for us?" Jordan asked.

"Yes, of course," Jemma said. "You can help yourself in the kitchen or wait until I finish."

Jordan wandered into the kitchen. "Where's Naomi?"

"Lying down with the baby in the other bedroom," Ciddah said. "Elyot and Kimi finally fell asleep, so hopefully Naomi is sleeping too."

Jordan pulled out the chair on Levi's left and sat down. "Harvey didn't sleep very well."

"New babies rarely do," Aunt Chipeta said.

Jordan grunted and took a huge bite of sandwich.

"Tell me about the new living arrangements," Levi said.

Jordan chewed a few times, then spoke over a full mouth. "It's weird. A bunch of tunnels hook everything together. And there's a park with real grass."

A park? "How do you have grass underground?"

"We have special lights that enable plants to grow," Ruston said. "There are ten empty homes in the basements. The list you and Beshup created only utilizes eight of them. Are you sure you don't want to spread the people out a little more? The houses are quite small."

"There aren't enough adults," Levi said. "As it is we had to divide up three families of Jack's Peak's children."

Beshup shrugged. "Once we are settled, I guess we'll discover what works and what doesn't."

Once they were settled Levi could focus on the important things, like finding Mason and Omar and helping Beshup free the Jack's Peak women from the harem: the Safe Lands' compulsory in vitro program. "When can we move down there?" he asked.

"Right away," Ruston said.

"Once everyone has eaten," Jemma added.

And so Levi ate, finishing long before most of the children, who were too busy laughing to eat. Finally, they divided into groups and, one at a time, descended into the basement. Levi's group went last.

His new household consisted of Jemma and Shaylinn, Levi's nieces and nephews—Nell, Trevon, Jake, Joey, and Carrie—and Grayn and Weiss, two little Safe Lands refugees who were friends with Trevon and Joey. It would be a busy house. When they finally went down the stairs and into the basement, Zane was waiting.

"I'm coming too," Zane told his father. "I'd like to see Tym and the girls."

Ruston gave his son a silent nod.

The basement was a small, cement room with a ratty old couch, a combination washer/dryer, and a long bookshelf that hid the entrance tunnel to the nest, where Zane worked.

But rather than moving the shelves that led to the nest, Ruston rolled the washer/dryer combo out from the wall, which revealed an airlock door similar to the one that led to the underground bunker where they'd lived for several months. This opened to what looked like a storm drain at first, but it wasn't round and the floor wasn't wet. Plus, the ceiling was much lower that the storm drains they used to travel under the Safe Lands.

Ruston led the way with a flashlight. Shaylinn went next with Joey and Weiss, holding a boy's hand in each of hers, and the other kids scampered after. Then Jemma, holding little Carrie. Levi followed his wife, and at the end of the line, Zane pulled the washer/dryer back into place and closed the gateway door behind them. The tunnel was just high enough for Levi to stand without crouching.

"Where light go?" Carrie said.

"Ruston has the light," Jemma said.

"It won't be dark for long," Ruston called back. "Maybe twenty yards."

"What is this place?" Levi asked, inching along.

"One of seven gateway tunnels the Kindred built over the years," Zane said from behind him. "Entrances to tunnels that weave above the storm drains and remain separate from them, which keeps our homes safe from curious enforcers and from flooding."

"The door to the bunker?" Levi asked. "Is that a gateway?"

"It was," Zane said. "It's been closed off from the basements for years. There used to be ten gateways, but we no longer use the three under the downtown Midlands."

"So, I'll come back out through this door when I need to go above?" Levi asked.

At the front of the line, Ruston stopped and shined the light back to Levi. "No one leaves without my permission. Even you."

That stopped Levi in his tracks. "You can't be serious."

"This isn't like the bunker," Ruston said. "The basements allow my people to live a somewhat normal life. You should know that there are some Kindred who don't want you to live with us. They fear I'm bringing corruption to our doorsteps. I explained that you're not Safe Landers but Outsiders. And, like us, you're descendants of Seth McShane."

"But we're trying to get out of here," Levi said. "We've been prisoners above. Now we're going to be prisoners below? That seems worse."

"You're not prisoners," Ruston said. "But you can't come and go from the basements to the Safe Lands whenever you choose. You must take care and let me know when you want to use the gateway. This is for all of our safety. Plus, this particular gateway empties into my house, and my wife wouldn't like people passing through our home at all hours of the day or night."

Ruston turned back toward the path and the line began to move again.

"She doesn't like much," Zane said. "My mother."

Wonderful. But Levi had no right to argue. He was tired of being totally dependent on others, though, and he wanted more than anything to get out of this place and back to Glenrock.

The tunnel ended at what looked like a regular wooden door. Up ahead, Ruston opened it, and dim light seeped into the corridor.

"You have electricity?" Levi asked Zane as the line started to move again. "How?"

"We have our own powerhouse," Zane said. "It was built right underneath the Highland-Midland wall. It's actually connected to the biofiltration system for Lake Joie, though the Safe Lands Guild doesn't know it."

"So, it's a dam?"

"A little simpler than that, actually. It's a series of waterwheels. Some are connected to the fountains and waterfalls in Lake Joie Park, some are hidden throughout the storm drains, and we've engineered the drains to send the water through them. It works quite well."

Levi followed Jemma through the door and into a living room that looked like any other. It had carpet and furniture and pictures on the wall. No windows. No wall screen.

Behind Levi, Zane closed the door.

"But what about in the winter?" Levi asked. "When the water freezes?"

"LPG-powered generators," Zane said. "Dayle gets us most of the gas through the Highland Department of Public Tasks office, or I work out the credits for emergency purchases." His gaze focused past Levi's shoulder and his eyes lit up. "Hay-o, Tym." Zane slipped past Levi and approached a boy who looked to be in his early teens.

"Hay-o." The boy embraced Zane.

"We try to keep power use to a minimum," Ruston said, "Take short showers or they'll get cold fast. Turn off lights you aren't using. There are space heaters for when it gets cold and lots of blankets. And we use ceiling fans or portable fans for when it's hot. We wash laundry in cold water and don't use dryers. Hang out clothing to dry it and—"

"Tym!" a woman yelled. "To your room. Now!"

The volume of that voice hushed the crowd. Levi looked over the heads of the others to where a woman stood in the doorway that led out of the living room. She clutched two girls, one to each side, and glared at Zane and the young teen.

"Obey your mother, Tym," Ruston said.

"Yes, sir." The young boy hung his head and walked through the crowd to a room on the left wall. He went inside and closed the door softly behind him.

"You must be Ruston's wife," Jemma said, hefting Carrie up her hip.

Zane's mother, who didn't like much.

Ruston squeezed through the crowd until he stood beside the woman and girls. "Yes, this is my wife, Tova, and my daughters, Resi and Luz. My son, Tym, just went to his room. And the new boys from the boarding school should be around here somewhere."

"They went to the park with Katz," Tova said. But that's all she said. No polite greeting or kind words. She simply stared at all of them like she wanted them to leave her house as soon as possible. She did eye baby Carrie with softer eyes though.

Her youngest girl reached out and took hold of Carrie's chubby fingers. "Hi, baby."

"Kids!" Carrie said in the thrilled tone of a two-year-old, waving her other hand. "Hi, kids."

"This is Carrie," Jemma said. "Her mommy is away right now, so I'm taking care of her. These are some of her brothers and sisters and their friends."

"None of them are yours?" Tova asked, frowning.

"No, Levi and I have only been married a few months. No kids yet." Jemma blushed, and Levi thought she was the most beautiful creature in the world.

"Let's get you to your new home, then," Ruston said. "Dathan? Are you coming?"

Dathan—Zane's given name. Those who went into the Safe Lands all had aliases to protect themselves. And if Levi remembered correctly, Katz was Nash's real name.

"Yep, I'm coming." Zane crossed the room to where his father stood by another door. "Bye, Mom. Bye, Resi. Bye, Luz."

"Bye, Dathan," the younger girl said.

Tova glared at Zane, then took the girls by the arms and led them into the kitchen.

Odd.

Ruston guided Levi and his household out the door and into a narrow corridor that was similar to the one that led from the basement of Zane's Safe Lands house to Ruston's underground home, though this one had lightbulbs hanging from the ceiling every five yards.

At the end of the corridor they met a crossroads. Straight ahead was a little alcove and another door, but to the left and right, the corridor stretched until it curved out of sight.

They walked to the left for maybe two hundred yards, passing by two alcoves with doors before Ruston stopped and turned into yet another alcove. There was a number on the door: 16–1.

"That one on the right we just passed leads to the library," Ruston said.

"Can we use the library?" Jemma asked, her voice so hopeful that Levi chuckled.

"It's always open, so feel free to go in and read books," Ruston said. "If you take them home, try not to keep them too long. Straight through the library is the school. If you decide to send the kids, that's the path they'd take. We have good teachers—volunteers, of course. We all do our part down here. If any of you see a place where you'd like to serve, speak up. We'd appreciate your help."

Levi wasn't convinced. If the way Ruston's wife had acted was any indication of how other Kindred might respond, Levi doubted anyone here would appreciate their help.

Ruston opened the door and walked inside a house that was similar to his own. It opened into a living room furnished with two cream-and-blue-plaid couches. The floor was worn brown carpet. Around a short wall, Levi found a tiny kitchen. There were four other rooms. Two doors behind the couches each led to a bedroom. And the two doors off the back of the kitchen led to another bedroom and a bathroom.

"As you can tell, this place will be a tight squeeze," Ruston said.

"It's wonderful," Jemma said, setting Carrie on her feet. "Thank you."

Carrie toddled to the sofa at a near run and threw her face into the cushions, then looked up, smiling, and did it again.

"It might be best if you ladies get everyone settled and I walk Levi around," Ruston said. "Then he can take you all out later."

"That sounds great," Jemma said.

Levi kissed Jemma good-bye and left with Ruston and Zane, back out into the corridor. "I don't understand these tunnels. They're higher than the storm drains?"

"Yes," Ruston said.

"So, these houses are actual basements of houses in the Safe Lands?"

"That's right. But we've closed them off. Not us, really, but our ancestors. My grandfather. Back then, things weren't what they are now. They lived in the houses above ground. But when the government threatened to take their children away, this was how my grandfather and his friends fought back. It took time, granted, to build all this..."

"No one found the secret doors to the basements?" Levi asked. "Once the houses above were abandoned?"

"Most houses don't have secret doors," Ruston said. "They built walls, closed off the basements entirely. The seven gateways are all in safe aboveground locations."

"Some got caught, though," Zane said. "One basement home was found when the property was demolished to build an apartment building. Thankfully, the Kindred who lived there at the time were able to destroy the tunnel leading off from the basement house."

"And that's another reason we've expanded under the warehouse district, away from downtown where they're always digging deep and building more apartment buildings," Ruston said. "Someday they'll likely stumble upon one of our houses again, but it's my hope we won't be here then."

"You want to leave too?" Levi asked.

"Of course. Though many of the Kindred—the women, especially—have gotten used to life as is. But your being here is forcing us to remember our long-term goal of escape. It's a good thing, even if everyone doesn't understand that yet."

The corridors were mostly in a grid that followed the city streets above—there were even graffitied street names on the walls, marking the routes overhead. Occasionally a corridor took a sharp curve, cutting across the middles of city blocks above. Every few yards, alcoves jutted off to one side or the other, leading to doors of houses or other locations.

"There are sixty-three habitable basement houses," Ruston said. "They exist under seventeen square city blocks. Besides the houses, library, and school, we also have a park, a gymnasium, a public square, a meeting hall, greenhouses, the powerhouse, and the trash dumpster area."

"What do you do with the trash?" Levi asked.

"Ever been to Bender's old warehouse on Fifth and Sopris?" Ruston asked. "We have a freight elevator that goes up into there. We raise dumpsters to the surface, inside the warehouse, of course, and trade them with empty dumpsters."

Interesting. Levi saw no other person until they reached what Ruston called Kindred Park. It was as if someone had built a park in a cave. The way the lampposts lit the area with bright white light reminded Levi of Champion Park at night. The grass was green and bright, and it filled the space of a whole city block. Dirt paths wove around benches, bushes, and playground equipment, and connected to corridors on all four walls.

Some children were climbing on a structure with various bars and steps and two slides. A man and woman stood watching, but their heads turned when Ruston, Levi, and Zane entered.

The woman walked forward until she stood between her children and Levi's view. She crossed her arms, eyes wary and sharp.

"Hello, Ruston," the man said, lifting a hand in a wave.

"Kirkland." Ruston nodded. "Olivia."

"Dathan." The man looked at Zane. "How are you?"

"Still alive, much to my mother's dismay," Zane said.

The woman rolled her eyes and turned her back on them. The man chuckled nervously, as if he wasn't sure if he should laugh at Zane's joke.

"This is Levi of the tribe Elias," Ruston said. "He's Elias McShane's great-grandson."

"That so?" Kirkland asked, casting his gaze on Levi. "Pleased to know you."

Levi nodded at the man. "You've got quite a place down here."

"Yes, it suits our needs," Kirkland said.

"*Kirkland.*" The woman had gathered her children and held each by the hand, a boy and a girl. "We should go."

"When I'm finished," Kirkland said, as if trying to prove who was boss. Yet he said to Ruston, "I should go. I'm sorry the women are, well..." He gestured to Zane. "I'm sorry."

"Keep working on them," Ruston said.

The man walked away with his children and his wife, who glared over her shoulder twice before they vanished into a corridor.

"What was that all about?" Levi asked. "You have some enemies down here or what?"

"Yeah. When I turned sixteen, I left the Kindred against the will of my parents and the councils. When that happened, the councils declared me a deserter and I was exiled."

Exiled? "But you can still come down here?"

"I can now. When I made peace with my father, the men's council voted to end my exile. But the women's council doesn't like flakers like me."

"Your own mother?" Levi asked.

"I vouched for his change of heart, and the men accepted that," Ruston said. "But since he refuses to move home—"

"And get rid of my nose rings..." Zane added.

"And the hair." Ruston gestured to Zane's blue hair. "His mother won't welcome him back. Which leaves no one to appeal to the women's council on his behalf. He's still officially exiled, though I can grant him asylum as long as he's in my presence."

Levi had once treated Omar with a similar prejudice. "Will she relent in time?"

"I doubt it," Zane said. "Even if she wanted to, doing so would make her look weak to the other women. So she'll continue to deny me to please them."

"Why do they insist on denying you at all?"

"They're afraid I'll corrupt the children. Make them want to leave too. You saw that woman glare at me just now. I'm a bad influence. My having the thin plague doesn't help, either. They're worried I might breathe on someone and infect them."

"Then why do you come back?" Levi asked.

"Because this is home. My family is here. And I love my mother even though she won't admit that she loves me too."

When Levi returned to his home at number 16–1, Jordan was waiting inside. And from the scowl on his friend's face, Levi knew something had happened.

"What's wrong?"

"I told the medic and her parents that they couldn't leave the house, and the parents freaked out. Yelled so loud they woke Harvey and the other baby. The medic said she wanted to speak to the man in charge, as if I were nothing more than a maggot that she could step on."

"Where are they now?" Levi asked.

"At my place, probably driving Naomi nuts."

"Lead the way."

Jordan's house was in the next block, around a big corner and right before one of the entrances to Kindred Park. 15–2. Levi found Ciddah and her parents inside, sitting on the couch. Ciddah was holding baby Elyot with his head above her shoulder, bouncing him and patting his back. Her mother, Losira, sat beside her, arms crossed. Her posture and the glare on her face reminded Levi of the wary Kindred mother he'd seen in the park. Droe, the father, was asleep in an armchair.

"What seems to be the problem?" Levi asked Ciddah.

Losira stood and stepped in front of him. "He said we can't leave this house! Ever."

"No, I said until you hear *differently*," Jordan said.

"The Kindred don't allow just anyone to live down here," Levi said. "My people were approved by both councils, but you three... Ruston had to fight to get you down here at all."

"What have we done to deserve this?" Losira asked.

"It's not what you've done or not done," Levi said. "It's just—"

"It's me," Ciddah said. "They don't trust me. And that's fair."

Losira turned to her daughter. "It most certainly is *not* fair."

"I've done some things I'm not proud of," Ciddah told her mother. "I—I'll explain later."

"That's my concern, I have to admit," Levi said. "That you're Renzor's spy."

Her oddly-bright blue eyes locked with his. "I'm not. I swear it on Elyot's life. On Mason's life."

The desperation in her tone gave Levi pause. His brother claimed to love this woman, had even talked about marrying her. Levi didn't get it. Not only was she a flaker, she was a flaker who'd been in a relationship with Lawten Renzor, a man who had approved the destruction of Glenrock. Why did Mason trust her?

"It's not only that, though," Levi said. "It's also you two." He nodded to Losira and Droe. "Non-Kindred are rarely given access to the basements. Only when the rebels see someone's loyalty and it's necessary to hide them, then the Kindred vote to extend asylum. And sometimes that vote is a no."

"But they said yes?" Ciddah asked.

"On the condition that you stay in this house," Levi said. "Unless accompanied by someone. One of us, one of them. And that has to be approved by me or Ruston."

"I understand," Ciddah said. "And I appreciate that they've taken us in."

"Ciddah!" Losira stared at her daughter.

"What are you doing to find Mason?" Ciddah asked Levi.

The dull ache returned at the mention of his brother. "Zane can still see through their contact lenses. Last I heard, they were being transported back to the Rehabilitation Center. But Omar's old enforcer friends have been assigned new tasks in the Midlands. And Zane doesn't know anyone who works in Surveillance." He sighed. "We can't get them out."

"You can't just let them be liberated," Ciddah said. "Mason did everything you asked him to."

"Except rescue you," Levi said. "I asked him *not* to do that. Had he listened, he'd be here right now."

"Levi, that's not fair," Naomi said, walking out of a door in the back of the house. "Shaylinn wouldn't be free either if it wasn't for Mason and Omar."

Levi had no response to that. "I'm sorry you're stuck here," he said to Ciddah. "We all are. And you can take my word that I'm doing everything I can to get us out." He gave them all his most sincere look, then left the house.

Jordan followed him into the corridor. "I don't like those maggots in my house."

Levi fought back the exasperation that often came with Jordan's stubbornness. "It's the only way. And she's a medic. If anything goes wrong with Naomi or the baby..."

"Well, you don't have to live with her. Or her weird parents. I swear, if that woman doesn't stop complaining... And Droe. All he talks about is teeth. It's mad weird."

Levi slapped Jordan on the shoulder. "Do what you can to survive, brother. Rest tonight. Tomorrow we'll meet with Ruston to talk about what to do next."

"We need to get out of here. What else is there to talk about?"

"The Jack's Peak women are still in the harem," Levi said. "Mason and Omar are in the RC. And we need to decide if we're going to help Ruston and Zane with their rebel plot."

"I thought that was Bender's deal."

"Not Operation Lynchpin."

"*Omar's* idea? We're actually going to take something he said seriously? His idea of fighting back was to wear an owl costume and spray paint threats on buildings."

"That's not all he did, and you know it. Plus, Ruston likes the idea. And Zane was on board from the start. Actually...we're going to need us a new Owl."

"Count me out," Jordan said. "I ain't wearing that stretchy suit."

"I didn't expect you would. But someone will have to."

The question was, *Hoo?*

Chapter 2

"Liberated without delay?" Mason glanced at his little brother, Omar, who was secured to the seat across from him in the back of the prisoner transport van. Both had their hands and ankles cuffed, and the ankle restraints had been clipped to a bolt on the floor. Their trial had just ended. They'd been sentenced to premature liberation by the Safe Lands Guild. "So, *without delays* as opposed to being liberated *with* delays?"

"It's perfect." A grin spread over Omar's face, which was sweaty and pale. Strange to see him smiling, since he'd just received the worst sentencing the Safe Lands had to offer. "Lhogan and Zane will see everything. And Zane can broadcast it as the Owl."

The contacts. Mason had forgotten he was wearing them. A little thrill shot through him at what this might mean. The greatest mystery in the Safe Lands, foiled by two rebel outsiders and some incredible technology. He couldn't help but return Omar's smile. Things might be looking up after all.

Omar waved at him. "Hello, Levi. Hello, Zane."

"They can't hear you," Mason said. "The contacts are visual only. No sound can be transferred."

"I know. I keep forgetting they disabled my SimTalk." The van went over a bump, and Omar groaned and clutched his stomach. "It hurts, Mase."

"I'm sorry." It was all Mason could say, and he'd been repeating it for the last two days. Omar was suffering withdrawal from his chemical dependency to who knew what types of substances. Omar probably didn't even know.

To make matters worse, whenever the guards were fed up with Omar's screaming in the Rehabilitation Center, the enforcers had come and administered what they called a "mercy vape." No more than one mercy vape per prisoner per day. Since they'd been in trial all day, Omar had not yet been given a mercy vape, and he looked it. And daily meds were administered during dinner, so Omar was also currently without whatever mystery stimulant might be included in his meds.

Another groan from his brother, this one even more pathetic. Less than twenty-four hours without some sort of stimulant and his brother was falling apart. Mason prayed the deprivation wouldn't kill him.

"Where do you think they're taking us?" Omar managed to pant out. "We should've been back by now."

The drive *was* taking more time than it should. It had been a five-minute ride from the Rehabilitation Center to Champion Auditorium that morning. They'd been in the van twice that long already.

Omar bit his lip and grimaced. "If they're just going to kill us, the fact that Zane can see isn't going to be much help. And it's not like they can see where the truck is taking us right now."

"Maybe liberation isn't death," Mason said, though he had no evidence to support that theory. Liberation was a mystery in the Safe Lands. It happened to everyone at age forty, though some were prematurely liberated when they died, reached three strikes on their record, or if the Safe Lands Guild decreed it must be so. Omar had three Xs, or strikes, after this last infringement. Mason now had one. But the Guild had voted in favor of liberating Mason too. Lawten Renzor's idea.

"But what else can"—Omar sniffled and panted, having difficulty breathing again—"liberation be, though?" Another pant. "Seriously."

"I don't know, but it reminds me of something I overheard when we were at Champion House. Lawten told Otley that if Otley killed him, Otley would be liberated. Otley said he'd never be liberated. Then Lawten said, 'It's that or the Ancients.' As if Otley had a choice between those two things."

"Ancients?" Omar squinted at Mason. Could withdrawal affect eyesight? Perhaps it was a migraine. "Those guys in the hoods?"

Mason nodded and shifted his weight as the van went around another turn. During their trial—or lack thereof—in the Champion Auditorium, there had been sixteen people sitting up on the platform wearing black hoods. Lawten had addressed them as the Ancients of the Safe Lands. "What if that's the ultimate promotion? Perhaps becoming a hooded Ancient is the only way to avoid being liberated at forty."

"Why would anyone want to wear a hood for the rest of their lives?"

"To escape something worse. Whatever liberation is."

Omar rubbed his temples. "You're saying that a select few who know the secret of liberation have a way out by becoming an Ancient? Wouldn't everyone sign up?"

"I don't think they can. Lawten said that he doubted the Ancients would accept Otley, knowing how treasonous he was—as if he needed to apply. And such knowledge is likely only open to the top government officials of the Safe Lands."

"That's good stuff, Mase." Omar sniffled. "The Owl should look into that." He gazed directly into Mason's eyes. "Look into those hooded Ancients." He pretended to pull a hood over his head, as if the gesture might help Zane decipher the message, but it just looked like he was scratching his ears. He slouched back against the wall. "Still, where would they live? I've never seen any old people walking around the city."

"Maybe they're forced to live apart from everyone else?" Mason suggested.

"Maybe they're not old, Mase. Maybe they're young. Maybe Luella Flynn was under one of those hoods."

"Their voices sounded old." Though Mason had only heard a couple of them speak.

"I don't know, brother. I still think liberation is a firing squad."

"That would be too messy for the Safe Lands. Death by lethal vaporizer is more their style of execution."

Omar smiled dreamily. "If they'd let me OD on brown sugar, it wouldn't be a bad way to go. It's almost like flying."

The comment pricked Mason's nerves. "Don't say that stuff, Omar."

"It just itches so bad. What if they don't give me any more? What if—" Omar straightened. "We're stopping."

Indeed, the van had slowed down, and now it stopped suddenly. Mason could hear the hum of a garage door, though he couldn't guess whether it was going up or down.

The back door of the van opened into darkness revealing a single enforcer, visible from only the waist up.

"Welcome to lib prep." He raised a SimScanner at Omar and fired.

Before Mason could think about offering sympathy to his brother, the enforcer shot him with the SimScanner as well. A pulse of electricity blossomed from the SimTag in his right hand and instantly spread through his body.

His muscles cramped at the electrical disruption of his nervous system, and adrenaline rushed over him in a flash of heat and pain. Being shot with the SimScanner didn't feel much different than when he'd been shot with a stunner. He'd lost all motor control but could still see and hear. The only difference was the steady sting at the location of his SimTag.

The enforcer climbed into the back of the van. "Bring the stretchers." He unhooked Omar's ankle cuffs.

Soon Mason and Omar were being wheeled under a high concrete ceiling with bright round lights. The current pulsing from Mason's hand stopped sending its charge, and his body relaxed. He still couldn't move, though, and his nerves seemed to throb along with the buzz of the overhead lights.

They wheeled him into some sort of laboratory, where two medics stripped off all his clothing and placed him on a paper-covered exam table. The table had no legs but stretched across the end of the room, attached to the walls at the head and foot. A round tube was imbedded in the wall at Mason's feet. It was about a yard in diameter and circled the end of his bed. Omar and his stretcher had apparently not followed them in.

The medics strapped Mason to the table and left. He was mortified to be lying naked, and his cheeks and chest burned. Mobility had returned to his fingers and toes, and he wiggled them, hoping it might speed the recovery to his limbs.

The circular tube released a mechanical hum and lit up blue, as if someone had turned it on. Something beeped. The tube emerged from the wall with a whoosh and stopped a few inches out, vibrating. Then it proceeded forward, slow and constant, sliding its way up and around Mason's body. It must have been scanning for something, though Mason couldn't imagine what.

When the circle passed over his head, it hissed, the blue light went off, and it sailed back to the wall by his feet. The door opened and the medics returned.

"He has them too," one of them said. A male. Mid-thirties, perhaps? He stopped at Mason's side and looked down. "Nothing goes with you into Bliss. No need for SimSight there."

SimSight? The contact lenses. The circle must have scanned his body for foreign materials and found the lenses.

The second medic—also a male, though slightly younger—stepped up beside the first and handed him a squeeze bottle. The first medic pulled on blue latex gloves. He held Mason's eyelid open and squeezed liquid onto the pupil.

Mason flinched at the coldness. The medic's finger easily swiped the lens to the side of Mason's eye and pinched it out. He repeated the procedure with the other eye.

So much for his friends being able to see what was going to happen to them.

"I'm going to unhook you now," the first medic said, pulling at the straps across Mason's chest. "There's clothing on the chair by the door. Once you can move, put it on. Then we'll take you to the liberator."

The liberator. Well, that certainly sounded foreboding.

The medics left, shutting the door behind them. Mason lifted his arm. It went only a few inches off the table. He turned his head, found the chair by the door with shoes and orange fabric folded on top.

Orange? A strange color choice for a journey to Bliss. It reminded him of what prisoners wore in Old movies.

Was he still a prisoner?

He caught sight of a yellow camera in the top corner of the room, pointed down at the paper-covered table. His nakedness was being recorded? Wonderful. That thought inspired him to try to sit, which he managed without too much difficulty. He swung his legs off the side of the table and found it was too high up for his feet to reach the floor. His gaze landed on the puckered scar on his thigh where Otley had shot him. Five days ago. Amazing what they could do with technology here. Bullet easily removed. No stitches. It still hurt to walk, though. As if he'd been badly bruised.

Mason pushed himself off the side. The concrete was cold under his feet, and his legs buckled under his weight. He turned and grabbed the table to keep from collapsing on the floor. Once his legs felt stable, he limped backward toward the chair—childish perhaps, but he felt more comfortable with the camera behind him.

When he reached the chair, he picked up the jumpsuit and sat down. A pair of underwear fell onto the floor. He sighed. Safe Landers did not likely expect such humiliation as part of the exciting journey to Bliss. Though perhaps this was merely for those convicted of crimes against the Safe Lands. Maybe upstanding citizens received better treatment.

Mason dressed and had barely slipped his feet into the thin shoes when the door opened. An enforcer pointed a SimScanner at Mason and waved him out.

Mason limped into the corridor. The enforcer had a partner, who was also pointing a SimScanner his way. With their blue uniforms and gray helmets, they looked almost identical. They didn't even have name patches.

The enforcers motioned Mason down the concrete corridor. A black rubber mat lined the floor. Bright lights and yellow security cameras hung down from the ceiling every few yards.

"Where's Omar?" Mason asked as they made their way along the endless hallway. "I came here with him."

"We can't tell you anything, peer," one enforcer said. "Save it for the liberator."

The liberator. Of course.

The corridor ended in a T, and the enforcers prodded Mason to the left, where a doorway opened automatically. One of the enforcers pushed Mason into a square chamber no wider than the hallway. A closed door stood opposite the one he'd entered through.

"This is where we leave you, peer," the enforcer said. "Find pleasure in life."

"Happy liberation," the other said.

The door slid shut with a clank of metal against metal. Inside, Mason looked for a handle and pushed against it. He tried the same on the other door. Nothing.

All right. What now? It occurred to him with a rush of heat that maybe liberation was death, after all. Perhaps gas would filter in through the ceiling and he would die in this little room.

He stood in the chamber for a span of thirty seconds before the other door slid open. Mason walked out and met two enforcers—older-than-forty enforcers, if he wasn't mistaken. They wore green uniforms with brown helmets rather than the navy blue uniforms and gray helmets that the city enforcers wore. "Let's go, shell," said one with a gray mustache. A name patch on his uniform said "Penn." "Time to see the liberator."

Mason followed Penn and the other enforcer, Blake, down another corridor. They passed through an automatic door and into a small lobby.

An elderly woman sat at a counter, tapping on a GlassTop computer. She looked up, frowned, and pushed a SimPad his way. "Tap, please."

Mason set his fist against the pad and it beeped. The woman focused back on her computer. Mason's face came up on the screen.

"Oh, dear. You did get into some mischief, didn't you?"

No reason to pretend otherwise. "Yes, ma'am, er—miss." Safe Lands women didn't like being called ma'am.

But this one didn't seem to mind. "Have a seat until you're called," she said.

The enforcers led Mason to a row of chairs. He went ahead and sat down, which made the gunshot wound in his thigh twinge until his weight was off it. The enforcers positioned themselves out in front of the chairs as if Mason might make a run for it.

He studied the lobby. There were four doors in the room: One behind the counter, one on each end of the lobby, and the one they'd entered through. A sign on the wall behind the reception desk said, "Taskers in this office may use sarcasm in a way you are not accustomed to. You might suffer severe mental damage."

Mason raised his eyebrows, surprised to find humor in a place like this.

The woman leaned over the counter. "The liberator will see you now, Mr. Elias."

"Let's go, striker," Penn said.

Mason got up, and the enforcers escorted him to the door on the left end of the lobby. They entered a small office. A man sat behind a steel desk with a built-in GlassTop. He too was dressed in a green enforcer's uniform, though he wore almost as many bars and medals as General Otley once had. He was older—late fifties, perhaps? His salt-and-pepper hair was cut short, and he wasn't wearing a helmet. A Wyndo screen hung on the wall behind his desk, and a yellow security camera perched in the corner by the ceiling.

"Another premie. Good," the man said. "We could use some more muscle down here, though it doesn't look like you've got much, striker. That'll change in a hurry. Sit down."

There were two metal chairs in front of the desk, so Mason pulled one out and sat. His enforcer escorts remained standing behind him. "You're the liberator?" Mason asked.

"That's right. I'm General Dannen, head liberator for the Safe Lands. You were sentenced to premature liberation by the Safe Lands Guild, which, frankly, is not good. It makes you a striker despite the fact you never Xed out. You probably think that ranks you higher than your Xed-out peer. Not so. For some reason, the task director general wants the worst for you. Put you in Livestock. Sector five. Frankly, I don't think the Tasker G knows what's what down here. If it were me, I'd have put you in one of the slaughterhouses."

A chill raced up Mason's arms.

The liberator looked Mason up and down and sighed. "Life in the Highlands and Midlands, that's all about pleasure. Task a little, play a lot. That's all over for you. We task here so that the young can play. Since you're a striker, you get to live with the other strikers. And, lucky you, the Tasker G put you in the men's bunkhouse. That's about as bad as it gets down here, so I guess maybe he does know something about this place." The liberator looked Mason over again, eyes lingering on his thin arms. "Good luck with that. You're in 2C. That's the second floor, block C. Bed 26. Your SimTag will let you in. Strikers have a curfew. You must be in your block by ten o'clock each night or your SimTag will shock you and let us know. You can't leave earlier than five in the morning or the same will happen. Blocks are locked at night."

Mason's mind raced. So many questions. "What do you mean by—?"

"I'm not done. Women aren't allowed in the men's bunkhouses or striker residences, and men aren't allowed in the women's bunkhouses or striker residences. You got that?"

"Yes, sir."

"When you're off shift, you can go most anywhere else, even into private residences if you've been invited. But if you're somewhere you're not supposed to be"—he motioned to the camera on the ceiling—"we'll see you and your SimTag will shock you. Then enforcers will drag your sorry carcass to see your warden. And you don't want to see your warden. Ever. Understand?"

"Yes, sir."

"I like your manners. You should keep that up. Now, you get ten credits a day to use however you want. We've got stores and clubs and restaurants and theaters in Cibelo. That's the shopping district. You need something, tell the block enforcers or your task director, who is..." He tapped on his GlassTop screen and squinted, pulling his head back like he needed glasses. "Gabon Gacy. He runs the cattle feedlot."

He was going to work with cattle? That wouldn't be so terrible. He'd worked with cattle back in Glenrock. "Are we still in the Safe Lands?" Mason asked.

The liberator grinned. "This is the Lowlands, shell. Welcome to the rest of your life." He looked over Mason's head. "I'm done here."

Before Mason could formulate a question, Penn prodded him out of the chair. "Let's go."

"Find pleasure in Bliss, shell," the liberator said as the enforcers ushered Mason out the door.

They left the office, walked down another hallway, then took an escalator that emptied into some sort of train station.

This "train" was more like a tram. It had an engine on the front that looked like a miniature truck with three cars attached to it, steel with no walls, just five benches in each car, all facing forward, all empty. The enforcers directed Mason into the front of the second car, then they climbed on three rows behind him, resting their SimScanners on the back of the seat in front of them. No one else got on.

The tram pulled forward and into a dark tunnel, which produced a cool breeze on Mason's face. Thirty seconds passed in the darkness until a light shone up ahead. It grew steadily until the tram passed through another station. There were a handful of people waiting, but the tram didn't stop. Painted on the wall beside an escalator were the words "Sector One: Drugs."

What could that mean?

A few minutes passed in the darkness until the tram sailed through "Sector Two: Produce." Since Mason was in sector five, which was Livestock, he surmised that each sector must produce some sort of raw materials for the rest of the Safe Lands.

It was even longer until "Sector Three: Textiles" flashed by, and it must have been five or six minutes until they passed through "Sector Four: Grains." Mason wanted to ask how many sectors there were, but he doubted the enforcers would speak to him.

So Bliss was a penal colony. *We task here so that the young can play*, General Dannen had said. Interesting way to set up a society. Make the elderly and the lawbreakers do the hard labor.

No wonder General Otley and Lawten Renzor didn't want to come here.

The smell of decompressed manure gripped him long before the tram stopped at the station for "Sector Five: Livestock." There had to be a lot of cattle up there to produce such a strong odor, but the station itself was deserted.

"This is your stop, striker," Penn said.

Mason got off the tram and limped alongside the enforcers. They went outside, which wasn't outside at all. They were still underground, yet there was a city here. The ceiling was black with a tangle of support beams and lamps. Many buildings stood as high as that ceiling, but there were lots of smaller buildings, too, especially in smaller street grids.

Mason could still smell cattle, though he didn't see any. They walked the equivalent of two city blocks and entered a gray-brick building that said "Men's Bunkhouse" over the door. Inside, the manure smell diminished somewhat, only to be replaced by the smell of disinfectant failing to mask the odor of sweat, urine, and excrement.

Life had just become very unpleasant on many levels.

But at least it was still a *life*. So, liberation didn't mean death.

The enforcers escorted Mason through a small lobby with a scuffed tile floor. A hall stretched out straight ahead for what looked like the depth of the building. To the right was a stairwell and elevator. To the left, a door beside a thick, scratched window with a circular hole cut at mouth level. Two enforcers sat at a counter inside the window, chatting with each other.

Mason's enforcers waved to the men at the desk, then took Mason up the elevator to the second floor. It looked identical to the ground level, with a scuffed-up lobby, the long hallway stretching back, and two enforcers behind another scratched-up window.

Penn knocked on the thick glass. The enforcers inside wore the same green uniforms, without the helmets. Hays and Ebler, according to their name patches. Hays was totally bald and had tiny, sunken eyes. Ebler had black hair and a beard to match. He was a full head shorter than Hays, though if Mason had to choose one not to cross, it would be Ebler. He had a mean look to him.

"New resident," Penn said. "He's in 2C."

"Ooh." Hays winced at Mason. "That's a shame. That's Scorpion's block."

Ebler frowned. He and Hays looked Mason over like he'd just lost a hand of cards.

"How old are you, kid?" Ebler asked. His beard was so thick around his mouth, Mason could hardly see his lips move.

"Eighteen."

Hays brushed his hand over his shiny scalp. "Dang."

"What'd you do to earn the orange pajamas?" Ebler asked.

"Uh... I upset Lawten Renzor."

Ebler snorted. "Now that wasn't smart."

"Yeah... well, that's irrelevant at this point, isn't it?"

Ebler chuckled, glanced at Hays then back to Mason. "Scorpion will love that mouth, kid. You better learn to shut it."

"Look, this bunkhouse is where they put the worst of the worst," Hays said, "the real bad shells. We bunk enforcers do our best to crack down on violence in the blocks, but..." He shook his head. "There's only so much we can do. If I were you, I'd cozy up to Rock Fist straight off. Him and Lethal are the only ones Scorpion won't mess with, but if you make a deal with Lethal, he'll own you, and you don't want that either. We haven't had any competitions for new arrivals in 2C since Rock Fist got here. So, trust me, Rock Fist is your new best friend."

"Rock Fist." Mason committed the name to memory. He'd never been one to spend much time with the men, comparing muscles and who'd caught the biggest fish. This seemed to be desperately worse than any of that. Not even comparable, really.

Ebler shook his head at Hays. "He doesn't understand."

"They never do," Hays said.

Penn squeezed Mason's shoulder, as if to offer some sort of support. "He will."

"Look." Hays leaned onto his arms on the counter. "Someone comes after you, yell out, 'I'm with Rock Fist!' and hope for the best. He sleeps in bunk three."

"It's all you can do." Ebler shook his head. "I'll tell the next shift to keep a close eye tonight."

Mason had started the day apprehensive about the trial. Then he'd felt hopeless when he learned he was going to be liberated. Hope*ful* when Omar had reminded him of the contact lenses. Then he'd despaired when the lenses were taken. He'd been curious when he'd met the liberator. Thankful when he'd realized he wasn't going to be killed. But now, in this place with these cryptic warnings... He was terrified.

"We'll take him back to the block, then out to the pens," Blake said.

"Good Fortune, shell," Ebler said. "You're going to need it."

The enforcers led Mason down the hallway, where the stench of unbathed humans intensified. They passed two doors on the right—both labeled 2A—and two on the left—both labeled 2D. The top half of each door had a thick, two-pane window with a wire grid inside. There were SimPads on the doors themselves. Inside, bunk beds filled the rooms. He saw no people.

"Where is everyone?" Mason asked.

"Tasking," Penn said. "Most everyone in the Lowlands tasks from eight to six, except those on night shifts."

"But all strikers work days," Blake said.

"That's right," Penn said. "Every once in a while, they take a group of you strikers out to do some late-night task, but mostly, they want your kind locked up when it's dark out."

His kind. Strikers. Lawten had purposely lumped Mason in with criminals. With the fairness of the Safe Lands justice system, he wondered how many men in the bunkhouse were despicable and how many were merely as unlucky as he was.

They passed by the doors for 2B and 2E and found block 2C at the end of the hall across from 2F.

"Give your tag a try and make sure it works," Penn said.

Mason set his fist to the door and the entrance swung in. Nothing but bunk beds, three rows of them. One row on the front and back wall, one in between. He quickly counted the bunks. Eight across... must be three deep... two beds per bunk. "Forty-eight people in this little room?"

"Naw, I don't think they put more than forty in a block," Penn said.

"And this is where I'm meant to live?" Mason asked. "For how long?"

"That depends on a lot of things," Penn said. "Your sentencing, your behavior, whether or not you work hard for your task director."

The smell wasn't so bad with the room empty. Add enough bodies, and it was sure to be ripe. "Where are the bathrooms?"

"In the back. I'll show you," Penn said, walking deeper into the room.

Mason followed and saw that the back row of bunks didn't have eight across, but six, separated by an opening in the wall that led to a tile room. Penn went inside, and Mason followed, stopping beside the enforcer. Ten shower stalls on the back wall—no curtains. He turned around. Four toilet-sink combos on one side of the entrance, four on the other. And on the ceiling, a yellow camera on each end of the room.

Blake was standing in the archway that separated the bunk room from the showers. He smiled wide. "Nice, huh?"

"Cameras in the showers?" Mason met Penn's gaze, and the look on his face must have showed his total horror because the enforcer jerked his head back to the bunk room.

"Don't let those cameras scare you," Penn said. "They're for your protection. And listen, a friend of mine started out in the bunkhouse. He didn't shower here. He didn't use the toilets. He waited until his tasking breaks or his free time. And he only showered at the car wash."

"What's the car wash?" Mason asked.

"Mandatory cleaning for strikers," Blake said.

"It's a shower, a change of clothing, and a quick word with a medic to make sure you're okay," Penn said. "Get patched up, if you need it."

Mason's stomach fluttered. "And that takes place...?"

"Basement. Second floor goes on Saturdays, I think," Penn said. "The bunk enforcers won't let you miss it."

"And there are no vehicles involved in this car wash?"

"Walls! It's not an actual car wash, shell. We just call it that because you move through and get clean, just like a car in a car wash." Blake shook his head, clearly unimpressed with Mason's intelligence.

"I see." Mason glanced around the bunks. "Which one is mine? Twenty-six?"

"Numbers start on that wall, so..." Penn pointed at the wall opposite the shower room, the one with the entry doors to the block. "Sixteen on the far wall, eighteen, twenty, twenty-two, twenty-four, twenty-six." He pointed at one of the bunks directly in front of the shower entrance. He walked toward it and moved a thin wool blanket off the bars on the end. "Twenty-six." He tapped the black number that had long ago been painted onto the steel frame.

"Someone's belongings are there," Mason said.

"Just claim an empty one later," Penn said. "After you find Rock Fist."

Yes, Rock Fist. Mason's only hope for remaining unscathed. "Which is bed three?"

"Over there." Penn pointed at to the corner by one of the entry doors, opposite the showers. "Second bunk on the bottom."

Mason walked that way and studied the bed. "You know him?"

"Naw. But you'd better, shell." Penn met his gaze, and the man's eyes were sympathetic. "You understand the gravity of the situation, I hope?"

"Yes," Mason said on a deep sigh. It was going to be a long night.

Chapter 3

Omar was dying. The medics who'd taken his clothes and the contact lenses had refused to give him any stims. Said someone would take care of that on the inside, whatever that meant. Then some enforcer minion took him to some enforcer rank who called himself the liberator. And that maggot wouldn't give him anything, either.

Now he was riding on some underground transport to who knew where. Sector six, the liberator had said, though Omar had barely been listening once he'd learned he wasn't getting any juice.

What had they done with Mason?

Omar turned in his seat. "What about my meds?" he asked the minions. He had to lift his voice over the sound of the transport, which made his already pounding head throb.

"Meds are distributed once a week at the car wash when you get clean clothes," one of them said.

"What does that even mean? Are there stims here?"

"Sure, but you've got to buy them, and they're not cheap."

"How not cheap?"

"You get ten credits a day. A level one hit of alcohol will cost you five."

Two hits of alcohol a day? "What about brown sugar?"

"User, eh?" The minion shook his head.

"How much?" Omar asked again, pressing his trembling fingers against his temple.

"Fifty for a level one, I think. Maybe five hundred for a level ten."

Walls! It would take Omar three weeks to save up enough credits for one vial of his usual. And he still needed to buy a new personal vaporizer, as he hadn't been allowed to keep his old PV.

"Look, vaping that stuff will kill you," the minion said.

"Yeah? Well, I'm liberated now, anyway, so what's it matter?"

"Don't you get it?" the minion asked. "There's no next life down here. Old people and strikers work until they die. Surprise, surprise. Welcome to Bliss."

Work? Yeah, that liberator had said something about Omar tasking in a slaughterhouse. Wonderful. Work prison was one possibility smarty-pants Mason hadn't seen coming. No wonder Otley hadn't wanted to come down here.

For some reason Omar started to laugh. Bliss equals work prison. He laughed long and hard until the tram stopped at sector six and the minions made him get off. They took him into an underground building called the Men's Striker Residence. This turned out to be his new home. He was in room 318, a closet with four bunk beds and a doorless bathroom with a doorless shower.

Whatever.

There was nothing Omar could do here. No way to continue being the Owl. No way to communicate the truth to Safe Landers. No way to help Shay or ever see her again. His SimTalk wasn't working. The lenses were gone, so he couldn't show anyone what he was experiencing. He couldn't even vape himself to death, so he'd likely die in slow agony. It was over. Done. God had finally punished him for his sins. Justice had prevailed.

Next, the enforcers took him up to the ground level, where a rotten stench hung in the air. They went to the slaughterhouse and left him in a dinky office with a grizzled man who called himself Taz Akers. Akers gave Omar a tour of the place. Turned out this was where they killed chickens.

The birds came into the first room in flat crates on conveyor belts, squawking and shaking. Some taskers opened the crates and hung each live chicken by their feet onto metal hooks on a moving rail. That rail carried the chickens along, then dipped them into a trough of water, which Akers said was electrified.

Omar hadn't seen that one coming. "Why don't you just chop of their heads with an axe?" That's what they'd done in Glenrock.

"We process too many chickens to kill them one by one," Akers said.

The rail rose up on the other side of the electrocution bath and carried the now-unconscious chickens through a hole in the wall, where a mechanical blade slit their throats as they passed by. Blood dripped down onto a shiny steel counter and drained into a trough. The rail kept moving, carrying the dead chickens into another room.

In this second area, two guys stood around watching to make sure nothing went wrong with the chicken killing machine. First, the chickens went through the scalding tank, where the birds were submerged in boiling "water," which was brown and filled with floating feces and feather shards. Akers said this bath scalded the skin and loosened feathers for plucking. Then it was on to the whirring rubber fingers that ripped out feathers as the carcasses filed past. Next, the machine lopped off heads. Another part cut out their guts.

It was gross and mad wild at the same time.

When the tour was over, Akers took Omar out to the yards, which was a group of four barns filled with chickens. The stench horrified him, and he instantly wretched. He pinched his nose and breathed through his mouth, trying to calm his stomach.

"Walls, you're a weakling," Akers said. "Here. Put this on." He handed Omar a little U of plastic. "It's a nose clip." He pinched the bridge of his nose. "Slides right on."

Omar slid the U over his nose and the stench diminished. Much better.

In the first barn, trucks dropped off crates of baby chicks that were dumped into the yard to fend for themselves. The floor of each barn was a grid of steel squares that feces could fall through. Still, filth was everywhere. Workers waded through the chickens and choose which ones were big enough to be killed. Those were gathered into crates that, when full, were set on the conveyor belt that carried them into the slaughterhouse.

Akers gave Omar a pair of thick boots and told him to put them on. Once he did, Akers led him out into the yard of Barn Two.

"Your job is to walk the pen and look for trouble. Pull out injured chickens or dead ones. Injured ones, if they're big enough, go in a crate for slaughter. Dead ones or ones that are too small go in the incinerator."

Omar followed Akers around the yard as the man showed him what to look for in regards to injury. "If you aren't sure, just ask one of the others. You'll get the hang of it."

"Do we ever clean out the yard?" Omar asked.

"No point. The chickens are always being rotated through, so the yards are never totally empty. Plus, most of it falls through the grid and gets washed out below. It's really not that bad."

Oh, yes it was. Back home, the chickens had lived in neat pens and could walk in the grass, eat worms, and sleep in little beds where they laid eggs. Here... Omar shuddered.

When Akers left, Omar kept his distance from the other men, not wanting to talk to anyone. His bones were aching, and he felt cold despite how warm it was. Feverish.

For hours, he walked the yard "looking for trouble" of the chicken kind, until a whistle blew, and the other men started for the exit. Omar followed, watching as they clocked out at a SimPad at the end of the barn. Omar did the same. He left the nose clip on and followed the men outside, not certain how he'd gotten to this place or where he was supposed to go next.

The men walked away from the buildings and down a sidewalk on the perimeter on the compound wall. At a sign for the tram station, they took an outdoor escalator down a level. Soon Omar saw the lights of an underground city. His temples throbbed at the brightness. He removed the nose clip, and the smell of food made his stomach hurt worse. There would be clubs here, he was almost certain. What had that enforcer said? Ten credits a day? Omar needed food, but food wasn't what he wanted. He had a curfew at ten o' clock, meaning he was free until then. Free to find some clubs and make friends. Friends who might get him some juice.

But the bouncers outside the clubs wouldn't let him in. "No strikers," they said.

Apparently, Omar was a striker. So how did strikers score juice? Should he use his ten credits on a beer? He wanted something, but a beer would only make him crave more.

He eventually bought a slice of pizza, which was the cheapest and biggest food he could find. He devoured it, which eased the pain some. He rejoined the flow of orange-clad bodies heading away from the city. He ached so badly, he hardly remembered the walk. As he passed by the men's bunkhouse and entered the strikers' residence, he wondered briefly what was the difference between the two and if his roommates would be home now.

Fingers crossed they weren't insane.

The enforcers showed Mason the strikers' cafeteria in his building where he could eat for one credit a meal, then they led him out of the bunkhouse. They crossed an underground street that took them back to the tram station, then they rode an escalator up to the surface, which deposited them on a narrow sidewalk that was fully outside—sky and clouds and everything.

From where Mason stood, he could see the perimeter wall of the Lowlands. A row of four-story brick buildings lined the wall for as far as he could see. Across the sidewalk, a waist-high railing overlooked a corral filled with cattle. The sight staggered him almost more than the smell. Black and brown steers, as far as his eyes could see. Tens of thousands of them.

"Astonishing," he mumbled.

"I never get used to that stench," Penn said.

"At least you're not in the slaughterhouse," Blake said. "I hear that's about as bad as it can get."

Mason didn't doubt it. He had seen enough animals butchered in his life to be able to imagine the horror of multiplying that times the number of cattle in that corral. What did they do with all the blood?

The men led Mason into the feedlot, and he marveled at the staggering size of it. The cows were all brown or black and looked to be male yearlings, far too crowded together. The pen was filled with dirt—no grass in sight.

Mason's escorts took him inside a red barn to an office, where Blake introduced Mason to his new task director, yard foreman Gabon Gacy.

"You're on your own now, shell," Penn said. "Stay out of trouble."

And the enforcers left.

Gacy was strong with short black hair. He was dressed in a blue shirt, brown pants, and thick boots, all of which were covered in a layer of dry dirt. He sat against the front edge of a steel desk, which was pushed against the wall. "Glad to have another farmhand." He put his boot on his desk chair and pushed. It glided on wheels toward Mason. "Have a seat."

Mason sat.

"I got a text tap on you this morning," Gacy said. "Said you tasked as a medic."

"A level two medic, yes."

"Well, the tap said you're to task as a farmhand. At some point, if you're good and the task director general thinks you've been punished enough, I could train you as a vet, since you have a medical background. You don't need to be a vet to learn how to vaccinate, though."

"Do the cattle have the thin plague?" Mason asked.

"Of course not."

"Then why vaccinate them?"

"We vaccinate with a five-in-one for the clostridial diseases—tetanus, malignant oedema, enterotoxaemia, black disease, and blackleg. We've got a separate vaccine for protection against botulism, if needed. We get a lot of BRD here—that's bovine respiratory disease. So, we vaccinate for that, plus— "

"Why would cattle get respiratory diseases?"

"They catch colds. They're close together. They're stressed. So, their immune systems are in high gear, trying to guard against everything that's coming at them. Other diseases crop up too. And since these animals are bred for meat, we give them antibiotics to keep the liver functioning long enough to reach slaughter weight. Part of your job is to segregate sick animals so the vet can take a look."

Mason wanted to raise the question why the cattle couldn't be given more space, but doubted Gacy cared to debate animal cruelty. "What else will I be responsible for?"

"Moving the cattle for the vets, moving the cattle for cleaning the pens, watching for damaged fences, helping the penriders or vets when asked. Think you can work with cattle?"

Work with them, yes. Slaughter them, no. "I took care of them in my village."

Gacy frowned. "You're an outsider?"

"Yes, sir."

"And you had your own cattle?"

"Not like this. Ours lived off grass."

"Is that a fact? Well, we don't have the space to let our cattle wander the prairie eating grass. We feed them grain with added growth hormones. How many head you have?"

"Head?"

"How many animals?"

"Oh, um, we had six milking cows, eight calves, six yearlings, and three bulls."

"Well, we've got about ten thousand head here. Fifty pens that house two hundred head each. Let's take you out and see how you do. You'll need a pair of boots. Check that room for your size and put them on." Gacy pointed at a closet by the entrance to his office.

Outside, Gacy showed Mason around the pens. There were three rows, each separated by a road for the feeding truck. As they walked down one of the roads, the truck passed by, pouring grain into a trough that lined the outside of the pens. The cows poked their heads between the bars on the fence and munched.

"This first row has pens one through eighteen. The second"—Gacy motioned to where the truck was dumping feed—"goes from nineteen to thirty-six. And the third row holds pens thirty-seven to fifty-four. We don't use those last few unless we need them. Off past the third row, that's where the manure stockpile is, and the terraces and retention pond. Down at the ends of the rows are the sick pens."

"Do you birth calves here?" Mason asked.

"Not on the feedlot. Calves spend six months with their mothers before being weaned. Then the trucks bring them here. We can finish a steer in twelve months. With the hormones in the grain, these animals gain an unnatural amount of weight in a short period of time. At eighteen to twenty-four months of age, the cattle are taken to the slaughterhouse."

Forced to grow as quickly as possible, medicated to remain alive until they gained enough weight, then killed for burgers at Café Eat.

Mason's stomach twisted.

When they reached pen eighteen at the end of the row, Gacy opened a gate and they went inside. Two cows that were standing nearby lumbered away.

"This is your row. Every day you walk pens one to eighteen. I want you to become aware of what's normal so you know when something is wrong." Gacy went on to list the things Mason needed to watch for to identify lame or sick animals, then said, "Farmhands task from seven in the morning to five at night. You get an hour lunch, but you got to work out the time with the others. We like to have a penrider and a farmhand on each row at all times during the day."

Before Mason could mention that he'd had no breakfast or lunch yet today, Gacy said, "In fact, let me introduce you to the others."

So, Mason met the first row penriders, Coy and Brondon, who each rode glossy brown horses. He also met Wayd and Prezan, the other two farmhands for the first row. They all wore orange jumpsuits like Mason. Strikers. The vet was busy working with the animals, so Mason was informed he would meet him later.

And with that, Gacy left Mason to it.

Alone, he wandered the pens, looking for sick animals. The cows were friendly, and Mason felt a kinship with them. They were all here against their wills, captives in this place. At least Mason would not be slaughtered, though he couldn't get the guards' warnings about his bunkhouse out of his thoughts. He wished he could spend his nights with the cows.

He was suddenly thankful for the task he'd been given. Lawten had meant to punish him, but Mason liked animals, stench or no. He thought of Omar, then, wondering where they'd taken him, how he was coping, if they'd given him a mercy vape yet. And Ciddah. Where was she? He scanned the horizon but could not see the city in the Highlands past the walls that surrounded the Lowlands.

The rest of his shift dragged by. When a bell rang out, Wayd, one of the other farmhands, walked up to Mason. "The bell means were done for the day."

So, Mason left the feedlot and followed the mob down a level toward the underground city. He walked around the shopping district that General Dannen had called Cibelo. It reminded him of the entertainment district in the Midlands. There were dozens of establishments, but they all looked a bit rundown. The smell of fried food reminded him how hungry he was. As he wove his way through the crowd, Mason noticed that very few people wore an orange jumpsuit. In fact, most people were dressed in regular clothing and seemed to be keeping their distance from the strikers.

Could Mason get ahold of some other clothes? He could use a friend who could explain how things worked in this place, and it might be easier to make friends without the hindrance of the orange jumpsuit.

He suddenly wondered if his mother was here and, if so, how he might find her.

His growling stomach took priority, and he returned to the bunkhouse cafeteria for dinner. The establishment clearly wasn't used to vegetarians, forcing him to scrounge up a plate of droopy lettuce and some peas and carrots. Mason sat at a table near the entrance with his back to the door, hoping that would keep people from noticing him or picking a fight. This turned out to be a valid concern—the other strikers were loud and rowdy, and started two food fights and one fistfight while Mason ate.

A Wyndo wall screen in the far corner was playing C Factor. Mason lingered in the cafeteria until they closed at eight o'clock and made him leave. He wandered back into Cibelo, trying to waste time. He didn't want to go to the bunkhouse until he absolutely had to.

Mason had just left a clothing store when his SimTag buzzed. A voice came over speakers in the store.

"Ten minutes to curfew. Ten minutes to striker curfew."

Mason took a deep breath. Time to go.

When Omar staggered into his room, he found that he wasn't the first to arrive. Three out of eight bunks were occupied. They all wore the orange jumpsuit, though a guy with dark hair had stripped his off to the waist, baring a muscled and hairy chest, and arms decked with SimArt. The sound of water spraying in the shower told Omar that it was occupied as well.

"Hay-o, newman. What's your name?" the half-dressed guy asked.

"Omar."

"I'm Prav," the hairy guy said. "This is Kurwin." He gestured to a man on the bottom bunk across from his. Kurwin had white-blond hair that had been shaved so short it looked like the fuzzy glow of a baby chick.

Omar shook off the thought. He'd seen too many chicks today.

"That shell up there is Jeorn," Prav said, "but he doesn't talk. Lost his tongue in a fight club match that got ugly. You must be above Kurwin, yeah?"

Omar was staring up at Jeorn, trying to decide if he should be afraid of the man or not. Prav looked much stronger than the mute. "Uh, are they assigned?"

"Liberator should've told you your bunk number," Prav said. "Take bed five. Over Kurwin."

Omar wasn't sure he wanted to climb anywhere. "When do we get our meds?" he asked.

"We got car wash on Friday morning," Prav said. "You just missed it."

Wait another whole week? "What's a car wash?"

"Showers and clean clothes for all strikers," Prav said. "Meds too."

"What you in for?" Kurwin asked.

"You don't have to tell us," Prav said. "Kurwin's a nosy shell."

Omar shrugged one shoulder. "I got on the task director general's nerves. Otley's too, but he's dead now."

"Stun me, Otley's dead?" Prav asked. "How do you know?"

"Saw him die. Got shot in the head with an Old pistol. Guess they couldn't bring him back from that." Papa Eli had shot Otley with his rifle once before, yet the MC had managed to save him.

"You some kind of rebel?" Kurwin asked.

"Some kind. Not anymore, I guess."

"Yeah, ain't no rebels down here," Prav said.

"Why not?" Surely rebels had been sent here.

"'Cause enforcers are always watching. Plus, they mark rebels. Don't let them get within two yards of each other for more than five minutes or their SimAlarms go off."

"Seriously? What's a SimAlarm?"

"Didn't you listen to anything the liberator said?" Kurwin asked.

"A SimAlarm is the stunner in your SimTag, peer," Prav said.

"Oh, right." *Duh, Omar.* "I just never heard it called that."

"Well, that's what it is, and it hurts," Kurwin said.

"So, what are you in for?" Omar asked Kurwin.

"Disorderly conduct." He cackled as if he'd made a joke.

"Kurwin gets drunk and acts like a shell. The Midlands bouncers throw him out, then he tries to fight them."

"So, basically, you're an idiot," Omar said.

Prav and the mute laughed. Not Kurwin.

"Shut your face, shell," Kurwin said, standing up. "At least I don't get credited to hurt people." He gestured to Prav.

"I only hurt people who ask for it," Prav said. "And sit down."

Kurwin sat.

It *would* be the strong guy who was in for hurting people. "How do people ask for it?" *So I can make sure I never do.*

"You'll be warned first," Prav said. "I'm a fair guy. But we all have to earn a living down here. And ten credits a day for watching chickens die doesn't cut it."

Maybe once Omar got to know Prav better, the guy would help him find a side job to make more credits.

There were seven men in bunk 318, which left one bed empty—the one above Kurwin. Omar showered, but since he had no clothing to change into, he had to put on the same clothes again. His new SimTag hadn't brought back his SimArt, and Omar missed it. He liked putting his feelings on his skin. Prav had SimArt, so perhaps Omar could start buying it again someday. But first, whatever credits he made were going one place: in a PV.

He awoke that night, unable to breathe. Clutching his chest, Omar wretched over the side of his bed. The vomit splatted to the floor in the darkness.

"What the...?" Kurwin.

"Sorry." Omar fell back on his matress. He should get up. Clean that mess before Prav found out and got angry. But all he could do was lie on his back and stare at the ceiling. His heart pounded against his chest, too fast or too slow. Too... wong. And his head was still throbbing.

He was going to die for sure this time.

"Hey, shell. Here." Prav's voice.

The familiar cool metal of a PV pressed against his cheek. His lips found it and he inhaled. He could tell right away it was grass. A high level too. Glorious grass. He let it in, let it soothe the itch, though it wasn't what he really needed. It wasn't—

"What's your stim?" Prav asked.

Omar sniffled, unable to see Prav in the darkness of the room. "Brown sugar."

"Walls. That stuff's ranked. What'd you task before to make that kind of credit?"

"Enforcer."

"*You*, a force? Come on. I'm no dim."

"Does it really matter anymore?" Omar asked.

"Guess not," Prav said. "Look, I see you got two options. You can save up, and if you're smart you'll switch to grass before you kill yourself. Or you can do what we do."

"Which is?"

"Task for Rain in our free time."

"Is that the enforcer you beat guys up for?"

"Oh, no. This is different. Both are special off-grid tasks."

"Rain will like you, peer." This from Kurwin, from the bed below. "You're young. That's all she cares about."

"Meet us in Cibelo tomorrow night," Prav said. "Eight o'clock. Place called Fajro. And once you calm down, clean this pile of puke. It reeks."

"Sure thing," Omar said, not wanting to anger his savior.

Chapter 4

The warnings from the block enforcers had Mason scared out of his mind to enter his bunk. *Look for Rock Fist,* he reminded himself as he walked back to the bunkhouse.

Inside the lobby, a mob of men around the elevator inspired Mason to take the stairs. He wasn't alone. A river of men clad in orange jumpsuits flowed up each flight. Mason kept to the side, limping up the steps. People occasionally darted around him, in some kind of hurry. A few bumped his shoulder on purpose. The body odor overwhelmed him, though after the day Mason had experienced, he bet he was doing his part to add to it.

One shower a week would not help the smell.

Mason studied the men's faces, trying not to look like he was staring at any one person. The majority seemed middle aged, though there were some younger people and many older ones. Which was Scorpion? Lethal? Rock Fist?

On two, he passed by the first door of block 2C and entered the second without drawing any attention to himself. The second door opened right into Rock Fist's sleeping area. Bed three, Penn had told him, which was the bottom of the second bunk from the wall. It was currently empty. No Rock Fist.

Okay, plan B. Mason walked into the narrow aisle between the first and second bunks and squatted against the wall, hoping no one was watching. He got down on the floor, as if looking for something, then slipped under the bed on his stomach.

Feet shuffled past. Lots of boots. Mason kept his breath quiet and peeked up though a space at the end of the mattress where the men loomed past. No one had seen him.

"Move it, Hobbles!" a loud voice jeered, every word a near scream.

An elderly man stumbled into the room and grabbed hold of the post on the end of Rock Fist's bunk, which jerked the bed to the left. Mason scooted over a bit.

"Don't fall now, you ancient." The screaming voice belonged to a skinny man, who pulled the back of the old man's jumpsuit. The old man held tight, and the bunk scraped to the right. Mason squirmed that way, trying to stay underneath.

Laughter spilled out from nearby bunks.

"Hey, who's that?" someone said. "On the floor."

Mason held his breath.

A pair of boots stepped beside the bed. A man crouched.

What now? Mason slid out from under Rock Fist's bunk and beneath the one in the corner.

"He went under Hobbles's bed!" someone else yelled.

Great. Mason had managed to get another person's attention.

Footsteps. "Out of the way, old man," the skinny man screeched. "What are you doing, sneak?" A fist hammered Mason's back. "Huh?"

Mason grit his teeth. "Just looking for something."

"No... I don't think you belong here." A hand seized the back of Mason's jumpsuit and dragged him out like he weighed nothing, lifted him to his feet, then spun him around. The skinny bully clutched the front of Mason's jumpsuit and gave him a shake. "Who are you?"

Mason grabbed the man's wrist and pushed it back, but his grip was ironclad. So, he seized the man's throat instead and pressed his thumbs over his carotid arteries.

The bully's eyes bulged, but only for a moment. He dragged Mason out into the main aisle and slammed him on the floor. Mason's head knocked against the tile and stung. The bully sat on his chest and pinned his arms against the floor.

A thrill of panic shot through Mason. He tried to knee the guy in the back. "Get off me!"

"What you got, Wicked?" a deep voice said from somewhere above.

"Block crasher," Wicked said.

"Let's see him."

Wicked sighed, slouching a bit, then climbed off Mason. A crowd had formed around them, some standing, some sitting on top bunks. Mason stood up slowly, trying to breathe and look calm, wondering if Rock Fist was here yet, praying he might be. He touched the back of his head. A lump was forming, but no blood.

A man pushed through the crowd. Pale and bald with horn implants, his face was tattooed in hundreds of puzzle pieces. He had inky-black eyes, even the iris. Mason knew it must be due to contacts, but the effect was hideous. Demonic.

"You packing?" the man asked.

Mason didn't understand the question.

Wicked pushed him. "You come here to take Scorpion out? Who sent you?"

Ah, the horned fellow was Scorpion. "I live here now. In room 2C, bed twenty-six."

"Ah, a newman." Scorpion grinned, revealing teeth colored black with SimArt. "Well, this *is* a celebration. We haven't got a newman since Hobbles limped his way up here."

Men were still filing inside the room. Mason eyed the bed that was supposed to belong to Rock Fist, but it was still empty.

Scorpion leaned his face close to Mason's. "Now, what'd you say, raven? Bed twenty-six?" He walked through the crowd, which parted for him like it was made of opposing magnets. Wicked pushed Mason after Scorpion, so he followed. Scorpion stopped at bunk twenty-six and tapped the side with his hand. "Strongboy sleeps here. Where you at, Strongboy? You been holding out on me, peer?"

A man stepped into view. He was as big as General Otley, like someone had inflated him two sizes larger than everyone else. "Leave him be." Strongboy's voice was deep and low.

"What'll you give me for him?" Scorpion asked.

Strongboy shook his head. "I thought we were done with this."

"I like him." Scorpion looked back to Mason, slid his hand down Mason's arm. "Yeah, I like him a lot. Maybe I'll trade Obi for this here raven. Get me a new lifer."

Mason shivered. "I'm with Rock Fist," he spat out.

Scorpion stepped closer, raised his eyebrows. "That so?"

"Yes." Mason inched back and bumped into someone, who shoved him forward.

Scorpion gently slapped Mason's cheek. Slap-slap. "Stimming block enforcers tell you to say that, huh, newman?"

Mason tried to stay calm, even though his heart felt like it was pulsing in his throat. He needed to appeal to Scorpion's humanity. So, he looked him in the eyes, those crazy arthropod eyes, and tried to get him talking. "So, h-how long you live here?"

Scorpion grinned, wide and black, and jerked his head to the side. "Bring him."

Hands gripped Mason's arms and dragged him after Scorpion. Mason yelled and went limp, which didn't even slow his captors for a second. He kicked the guy on his left, trying to break his grip. When they reached the open space before the entrance to the showers, the guy holding Mason's right arm screamed and released him, doubled over. Then Wicked fell to the floor as well. Both had clearly been stunned.

The bunk enforcers were watching. Good.

Mason stood alone in the open space, heaving in gasps of air, his entire body trembling.

Scorpion had relocated to the foot of the bed in the opposite corner of the room from where Mason had first hid himself. He straightened his spine, pointed to the bottom bunk. "You sleep here, raven."

But Mason knew he was safe, for the moment. "I don't think so." He backed his way past Strongboy's bunk. His legs were shaking so badly he feared he might collapse.

A muscular guy tapped his shoulder. He had a thick, black chin beard. "Me and mine will protect you, newman. But it'll cost you. They call me Lethal."

Mason shook his head and kept moving. "No, I-I'm with Rock Fist." He returned to where he'd started, and this time, sat against the wall between bunks one and two.

"I'm-a get you later, raven!" Scorpion yelled across the room. "The BEs can't be everywhere at once. Just you wait 'til dark."

Mason was certain his stress had blocked enough blood flow to his heart that the muscle would stop working at any moment. He took slow, calming breaths and thanked God for the yellow cameras.

"You okay?"

Mason looked to his left and the source of the voice. The old man named Hobbles, sitting on the bottom bed. "Yeah. What does he want?"

"It's about power. Dominance. Plus, Scorpion can make credits off you."

A boy who looked younger than Mason hung his head down from the top bunk. "You don't need him," he said. "You can sell yourself. Plenty will pay."

Mason wanted to puke. "Why don't they just go pay at a club in Cibelo?"

"Not enough women," Hobbles said. "And most clubs don't allow strikers."

"Ah." So, *this* was why Lawten had sent Mason here. Mason had underestimated the man.

"Who's this?"

A man stood in the opening between bunks one and two. He had green eyes, chin-length graying black hair, and a short, black beard. His hair was swept back over his head, making his forehead look nearly half the size of his face.

"Hay-o, Rock," the boy said. "This here's Mason. Scorpion tried to claim him, but he said he's with you."

"I don't know you," Rock Fist said.

"I realize that." Mason pushed to standing, wincing at the tightness in his thigh. "The block enforcers said you'd help me."

"I don't have any more beds for helping people," Rock Fist said.

"I don't need a bed," Mason said, slightly panicked that this man might reject him. "I can sleep on the floor."

Rock Fist's hair fell into his eyes and he pushed it behind his ear. "What'd you do to get here?"

Mason thought of the best way he could word this. How could he be honest, yet impress a bunch of tough prisoners? "I stole Renzor's girl."

Rock Fist barked a laugh. "Oh, that won't do. You need a better story than that or the men will start calling you love names. You don't want that. How'd you get caught?"

"I broke into Champion House and rescued her. She got away. Into hiding with Baby Promise and the latest Outsider Queen. Renzor wasn't happy."

Rock Fist's eyebrows rose. "This girl of yours an Outsider?"

"No, sir. A medic in the Surrogacy Center. I tasked there too."

"But you're an Outsider." It wasn't a question.

"What makes you say that?" Mason asked.

"You're far too pretty, boy. And you couldn't have enough credits to buy any Roller Paint yet. From which village?"

"Why would you assume I'm from a village? Why not Wyoming?"

Rock Fist merely waited for Mason to answer.

"Glenrock."

Rock Fist smirked. "They liberate you as a rebel?"

"I don't know. They didn't say."

"Then they didn't. *Mason.*" Rock Fist said the name as if many pieces of a puzzle had come together in his mind.

Mason's name on this man's lips raised so many questions. "How do you know me?"

"Later. You're one lucky shell getting put in here with me, you know that?"

"That's become abundantly clear in the last ten minutes."

Rock Fist chuckled. "Mason. The smart one. The medic. Yeah, I'll claim you, boy. I got your back." And with that, Rock Fist turned around and shouted, "Listen up, you sick shells. This boy Mason is mine. You hear what I'm saying, Scorpion? *Mine.* Hands off. Don't even look at him. Don't even brush up against him while you're coming in the front door. You do, I will make you scream. That clear?"

Mumbles of affirmatives rolled around the block.

A chill ran over Mason.

"Why you want his skinny butt anyway?" Scorpion asked.

"That's not your business," Rock Fist said. "It's just a fact. Deal with it. Now, I'm going to need a mattress over here, so someone better cough up."

Mason's gaze swept the room. No one was moving.

"I'm not going to ask again," Rock Fist said.

Movement over by the first door caught Mason's attention. A man on a bottom bunk stood up and drew back the covers on his bed, revealing two mattresses stacked together. He pulled off the top one, dragged it between two bunks in the middle, and dropped it in the aisle in front of Rock Fist's bunk.

Rock Fist waved at the boy on the top bunk. "Get down here and help me, Teardrop. You too, Mason."

The boy climbed down, and he, Mason, and Rock Fist pushed the bunk over until it nearly met the one on the other side. Then Rock Fist arranged the mattress on the floor in the now wider gap between bunks one and two.

"Just 'til they get used to you being here," Rock Fist said. "Then we'll find you a bunk."

"Thank you, Mr. Rock Fist," Mason said.

The man fixed his gaze on Mason, staring so indensely Mason had to fight not to look away.

"Call me Rock. And I hope you'll remember this, boy. There might come a time when you decide you don't like me very much."

"I doubt that." But Mason did wonder. How had this man known his name? Was he only helping him in exchange for something? And if so, what?

Chapter 5

"Shh, it's okay." Shaylinn paced in front of the couch, bouncing baby Harvey with every step. She'd come to visit and had volunteered to watch the baby so Naomi could take a nap. But little Harvey wouldn't stop crying, and Shaylinn didn't know what to do.

Levi and Jordan acted like all was well now that the kids had been divided into homes and were, as they put it, *safe*. Shaylinn didn't mean to complain; she was thankful to be able to live in the basements. But what neither man seemed to understand was that this place was scary for some of the kids, many of whom had just learned that their mothers had been liberated. And then there were the Safe Lands children, who knew only fun and had been dismayed to find no electronic toys here.

There was nothing to be done for any of it, though, but to pray and to comfort the grieving children and discipline the naughty ones as best they all could.

Little Harvey, however... "Hush, baby. Your momma needs a nap." She bounced the infant boy, beyond frustrated. Maybe she should put him down. Maybe he didn't want to be held.

"He's not very happy, is he?"

Shaylinn spun around, startled, though she'd recognized Ciddah's voice. "You scared me." Harvey cried louder, unhappy with the sudden movement.

"Sorry," Ciddah said. "Want me to take him a moment? Elyot is sleeping."

Elyot is sleeping. Shaylinn's cheeks flushed at the mocking tone of her thoughts. It wasn't Ciddah's fault that Shaylinn was clueless with babies. "I guess you'd better, or Naomi won't get her nap."

Ciddah lifted Harvey into her arms. "Hello, my sweet boy. Are you unhappy? I'm so sorry. Yes, I am. But your momma needs some sleep. Yes, she does." Ciddah said all this in a gushy baby voice.

"I hadn't thought to talk to him," Shaylinn said. "He wouldn't understand me, anyway."

"Mason once told me that scientists of Old claimed that babies as young as six months can understand a wide vocabulary." Even as she said it, Ciddah kept talking in that gushy voice, eyes locked on Harvey's. "He said that speaking to them normally could improve their language skills later on."

Yes, well, speaking *normally*. Not like the baby was a puppy. "Harvey is only a few days old." But Harvey wasn't crying anymore, just staring at Ciddah's face.

"I think I've intrigued him. You know, it might be my light hair. Your coloring is so close to Naomi's that maybe he thinks you're his mother and wonders why you won't feed him."

Shaylinn hadn't thought of that, either. Ciddah was the medic responsible for the procedure that had made Shaylinn pregnant with twins. But that wasn't why Shaylinn was so upset. She rested her hand on her stomach. It didn't look any different than it ever had—still chubby—but she knew the babies were in there, almost nine weeks old. "I don't think I'm going to be a very good mother."

Ciddah looked away from Harvey, her cool blue eyes staring straight into Shaylinn's soul. "Shaylinn, you're so sweet, that's just not possible."

"But some people have difficult babies. My aunt Mary had a lot of trouble with Nell, so she knows. And she told Jemma that Harvey was a good baby. I can't even handle a good baby, and I'll have two of my own." Plus, she was only fourteen years old—fifteen when the babies came, but still.

"You'll learn quickly."

"Jemma said my babies are hearing my voice all the time, getting used to the sound of me. Maybe that will help."

"I never thought of that. It's lovely."

"Shay."

Levi's voice made Shaylinn look to the doorway. "Hello, Levi."

"It's time to go."

"Already? That went fast." Shaylinn sighed and walked toward the door. Jemma insisted that Shaylinn shouldn't go anywhere alone in her condition. They were babying her as if they also knew she couldn't do this. She waved to Ciddah. "Good-bye, Ciddah. Thanks."

"Bye-o, Shaylinn."

Shaylinn walked beside Levi in silence in the creepy underground corridor. She didn't like it here. The air was stuffy, and she felt buried alive. She knew they were supposedly safe, but she missed the breeze and trees and sky.

"Ruston and I have arranged for the children to go to school tomorrow," Levi said.

"How wonderful!" The children needed something to do. Being cooped up underground seemed to be making them all extra hyper.

"Eliza and Mukwiv are going to take them," Levi said, "but I'd like you to go along. Ruston said they divide the children into smaller classrooms. And I don't want any of our kids to be without one of our adults."

Ah. She was going as a chaperone, not a student. "So, I'm an adult now?"

"Yes, Shaylinn. And I need you to be my eyes and ears."

But she was an adult who couldn't be trusted to walk two blocks alone. She tried to hide her frustration from Levi. At least she would get *some* responsibility. "I'll do my best."

The next morning, Shaylinn, Eliza, and Mukwiv led thirty children to the underground school. They crowded into a hallway that stretched the length of the building. Shaylinn could barely see the door on the other end over the tops of the heads of their group. The walls were covered with children's creations: coloring pages, paintings, and other assignments. There were doors between as well—three on one side of the hallway, three on the other. The outsider children were making a lot of noise, and Shaylinn shushed them as best she could.

A door opened, and Ruston's wife, Tova, stepped out. She surveyed them with a thin-lipped expression. "Can you silence your children?"

Shaylinn shushed the kids again, Eliza put her fingers to her lips, and Penelope whistled sharply, like Jordan always did. Penelope was Levi's cousin and liked to act like she was in charge.

The noise died down instantly, though Tova frowned at Penelope as if she had done something wrong.

"The children must be divided by age," Tova said. "Five- to seven-year-olds will be with Samara in the first classroom there." She pointed to the door nearest Eliza. "Eight- to ten-year-olds will come into my classroom here. Eleven- to thirteen-year-olds will enter the class there." She pointed to the door on Eliza's other side. "And the older children, aged fourteen to sixteen, will go into this class." She gestured to the door across the hall from her classroom.

"Jake, you go in here," Shaylinn said, pushing him toward Tova. "Joey, go with Eliza."

"But I want to be with Jake," Joey said.

"You'll be with Weiss and Kaylee," Shaylinn said.

The frustrations continued as children were divided from friends and family. Mukwiv went with the eleven- to thirteen-year-olds with his son Ian. Eliza chose to go with the smallest children and her daughter Kaylee. And while Shaylinn was young enough to enter the fourteen- to-sixteen classroom as a student with Penelope, Eliza bid her go with the boys into Tova's class.

"Are you not still a child, Shayleen?" Tova said when Shaylinn came into her classroom.

"I'm here to observe," Shaylinn said, then swept past Tova into the room.

Shaylinn found the outsider children—there were seven—standing in a line against one wall, looking uncomfortable. The classroom was furnished with two long tables. Six students were sitting around each—girls at one desk, boys at the other. There were no extra chairs. A small desk stood in the front corner of the room to the side of a chalkboard. The teacher's desk, Shaylinn assumed.

"Didn't you know we were coming?" Shaylinn asked Tova.

"My husband told me." Tova turned away from Shaylinn and strode to the front of the class. "You may sit or stand in the back of the room."

Shaylinn's cheeks burned. But she needed to set a good example, make the best of things. Besides, it might take time to find more tables and chairs. It was unfair to expect the Kindred to provide for every need so quickly.

Shaylinn waved the children to follow her. "Come and sit," she said in a cheerful voice.

She settled them on the floor along the back wall, though she soon realized they were unable to see the chalkboard over the heads of the students. So, she put the boys in one corner and the girls in the other where they could see down the space between the tables and the walls.

Tova sat at her desk in the front. "Open to page twenty-six in your history text. Resi, will you read, please?"

Pages rustled as the Kindred children opened books. Shaylinn looked around the room for more of the blue texts but saw none.

A little girl on the side near the door cleared her throat and wiggled in her chair. Shaylinn recognized her as Tova's older daughter. "Though Seth wanted to leave, he was now in prison, where he would remain for two years. When the day came that he was released, the fences around the city were now stone walls. He was trapped. But at least his son was free."

"Thank you," Tova said. "Hart?"

A soft voice came from the boy table. "Seth found a task as a car... car-pen-ter. He learned to build many things. He made friends and met Reb... Reb-ecca Webster. They got married and had seven children. In the year 2029, the Safe Lands Guild est-ab-lished a boarding school for all min-ors. Seth and Rebecca did not want their children to go, so Seth made a way for his children to hide in their bass... ment?"

"Basement. Thank you, Hart." Tova stood and walked to the center front of the classroom. "That was the beginning of our people, the Kindred. We were chosen to go below. We alone were saved from the evil that takes place topside. Thank the Lord and our forefather."

"Thank the Lord and our forefather," the children murmured.

"You weren't the only ones saved," Trevon said, sitting up on his knees. "We didn't grow up in the Safe Lands. We're from outside the walls."

"You will speak only when called on," Tova said.

Trevon frowned and looked to Shaylinn. "But she said a lie, didn't she?"

Shaylinn lifted her hand. "May I speak?"

Tova's chest heaved with an intake of air. She seemed to hold it, looking down her nose at Shaylinn from across the room. "You may not refute what I teach in my classroom, Shayleen. But if you have a question, I will answer."

My, my. Shaylinn phrased her question carefully. "Have you told your class who we are and where we came from?"

"You are refugees that our councils saw fit to offer asylum. You will learn our ways and adapt to them. Only if you are uninfected and join the Kindred may you marry with our people."

Marry? "These are only children, Ms. Tova," Shaylinn said. "And we won't be here for long. Our elders will find a way out of the Safe Lands and we'll go back to our village in the woods."

The children at the tables murmured.

"That was not a question, Shayleen," Tova said, her voice a scolding yell. "If you break the rules again, I will ask you to leave."

Shaylinn's eyes widened. How could anyone be so mean?

At that moment, the classroom door opened and Eliza leaned her head in the opening. Behind her, Shaylinn could see the outsider children filing past. "We're leaving. Shaylinn, bring our children, please."

Leaving? Good. Shaylinn pushed herself to standing, which was harder than she had expected. Her body was getting heavier, even if her belly hadn't grown yet. She ushered the children to stand.

"Where are you going?" Tova asked.

Eliza opened the door all the way and stepped inside the classroom. "Our children will not be attending your school. We won't allow them to be treated as if they're of lower value. Nor will we allow them to be lied to."

"Who has lied?" Tova asked.

"This is not the time." Eliza glanced at the children. "Samara can explain my concerns, or I'd be happy to talk with you about your *curriculum* later."

"This school is not yours to run," Tova said. "Our councils approve our curriculum."

"I mean no offense," Eliza said. "But why should your councils make the decisions for the children of Glenrock, Jack's Peak, and the Safe Lands? If you simply taught reading and math, we might be able to work together."

"This is *my* school," Tova said. "I will decide what and how to teach."

"I thought this was the councils' school," Eliza said. "But never mind. We'll start our own school."

"If you feel you must."

"You've given us little choice. Come, children!" Eliza waved the kids out the door. "We'll learn in the park today."

They left the school and walked to the park, single file down dark concrete corridors that smelled of soil. By the time Shaylinn reached the park, the children had already raced ahead to the playground.

Eliza sat on a bench. "I'm going to let them play a bit. In fact, maybe we should bring them here during school hours so they can have this place to themselves. Then have our studies in the afternoon."

Shaylinn knew what Eliza wasn't saying. She wanted to keep the children away from the Kindred children as much as Tova wanted to keep the Kindred children away from them.

It didn't seem right.

She sat beside Eliza on the bench. "Once we're free, we'll all move away from this place, the Kindred included. Shouldn't we try to get along?"

"Once we're free, they'll find a place to build their own village," Eliza said. "They still won't want to live near any *evildoers*. You should have seen what happened in that classroom, Shaylinn. Samara made our children stand in front of the class, then she told them that everything they had been taught up until now was a lie. As if she even knows what the children had been taught. Even Safe Lands children learn that one plus one is two. Is that a lie as well?"

Shaylinn shared how Tova had scolded Trevon for speaking out of turn and what had happened when Shaylinn had tried to defend him.

"If you're not one of the Kindred, they think you're evil," Eliza said.

"But Ruston isn't like that," Shaylinn said. "And he said the Kindred believe in the Bible."

"Well, maybe they're not all as strict as Tova," Eliza said. "I'll have to watch their actions to see what they truly believe."

"Tova's actions don't match the selfless love Papa Eli taught about," Shaylinn said.

"Yes, and Papa Eli warned us never to come here," Eliza said. "He was trying to protect us. To keep us away from the thin plague. I guess Tova is only doing the same for her children."

The fear was understandable. Shaylinn didn't want her babies to be born sick. "But Omar and Mia have the plague and we still love them. So, I think we should be kind to the Kindred, even if they treat us badly."

Eliza smiled and put her arm around Shaylinn. "You're right. I'll work on forgiving Tova for judging us. But that doesn't mean I'm going to send my children to her school."

Shaylinn couldn't blame her for that. "It's not easy to love people who hate you."

"No, it's not, but we're supposed to do it anyway."

They sat together in silence awhile, watching the children play. Shaylinn thought about the messages she had been sending to people when she'd been in hiding. She had wanted to give people hope and let them know that they were loved. She wondered if she might still be able to send messages from the basements.

"The elder council will have to talk about all this," Eliza said finally. "I'll ask Levi if you could come and share. I like what you said about trying to love the Kindred."

"I'm too young to be on the elder council," Shaylinn said.

"You're not that much younger than I am. And now that Mason is gone, well... we could use a logical perspective. You don't tend to get emotional like me."

The very idea of speaking to the elder council scared Shaylinn. But it also filled her with a surprising thrill. It was important to educate the children. But Shaylinn felt it was even more important, while they were here, to be an example of selfless love to the people in this place, be they Kindred or Safe Lander.

Chapter 6

When Omar awoke the next morning, he still hurt, but he managed to get up and walk to the slaughterhouse. By the time his lunch break came, he must have boxed up a hundred chickens. He'd put seven carcasses in the incarcerator too. He sort of liked watching the iron door heat up until it glowed a reddish black.

Kurwin had told Omar about the strikers' cafeteria where the meals were only one credit, so Omar went there for lunch. He didn't see Kurwin or Prav in the cafeteria, so he ate as much as he could and wandered back to the slaughterhouse. He still felt weak and feverish, but at least his stomach was full.

Another thing he was thankful for: working out in the yards. It stank. But with the nose plug, it was tolerable, and not nearly as gross as working inside the slaughterhouse would be.

Omar walked the yard. He found a dead chick and carried it to the incinerator. There was still ash inside from his last burn, so he grabbed the hand broom and swept the remaining ash into the ash pit. He tossed the chick inside, then crouched down at the bottom of the incinerator and pulled out the sump trap. As many chickens as they burned, it needed to be emptied several times a day. By the time Omar had managed to pull out the drawer and carry it to the ash dumpster, his hands and arms—the whole front of his jumpsuit—were covered in pasty gray soot. Soot almost like charcoal.

It made him want to draw.

Could he draw with chicken ash? Was it unsanitary? He was already dying, so what was the worst that could happen?

Maybe he could find a container to collect the ash in. Then he could experiment with this new medium. He'd need black paper, though, since the ash was so pale. Unless he could find a way to color the ash. An ink pen, maybe?

He tasked out at six o'clock that night, exhausted, his limbs trembling with every step. He hated feeling weak. What little muscle he'd built up wouldn't stick around if he didn't get his act together. Did it really matter though? He was as good as dead here. At least he'd managed to free Shaylinn from Otley and Bender and Rewl and the Tasker G after they'd kidnapped her. He'd have to entrust her and the babies to Levi and Jordan. His babies, if Mason was right about the donor sample.

Levi and Jordan would do better for them than Omar ever could.

He sighed heavily, breathing out his depression and pain in one long exhale. He had two hours before he had to meet Prav and Kurwin to learn about the off-grid tasking, so he wandered around Cibelo, wishing he had the credits to buy whatever he wanted. He'd come to the Safe Lands with millions of credits and big, naive dreams.

Now he was here.

He'd tasked two days now, so he should have twenty credits, minus the two-credit slice of pizza he'd eaten last night and the one credit lunch he'd had in the strikers' cafeteria. He was starving. For food *and* juice. And he no longer knew which was more important.

He was walking past a bar, smelling the hint of alcohol on the air, when he saw a man toss a half-eaten sandwich into the trash. Omar walked by the trash can and looked inside. The sandwich was just sitting there on the top, still partially wrapped in foil. It looked to be shredded steak with green peppers and onions. He snatched it out of the trash and took a bite.

It was still warm.

Afraid someone had seen him, he strode back the way he'd come, scarfing the sandwich down. He slipped into the narrow alley between a Sparkle cosmetics store and a SimTalk dealer. He slid down against the brick wall of the Sparkle shop and savored the last few bites of the sandwich.

He was pathetic. This was what life had come to. The Owl eating trash.

The Owl was dead.

When he finished the sandwich and licked the juices from the foil, he folded the wrapper carefully and put it in his pocket. He might be able to collect ash in it from the incinerator and find a way to draw.

Omar forced himself to get up. He went inside the SimTalk dealership, but the man told him strikers were forbidden access to SimTalk. So, Omar left and headed toward the club district. He passed a Sweet Spot store, which sold a million types of candy. He went in and walked around. There were lots of machines where you tapped the pad to pay and the candy rolled down into a little slot. Omar checked all the little metal doors for forgotten candy and found a gumdrop, a chocolate caramel, and a minty gumball. He ate the two pieces of candy and was about to walk down the second row when a tasker from the shop yelled at him.

"Either buy something or get out."

"Sorry," Omar said. "I was just looking."

"I know what you were doing. Stop spending all your credits on juice and maybe you could afford to buy food."

The words shamed Omar and he fled, chomping on the tiny nub of gum. The club district was quiet. Most places probably didn't open until at least nine or ten. Why had Prav told him to come at eight? Maybe that was when taskers got the club ready for the night.

Would this Rain woman care that Omar was a striker? Prav didn't seem to think so. If Omar could get a second task, he might be able to afford what he needed to survive. Hopefully, it would pay better than ten credits a day.

He found Fajro, but it hadn't been easy. The place was deep in the heart of Cibelo, down several twisting roads and alleyways. Omar had had to ask five people for directions, and several had given him a look—a glare, really—before answering. He blamed the orange jumpsuit.

Fajro was a door in the wall between two bigger clubs. One called Ludo, which had a marquee with fuchsia and chartreuse neon lights that flashed silhouettes of curvy women. And the other called Zendax, which had piped stripes of white and black light alternating along the front, like pinstriped fabric. The lights flashed on and off, one after the other, which made the club front look like it was made of water. Watching it made Omar dizzy.

Yet Fajro was nothing more than a bright sanguine-red door, solid and glossy, set in a black wall. No lights. The word "Fajro" had been painted on the black wall above the door in letters that looked like fire.

Someone might hire an artist to do such things in Cibelo. Maybe Omar could make credits painting signs.

He knocked on the door, but no one answered. He looked for a SimPad but found none. After a blank moment of confusion, Omar noticed the doorknob. He hadn't seen one since Glenrock. It seemed so foreign here. He took hold of it and turned.

It was dark inside Fajro, and though he couldn't see at first, the air smelled like incense and stims and alcohol and sweat. Omar's stomach clenched at the very idea that he might find a breath of brown sugar here.

A bar edged in red lights ran down one side of the very narrow room. Tiny round tables and a few booths on the other side. No one stood behind the counter, but the shiny bottles of liquor made Omar's mouth water, spoke to him.

Come to us, Omar. Drink us.

He walked toward the bar, chewing on the nub of gum.

"Can I help you?"

Omar jumped and clenched his fists. A woman had stepped out of a doorway at the far end of the bar. Not a door, really, but an opening where a door should be that was covered in long shimmering strands of red and orange and yellow crystal beads. The woman was wearing a red and black animal-print dress.

"I'm looking for Rain," Omar said.

"Rain quenches fire," the woman said.

"Okay." Whatever that meant. "Do you know her?"

"You look too young for her. You look lost."

"I'm not lost, not literally anyway."

The woman cackled, baring a wide smile and very white teeth. "Aren't you funny? Who sent you?"

"Prav and Kurwin. They said to come at eight."

"It's only seven."

"I couldn't find a clock." Omar tucked his hands into the pockets of his baggy jumpsuit. His head throbbed then, and he fought the urge to rub his temple.

The woman stepped away from the curtain of beads, leaned one hip against a bar stool. "How long you been here."

"In the club? I just walked in."

"In the Lowlands."

"Oh, this is my second day."

"Come on back here so I can get a good look at you."

Was this Rain? Omar walked the length of the bar. He tried not to look at the bottles of alcohol on display just out of his reach, but they were too beautiful.

He reached the woman and stopped. She was pretty, though desperately thin with a gaunt face and hollow green eyes. Too green. Fake. She reminded him of Red back in the Midlands. All bones. Nothing soft left to her. Though unlike Red, this woman had thin, straight black hair that ran over her shoulders and curved past her breasts to her waist. Her skin was tan and flaky and decorated with lacy black lines. SimArt. Her lips were thin too, and painted maroon. The shade was off from the red in her dress.

She walked around him, swaying as she went. When she stopped before him again, she reached out and touched Omar's face with the tips of her fingers, making him shiver. He found her kind of creepy and chomped harder on his gum.

"Walls, you're soft," she said. "What's your name?"

"Omar." His voice was suddenly hoarse, and he cleared his throat.

"Can I get you a drink, Omar?"

"Can I get a vape of brown sugar?" *Please say yes.*

She stared at him a moment, then her lips curved into a slow smile. "Brown sugar is not a drink, Valentine."

He sighed, thirstier now that the options had been narrowed. "I'll have a drink. Anything is fine."

She swayed past him and behind the bar. She set two shot glasses on the counter and picked up a bottle of something clear. She filled only the bottom of the glasses, an inch of liquid. He was an idiot. He should have asked for a beer.

She pushed one glass toward him. It scraped across the shiny counter, and the sound made him twitch. Her fingers were long and thin and tipped with red, which made him think of Belbeline.

The memory made him grimace. He grabbed the glass, tucked the gum in his cheek, and swallowed the contents. The liquid burned as it trickled down his throat. He set the glass on the counter and wiped his mouth with the back of his sleeve.

"You're a hungry one."

He didn't know what she meant. "You're Rain then?"

"Like water from the sky, Valentine."

Um... okay. "Prav said I could get brown sugar if I tasked for you."

"If you task for me, you can get anything you want."

She was teasing him. "So, what's the task? Is there an application?"

"It's hardly a task at all, really." Rain scratched her fingernail along the neckline of her dress and looked deep into his eyes. "Women in the Lowlands are lonely, Omar.

The men would rather go to the clubs and pay young striker women to play than look for companionship amongst women their own age. Don't all women deserve the same pleasures in life? Hmm?"

What did that have to do with anything? "I suppose. But aren't there clubs for women to—"

"Yes, yes." She waved her hand. "They have them, of course. But women like being treated special. And those clubs... It's shallow there, Omar. Women want more. I provide them with more."

Oh. He didn't like where she was going. "What exactly would I have to do?"

"Again, you're missing the point. You don't *have to* do anything. You have a right to enjoy life as much as the rest of us."

He was tired of her games already. "Stop saying nothing. Just tell me the truth."

"It's simple, really. I've created the ultimate dating service."

Omar's stomach tightened. "Would I get to pick who I date?"

"No, Valentine. I pick." Rain pointed at her chest. "And only when I get confirmation from my client that things went well, will I pay you."

Omar felt very small then. She'd give him the stims he wanted—*needed*—but only if he traded paint with whomever she said. He couldn't believe anyone would consider a task to sleep with someone. Or that he was still standing there. "It's not right."

"Now, why would you say that? It is what you make it, Valentine. Good attitudes are contagious, you know. You don't have to be so negative."

He wasn't being negative. This was twisted. There was no way he could do such a thing. Unless... "Could I vape first?"

Rain laughed, and it almost sounded like music. Omar bet she could sing. "My clients don't pay to play with juiced-up men. And you've already admitted to being a sweet tooth for brown sugar. That stuff makes you nod into a coma."

"I could do grass first."

She shook her head. "Not from me. My offer stands. Your choice. Take it or leave it."

Leave it, Omar, you fool. But the red lights reflected off the bottles along the wall, making the liquid inside shimmer. "Can I think about it?"

"Sure. Think all you need to, Valentine." She reached under the counter and pulled out a PV, which she set on the surface and rolled from one hand to the other. He watched it, mouth watering. It was black and thick. A man's PV. He swallowed. He could take it from her. He had to be stronger than she was. He glanced around the room for yellow cameras and instead saw a black one looking down on him.

"You're not thinking of being naughty, are you? My bodyguards wouldn't like that."

Omar looked into her eyes, winced a little as a bone-aching shiver attacked. He slouched onto the nearest barstool and watched the PV roll back and forth, back and forth. He wished Mason were here to haul him out of this place. He knew he should leave, but the PV had hypnotized him.

"I'll tell you what, Omar. You spend an hour with me, I'll not only give you a vial of brown sugar, I'll let you keep this here PV as a present. Do you like presents?"

"*With* you?"

"I have to know what my boys are capable of, don't I?"

Omar should leave. Or pray. Or do something sensible. But all he could do was watch the rolling PV, the way the black cylinder reflected on the shiny gold counter. He felt sick in so many ways. Sick to his stomach, sick in his mind, sick in his very soul. He was dying. If she'd give him a ten of brown sugar, and if he took it fast, he could end everything, finally be at peace. Unless he went to hell, of course.

Shaylinn would say that heaven and hell wasn't about his actions but his relationship with God. But maybe she was wrong. Maybe there was no hell. Maybe everyone went to heaven. Or maybe there was no heaven, no God, just nothingness. Darkness. Emptiness.

"Okay," he said, hating himself more than ever. He wanted to cry at that thought, but he shook it off. He didn't have to like himself. He just needed to survive long enough to get that PV filled with brown sugar.

She smiled at him, like she'd won a great victory, then came out from behind the counter and reached for his hand. She held the PV in her other hand where he couldn't reach it. Yet.

He slid off the stool, took her hand lightly, and she pulled him through the beaded curtain.

Chapter 7

Someone grabbed Mason's ankles and pulled. His body slid off the mattress and onto the floor. He looked up into Scorpion's angry face.

Mason's eyes flashed open, his pulse throbbing in his ears, his hand stinging from the effects of his SimAlarm. It had been a dream. Only a dream. Still, anxiety gripped him, and he lay staring at the bunks above and the ceiling, breathing slowly to calm himself down. People were moving in the room.

"Time to get up, boy."

Mason's head twitched as he found the source of the voice. Rock was sitting up on his bed, looking down on Mason.

Mason stretched until he could see the glowing blue digits of the clock above the door. It was 5:27 a.m. "I don't need to wake for another hour."

"We've got the car wash on Saturdays. It's mandatory."

"Oh." Mason sat up. "Where do I go?"

"Just follow the crowd."

Yeah... Mason would follow *Rock*, not the crowd. Many of the guys were already leaving. Mason made a project of standing up, stalling in hopes that Rock would get up and walk to the door. But the man appeared to have fallen asleep sitting up.

Then he saw that Rock's lips were moving. Could he be meditating? Praying? The very idea chastened Mason at how little time he'd devoted to prayer since they'd come to this place. Sure, he prayed, but they weren't prayers of devotion or meditation on Scriptures. His were a string of selfish, "Help me with this" or "Help me with that." Before he had the chance to bow his own head, Rock opened his eyes and stood.

He pulled the sheet off his bed. "Better go now. Bring your sheet if you want a clean one."

Mason gathered his sheet and followed Rock out into the hallway and to the stairwell. They went all the way to the basement, stopping just past the cafeteria, where a line of men stretched down the hallway.

Rock turned around in line and faced Mason. "Where you tasking?"

"I'm a farmhand on the feedlot," Mason said.

"Know what time you take lunch?"

"I have to work it out each day with the others."

"Try to come eat with me today," Rock said. "At two, if you can. No one should complain about that. There's a Café Eat in Cibelo over by the entrance to sector one. Behind that is a place called the Get Out Now Diner. Meet me at the table in the back. I'll buy."

Mason couldn't think of a reason to refuse. He didn't want to risk angering his protector. "Okay." He only hoped that Rock Fist's ideas of payment were something he could agree to.

The line was moving fairly quickly, and soon Rock and Mason turned into a steamy room tiled in one-inch turquoise and white squares. Inside, the line split into ten shorter ones that were queued up behind tile privacy walls. An enforcer stood at the door in front of a SimPad that was mounted on the wall.

Rock touched his fist to the pad. It beeped.

The enforcer read the screen and said, "Line three."

Rock winked at Mason and walked to line three, standing behind four other men.

Mason set his fist against the SimPad. When it beeped, the enforcer squinted at the screen.

"Huh. Line one, shell, and don't forget to use soap."

Mason joined line one. He tried counting the days since he'd last showered. It had to have been the morning before he and Omar helped Kendall move up to the cabin. A full week, he guessed.

Ahead of him, two men were lined up behind a semitransparent shower curtain. He could see the peachy shape of a body inside. A few minutes later the body exited the other side. The man at the front of the line already had his socks and shoes off. They were sitting on the floor between his feet and a wadded-up bed sheet. He stripped off his orange jumpsuit and underwear, dropped everything in a chute before the shower, then went inside.

Car wash, indeed.

Mason wasn't thrilled with the idea of undressing in front of anyone—cameras included—but by the time his turn came, there was still no one in line behind him. He didn't know why his line was so short, but he was glad for it. The camera, he'd have to get used to.

When he saw the man in the shower exit, Mason took off his clothes, dumped them down the chute, and went in, annoyed to see a camera overhead in the shower itself. Eyes were everywhere for the strikers. He quickly discovered the water was a single push button that sprayed high-powered streams of steamy water down on his head for ten seconds at a time. The soap was also a button that dispensed a glob of liquid. He lathered and rinsed quickly, then peeked around the second curtain into another curtained area with bins on both sides. Clean towels on the right, wet towels on the left. Then five bins of orange fabric on the right and five bins of white fabric on the left. Clean jumpsuits and underwear. Each bin was marked with a letter to indicate size. After that, stacks of clean bed sheets.

Mason stepped out of the shower and grabbed a towel. He wrapped it around his waist, then grabbed a pair of underwear out of the medium bin.

Behind him, the shower started. Someone was coming through. He pulled on the underwear as fast as he could over his wet legs, then ran the towel over the rest of him and tossed it in the bin, not bothering to do a very good job. He was too panicked with the idea of someone stepping into his area of the curtain before he left it. He grabbed a medium jumpsuit and put it on. He'd barely zipped it up when the shower curtain behind him slid aside. Mason grabbed a bed sheet and darted around the next curtain. The jumpsuit clung to his arms and back where his skin was still wet.

A medic sat on a small desk, swinging his legs. He stared at Mason a moment, then gestured to a SimPad on the desk. "Tap, please."

"Oh, right." Mason tapped his fist.

The medic watched the results screen and hummed. "No plague?" He looked up, his gaze roaming over Mason's body. "Wow, okay, then. No meds for you. Any health issues to report? Injuries?"

"No, sir."

"How long you been here?"

"Just one night."

"You okay in your bunk? No one assaulted you?"

Mason swallowed. "Someone tried to, but, uh, someone else helped me."

The medic hummed again. "Be careful making deals. Protectors usually want something in exchange for protecting you. Tell the block enforcers if someone is harassing you. Most try to help if they can. This isn't a nice place to live, I'm sorry to say."

"You live here?"

"No. I live in a shoebox of an apartment two blocks away. But that's a hundred times better than what you've got."

That figured. *Lawten*, anyway. Mason only hoped that Ciddah was safely hidden from that miscreant. "Do you need more medics? I tasked in the SC before I came here."

The medic shook his head. "That's not for me to decide. They know your skills. They put you where they want to put you. Strikers don't get the luxury of retask testing. Work hard, and maybe they'll move you someday. I'm sorry, but you need to keep the line moving. Shoes and socks through that curtain."

"Thanks," Mason said.

"Find pleasure if you can," the medic said.

"Yeah, sure." Behind the next curtain Mason found a bench on one wall and a metal cupboard on the wall opposite. There was a SimPad beside the cupboard door, so he tapped his fist against it. Something inside clicked like gears shifting, followed by a loud clump. Mason slid open the door. A pair of boots and a pair of socks sat inside.

Convenient. Mason grabbed the socks and boots and sat down to put them on. He was tying his second boot when voices rose in the medic section behind him.

"Well, I need something! Why don't you have mercy vapes here?"

"It will be better for you to get clean," the medic said.

"I don't want to get clean. I want some golden ice. I *need* it."

Mason wondered if Omar's sessions with his car wash medic sounded similar. He stepped past the next curtain and found he'd reached the end. A narrow corridor led back to the basement hallway.

And that was that. Thoroughly demeaning yet efficient.

Mason stopped in the cafeteria and drank a glass of orange juice. He also grabbed an apple, which he ate on his way to the feedlot. It was his first full day on the field, and he didn't mind it, the stench notwithstanding. The cows were in good humor despite their crowded living conditions. He walked the first row from pen one to eighteen and back, checking the cows for sores, pink eye, or injury, trying to get a feel for normal behavior. He found nothing odd.

He tried to forget what the medic had told him about protectors wanting something in return but couldn't stop imagining the horrors Rock Fist might demand of him. Wondering how the man had known his name.

The lunch hour arrived quicker than he expected. Coy and Wayd went first, and when they returned, Brondon and Prezan left.

Coy found him in pen six. "You can go to lunch now. Wayd and I can watch the pens."

"I'd like to wait until two, if that's okay." Though after Mason's morning of imagining the worst, he'd rather not see Rock at all.

"Sure you can last that long?" Coy asked.

"I can last," Mason said. "I'm meeting someone." Hopefully a friend and not a pervert.

At a quarter 'til two, Mason left. He found the Café Eat easily enough, but it took him longer to locate the diner. It turned out to be a dark doorway between a Lift coffee shop and a place called Garrick's, which looked like some sort of dance club.

Mason slipped inside the diner, very much on edge. A counter ran along the left-hand wall. Booths on the right. Only five. Small place. He spotted Rock Fist sitting at the booth in the very back on the side facing the door. He waved Mason to join him.

Mason walked toward the table, limping slightly, wondering with each step if this were a mistake. Framed posters hung on the wall above the booths. A sandy beach. A massive waterfall. A crowd of people in an Old city. All locations outside the Safe Lands.

As Mason approached the booth, he saw that Rock wasn't alone. He was sitting with two women, though Mason could only see the backs of their heads. He was three steps away when they turned.

He had to grip the top of the booth not to fall over. "Mother?"

And Shanna, who was Jordan's, Jemma's, and Shaylinn's mother. Alive and well. He could only gape.

"Mason! Thank God!" His mother jumped out of the booth and crushed Mason in an embrace. Her familiar smell stunned him. His mother.

She pulled back and stroked his face, hair, shoulders. "You look well. Are you?" Her eyes filled with tears. "Are you okay?"

"I'm fine. Terribly mortified at my new living arrangements, but Mr. Rock Fist has, thankfully, come to my aid." He gestured to Rock, his arm shaking with adrenaline.

He hadn't realized just how terrified he'd been of Rock Fist until now. But instead of a slaveholder, God had provided a guardian angel.

Mother took hold of Mason's hand and grinned at Rock. "Yes, he's wonderful, isn't he?" The sound of adoration in her tone gave Mason pause. "Sit down. Here." Mother all but pushed Mason into the booth beside Shanna, who slid farther in. Then his mother sat next to Rock, across from Mason.

"Mason, my children?" Shanna asked. "Are they okay?"

"And Levi and Omar," Mother added. "Everyone, really. We never thought we'd see any of you again. Tell us everything."

"Okay, well, everybody is fine, the last I heard. Naomi had her baby. A boy they named Harvey."

"Oh!" Shanna cupped her hand over her mouth as tears instantly materialized and rolled down her cheeks.

"And Jordan performed a wedding for Levi and Jemma about a month ago."

"Good," Mother said. "Are the women still in the harem? Rich told us about it—said Levi and Jordan had been trying to get them out."

Rich? Or Rock? Mason paused, wondering if he'd misheard. "Um, no, we helped the women escape the night of Lonn's liberation ceremony, which was almost two months ago."

Rock grunted. "*Two* months ago?"

"That's right. And the children are free as well," Mason said. "We helped them escape from the boarding school just last week. Levi befriended some rebels, and though some betrayed us, some did not. Last I heard, everyone was moving underground into some kind of basement."

"And Omar?" Mother asked.

"Omar is here in the Lowlands, though they didn't tell me where, and I haven't seen him. We were liberated together. He's... struggling. He's addicted to opiates and likely in a great deal of pain. He'd been suffering from withdrawal while we were in the RC."

His mother turned to Rock. "Can we find him?"

"He won't be in sector six," Rock said. "They never put friends together."

"What's worse than the feedlot?" Mason asked. "The liberator let on that the task director general was punishing us."

Rock chuckled. "You lucked out then. The feedlot isn't all that bad. Though you do have the worst housing. As far as worst tasks, I'd say sewage cleaner or tasking in the waste treatment plant. Chimney sweep is a pretty rough job. And any slaughterhouse. The dairy isn't too pleasant, either."

"What sectors are all those?" Mother asked.

"Dairy is eight and there are slaughterhouses in five, six, and seven," Rock said. "Chimneys and sewage tasks in all of them."

"Is the Lowlands fully a prison for Xed people? Strikers?" Mason asked. "Where do the other liberated people go?"

"Everybody is here," Rock said. "See, Loca and Liberté, the founders of the Safe Lands, they decided it would be better to play when you're young, then work when you're old."

"How did they get the populace to go along with that?" Mason asked. "Especially the elderly?"

"Don't know for sure," Rock said, "but there's a rumor. Back before liberation, prisoners were sent to the Lowlands. This got them out of the city and put them to work."

"That seems reasonable," Mason said.

"Yes, except there weren't enough prisoners to do the work. Not long after this problem arose, there was an outbreak of an airborne strain of the thin plague. Every man, woman, and child was quarantined, and before they could be released, they were injected with a number and sorted. The young were sent home. The old were sent to the Lowlands."

"You think the Guild faked the outbreak?" Mason asked.

Rock nodded grimly. "That's the story."

"Why were you and Omar liberated?" Shanna asked Mason.

"We broke into Champion House." At the blank look on his mother's face, he elaborated. "That's the task director general's home. General Otley and a rebel named Bender were trying to frame Lawten Renzor for several crimes. To do so, Bender kidnapped Shaylinn to make it appear that Renzor was helping the pregnant outsider fugitives get medical care. So, we went in to rescue Shaylinn." And Ciddah.

"Shaylinn is *pregnant*?" Shanna asked.

"Oh, sorry, yes," Mason said. "With Omar's twins."

"*Omar*?" Mother choked on her water and set down the glass. Rock rubbed her back Mason berated himself for his lack of tact. "I'm sorry. I should have said that first."

"Omar and Shaylinn?" Shanna asked. "I didn't even know they were friends."

"It didn't happen like that," Mason said. "Shaylinn was in the harem. Do you know how things work there? Women can be impregnated by an embryo transfer procedure."

"Yes, Rich explained it." His mother took hold of Rock's hand, though she kept her eyes on Mason, waiting for him to continue.

Mason cleared his throat. "Yes, well, Omar was the donor whose sample they used to... create the embryos that were transferred into Shaylinn. He was the only man from Glenrock who complied. I expect at least one woman from Jack's Peak will be matched with his donation as well. The medics try to vary the DNA pairings, though I checked Jennifer's chart, and she was not matched with Omar's sample. Nor was Mia."

"That boy," Mother said. "What has he done to himself? To all of us?"

Mason hadn't meant to make Omar look guilty. "You should also know that Omar came back to us. It's still difficult for many, Eliza and Jordan especially, but the new elders of Glenrock offered forgiveness to Omar, and he's been working with us against the Safe Lands. Shaylinn's pregnancy has given him purpose, I believe. He risked his life to save her from the task director and General Otley."

"Did General Otley succeed in framing Renzor?" Rock asked.

"No. Bender shot and killed General Otley after Otley killed Bender's son. And we helped Shaylinn and Ciddah and Baby Promise escape before Otley's men could find them. In fact, Bender should be down here too. He was alive when I last saw him."

"Baby Promise is Kendall's child, right?" Mother asked. "That girl on the ColorCast? The last queen?"

"That's right," Mason said. "You get the ColorCast news down here?"

"Strikers can watch in the cafeterias," Rock said. "But your mother is a reputable and has a Wyndo in her apartment."

"Who is Ciddah?" Mother asked.

Mason glanced at the tabletop, hoping to look indifferent. "She was the medic in the Surrogacy Center—the place I tasked."

"The blonde girl—Kendall's medic." Mother chucked and pulled Rock's hand into her lap, leaning against him. "She told me I was too old to conceive. As if I didn't know that already."

But Rock's eyes were on Mason. "*She* was your medic? The one you stole from Renzor?"

Mason cheeks filled with heat. He'd forgotten that he'd told Rock he'd been liberated for stealing Lawten's girl.

"Who did you steal?" Mother asked. "What does that mean?"

"How did the medic play into Otley's plan?" Rock asked. "And Baby Promise?"

Mason was happy to answer Rock's question over his mother's. "Right, well, Renzor had taken Ciddah to be his lifer—against her will," he added, reminding himself of the fact. "Otley accused Lawten of using Ciddah to provide medical care for outsider women. And Baby Promise is Lawten's own blood, a child he conceived with Kendall Collin after purchasing her from Wyoming. Ciddah says Lawten has always wanted a family of Old, but someone else told me Lawten saw it as an experiment. Neither makes sense to me."

"What rebel is Levi working with now?" Rock asked.

"Ruston Neil and his son Zane."

Mother turned to Rock, her eyes searching his.

"Good men. Honest," Rock said to her, and she seemed to relax.

"Is anyone else pregnant?" Mother asked. "You said Mia and someone from Jack's Peak?"

"Yes. I don't know which of the Jack's Peak women, as I wasn't able to confirm that before I went into hiding. But Jennifer and Mia are. Mia by natural means, as she fell in love with a piano player. She and her child are infected. Jennifer became impregnated because Mia refused to be rescued when we freed the women from the harem—Jennifer insisted on staying with her daughter. Jennifer's donor is from Wyoming, and I don't believe she or her child are infected."

"Foolish women," Mother muttered.

"Mason, I'm so sorry." Shanna touched his shoulder. "I know that you and Mia were to be married."

Mason had nearly forgotten. "Marrying Mia was my father's idea, not mine."

"And now you have the medic," Rock Fist said.

Mother looked at Mason, eyebrows raised. "You *have*?"

"No, now I am here," Mason said, hoping to again bypass the subject of Ciddah Rourke. "And I discover that liberation is nothing more than a penal colony."

"Someone has to do all the hard labor so that those in the Highlands and Midlands can task and play," Rock said. "Did you never find it odd that Safe Lands nationals only tasked four to six hours a day, four days a week?"

Mason should have. He'd been too busy worrying about finding a cure for the plague to think about the economy. "I did notice the exorbitant wealth, but I didn't take the time to consider where it was being manufactured. Ruston mentioned factories in the Midlands, so I assumed..."

"Oh, there are factories there, sure," Rock said. "We can't do everything down here. But we do the hardest labor. Without us, there'd be little for the people to find pleasure in."

"Mason, you need to eat," Mother said. "And then I want to find Omar. He might not be as lucky as you to find a rebel in his prison block."

"Wait, you're a rebel?" Mason asked Rock. That explained how he knew Ruston and Zane.

"He was their leader!" Mother exclaimed, her expression beaming with pride. She clutched Rock's arm, and a chill settled over Mason. His mother and this man were together. Romantically. A couple.

"Rock Fist isn't my name, boy. Scorpion and the rest of 2C, they give everyone nicknames. I got mine when Scorpion tried to claim me, and I turned his face into road kill."

Mason shuddered at the very thought. "So, your name is...?"

"Richark Lonn."

Mason limped back to the feedlot in a daze. Rock Fist was Richark Lonn, the Safe Lands rebel he'd been researching back in the Midlands. Worse: His mother was romantically involved with Richark Lonn. He wanted that story, for sure, but there was so much else Mason wanted to ask the man. About the thin plague and why he'd been fired from his medic task and what he'd been looking for in the MC. There hadn't been time. Lonn had said Mason would get in trouble if he were late getting back to the feedlot. So, Mason had left with plans to return to the diner for dinner.

He was making his way up the feed alley between the first and second rows when he caught sight of a penrider in row two. A bald one. With SimArt all over his head. The closer Mason got, the clearer the artwork became. Puzzle pieces.

It was Scorpion.

Mason stared across the pens, shocked to see his persecutor outside their bunk. Then Scorpion looked his way and grinned. And not in a friendly way.

"That's one you don't want to mess with," someone said.

Mason looked behind him and found Wayd standing beside a wheelbarrow, holding a shovel.

"Who is he?" Mason asked, curious to learn how those outside bunk 2C viewed the man.

"Score Pinon. But people call him Scorpion."

Mason shuddered at the sound of that name. "Does Gacy like him? I mean, he got promoted to penrider, right?"

"I don't think anyone likes him. But believe it or not, he's a hard worker." Wayd scooped up a shovel full of manure and dumped it into the wheelbarrow. "I heard he was a murderer in the Midlands before coming here. And not because he was angry or vengeful. He just likes killing. Be thankful you're not in the second row."

Mason was desperately thankful he wasn't in the second row and that Richark Lonn was in bunk 2C, and he spent the remainder of his shift telling God just how thankful.

That evening, Mason returned to the Get Out Now Diner, where Lonn had promised to tell him something worthwhile. Mason didn't think anything could top the discovery that his mother was alive and well and romantically linked with the former leader of the Black Army, but who knew? Besides, he wasn't about to spend another meal in the strikers' cafeteria when he could be with family.

Mason entered the diner and found his mother, Shanna, and Lonn sitting in the back booth—his mother beside Lonn, of course. Had they even left?

"Sit, Mason," Lonn said. "I want to explain how our rebellion works in the Lowlands."

Mason sat beside Shanna, the vinyl seat crackling under his weight. "You have a rebellion here?"

"Of course," Lonn said. "Were you told about rebel tags?"

Mason shook his head

"Rebel tags keep former rebels from gathering," Lonn said. "If two or more rebels are within ten yards of one another for more than ten minutes, their SimAlarms go off.

An ingenious strategy. "Must make going to the movies troublesome."

"Most theaters will let a rebel know if another rebel bought a ticket before you," Lonn said. "It's all in their computers. But you get the idea. It's forced us to get creative."

"How?" Mason asked.

The same waitress from lunch walked up and set plates of food before Lonn, his mother, and Shanna. She smiled at Mason. "What can I get you?"

"Get whatever you want," Lonn said. "It's on me."

Mason looked up to the waitress. "Same as I had at lunchtime. Bean soup and a salad. Vegetables only, please."

"With the avocado dressing?"

"Yes, thank you."

"You got it." She walked behind the counter.

"You asked how we get creative," Lonn said, pulling Mason's gaze back to him. "For one, this diner is our base. That waitress is Cori. She's one of us. As is the cook and the rest of the kitchen and wait staff."

"Your aunt Janie works here too," Shanna said," but she's off today."

"By some miracle, the outsiders weren't tagged rebels, not even you, who broke into Champion House. That's fortunate—for all of us."

"Did you find Omar?" Mason asked.

"He did." Mother beamed at Lonn.

"He's in poultry. Sector six," Lonn said. "And he's living in the sector six strikers' residence, which is safer than the bunkhouses. I'm going to try and contact him. Just need to figure out exactly where they have him tasking."

"Why did Mason get put in maximum security?" Mother asked Lonn. "Omar had three strikes, right, Mason? And you only have one. Shouldn't Omar be in a bunkhouse?"

"Task director is punishing him," Lonn said.

"Why? What did you do to make him so angry?"

A smile broke out on Mason's face. He tried and failed to fight it. Though it was kind of funny, he supposed.

"We talked about this at lunch," Lonn said. "He stole Renzor's girl."

"*You* stole a girl?" Shanna shot Mason a skeptical glance.

For some reason that made Mason defensive. Perhaps because it was a very Jordan-like comment. "She likes me. Is that really so difficult to believe? She's a medic—fairly brilliant, if that helps you."

"That does, actually." Shanna took a bite of her sandwich.

"But Mason, a Safe Lander?" Mother stared him down. "You don't actually care for this girl, do you?"

Mason was nearly certain he loved Ciddah Rourke, not that he was experienced enough in such things to know for certain. But his feelings for Ciddah were private. He wasn't about to tell his mother any of it. "How do the rebels make plans if you can't meet?" he asked Lonn.

"The conversation about the medic is not over," Mother mumbled.

"Is that a fact?" Mason pointed from his mother to Lonn and back and forth. "Then why don't you two go first."

Lonn chuckled, scraped his noodles over his plate. "We make *plans*"—he raised his eyebrows at Mason's mother—"very carefully. It's not easy. And everything takes a long time. We use the meeting chain. Each rebel is assigned another. When a message needs to be spread, it starts at the top and works its way down."

"Does it work in reverse?" Mason asked. "If someone wanted to talk to you?"

"Yes," Lonn said, "though it's not as fast that way. There are no transmitters down here. Reputables can communicate through their Wyndo wall screens and if they purchase SimTalk plans, but everything is monitored heavily. So, we've learned the art of patience. We're working on a plan now, but it's taking a while to get everything in place."

"What's the plan?"

"Trucks take raw goods into the Midlands for distribution," Lonn said. "From what I've learned, those drivers move the goods as far as the wall. Then there are the turnstiles."

"Which are...?" Mason asked.

"Remember that chamber when you came in? The one with a door on each side? The Midland enforcers put you in, and the Lowland enforcers took you out. Like that, only big enough for a truck. They use the turnstiles to keep Lowlanders from speaking with anyone else. They're what keep us from getting back to the Midlands. There are no other doors. There are no storm drains down here, at least not big enough to crawl through. And we can't get into the tube."

"The tube?" Mason asked.

"The road that cuts through the Lowlands from the entrance to the Safe Lands all the way to the Lowland/Midland Gate. The Lowlands is a prison, even for reputables. And the Safe Lands Guild can't afford to let that secret get out, or their way of life is over."

The waitress returned with Mason's soup and salad. He picked up his fork and he the lettuce. "You said that before. What's a 'reputable'?"

"Someone who was liberated at forty," Lonn said. "Or in your mother's case, because she was an outsider and could no longer bear children."

"Same with me," Shanna said.

"You plan to sneak into one of the turnstiles?" Mason asked.

"We figure a man can hide in the back of a truck, buried under a shipment of produce. As long as we cut out his SimTag first."

Mason thought it over as he ate. It could work in theory. "Someone must have tried that already."

"People have cut out their SimTags, yes," Lonn said. "They've tried to sneak through the turnstiles. And they've even tried to scale the walls. But the walls have motion detectors and they're much higher here than in the Highlands and Midlands. From what I've been able to learn, no one has tried to hide in a truck. So, we're going to."

"When?" Mason asked.

"In a few weeks. We're sending a guy by the name of Grady. He was one of my men. Liberated a few years before me. He's earned the right to be the one to go."

"What's his plan after he gets through?" Mason asked.

"To let the people know the truth," Lonn said. "If the people up there knew what really went on down here, things would have to change."

"I hope it works," Mother said.

"I think it will," Lonn said. "Unless there's technology I don't know about, which is always a possibility. I don't have a Zane down here."

Mason ate his salad in silence for a few bites and thought about the technology in the Safe Lands, which made him think of the advanced health care and his failure to find a cure for the thin plague. "I have some questions for you," Mason said to Lonn.

Lonn narrowed his eyes. "About what?"

"Why you got fired from the MC. What were you looking into? And what part did Lawten Renzor play in the whole thing?"

"Another time," Lonn said. "I've got to meet Grady tonight."

When everyone had finished eating, they stood to leave. Mason walked to the door beside Shanna, but when he turned back, he saw Lonn and his mother lingering beside the table, holding hands and talking to each other. Lonn kissed his mother on the lips and they embraced.

Mason could only stare.

"I know it's only been a few months since Justin was killed," Shanna said, "but... Rich is very good to her."

Rich. Mason stared at Shanna, eyebrows raised.

"It's only that Justin..." Shanna frowned. "He never..." She twisted her lips. "Sometimes arranged marriages are difficult, Mason. I'm glad you didn't have to marry Mia, though I'm sorry over what's become of her. But perhaps you both have a chance at happiness now."

Happiness? Mason didn't want to be negative, but he doubted such a thing was possible. He'd been liberated, for crying out loud. Though as he looked back to his mother and Lonn and saw the man hold one side of his mother's face in his hand, smiling as he spoke to her, their foreheads touching, her lips curved in a smile, Mason did wonder. He couldn't recall ever seeing his parents kiss, though they must have since they had produced three sons.

Much had changed about romance in Mason's mind, though he still had plenty to figure out. But if his mother could choose love with a Safe Lands national, why couldn't he?

For one simple reason. Because he was here, in the Lowlands, and Ciddah was not.

Chapter 8

"There's wisdom in Shaylinn's words," Aunt Chipeta said. "But I still don't feel comfortable letting our children go to their school. Not if the teachers belittle them."

"I agree." Levi had gathered the adults from Glenrock and Jack's Peak in the underground library along with Ruston, Zane, and Nash. "Can you ladies create your own curriculum?"

"We'll manage," Eliza said. "But we should heed Shaylinn's advice and find other ways to befriend the Kindred."

"Think on it, all of you. I will as well." But at the moment Levi had more important things to worry about than whether or not the Kindred liked them. "That moves us to the subject of the Jack's Peak women in the harem."

"We need someone who's been there," Zane said. He was sitting on top of a table, his feet dangling. "I mean, even if I could turn off the cameras, I don't know my way around the place. None of us do."

"I know where to go," Jemma said from the chair beside Levi's. "I could come with you and—"

"No." As if Levi would put his wife back in danger.

"Don't just say no without thinking it through," said Ruston, who was standing against the end of a bookshelf. "I realize that sending any of the women back there is not ideal, but she could be a great help."

"*No,*" Levi said again. "That's not an option. Can we get a message to the women in the harem?"

"Everything is monitored," Zane said.

"Who else can go, Levi?" Jemma said softly. "Hazel needs Chipeta. Aunt Mary's knees are too bad. Eliza's children need their mother. Naomi has the baby and is still recovering from childbirth. And Shay... she can't go back there, Levi. I'm the only option. Unless you're willing to use Ciddah."

Levi gritted his teeth. "We can't trust Ciddah."

"I think we can," Naomi said. "She's been such a help with the babies. And she's so sweet."

"She lied to Mason, and very convincingly, if I understand things correctly," Levi said. "She's good at fooling people. She stays here."

"Then let me help," Jemma said.

Levi glared at his wife. "We'll talk about this later."

"I want to get my wife out now," Beshup said. Levi's old friend from Jack's Peak was sitting crosslegged on the floor besides Mukwiv. "It might already be too late for her."

"I agree," Mukwiv said. "My wife is not as young as the others. If something goes wrong, she could be liberated."

"They took the lenses from Mason and Omar before we could find out what that means," Jemma said. "I could—"

"You could draw a map," Jordan said to his sister. "Then we'll know where to go and you can stay here."

"Jordan, I can't draw," Jemma said.

"It doesn't have to be Omar art," Jordan said. "Just a simple map with arrows and stuff."

The tension eased from Levi's shoulders. This was a much better idea. "Between the six of you ladies, I'm sure you can manage," he said.

Now Jemma glared at him. He could tell she wanted to go on the rescue mission. Why, he couldn't guess.

"Can you at least try the map first?" he asked, pleading with his eyes. "Please?"

So, the women set to work drawing a map, and when they finally somewhat agreed on how it looked, they handed it over to Levi. The only problem was that no one knew which rooms the Jack's Peak women might be living in. According to Jemma, there were two floors with suites.

But at least his wife would be safe.

However, later that night as they were getting ready for bed, Jemma still hadn't given up.

She came into their bedroom, toothbrush in hand. "It's silly, Levi," she said, closing the door behind her. "Just let me come with you. We'll be twice as fast with me as a guide."

Levi set the harem map he'd been studying on his bedside table. "You're *not* coming with us."

She folded her arms. "Why? Why do you get to decide?"

"Because I'm the village elder, and I'm your husband."

"And that makes you my boss?"

"No. I just..." He crossed the room, took her hand. "I don't want anything to happen to you."

She pulled away and stomped down her side of the bed. "You think you can control me? Keep me here? Obey your every word?"

"Jemma, that's not what I—"

"You think women aren't capable of doing heroic things. You think we're weak."

"I don't think that." Had he said that?

"You're going to be like your father, is that it? Boss me around? Yell at me? Are you going to hit me too?"

Levi could only stare. Her comment made him so angry he wanted to shake her. Did that somehow prove her point?

So, he turned and left the room, then the house. He stormed through the corridors, feeling desperate… angry… and hurt. People had talked about his father's temper. But he'd always believed no one really knew that Elder Justin had ever struck his wife. And he hadn't… often.

Maybe his mother had told someone.

But that didn't mean Levi would harm Jemma. Ever! Why had she said that? Did she think he would? Was she afraid of him? Had he given her reason to fear him?

He hadn't. Had he? Surely, he hadn't.

He couldn't fathom why she'd said such a thing.

Hours later, when he was certain he'd walked every inch of the underground corridors, he ended up at Ruston's house. The man invited him in, gave him a piece of some kind of cake his wife had made. Levi sat at the kitchen table across from Ruston and stared at it, not really hungry.

"I like to go on walks when Tova and I have a fight," Ruston said.

"What makes you think Jemma and I fought?"

Ruston chuckled. "Didn't you?"

Levi stabbed the fork into the cake. "She said so many cruel things."

"Women do that. Men do too, I suppose, but men are usually quiet in a fight. Women do most of the talking."

"Yelling, you mean. She cut me with words. I swear I must be bleeding." Levi looked at his arms, turned his hands over.

"I doubt she meant any of it. Women, they get emotional. Half of the fight takes place in their imaginations."

"Yes," Levi said. "She yelled at me for things I hadn't done."

"What's she really angry about? That's what you need to focus on."

That much Levi knew. "She's mad I won't let her help with the harem rescue."

Ruston smiled at him kindly. "And why won't you?" At Levi's glare, he added, "Humor me."

"Because she could get hurt or arrested. I could lose her. I lost her once." He set down the fork on the table. "It was agony."

"What do you love about her?"

Levi frowned. "What's that have to do with—?"

"Humor me again, please."

Levi sighed and rubbed his temple. "Fine. Jemma, she's kind. And smart. And when I look at her, it's always a shock that *she* loves me. Such an amazing, beautiful creature… and she's mine."

"And you're hers," Ruston said. "You're a team. That means give and take. Why should you get to be the only brave one?"

Was the man not listening? "I told you, it's not safe."

"Nor is it safe for you."

Levi had no reply to that.

"You're going to have to let go of control, Levi," Ruston said. "That can be a difficult thing. And I'm not necessarily saying that Jemma *should* come with us. But if you want peace in your house, if you want to *keep* that woman in love with you, you're going to have to trust her. Otherwise, her love will slowly turn into resentment."

When Levi went home, the lights in the house were out. He walked carefully so he didn't wake Trevon and Grayn, who had taken to sleeping on the couches to be apart from the little boys in the boys' bedroom.

The lights in his bedroom were off as well. He changed in the dark and climbed into bed, trying not to wake Jemma.

"Where have you been?" she asked.

So much for not waking her. "Walking. Went to Ruston's house."

"Why?"

"Don't know. He says I need to let go of control."

A pause. "Interesting."

"You think I'm controlling?"

"I think you worry too much."

Levi stared into the darkness above. "The village elder has a lot of responsibilities."

"And you handle them well. But fretting isn't going to change anything. It's only making you cranky and impossible to be around."

He didn't want to be his father. He wanted to lead like Papa Eli had. "Why do you want to come on the harem rescue?"

"Because I can help. My presence can shave ten minutes off your time. I promise you."

That sounded good. "That's it? You just want to help us be fast?"

There was silence again for a long moment, and Levi wondered if his wife had fallen asleep. But then she spoke. "I'm trapped here, Levi." And there were tears in her voice, like she was struggling to say these words. "I want to help. And this is a place where I can help. I'm the best one for the job. Me. Only me."

He found her hand in the darkness and took hold. "It means a lot to you? To come?"

She squeezed back. "Yes."

Levi felt like saying the next words might kill him, but he said them anyway. "Then come."

"I don't like it," Levi said. He and Jemma were in the nest with Zane, sitting beside him at his GlassTop computer, where Zane had somehow pulled up a real floor plan of the harem.

"It's the best we can do," Zane said. "I can't find a camera for that back stairwell. So that's how you go in. Jemma leads the way. Once you're inside, you might have to stun the matron and an enforcer or two, so be ready. Then you come out the way you went in. It's pretty simple, really. What don't you like about it?"

Having Jemma involved, but it was too late to change that. "Why wouldn't they have installed a camera there after two different escapes happened that way?"

"I don't think they know the women went that way," Zane said. "The first time, they didn't get caught until they were in the gardens. The second time, they never got caught."

Could they really not know? "Still, after losing the entire harem, you don't think they'd investigate? See how the women had escaped?"

"The power was out that night," Zane said. "It was chaos. They likely assumed the women had walked out the front doors."

"It'll be fine, Levi," Jemma said. "I'll be beside you the whole way."

Which made him useless. How could he be alert and watching for enforcers when he'd have his eyes on his wife? "How many men do we have?"

"All five from Jack's Peak, plus you and Jordan, and Farran and Nash," Zane said.

"And were looking to free how many women? Ten?"

"Eleven," Jemma said.

That was fairly even. Still, that Jemma was leading the way, that his wife would be in danger...

The whole scenario was completely unfair. Levi couldn't imagine any of the other men allowing their wives to come along. His instincts told him that he'd rather have Jemma safe and resentful than in harm's way and happy that she'd tried to help. But he'd made his choice, and he couldn't go back on it now.

That night in the library, after Zane and Levi gave instructions to the group, Levi added one more. "If anyone is captured"—he forced himself not to look at his wife—"do whatever you can to stay out of prison. Pretend to switch sides, offer false information about the rebels, make the best of living your life as a good Safe Lands national, whatever it takes. We'll come for you when things calm down."

"What false information could we give?" Beshup asked. "Anything we say will be tested."

"Theater nine still hasn't been discovered," Zane said. "I could take some supplies over there and set up a fake rebel headquarters. I could even make it look like that's where we film the Owl. And Omar had an early mask that didn't turn out well. I can leave it there as a clue."

"Good. Do that, Zane." Levi looked at the faces of his team. "If you're caught, don't give up the theater right away. Hold out for a day or two, like it's important information. Don't let them torture you, though. Just let them ask a few times first. Understand?"

He watched Jemma nod along with the others. She wouldn't get caught, though. Because Zane had reassured him that this would be simple.

Ten rebels entered the Safe Lands through a storm drain in Champion Park. They walked in pairs, a few yards from each other, to Gothic Road. Levi walked hand in hand with Jemma, following Nash and Farran. Behind him were the men from Jack's Peak: Beshup, Mukwiv, Tupi and the teenaged boys Nodin and Yivan.

They followed Gothic Road into the downtown Highlands. Zane and his father were watching through the street cameras, though Levi couldn't speak to Zane since he'd never gotten a SimTalk implant. Zane had offered to take Levi to get one, but Levi didn't want any Safe Lands technology in his body. That put him at Nash's mercy tonight.

Levi's senses screamed to turn back. He felt like he was walking into a den of mountain lions with no weapon. They were carrying stunners, but he still felt on edge.

As per the plans, Dayle, a rebel who lived in the Safe Lands, should have parked a Department of Public Tasks truck beside the Green Cactus Grill. Farran and Jordan split off to walk that way—they'd drive around to the back of the harem. The other men continued on foot.

Nash stayed with Levi, repeating everything Zane said. Beshup walked on Nash's other side. Levi knew his friend from Jack's Peak wanted to be in charge of this operation as much as Levi did. Working with so many leaders was more difficult than Levi would have ever imagined.

When Zane agreed the roads were clear, Jemma led them to the loading dock and into a warehouse of sorts. They moved quickly through the warehouse and up a stairwell—all but Jordan and Farran, who were hopefully parking the truck to wait for their exit. Levi wanted to tell Jemma that he could find the way from here, make her go back and wait with Jordan, but he knew where that would get him.

They climbed to the fifth floor and Jemma stopped at a door. Locked, of course. While Nash and Zane talked about reprogramming Nash's SimTag to get the door open, Levi grabbed hold of his wife, slid his arms around her waist, and pulled her close.

"I'll be fine," she said.

But Levi didn't want her reassurances. He just wanted to hold her. He buried his nose against her neck and hair and prayed that God would keep her safe, that he'd put an end to all their misery and let them escape this place so they could be free to live their lives the way they wanted to.

The door clicked open. "We're in," Nash said. "Jemma?"

Levi fought back a sigh and released his wife, took hold of her hand.

She pulled him through the door and into a dead-end hallway, motioned to another locked door on the right. "This leads into the back of the kitchen."

Whatever magic Zane had worked on the last lock was still in Nash's SimTag. He set his fist against the SimPad and the door clicked open.

And into a kitchen they went.

The room was dark, lit only by a white light above the stove and a glowing green exit sign over the door they'd entered through. Jemma pulled Levi across a tile floor to a set of two-way swinging doors. She pushed them open enough to peek through, then she and Levi slipped inside the harem.

It too was dark, though distant street and city lights gleamed through a wall of windows on the left that stretched three stories high. Levi had stared at those windows so many times from the outside, pining for Jemma. Even in the dim light, Levi could see the extravagance. The place looked like a palace. Thick white carpeting, draping crystal chandeliers, gold sconces, elaborate paintings, fancy furniture.

Jemma led him toward a staircase that ran along the wall opposite the kitchen doors. Nash remained downstairs to act as a scout. The rest followed Jemma. Up they went, the stairs creaking underfoot. Jemma had said the matron lived in the suite under the stairs, so he hoped the creaking stairs wouldn't wake her.

Since they didn't know who was where, the plan called for Jemma to go to the seventh floor, hoping to avoid Mia's room for as long as possible since Mia had been on the sixth level.

The seventh floor was a long hallway with two doors on each side. The doors had nameplates: Black Sapphire, Citrus Blossom, Fire Opal, and Imperial Topaz. Jemma knocked softly on the door that said Fire Opal.

"Beshup," she whispered, "you knock on one of these other doors, but be ready with your stunner just in case."

So Beshup knocked on the Imperial Topaz door and waited. Still no answer from Fire Opal.

Beshup's door opened first. "Beshup?" The voice was female and high-pitched.

"Shh, Chowa," Beshup said. "We've come to free you of this place. Where is Tsana?"

Levi had never met Chowa. She looked to be in her mid-forties.

"Tsana is downstairs in the Moonstone Suite," she said. "Must we hurry?"

"Yes, do you need help?"

"No, I'll get Paa and Kwis."

"Kwis is in there?" Tupi asked, his eyes hopeful.

"What other rooms are our people in?" Beshup asked Chowa.

"Kwis is in here with me. Ani, Sunki, and Mamaci are in Fire Opal." She nodded across the hall to the door Jemma had knocked on. "The others are downstairs in Moonstone and Blue Diamond."

Beshup turned to Mukwiv. "Then we should go down—"

"Jemma!"

Levi turned back to the Fire Opal door and there stood Jennifer, hugging Jemma.

"You've come for Jack's Peak, haven't you?" Jennifer asked.

"Won't you and Mia come too?" Jemma asked.

"Mia won't leave. In fact, if she sees any of you, she might call the enforcers." Jennifer waved Jemma inside the Fire Opal Suite. "Go and wake the women. They're all from Jack's Peak in here. I'll go down to the Blue Diamond Suite and wake the girls there. Hopefully Mia will stay asleep. Levi, you and some of the men could come with me."

"I'll stay with Jemma," Levi said. "Beshup, take a man down with Jennifer."

"Where is Samantha?" Mukwiv asked.

"Down in Moonstone with Tsana," Jennifer said. "What about the SimTags?"

"Nash will remove them once we get out," Levi said. "He's one of the rebels."

Jennifer nodded, then she, Beshup, and Mukwiv headed for the staircase.

Levi made to follow Jemma into the Fire Opal Suite, but she turned and stopped him with her hand against his chest. "Wait here. There's only one exit from this suite. I don't want you scaring these women in their beds."

And just as he'd feared, Jemma was parted from him. Yivan stood beside him, an eager look on his face. Nodin paced the hall behind them. Tupi stood outside the door to the Imperial Topaz room.

Seconds later, the Imperial Topaz door opened again and Chowa returned with two other women. Tupi embraced one of them. Must be his wife. The couple looked no older than Jordan and Naomi, though they already had three children.

"Take them into the kitchen and be quiet," Levi said. "Nodin and Yivan, stay with me."

Tupi led the women toward the stairs.

Jemma came out of the Fire Opal Suite with two women and a girl who looked no older than Shaylinn. Yivan greeted the girl by taking her arm and whispering to her. She hugged his waist.

"That's all," Jemma said. "Let's go."

"Gladly." Levi took Jemma's hand and motioned for the women to go first. "Into the kitchen as silently as you can." He and Jemma brought up the rear.

"Where is Alawa?" Nodin asked the girl with Yivan.

"She's in the doctor place."

"Why?" Nodin asked. "Is it far?"

"Shh," Levi whispered. "Wait until the kitchen to talk."

They reached the sixth floor, and Jemma tugged him to stop. "I need to make sure they got everyone from here."

Levi frowned and let Jemma pull him into the sixth-floor hallway. Beshup and Mukwiv were waiting there.

Levi joined his friends. "Well?"

"The one called Jennifer came out of Moonstone and went into Blue Diamond along with Ani, whose daughters are in there," Mukwiv said. The Moonstone door opened. "Ah, here comes someone."

"Beshup!" It was Tsana. And another woman who ran to Mukwiv and embraced him.

Reunions everywhere. But it was past time to go.

Finally, the door to the Blue Diamond Suite opened, and a Jack's Peak woman came out, helping a young girl along.

"I want to stay with Alawa." The girl looked pale but didn't seem to have any injuries.

Jemma ran to the girl's other side and supported her. "Is she okay?"

"She and her sister had an allergic reaction to something in the meds," the Jack's Peak woman said. "Shootsi has mostly recovered, but her sister is still in the SC."

Levi's heart sank. They had no way to get to the SC tonight, and enforcers would increase security once they learned of the escape.

Jemma and the woman helped the girl toward the stairs. Finally, they had everyone. Levi followed and waited at the top of the stairs for the ladies to start down.

"*Behne*, Levi."

He nearly jumped out of his skin. He turned around. Kosowe stood just outside the Blue Diamond Suite's door, her dark eyes fixed on his.

Well, he'd *thought* they had everyone. "Head on down the stairs, Kosowe. That's the last of you. Right?"

"Jennifer and Mia are still in there." Kosowe walked toward him. Levi backed against the wall and waved her past, not wanting to touch her. He was overreacting, sure, but he well knew that she was trouble. And the history the two of them shared...

She walked past, and he followed her slowly, wishing she'd move faster. "Hurry, Kosowe. There's not much time."

She turned around, facing him. "But Jennifer and Mia—you can't leave them."

"They're not coming," Levi said. "They don't want—" Something tickled his waist. He reached down, patted his hip. No gun. He spun around.

Mia, grinning at him. His own stunner trained on his chest.

What? Why? "Mia, don't be—"

She fired. The stunner cartridge struck Levi's chest and knocked him back a step. He slammed against the wall and slid down it like a broom handle, stiff and hard, sharp pain immobilizing his body.

"What are you doing?" This from Kosowe.

Levi couldn't move. He lay staring at the ceiling, straining to hear the whispers of Mia and Kosowe from the doorway. Kosowe leapt over him and ran toward the stairs.

Mia's face appeared over his. "You left me here, like I didn't matter. Mason said they made you elder, and then he left me too. Kosowe told me about the terrible things you did with her, *Elder* Levi. Not so perfect, are you? Wait until I tell Jemma what I know about..."

Mia vanished.

"He's here on the floor." Kosowe had returned. "He fell over."

"Levi!" Jemma knelt at his side, took his hand in hers and pressed her other fingers to his neck.

"We must carry him away," Kosowe said to Jemma. "Mia will return with enforcers."

"You get his feet," Jemma said.

Behind Jemma, a shadow shifted on the wall. *No!* Not Jemma. *Please not Jemma.* Levi tried to open his mouth to speak. *God, help her!*

But God did not help. Jemma gasped as the stunner's cartridge struck her back. She stiffened and fell on top of him. He could smell her hair under his chin.

Mia dragged Jemma off of him and into the Blue Diamond Suite. Kosowe grabbed Levi's ankles and pulled him toward the stairs. His body tugged over the thick carpeting. Somewhere nearby, a door slammed.

Jemma!

Beshup came into view above him. "What happened?"

"The one called Mia took his weapon," Kosowe said. "She shot Jemma and Levi. She has Jemma in her room and is calling the enforcers to come. I could not open the door."

Beshup looked down on Levi, his eyes wide. Shocked. Filled with conflict. Levi knew what he was thinking. Save the women or go after Jemma? Enforcers on the way. What to do?

Levi needed his body to move. Now! At least to speak. He willed his voice to make sound. To fight the numbness. His body ignored him. All but a tear that rolled down his cheek and pooled cold and wet in his ear.

Useless tears!

"I'm sorry, my friend." Beshup crouched and lifted Levi's limp body over his shoulder. He carried him down the stairs, into the kitchen, out into the dead-end hallway, and down the dark stairwell, with Kosowe following. Down, down, down, leaving Jemma—his life and heart—behind.

Chapter 9

Shaylinn joined Eliza, Chipeta, and Aunt Mary at Jordan and Naomi's house to pray for the harem rescue. Though the night wasn't going as Shaylinn had expected. Naomi had taken Harvey out to feed him, and Ciddah and her parents were in their rooms. And somehow the topic had drifted to the school situation again.

"We need to get started teaching," Eliza said. "I love having my kids back, but with the additional three Safe Lands girls, it's nuts in my house. The kids need something to do all day besides run wild."

Shaylinn agreed. "The boys are driving Levi crazy."

"He should send them to the park," Chipeta said.

"He did," Shaylinn said, "but they left the park and got in trouble, snooping around the greenhouses. Someone complained to Ruston, who passed it along to Levi, and now Levi's grounded them to the house."

"Oh, dear." Aunt Mary frowned at Shaylinn. "It's got to be hard on the older boys, who had so much freedom in Glenrock."

"There are plenty of books in the library," Eliza said. "Why not assign them all books to read and report on? At least until we can get a curriculum together."

"It might be worth trying. Though they're such a wide range of ages," Shaylinn said. "I mean, how will I know if the book is too easy for them?"

"How fast they read it," Chipeta said. "But honestly, if they're quiet and happy, I wouldn't worry about it. Let them read whatever they want as long as it's appropriate."

"And don't forget, we won't be here much longer," Eliza said. "Once the Jack's Peak women arrive, we can focus on getting outside the walls."

"But we still don't know the secret of liberation," Shaylinn said. "Don't forget my mother and Omar and Mason."

Eliza looked like she was trying to find a way to say something delicately. "Shaylinn, no one knows what liberation is. Not the rebels, not the Kindred, no one. We'll likely never know. Don't you think we'd be wise to consider them lost?"

Tears filled Shaylinn's eyes. "I can't." The very idea of never seeing her mother again. Never seeing Omar. "I *won't* give up hope, and neither should you!"

"Your tone, Shaylinn," Aunt Mary said. "You must not speak disrespectfully to your elders."

Shaylinn took a deep breath. She could never control her emotions these days. "I'm sorry. But I can't just forget them. We have to believe they're okay..."

"Let's pray again," Chipeta said, taking Shaylinn's hand. "I fear we've gotten distracted from our purpose."

So, they went back to praying for the rescue and didn't stop until Naomi returned, carrying little Harvey in her arms.

"Is he sleeping?" Chipeta asked.

"No, just waking up," Naomi said.

Shaylinn watched Naomi with her child, and fear overwhelmed her at the knowledge that she soon would have two babies to care for.

What if she couldn't do it? What if she failed? What if Omar really was gone?

The front door opened then, and Jordan and Nash entered, carrying Levi between them. Levi's head was limp and he was muttering, whimpering. A beautiful, dark-haired woman entered behind them. She looked like someone from Jack's Peak.

Shaylinn stood to make room for Levi on the couch. "Someone should get Ciddah."

"I will." Chipeta jumped up and ran to Ciddah's bedroom.

Jordan and Nash settled Levi on the couch.

"What happened?" Aunt Mary asked.

Ciddah's bedroom door opened and she ran out.

"He was stunned," Jordan said.

"How long ago?" Ciddah asked.

"An hour? A little less maybe? It took Nash a while to cut out all those SimTags. Kosowe said it was Mia."

Mia? Shaylinn looked to the Jack's Peak girl, Kosowe. "Why would Mia do that?"

"I know not," Kosowe said, "but I was the last to leave. I blame myself. I will care for him as a debt."

"That's not necessary," Jordan said. "He has a wife to care for him."

Shaylinn looked back to the front door, saw it hanging open, then walked out into the dark corridor. Empty. She went back inside and closed the door. "Where's Jemma?"

"Jemma," Levi said, his lips still not fully working. "Mia Jemma. Mia Jemma."

"Finally, he's talking." Jordan stared at Levi, hands on his hips. Angry. At Levi? At someone else?

"Relax, Levi." Ciddah knelt on the floor beside the couch. "Your voice will come back, and then you can tell us everything."

Shaylinn frowned, overcome with emotion she couldn't explain. She grabbed Jordan's arm. "Where's Jemma? Jordan, tell me."

"I don't know."

"What does *that* mean?" Naomi asked.

"It means I don't know." Jordan was stormy, his eyes dark and wild. "I didn't go inside. I was waiting in the truck with Farran when they all came out. Beshup and Mukwiv were carrying Levi, and there was no time. Kosowe said Mia had stunned Levi and called the Enforcers."

"Mia also stunned Jemma," Kosowe said.

"Couldn't move." Levi's voice was hoarse. "Jemma."

"She's lost to you now," Kosowe said.

Her words brought a keening sound from Levi that made Shaylinn shiver.

"Get her out, Nash," Jordan said. "Take her to Beshup."

"I want to help," Kosowe said. "Don't make me leave. He needs me."

"You heard the man. Let's go." Nash stretched his arm toward the door and waited for Kosowe to move, but she did not.

"I owe you my life, Levi of Elias," Kosowe said. "I will pay my debt."

"You own him nothing," Jordan said. "Get out."

Shaylinn's eyes widened at such harsh words. Finally, Kosowe turned and walked out the door, head held high.

"I'll be right back," Nash said, closing the door behind him.

"What happened, Levi?" Shaylinn asked.

His gaze settled on Shaylinn's, though his eyes seemed out of focus. "Mia. Behind me... Must have taken my stunner. Stunned me. Said she'd tell Jemma about... Then Jem came. Tried to help, but Mia stunned her too. Took her away. Kosowe dragged me to the stairs. Told Beshup that Mia had called enforcers."

Jemma captured? Shaylinn's chest constricted, and she asked a question to keep from being overwhelmed. "Why does Kosowe want to help so badly?"

"Kosowe has wanted to marry Levi for years," Jordan said. "I guess she thinks this is her big chance."

"It's not. I have a wife." Levi sighed and, with an effort, brought his hand to his face and covered his eyes.

For a moment everyone remained still. Shaylinn looked from face to face, but everyone seemed to have taken great interest in things like the rug, the ceiling, and the wall fixtures. Jordan was picking at his hand. Then Aunt Mary started to cry, which made Shaylinn cry too.

Jemma gone. In the harem again. It was really too much to bear.

Over the next few days, Shaylinn and Nell did all they could to keep the children quiet and give Levi space. Shaylinn couldn't just sit and stare as Levi did, though. Didn't he know that she was sad too? That she loved her sister?

She went over her old message list, wondering how the people she wrote to were doing. She wanted to continue writing to them, but she had no way to deliver the messages without Omar.

Shaylinn decided to visit the library. She needed something to read—to distract her from her sorrow. Ciddah asked to come, so Shaylinn went to Jordan's house to fetch her, since Ciddah needed an escort to leave. When they walked inside the library, Tova was there.

"Good afternoon to you, Shayleen. Who is your friend?" Tova seemed to be overly cheerful today, though she was giving Ciddah a wary glance. It was probably Ciddah's flaking skin. There was no Roller Paint in the basements. Without the special lotion, people who had the thin plague couldn't hide their disease.

"It's Shay*linn*, Tova. And this is Ciddah. Ciddah, this is Tova, Ruston's wife. Ciddah is a medic."

Tova pursed her lips. "I see."

"Nice to meet you," Ciddah said.

Ciddah walked over to the nonfiction books. Tova just stood there in the middle of the room, looking through a book. Shaylinn wandered to the fiction section. Oh, they had Jane Austen books! Jemma would have been so excited about that.

"I've been meaning to apologize to you," Tova said.

Shaylinn looked over her shoulder at Tova. "Really? What for?"

"My husband was not pleased that your children left the school and so soon. I should have tried to mend the argument. And I spoke unkindly to you, as well. I'm sorry."

Well, that was nice of her to say. "I'm sure our being here is difficult for you." It was difficult for them all.

"Yes," Tova said, "but it's good too. It will be, anyway. Once your people understand what's at stake and agree to our terms, you can apply to become Kindred. Did you know that?"

"No." But why would they want to? The Kindred wanted to stay underground forever. Why would she agree to that?

"We should have started there, I think," Tova said. "If we teach you what it means to be one of us, you can choose to be cleansed."

As if they were dirty? Inferior? Was Tova referring to biblical baptism? But that was between a person and God. Who did the Kindred think they were to have the power to clean any person? "Why must we conform to *your* ways? We have no intention of staying here."

Tova laughed. "You're in denial, I think. It's not possible to leave this place, unless you're a man looking to bring back food."

"What about the rebels?" Ciddah asked. She had walked back over to Shaylinn's side and crossed her arms. Two against one. "They come and go."

Tova's face went stony. "To rebel against our safety here is to rebel against Providence. Our home is a gift. We were chosen to live here, free and away from the evils above. Those who leave are not welcomed back."

"But isn't your husband, Ruston, one of them?" The leader, if Shaylinn wasn't mistaken.

"My husband, *Shane,* speaks with the rebels under the name Ruston, but he takes no part in their schemes. He helps where he can but doesn't put himself in harm's way."

Yet Ruston had gone with Levi and Mason the night they'd freed the children. And according to Jemma, he'd also gone out to help Omar and Mason borrow the invisible suits. Could Tova not know? Shaylinn didn't dare get in the middle of this woman and her husband's communication problems, so she tried to end the conversation. "Well, thank you for apologizing, but I still don't think we'll be attending your school or participating in your Kindred cleansing."

Tova raised an eyebrow. "In time you will, Shayleen. Or you will be asked to leave. We will not tolerate permanent residents who refuse to seek the truth."

"What truth? Yours?" Ciddah said. "What you believe may not be truth to me."

"There's only one truth," Shaylinn said to both women. "If truth is what each of us believed, and we each believe differently, there would be no such thing as truth. Truth stands against what's false. If there is no true and false, light and dark, right and wrong, then there is nothing to guide human morality."

"You speak in riddles, Shayleen," Tova said. "But I agree with what you say about truth. You would be wise to be cleansed." She turned and left the library.

Shaylinn's hands were trembling. What right did that woman have to judge her so harshly?

A slow smile crept across Ciddah's face. "You sounded like Mason. He loves to argue about such things."

"I hate to argue," Shaylinn said. "But I can't stand by and watch someone hurt others. And Tova is hurting people with her 'truths.' Zane, for one. If I can convince Tova that the Kindred truths come from fear and a desire to control people's behavior, then I might actually have a purpose in this place."

"She'll never change, but I'd love to see how you try and convince her," Ciddah said. "Mason talked about what you outsiders believe, and I'd like to understand it better."

Shaylinn threaded her arm with Ciddah's. "I'd be happy to talk to you about it anytime. But first let's find some books and get out of here before Tova comes back for round two."

Shaylinn picked out some picture books for the children, and Ciddah chose a stack of books about medical things: *Herbal Medicine*, *Natural Childbirth*, and *Story of a Modern Midwife*. Shaylinn should probably be reading books like that, but just thinking about giving birth terrified her.

They left the library, which was only two doors away from Levi's house, but Shaylinn had to walk Ciddah back to Jordan's home, which was farther down and around a corner. As they rounded that bend, a man was coming toward them. Though it seemed silly, Shaylinn panicked. Cold fear trickled up her spine, down her arms, and pooled in her belly. The interaction with Tova had taken all her effort. She didn't want to have a run-in with a Kindred man too. She stepped closer to Ciddah, which gave her a bit more comfort, until she recognized the person. It was Nash. Ruston and Tova's eldest son. Oh, good.

Nash was a few inches taller than Zane but had the same shape to his face. Where Zane often dyed his hair strange colors like blue and orange, Nash's hair was a natural brown, as were his eyes.

"Hello." He stopped and smiled at them both. "We've not officially met. I'm Katz, though you probably know me as Nash."

"Yes, hello," Shaylinn said. "This is Ciddah, and I'm Shaylinn."

"Do you prefer to be called Katz?" Ciddah asked.

He shrugged. "I answer to both, though don't call me Nash when my mother's around." He raised his eyebrows and widened his eyes, hinting at the danger that might result from such a mistake.

"I don't think your mother likes me," Shaylinn said. "Any of us, actually."

"She's afraid. If enforcers were to find this place, it would be the end of our way of life."

Shaylinn knew that was true, but it didn't seem like an excuse to be judgmental. Nash/Katz wasn't being judgmental. He was very friendly and had a low, soothing voice. "Do you like living here?"

"I like being free from the Safe Lands regulations. But I like the breeze too, and the feel of my feet in the bottom of Lake Joie, and the sun shining on my skin. I like watching birds fly. They get down here sometimes and flutter about until one of us catches them and takes them to the surface. I guess I'm like the birds: I'm stuck down here, but I know that this isn't where I was created to live."

"I like that," Shaylinn said. "Do you go to the school?"

"I'm twenty."

"Oh." He didn't look that old to Shaylinn, but Zane was eighteen and Nash was older, so she should've known.

"Is twenty bad?" Nash asked, wincing slightly with such a cute expression.

"You look younger, that's all," Shaylinn said.

He smiled, had a nice smile too. "You look older than... fourteen, right?"

"Fifteen in another month." Why had she said that? Did it really matter?

"Almost a grown woman," Nash said. "With me looking younger than twenty and you looking older than fourteen, we're almost the same age."

The comment made Shaylinn blush, and she suddenly felt uncomfortable again. "We should go." She looked at Ciddah, whose eyes widened, as if getting Shaylinn's hint.

Ciddah smiled at Nash. "Good-bye."

"Good-bye," Nash said.

They hurried on, but Shaylinn looked back over her shoulder. Nash was standing in the corridor, watching them. "He's watching us."

Ciddah looked over her shoulder. "He likes you."

Shaylinn almost tripped over her own feet. "Me? Why?"

"Why not?"

Shaylinn all but ran the rest of the way to Jordan's house, eager to put a door between her and Nash. She didn't know why she'd wanted to get away, but Nash had made her uncomfortable. And now she missed Omar more than ever.

Chapter 10

Omar stood in front of the incinerator, feeding it dead chickens one at a time. He wasn't supposed to let it burn with the door open, but he liked the heat on his face and the way the feathers shriveled into flame and ash. Some of the smaller feathers didn't burn right away, but danced around in the hot air above the flames, floating in the heat.

It reminded him of a story Jemma had once told the children about a balloon that flew through the sky and carried people. He remembered the debate Mason had gotten into with Uncle Colton when the older man had mocked the story as impossible. Mason had disagreed, said that hot air was lighter than cold air, or some such scientific answer. Omar didn't understand it, but he wondered if such a thing might help the Owl fly again.

The Owl. He should forget such fantasies. The Owl was dead. As was Omar. The sooner he resigned himself to that, the better. Hope was deceitful. Hope was for fools.

Yet he watched the feathers fly, wondering.

When his shift ended for the day, he trudged along with the other strikers to the strikers' exit. There was segregation in this place. Strikers' bunkhouses and residences, strikers' exits, strikers' restrooms. There were even some restaurants, shops, and clubs that prohibited strikers from entering. Strikers were filth here. Criminals. Failures. Chickens in a slaughterhouse.

But everyone had been duped by the Safe Lands government. If only the Owl could fly over that wall and tell the truth to the people.

Liberation isn't death. It's a prison sentence, even for "reputables." The Owl speaks the truth. Trust the Owl.

Omar clocked out and headed for the strikers' residence. He'd decided to spare one credit a day for a cafeteria meal and gorge himself. Eating out of the trash was too low, and Omar felt low enough as it was. So far, he'd managed to ration the vial of brown sugar Rain had given him. But one vape a morning wasn't enough to keep the shakes from coming late in the day.

He staggered across the street to the sidewalk that led to his building, and a man stepped in his path. A large man in orange. Omar made eye contact with him and was startled to find a pair of dark eyes already fixed on his.

Omar stepped aside and muttered, "Excuse me."

The man turned and walked alongside him. "You Omar?"

Omar stopped walking. "Who wants to know?"

"Tamera of Elias."

His mother's name froze time. Omar's mouth opened, and it took him a moment to formulate a reply. "You know my mother?"

"She tasks in sector one. Wants to see you."

His mother was alive?

"Come with me," the man said.

Omar nodded dumbly and followed. "How do you know her? And how did you find me? How did you even know to look for me?"

"I live in the sector five bunkhouse with your brother Mason. He told us you were here. As to how I found you, that's my business."

Sure. "But how do you know my mother?"

"I first saw her in a café. A man started choking and she helped him. Saved his life. I'd tasked as a medic for years, so I recognized her medical training and decided to start up a conversation."

Which only left Omar with more questions. "When did this happen?"

"The end of June. I'd been here for just a few days when we met. She hadn't been here long before me."

That fit the timeline.

His mother was alive!

The last words she'd said to him ran through his memory. *"Omar, why? You plan to work for them? And live with them?"*

Omar's steps slowed. "Why does she want to see me?" He had enough problems. He didn't need to add motherly lectures to the list.

"Your mother loves you," the striker said. "Isn't that reason enough?"

No, she couldn't still love him after everything he'd done. Omar stopped walking. "I deserve to be here. But my mother doesn't. And Mason doesn't. Seeing them... It will only make me feel worse. Tell them I'm sorry." He turned to walk away.

But the man grabbed Omar's arm, his grip squeezing to the bone. "I'm not asking if you want to come, boy. You'll come. And you'll be respectful. You hear me?"

The intensity in that that voice... Omar could only say, "Yes, sir."

The striker tugged Omar's arm. "You going to walk on your own, or do I have to drag you?"

"I can walk fine." Being startled had unnerved him. That, coupled with his fatigue from a long day in the pen, brought on the shakes. And he'd left his new PV in his room where he wouldn't be tempted to vape it all at once.

The man released Omar's arm and nudged him to a nearby bench. "Take a seat. Rest."

Omar sat.

The man stood over him, looking down. "What's your juice?"

"Brown sugar."

"Walls, boy. Best to let that go, all right? Don't go looking to find more. I've worked with a lot of addicts. The good news is, it's hard for strikers to get juice down here. That'll help you get clean."

Omar looked at his shoes. The thought of losing his PV was more than he could bear. He wouldn't tell this man about the PV or Rain or the deal he'd made with her or what he'd already done. It would be his secret.

"I know," the man said, "you don't want to get clean. But you'll be happier when you do. Trust me."

When Omar's strength returned, he followed the man into Cibelo. "Who are you, anyway?"

"My name is Richark Lonn. Most people call me Lonn."

Omar perked up. "The rebel leader? We saw you get liberated!"

"That's right, boy. And the rebels haven't stopped fighting."

Really? Omar hadn't thought there was a way to fight from down here. He wondered what Lonn had meant by that. Was there a chance for the Owl to soar again?

Lonn opened the door to a dinky little restaurant and held it, motioning Omar to enter first. He stepped inside, thankful for the cool air-conditioning.

"Omar!" Mason stood from a table in the back and strode toward him, beaming. "Come on." He pulled Omar back to his table, but their mother was already running toward them.

She met them halfway and embraced Omar, squeezed him. Behind her, Shanna and his aunt Janie stood beside the table, staring at him.

Tears flooded his eyes. He was guilty. They all thought so. And he couldn't deny it. Their husbands were dead because of him. They were in this place because of him.

His mother kissed his ear, his cheek, his forehead, then pulled back and took hold of his cheeks and really examined him. She looked well. Healthy. Her eyes were filled with tears, some of which had already spilled down her cheeks. She was tanned, as if she'd been working outdoors every day all summer. "My son," she said.

Omar shook his head. "I'm so sorry."

She took his hand and pulled him toward the table. "Sit here." She nudged him into the booth. There were white paper placemats on the table, the first paper he'd seen in days, and Omar longed for a chance to draw. "Shanna? Will you order Omar a chicken dinner? Chicken was always his favorite."

"Not chicken," Omar said. "I'm working in the slaughterhouse now and..." He shuddered.

"Say no more," Mother said. "What would you like to eat?"

He was tempted to ask for a salad, which was the only meal he could think of that might be created in a way that wasn't horrifying. But he was too hungry for lettuce. "Is there soup? Tomato, maybe? And some bread?"

"I'll ask," Shanna said.

Aunt Janie slid into the other side of the booth. She reached across the table and squeezed his hand. "How are you, Omar?"

"I've been better."

"Is it bad in your residence?" Mason asked.

Bad? Omar frowned at his brother. "Not really. Why? Is yours bad?"

"Yeah, the liberator said Renzor wanted the worst for me," Mason said.

"I hate Renzor," Omar said. "I wish Otley would've shot that maggot."

"I know it seems bad, but there are a lot of things to be thankful for," Mother said. "Rich is able to keep Mason safe. We've all found each other. Don't give me that look, Omar. I think we're here for a reason."

"Why would you say that?" They were here because of Omar's selfishness. Nothing more.

"These people are trapped," Mother said. "But we came and reminded them that there's something else out there. Hope."

There it was again: hope. Haunting him. Omar wanted to say, "Hope for what?" but he held his tongue. He didn't want to fight.

Shanna returned with a bowl of soup and a plate of bread. She set it before Omar, then sat next to Aunt Janie.

"Thanks," Omar said, tearing off the end of the bread and dunking it. He bit into it, and the warmth and tartness of the soup was delicious.

"If we can get a man to the Midlands, we can change everything," Lonn said, then told Omar about the Lowlands rebels and their plan to try and get a man through the turnstiles.

"I still think it's too dangerous," Mason said.

"Your brother doesn't like my plan," Lonn told Omar. "But there's no way to get over the wall."

"If only the Owl could fly," Omar said.

"The Owl?" his mother asked. "That rebel in the mask who interrupts the ColorCast?"

Omar grinned and told the story of how the Owl had come to be and all he had done in a few short weeks before being caught and liberated. The feathers in the incinerator came to his mind then. "If we could make a balloon with hot air, I could fly over the wall."

Mason lit up. "That's a great idea, Omar. Perhaps we *could*."

"A balloon can't lift a man," Lonn said.

"A big enough one could," Mason said.

"So, we make a big one. Or more than one," Omar said. "Or we attach a rope to a smaller one, and it carries the rope up the wall. Maybe with a grappling hook."

"There are no grappling hook stores in Cibelo," Mason said. "Plus, there are motion detectors on the wall. Still, a hot-air balloon—or a collection of small ones bound together—could be done, in theory. It would be a lot of work."

"We already have a plan," Lonn said. "And it's a good one."

No more was said about hot-air balloons.

When it was time to leave, Omar collected the paper placemats from the table and took them with him. Mason was waiting outside the restaurant. Omar stopped and looked back through the glass door, saw Lonn kiss their mother.

What? "They're together?"

"Strange, isn't it?" Mason asked.

"Beyond so." Omar shook his gaze away. "Why are we standing here?"

"I don't dare enter my bunkhouse without Lonn," Mason said.

Omar wanted to ask why, but he wasn't certain he wanted to know. "Meet me tomorrow at one at the poultry slaughterhouse and we can walk to lunch," he said to Mason, then explained how to get to the strikers' entrance to the chicken yards and where he'd be working.

If his brother came to the slaughterhouse, he could show him the incinerator. Because if anyone could build a hot-air balloon, it was Mason.

While Omar wanted to obey Lonn's advice and refrain from brown sugar, he couldn't. When Prav and Kurwin left for Fajro that night, Omar went with them.

There was a back entrance to Fajro that led to an area with dressing rooms. Rain made them change clothes when they arrived. She didn't want her customers knowing they were playing with strikers, though she didn't try to hide the Xs on their faces or hands.

Omar found a pair of black pants and a dark brown satin shirt that made him think of Shaylinn's eyes. Burnt umber. All the men's clothing in Rain's closets was flamboyant and never had enough buttons. This brown shirt had only three buttons at the bottom. Ridiculous.

There weren't many customers at Fajro that night. Two men sat at the bar, apart, one drinking, the other vaping something with lime green fog. Omar sat with Kurwin at a booth in the corner as he had every night since his encounter with Rain last Saturday. Prav always went out with a woman. Kurwin and Omar did not. Prav's muscles had intimidated Omar at first, but he was glad for them now because women liked them. Hopefully they'd continue to choose Prav and leave Omar alone.

Though he wouldn't earn any brown sugar that way.

"Do you get chosen much?" Omar asked Kurwin.

"Two or three times in a weekend. Reps rarely come out on a weeknight."

"Oh." Today was Wednesday. The weekend was coming. Omar took a gulp of his beer, trying not to think of Friday night when the reputables would come looking for pleasure.

The mere thought didn't feel all that *reputable* to him.

Rain let her ravens—as she called them—drink as much as they wanted, so Omar was drinking, trying to keep his mind off the half-full PV in his pocket. He needed to make it last until he could afford to fill it himself. There must be ways he could earn credits without being one of Rain's ravens. Maybe he could sell some art or learn how to apply ash ink tattoos to strikers. They might pay him in vials of brown sugar for such things.

Or maybe Mason would see the feathers and know how to make a hot-air balloon, and they'd all fly away.

"What's so bad about the bunkhouses? Omar asked, thinking of Mason.

"Those are the maximum-security cages," Kurwin said. "Where they put the real rotters. Be thankful you don't live there, peer. They're a nightmare. And it's even worse for the strikers in sectors five and eight."

Mason was in sector five. "Why?"

"Cows, peer. They're heavy. Like fifteen hundred pounds. This one time, a cow busted through the ground, which was the ceiling of the top floor of the strikers' bunkhouse in sector five. Killed three men in their sleep."

"No way."

"That beast crushed them in their beds. Sector six is safe, peer. Ain't no chicken that big."

Giant chicken. Omar laughed.

"Omar."

He jumped at the sound of Rain's voice and looked up.

She was standing across the table, looking at him. "I have a customer for you."

A chill ran up his arms. "But it's only Wednesday."

She frowned. "So? Come on." She turned and walked away.

"Well, there you go," Kurwin said, elbowing him. "Have fun."

Omar felt dizzy. He downed the remainder of his beer and slid out of the booth. Rain was waiting for him beside the bar.

"She's new," Rain said when he reached her. "And she's scared. She only wants to talk to someone, so I figured it would be a good first for you. I didn't charge her the full price, but if you make her happy, I'll pay you in full."

A thrill kindled in his chest at the idea of a full vial of brown sugar. "What do you want me to do?"

"Figure it out." Rain nodded to a booth in the back corner. "She's in the blue shirt."

Omar walked toward the booth. The woman looked about his mother's age. She was pale and bone thin, and she watched him approach with wide green eyes.

Omar sat across from her in the booth. "Hey."

"Hay-o," she said. No smile.

What am I doing here? Omar stared at her for too long, until she looked to her lap. Then words came out of his mouth. "What's your name?"

"Cacia."

"I'm Omar. Where do you task?"

"Sector three. Textiles. I like your shirt."

Of course she did. "Are you sad, Cacia?"

"Why do you ask?"

He shrugged, feeling like Mason trying to be a doctor of the brain. "Something in your eyes."

She blinked, and tears fell to her lap, tears that hadn't been there seconds ago. Nice job, Omar. At this rate, he wasn't going to earn a vial of anything.

She slouched down in the booth, and her feet hit his under the table. "I just feel really alone."

Join the club. "Yeah, well, this isn't a world that encourages real friendships."

"That's so true," she said, suddenly eager. "I thought I had a friend, but she blamed me for something that went wrong at the office. She did it because our task director liked me, but she liked him too. So, she made me look bad to make herself look good. He believed her. And I was demoted." She gasped, choking back a sob.

"I'm sorry," Omar said. "That's horrible." And it was. People here didn't care about anyone but themselves. Maggots. All of them.

"They were my best friends, but she betrayed me and he believed her. So, I never really had any friends, did I? It was all a lie."

Omar shrugged one shoulder. "I don't know. Maybe not a lie. People do stupid things sometimes. He'll find out what she did, eventually. Then he'll know he can't trust her."

"But that won't fix things with me."

Yeah. "Probably not."

"So, what can I do?"

Omar recalled the advice Zane had given him a few weeks back. "Forget them. You have to decide who you want to be. And you have to like that person and believe in that person no matter what anyone else says." He paused, thinking over how that had sounded, then added his own thought. "But you still need other people. There's no pleasure in a life lived alone."

"Being alone means you have fewer problems," she said.

"Then why are you here?"

Cacia smiled through the tears. "Because I wanted some company."

She'd come here and paid for company. That was so sad. Though not as sad as the guy who got paid to hang out with people because he was hooked on stims. "I used to think being alone was good because I could do what I wanted and I didn't have to answer to anybody. But looking back, my family was only trying to protect me."

"I don't understand that word. Family."

Wow. It was so easy to forget just how different these people were. No families. Omar thought of his mother and Mason and Aunt Janie. His mother was right. He should be more thankful. "Family is people who love you no matter what. And if you mess up, you forgive each other." He pictured Shaylinn and all the ways he'd hurt her and how she'd always forgiven him. Did she believe he was dead right now?

"You think I should forgive them?" Cacia asked.

"Maybe. Because life doesn't work so good without family—or friends, anyway. You become selfish, concerned only with your own needs. I lived that way. I've taken from others all my life. And I whined. 'Poor me. Look at what everyone else has.' But in my search for happiness, I lost what little good I had. And I figured out that love is about giving, not taking. It's about loving others more than you love yourself." Omar could barely believe he was telling her this stuff. He felt like a hypocrite, and yet the truth of his words suddenly felt more real to him than ever before.

Cacia sniffed, rubbed her nose. "You're so weird. There's no such thing as love."

Omar leaned forward, folded his arms on the tabletop. "No such thing? Now, I can't let that comment slide. Love covers all wrongs. Love is kindness and patience and discipline and trust. Waters can't quench it or wash it away. It binds us together in unity. It covers endless amounts of mistakes. And perfect love—ah, perfect love drives out even the darkest fears. Love... Cacia, love never fails."

She laughed. "You're a songwriter, raven. How do you come up with that stuff?"

"Because I've made a ton of mistakes. And people love me anyway." Shaylinn, Jemma, Levi, Mason, and now Mother, Shanna, and Aunt Janie. They shouldn't love him, but they did. Why?

A verse came to him then from deep inside his memory. *"We love because he first loved us."*

"I'll tell you a story," Omar said. "Once upon a time there was darkness. And a voice said, 'Let there be light.' And there was light."

"Had the power gone out?"

"Just hush and let me tell the story, okay?"

Cacia fell back in her seat. "*Okay*. Walls."

And Omar told her the oldest story he knew about love.

Chapter 11

It was time for vaccinations, so Mason started at pen one and drove the cattle, six at a time, out of the pen and into the cattle lane. They were good-natured and went where Mason urged them to go, moving quickly down the lane, past all eighteen pens, all the way to the end of the row.

Mason caught sight of Scorpion on his enormous black horse in the second row, but thankfully Scorpion's back was to him.

Mason couldn't bring more than six head at a time into the crowding tub, because if it was too full, the cattle couldn't move. When the first cow reached the tub, Mason had to squeeze past them and open the heavy iron half-door that squeaked on its rusty hinges. Once the door was open, Mason herded the animals inside. The cattle bumping against the chute walls sounded like the tribal drums from Jack's Peak. He chased the animals from the tub into the chute system. This wasn't difficult—they knew where they were going.

The hum of the hydraulic chute motor purred like one of the Old generators in Glenrock. Wayd was ahead of Mason and helped move each cow up to the chute. Over and over, a cow ran inside until his head came out the other end, where the press caught and held him until the vet could check him over and administer the vaccine.

Then the vet released the cow, and Wayd steered it back into the cattle lane.

The constant motion made the hours pass by quickly, and soon Mason was on his way to sector six to visit Omar at the poultry slaughterhouse.

Mason had just about gotten used to the smell of cow manure. But sector six had a different stench. The chicken manure was unpleasant, but there was a rotting smell too. A smell of death that hung on the air.

He entered the poultry slaughterhouse through the strikers' gate as Omar had instructed. The sounds of birds squawking carried through the walls, and the brutal stench assaulted his nostrils. He pinched his nose, his revulsion increasing with each step into this house of murder.

And then he stepped into the pen and his breath left him.

He stood on the edge of a field of white birds. There must have been thousands, packed solid. Clucking, bobbing, shifting on a floor made of metal wire. Feces fell through the holes and gathered below—and blood. Mason could only guess that some of the birds got stepped on and were crushed by the workers as they waded through the mass.

He had to ask several people before he found his brother wrestling some chickens into a shallow rubber crate. Every time Omar tried to close the lid, a bird escaped and he had to chase it down. With Mason's help, he managed to shut the lid. Then Omar set it on a conveyor belt, which pulled it inside a dark chute in the building.

Mason pinched his nose again and his voice came out nasal. "Where does it go?"

"The slaughterhouse. Trust me, you don't want a tour, Mr. Vegetarian."

Mason shivered. He wouldn't have survived tasking here. "I'll take your word for it. Let's go." Though he wasn't certain he could eat after this.

"I want to show you something first. Here." Omar handed Mason a piece of plastic. "Put it on your nose, like mine."

Mason slid on the nose-pincher, which helped immensely. "If the smell is so bad that one must invent a device to plug one's nose, perhaps there is a bigger problem."

"It's the Safe Lands, Mase. No one cares."

Omar walked in the direction of the incinerator, and Mason followed reluctantly. The birds scattered before them as they crossed the strange metal floor. Mason tried not to retch at the sight below. He lifted his chin and focused straight ahead.

Omar gestured to a bright red barrel the size of a Safe Lands car. Blue and silver pipes curled out from the sides and ran toward the ceiling. "This is the incinerator. Good timing too." He put on a pair of thick gloves. "We burned some birds a while ago, so it's cooled down enough that I can open it."

Mason didn't want to know why they burned birds. Nor did he want Omar to open that door. "Let's just go."

But Omar gripped the handle, pulled down until his actions produced a loud clank, then opened the heavy metal door.

Inside was a chamber of smooth, sooty steel walls, like some sort of massive oven. Light gray ash was scattered on the bottom in clumps.

Omar gripped a rectangular hole in the front with his gloved fingers. "This is the ash pit." He grabbed what looked like a large hoe and raked the ash into the pit. The hoe made an awful sound scraping over the steel surface. When he got most of it, he traded for a hand broom and brushed the rest into the hole. Then he crouched on the side of the incinerator and pulled out a long drawer that also sraped horribly. This held these the ash. Omar carried the drawer to a dumpster and emptied it, tapping it until all the ash fell out. Particles danced in the air around him.

"They use this ash to make cinderblocks," Omar said.

"That's interesting." And disturbing. That some of these buildings could be made from the remains of chickens and who knew what other animals. And Mason had never seen a graveyard in the Safe Lands either, so they likely cremated people as well. He shuddered at the nightmare of this place.

Omar replaced the drawer, then walked around Mason to a waist-high bin on wheels, which he rolled over to the incinerator. Mason saw that it was full of dead chickens or chunks of dead chickens.

He gagged and covered his face with his hands. Took a few quick breaths. This place. Every time he thought it couldn't get worse... He peeked between his fingers and saw Omar tossing handfuls of bird parts into the incinerator. "What are you *doing*?"

"Back up." Omar wheeled the bin to the side. He pulled Mason's elbow—Mason still had his hands over his face—until they were a good ten feet from the open incinerator door. "Stay here." Then Omar walked to the side of the incinerator. "Okay, watch this." He pressed a button.

The incinerator growled, then flame gushed out of the side of the chamber, engulfing the pile of bird parts. It sounded like a waterfall of fire and looked like an oversized blowtorch. Omar released the button, but inside the birds still smoldered.

Mason whimpered. Why? Why had Omar made him watch this?

"Come closer," Omar said.

Mason inched toward the open door, wary of what he'd see next.

His brother stepped up beside him. "See it? See the feathers?"

Mason did see. Bits of feathers and ash circled in the air above the flame, the hot air a current for them to ride on.

"Well?" Omar asked. "Do you know how to do it?"

The hot-air balloon. Mason closed his eyes, exasperated that Omar had put on a full demonstration—burned chicken carcasses—to show Mason something he already understood. "In theory, yes. But it will take some trial and error. And I'm not sure where we'd get the supplies. We'd need a lot of fabric."

"But it's a good idea, isn't it?"

Mason patted Omar on the back, keeping his other hand over his mouth to act as a filter. "It's a great idea, brother. Let me think on it. And let's get out of here."

When Mason's task shift ended for the day, he went into Cibelo and found a G.I.N. store. He'd been tasking only six days now, so he didn't have many credits to spend. But he didn't need much. Just enough to test the theory for Lonn.

As Mason began searching the shelves for materials, he was reminded of the Old book of children's experiments Papa Eli had given him for Christmas one year. He'd performed each experiment many times, using whatever materials he found around Glenrock. Mason wished Papa Eli could see how his great-grandson was putting all that practice to work. It might just get them out of the Safe Lands.

The first thing he needed was a fire source. Smoking was illegal in the Safe Lands, but he found a small box of matches in the cooking aisle next to the birthday candles. He bought the matches, as well as the birthday candles, a box of bendable straws, a roll of tape, and a package of dental floss. It all came to eight credits, nearly a full day's work. He sighed, hoping this wouldn't be a waste of time.

He paid and asked the clerk for a few extra plastic bags. The clerk was more than generous, shoving a handful into the one holding Mason's purchase.

Mason carried it all to the Get Out Now Diner. The place was empty for the moment, so he sat at the table in the back and asked Cori for a salad, which would likely be put on Lonn's tab. Mason wasn't sure how Lonn paid for all the meals here. Maybe he didn't.

While he waited for his salad, he started his balloon. He took five straws, pinched one end of each, and tucked it into the open end of another, bending the straws until he had a misshapen ring. He then ripped off four foot-long strips of dental floss, tying one end of each evenly spaced around the straw ring. Next, he taped the ring around the opening of one of the plastic bags, pleating the excess bag here and there, careful to leave no gaps.

His salad arrived, so he took a break and ate. When he finished, he tore apart the box that held the birthday candles, separating the back square. He used a tine of his fork to poke a hole in each corner. Then he tied the loose end of each piece of dental floss around each hole.

He'd just completed that step when Lonn and his mother arrived.

"What are you doing?" Mother asked, sitting across from him with Lonn.

"An experiment." Mason looked to Lonn. "Do you think the cook would mind if I lit a few birthday candles?"

"No. What kind of experiment is this?"

"You'll see." Though Mason was nervous now that he had an audience. He used his fork to poke four closely spaced holes in the center of the cardboard. He pushed a birthday candle through each until they were about halfway through. Then Mason slid out of the booth, pulling his "balloon" with him. "Will you help me, Mother?"

Lonn got up so that Mother could get out.

"What am I doing?" she asked.

"Hold the top of the bag, please, while I light these candles." Mason pinched the top of the bag to show her what he wanted, and she took it from him. Then he grabbed the matches from the table and squatted under the bag. By then, Cori and the chef had come out from the kitchen to watch.

Mason tried to remain calm. He had done this before. But his hands were trembling as he put his hands near the candles and struck a match. He had two candles lit before the match burned too close to his fingers, forcing him to drop it on the floor. He struck a second match and lit the other two candles. "Okay, let's give it a moment," he said, taking the bag from his mother.

His sympathetic nerves had him sweating. He let go of the bag and it sank, so he grabbed it again and waited longer. He continued to release and catch the bag until it hovered in place.

Okay, good. He stepped back and watched as the bag slowly rose into the air, drifted higher and higher, and finally bumped against the ceiling.

Cori and cook cheered and clapped for the balloon. Mother joined in the applause. Mason grinned at them.

"You wanted to show this to *me*, didn't you?" Lonn asked. "Omar's balloon?"

Mason sat across from Lonn and leaned over the table. "What if we could build one big enough to lift a man? Carry him over the wall where he could get a message to the rebels in the Midlands?"

Lonn didn't look convinced. "How big would it have to be to lift a man? And how would you get the controlled flames big enough?"

"I don't know yet," Mason said. "But I think it's possible."

"I can see that it *might* be possible." Lonn gestured to the balloon, which was already starting to sink. And the bag had shriveled, meaning the flames had gotten too hot. "But I doubt it will work."

Mason pursed his lips, then got up and blew out the candles on his balloon. He wanted to say that he doubted Lonn's plan to sneak a man through the turnstile would work, but there was no point. Lonn would do what he would do.

And so would Mason.

"You have no objections to me trying, do you?" Mason asked.

"Of course not," Lonn said. "Just don't get caught."

Mason grinned. The game was on. He wadded up his balloon and put it in the trash, then came back and sat across from his mother and Lonn. As he picked at the remains of his salad, he watched the two interact. He knew very little about his guardian angel—and possible future stepfather. "Why did you get fired from the MC?" he asked Lonn. "What were you researching?"

Lonn's eyes bored into his. "What makes you think I was researching anything? Or that I got fired?"

"I read your bio in the History Department. They didn't say you were fired, by the way. It says 'forced retirement.'"

"Forced." Lonn huffed a laugh. "It was indeed forced."

"What happened?" Mason asked.

"I'd been doing experiments. And I hadn't told anyone about them."

"Not even Lawten?"

"Not at first. It all started with Martana's death in sixty-eight. She was hypoxic, and I felt like she wouldn't have had an oxygen deficiency if she'd been healthy. The plague causes anemia, which decreases the amount of red blood cells in the body and therefore decreases the amount of oxygen in the blood. I set out to find a way to increase red blood cells. I got nowhere for the first few years. Most my free time was spent with the growing rebellion anyway.

"But I got thinking about trying to filter blood. To create a sieve. We did that for dialysis patients, so why couldn't we do something similar for the plague? I started talking with a man in technology design. I also brought in a biologist, and we used a dialysis machine as a prototype. Together, we found a way to filter the virus from the blood."

"That's amazing!" Mason said. "Why wouldn't they want that?"

"Well, it didn't work. I mean, it did, but the problem was that the blood is not the location of the infection. Blood carries the infection throughout the body. It's a transmitter of the virus. But the replication of the virus happens in the lymph nodes and the spleen. While transfusion might have filtered the virus from the blood, it didn't stop the virus from entering the blood all over again."

Oh. That made sense. Frustrating, though. "So, what did you do?"

"I tried another theory. I tasked in the MC, where we occasionally worked with bioengineering on transplant patients. My first instinct was to grow new organs—a spleen, lymph nodes, intestines, whatever was needed—to flush out the plague. I hoped the combination of new organs with filtered blood would provide the cure. We could rebuild the body, so to speak, replacing the infected areas one at a time."

The very idea enthralled Mason. "How can you grow a new organ?"

Lonn smiled at his mother. "You ask the same questions Tamara asked. Another time on that one, okay? It's a complicated procedure. If we ever get out of here, I'll take you both over to bioengineering. You'll love it."

Mason already felt a tinge of excitement. "But your plan didn't work?"

"The virus is too complex," Lonn said. "It latches on in so many places that what works for one person might not for another. And growing organs is time-consuming, and transplants are hard on patients. None of this was ideal. So, I came up with yet another idea: Grow a womb."

Mindboggling. "You can do that?"

"I didn't see why not. I approached the bioengineering department, and it turned out they'd been trying to do this for years. They had successfully grown and implanted a womb for a woman who couldn't conceive, but it didn't keep the virus from the fetus. Learning this sent me back to the virus itself and the meds we were already using."

"And you found out there was a stimulant in the meds?" Mason asked.

Lonn furrowed his eyebrows. "No. What makes you ask that?"

"That's kind of how I got here," Mason said. "Ciddah learned that there was a stimulant in the meds, and she and I were testing my blood to find it."

"Why your blood?"

"It was just a wild guess on my part. She told me she'd tested a variety of blood types, but it was all infected blood."

"And if the meds catalyzed with the virus, it would be impossible to detect what was in the meds."

"Exactly," Mason said.

"But they stopped you before you could do this test?"

"Almost. The enforcers came just as the blood meter was running the test. I hid in a closet while Ciddah went out to talk with the enforcers. They took her away but didn't find me. And when I came out, I checked for a result. The blood meter said Xiaodrine."

Lonn wrinkled his nose. "Odd. Why put that in the meds?"

Lonn knew this drug? Maybe Mason would finally get some answers. "What is it?"

"It's an amphetamine designed to fight obesity. It speeds up the metabolism. Now, the plague does slow the metabolism, but I'd think Xiaodrine would be a dangerous combination with the plague's meds."

"Why?"

"Xiaodrine is processed in the liver. It would interact with other medications and reduce the benefit of the antivirals in the meds. Plus, I've read studies from bioengineering that say dependency on amphetamines has a physiological impact on the immune system."

"So why put Xiaodrine in the meds?" Mother asked.

"I don't know." Lonn looked back to Mason. "Whose meds were you testing?"

"Ciddah's old prescription. Once she learned about the stims, she started compounding her own meds."

"Clever girl," Lonn said.

Mason thought so and couldn't help smiling.

Lonn leaned back in the booth and folded his arms. "But I'm surprised they allowed it."

"Why?" Mother asked.

"Because meds for the plague aren't compounded in a regular Pharmco. They're made in the compounding pharmacy located in the main lab. Every medic knows that. How would she have gotten the recipe?"

A connection clicked in Mason's mind and his heart sank. "This was the Pharmco in City Hall. And Ciddah... she's... she was together with Lawten Renzor."

"Ahh... yes. Renzor's girl. The plot thickens. That Pharmco... and the SC... things go on there that no one is supposed to talk about. Some do, of course, which only adds to the legends. If Ciddah was one of Lawten's femmes, he'd probably given her a golden ticket to do whatever she wanted."

Mason didn't like thinking about Ciddah as one of Lawten's femmes. "But she stole things from the Pharmco to compound meds for her parents—wait. You knew her parents, I mean, one of her donors, anyway. Droe Rivan."

"Droe the dentist." A slow smile parted Lonn's lips. "He was with the rebellion early on." His smile faltered. "We had a major setback and he left. I didn't hold it against him. It was a hard thing. But, walls, he was a smart fellow. Not surprised his daughter is too. Both of you got further than I did. I'd tried to take a closer look at the meds, but I didn't have any reason to wonder what was in them so much as to wonder why every patient's prescription was so different."

"I don't understand," Mason said. "Don't medics write the prescriptions?"

"For everything *but* thin plague meds," Lonn said. "It's one of the biggest questions every medic has."

"Do you think there was some difference to the recipe other than the volume of compounded suspension based on the patient's weight?" Mason asked.

Cori came and whisked away his empty salad plate.

"They've lost me now," Mother told her.

"They always lose me," Cori said.

"It's more than simply consulting a dosing chart," Lonn said. "Some of my patients had to vape meds three times a day. Some only once a week. And some were far healthier than others. I wanted to find out why."

"But that's wasn't a safe question to ask," Mason said.

"It was not. And I made the mistake of talking about it with Lawten. Looking back, I know they'd been watching me, put Lawten up to it. He recorded our conversations. He took the recordings to the Guild, and I was—how did you put it?—promoted to 'forced retirement' for task infraction."

"What's task infraction?" Mother asked.

"All taskers sign an oath when we graduate from our mentoring programs," Lonn said. "We're not to ask questions outside our task. We're not to meddle in another task area. And that's what I'd been doing. I wasn't tasked as a bioengineer or a technology designer, after all. It wasn't my job to look for a cure. I was fired. And Lawten got my job."

"And a seat on the Safe Lands Guild," Mason said.

They sat silently for a moment, until Lonn said, "We need to find a way to test more meds. A wider variety. See if they all contain Xiaodrine. See what else they contain. I wish we could talk with your Ciddah."

Your Ciddah. A nice thought. Mason wondered if she missed him, believed him dead. Was she still with Levi and the others?

"I also wish we could visit the compounding lab. Or the blood lab," Lonn said. "I'm sure you know that medics take a blood draw of every patient at every visit."

"Yes. Why?" Mason asked.

"I always assumed they were monitoring the meds to make sure they'd prescribed the best dosage. But who's to say that's what they're doing."

That thought was a little scary. "What else could they be doing?"

Lonn chuckled. "Oh, Mason, it won't do to have you trust our government so easily. The fact is, they could be doing anything."

Chapter 12

Jemma spent several nights in the Rehabilitation Center, inside the same cell she'd been in last time, cell 40, at the very end. She had a wall to her left, and the cells on her right and across the aisle were empty. Her nearest neighbor was four or five cells down. She didn't bother trying to speak with him through the bars. Levi didn't seem to be here. Hopefully he'd gotten away.

She'd had days to wonder why Mia had betrayed her. Mia had said such hateful things after she'd stunned her. It seemed like she blamed Jemma for something, though she didn't know what it might be.

What would they do with Jemma? Or more importantly, what would she do? Levi's instructions before leaving the basements wore heavily on her mind. She must pretend to betray the rebels, give up the location of theater nine. But not at first. She had to hold out for a bit, then she could pretend to switch sides in order to protect herself.

Protect her from what, though? They wouldn't kill her. If anything, they'd put her back in the harem and make her pregnant.

Again, she wondered why Mia had done this. A reward, perhaps?

Sometime that afternoon, an enforcer came for her and transported her to the lobby, where Matron Dlorah was waiting with Ewan, one of the harem enforcers.

So it was back to the harem, then.

"We have a meeting with the task director general," Matron said. "We mustn't be late."

"What does *he* want?" Jemma asked.

Ewan held open the door and Matron waved for Jemma to exit first. "You'll find out when he tells you," Matron said.

A short ride in Matron's fancy black car brought them to City Hall. The task director general's office was on the top floor of the building. An elevator took them there far too quickly.

Jemma had never been in the task director's office. It had the same opulence of the harem, though the colors here were black and red with dark hardwood floors. Three of the four walls were made of floor-to-ceiling windows that offered a vast view of the city and surrounding area. And as her gaze fell to the man sitting behind a large desk, she almost felt as if she were standing in a throne room.

Jemma had seen Lawten Renzor before, in Champion Theater right before the entertainment orientation. He looked older now, though he wasn't wearing makeup like he had been the night he was on the ColorCast. He was a hunched man with flaking skin and a large nose that claimed most of his face. The size of his nose made his dark eyes seem smaller and more intense. A pale number nine glowed on his cheek, which made Jemma glance at the number four that had returned to her own hand.

Kruse, whom she remembered was the personal assistant to the ruler of the Safe Lands, stood next to the task director general's desk. He was bald with smooth pinkish skin and a funny black SimArt tattoo that looked like a hand slapping the side of his head.

Jemma could think of a few heads she'd like to slap right now.

"Ms. Levi, welcome," Kruse said in a happy voice. "Please have a seat." He gestured to a chair in front of the task director's desk. "Matron Dlorah, would you mind waiting outside?"

Matron shot Kruse an indignant glare. "Ms. Levi is my charge. What concerns her, concerns my harem."

"If there is something you need know, Matron, I will inform you," the task director said. Where Kruse's voice was pleasant, the task director's was grating and deep.

Jemma shivered at the looks Matron and the task director exchanged, but Matron left the room without another word.

Once the door closed, the task director spoke. "Ms. Levi, you and your rebel outsider friends have deprived our nation of nine surrogates."

"Ten, at my count," Jemma said, lifting her chin.

"Perhaps you didn't factor yourself into my equation," the task director said. "You helped ten women leave the harem, indeed, but you remained behind, a valuable replacement surrogate."

"I will not be a surrogate," Jemma said, though there was little she could do to keep from becoming one.

"You *will* carry a child," the task director said. "I leave the method of conception to you. Though I am looking to have another child of my own, should you prefer more natural methods over the SC's embryo transfer program."

Jemma gasped at his rudeness. "I would never do anything with you." She was glad little Elyot would not be raised by this man.

"I think that, in time, you'll change your mind. I can be very persuasive."

She opened her mouth to tell him what he could do with his persuasive ideas, but she remembered she was supposed to pretend to turn traitor. How could she do that without encouraging this man's advances? "What do you want from me?"

"You will be a queen, of course," the task director said. "And since the leader of your outsider clan claims you as his, I will claim you as mine. In this, I'll show my people that no rebellion is stronger than our government. And once you conceive, they will also see that there's still no greater privilege for a woman than bearing a child for the Safe Lands."

Childbearing. That was what they'd wanted from the Glenrock women from the start. But allowing the task director general to claim her? Perhaps this was the way to get on his side. To make herself appear to be the traitor Levi wanted her to be.

"I'll be a Safe Lands queen," she said, a plan formulating with each word, "on one condition."

The task director raised his eyebrows. "A condition? I'm intrigued."

"I want to be the only queen. Mia doesn't get to be on the ColorCast, nor does Jennifer or any other pregnant woman. Only me, until I deliver my child."

He sat back in his chair, folded his arms. "Why do you ask this?"

"Because Mia betrayed me." That much was true. "And if I'm going to have a baby, I want to be the famous one. I want to be the one on all the posters and ColorCast programs."

"All our queens get that, femme," Kruse said.

"But not Mia," Jemma said. "Not anymore."

"Why should I agree?" the task director asked. "You'll do what I say when I say it."

"I know you can make me do whatever you want. But wouldn't you rather work with someone willing?"

"Mia has been very willing," the task director said. "And I don't see that you have any right to make demands."

Good. Now was her chance. "What if I give you something?"

The task director chuckled. "I like your bargaining spirit, Ms. Levi. What will you give me to leave Mia and the others off the ColorCast?"

Jemma swallowed, and her eyes filled with tears, which she hoped made it look like her decision had been a difficult one. "I'll tell you where the rebels meet in the Midlands. I'm not very good with directions, but I know enough that your enforcers will be able to find it."

The task director raised one eyebrow. "Why would you give this information?"

"Because they haven't helped us!" Jemma yelled. "And they won't help us. We just wanted to get outside of these walls, back to our home, but the rebels have their own plans. The Owl. Taking over the government. We don't care about your political problems. We only wanted to leave. But now I'm back in the harem, because the rebels wanted to free the other women and because Mia stunned me. The rebels and Mia... they ruined my plans. So, now I'll ruin theirs."

He stared at her with those beady little eyes. "Very well," he said at last. "Where do they meet?"

Jemma shook her head. "First, you make me queen."

"Walls, femme. You aren't even pregnant yet," Kruse said.

"Your people are living with the rebels, you said?" the task director asked. "You're dependent upon them?"

"Yes," Jemma said, not understanding why he would ask such a thing.

"I'll need time to think this over. For now, you'll move into the harem. You'll have your appointments in the SC. Then we'll talk again."

Kruse walked her to the door and winked. "Don't you worry, femme. Everything is going to work out fine."

"I'm not worried. 'I will not give way to useless alarm,'" she said, quoting a favorite story. "'It's right to be prepared for the worst, but there's no reason to look on it as a certainty.'"

Jemma would not live in this place forever. She could not.

Matron took Jemma directly to the Surrogacy Center for an appointment. Rimola, the receptionist, still tasked there, but she seemed to be doing Mason's old task of assisting the medics in addition to her own. And instead of Ciddah, a man was now the medic. Medic Vallen, Rimola called him. When Rimola took Jemma into the exam room and asked her to put on the blue robe, Jemma refused.

"Why are you being difficult?" Rimola asked. "Matron said you were eager to become queen."

"I just don't want to have a male doctor." She winced at her words. She'd always been supportive of Mason's interest in medicine. But she wasn't pregnant yet and therefore didn't require a doctor. "Is there no female medic?"

"Not since Ciddah left," Rimola said. "If you won't cooperate, I'll have to stun you."

Tears flooded Jemma's eyes. She didn't want to get stunned, but maybe that would be better. Then she wouldn't remember what had happened.

But that was cowardly. "Fine." She snatched the blue gown from the exam table and waved Rimola out the door.

"Thank you, femme," Rimola said, smiling as if they were friends.

Jemma changed into the robe and fought back tears. She didn't want to do this, but if she were going to be convincing as a Safe Lands queen, she'd have to do a better job of acting.

Rimola returned and took Jemma's weight and blood pressure, then asked her to go into the bathroom and urinate in a plastic cup. Once Jemma did all that, she was sent back to the exam room to wait—and dread—the medic's arrival.

He came finally, dressed in bright blue shirt and pants. He looked to be in his early twenties. Short with a square face and green eyes. But Jemma's gaze was drawn most to his skin—it was flaking, and he hadn't bothered to use Roller Paint. Wasn't that unsanitary for a medic?

"Ms. Levi, hay-o." He was too busy reading the CompuChart to look at her. When he finally did look up, his eyes widened, and his leering stare slid across her entire body. "*Hay-o.*"

She tried not to express disdain at the sultry tone of his second greeting. "Hello."

He swallowed, his throat bobbing. "I... You... I'm sorry." He actually flushed and looked back to the chart, scratched the back of his head. "It, uh... may interest you to know that you're pregnant."

Pregnant? "But you haven't done anything to..." Her words trailed off as understanding settled over her in a thrilling rush. "On my own?"

"Yes, well done." He smiled. He had very small teeth. "Procedure dictates that you ask the donor to come in so we can check his blood and DNA. If we can get you on the right combination of meds now, there's a chance we can stop the virus from reaching the child. It's a new procedure. Still being tested. So far there have been no successes, but we're hopeful that—"

"My husband and I aren't infected," Jemma said. "I will take no meds. Nothing, is that clear?"

"*Not* infected?" Medic Vallen looked back to the chart, scrolled back a page. "Oh. Forgive me, Ms. Levi. I didn't think to check that. I apologize." He looked at her again, frowning. "*Both* of you uninfected? Are you certain? Men sometimes say things that aren't true to, you know, to..."

Jemma beamed at him. "I'm positive." Pregnant! Ha! There would be no embryo transfer procedure for her, no having to deal with the task director and his persuasive ideas. Wait until she told Levi! She tried to imagine the look on his face. Surprise first. Then a wide smile and—

"Well, I, uh... I see Rimola didn't fill in the last date of your menstrual cycle. Do you remember? It will help me to determine the birthdate. An ultrasound will confirm it, but it's a little early for that."

"I don't know." Jemma tried to remember. "I was here. In the harem," she said. "I was only days away from an embryo transfer appointment. That's probably written in your chart."

He frowned and studied the CompuChart, tapped around a bit. "Ah, yes. Here it is. You've skipped, it looks like... two. You're likely seven or eight weeks along already."

"Are you sure?" That put Jemma only a few weeks behind Shaylinn.

"Fairly certain, yes. Like I said, an ultrasound will confirm it, but I'll need to notify the task director first." He looked up from his chart and smiled wide. "Congratulations, Ms. Levi."

Jemma couldn't help but return his smile. "Thank you. And it's *Mrs.* Levi.

Jemma stormed into the Blue Diamond Suite, furious that Matron Dlorah had put her in the same area as Mia. She wouldn't be here long. Not if she could negotiate a room change with the task director. There were plenty of empty rooms in the harem now.

Only one person was sitting in the living room when Jemma entered. A very young girl with long, dark braids. From her coloring and hair, Jemma guessed she must be from Jack's Peak, though she knew very few women from that village. She'd met Tsana before. And she knew of Jack's Peak's medicine woman, Shavingo'o, and of course Chief Kimama, Jemma's great-grandmother.

The girl jumped up and ran to meet Jemma by the door. "You're Jemma, aren't you?" the girl said. "You're the one Levi of Elias chose."

That brought a smile to Jemma's lips. "Yes, that's right."

"I'm Alawa. My mother and sister were here too, but they escaped when I was in the SC." Her voice became wistful and tears filled her eyes. "I'm sorry you're here, but I'm glad."

Jemma took hold of the girl's hand and squeezed. "It's nice to meet you, Alawa. How old are you?"

"Seventeen." She took a deep breath. "Jemma, did you see any of my people, besides the women and girls in the harem, I mean. The men and boys?"

"I've seen many of them. Who are you curious about?"

"My brother Yivan and his friend Nodin."

"Yes, I've met them both. They helped rescue the children from the boarding school, and they were here the night we freed the other women—all except you and me, that is."

Alawa gasped in several relieved breaths, a huge smile on her face. "Oh, thank you, Jemma. I was so worried about them. I-I saw my father die. He was so brave. But when I was taken, Yivan and Nodin were still fighting."

Jemma put her arm around the girl. "I'm glad to be able to tell you that they are well—though missing you, I'm sure."

"Nodin and I were planning to get married," she said. "But now..."

"You mustn't give up hope," Jemma said, giving her a squeeze. "We won't be here forever."

"But they made me pregnant with another man's child! What will Nodin say when he learns that? Why would he still want to marry me?"

Nodin was a quiet young man. Jemma really didn't know much about him. "If he loves you, he'll still want to marry you."

"Sure, he will." Mia. She was standing at the mouth of the hallway, leaning against the wall, arms folded. She looked lovely as always and not at all pregnant, though she likely wasn't that far along. "Jemma has a lot of silly ideas about men and love."

"There is nothing silly about a man who loves a woman, Mia," Jemma said.

"There is because it's a lie," Mia said. "Men are incapable of loving one woman."

"Did your piano man hurt you?" Jemma asked. Maybe that was why Mia was trying to ruin Jemma's life, because her man had run out on her. Could she be jealous that Jemma had a husband who loved her?

"No," Mia said with a hint of disgust in her voice. "I didn't want him anyway."

"If you're patient and wait for the right man," Jemma said, "you'll find one who'll love only you."

"Like you can talk," Mia said. "Levi can't decide whether he loves you or Kosowe."

Jemma straightened her posture. "Who?"

"Kosowe is from my village," Alawa said. "She has always longed to marry Levi."

Jemma had never even heard Levi mention this Kosowe before. "Was she in the harem?"

"You met her," Mia said. "Last night. She went and got you when I stunned Levi. And after I stunned you, she's the one who dragged him away."

Jemma could hardly breathe. Had Mia and this Kosowe woman conspired against Levi and Jemma? "You did this to break up our marriage?"

"You got married?" Mia chuckled, as if Jemma was a fool. "It won't last. Kosowe is gorgeous. And Levi loved her long before he loved you."

Though Jemma tried to fight it, tears filled her eyes. "That's not true." But could it be? Levi had spent a lot of time trading in Jack's Peak. No. Surely it wasn't true.

"Why do you think he was always going out on those trips, spending the night? He was sleeping with her."

Heat flashed through Jemma's chest. "Mia, you are a horrible person. I can't imagine how being this cruel could give anyone joy. I feel sorry for you." She turned and tried to open the door, found no knob, remembered the SimPad. She slammed her fist against the pad on the wall and the door popped open. Jemma wrenched it open wider, faster, and fled down the stairs, past the enforcers who were posted inside the front door, and across the main sitting area until she was standing at the vast picture windows that overlooked the harem gardens.

And she cried.

She didn't know how to respond to Mia's declarations and could only pray God would send her the strength and conviction she didn't feel. One thing was certain: Jemma was leaving the Blue Diamond Suite as soon as possible. And she would take Alawa with her.

Chapter 13

A bang jerked Levi from sleep. He sat up on one elbow and blinked, confused. It was dark, but bright light streamed through the open doorway. Someone stood there, silhouetted in the doorframe.

"Time to get up, you lazy maggot."

Jordan. Levi rolled over and burrowed under his pillow. "Go away."

"You've wasted enough time moping around like a girl. You're going to get up, you're going to eat a real meal, then we'll go talk with Ruston and Zane and figure out how to get her back."

"You know we can't rescue her." After losing ten harem women, there was no way they'd give up the last few they had. "They've probably got enforcers sleeping outside her bedroom door."

"You think I'm not hacked about this? She's my *sister*. If we can't get into the harem, then it's time to put down this psycho nation. The sooner we do that, the sooner we all go free."

Free. As elder of Glenrock, this was Levi's job. He couldn't afford to hide in his cave and mourn the loss of his wife. He had people looking up to him. And he'd wasted a week.

"Okay." He rolled over and threw back the covers. "I'm getting up."

"Mad good. Shay and Nell made breakfast. Come eat."

And that was how Levi found himself at the kitchen table with his household, minus one.

Minus Jemma.

"Good morning, Elder Levi," Trevon said, and the other children around the table parroted him.

"Good morning," Levi said, looking around at their faces. All boys, except for little Carrie, who was squeezing chunks of pancakes into mush with her fists. Trevon, Jake, Joey, Grayn, and Weiss all watched Levi with wide eyes, like he might explode at any moment. He looked to his plate, which was empty. "Did someone give thanks?"

"Jordan did." Shaylinn walked to the table, holding a frying pan and spatula. She scooped a large pancake out onto Levi's plate. "We didn't know you'd be joining us. It's nice to see you."

Levi nodded, glanced around the table again. While he'd been feeling sorry for himself, Jordan had been taking care of two households. Yet now that he was here, all eyes were on him. "Well? Go ahead and eat then."

The children started shoveling food into their mouths.

Levi didn't feel comfortable at the head of the table without Jemma here. What if they never freed her? What if they never learned what liberation truly was, and his mother and aunt Janie were gone forever? What if he had to raise his cousins without a wife? He was suddenly thankful they were mostly boys. He could raise boys, but Naomi or Shaylinn would have to help with Carrie.

Levi pushed the defeated feelings aside. Let the women care for the children for now—he and Jordan were going to war against this place. And he *would* get his wife back.

He kept his eyes on the table as he ate. The food was good. He reached for a slice of bread that was sitting on a platter before him. His movements slowed as he took in the familiar round shape of the loaf. "Shaylinn, did you make this bread?"

Shaylinn met his gaze from her seat across the table, set down her fork. "Kosowe brought that by. She's been bringing us food. Jordan said not to let her in, though."

"She keeps talking about the debt she owes you," Jordan said. "I told her she owes you nothing."

"Good, thank you," Levi said.

"I did let her take a load of laundry," Shaylinn said. "Was that wrong?"

The slight wince on Shaylinn's face... what she wasn't saying... She'd never admit that she needed the help because Jemma was gone.

"It's fine," Levi said. "We have nothing to fear from Kosowe." Unless she started telling people her version of what had happened in Jack's Peak two years ago.

He ate in silence and tried to decide if he should ignore Kosowe completely or tell her to leave him alone.

Neither option seemed best.

When he finished eating, he showered and dressed then went with Jordan to Ruston's house.

Tova opened the door and, unsurprisingly, didn't seem pleased to see them. "My husband is not here."

"Can you contact him?" Levi asked. "Tap him?"

"The technology of the devil is not allowed in the basements."

"Even the stuff Zane makes safe, like the Wyndos?" Levi asked.

Her face flushed then. "Whoever is a friend of the world is an enemy of God."

Wow. The rage in Tova's expression and tone chastened Levi for his fears of flakers. Had he ever been so judgmental toward Zane? He hoped not.

"Zane isn't a friend of the Safe Lands, Tova," Levi said. "He's a rebel. Which means he's fighting the same enemies you are. That we all are."

"You know not of what you speak. The Kindred know we are from God and that the rest of the world lies in the power of the evil one."

"You're as psycho as they are," Jordan said. "Last I checked, simply saying someone is evil doesn't make it true."

Tova's face hardened. "Further proof you cannot accept the ways of God. One who does not know God deems his ways to be foolishness."

Levi realized this woman was truly unwilling—or unable—to be proven wrong when it came to her Kindred. But why?

"Is something wrong?" a male voice asked from behind Levi. He turned and saw Nash standing in the corridor behind him.

Thank goodness. Sanity had arrived. "We were hoping to speak with your father," Levi said. "Tova says he's not home."

"I'll take you to him," Nash said. And he stepped past Levi and into the house.

Tova backed up a step, out of her son's way. "I'll not have my home turned into a common passageway."

"Of course not, Mother," Nash said, crossing the living room, "but we must be flexible in this transition time."

Tova followed at his side, continuing her rant. "This is no transition. All will return to normal soon enough. I will not have these upsiders putting ideas into my children's heads."

Nash pulled his mother aside and waved Levi toward the door that led to the gate to Zane's Midland house. "Peace, Mother. Perfect love casts out all fear."

"Don't talk to me about perfect love," Tova said. "I have loved you all, and what has it gotten me? You all go upside, against my wishes!"

"Mother, please. We'll talk more on this later."

Nash kissed her forehead and joined Levi and Jordan at the door. They went through and followed the corridor to Zane's basement. From there, they moved the shelves and curtain and went into the nest: the small, underground room from which Ruston and Zane commanded their rebel activities. There they found the pair hunched over Zane's GlassTop computer.

Ruston straightened to greet them. "Levi, it's good to see you awake. How are you?"

"As well as any man whose wife has been taken to that place," Levi said. "I don't suppose there's any hope of going back for her?"

Zane twisted his chair around. "It's not looking good. They've installed cameras in all the rooms now, added an enforcer shift inside the harem, and they've sealed off that door in the kitchen. I guess they don't care if there's a fire exit or not. Now, if we had those SimSuits, we might have a chance. But Lhogan isn't returning our taps."

"I owe *him* now," Ruston said. "He's not going to take such a risk again if he doesn't have to."

"Could we start a fire? Then try and free them when they're outside?" Levi asked.

"I wouldn't want to risk them getting trapped in there," Zane said. "It's too dangerous."

It was. Levi pressed back his frustration and, in desperation, grasped the one straw he had never taken seriously. "So, we focus on Omar's old plan: Operation Lynchpin."

Which was all about controlling the food and water sources in the Safe Lands. "The sooner we can take down the government, the sooner we can get to Jemma."

"This isn't a thing that can be rushed," Ruston said. "Such a plan might take years."

Levi couldn't wait years to get Jemma back. He sat on one of the chairs against the wall, ready to finish this fight once and for all. "What do we know?"

"Much about enforcer protocol, how enforcers get their orders from the guild," Zane said.

The Safe Lands Guild that had sentenced his brothers to premature liberation. "What do you know about those hooded people?"

"The Ancients?" Zane turned back to his computer and pulled up a map. "They live in Teocalli Manor—a mansion in the forest at the northern curve of the bell." He zoomed in to the location and pointed to his screen. "They're not allowed to come and go as they please. They have servants who see to their needs and enforcer escorts for when they're permitted to leave the manor."

"So, they're prisoners too," Jordan said. "Who are they?"

"Safe Landers believe they're the wisdom of the past," Ruston said. "They've forsaken moving on to the next life in order to stay here and advise the people."

"But what about what Mason overheard?" Levi said. "That they wouldn't have accepted Otley? Do you think they become Ancients to avoid liberation?"

"It makes as much sense as anything," Ruston said.

"Which means liberation is death," Jordan said.

"Or something unpleasant," Zane said. "Though it doesn't seem pleasant to have to keep your face hooded and live in confinement. Yet these people choose it."

"We've tried to figure it out for years," Ruston said. "But we've never known what to look for. Now that we know liberation ceremonies are prerecorded and that those who go through it are taken directly from the Champion Theater to wherever they're liberated, perhaps next time we can have some vehicles waiting to follow the van when it leaves the amphitheater."

"I wish I would have thought to follow Mason and Omar's van on the traffic cams," Zane said. "Then I could have seen where it went. I just assumed they were going back to the RC."

"Next time," Ruston said.

"Isn't there a liberation tonight?" Jordan asked.

"Liberation ceremony, yes," Zane said. "But it's only the recording. And there are never trials at night. We need to monitor the trials somehow. Then we can try to track the vehicles that leave the amphitheater."

Levi needed do do something now. "We can't wait around for a trial," he said. "What about the Owl? The kids are still talking about him. Did he have as much impact with adults?"

"At first," Zane said. "But the ratings are dropping fast. I've had to cobble together different videos and backgrounds to make it seem like new material, but the people are getting bored. We need a new Owl."

"I'll do it," Levi said, feeling reckless.

"I'm not sure you'll fit in the suit," Zane said. "Omar's a lot smaller than you."

Levi stood. "Where is it?"

"Upstairs. After Otley died, I went to Omar's apartment and grabbed whatever I could before they came and cleaned it out. I went to Mason's too, but he didn't own anything but a suit and some medic scrubs." Zane shrugged. "I thought Omar would want his paintings."

Such a thing had never occurred to Levi. "Thanks for doing that for him, Zane. What else did Omar have? Any weapons?"

"No. He had the Owl costume and a bunch of art and paints, brushes and canvasses. A few letters from Shaylinn."

Jordan narrowed his eyes. "What kind of letters?"

"I didn't read them. They were from the Messenger, which I know was Shay, so... you know how she is."

"No, I don't," Jordan said. "She never sent me any Messenger letters. Why would she mail some to Omar?"

"If I can fit into that suit," Levi said, hoping to distract Jordan from his nonsensical issues with Omar, "what do I have to do?"

"I'll work on a script," Zane said. "We can say some of what we saw happen through the contact lenses. That Mason was liberated with only one X, that they were given an unfair trial. Stuff like that."

"And for Operation Lynchpin?" Levi asked. "How do we move that along?"

"All the food comes from the Lowlands," Ruston said. "We'll need to figure out how to stop the shipments. Water comes from the dam."

"So, we drive down to the Lowlands and see what's what," Jordan said. "See what we can burn."

"We're not going to *destroy* the food," Levi said. "I don't want to be responsible for thousands of people starving to death this winter. We just need to take control of it somehow."

"It won't be easy," Ruston said. "No one just drives to the Lowlands, not the way Highlanders can come into the Midlands, anyway. The road to the Lowlands leads outside the walls, so it's heavily guarded."

"Can you make fake SimTags with Lowlands information?" Levi asked Zane.

"Conceivably," Zane said. "I've never seen a Lowland SimTag, though. I'll ask my contact in Registration."

"Do you have any friends up at the dam?" Levi asked.

"No," Ruston said. "The dam is so far away from where we recruit that none of us have ever gotten to know anyone who tasks there."

"As I see it, we've got three goals," Levi said. "The Owl, the Lowlands, and the dam." It felt good to have a plan.

"It's a start, at least," Ruston said. "And if Jemma gave Renzor the information about the theater, that should distract the Guild from what we're really working on."

Levi took a deep breath through his nose, hating that Jemma had been the one to get caught. He should've insisted she stay behind. He shook his head—no use going over that territory again. She'd wanted to go. Had she leaked the location of the theater? They'd better not have hurt her.

Zane stood and walked toward the exit. "Let's go see if you can fit into that suit."

Levi followed him upstairs. The Owl suit was tight, but Omar had made it from an Old wetsuit, which was stretchy. It fit, and Levi was able to move surprisingly well. Once it was clear the mask also fit, he and Zane returned to the nest to record a new statement.

Once they finished the recording, Zane said, "I'll broadcast it tonight, in the middle of the liberation ceremony. The task director general will *love* that."

A chill ran up Levi's arms. This month's ceremony should include the prerecorded footage of Mason and Omar. And Bender and Rewl and General Otley, as well. Time was going by faster than Levi wanted it to. They'd been in the Safe Lands two and a half months already.

"Make sure to interrupt someone we don't know," Levi said. "I'd like to watch this one." Though he didn't know why. It would only make him upset.

That night, Levi and Jordan returned to the nest to watch the liberation ceremony. Levi sat in a chair beside Zane and focused on the big screen. Watching would provide no clue to his brothers' whereabouts, yet he stared at the screen, eager to see their faces.

The announcers, Finley Gray and Luella Flynn, both had silver hair and were wearing matching purple outfits, which meant that by tomorrow morning, purple would flood the streets and storefronts for mimics everywhere. Levi was glad to be underground.

The show opened with a tribute to Kendall Collin. Dozens of pictures flashed across the screen as Finley and Flynn took turns talking about the great times they'd had with the former Safe Lands queen. It was tragic that she'd been liberated so young, they said, but being a number one, she had many more lives to get it right. Best of luck to Kendall Collin in the next one.

It had been two and a half weeks since Kendall died and Levi's brothers had been captured. And two weeks had passed since Mason and Omar had been sentenced. But to everyone else watching, this was happening live.

"We should kidnap Luella Flynn and see what she knows about liberation," Jordan said.

"Now there's an interesting idea," Zane said. "Maybe the Owl should pay her a visit."

"I'm game." Levi bet that woman knew more than anyone about what went on in this place.

Luella brought out a man named Garber Bloom, the dancer who had taught Maroz Zerrik everything he knew—whoever Maroz Zerrik was. She introduced a video montage that showed clips from movies he'd been in, dancing and singing.

"Why are we watching this dung?" Jordan asked.

"It might be your last chance to see Mason and Omar," Zane said.

Jordan grunted, and Levi knew what he was thinking. "If by some miracle they're still alive, until we can learn the mystery of liberation, we can't help them." And maybe never could. Maybe whatever lay beyond liberation was a death camp. Welcome to Bliss. Mass murder. "But I still want to watch. That way I can know how to word what I say as the Owl so that I contradict what they say here."

"Fine," Jordan said. "It's a lot of fluffy nonsense, though. I can't imagine Luella Flynn interviewed Mason or Omar."

"She couldn't have. You never saw anything like that in their contacts feed, did you?" Levi asked Zane.

"Nope. They weren't important to the Safe Lands," Zane said. "We'll see their faces at the end and that's about it. They don't usually interview Xed people. Lonn was an exception."

"More like a warning," Levi said.

"Liberation has to be death," Jordan said.

It can't be death, Levi thought, trying to convince himself.

They suffered through another twenty minutes of the dancing man before Luella Flynn brought out a woman who'd tasked as a costume designer for twenty-two years. She got a standing ovation.

Jordan threw an apple core at the screen. It bounced off and left a wet mark across the glass.

Zane stood up. "Whoa!"

"*Jordan*," Levi said.

"Sorry, but why does this place think dancing and acting and fashion is better than every other job? Seems to me it's more work to task in construction or street cleaning or picking fields in the Lowlands. Why don't we ever see a pig farmer getting interviewed by Luella Flynn, huh?"

"Because pig farming and construction and street cleaning aren't glamorous," Levi said. "And perception of pleasure is all that matters here. They show us what they want us to like, hoping the viewers will love it and not ask where bacon comes from."

"That's not exactly true," Zane said, wiping the apple core streak from the wall screen with a rag. "There are some who are that naive, of course, but most know the guild is hiding things. They just go along with it because it's in their best interest not to ask questions."

"The truth is in everyone's best interest," Levi said. "And we have to find it."

"Shh!" Zane said. "It's General Otley."

A still image of Otley's face filled the screen. "Tyr Otley," Finley Gray said. "Best known as the young enforcer who took down the rebel group VIRUS in 2076, Otley kept our land safe as Enforcer General for the past nine years."

Jordan groaned. "And I wasted my apple core on the clothes woman."

"Why is Otley so far down the list?" Levi asked.

"Don't know," Zane said.

"Because he doesn't sing and dance," Jordan said.

Finley went on for a long while about how great Otley had been and how much the Safe Lands would miss him. Levi wondered how many Safe Landers were secretly glad Otley had been premie libbed.

When the Otley tribute ended, the camera showed a close-up of Luella Flynn's face. Her skin was silver and glittery, her eyes lime green. What a freak.

"Safe Landers, join me in a moment of silence to honor the following nationals who have passed on to the next life, including some nines who are entering Bliss. We send them our love and know that we'll see them soon."

Luella faded away, and the camera showed a wide shot of the amphitheater and the distant Wyndo stage screen, slowly zooming back in. The first face appeared on the screen. A man with dark hair and SimArt lines on his forehead.

"Jesmin Harres, six," Finley Gray said, "tasked in engineering and design. The Safe Lands bids you pleasure in the next life, Mr. Harres."

"August Liv, three," Luella said, "tasked as a level sixteen medic in the Men's Health and Wellness Department. The Safe Lands bids you pleasure in the next life, Mr. Liv."

"This is stupid," Jordan said. "How long are they going to make us wait?"

"I told you, they'll be on last," Zane said. "Nationals are ranked by celebrity status, so the Xed come at the very end."

"Bertram Grice, five," Finley Gray said, "enforcer, wall patrol unit. The Safe Lands bids you pleasure in the next life, Mr. Grice."

"Nella May, two," Luella said, "tasked as an educator in the Safe Lands boarding school. The Safe Lands bids you pleasure in the next life, Ms. May."

"Leon Jaff," Finley Gray said, "tasked as an educator in the Safe Lands boarding school. The Safe Lands bids you pleasure in the next life, Mr. Jaff."

"Do you think those teachers got liberated because we took the kids?" Levi asked.

"I wouldn't doubt it," Zane said.

Levi didn't know if he should feel sorry for them or not. He guessed not.

"Angel White," Luella said, "tasked as a matron in the Safe Lands nursery. The Safe Lands bids you pleasure in the next life, Ms. White."

"A nursery worker too," Levi said. "I bet she was the one who killed Kendall."

"More likely she's the one who didn't. Killing Kendall would have been seen as heroic by the guild," Zane said. "I doubt they liberated whoever pulled the trigger."

Jordan looked at Levi and frowned. "Can you believe that?"

In this place, Levi could believe just about anything.

Then Omar's face claimed the screen. The picture had been taken back when he was wearing an enforcer's uniform, complete with the hat. It reminded Levi of the Old Colorado State Patrol hat Omar used to wear every day. The look on his face was smug, captured back when he thought the people of Glenrock would benefit from life in the Safe Lands.

"Omar Strong, nine," Finley Gray said, "tasked with the enforcers, in SimArt design, and in construction. The Safe Lands bids you enjoy Bliss, Mr. Strong."

"Cavek Rose," Luella said, "tasked as a cook for Café Eats. The Safe Lands bids you pleasure in the next life, Mr. Rose."

"That's it for Omar?" Jordan asked. "He deserves more words than that! Those stinking maggots and their—"

"Jordan, look!" Levi gestured to the Wyndo screen.

"Bender," Finley Gray said, "a known rebel from the Midlands. No tasks on file, no full name, no number. The Safe Lands bids you pleasure, Mr. Bender, wherever you next find yourself."

"Wow," Levi said. "Not a word about his killing Otley." This place was bizarre. He'd never understand it.

Then Mason's face filled the screen.

"Mason Elias, nine," Luella said, "tasked in the Pharmco Pharmacy and as a level two medic in the Surrogacy Center. The Safe Lands bids you enjoy Bliss, Mr. Elias."

Tears filled Levi's eyes, and he blinked them back. He never should have let them go after Shaylinn without him. He'd known they weren't ready. But Ruston had convinced him. What did Ruston know about anything? His people hid underground with no desire to leave, shutting their eyes to the horrible realities above.

From now on, Levi would trust his own instincts.

"Time to interrupt the show," Zane said, tapping on his GlassTop keyboard.

The liberation broadcast blinked to black, then the Owl filled the screen—Levi, the Owl. Zane had given him a video background of the footage captured through Omar's eyes. It showed him getting stunned in the back of the truck and taken out on a stretcher.

"This is not an error," Levi's distorted voice said. "The Messenger Owl has truth to deliver to the people of the Safe Lands. Truth brings freedom. Listen well. Liberations are not peaceful. You are taken to a facility where you are strip-searched before being led into the unknown. This ColorCast is a tool for the Safe Lands Guild to tell lies. The Messenger Owl speaks the truth. There are not nine lives, but only one. Make yours count."

Behind Levi, the video through Omar's eyes continued to roll as he was set on the strange exam table and the enforcers started to undress him. The footage faded to black just as Levi stopped talking.

Zane tapped back to the liberation ceremony where Finley Gray was on screen.

"On this, the first day of September," Finley Gray said, "there are still fourteen people in the Safe Lands who will be celebrating their liberation in what remains of 2088. If you know one of them, take the time to enjoy them while they're here. For it won't be long until they head into the next life."

"From us to you, Happy Liberation Day, Safe Landers," Luella Flynn said. "We'll see you next month. And as always, find pleasure in life."

Zane muted the volume as the broadcast went to commercial.

"That was incredible," Jordan said. "What you did with the contacts video..."

Levi had to agree. Zane's abilities never ceased to impress. "Surely it made Renzor mad."

"Well, it's all we had," Zane said. "I can use it again with different words, but you're going to have to find something just as good to keep people watching."

How was Levi going to find something new? "Don't we have what Mason's eyes saw?"

"Lhogan isn't answering my taps," Zane said. "So, I only have what was on my screen at the time, which was Omar's viewpoint."

Levi would have to don the Owl suit again, and soon.

"We must have missed Rewl's picture," Jordan said. "Bender was a natural, and they put him on the show."

"As a warning," Zane said. "And because Bender was alive when they recorded this. Rewl is a dead ghost no one will miss."

Which was what they'd all be if they got themselves killed.

"Levi!" Shaylinn ran toward him as he entered his underground house, her face tear-streaked. "The liberation ceremony was on. We watched on my Wyndo. They showed Omar and Mason and Bender and Kendall."

Levi looked around the living room. Everyone was sitting on the couches, staring at a portable Wyndo that was propped up on the coffee table. "All of you watched it?"

"I thought they might have said something about the Owl," Trevon said, "but then the Owl came on! That means wherever Omar is, he's okay!"

Levi bit his cheek. Should he tell the kids that he was Omar's Owl now? No, he couldn't take away their hope. "Listen, I don't want any of you watching the ColorCast. There's not supposed to be any technology down here. It could be dangerous."

"I'm sorry," Shaylinn said. "Am I supposed to give back my Wyndo?"

"Ruston didn't say. Either way, showing the children the ColorCast wasn't a responsible thing to do."

Tears pooled in Shaylinn's eyes. "I wanted to see Omar."

"I understand," Levi said. What else could he say? "But I don't want anyone watching Safe Lands TV. Including you." He snatched up the Wyndo from the coffee table. "I'll just hold on to this until I talk with Ruston. He may not want this down here. I know his wife wouldn't."

"But how will I research people to send messages to?"

"Shaylinn, forget sending messages, will you? Focus on helping Eliza teach these kids."

"Okay." Her voice sounded so desperately sad that Levi felt like a jerk. Still, he carried the Wyndo into his room and tossed it on the bed. He needed to keep his people from indulging in Safe Lands entertainment. The more they liked this place, the harder it would be to leave when the time came, which, Levi hoped, would be very soon.

Chapter 14

Friday night, Omar climbed into his bunk and pretended to be sick. He didn't want to go to Fajro anymore, but he was too chicken to just up and quit.

Faking illness wasn't all that difficult. He'd earned a second vial of brown sugar from Rain last Wednesday for talking with Cacia. So, he'd let himself finish off his first as a reward for a job well done. But that had only increased his craving. He hadn't loaded his new vial yet in fear he'd down the whole thing. Instead, he'd spent all his credits on a hit level two of grass, which he'd nursed for the past two days and was almost gone. The aches and trembling had returned as his body cried out for the sugar.

Kurwin peeked over the side of Omar's bunk. "You can't just skip."

Omar answered with a pathetic moan.

"Rain isn't going to like it. Prav either."

Prav? What did he have to do with it? Omar wanted to ask. Instead, he waited, hoping Kurwin would leave and give Rain the message that Omar was ill.

"You better not make a habit of it," Kurwin said and left.

Omar stayed in bed, taking little puffs of grass and letting it calm his nerves. He didn't dare leave the room in case someone saw him out. He was exhausted anyway, so going to bed early was probably for the best.

He lay there savoring each breath of grass and thinking about Shaylinn, wondering where she was, how she was doing, if her belly had grown yet, if the babies were okay, if they were boys or girls or one of each.

He fell asleep with those thoughts lingering in his mind, thoughts of Shaylinn and children and a life he'd never live.

"Get up, you shell!"

Pain blasted through Omar's jaw. He opened his eyes. Prav was straddling him, hand raised to strike again.

"Don't!" Omar cringed and lifted his hands between them.

"Don't you tell me don't, you lazy juicer." Prav slapped Omar's chest. "I don't care if you're puking your guts out. Tonight, you come to Fajro. No excuses."

"Okay!"

Prav gave him one last shove before climbing off and jumping to the floor. Omar massaged his jaw as he watched Prav stride into the bathroom. Walls, that guy was intense.

Omar's SimAlarm buzzed, telling him he had ten minutes to be up and out of the building. No time to shower. He'd slept in his jumpsuit, so he climbed down and shoved his feet into his boots.

"You shouldn't have skipped," Kurwin whispered. "I told you Prav wouldn't like it."

"Why should he care?"

"Because he brought you to Rain. He stuck his neck out for you, and she invested in you. If you turn out to be worthless, she'll get mad at Prav for wasting her time."

"Oh." Omar didn't want to be anywhere near Prav right now. "See you later." He darted out the door. His jaw ached, and his stomach roiled with hunger. Credits were applied each morning for the previous day's work, so Omar jogged down to the cafeteria and went through the line for two dry pancakes and a banana. He ate them on his walk to the pens.

It looked like he was going to have to go to Fajro tonight. That, or deal with Prav. Neither option sounded very pleasant.

When Omar entered Fajro that evening, he was surprised to find it crowded so early. He stood in the doorway, paralyzed, uncertain if he should stay or run. He glanced back to the table where he and Kurwin always sat and drank. It was filled with people he didn't know. Customers.

"You're late."

He jerked out of his thoughts, and his gaze fell on Rain. She was wearing purple tonight, and once again her lipstick didn't match. That suddenly annoyed him. Why couldn't she see how the shades clashed?

"Go change."

Omar walked past the beaded curtain. He changed into a waxy blue shirt and black pants. When he came back out, Rain was standing at the doorway, holding the beads aside.

She nodded across the room. "She's waiting for you."

Omar followed her gesture to a booth where Cacia sat. Omar sighed as weight melted away from his heart. Another night of talking? No problem.

He ducked under the doorway, and Rain let the beads fall shut. They clicked against each other and the doorframe, oddly sounding like rain on a window.

Omar walked over to the booth and sat down. "Cacia."

"Hay-o, you." She grinned and bounced in her seat. Omar didn't like her flirty tone. She hadn't been like that last week. "I'm feeling better, thanks to you."

"That's good."

"I thought we could go out. There's this dance club I like called the Dexx. Then we can go back to my place."

Omar tried to keep his expression calm, but he felt his eyes swell. He hoped she hadn't noticed. "Uh, I haven't been feeling well. I'd hate for you to catch something."

She leaned back in the booth and crossed her arms. "I'm not that old, you know."

"I never said you were old."

"I know an excuse when I hear one. Well, guess what, raven boy? I paid for you, and I paid until your curfew."

Oh, walls. Omar's stomach turned to stone. He gritted his teeth. "My mistake. Dancing it is." He got up and strode to the bar, where he ordered a beer. The barkeep had just pushed it toward him when Cacia appeared at his side with Rain.

Omar picked up the beer and took a big gulp. He held the glass at his chest and looked at the women. "What? I need a beer before I dance, okay?"

Rain raised one eyebrow, then glanced at Cacia. "He'll behave."

Behave. As if this woman owned him. She may as well get a collar and leash.

He chugged the rest of his beer and left the glass on the counter. "So where are we going?"

"I told you," Cacia said. "The Dexx. It's on the classy side of Cibelo."

The Lowlands had a classy side? Omar went with Cacia to the club. It was dark, with red lights shining down from the ceiling onto a packed crowd, the silhouettes of waving arms and bobbing heads all facing the stage where a live band was playing.

Cacia pulled him by the hand along the back of the crowd. "The dancing is over here."

He plodded along behind her, but his attention was on the stage. There were four in the band. Two men and two women, all in their mid-fifties, perhaps? They had chartreuse-and-violet FloArt tattoos that glowed like light under their skin. Three of them played guitars, though the instruments looked nothing like the one Uncle Ethan used to play in Glenrock. These were thin glass. The fourth band member—a woman—was sitting down at a GlassTop, tapping her hands on the surface in the beat of the percussion. They all must have had some sort of amplified SimSpeak, as their voices rang out from all sides of the club.

Cacia stopped suddenly and started to dance—at least that's what Omar suspected she was trying to do. He tried not to laugh at her obvious lack of rhythm. She wiggled and kicked and waved her arms, but it looked more like she was trying to shake out an itch than dance.

She looked happy, though. Maybe if he could keep her here long enough, she'd forget about going back to her apartment.

Omar tried to enjoy himself. And there were moments—brief ones—where he completely forgot that he'd sold himself for brown sugar. Like when he thought about

Shaylinn or when the band played a slow song and the man's voice seemed to carry him into a dream.

Cacia said she wanted a drink, grabbed his arm, and dragged him toward the exit.

"But the bar is that way," Omar yelled, pointing behind him.

"I have drinks at my place," she said. "We're running out of time."

Right. Because Omar had a curfew. If he wasn't back at a certain time, his SimTag alarm would go off.

Omar followed her, dumbly, a slave to his vice. Would he never make the right choice?

She didn't live far from the club. Her apartment was small—all in one room. But it was clean, and she didn't have to share it with anyone. Not like Omar did, anyway. Or poor Mason.

She gave Omar a bottle of beer from her fridge and urged him to sit on the couch. They sat side by side, drinking.

Omar stared straight ahead. He wanted to leave, but how could he? What were his options? Stay with her and get paid with a vial of brown sugar, or leave and get beat up by Prav—and get no brown sugar.

There had to be another way.

She took the beer from his hand and set it with hers on a table beside the couch. Then she turned back to him. "Kiss me."

To be fair, she wasn't ugly, not like some of the women he'd seen Prav leave Fajro with. Maybe if he didn't think about what he was doing… Or he could pretend she was someone else. Shaylinn?

No, not Shaylinn. Someone who didn't matter. Red or Belbeline. If he pretended he was with one of them, perhaps he could get through this.

He closed his eyes and pressed his lips against hers. She grabbed his head, his neck, his shoulders, pawing at him with clammy, bone-like hands. He recoiled at her touch.

Lord, help me, please. I'm sorry I got myself into this.

Cacia pulled away from him and groaned like he was the most disappointing date she'd ever had. "Don't just sit there. Do something. Why are you such a prude?"

He stood up. "I'm going to leave."

"What? Why? You can't."

"I'm sorry, Cacia. You're a nice person, but I can't do this. Besides, I like someone else."

"So?" Her tone dripped with indifference.

"Don't you remember what I said about love? Well, this isn't it. You and I, we can be friends. But you can't force it to be something it's not."

She stood up, toe to toe, and glared at him. "I can do whatever I want. I paid good credits for you. And I own you for another forty-five minutes."

"Nobody owns me." Omar walked to the door and opened it. "I'm sure Rain will give you a refund." And then have Prav turn Omar's face into a pile of guts worthy of the incinerator.

He slipped out into the hallway and quickly shut the door behind him. He grinned, which was stupid, because now he was in trouble.

The door to Cacia's apartment opened, and Omar jogged down the hall.

"Get back here!" she yelled after him.

But he slipped down the stairwell and out of sight. He didn't slow down. He had no desire to have her chase after him and make a scene.

What now? He headed across Cibelo on his way to the strikers' residence. But going back would only put him in Prav's path. He wandered around, trying to decide what to do. Maybe he should just go back and tell Rain he quit? Take his beating and be done with it.

He found himself outside the Get Out Now Diner, but he didn't recognize anyone inside. He wondered if these people were rebels. The thought made him think of the RC. If he missed curfew, they'd take him there, right? He'd have a private cell and maybe even a mercy vape.

He never thought he'd actually look forward to spending a night in prison. But right now, prison looked pretty good.

Since he was wearing Rain's raven clothing, he entered a club on his own and watched people dance, knowing it was close to curfew. He sat at the bar for a bit, but he didn't want to spend what little credits he had on anything, so he went back to the dance floor rather than have to deal with dirty looks from the barkeep.

He wished he had his PV. He'd left it in his pillowcase so he wouldn't be tempted to finish it, saving his meager puffs for long nights. But he was wound up now from stress and fear and not knowing what was going to happen when he didn't go back to his bunk.

His SimAlarm pulsed with the ten-minute warning. Ten minutes and he'd break curfew. Thankfully, he wasn't wearing an orange jumpsuit, so he wouldn't stand out as a striker to the reputables. But where should he go?

He decided on a bench at the end of a narrow street of shops since it was somewhat secluded. That way when his alarm went off, he wouldn't make a scene. Most of the shops were closed as they weren't the kinds of places that got a lot of customers at this time of night. A cleaner, a cosmetics store, and a messenger's office.

He thought of Shaylinn and wondered if she was still sending her messages. He suddenly ached with indignation at his lot in life. Sure, he'd done it to himself. But he'd been trying to fix his life, and now he was here. And Shay was there. It was probably for the best. He'd hurt her enough. He hated the idea of her raising the babies on her own, but maybe Nodin would marry her. Or Yivan. They were decent-enough fellows.

The SimAlarm went off then, delivering as much current as any SimScanner or stunner could. Omar's body seized, and he fell onto his side on the bench. Little grunts came out of his throat, though he was trying not to make any noise. He closed his eyes and pictured Shay's burnt-umber eyes until he passed out.

"Hey! What's the problem here, shell? You OD?"

Omar opened his eyes and found an enforcer looking down on him. He jerked, slid on the bench a little, and pushed himself up. He could move. What time was it? How long had he been here?

The enforcer held out a SimScanner and Omar heard it beep. "Omar Strong. He's a striker."

"Where's your jumpsuit, striker? Those are awfully nice clothes."

"You got a girl buying you glossy things? Or are you a streetman?"

"Can't you talk?" the other said. "Stand up. We need to search you."

Omar pushed up on shaky legs. The weakness hadn't fully faded yet.

The enforcer patted Omar's body, running his hands along Omar's back, sides, hips, pockets, and legs. "No PV. No vials either. Shame, I was looking to help myself to some treats tonight, striker boy."

"He can still buy us something," the other enforcer said.

The one with the SimScanner read Omar's SimTag again. "He's got nine credits."

"That's it? That's pathetic. You spend it all on that fancy outfit?"

"I thought you were going to take me to the RC," Omar said.

"Oh, you want to go to the RC, is that it? Someone back in the bunkhouse have you scared?"

Clearly, he wasn't the first striker to try this. "No. I just thought that's what happens."

"What's your address, shell?"

Omar didn't say anything.

"Stupid, stubborn strikers."

The other chortled. "Say that three times fast."

The enforcer used his SimScanner again. "Sector six. Strikers' residence. 318. Cohabs are Vita, Jeorn, Arling... Prav." He grinned. "Oh, yes. It's Prav who's got you scared, I bet."

"Then let's take him to Prav."

"What? No! I missed curfew, and the liberator told me I'd have to see the warden."

But the enforcers didn't care. They dragged Omar to the strikers' residence and right up to the door to his room.

Where Prav was waiting.

"Missing someone?" the enforcer asked.

"Yes, actually." Prav lifted one fist and, with a squeeze, cracked several knuckles. "I've been waiting for this shell."

"You want to do it out here?" the enforcer asked.

Omar caught sight of Kurwin's wincing expression through the cracked-open door. "Do what?"

Prav held out his hand. "I would, thanks."

"Do what?" Omar asked again, fear making his pulse throb. "Prav, what's this about, peer?" Buddy? Pal?

The second enforcer used his SimScanner on Prav's hand, and Prav walked out into the hallway. His SimAlarm didn't go off for being out of his room after curfew.

"I warned you, didn't I?" Prav asked.

Omar swallowed. "Prav, come on. I just can't do it, okay? I gave it a shot but..." He tried to pull away from the enforcer. He pushed. Grabbed at the man's hands and pried his clamped fingers open. Just as he slipped free, Prav grabbed Omar's shoulder, turned him, and his fist shot out and clipped Omar's jaw.

Omar's head jerked back. Throbbing fire engulfed his face. He stumbled against the wall and grabbed it to keep from falling.

Once his footing was steady, he palmed his jaw. Okay... pain, but nothing seemed broken. He glanced up.

Prav was staring down, a sneer on his face. "You don't get off *that* easy."

Omar lifted his arm to block his face, and Prav's fist rammed into his stomach. Omar groaned and doubled over, hugging his gut. He gasped for breath, but had barely managed to inhale when Prav struck him again, this time in the side. Omar tottered, off balance, and fell on the floor. The cold tile felt nice on his cheek but stank of urine and bleach at the same time.

Why did the enforcers just stand there? And why did no one watching through the yellow cameras come to help?

"You're pathetic," Prav said. "Aren't you even going to try to fight back?"

"Do... what... you have to." Omar choked in a breath. "I'm not... tasking for Rain again."

"If you insist." Prav grabbed Omar's sleeve and dragged him into the middle of the hallway. "Why don't you give me a hand with this, peers."

Without mercy, the three men beat Omar with their fists and feet until every inch of him had been bruised or jabbed or clawed or kicked. He curled into a ball and tried to make himself smaller, but that didn't end the pain.

At some point he awoke. He was being carried through the door of his room. The enforcers had his legs, Prav the underside of his arms. They pushed him up onto his bunk and left him there. The door opened and closed. Then the lights went off.

Omar lay in the darkness. Over his own choked breaths, he could hear Prav settling into his bunk. He dared not move. His body felt like someone had peeled off the skin and dipped him in salt. He burned. He ached. Something was bleeding. He was pretty sure he was dying.

Why die in pain when he could fly?

Though his muscles protested, he reached up inside his pillowcase and found his PV and the vial of brown sugar he'd earned last week talking to Cacia. He couldn't see, but he'd done this enough that he didn't need light. He popped out the nearly empty vial of grass and replaced it with the brown sugar.

He couldn't take it all in one breath, but two should do the trick. Then it would all be over. His hand was shaking as he lifted the PV to his lips.

Good-bye, Shay-Shay.

His first vape was long. He breathed the juice all the way into his toes. He held his breath through the nausea, waiting for it to carry him into the blissful warmth. The rush had never been as good as that first time, but when it finally came, it melted all the pain off his body. He was safe in this place. Nothing hurt here.

A flash of white mist formed around him, so thick he couldn't see past the edge of his bed. Above, the ceiling sparkled and glitter began to rain down. He closed his eyes, and he was driving his old motorcycle down the forest road toward Glenrock. Going home. The sky was white above stark branches. Suddenly the road was covered in snow.

Up ahead, a man was standing on the road. Not a man, but a face. A giant face twice as big as Omar was tall. It was God's face, he somehow knew, frowning, daring Omar to stand before him and be judged. A path branched off the road, and Omar steered the motorcycle onto it, leaving God behind him.

Something clumped on the floor across the room. He opened his eyes and found himself still shrouded in white mist. His bed shook. Someone was climbing up the ladder. No! He would do this his way. His heart fluttered, and he vaped another long drag.

As he clenched against the nausea, the white mist darkened to gray. Then black. Smoky tendrils drifted toward him, coiled around his legs and arms, his waist. He thought about his motorcycle again, closed his eyes, tried to picture the road in the forest.

The tingling came, and he was riding again down the dark road. Something was racing him, trying to fly past. An owl? It was big and black. Not a bird. It had arms. The sky was dark now and there was no snow. He sped down a dirt path, his headlight casting a faint glow. And still the creature came, sometimes on his right, sometimes on his left, sometimes above, behind, down by the tires. A flying, hooded shadow. Faceless. Chasing him. Reaching out.

The road vanished and the motorcycle dove into a chasm. But the chasm became the shadow monster, arms grasping, prickly and clawed.

And Omar saw no more.

Chapter 15

“I don’t understand why you’re still so upset.” Penelope was sitting beside Shaylinn on a bench in Kindred Park, watching the children play. “You never really watched the ColorCast, did you?”

“No,” Shaylinn said. “But I used it to research people so I could write them messages that gave them hope. And now I can’t.” Levi had taken away her link to the Safe Lands. Writing messages had given her a sense of purpose and meaning in this place. Granted, she hadn’t written any in almost three weeks. The move underground had distracted her. But now that she couldn’t, she was angry.

“Just tell him you want it back.”

“I tried. He said I didn’t need to be writing messages anymore.”

“Sounds like *he* needs a message,” Penelope said. “It’s not fair. He treats us like children, but he makes us take care of the little kids. We’re doing the work of mothers, but we’re not getting any of the respect. He never used to be like this.”

“I think he’s afraid. For Jemma. For all of us. And fear makes people think that if things are done a certain way, bad stuff won’t happen. But that’s silly, because we aren’t the ones in control. We just have to have faith everything will work out.-hat scum can manipulate the words and images from her experience before.s coming?s her blush at the fact all the envelopes hav”

“Like with you and Omar,” Penelope said. “Did he really kiss you?”

It hurt to think about Omar. “I told you, I kissed his cheek. That was all.”

“Right. And he kissed Kendall. Do you think he loved her?”

What an irritating question. “He said he didn’t. But, Penny, it doesn’t matter. He’s been liberated. Maybe he’s dead.” Shaylinn didn’t want to talk about this again, but Penelope kept bringing it up.

“Of course it matters! You have to have faith, like you said.”

“I have faith… mostly. But if he isn’t— Until Omar comes back, there’s no point in dwelling on everything that’s happened. That would be like torturing myself.” Not that she hadn’t been, but she was trying not to. “But that’s why I need to write messages. Even if I take care of the children all day and help Eliza teach and cook all the meals for Levi’s household, there’s that time when I first wake up or right before I go to bed. I could write messages then. I want to.”

"Then do it for the people you've already written to. Don't worry about trying to find new addresses. Just be loyal to the ones you've got."

That was a good idea. "But how will they get delivered? Levi won't help me. And forget Jordan. He thinks I should be sewing baby clothes for my children twenty-four seven. I already used the entire bag of fabric Omar gave me." The memory of him giving her the fabric made her eyes prickle, and she blinked to keep the tears away.

"How many clothes does Jordan think a baby needs?"

Shaylinn shrugged. "Plus, I'll have his son's hand-me-downs."

"Why don't you ask that guy to help you?" Penelope pointed at the playground. On the other side of the slide, having just walked in through the corridor on that end, Nash stood talking to Trevon and Grayn.

"Zane's brother? I suppose I could." But Ciddah thought Nash liked Shaylinn, so she didn't want to encourage him. The few times they'd met, he'd been overly friendly.

He saw them then, and waved, though he continued talking to the boys. Shaylinn waved back.

Penelope grabbed Shaylinn's arm. "He'd be perfect, Shay, because he can go upside but he's not from Glenrock."

Which likely meant he wouldn't feel obligated to tell Levi. Not that Omar had told Levi about Shaylinn's messages, but Omar had liked keeping things from his brother.

"He's coming!" Penelope whispered. "Quick, talk about something interesting."

"Was I boring you before?"

Penelope started to laugh, a strange, fake laugh that was overly loud and turned the heads of most of the kids on the playground.

Shaylinn stifled a groan. "You like him, don't you?" Penelope used to act this way whenever Levi had brought Nodin to the village. "I thought you liked Nodin."

Penelope's eyes bulged. "Shhh!"

Shaylinn couldn't believe how silly her friend was being. "Hello, Nash," she called out. "We were just talking about you."

"No!" Penelope tried to put her hand over Shaylinn's mouth.

"Stop it." Shaylinn shot Penelope a glare. Why would she assume Shaylinn was going to try to embarrass her?

Nash stopped in front of them and looked from Penelope's face to Shaylinn's, back and forth. His lips curved in a slow smile. "It was all good, I hope?"

"We weren't talking about you." Penelope's cheeks were beet red.

"Penny suggested I ask you a favor," Shaylinn said. "When I was hiding in the Midlands, I wrote messages to people who'd expressed interest in the rebellion. I wanted to do something that would cheer and inspire and give hope to those who needed it. Omar delivered them for me, but now that I'm down here and Omar... I have no way to deliver them."

"You're the messenger girl?" His eyes lit up, and his smile grew even wider, though that seemed impossible. "Zane told me about you. I think that's amazing. I'd love to help. On one condition."

Shaylinn held her breath and glanced at Penelope.

"You have to write me a message too," Nash said. "I want to see for myself what's so powerful about these words of yours."

Relief settled over Shaylinn. "Of course I'll write to you. Thank you."

Again the wide smile. "Well, my mother is waiting for me, so I should go. But, hey, I have my own house. It's in block eight, between the greenhouses and the gym. The number is 8–2. Bring your letters by anytime. I don't lock the door."

"Thank you," Shaylinn said, excited that she'd have a way to deliver her messages again.

"I look forward to that message." He winked, then waved and walked away.

"'I look forward to that message,'" Penelope said in a mocking voice. "'Bring your letters by anytime. I don't lock the door.'"

Shaylinn glared at her friend. "Why are you doing that?"

Penelope folded her arms. "Because it's obvious that he's in love with you."

"He is not."

"Is too."

"Penny, I can tell that Nash likes me a little. But he doesn't know me at all."

"He wants to."

"Perhaps. But that's not love. Jemma told me love is hard work, not just thinking someone is cute. I love Omar." And that really *was* hard work.

"No one will ever love me," Penelope said. "Nodin is pledged to marry Alawa, and Nash likes you."

And Shaylinn suddenly knew why she was so frustrated. Penelope hadn't changed. But Shaylinn's time in the harem, the babies, Omar... those experiences had forced her to grow up sooner than she might have liked. Penelope had gone to the boarding school with the other children and had seen girls and boys in superficial relationships. Shaylinn could try and offer advice, but she wasn't sure Penelope had the experience to understand.

"Penny, love isn't all butterflies in your stomach and staring into each other's eyes. Eventually, someone will mess up. And that hurts, trust me. Loving someone means accepting him, faults and all."

"Don't lecture me, Shay. I'm not stupid. Just don't steal Nash from me. I saw him first."

Which was totally untrue. Shaylinn had seen Nash while Penelope was still living in the boarding school. "I have no intention of stealing Nash. I told you: I love Omar."

"I know. But Omar is... If he doesn't come back, you'll want a husband to help with the babies."

"Stop it! You already promised to help me with the babies. Why are you doing this?"

"Don't yell at me. You're not that much older."

Shaylinn took a deep breath. "I'm sorry I yelled. I promise I won't steal Nash, okay?"

"Thank you. And I'm sorry I said Omar might not come back. Hug?"

Shaylinn accepted Penelope's peace offering and the two embraced. It seemed to heal all of Penelope's worries, but for Shaylinn, it only confirmed how much they'd changed.

The thought made her feel tired and lonely. But at least she'd have her messages to occupy her mind.

Two days later, Shaylinn had her letters ready to send. She wasn't supposed to wander the basements alone, but she couldn't risk anyone knowing what she was doing—especially not Nell, who couldn't keep a secret to save her life. From the tour Levi had given when they'd first come to the basements, she remembered that she could get to the gym from the corridor by Ruston's house. So, she walked that way, seeking to avoid the park and school and the other houses that people from Glenrock were living in.

Unfortunately, there were boys in the gym playing basketball. Shaylinn recognized some of the older boys from her day in the Kindred school. She clutched her package of letters tightly and jogged across the center of the gym.

Someone whistled, which made the hair stand up on the back of her neck.

"Hey, upsider. Over here!"

Shaylinn didn't stop, didn't look his way. She reached the other side of the gym and yanked open the door. Once she was on the other side, in the dimness of the corridor, she relaxed. She hoped no one had recognized her or would tell Ruston they'd seen her.

The first alcove on her right was numbered 8–8. Then 8–7 on her left. She passed by 8–6 and 8–5, then 8–4 and 8–3. She could see the door at the end of the corridor and the word GREENHOUSE written above it, but right before it was the final alcove, 8–2. She knocked, hoping Nash wasn't home and that she could slip inside and leave the letters on his table or something.

When no one answered, she turned the knob. Sure enough, the door opened. Shaylinn went in, but it was too dark to see. She caught the door that was swinging shut behind her and held it open until she found a light switch. The lights flickered on overhead. She let the front door shut completely and stepped inside.

She was standing in an enclosed entryway. It was no bigger than a half bathroom, and had a coatrack on one side and shelves on the other that were filled with planters in dozens of sizes. There must have been a thousand the way they were stacked and crammed on the shelves.

There was a second door, so Shaylinn knocked on it before entering. She cracked the door a little, and a sweet and powerful smell enveloped her. "Hello?"

This next room wasn't dark, but it glowed with electric white light. She crept inside and lost her breath.

Flowers and plants. On every surface, on the floor along the walls, and even hanging from the ceiling. The heady smells of blossoms mixed with the tangy scents of greens. She could smell hyssop, basil, and lavender the most. She wandered inside, scanning the room for the purple blossoms she loved so much.

She found a pot of lavender hanging against the wall where the kitchen counter ended. She buried her face in the slender stalks and breathed them in. Lovely.

She stepped back and tried to take in the house itself. The first thing she noticed was that it was clean. Spotless, really. Not a dish in the sink or the dish rack. The floors were swept, even under the plants on the floor that were growing in big pots of soil. Electric lights lit the room in a soft white glow. Some hung from the ceiling, some were floor lamps, and some hooked to the wall with cords running down to the plugs that were closer to the floor. There was no Wyndo wall screen here. No electronics of any type.

She wasn't sure what she'd expected Nash's house to look like inside, but this wasn't it.

Curiosity pulled her feet into the kitchen. Even his sink was empty. Beside it, a few still-wet dishes lay drying on a towel. A potted freesia sat on the other side of the sink. Shaylinn bent to smell the blossoms and noticed a portable Wyndo tucked between the freesia pot and the wall. Levi said such things weren't allowed in the basements.

"Looking for something?"

Shaylinn screamed and dropped her package of messages. She spun around and saw Nash standing behind her.

"Shaylinn, I'm sorry." He lunged to her feet and picked up the package of messages, studied it, then looked at her, eyebrows raised.

She'd wrapped all thirty-two envelopes in a scrap of the printed ducky fabric Omar had given her for making baby clothes. Did Nash think that was silly? Why did she care?

Nash held out the package, but she waved him back. "Those are my messages. I'm sorry I came in here when you weren't home. Your plants are so beautiful. Did you grow them yourself?"

"Yes. I picked this place since it was closest to the greenhouses. I work there when I'm not running errands for my dad or Zane. Or my mother."

"How long have you lived on your own?"

"Two years. Since I turned eighteen."

He was twenty. He'd told her that already. He was six years older than Shaylinn. Five and a half, really. It was still a lot. But Eliza had married Mark when she was eighteen and he was twenty-seven. That was nine years' difference.

Why was she thinking about marriage? Penelope had turned her back into a silly child. "Do you have any favorites? Of the plants, I mean."

"The ficus." He gestured to a green fern-like tree beside the sofa. "It was one of the first things I ever planted myself. It's sort of my baby. And the freesia." He pointed behind her. "I had two that turned out that nice. Gave the other to my mother."

"It's really beautiful."

"Thank you. Did you see my lavender plant?"

"I did. Lavender is my favorite, so my nose led me right to it."

"You should take it, then. I doubt there are any plants in Levi's house."

"Oh, I couldn't take your plant."

"Don't you think I have enough?" He winked. "I'm happy to share." He set the package of messages on the kitchen table and walked to the lavender plant. He unhooked it from the ceiling, then set it on the low table between the couch and chair.

"There. You take that with you when you leave."

"Thank you." She should leave now, but she didn't want to be rude.

"So, show me these messages," Nash said. "And you have one for me, right?"

"Yes." She walked to the table and pulled the yarn string that held the package together. She unwrapped the stack of letters. "Yours is on the top, but you can't read it while I'm here." That would be so embarrassing.

He took the letter in his hands and stared at the front. It was a plain white envelope like all the others, but rather than an address on the front, his simply said "Nash" in Shaylinn's loopy handwriting. "Shaylinn, I wonder if you'd be willing to write to my brother."

"Zane?"

"Well, him too, if you'd like, but I meant Tym. He's at a fragile age, and he's being pulled between my mother's fear and his love for Zane. I'm not asking you to take sides, but you said you like to give hope and encouragement, and, well, I think he could use some."

"I'd be honored to write to him. Do you think your mother would mind?"

He shrugged and gave her a shy smile. "She won't know. And even if she finds the message, she won't know it's from you."

Shaylinn didn't want to start another war with Tova. "Will you at least ask your father? I don't think it's appropriate for me to write messages to children I don't know unless one of their parents gives permission."

"I'll ask him." He set down his letter and met her eyes. "I appreciate your caution. Down here, most people are concerned with the rules but not because they care about people's feelings. They only care about obedience. You care about people more than yourself. And I like that very much."

CHAPTER 16

Before Mason could start building a hot-air balloon, he needed to determine two things: what type of fabric would work best and how much he would need. The ideal fabric would be lightweight, nonporous, and heat- and flame-resistant, like the kind of fabric once used in tents or umbrellas but with protection against fire.

Mason had no idea where he could get such fabric.

And then there was the amount. He needed only to lift the weight of one man and only as high as the wall, which he estimated to be about one hundred feet high. But there were a lot of other factors to consider, like the temperature outside, the wind, how the rider would keep the balloon from rising too high, and how he would land it.

For now, he concentrated on the size of the balloon. It was the second week of September, and while it was still rather warm during the days, the nights were cool. Yet it would take some time to sew together the balloon—at least a month—and the October nights would be even colder. Mason guessed it would be between 20ºF and 30ºF. Such cold air would also affect the lift rate of a hot-air balloon.

All that, Mason had figured out rather quickly, but it took him much longer to work out the equation to determine the size of the balloon. After much trial and error, he surmised that the volume of the balloon that would lift one man would need to be about $500m^3$. That would give him a radius of about four meters, which would give him a surface area of around $200m^2$.

That was a lot of fabric. Mason had no idea how to get so much of it, short of purchasing two hundred umbrellas and dismantling them.

That was a lot of umbrellas too.

He went back to the G.I.N. and scoured the store. There was no fabric at all. Plenty of umbrellas though. But then he spotted one item that might change everything: waterproofing spray. It wasn't cheap, and it wouldn't protect against fire, but perhaps Mason could use it on cotton bed sheets. It would be heavier than the nylon, but it just might work.

A week later, Mason was walking pen twelve when a human scream rose over the braying cattle. Mason scanned the browns and blacks until he caught sight of an orange jumpsuit on the ground in the second row, surrounded by four-legged animals.

Mason ran out of the pen, climbed over the cattle lane, and sprinted across the feed alley. He slipped inside pen thirty, taking a wide berth from the victim in hopes that he wouldn't herd the cows closer to him.

"What happened?" a farmhand yelled, running up to the fence between pens twenty-nine and thirty.

Mason hadn't met this farmhand. He knew only the taskers in the first row. "I don't know. I heard a scream and saw him on the ground."

"Miks ran for help, but I didn't hear what he yelled at me."

Mason started along the fence on the far side. Cows ambled out of his way. As he closed the gap between him and the injured farmhand, he heard the moaning. The man was alive and conscious. Then he saw the familiar tattooed head. The sight stabbed a thrill of fear into Mason's gut.

Scorpion.

He crouched at the man's side. At first glance, he couldn't see any injuries. There was no blood. No rips in his jumpsuit or dirty hoof prints. "Where does it hurt?"

Scorpion gasped, his face drawn with pain. "My foot."

The other farmhand had climbed over the fence and joined Mason. "What happened to your horse?" he asked.

"Miks needed a hand," Scorpion said. "A steer had its leg caught in a coil of wire."

"Which foot did you injure?" Mason asked.

"My right."

Mason took a good look at Scorpion's boot. It was flattened unnaturally at the heel. He didn't dare try and take it off. He needed to get the man out of here. But did he really want to help *this* man? He bit back his hesitation. It didn't matter who was hurt. Doctors took an oath to help others. Mason was no different.

"Should we take off his boot and see what's wrong?" the farmhand asked.

"No," Mason said. "His heel looks crushed. I don't want to touch anything until a medic can take a look. We need to take him to the medical center. Help me get him up." Mason moved to Scorpion's left and put his arm around the man's waist. The farmhand crouched on his other side, and together they managed to get Scorpion standing on his good leg.

Scorpion had to hop, but they moved, slowly, toward the fence.

Gacy was waiting for them. "Should I call Enforcer 10?"

"No!" Scorpion said. "It's no big deal." Though he looked paler than usual beneath his SimArt, and his face was sweaty.

"He's pretty bad off," Mason said.

"Then take him to the MC," Gacy said. "I'll drive you to the tram."

Mason helped Scorpion into Gacy's truck, and Gacy drove them to the sector five tram station. Then, step by step, hop by hop, Mason helped Scorpion down to the station.

Once they were settled on the tram and had some space between them again, Scorpion spoke up.

"How'd you know not to take off my boot?"

"I tasked as a medic before."

"Ah."

Scorpion said no more the rest of the ride. Following Gacy's instructions, they got off at the Midland Gate station and took the escalator up to the ground floor. There they followed the signs to the MC—step-hop, step-hop—which turned out to be on the second floor.

Inside the MC... chaos. Medics bustling to and fro, some pushing wheelchairs, some clutching CompuCharts. Mason helped Scorpion to the front desk.

"Excuse me, but this man is injured. A steer trampled him."

The woman at the GlassTop glanced up, looked Scorpion up and down, then motioned to the elevators. "Take him to General. It's on four." She looked back down to the GlassTop. "Midland Gate Emergency Medical Center, how may I help you?... Is he breathing?... What's your sector?"

Mason helped Scorpion back to the elevator. It took them another ten minutes to reach what Mason guessed must be General. The waiting room was overcrowded, four rows of chairs—all filled. There must have been fifty people waiting. Another dozen stood in line at the front desk occupied by a frazzled-looking receptionist. Behind her, a single medic in blue bustled from bed to bed. Not even private exam rooms here?

"Will anyone give up a chair for this man?" Mason shouted. "He can't stand."

No one moved.

"Will you shut it?" Scorpion hissed, though he looked like he might pass out.

Mason tried again. "His foot was crushed by a steer. A cow. A thousand-pound cow."

A woman three rows back stood. "He can sit here."

"Thank you," Mason said, helping Scorpion in that direction. It occurred to him then that they were wearing the orange jumpsuits that marked them as strikers. Perhaps that was why the people had been hesitant to help. Perhaps not.

Once Mason had settled Scorpion into the chair, he got in line to check in. The woman ahead of him was clutching her arm and sniffling. She glanced back at Mason, wide, bloodshot eyes taking in the color of his jumpsuit. Dried tears streaked her cheeks.

"What happened?" Mason asked.

Those wide eyes settled on his again. She glanced down at her arm, then quickly moved her other hand off the wound and back in a flash. A gash, three inches long. It hadn't looked terribly deep, though Mason had seen it for only a quarter of a second.

"Where did it happen?"

"Sector seven. Salmon packing plant."

"Was it a knife?"

She shook her head "The blade on the gutter."

Gutter, eww. "So, clean, though likely not sterile?"

"I don't know."

There was no reason for this woman to wait in line when Mason could easily assist her. He looked over the front desk, his gaze searching for what he needed. He spotted a box of alcohol pads on a counter against the side wall. Liquid adhesive was likely nearby... There. The familiar purple tube was sitting on the shelf below the counter. And a bottle of sterile water to clean it. Excellent. Now, if only the receptionist would not panic.

He left the line and darted through the swinging half door that separated the waiting area from the medical side. He had the bottle of sterile water in hand before he heard the first protest.

"Excuse me, you can't be in here."

He grabbed a pair of gloves, the liquid adhesive, and the box of alcohol swabs, then jogged back to the swinging door. The receptionist was standing beside her chair, scowling at him.

"I tasked as a medic before," he said. "I can help shorten your line." Then he pushed through the door and set the materials on the desk.

"Sir, that's really not necessary," the receptionist said.

"I tasked as a medic in the Highlands," he told the woman with the gash, pulling on the gloves. "Would you allow me to help you?"

The woman glanced at the line, then at the receptionist, then back to Mason. "I guess."

Gloves on, he waved her to him. "Come here, please."

The woman walked to his side. Mason took hold of her elbow and turned her hand palm side up, which revealed the still-bleeding cut. He squirted sterile water over the wound, then opened an alcohol swab and wiped the cut. It wasn't deep. The liquid adhesive would be enough to heal it without a scar. Mason pinched the wound closed with one hand and squeezed the tube of liquid adhesive over the cut with his other.

He met the woman's eyes and smiled. "Now we count to twenty. It dries quite fast."

"He just took things and started to help that woman." The receptionist's voice, behind him. "Said he tasked as a medic in the Highlands."

Mason looked over his shoulder. The receptionist stood with the medic, a man with white hair and a tired but curious expression.

"This is your friend?" He nodded to the woman Mason was helping.

"No, sir," Mason said. "My, uh, friend's foot was crushed by a steer in sector five. I saw how long your line was and thought I could be of some help."

"Where did you task in the Highlands?"

"The SC. Under Ciddah Rourke."

"Never heard of her, but I've been down here for fifteen years. Who's your task director?"

"Gabon Gacy in the sector five feedlot." The adhesive had dried, so Mason released the woman's arm. "That should do it. I could wrap it in gauze if you'd like. It would keep you from scraping the cut until it has time to fully heal."

"Yes, please," the woman said.

Mason looked to the medic. "May I fetch some gauze?"

The medic nodded. "Reena, tap Gabon Gacy at the sector five feedlot and tell him that I'm borrowing his… What's your task?"

"Farmhand," Mason said, pushing though the swinging half door to find gauze.

"I'm borrowing his farmhand for the rest of the day. See if he cares and let me know."

And so, for the rest of the day Mason tasked in the General Medical Center under the medic, Kam Cadell.

Mason helped administer meds to bedridden patients, patched up a dozen more cuts, helped Cadell wrap Scorpion's foot until he could be sent for surgery, and took vitals on dozens of patients to prepare them for Cadell.

"Mason, get a blood sample and test for opiates on bed twelve."

Mason drew a vial of blood from the patient, then located the blood meter. As he waited for the results, he recalled the experiment he and Ciddah had been doing when the enforcers had interrupted them. Lonn wanted to try and test more meds. Could Mason steal the supplies for that? He didn't see how.

He tapped the results from the blood meter into the CompuChart, then cleaned up his mess. The GMC was like some sort of triage area. He counted sixteen beds, all of them full. Where would they put the rest of the patients who were sitting in the waiting room?

Cadell approached him. "An aide is here to move bed six down to long term. I can't go with him right now. Can you walk down and make sure everything is hooked up correctly? They're busy down there too, and I don't like moving someone like this without a medic involved."

"Sure. Can you show me what I need to hook up?" Mason had never moved beds before. There had never been a need in the SC.

Cadell waved him over to bed six. Mason followed. As he neared and the person in the bed came into view, he slowed to a stop.

Omar.

His little brother lay there, unconscious and intubated. A nasal cannula delivered supplemental oxygen through his nose. His face was covered in bruises and cuts that had been patched up with liquid adhesive.

"The beds have everything the patient needs," Cadell said. "They even have a small battery, but it won't last long. The patient's SimTag is registered to the bed, so if the breathing or heart stops, it will set off an alarm and the medics will come running. Still…" He tapped the top side of the bed. "The cords are here. Just wheel the head up against the wall and plug it in. Be sure and bring me back an empty bed to replace this one."

Mason was still staring at his brother. "What happened to him?"

"OD'd. Can't be sure, but his bunkmate who brought him in thinks he was trying to end it. Took a whole vial of brown sugar at once."

Oh, Omar, why? "What about the bruises and cuts?"

"Someone beat him up pretty badly. But he did worse to himself with the PV."

Indeed. "He's comatose?"

"Yes. He should recover once the substance clears his system, though."

Relief flooded through Mason. "How long will that take?"

"Most overdose comas last between two and four weeks, sometimes longer. Recovery is usually gradual. The patients become more aware over time and will wake for longer periods. His coma scale score was an eight, so that's not terrible. Since he OD'd, and likely on purpose, I'll probably keep him sedated for four weeks, then see if he'll wake on his own. I like to detox juicers. Force them to get clean. What he does after that is up to him. Now, take him down there for me, will you? And hurry back."

"Yes, sir."

Mason and the aide moved Omar down to the third floor and made sure the bed was plugged in. As Mason pushed an empty bed back to the GMC, he prayed that this would be a good thing for his brother, that being here would keep him away from the stims, that his body would heal, and that when he woke up, all the cravings would be gone.

When lunchtime came and Cadell told Mason to go eat, he ran to the diner and told his mother the news. Lonn wasn't there yet.

"He tried to kill himself and you think it's a good thing?" she asked.

"Just that when he wakes up, it'll be out of his system. He'll have a new start," Mason said. "I know he wanted to beat it, but I saw the cravings in his eyes. He would have done anything to get more. It was scary."

"My poor boy. Everyone goes through a stage where their curiosity is stronger than their common sense. But I've never seen anyone take it as far as Omar has."

"He's not as lost as you think, Mother," Mason said. "If we ever get out of here, I think he'll turn out fine."

"Rich's plan is almost ready. If we could get just one person to the other side, he could take the truth to the people."

"Yes, but their plan is reckless. I'm working on Omar's balloon idea. I've been taking three bed sheets when I visit the car wash. It's not the ideal fabric, but it should work with the waterproof spray I saw at the G.I.N. If you help me sew, we could have the balloon ready in three or four weeks. There's no need to risk any lives."

Mother sighed and took hold of Mason's hand. "Rich doesn't believe your balloon will lift a man. I've tried to tell him not to underestimate how clever you are, but his mind is set. He's going to do this. We must pray that it will succeed."

Mason gritted his teeth. "And if it doesn't?"

"Then we pray that no one will be hurt."

"Mother, my idea risks no one." But Lonn arrived before he could say anything else.

"Mason worked in the MC today," Mother told Lonn.

"Really? How?"

Mason relayed the morning's events and how Kam Cadell had gotten permission for him to stay.

"This is excellent," Lonn said. "You have access to meds there. You could test them."

"I thought about that, but it's only for today," Mason said. "I don't think I could manage any tests when it's so busy, and I have no way to steal the supplies, either."

Lonn grabbed Mason's shoulder. "You've got to try, boy. You've got to! This chance might not come again."

When Mason returned to the MC, Cadell had a surprise for him.

"You've been reassigned," he said. "You're my assistant now."

"What? No more feedlot? How?" It was too good to be true.

"It was purely selfish, I promise you," Cadell said. "I've been asking for an assistant medic here for ages, but medics don't tend to be prematurely liberated, so... I'm sure the liberator was simply tired of hearing me whine. But I couldn't let someone with your skills and bedside manner be wasted on cows."

"Thank you," Mason said. "I greatly appreciate this." Surely, he could find a way to conduct tests now that this was his permanent task.

"I wasn't able to move your residence, unfortunately. I'll keep trying, though. Striker bunkhouses are filled with disease. If you're working here, I need you healthy."

Mason hadn't minded tasking on the feedlot. But this news took the pressure off Lonn's demand that he steal meds and a blood meter this very afternoon. He now had time to conduct his investigation. And being here would allow him to check up on Omar as well.

This felt like a new beginning. He and Lonn could look for a cure for the thin plague. And if they found one, it would change everything.

Chapter 17

Once the task director learned that Jemma was pregnant, things started to happen quickly. She met with Tyra to discuss wardrobe, a makeover, and to schedule initial ColorCast interviews with Luella Flynn. Jemma demanded that she and Alawa be moved into their own suite, and Matron Dhlorah gave them a tour of the rooms.

Jemma and Alawa chose the Citrus Blossom Suite on the seventh floor, as the colors were bright and cheery and it was completely empty, so they didn't have to share it with anyone. That also made it easy for the girls to discuss ways to use Jemma's position to help the rebels or how they might escape altogether.

So far, they'd come up with nothing.

On the day of Jemma's first ColorCast appearance, Tyra took her to a hairdresser in the morning, then Matron and Ewan escorted her to the ColorCast Studio lot and into the small theater where they filmed the *Finley and Flynn Morning Show*. It had maybe fifty seats, which was much smaller than it looked on TV. Only the first two rows were filled.

Matron took Jemma to a dressing room where a red ball gown hung on the wall. It had a V waist and a full skirt that poofed out and swept the floor.

Jemma tried to hate it, but it made her feel like a princess.

Once she was dressed and a woman had painted her face with makeup, Matron led Jemma back out to the stage. There were two little white couches in the center, angled so that they faced each other. Lights from the ceiling were pointed down at the couches, making them glow in comparison to everything else.

"Jemma, lovely!" Byran Kester, a director Jemma had met the first time she'd been in the harem, walked out on the stage and greeted them. Two kisses for Matron and two more for Jemma. She felt strange to greet this man like they were friends when he had betrayed her.

Byran was a short man with dark hair and a scruffy face. As per the current mimic trends, he wore a loose purple shirt with several thick silver chains around his neck.

"I hope you plan to film an honest interview today, Mr. Kester," Jemma said.

Byran chucked. "Now, where's the pleasure in that?"

Jemma glared at him, and his expression sobered.

"In all seriousness, this will be a very simple interview. Your words are on the teleprompter. Just read what's there. Try not to adlib. We'll do it once and then maybe run a few places where I think we need a little something extra."

Jemma knew all about the something extras they used here. The last time she had acted for him, they'd edited the footage to make it seem like she was being held hostage. Then they'd used it to blackmail Levi.

Well, they didn't have Levi this time, so she doubted they could do anything too terrible.

"I just need to read the teleprompter. That's it?"

"Mostly," Byran said. "Luella will come out first. She'll introduce you both. You'll come in on the right, Mr. Renzor will enter on the left."

She stiffened. "The task director general is going to be here?"

"That's right. I'd like you to take hands when you reach center stage, right in front of the couches. Smile, act like you like him. This is to show the people that the rebels aren't what they claim to be, so you need to look thrilled to be here. Think you can do that?"

"Yes." But Jemma's heart sank. She would truly have to become an actress to pull this off.

"Once the applause dies down, you'll sit together on the couch on the left, on Mr. Renzor's side. Luella will sit on the other couch. Then just follow her lead and read the prompter. If Mr. Renzor touches you, don't move away. Look like you want to be here."

Jemma fought back a sigh. "I understand."

"Great," Byran said. "We'll get started soon."

"Ready in five!" a man yelled from the back. A cameraman.

"Well, there you go." Byran walked to the edge of the stage and jumped down.

Matron led Jemma over to the side of the stage, similar to where Naomi had stood a few months ago when she'd been introduced as the Safe Lands Queen.

"Hay-o, femmys!" Luella Flynn tottered up the three steps to the side stage, bringing a burst of spicy perfume with her. She was wearing a tight black skirt that ended just below her knees and a fluffy purple top that made it look like she had climbed inside a gigantic flower. Her hair was silver tinsel that must have been some kind of wig.

Luella kissed them both on the cheeks and looked Jemma up and down. "My, don't you look gorgeous! Lawten chose that dress, you know. He has a thing for red. I wouldn't be surprised if you gain some mimics over that outfit."

"We're on in sixty!" the cameraman said.

"I'll see you up there, femmy!" Luella trotted past Jemma on spiky platform heels.

Jemma's stomach twisted. She didn't want to be on TV. She wished she were in the basements with the others, taking care of Shaylinn. She wondered how her sister was coping with her morning sickness and being alone with Levi and all those kids. She hoped Levi was being sweet to her.

Levi.

"In five, four, three, two..."

Luella Flynn was standing in the center of the stage, touching her ear with one finger. She released it and beamed at the center camera. "I'm right here, Finley. And I'm simply juicing to introduce you all to our brand-new Safe Lands Queen. But she's not alone today. She brings with her a very special guest, our own task director general. Please welcome Ms. Jemma Levi and Task Director General, Lawten Renzor!"

Music burst out from overhead speakers. The crowd clapped. Matron nudged Jemma and her feet started to move. She walked across the stage toward the couch. The task director entered from the other side and walked toward her. They met in front of the couches, and Jemma let him take her hand. He held up their joined hands, faced the crowd, and waved. Jemma waved too. The applause increased.

It seemed like an eternity before he lowered their hands. Luella gave them both cheek kisses, and they sat down, Jemma and the task director on one couch, him still holding her hand, and Luella on the other.

"Jemma, darling. Tell us, how far along are you?" Luella asked.

"Last I saw the medic, he said I was eleven weeks along," Jemma said. *Over a quarter of the way there, already!*

"Tell us what this means for you?" Luella asked.

"I'm very excited." That much was true.

"And this is a miracle baby! Conceived in the natural way, right?"

The question startled Jemma. She'd been certain they would claim the baby was produced in their surrogacy program. "Yes." She looked into the camera and said, "You're going to be a father, Levi!" Though she was sure they would cut that out.

"Indeed," the task director said. "Levi served as the best kind of donor. He's an example to all of us." Lawten put his arm over Jemma's shoulders and squeezed.

Jemma gritted her teeth and tried to keep her expression plain.

"Jemma, why did you return to the harem?" Luella asked. "Weren't you in hiding?"

Why did she return? Because Mia had stunned her. She suddenly remembered the teleprompter and read the words there. "I felt it would be a good gesture to the people to show my support of the Safe Lands government. I was a rebel, but I am no longer."

"I'm very glad to hear that," Luella said. "Rebellion tears our nation apart where we should be trying to work together."

Jemma would have loved to have made a comment about how forcing people do to something wasn't working together, but she held her tongue.

The interview went on. Lawten said Jemma's pregnancy was a sign of good things for the future of the Safe Lands, which to Jemma meant they intended to steal her child. Luella gushed over Jemma's dress, and just as Jemma started to relax, Luella said good-bye.

"We're clear," the cameraman said.

"Oh, well done, Jemma," Luella said. "She's going to do fine, Lawten. Much better than the others."

"She's humble," Lawten said.

"The audience loves humble," Luella said. "Especially after that Mia. Oosh."

Kruse walked up to the stage from the audience, looking short the way he stood below them. "Mr. Renzor, you have an urgent tap."

"Excuse me for a moment, ladies," Lawten said, and left Jemma alone with Luella Flynn.

"So, this wasn't really live, was it?" Jemma asked.

"Not this time, femmy, no."

"When will it air?"

"Byran? When will this air, trig?" Luella yelled.

Byran's voice came from the back of the room. "On tomorrow's morning show. Then we'll run it again throughout the day."

"Tomorrow morning you can watch," Luella said, then raised her voice again. "Are we done?"

"I'm taking a look at the footage," Byran said. "Just hold tight for another couple minutes."

"Hold tight, hold tight," Luella muttered to herself. "So, Jemma. You must know the identity of the Owl, no?"

"Who?" Jemma had said it too quickly, though.

Luella grinned knowingly. "*Hoo*, indeed. His little broadcast interrupted this month's liberation ceremony."

"I didn't see it."

"Oh, well, you missed something spectacular, then." She lowered her voice to a whisper. "The Owl had footage of two outsiders being liberated. It was *incredible.*"

Jemma's eyes widened. "Which outsiders? What is liberation, anyway?"

Luella sighed dramatically. "Lawten keeps it from me. But that footage was amazing. It followed the two outsiders who share the same donors as your lifer. Surely you know who I mean. They were liberated for crimes against the Safe Lands? One was the medic who tasked in the SC."

"Mason and Omar," Jemma said. "They're Levi's brothers."

"Yes, well, the Owl intrigues me. I'd love to do an interview with him. Think you could put in a good word for me?"

"I don't really know who the Owl is," Jemma said. "I'm not sure that it's one person." That much was true. Omar had been liberated, so someone else had to have put on the costume to do that recording.

"Of course." Luella's eyes were wide as she considered that information. "That's truly brilliant. A flock of owls. Oh, I love that."

"Luella, femme," Byran called, "I'm going to need you for a few more shots. But Jemma, you're free to go."

Jemma stood, anxious to be away from Luella Flynn and all of her questions. "Good-bye."

"Yes, indeed, bye-o, femmy. I'll be seeing you soon enough, I'm sure."

Jemma wobbled across the stage on the heels that had started to pinch her feet terribly. Matron was waiting.

The next morning, Matron and her two enforcers escorted Jemma and Alawa to the main sitting room to watch the broadcast. The massive wall of picture windows had already been converted into a Wyndo screen, which, combined with turning off all the lights, made the sitting area dark. The Finley and Flynn show was on, muted, though Jemma recognized it as yesterday's program, which always aired before the current day's show.

The other harem women were already seated, though with the ladies from Jack's Peak set free, there were only four others: Jennifer, Mia, and two Safe Lands women Jemma only knew by name.

"Why do we have to watch this?" Mia asked. "I wanted to sleep in this morning. This pregnancy has me exhausted."

"Because this is a historic occasion," Matron said, taking a seat in a high-back chair, "and because the task director demanded it."

"He demanded we all watch Finley and Flynn's morning ColorCast?" Mia asked.

"Yes," Matron said. "I think it will be the best way to show you what's possible to achieve with your position here."

"Cryptic," Mia murmured to Jennifer, her mother.

"It's starting," Matron said. "Wyndo: Volume: Twenty."

The opening music and montage began, showing candid clips of Finley Gray and Luella Flynn on various interviews or with Safe Lands celebrities. When it ended, the screen flashed to Finley Gray sitting behind his desk.

"Good morning, Safe Lands nationals. We have an incredible morning planned for you. Bick from the To Dye For Salon is here to give my hair a new style. I've got to say, I can't wait to see what he does. It's time for a new look. We're also going to hear from *Big is Beautiful* star Melana Georjan. I just love her show. Look, I'm even wearing my *Big is Beautiful* T-shirt." He opened his jacket, revealing a white shirt with two fancy letter Bs on it. "Decked, isn't it? But first we're going to go live to the ColorCast Theater, where Luella is waiting to introduce you all to a very special guest. Luella? You there, femme?"

The image on the screen switched to Luella, who was standing on the stage in the ColorCast Theater in front of the white couches. "I'm right here, Finley. And I'm simply juicing to introduce you all to the brand-new Safe Lands Queen. But she's not alone today. She brings with her a very special guest, our own task director general. Please welcome Ms. Jemma Levi and Task Director General, Lawten Renzor!"

"What?" Mia shot Jemma a glare.

Applause and whistling came from the speakers as the camera angle changed to show a packed auditorium, way larger than the amount of seats that really existed in the ColorCast theater. The crowd was clapping and cheering, some on their feet as, in the distance on the stage, the task director general and Jemma walked out.

"That's so weird," Jemma said. "There were only a few people there." They were doing it again. Changing things. Making a movie from what really happened. It made Jemma nervous as to what else they might have changed.

"You probably didn't notice," Matron said. "Nerves and all."

"I *did* notice," Jemma said. "There were only twenty people in the crowd. They change things. I mean, clearly this isn't being taped live since I'm sitting here and not there."

"Shh." Matron waved her hand at Jemma and looked back to the wall screen, where Jemma was walking across the stage in that gorgeous red dress. She took Lawten's hand, and the two of them stood there. Jemma hadn't paid all that much attention to what the task director had been wearing, but she did now. He was in a white suit with red accents. They matched. Like a couple.

Her stomach churned as she watched them sit side by side on the sofa across from Luella.

"Jemma, darling," Luella said on screen. "Tell us, how far along are you?"

"Just a few weeks," Jemma said.

"Oh no." The real Jemma froze. That wasn't what she had really said.

"And isn't it true that this is a miracle baby?" Luella asked. "Conceived in the natural way?"

"Yes." Jemma smiled. But, of course, they had cut her message to Levi.

"The baby is ours," Lawten said, and his hand lowered onto Jemma's shoulder. The camera zoomed in on the task director's lined face. His eyes were teary, as if he were emotional over the news.

"No!" Jemma clutched the arm rests on her chair. "That's not what I said. I said it was Levi's baby." She should have known they would do something like this.

The camera flashed back to Luella. "Tell us what this means for you?"

"I'm very excited," Jemma said.

And back to Lawten, the close up on his face. But his eyes weren't teary now. "I know there's much controversy over the subject of lifers. But Jemma and I, we share a bond that's stronger than pleasure alone. This child. We created this child through our passion for each other."

At the harem, Jemma cried out and stood. "That's not what happened!"

"Jemma, please sit down," Matron said.

On screen, the task director said, "In fact, I am so in love with this woman, I want to exchange vows with her."

Jemma lost her breath and sank back to her chair, staring at the screen, horrified at what was happening.

"What kind of vows?" Luella asked.

"In the Old days, couples who wanted to spend their lives together exchanged vows of promise before witnesses," the task director explained. "Jemma and I have decided to do this."

The camera switched to Jemma's face. "I felt it would be a good gesture."

No! "They've twisted things around. That's not how it happened." But she'd known they would change something. Tears rolled down her cheeks at the thought of Levi seeing this.

On screen, Luella looked into the camera. "And so, Safe Landers, we're going to have a party. The date has been set. January twenty-fourth. You won't want to miss it."

The camera changed to a view of the couches with the task director holding Jemma's hand. Animated letters flew across the screen like a spilled puzzle and arranged themselves to say "Vow Exchange, January 24, 2089. Don't miss it."

"They changed things!" Jemma cried. "He made it seem like I'm going to marry him." Why would he do that? What was his angle?

"I don't understand," Alawa said. "How could they change it?"

"It's recorded, isn't it?" Jennifer asked.

"It said it was live," one of the enforcers said. "But like the femme said, she's sitting right here."

Jemma wrung her hands together. "They rearranged the things I said, played them out of order to make it sound like I said something else. And that part when they zoomed in on the task director's face, they must have recorded that another time. He never said that while I was there."

"You should be happy," Mia said. "You like romantic things."

"This is *not* romantic."

"Sure it is. It's like that story in the Bible you like so much. You know, the orphan Hadassah, living in exile with her uncle in Susa after King Nebuchadnezzar conquered their home."

"That's romantic?" Alawa asked.

"Only because of how the story ends," Mia said. "Hadassah becomes Queen Esther, marries King Xerxes. He chose her out of all those others."

Jemma glared at Mia. "This is *not* the same. Hadassah wasn't already married. I am. And this baby is Levi's, not the task director's."

"It really doesn't matter who the donor is," Mia said. "The child belongs to the Safe Lands."

This comment poured ethanol on Jemma's anger. But she stopped herself before she lit into Mia. Jemma was failing to play her part. She took a deep breath and forced aside her anger. "He could have at least told me what he was going to do." Jemma stood up and walked to Matron's chair. "I want to talk to him. Take me to the task director's office. Now."

"You can't see him without an appointment," Matron said.

"I'm the new Safe Lands Queen. I can do whatever I want." Right?

Matron's eyebrows furrowed as if she wasn't certain what to do. "Jemma, dear, let's not get upset. Why don't you use the Wyndo wall screen in your suite to tap him? That way, you can talk to him now or at least make an appointment. He's a very busy man."

"But I don't know how to tap anyone," Jemma said.

"I'll help you. Come along."

Jemma and Matron went up to the Citrus Blossom Suite. Inside, Matron spoke to the wall screen.

"Wyndo: power. Tap: Lawten Renzor." The screen brightened to show a list of text. "Wyndo: zoom. Wyndo: zoom." The text got larger, then larger again. It said:

Renzor, Lawten. 79 Summit Road.

Renzor, Lawten. City Hall.

Renzor, Lawten. Safe Lands Guild.

"Wyndo: select: City Hall," Matron said.

The wall screen went black and the logo of the Safe Lands rotated on the dark screen.

Then a woman's face appeared on the screen, slightly misshapen as if the camera was at an odd angle. "City Hall. Lawten Renzor's office. How may I help you?"

"This is Matron Dlorah at the Highland Harem. Our queen, Jemma Levi, would like to speak with the task director. Might we set up a tap appointment?"

"Just one moment and I'll see if he's available," the woman said.

The screen went black and silent again, and the rotating Safe Lands logo filled the screen.

"See now?" Matron said. "Isn't this easier than driving over there?"

Jemma shrugged, though she had to admit it was. She wondered if there was any way to talk to Levi on this contraption.

The task director's face suddenly appeared on the screen. "Jemma, shimmer, I thought I might hear from you. Hay-o, Matron."

"Hay-o, Lawten. I hope you're finding pleasure this day."

"Indeed, I was, until I this tap came through. My queen's expression weighs heavily on my mind. She seems upset. Would you give us some privacy, Matron?"

"Of course." Matron nodded to Jemma and left the room, closing the door behind her.

"Why did you do that?" Jemma yelled. "You said so many lies!"

"Everything I did was for your benefit, shimmer."

"Don't call me that! You don't have any right to call me anything."

"I don't understand why you're so angry. You asked to be the Safe Lands Queen."

"Yes, the queen. But you made it sound like I'm going to marry you. I'm already married to Levi."

"Oh, that doesn't matter."

"Of course it matters!" She stopped talking and took several deep breaths. How could she do this? Share her anger yet still play the part of a rebel who'd changed sides? "I might not believe in the rebel cause, but I still love my husband. I mean to see him again someday."

"You will. This whole broadcast was for his benefit. When he sees it, he'll have no choice but to comply with my demands."

His words made her shiver. "What demands?"

"That's not your concern. If there's nothing else, I have much to do."

Questions jumbled in Jemma's mind. "Nothing else now, no," she said, almost to herself.

"Then we understand each other. Good. Oh, and don't wear that muddy color again. It completely washes you out."

The screen went blank. She glanced down at her shirt. It was dark tan, almost the color of her skin.

Did he think he could tell her what to wear? She sat on the couch and thought over what had happened. The task director was up to something. He was using her to blackmail Levi, but how could he even communicate with the rebels?

She still smarted over Mia's comparing this situation to the story of Esther. Mia had no doubt said it out of her own anger over Jemma having taken her place as queen, but what if there was some truth to it? If Jemma could play this role of Lawten Renzor's lifer, perhaps she could learn things that not even Luella Flynn knew. Like what he wanted from Levi and maybe even the truth about liberation. Maybe this was the chance Jemma and Alawa had been waiting for. Maybe Jemma could use her position to save her people.

Maybe she had been brought to the harem for such a time as this.

Chapter 18

"Where did you get this?" Levi asked Zane. He and Jordan had come to the nest the moment Nash had brought word that Lawten Renzor had left Levi a package. It was an envelope made of gold foil with Levi's name on the front in black type. Inside was a little square of plastic with a metal strip on one end, like a tiny Old video game cartridge.

"It was left in theater nine," Zane said. "We decided to open it there just in case there was some sort of tracker on it."

"You sure it's safe?" Jordan asked.

"I looked it over, shot it with a SimScanner, put it in an off-grid GlassTop to scan it for spy adds. There's no other way I can think of to put a trace on a data card. It's clean."

"So, what is it?" Levi asked.

"It's a video—two, actually. One is footage from this morning's *Finley and Flynn Morning Show*. Jemma was on it. The other is a message to you from the task director general. He's trying to blackmail you."

Figured. "How?"

"Best if you watch." Zane took the plastic from Levi and inserted it into a slot in his GlassTop computer. A few taps and the video filled the GlassTop screen. Another tap and the video appeared on the wall screen as well.

Jemma had been a special guest on the ColorCast program. They'd dressed her up in a fancy gown and had her sitting with Renzor. And Renzor was touching her. Holding her hand and putting his arm around her. Levi's stomach clenched. Then that Luella woman said Jemma was pregnant with Renzor's baby. And Jemma looked happy about it.

Why would she look happy?

"That scum-licking maggot," Jordan said.

Then Renzor announced that he and Jemma were lifers and were going to exchange vows. "This isn't real," Levi said. "Right? Tell me this is a fake."

"The video is fake, sort of," Zane said. "But it's what they showed the nation this morning. Jemma was there when they recorded this, but there are discrepancies. Like when they zoom in on Renzor's face, the lighting is off, as is the position of his body. I don't think Jemma was sitting beside him when they shot those lines."

"Just like those videos they made of Jemma and Naomi," Jordan said. "The ones they showed us in the RC. Naomi told me she never said those things, that they'd been told they were acting a part in a play."

"Jemma told me too," Levi said. "Okay, good. So, they edited this to tell the lie they wanted to tell, right?"

"That would make the most sense," Zane said.

"She's probably not even pregnant yet." Levi grabbed a chair and sat down, relieved. "He's just messing with me."

"Let me show you the second file." Zane tapped around his GlassTop, and soon Lawten Renzor's face replaced the image of Jemma.

"Mr. Justin, it pains me to greet you in such a way after I've taken your lifer from you. I'm sure you'd like her back. So, I propose an exchange. Your Jemma for my Ciddah. It's that simple. Leave your reply by Monday morning in the same place this package was found."

The screen went dark.

A chill ran up Levi's arms. "That's it? He wants Ciddah?"

"Do it," Jordan said. "And send her *donors* along. I'm tired of having to watch them."

Oh, how Levi wished he could. "It's not that easy, brother. She knows too much. Everything. She could lead them right to us, and we still don't know that her presence here wasn't Renzor's plan from the start. Plus, Shaylinn needs her."

"The other women delivered Harvey Jr. just fine on their own," Jordan said.

"But they had Jemma, who was learning about that stuff from my mother," Levi said. "Jemma's not here. And the twins might come early."

"Why would they come early?" Jordan asked.

"I don't know," Levi said. "It's just something Ciddah said. Look, none of that matters. I don't trust Renzor. What's to say he'd really give us Jem? We took their other surrogates. They're not just going to give her up."

"So, what do we do?" Jordan asked.

"We've got to get her out of there," Levi said. "That video said she was at the ColorCast Theater. You think that was true?"

"It looked like it," Zane said, "only the theater doesn't seat that many. But they often fake the audience."

Levi thought that over. "So maybe Jem leaves the harem sometimes to do this stuff. And if they've made her queen, she'll have to leave more often, right?"

Zane nodded. "I guess."

"Then we attack when she's in a vehicle," Levi said. "There can't be more than two enforcers that would go along. We could take down that many."

"Yeah, but I can't sit here twenty-four seven monitoring the harem and waiting for her to leave," Zane said.

"I could," Jordan said.

"You have a wife and kid, brother," Levi said. "But we could take shifts. Can't you train someone else to watch the cameras?"

Zane sighed. “My father won’t let just anyone have access to this room.”

“What if you and your dad and Nash helped out, just for a day or two of constant surveillance?” Levi held his breath. *Please say yes.*

“You’re going about this the wrong way,” Zane said. “We need to get her schedule—or better yet, Luella Flynn’s schedule. She’ll be doing all the ColorCast interviews monitoring this supposed pregnancy. If we can get a peek at her schedule, we’ll know when and where she’ll be seeing Jemma.”

A surge of hope swelled in Levi’s chest. “How can we get it?”

“We break into the ColorCast offices,” Zane said.

“*We* do?”

Zane tapped Levi’s chest. “You do. I’ll help.”

Levi batted Zane’s hand aside. “Yeah, that’s what I figured.”

“And for fun,” Zane said, “why don’t you go as the Owl?”

A week later they were ready. Nash dressed in an enforcer uniform. Levi dressed as the Owl. He also had a tiny device inside his ear that allowed Zane to speak to him. Zane had insisted on it after Levi had again refused a SimSpeak implant.

They’d come through the storm drains into the Highlands. The night air was icy, the sidewalks slick under Levi’s feet. October already. The nights were getting cold. Winter was coming. Halfway up Snowmass Road, they got into one of Dayle’s Department of Public Tasks trucks, which Nash drove to a garage near the back of the ColorCast Studio lot.

“I’ll be waiting right here,” Nash said. “Don’t take your time.”

“Don’t worry.” Levi climbed out of the truck and crept through the dark garage. There were only two vehicles inside, and the one he walked past was covered in a layer of dust.

The overhead lights spread his strange shadow out on the concrete. He couldn’t believe he was wearing a cape and an owl mask. Doing the video had been one thing, but going out in public... Only Omar would come up with a plan like this.

At the back of the garage, he found the corridor that led to the ColorCast building. Zane should have taken over the Surveillance Department’s camera feed so they wouldn’t see Levi, but later, the enforcers would be able to play back the footage and witness the Owl’s confident entrance. To make this look like just another Owl act, Levi would spray the Owl’s mark on the set of *The Finley and Flynn Morning Show*. Either Luella Flynn would have it painted over before the show aired tomorrow or she’d leave it for shock value. Regardless, Zane was recording so he could play this later on one of the Owl’s broadcasts.

Levi reached the back entrance to the building and stopped at the door there. No handles.

He touched his gloved fist against the SimPad and the door popped open. Thank goodness for the ghoulie tag inside the glove. "It worked."

"I see that," Zane said.

Levi slipped inside. So far, he'd seen no one. It was dark, and he paused for a moment while his eyes adjusted. He stood in the corner of two perpendicular hallways. The only light came from an emergency sign down the left hall.

"Walk into the light," Zane said in a low singing voice.

"Ha, ha." Levi crept toward the left until he reached another corner. This turned into the back stage of the theater.

"Go ahead and leave some marks on the stage," Zane said. "Maybe a nice big one in the middle of those white couches."

Levi climbed onto the stage and set to work, using cans of spray paint and Omar's Owl stencil. When he finished, he put away the stencil and paint. Zane directed him up the center aisle of the theater and out the front doors. That led him to a lobby with red carpeting and white walls.

"Take the elevator to the fourth floor," Zane said.

On four, the elevator opened to another lobby, though this one was more of a waiting room filled with chairs and a reception desk. A sign on the wall said Communication Department.

"Walk to your right, down that hall," Zane said. "Now, I'm not sure which office is Luella's, since there are no cameras in any of the offices. But I've seen her enter two rooms more than any other. The third door on the right. And the one across from it."

Levi walked past the reception desk and down the hall. He passed one door, a second, and stopped outside the third, which was wide open. He stepped inside a narrow room. One long table sat in the center and was surrounded by chairs. A white board covered one wall and was divided into a four-month calendar. Levi caught sight of Jemma's name and paused.

"I found something," he said to Zane. "A show schedule. It's a four-month calendar and Jemma's name is on it in dozens of places."

"Take a picture," Zane said. "But if it's only the schedule for when episodes air, it's not proof of where Jemma will be for each filming. We need exact locations. See if you can find Luella's office next."

Levi pulled Zane's portable Wyndo out of the satchel on his Owl belt and took several pictures of the calendar. Then he walked across the hall and into the office there. It had two GlassTop desks, a round table, and some couches over by the windows. He paused at the first desk and looked over the papers on top. He spotted the name Finley Gray on a nameplate, then walked to the second desk. He scanned for a similar nameplate and found it on the very back of the desk. Luella Flynn.

"Here we go."

"What?"

"Luella Flynn's desk. And her calendar." Levi took a picture of the open desk calendar, which was for the month of October. He flipped the page to November and photographed that page too. He kept going until there were no more entries. Then he flipped back to October and found the entries with Jemma's name. "I think some of these will work." There was an appointment at the To Dye For Salon next Friday and a shopping spree scheduled for two Saturday's from now. And weekly appointments at the SC.

His stomach twisted. Jemma really was pregnant.

"Great," Zane said. "Time to go."

Levi pocketed the portable Wyndo, trying not to think about Jemma. "On my way."

"Who *are* you talking to, trig?" a female voice asked.

Levi jumped. He squinted, his eyes seeking out the bearer of that voice.

A click. A lamp lit the room. Luella Flynn was reclining on a couch on the other side of the table.

Maggots! Levi backed slowly toward the door.

Luella straightened but didn't stand. "Don't leave so soon! Are you looking for something specific? I was asleep and missed the beginning of your conversation with yourself."

"Get out of there," Zane said. "She's trying to stall you."

"What's liberation?" Luella asked him. "At least give me a clue."

"What do you care?" Levi said. "You're nothing but a spokeswoman for the Guild. And didn't you say that 'Rebels are a blemish that must be painted over?'"

"I do what I have to do to keep my task and make my audience happy, but there are things that go on around here that don't add up. I want the truth as well."

"You honestly don't know what liberation is?" Levi asked.

She shook her head. "It's the one story that's always evaded me. Well, that and you. But here you are. What do you say? How about an exclusive? We could do it now. I just need to tap my cameraman."

"No thanks," Levi said, inching toward the door. "I'm well aware of how your exclusives are edited."

"Only when Lawten insists," she said, "or when the camera makes me look fat. A girl has a right to look her absolute best, you know."

Levi took another step toward the door. Two more and he'd turn and run.

"Wait!" She scooted to the end of the couch. "How did you get that footage of Mason Elias and Omar Strong? Did that happen in the RC?"

"You'll have to find out like everyone else," Levi said, then for the fake mission added, "The Owl sees all. Trust the Owl." Then he ran out the door and to the elevator.

"Take the stairs this time," Zane said. "That cameraman of hers is in the downstairs lobby, waiting for the elevator."

Levi ran toward the glowing green exit sign. He bashed his glove against the SimPad, and the door swung open.

Down, down, down he went. He paused to make sure the lobby was empty, then ran back through the theater and out the long corridor to the garage, where he found the DPT truck. The passenger door was already opening.

Levi climbed inside.

"You get it?" Nash asked.

"Yeah, I got it. Luella Flynn was there, though."

"I swear I saw her leave earlier today," Zane said through Levi's earpiece. "I'm really sorry."

"You think that's true what she said?" Levi asked Zane. "That she really doesn't know about liberation."

"Sure," Zane said. "The woman can't keep a secret. If she knew, so would everyone else."

They got back to Zane's house, and Levi changed out of the Owl costume. Then Zane loaded the pictures Levi had taken onto the Wyndo wall screen and they studied them.

"Lots of opportunities," Zane said. "But I don't like any of these locations. Except that one. On December twenty-six."

Levi read the entry aloud. "Dedication of the Prestige?"

"They've been rebuilding a new theater for the past year in the old Entertainer building," Zane said.

"But that's two months away." Levi didn't think he could wait that long to see his wife.

"The Midlands is my backyard," Zane said. "I can help you here much better than I can in the Highlands. I mean, we could try to hijack her car as they head to any of these other appointments, but they're all during the day. If there's a chase, there's no place for us to go. The only storm drains I trust in the Highlands are nowhere near these places."

Levi understood. If they tried to rescue Jemma and failed, the security around her would increase. They might not get a second chance. She was already pregnant. She'd be safe for two more months.

Though Levi might go insane.

Chapter 19

Shaylinn sat on her bed holding the letters Nash had given her. Letters that had been sent to her—to the messenger. Three of them. It had been over a month since she'd started writing again. A month in which Shaylinn had turned fifteen years old and her pregnancy now showed with a very small lump. And here were three answers to all her hard work. A thrill pulsed inside her. What was she waiting for? She should open them.

She ripped the first envelope and found a single card inside, the same size as the envelope.

To the Messenger—
Who asked you? Don't send your sentimental musings again.
C. Hydel

Shaylinn's breath shuddered. Tears flooded her eyes. She hadn't expected such a response. Had she been wrong to write people? Omar had liked her letters. But he'd known they were from her.

She wasn't sure she wanted to open another one, but she did it anyway.

Are you spying on me? Is this Ranj? Leave me alone. My life is none of your business.

A tear rolled down her cheek. These people hadn't liked what she'd had to say at all. She tore open the last one, eager to get it over with.

Mystery Messenger,
Thank you for your note. It made me cry. In a good way, though. I do feel alone, but not so much now that I know you're out there. Please write back.
Your friend,
Elani

Shaylinn cried even harder, thankful that she'd made a difference in one life.

Something flicked inside her stomach. She looked down just in time to see a slight protrusion sink away. She gasped and put her hand over the place where the little hand, elbow, knee, or foot had poked out, but it didn't happen again.

Time was going by quickly, and Shaylinn wanted to make the most of it.

She immediately got out her paper to write back to Elani. But without her Wyndo, she couldn't remember which person Elani was. She sat pondering what to say when it suddenly occurred to her that Levi had gone out with Zane.

She left her room and tiptoed across the living room where Trevon and Grayn were sprawled out on the couches like shirts to dry.

It felt wrong to invade Levi's bedroom, but she did it anyway, quickly spotting her Wyndo on his bedside table. The smell of his room made her wrinkle her nose. A pile of laundry against the wall and the smell of his sheets were the obvious culprits. She would offer to do his laundry tomorrow. The poor man was hopeless without Jemma.

Shaylinn sat on the edge of his bed and powered on the Wyndo, surprised to find that it wasn't off but only asleep. Levi must have been using it.

The screen faded into view on the grid page for *The Finley and Flynn Morning Show*. The title said "Safe Lands Crowns New Queen," and there was an image of Luella Flynn, the task director, and Jemma sitting on two couches.

Jemma... pregnant?

She couldn't help herself, she tapped play. The volume came through low enough that no one could hear outside the room. What she saw was horrible—couldn't be true. Why would Jemma ever look happy holding that man's hand, claiming to carry his child?

She didn't understand.

"What are you doing?"

"Oh!" Shaylinn jumped, shocked to not have heard Levi open the door. He was staring at her but didn't look angry.

"This can't be true." She held up the portable Wyndo.

"Give it to me." Levi walked to where she sat at took the Wyndo away. "I asked you not to use this thing anymore."

"I needed to look up someone I wrote a message to. She wrote me back, see?" She held up the letter and wiped her eyes. "That's not true about Jemma, right?"

"Zane says they faked some of it. There's no way to know what was really said until Jemma tells us."

Shaylinn sniffled. "You're not mad at her?"

"Mad at Jem? How could I be? She's only doing what I asked of her."

"What do you mean?"

Levi sighed heavily. "If any of us got caught, we were supposed to pretend to switch sides, to try and learn anything we could about the government or liberation. Anything."

And now Jemma had to play the traitor. "I'm sorry, Levi."

"It's fine. Just, please don't come in here again."

"No, I mean, I won't. I'm just sorry this happened. To you and Jemma."

"I'll get her back."

And Shaylinn knew he would.

The next morning, after she'd started Levi's laundry and she and Nell had taken the kids to the park, Shaylinn walked to Nash's apartment, let herself into his foyer, and knocked on the inside door.

Nash answered wearing a tank top and shorts. His feet were bare, and his hair was sticking up. He also had creases across his face.

Oh, dear. She woke him up. "Were you sleeping?"

"Just got up seconds before you knocked. Want to come in?" He stepped back and opened the door wider.

For some reason, she felt embarrassed. "Um... I was hoping to borrow your Wyndo."

"Electronics aren't allowed below."

She smirked at him. "Yeah, but I know you have one. I saw it in your kitchen."

He pursed his lips and cocked his head to one side. "That's what I get for letting a girl into my house."

Was he flirting with her? "You didn't let me in. I let myself."

He smiled and folded his arms. "What do you want it for?"

"The answers you gave me? The answers to my messages? One of the people wants me to write back, but I couldn't remember who she was. I wanted to look up her profile on the grid."

"Only one wants you to write back?"

"Yeah... The others weren't very happy with my letters."

He waved her inside. "I hope you won't let that discourage you."

"Only from writing to them again." Shaylinn walked into the living room, greeted by the sweet smells of Nash's garden, which was so much more pleasant than the stench of Levi's room.

"I have another letter for you. From Tym. You've really lifted his spirits." Nash jogged into the kitchen and returned with a message and his Wyndo.

She took them and smiled at Tym's childlike handwriting. "Do you mind if I read it now?"

"Not at all. Sit down, though. Here, let me move that." He darted past her and moved a stack of planters off the couch and set them on the floor.

Shaylinn sat, feeling shy with him staring at her. Why did he always have to stare? Was it wrong for her to visit? He was the only person willing to help her with her messages. What else was she supposed to do?

She opened Tym's letter.

Dear Messenger,

Thanks for writing to me. Where I live is probably different from where you live. I can't say more than that, but I'd like to leave someday. Not forever. I just want to know what's out there. Does that make sense? Sometimes I feel really alone here.

My mom doesn't understand. I know, my dad will support me whatever I decide, but not Mom. She's stubborn about anyone leaving. She thinks I'll mess up like my brother. So she's always watching me. I feel like a prisoner. I can't do anything without her thinking it's bad. I'm not a bad person. Just curious. Is it bad to be curious?

One other thing. I met a really nice girl. She's pretty too. But I know my mom wouldn't want me to talk to her. I said good-night to her once when I saw her walking with her friends. And she said it back. Anyway, I'm afraid my mom will be angry if I make friends with her, since she's not like us. What do you think I should do?

Write back soon!

Tym

Sweet Tym. She ached for him, but she also understood Tova's fear. It must have crushed her when Zane left home. And when she found out he'd contracted the thin plague... Shaylinn couldn't imagine a mother getting such news.

She wondered what girl Tym had met. "I'll write him back tonight," she told Nash. She set down the letter and picked up the Wyndo. "I need to try and be quick. I left Penny and Nell alone in the park with all the kids, and I don't want to be gone too long."

"I'm sure they can handle it." Once again, he gave her that wide smile.

Shaylinn looked down, focused on finding Elani on the grid. She recognized her right away. She was the girl who'd been depressed, who'd suffered two miscarriages. Shaylinn would write back tonight—Elani *and* Tym. She'd bring both messages to Nash first thing in the morning, before the kids woke for breakfast. Though maybe she shouldn't bother Nash so early. Perhaps she'd just slip the messages under his door. That way—

"Hello, Katz? Are you here, son?"

Tova.

Nash looked over to the door, eyes wide as his mother's voice came from his foyer. "Oh... She won't be pleased to find you here."

Shaylinn scooted to the edge of the couch. "Should I leave?"

"It makes no difference now."

Oh, dear. "I'm sorry."

His eyes latched onto hers. "Absolutely not your fault."

The inner door opened and Tova let herself in.

"Hello, Mother," Nash said. Shaylinn started to stand, but Nash waved her back in her seat. "Please don't trouble yourself, Shaylinn. You should rest whenever you can."

"I'm not an invalid, you know."

Tova stopped in the doorway, staring at Shaylinn. "Why is *she* here?"

"She's borrowing my... uh..." His eyes narrowed, looking at the Wyndo in Shaylinn's hands.

Shaylinn shoved the Wyndo under a couch pillow.

"She's just visiting," Nash said.

Well, that hadn't been at all suspicious.

Tova slammed the inner door. "This cannot be, Katz. I will not have my son breed with an upsider."

Breed? Shaylinn's cheeks burned.

"*Mother!* Please. You're embarrassing yourself."

She walked up to him. "I'm making myself clear. Haven't I lost enough? If you do this, what will become of Tym? With two older brothers leading him astray? Becoming exiles?"

"Mother, Tym won't go astray. Nor will I."

She poked his chest. "You both must obey the law. Only then will God protect you."

"That's not true," Shaylinn said. "Kindred laws are not all the same as God's laws."

Tova turned her glare on Shaylinn. "Don't tell me about the law. I know the law."

"Your law, perhaps. But nowhere in the Bible does it say that a man must live underground all his life."

"The law protects our people," Tova said.

"I understand that. But stop judging your sons for mistakes they haven't made."

Tova's eyes lit with fury. "You have no right to speak to me that way, Shayleen, especially about my children."

Shaylinn hadn't meant to pick a fight. "You're right. Forgive me. I was out of line. Nash, I'll visit you another time. Thank you for your help." Shaylinn got up and walked to the door. Tova was standing in her way. She met the woman's eyes. "Excuse me, please."

Tova pursed her lips and stepped aside. And Shaylinn left.

She chastised herself on the walk back to the park. She shouldn't have fought with Tova. She shouldn't have spoken to Tova at all. For some reason, that woman continually needled her.

Shaylinn suddenly found herself at the door to Levi's house. Why had she come here? She went inside and put her letters in her room, then pulled out a chair at the kitchen table and flopped down to rest a moment.

And sat in something wet. She jumped back up and looked at the chair. A smear of blood over the metal, and her pants were soaked.

The babies! It was way too early.

"Hello?" Her breathing grew agitated as fear settled over her. Apparently, she was alone in the house. Should she move or sit down? She felt no pain and didn't think she was in labor. But this wasn't supposed to happen. She knew that much.

She'd just have to go and fetch Ciddah. She took one step toward the door. Her pants clung to her thighs, feeling thick and heavy. Was she still bleeding? She pushed down her fear and inched her way to the door. She'd just about reached it when someone knocked.

"Shaylinn? It's Nash?"

"Come in!" The door opened and she grabbed hold of the end of it to steady herself.

Nash towered above her. She'd never been so close to him before, and he smelled like a garden. "Hey, I'm sorry about my mom." He smiled down on her and his expression quickly faltered. "What's wrong?"

"I think the babies are coming."

His eyes focused on hers, wide and bulging. "Now?" He glanced down and sucked in a sharp breath. "Oh."

"Can you find Ciddah or one of the women from my village?"

He stepped back, then forward again. "I don't want to leave you here alone."

"Please hurry!"

"Okay." He backed out into the corridor. "I'll be right back." And he ran away.

"I've never seen this happen," Ciddah said.

They were in Shaylinn's bedroom, Shaylinn tucked under the covers now that Ciddah had completed her examination. Ciddah stood at the end of the bed, arms crossed, brows furrowed in thought.

"I believe you've experienced placenta previa," she said.

Eww… "What does that mean?"

"That your placenta is partially covering the cervix. The placenta should be on top of the babies, but instead, it's under them."

Shaylinn's chest burned. "Is that bad?"

"It can be. But you haven't lost all that much blood. And it's still early, so it might not be true placenta previa. The placenta tends to move up and away from the cervix as the uterus grows. That's called placental migration."

It was like she was reciting from a textbook she'd memorized. No wonder Mason liked her. "Why did it happen? Did I do something wrong?"

"Not necessarily. You're having twins, and that can put more pressure on you. You've not gone into labor, though. And the bleeding seems to have stopped. I'm putting you on bed rest. That means you stay in bed until the babies come."

"But that could be months!"

"I know, and I'm sorry. But the babies need time for their lungs to grow before they're born. I'd like you to last at least until thirty-two weeks."

"But I can't stay in bed until February. That's over three months away!" Tears blurred her vision. Why was this happening? What was she going to do?

"I'm sorry, Shaylinn. I wish I had some antibiotics to prevent infections or even steroids to help them grow faster."

"I don't want to give my babies steroids. I want them to have the time they need."

"Then you need to stay in bed. I'm sorry."

Shaylinn hugged herself. It was like she'd just been sent to prison.

She was sorry too.

Chapter 20

Eight weeks had passed since Omar had tried to take his life. Medic Cadell had taken him off the sedation at four weeks, but Mason's little brother had yet to wake up.

Mason had kept himself busy. He visited Omar daily, moving his brother's arms and legs to keep his muscles working. He'd been plotting ways to test different meds without arousing Cadell's suspicions. But he'd spent most the last two months at his mother's apartment helping her sew together a balloon made of bed sheets. When they finished it, he exhausted his credits on waterproofing spray. But he still needed to find a way fill it. His attempts to build a burner had failed, but he thought it might work to fill the balloon with chimney smoke.

One night, as soon as it got dark, he set out to do a test in sector three, where the biggest factories were. November had brought snow and a coldness that Mason's striker coat didn't ease much. But at least the coat was brown and not orange. Cadell had given him several pairs of scrubs to wear at the GMC, and Mason hadn't worn his orange jumpsuit since. He doubted many people in sector three would like having a striker in their midst.

He snuck up to the roof of the steel plant with enough cement blocks to equal a man's weight. He arranged the balloon's opening over the mouth of the chimney. The fabric filled with heat and rose—it was working! Until the fabric at the base of the balloon caught fire. Mason barely managed to get it put out without going up in flames with it.

Now the balloon was damaged. He took it to his mother, who promised to sew patches over the burned spots. But Mason needed to work out a way to keep that from happening the next time around.

"I've got an injured enforcer here," Reena, the GMC receptionist called to Mason.

Enforcers were always priority patients. "I'll be right there." Mason finished the blood draw he was taking from the man in bed seven, then jogged to the reception counter.

Reena pointed to the enforcer, who was standing against the wall. "His name is Gryffel."

"Mr. Gryffel?" Mason said, looking toward the man. "Come on back." The man followed Mason to station fourteen. "Have a seat on the bed, if you don't mind."

"I'd rather sit in the chair, thanks. It's not a big deal. I'm only here because my captain insisted."

"The chair is fine," Mason said. "What seems to be the problem?"

Gryffel sank onto the chair and held up his right hand, which was already wrapped in gauze. "Stimming rebels, that's what. Five of them jumped me in the bathroom, cut out my SimTag. But they didn't get far."

Mason's pulse rose. This must've been Lonn's escape plan. And it sounded like it had gone badly. "Five of them? They were captured?"

"Not all of them. They knocked me out, see, so I didn't know what happened until I came to and the guys on my squad filled me in. One of the rebels took my clothes and somehow used my SimTag as his. Stuck it in a glove, so my squad told me."

Mason unwrapped the gauze from the cut, which was unnecessarily big and deep for simply removing a SimTag. "To what end? What did he try to do?" Mason knew, but he was hoping to learn whether or not Lonn's man had made it through.

"One of his rebel buddies had sneaked into the back of an onion truck. The shell who took my SimTag, he let the truck pass through, said the back was clear when it wasn't."

An onion truck. "What happened?"

"He got caught. I guess the trucks are inspected again before they go into the Midlands. Once they caught that striker, they used the cameras to track down the guy who took my tag. They've got the two of them in the RC now."

Mason cleaned out the cut, but it needed stitches. Even though Mason knew how, he'd have to call Cadell over to finish since only level six medics or higher were permitted to do any type of surgery. "But didn't they see them attack you on the cameras?" Lonn didn't have the ability to take over the cameras down here like Zane could in the Highlands and Midlands.

"Naw, cuz I was in the bathroom."

"But aren't there cameras in the bathrooms here?"

"In the striker bathrooms, yeah. But not for reputables."

Mason called Cadell to sew up the wound, and when the medic finished and sent the enforcer on his way, he came over to where Mason was gathering materials to administer meds to the patient in bed four.

"Did you hear what that was all about?" Cadell asked.

"With the rebels, yes."

"I know it's a hopeless cause, but I admire their spirit. The way the government lies to us, it's not right. I fear I'll die here with more questions than answers."

Mason had worked with Cadell for over two months. It was no secret that he had no love for their situation down here, but Mason had never heard him say anything so subversive. Maybe it was time to sniff around to see whether or not Cadell could be of any help.

"Part of why I was liberated early was because I was looking for answers."

Cadell cocked his head. "What kind?"

"Firstly, I was looking for a cure for the thin plague."

The medic snorted. "Well, there's your first mistake. There is no cure."

"Not yet. But it all started with this." Mason held up a vial of meds. "Did you know there are stimulants in the meds?"

Cadell looked skeptical. "Why would there be?"

"That's what we wanted to know."

"Who's 'we'?"

"Ciddah. The medic above me. She discovered it and had started compounding her own meds as a result. We had an idea to test the meds to find out what was in them. That's what we were doing when the enforcers came for us. They arrived just as we were conducting the experiment, which leads me to believe that we were on the right track."

"What was this idea of yours?"

"We'd mixed a sample of my blood with Ciddah's old meds to try and identify the stimulant."

"Why would you do that?"

"Because Ciddah found nothing when she tested her own blood. The theory was, perhaps the stimulant converted in some way when it reacted with the virus, and that's why Ciddah had been unable to isolate it. We decided to test it on my blood, since I'm uninfected."

"Uninfected? How can anyone be uninfected?"

"I'm an outsider. Safe Lands enforcers raided my village and took the young women into the harem."

"I saw all those new nationals on the ColorCast a while back. I had no idea they'd been taken from their homes. You know, I'd heard there were fertility problems up there lately, but all we get is hearsay from the newly liberated."

"I'd give more credit to hearsay than anything the task director general approves as news," Mason said.

Cadell smiled ruefully. "Yes, I suppose there's truth in that. What about your medic friend? She down here too?"

"No, she got away. Went to live with rebels ghosts in the Midlands."

"Too bad. I could use someone like her." He waved his hands at Mason. "Not that you aren't great, but it would be nice to have another surgeon."

Mason thought of Lonn. He hoped Lonn wasn't the second rebel who'd been caught. Maybe Cadell could get Lonn assigned here.

"I guess I don't understand the point of your investigation," Cadell said. "Even if you did learn something, what good would it do? We're still here. They're still there. We're trapped in this place, slaves to a system that has been working for the past fifty-some years. You heard what happened to those rebels who tried to get out today. How can any machine so tightly oiled break down?"

"Truth has a way of changing everything," Mason said. "We must never give up hope that the truth can set us free."

"Yes, well, right now we have work to do. Give that man his meds, please."

"Yes, sir."

And Cadell walked away, leaving Mason wondering whether he'd found an ally in the man or not.

Once his shift ended at the MC, Mason ran all the way to his mother's apartment building in sector one, slipping every few steps on the icy sidewalks.

His mother opened the door, and before he could speak, she asked, "Is something wrong?"

"That's what I came to find out." He came inside the warm apartment and shrugged out of his coat.

Lonn was there, sitting on the armchair in the living room.

"Oh," Mason said, relaxing at the sight of the rebel leader, "you're okay." He fought to catch his breath. "I heard about the mission. An enforcer came into the GMC today. The one who'd had his SimTag cut out."

"It's awful," Mother said, closing the door.

"It's a setback, Tamera, but we can try again," Lonn said.

"How? Show Mason your neck. Show him."

Lonn and Mother stared at each other, both too stubborn to say another word. Mason walked behind Lonn's chair, and Lonn lifted the hair off the back of his neck.

Mason leaned close and examined the red welt on his skin. "A SimTag?"

"Our punishment for trying to escape," Lonn said.

"And everyone is to get one," Mother said. "There will be no escaping now. I'm a doctor, and I wouldn't dare try to cut a SimTag out from behind someone's spine."

Mason couldn't have imagined a bigger blow to their plans. To his plans. How was anyone going to ride in his balloon now? "When do we get them?"

"Strikers will get theirs in the car wash," Lonn said. "Everyone else in their weekly medic appointments."

Within a week, the entire population of the Lowlands would have unremovable Sim-Tags.

But there was still one option. "Omar," Mason said. "I bet they won't administer new tags to coma patients until they're released."

"But he's unconscious," Mother said. "What can he do?"

"Nothing yet," Mason said. "But when he wakes up, he can ride in my balloon."

Lonn's jaw hardened.

"You didn't see me test it, but it was working." Until it caught fire.

"No, I didn't see it. No one did," Lonn said.

"Well, take my word for it," Mason said. "It could be ready by the end of next week."

"You have one problem, boy," Lonn said. "Omar is in a coma. What makes you so sure he'll ever wake up?"

"*Richark*," Mother said.

"I'm just being honest here, because that's what Mason likes."

Mason inhaled, fighting the urge to be offended. "True, he might not wake up in a week," Mason said, "but he *will* wake up. And when he does, I'll be ready."

Lonn looked to Mason's mother. "What do *you* think?"

"You already know what I think. I've told you not to underestimate Mason. He's very clever."

"Fine," Lonn said. "We'll try it your way. What have we got to lose?"

"Thank you." Mason couldn't help it. He smiled so wide he chuckled. "It'll work. You'll see."

The next day was Saturday, and when Mason went through the car wash, the medic was waiting with a SimTag gun. It stung worse to get a SimTag in the back of the neck. As Mason sat to put on clean socks and shoes, the thought occurred to him that he would likely have this SimTag for the rest of his life, even if they escaped.

That evening after his shift, Mason went to the G.I.N. store and bought a pen and a blank card that had a picture of Joie Park on the front. He took it to the Get Out Now Diner and sat down to write Ciddah a letter that he would ask Omar to deliver.

Ciddah,

I hope this letter finds you well. You'll be pleased to know that I have befriended Richark Lonn. He is a good man, ~~and he is still running the rebellion even from here.~~

No. It wouldn't do to send his brother with a letter that divulged any information on the Lowland rebels, in case Omar were caught. He erased the last two sentences and tried to be more careful with his words.

Ciddah,

I hope this letter finds you well.

You'll be pleased to know that I have befriended a certain medic. One whom we once researched together. He's an interesting man.

Before I left the City Hall SC, I saw the results of our experiment on the blood meter. The stimulant in your blood was Xiaodrine. My new friend said it was an amphetamine. We're still trying to figure out why they'd put an amphetamine in the thin plague meds.

I started out tasking in a cattle feedlot. Lawten's way of punishing me. But I've been reassigned in a medical center and made another important friend. I think I'm close to again donating my blood to a good cause.

He wanted to tell her that he missed her and was worried about her, but he wasn't sure how to word such a thing, so he ended the card with:

I don't know what the future holds, but I hope that you are part of it.
Love,
Mason

Chapter 21

"There. His eyes twitched."

"I didn't see it."

"Oh, yes. Here he comes."

Omar opened his eyes to blinding light. Shut his eyes. Why was it so bright? Even with his eyes closed, the light made his eyelids red.

"Omar? Are you there, brother?"

Mason's voice. How had Mason gotten into his bunk?

Omar opened one eye, squinted it, then blinked rapidly to get used to the brightness.

He wasn't in his bunk at all. This looked like some sort of medical center. Sure enough, a medic was standing across the bed from Mason.

Apparently, he hadn't died.

"Wh... wha..." His voice didn't work. He cleared his throat and tried again. This time his question came out in a whisper. "Where am I?"

"In the Lowlands MC," the medic said.

"You OD'd," Mason said.

Why did Mason always deliver that news? It was *so* like his brother to rub it in.

"Why'd you let me live?" Omar asked.

"That kind of a question doesn't deserve an answer," Mason said.

"I'll leave you for now," the medic said. "I'll be back to check on you later."

"Can't wait," Omar said.

"Yes, well. Good day." The medic left.

Mason sat on the edge of Omar's bed. "Don't be rude. That man saved your life."

"Not really. He only prolonged my death," Omar said. Mason folded his arms and shot Omar a dirty look. Oh, he hadn't liked that comment, huh? "You forgot I'm already dying, did you?"

"Omar, I'm not here to talk about your death wishes. Whether or not you care, there have been some developments while you've been... sleeping. I'd like to convey those to you."

Omar rubbed his eyes. "How long was I out?"

"Ten weeks. The Lowlands have a forced detox program. You shouldn't be craving stimulants anymore. Do you?"

Ten weeks? Forced detox? "Seriously?" Omar thought about it. He was hungry, but that ache in his bones was gone. "Why don't they do that in the Highlands?"

Mason shrugged. "I suppose because forced detox isn't very fun. You're lucky you were in a coma for it. Now, listen. I need you to try and stay here as long as you can."

Stay longer? Had he messed up his body? He shifted in the bed, testing his limbs. A little weak, but everything seemed to work fine. "Why?"

"Remember Lonn's escape plan?" Mason asked.

"The turnstile thing."

"Well, it didn't work. Two rebels are in the RC. Not only that, but they've reapplied SimTags to all Lowlanders. In the back of the neck, right along the spine and deep enough that I wouldn't dare trying to cut one out."

"Walls." No more walking around off grid. No more Owl.

"Yeah, *walls*. Anyway, the good news is, because you've been here, you haven't gotten the new tag yet. They gave them to us at the car wash."

"Okay..." His brother was working up to something; Omar could tell by his agitated tone.

"You remember my special project? Your idea."

"The balloon?" Omar straightened, eager to hear more. "You got it to work?"

"Just about. Mom says there's a little sewing left. I've made friends with Medic Cadell, and he says that once you've recovered, which will likely be several more weeks, he'll help you leave at the right time."

"At night."

"Yeah. So, no hurry, or anything, but with the new neck tags, there's no one else who can go over. You're it. Everything depends on you. So, I know you wanted to die, but we need you to live a little longer. Think of all the people stuck in the Lowlands. Think of Shaylinn and your future kids stuck underground somewhere. Get better, Omar, and help us."

Shame fell over Omar like a downpour of rain. He'd really tried to kill himself. He was such a coward, giving up like that. Now they needed him. There was no one else. This was his chance to make a difference. To help. To do something heroic. He'd been given a second chance, and he would make the most of it. "Yeah." For Shay. For his kids. For everyone in this rotten place. "Okay, brother. I'll do it."

Four weeks passed. Omar worked to strengthen his muscles and his mind, while Mason and their mother finished the balloon. Five days before Christmas, Mason was ready.

So was Omar.

Shortly after seven that night, the aide came to collect Omar's dinner dishes. As soon as the aide departed, Medic Cadell arrived. He moved Omar to a chair underneath the room's security camera where the surveillance department wouldn't be able to see what he was doing. Then he cut the SimTag from Omar's hand.

"I guess this officially makes me a rebel now," the medic said, applying a bandage to the small cut. He wrapped Omar's SimTag in a cotton ball and used some medical tape to stick it on the backside of Omar's chair. "So they think you're still here. I brought a set of clothes for you. They're on the chair by door. Change into them and meet me in the hallway."

The medic left, so Omar changed into a black shirt, black pants, and black shoes. When he was done, he stepped out the door and found Cadell leaning against the wall across the hall.

"Won't I look suspicious dressed like this?" Omar asked.

"Oh, right. There's the coat." Cadell walked back into the room and removed a brown coat from a hook beside the door. He handed it to Omar. "There's a pair of leather gloves in the pocket. You'll need those."

Omar put on the coat, which was thick and warm. Medic Cadell walked him down to the front entrance of the building. Through the glass doors, he could see they were on the underground level.

"Where am I going?"

"To sector one, though I don't recommend you take the tram since enforcers heavily patrol the stations. Avoid enforcers at all costs. If one should try to ID you and find no reading, he'd arrest you. Take Circle Drive about seven blocks, then turn right on Sigland Street. Your mother lives in the Borderland Building, apartment 212. You should be able to tap her through the gate. That's all I know."

"Thank you." Omar held out his hand to the medic, who grasped it tightly.

"You just come back for the rest of us, you hear?"

No pressure there. "I'll do everything I can. I promise."

"I'll hold you to that."

Omar left the medical center and headed down the street at a brisk pace. Even underground out of the wind, it was freezing. His breath puffed out before him. It felt good to walk again. His legs were stiff, his muscles sore from so many days in bed. Omar removed the gloves from his pocket and put them on. They were leather, lined with soft fuzz. Soon his cheeks and ears were stinging from the cold. He wondered if there was snow aboveground.

He'd never walked in this part of Cibelo. Sector one was a lot cleaner than sector six. He didn't see any strikers' residences, either. Maybe they didn't have strikers in sector one.

He spotted Sigland Street up ahead on his left. Halfway down the street, he came to the Borderland Building. He punched the numbers 2, 1, 2 into the gate.

"Hello?"

"It's Omar."

"We'll be right out."

A few minutes later his mother exited the gate, followed by Lonn, Mason, and some old guy who walked funny. Mason carried a thick blanket under one arm. Lonn wore a backpack that hung low on his back.

Omar's mother kissed him. "You look well. How are you feeling?"

"Good. Cold. Where are we going?"

"Sector three," Mason said. "Steel factory."

"Then we need to go to the surface," Omar said.

"Yes, but it will be safer to walk there underground," Mason said. "There's more people for us to blend in with."

As they walked through Cibelo and passed various restaurants and clubs, Omar's stomach growled at the smell of fried food. He'd been living off bland hospital food for too long.

At the sector three tram station, they took the escalator up to the surface. They stepped outside into the dark night, and an icy wind clapped around Omar. A thin layer of packed snow covered the ground. Omar followed Mason and Lonn over the slippery surface. He liked the feel of the crisp, fresh air in his lungs. He squinted into the distance and could just see the red lights that edged the Lowland-Midland wall. "Shouldn't we launch closer to the middle wall?"

"Nope," Mason said. "We need the steel factory. Plus, the wind will help us tonight."

Omar looked up at the dark sky. Was he really going up there in a hot-air balloon? All of a sudden, it seemed pretty crazy.

They walked down a narrow street that cut between a row of buildings that Mother said was where they wove fabrics. Apparently, Grandma Sarah tasked in one of them. At the end of the street they turned, walked another two blocks, then turned again, approaching a big building with multiple chimneys that poured white smoke into the dark sky.

They passed under a streetlamp, and Omar caught sight of a yellow camera on the front of the building. "Aren't they going to see us?" he asked.

"They might," Mason said. "But we hope they won't pay too close attention since it's before curfew and we're just walking. And, believe it or not, there are no cameras in the back alley. That's why I chose this building. That and the chimneys."

Again, Omar wanted to ask why they needed a chimney, but Lonn said, "Quiet now," and Omar said no more.

Mason led them around to the back of the building. There they turned into a narrow alley that separated this building from the back of the one behind it. The snow was deeper here where there was no reason to shovel a path. They trudged through it for about fifty yards until Mason stopped at a metal ladder that ran up the side of the wall.

"Up we go," he said, then started to climb awkwardly with the blanket pinched under his arm.

Omar watched him, then looked to Lonn. "Is he kidding?"

"Shh." Lonn motioned for Omar to go next, so Omar started climbing. He wished Mason would have bothered to clue him in on the plan. None of this made sense.

Once they were all on the roof, Lonn slipped off his pack and Mason unfurled the blanket, which Omar saw wasn't a blanket at all, but an oblong shape.

The balloon. "Why's it so big?"

"It has to be big enough to lift you," Mason said.

Omar's stomach twisted. Maybe this wasn't such a great plan after all. "Are you sure it will work?"

"Mostly," Mason said. "I *did* test it. And tonight the wind is blowing the right way." He crouched and held out a harness for Omar. "Put this on. Legs in the smaller holes."

Omar stepped into the harness, then took it from Mason and pulled it up his legs. It was orange. Looked to have been made of a striker's jumpsuit.

Lonn, the old guy who walked funny, and their mother, spread out the balloon beside a smoking chimney. Mason tied a bunch of knots on Omar's harness and held up a long rope. "This is for us to hold, to keep the balloon from going too high and to pull it back to us once you're on the wall." He hooked a coil of fine rope to the back of Omar's belt. "This is for you to use to rappel down the wall into the Midlands. These two here..." He grabbed a wide strip of orange that was part of Omar's harness and raised it until it was up near Omar's eyes. "There's one on each side of you. See the black X?"

It had been drawn with a marker. "Yeah."

"That's where you're going to have to cut it. On both sides."

"I'm sorry, what?"

Mason crouched back by the pack and pulled out a knife. "I got it from the diner. The knife goes here." He slid it into a sheath on the leg part of the harness. "When you reach the roadway, you must catch the railing. Then cut yourself free. If you go too high, we'll try and pull you back. To get free from the balloon, you'll need to either take off the harness completely or cut it. Whichever is easiest."

"Easiest. Right."

"We need to talk about communication," Lonn said. "You get back to the rebels, you make a plan to expose this place. But we want to help. If you can't find a way to communicate with us directly, Mason came up with a series of light signals."

"Optical communication," Mason said.

"For the next week," Lonn said, "every night from eight to nine, one of our rebels will be waiting for your message beside the greenhouses in sector one. After that, we'll have someone there on Tuesdays and Fridays. This is all in the notes, so don't lose them."

"Also in the notes are our scenarios and the corresponding light codes that will deliver a message back to us," Mason said. "No matter what the rebels decide, we're hoping that someone will come back, at least to the top of the wall, and give us an answer. This is very important." Mason removed some folded pieces of paper from his pocket and held them out. "These are the notes. Put them somewhere safe." Before he handed them over, he added another paper to the stack. "And this is for Ciddah. Would you mind?"

"Not at all." Omar took the papers and stuffed them into his back pocket.

"Keep the gloves on," Mason said. "You're going to need them to rappel down the wall. The rope will burn your hands otherwise."

Mason went to Lonn's pack and dug out a big coil of wire. He pulled at it in various directions, like he'd already shaped it into something, but it had gotten bent. "The wire will get hot, so try not to touch it. It shouldn't be anywhere near you, really." He carried his wire sculpture to the balloon and tucked it inside the narrow opening, which tugged at Omar's harness. Whatever Mason was doing slowly added a third dimension to the fabric, but it didn't look like a balloon to Omar. It looked more like the floppy hat of a giant.

Mason picked up the base of the floppy hat. "Follow me, Omar." He walked over to the chimney. "Sit down, close to the pipe, but don't touch it. It will burn you.

"Gee, really? I wouldn't have guessed, brother." Omar sat cross-legged near the pipe, which warmed his right arm and cheek. Mason was holding the balloon behind Omar, opposite where the pipe was. "Why am I sitting here?"

"Because we need to fill the balloon with hot air, and it will help to have you out of the way. Lonn, Mother, Hobbles? Come and hold the ties."

The old guy's name was Hobbles?

The four of them each took hold of a different long strip of fabric, each evenly spaced themselves around the sides of the balloon. The way they held it, spread out between them, Omar could actually see that there was indeed a balloon there. Mason's wire had put a round shape in the narrow opening of the balloon, making a stiff circle. Other pieces of wire stuck up inside the balloon, holding the fabric away from the bottom hole.

"Okay, let's get it over the chimney on the count of three," Mason said. "One, two, three!"

They moved at once until the hole was over the pipe. The chimney smoke disappeared up inside the balloon.

His brother was filling the balloon with chimney smoke? Huh. Omar wasn't at all convinced that it would work, but to his surprise, the fabric started to swell and take shape.

Mother giggled. "It's working!"

"Mason, I'm sorry I doubted you," Lonn said. "It's huge."

It was. As the balloon started to fill out, Omar could see that the thing was easily twenty feet wide at the center. And made of white fabric.

"They're going to see it," Omar said.

"They're not going to be looking for it," Mason said.

"But on the wall. The patrols will see it."

"We're just going to have to hope they don't," Mason said.

Omar wanted to argue, to say, "Really? That's your plan?" But it would serve no purpose at this point.

The first tug took him by surprise. It wasn't until then that he realized he never really thought his plan would work. But the force of that tug... He was really going to do this. Like it or not, the Owl was going to fly.

The balloon was huge now, a lightless moon over his head. It suddenly lifted Omar off the ground. Just a little bounce. He put down his hands to steady himself. "It picked me up."

"Lonn, grab the tether," Mason said.

Lonn left his post on the side of the balloon and studied the pile of rope. "Where's the end? I don't want to tangle this."

Mason left his post as well and grabbed the coil. "It's on the bottom. It should unwind as he rises. Just hold this end and don't let go."

Any second now and the Owl would take flight. "How much longer?"

"When you're floating up the wall, you'll know," Mason said.

Then Omar rose off the ground. Another bounce, but this time he didn't land. He put down his feet and stood.

Mason took hold of the tether that hooked to Omar's waist and ran a few yards of it through his hands. "Mother, Hobbles, let go of the ties. Let's see what happens. I've got the tether, so he won't go far."

Mother and Hobbles let go. The balloon rose slowly until the cords attached to Omar's harness pulled taut and his feet left the ground. His stomach flipped, and he grabbed the harness cords for lack of anything else to hold on to. He stopped a few feet off the ground, held by Mason's tether. His feet dangled at his brother's waist.

Why had Omar agreed to this?

"Okay, I'm going to let go," Mason said. "The wind should take you right up over the wall. We're going to hold the tether to try and keep you low until you get there and can unhook yourself. Once you're off, we'll pull the balloon back."

"I'm ready," Omar said, which was a total lie.

A hand touched his leg, his foot. Mother. "I love you, son. I'll be praying for you."

"Thanks." Omar wanted to say he loved her too, but he was trying to look brave and too many words would reveal the quaver in his voice.

Mason let go, and Omar rose in the darkness, much slower than he'd imagined. The wall stood about ten stories high. The factory roof was two stories, so they'd gotten a head start. Omar looked down and could see nothing at all, his companion's faces obstructed by the darkness and distance that separated them. All around, sparse lights of the Lowlands were divided by acres of black fields. Maybe no one *would* see him.

He looked up but saw only the balloon. The queasiness left. He was flying. He was the Owl, and the Owl was coming back.

Chapter 22

Omar continued to rise, but in the darkness, it was impossible to know how high he was. He looked for the red lights that were spaced along the top of the wall. Once he located them, he had his bearings. He wasn't far from the top now; he was really close, actually. The balloon was taking him the right way too. Mason was a genius.

Omar was high enough to see the road that ran along the top of the wall. A set of headlights swept past him as an enforcer patrol car turned around at the northernmost corner of the wall. Turned? Omar squinted in the darkness. Sure enough, the road didn't go all the way around the bell-shaped top of the Safe Lands compound. On this side of the Lowlands/Midlands wall, the road ran only around the perimeter of the Lowlands. Where the road could have continued into the Midlands—where Omar and Mason and everyone else had *thought* it continued—a partition wall stretched across the road, blocking the way. Now that Omar knew how segregated the Lowlands was, he shouldn't have been surprised.

But how was he going to get over that extra wall?

He was headed toward the perimeter wall, but if he let himself drift a little farther, he'd get over both. He'd also be dangling out over the forest. But Mason would pull him back, and perhaps then he could catch himself on the Midlands side of the partition wall.

He didn't see any other way.

He swung his legs and even tried swimming with his arms, but it didn't seem to help his trajectory. So, he waited and drifted higher until he sailed right over the perimeter wall. And a few minutes later, the inner partition wall. Sure enough, he felt a tug on the tether rope. They were trying to pull him back, but the rope must have been sagging, because he was well out over the forest before he finally stopped.

From his position, he could see both sides of the Safe Lands. To his right, the bright, flashing lights of a city of pleasure and self-indulgence. To his left, the dark secret that was the Lowlands.

If only he knew how to make the balloon sink a little.

He drifted backwards again, likely from Mason and Lonn's pull. He was still too high to catch the partition wall. He needed to cut a hole in the balloon somehow. That should make him sink.

He drew the knife from the sheath and pulled at the harness that attached him to the balloon. It barely moved, so he stuck the knife in his teeth and pulled with both hands until the balloon's opening was within arm's reach. One of the ties from the side of the balloon slid past his face, and he grabbed it and let the harness go. The sudden and crooked rise of the balloon made him jerk to the side. Once he was steady, he climbed the safety tie, hand over hand until the side of the balloon was within arm's reach.

He held tight with one hand, grabbed the knife with the other, and stabbed it into the balloon. He had to really push to get the knife to pierce the fabric, but when it did, he sawed down about a foot then released the tie.

The balloon straightened, and his body jerked as he fell back. He looked around. They were still towing him back, but now he was falling too. The partition roadway wall was coming at him fast. He was just slightly lower than it—and on the Midlands side too.

He struck the partition wall much harder than he'd expected. But then started to rise. No, stop! They were still pulling. He had to cut himself free before they dragged him back to the Lowlands, but he was also a good twenty feet above the roadway. Too high to fall. He needed the balloon to let him down slowly.

Maybe he could cut the tether.

But then Mason would lose his balloon.

Omar getting to the rebels was more important than the balloon, right?

No time. He started sawing at the tether rope. Mason and Lonn's pulling lifted him to the top of the partition wall. He grabbed it with one arm, trying to hold himself there long enough to cut the rope.

Just a little bit more.

Below him was the corner of the Midlands road where the perimeter road ended and turned along the Midlands side of the interior partition wall. As he continued to hack at the rope, the tether pulled him to the very top of the wall. He scissored his legs over the top edge, one on either side, and squeezed with his knees, sawing frantically.

And, finally, the knife severed the rope.

The tether fell away. Overhead, the wind blew the balloon, pulling him away from the wall. He threw himself along the top edge, hugging with his arms as well as his legs. He couldn't afford to get carried outside the compound.

He needed to move farther in before he tried to float down. That way, it wouldn't matter where the wind carried him because he'd be below the walls, inside the compound. He slid the knife back into the sheath, then twisted around on the top of the wall, hoping to straddle it facing the other way so he might crawl along the top. A gust of wind tugged him hard, however, and he lost his balance. He slipped off the wall and just managed to catch hold, hanging off the side by his hands. Behind him, the balloon was lower than it had been. He tried to pull himself back up, but it wasn't going to happen. Time to let go and hope for the best.

He let go and slid down the partition wall a good six feet before the balloon pulled him back from the surface. He was sinking fast, more like a guy in a parachute. Good. He jerked at the harness above, hoping to keep himself over the roadway below him.

So close.

The tips of his shoes touched the asphalt and slid sideways, too fast. The balloon was way ahead of him, dragging him toward the far side of the perimeter roadway. He just managed to hook his foot around the guard rail to stop himself before he floated out of the compound and into the forest.

The balloon's force tugged at him. He reached down with his hands until he got them around the guardrail too. Both arms and legs hugging the metal like it was the source of life. He let go with one arm, slipped the knife out of the sheath, and started cutting the harness at Mason's black X.

By the time he managed to cut through the first X, his hand was shaking. The balloon continued to tug at him. It was sinking, but it was still stronger than he was. A few seconds later, he cut through the second X, and the balloon sailed away into the dark night.

Omar let himself fall onto the icy roadway on top of the perimeter wall. He'd made it. He'd escaped the Lowlands. Mason was a genius. Sort of.

From where he lay, he could see the city in the Highlands, glittering and bright. He used to obsess over that city, desperate to come in and experience it.

It had nearly killed him, but he wasn't dead yet.

And he still needed to get down.

Omar got up and jogged across the road. He removed the coil of rope from the back of his harness and tied one end to the guardrail. Then he climbed over.

But once he was lying on his stomach on the guardrail, legs dangling over the edge, he found it hard to go all the way. No balloon to keep him from falling now.

The Owl wouldn't hesitate, he told himself.

He tugged on the cord, making sure it was securely attached and that he had a good grip, then slid back. The guardrail caught on his coat, snagging a bit, but he pushed past it until his body was completely over the side and he was holding his own weight by his grip on the cord.

He moved his feet until he got his toes on the wall, then let himself down a hand. His feet slipped, and he tried to get them on the wall again. No use. It was coated in frost and too slippery. So, he twisted his body around until his back was against the wall, then he lowered himself, hand under hand, toward the ground.

About halfway down, his arms cramped. All he could do was hold tight and slide down the rope. His gloves heated at the friction, but he didn't dare stop now.

He hit the ground and collapsed, but a ringing alarm sent him running. Ten feet out from the wall he met a chainlink fence topped with barbed wire. It ran parallel to the wall, trapping him. He knew he didn't have much time, so he scrambled up the fence at one of the posts. The barbed wire ran on an angled strip that faced the ground on the other side. If not for that small blessing, he wouldn't have dared trying to climb over. When he reached the top of the fence, he carefully gripped the arm that held the barbed wire, and placed his foot along the top edge of the arm.

Then he jumped.

He cleared the fence and hit the asphalt road, lost his balance and skidded several feet on his left side. A raw sting throbbed along his arm and leg, but he didn't have time to stop. He pushed to his feet and ran. He couldn't tell exactly where he was. Way past Midland West. Could he take the train? Were there still ghoulie tags in locker 127? He sure hoped so, because that was the only plan he could think of.

By the time Omar knocked on the door to Zane's house in the Midlands, his heart was beating so hard and his body was so sore, he wished he had his PV. But he was done with that now, he reminded himself, and, hopefully, very close to seeing Shaylinn again.

Would she forgive him?

He heard footsteps behind the door. A deep mumble. The door swung in.

Zane. Looking totally shocked. Like he was seeing a ghost. "Now, I was *not* expecting you. How?"

Omar grinned, despite his fatigue. "Unhappy to see me?" He slipped inside and Zane shut the door behind him.

"Omar?"

Omar barely saw Levi coming before he was tackled in a tight embrace. Levi's body trembled, but it was laughter that he heard, not tears. When Levi finally released him, he looked around the room. Besides Levi and Zane, Ruston stood staring.

"Hello, Ruston."

The man blinked and shook a smile onto his face. "You're not dead!"

"You look almost dead," Zane said. "Are you okay?"

"Just a few bumps and bruises." Omar took a good look at his arm and leg now that he was in a well-lit place. He'd scraped a nice swath of skin off his arm and leg, tore holes right through his clothing. But nothing was broken.

"I don't understand," Levi said. "Where have you been? You were liberated, weren't you?"

The three men stared at him, eyes eager for the answer to the biggest mystery in the history of the Safe Lands. "Yes, but liberation isn't execution." He sat down to rest his aching body and to drag it out a little longer. "Everyone who gets liberated is sent to the Lowlands."

"The Lowlands?" Levi and Zane exchanged a look of confusion. "But... why?"

"Have any of you ever tried to visit the Lowlands?" Omar asked, pulling off his gloves. "You can't. Because it's a task prison. Mason called it a penal colony."

"*Penal?* What's that mean?" Zane asked.

"Something to do with punishment, Mason says. Of course, he knows more vocabulary words than any normal person." But Omar was thankful for his brother's knowledge and the wisdom to apply it.

"Liberation is punishment?" Ruston asked.

"It's where they send strikers and old people—they have for decades. They task so the young people up here can find pleasure. And, Levi, everyone is there. Our mother and Aunt Janie, Avaci, Grandma Sarah, Granma Marian, some older men and women from Jack's Peak. Mom said Chief Kimama was down there with Shavingo'o. And Elsu too."

"Elsu!" Levi cackled and clapped his hand. "That's wonderful. Beshup will be thrilled."

"And Richark Lonn is there," Omar added.

"Lonn is alive?" Ruston said.

"And still running the rebellion. Guess what, Levi? Him and mom are, you know, together."

Levi's face went slack. "Together?"

"To-geth-er." Omar crossed two fingers and held them up. "Yeah. Weird."

Levi frowned, looked at Zane, who shrugged. "But—"

"If it's a prison," Ruston asked, "how did you get out?"

All three men looked at him, mouths gaping slightly in anticipation.

Omar couldn't help but smile, knowing that what he was about to say would sound impossible. "I flew. Mason sent me over the wall in a hot-air balloon he and Mother made."

Zane's eyebrows sank, and he looked at Levi. "I don't even know what that means."

So, Omar did his best to explain how Mason's balloon had worked. Then he gave Levi the stack of papers from Mason and Lonn and explained about how they might communicate with the Lowlands rebels. After that, Levi insisted they go underground right away so that everyone could hear the good news.

Omar followed Levi, Zane, and Ruston down to the basement where they entered a second secret storm drain. While they walked, Levi told Omar that Jemma had gotten caught.

"We're planning a rescue, though," he said. "Soon. And now that we know the secret of liberation, the Owl can tell the people. Oh, this will be good."

"I don't even have my costume," Omar said. "I think I left it in my apartment."

"Yeah, Zane got it. The Owl has been hard at work," Levi said.

"What? Who's running around in my costume?"

"Me." Levi offered a sheepish smile. "It's actually kind of fun."

Omar gave Levi what he hoped was a stern look. "That doesn't sound very practical *or* safe."

"I know, brother, but desperate times... Once they'd taken you and Mason, and once Jemma was caught, it was the only thing I *could* do. I was wrong to try and talk you out of it before. It was a good idea. I see that now."

"Thank you." Omar smiled at Levi, happier than he'd been in a long, long while.

Ruston came to a door, and they all entered someone's living room. The space included an open kitchen on the far wall, separated by a counter. A woman and small girl stood behind it.

"Father!" The girl ran up and hugged Ruston's waist.

"This is Ruston's house," Levi said. "His real one."

"Another upsider?" This from the woman, who was glaring at Omar.

"Omar, meet Tova, my wife," Ruston said. "Tova, this is Levi's youngest brother, Omar."

"The father of Shayleen's babies?" She squinted at him and her mouth quirked up at the corner. "Good. That's excellent news."

Omar looked to Levi. "Is Shay okay?"

Levi patted Omar's shoulder. "She's fine. Let's go say hello."

They made plans to meet up with Ruston and Zane in the morning to discuss what to do next, then left Ruston's place and walked down a concrete passageway. At a door marked 16–1, Levi went inside. It was dark, lit only with a pale light over the kitchen stove. This home had a similar setup to Ruston's, though the kitchen was partially hidden by a short wall rather than an open counter. There were two couches in the living room, and sleeping bodies occupied both. Omar recognized Trevon but not the other boy.

Levi nodded at the door behind Trevon's couch. "That's Shaylinn and Nell's room there."

Omar skirted the couch and peeked inside. The dim light that seeped through the door's opening barely illuminated two forms under blankets on a narrow bed.

He closed the door. "I'll wait until morning."

"Good idea," Levi said. "Now let me take a look at those scrapes."

"He's not really the Owl."

"Yes, he is! And he's my cousin too, which means were related."

"What's related?"

"I swear you don't know anything."

"He looks dead."

Omar opened his eyes to a pair of blue ones with thick lashes. Jake.

"Hay-o, Jake." Omar rose up onto one elbow and saw another boy peek out from behind Jake. A smaller boy.

"Trevon said you were bad because you brought the enforcers to Glenrock," Jake said, "but then he said you tried to fix it by being the Owl. Is that true?"

"I suppose, though Levi has been the Owl lately, since I've been gone."

"Levi?" Jake practically screamed. The boy behind him gasped, and they both burst into shrieking laughter.

The front door opened then, but it wasn't Levi who came inside. It was Nell and a woman with blonde hair.

"Ciddah?" The medic.

Her eyes widened. "You... you're not dead?" She crouched beside where he lay on the floor. "Is Mason here too?"

"He couldn't come," Omar said.

She paused, gave a quick nod. "But he's alive? He's okay?"

"Yes. In fact, he sent a letter for you." Omar sat up and reached into his pocket. He had to lie back down to pry the envelope out, and when he sat up and handed it to Ciddah, it was all bent out of shape. "Sorry. I didn't want to risk losing it."

She took it from him gently, like it was fragile in some way. "Thank you." Then she stood and went into the kitchen, clutching the letter to her chest.

"Girls are weird," Jake said.

Omar couldn't deny it. "Sometimes," he said.

"Not nearly as weird as boys."

Omar twisted around. Nell had moved behind the couch that Trevon was still sleeping on. "Good morning, Nell."

She stared at him, and he had no idea what she might be thinking. "Levi just told Jordan that you're back," she said. "Ciddah and her parents live at Jordan's house, and she wanted to know about Mason, so I brought her here since she needs an escort. Shaylinn said Ciddah loves him, but Levi doesn't believe it."

"Why would Ciddah and her parents live with Jordan?" Omar asked.

"Because Levi and Jemma had all these kids to take care of, and someone needed to keep an eye on Ciddah in case she's the task director general's spy. Jordan thinks they're all spies."

"Ciddah is not a spy," Omar said.

"How would *you* know? Shaylinn is waiting for you, by the way. I told her you were back. She's awake, in the bedroom, but she can't get out of bed, so you'll have to go in there to see her."

Omar pushed up to his feet, a little dizzy with the sudden movement. "Why can't she get out of bed?"

"She had some problem, and Ciddah put her on bed rest because if the babies come early, they'll probably die."

"What?" Omar strode around the couch, but Nell was standing between him and the door to Shaylinn's room and apparently had more to say.

"Did you know Jemma got taken?" Nell asked. "It was Mia's fault. She stunned Levi so Jemma would come running. Then Mia stunned Jemma. And Kosowe seems to think Levi should marry her now, at least that's what Penny and I think since Kosowe keeps bringing Levi food."

Trevon threw the blankets off his head and sat up. "Stop gossiping, Nell."

"He should know what's going on," Nell said.

Omar grabbed Nell's shoulders and twisted around so that they traded places. The door to Shaylinn's room was open a crack, so he knocked. "Hello? Shay?"

"I'm here."

Her voice brought goosebumps all over his arms. He pushed the door in and peeked inside. Shay lay in bed under a thin blue-gray blanket, her belly a small bump. Omar's painting of Shay, Nell, and Penelope hung on the wall over the bed. That she'd kept it made him smile.

He swallowed. "Can I come in?"

"Of course."

He closed the door behind him and walked to her bedside. "Shay, what did you eat? Something doesn't look right."

A shy smile broke out on her face. "Ha, ha."

She looked different. Rounder everywhere. "How much longer?"

"Well, they're not supposed to come until the end of March, but Jemma said your mom told her that twins are always early. And Ciddah says that she normally induced labor with twins at thirty-seven weeks, so that would be the first week of March. But then my... I had a problem, and Ciddah said it's way too early, so I have to stay in bed until they come. It's so boring."

There were so many things he wanted to say. "Shay, I know you think I—"

"How are you?" she asked. "You look tired."

"I am. But I'm good. I got clean. From the PV."

"That's wonderful." And her eyes seemed to come alive. "Nell said you were in the Lowlands?"

"Yeah." He explained a bit more, how Shanna was there and excited about her three new grandchildren.

"You really saw my mom?" Now she had tears in her eyes.

Happy tears, he reminded himself.

"She's fine, Shay. And I'm back to tell everyone the truth. It won't be much longer until we're all free."

Shaylinn took a deep breath, slouched a little. "And then what?"

"I know you think I... that I cared about Kendall."

"You kissed her."

By her tone Omar could tell that she was still upset about that. "Yes. I told her to stop, but she said you wouldn't want to be with someone who was infected."

"That's my choice, not Kendall's or yours."

"Not Kendall's, true, but it's partly my choice. Shay, I couldn't live with myself if I somehow infected you. I already have so much guilt: those who died in Glenrock. But to see your face every day, to see you get sick and know that it was my fault... I didn't think I could handle that."

"So, you were going to pick Kendall? Because of that?"

"No," he said. "But that's why I let her kiss me. She got me thinking about what it would mean to marry you. And I was scared. But mostly I was stupid. I should have been stronger. And then you were there, and I'd hurt you again. So, I just..."

"Ran."

Like always. He nodded. "I was a coward. I'm sorry. Everything was just so intense. And I didn't know how to handle it." His time with Rain came to mind and sent another stab of guilt through him, but he couldn't tell her about that. Not yet. "But I've been thinking a lot about it. About... everything. And I want to be there for you. I want to be a father to these babies. But I'm dying and I... I can't ask you to die with me."

"Omar, I'm dying too."

His heart hitched at her words. "What do you mean? Mason said you weren't infected."

"The moment we're born, we start to die. So, you have an infection. So, you might die younger than me. Well, I might die younger than you. You never know."

"*Shay.*"

"You can't know. So why live your life in dread? Embrace life while you have it. Trust that—"

Someone knocked on the door.

Not now! Omar gritted his teeth.

"Yes?" Shaylinn called.

The door opened and a man stepped inside. Nash. Holding a bunch of bright orange and yellow flowers. They filled the room with sweetness.

Omar started for the door. "Do you need something?"

Nash stared at Omar as if he had come back from the dead. "Uh..." He looked at the flowers in his hand. "I..."

"Oh, thank you." Shaylinn waved Nash over.

Nash walked past Omar. Their eyes met.

Shaylinn took the proffered flowers and smelled them. The colors were amazing next to her tan skin. Omar wished he could paint her like that, eyes closed, nose buried in blossoms. She opened her eyes and they were focused on Nash. Not Omar. She did glance his way, though.

"Nash tasks in the greenhouses," she said. "You should see his apartment. It's filled with plants and flowers."

Omar's stomach tightened. Shaylinn had visited Nash's apartment. How foolish of him to assume she'd be waiting for him all these months. "Oh," he said. "I see. I, um... I'm going to go." Omar pointed at the door, backed up a step.

Shaylinn frowned, reached out a hand. "No, Omar, please stay."

"I bring new flowers every week," Nash said as if it were no big deal. "You were here before me."

Omar looked from Nash to Shay. "Really, it's okay." Though his chest felt thick, like a weight had been pressed down on it. "You two talk."

"*Omar.*" Shaylinn's voice was deep and firm.

But Omar was already out the door. A breath shuddered past his lips. It was better this way, really.

"Omar!"

He ignored Shay's yell, strode through the living room, dodged little Carrie, who toddled out of nowhere.

"Omar, Shay's calling you," Nell said from the kitchen.

He pretended not to hear, opened the front door, slipped into the cool corridor, shut the door behind him.

He stood in the alcove, shaking. He patted his pockets, looking for his PV.

No more PV. Sober. Clean.

He had to deal with pain and disappointment on his own now. Walls!

The door opened, striking the backs of his shoes. He lurched out of the way and turned around to see who was coming out.

Nash.

Nash shut the door, grabbed Omar's shirt, and shoved him against the wall.

"Whoa!" Omar grabbed Nash's wrists and tried to push them away. The memory of Prav hitting him flashed through his mind. "What is this?"

"I have a message from Shaylinn for you. You ready?" He gave Omar a little shake. "You listening? Because I'm only going to give it once, then you're on your own. Because I love that girl. And I think I could make her happy."

Omar didn't want to hear this. Who did Nash think he was, shoving Omar around like this and saying such things? "Then you should marry her. Because Shay's a nice girl. She doesn't pair up or anything like that."

"Shut up." Another shake. "You're an idiot, you know that?" He released Omar with a shove. "Shaylinn doesn't love me. She loves you. Do you even get what that means?"

What? No, Nash was wrong. Omar had seen the way she'd brightened when the guy had given her the flowers. "You said Shaylinn had a message for me?"

Nash shot Omar one last dirty look, then grimaced. "She said, 'Don't you dare run away from me again.'"

The words were like a punch to the gut. Omar closed his eyes, wanting to defend himself. He met Nash's dark eyes. "I just thought she would be better off with you, you know? Without me."

"Yeah, well, I do too. But you don't get to decide that, unfortunately. And neither do I." He opened the door to Levi's house and pushed Omar back inside. "Be good to her." And he slammed the door in Omar's face.

Well, then. That had been nice and awkward. And so would be going back to Shay.

So, Omar didn't go back. He stayed put, leaning against the front door, watching Joey and his little friend play the Owl. Joey was the Owl, of course, and the other boy was an enforcer.

"You won't get away with this!" the boy said.

"Enforcers can't stop the Owl!" Joey said. "The Owl speaks the truth. Trust the Owl!"

Omar smirked, a little twinge of pride swelling in his throat.

A booming knock on the door made Omar jump. He turned and opened it.

Ruston's wife pushed past him. "Where is she?" The woman shook a crumpled piece of paper in his face. "Where is that girl?"

"Which girl?" Omar asked.

"Shayleen. I will speak to her right now."

"Shay*linn* is in bed like always," Trevon said from the couch.

The woman started for Shaylinn's room, but Omar grabbed her arm. "Wait. What do you want? Tell me first."

"Remove your hands from me this instant!"

Omar let go, taken aback by the anger in the woman's voice. She strode through the living room, around the couch, and knocked on the door to Shaylinn's bedroom.

Omar chased after her.

Chapter 23

An ache pulsed through Shaylinn's abdomen, starting in her back and ending at her belly button. She gritted her teeth and wondered what Nell had put in her oatmeal this morning that had given her such indigestion.

She stared at the doorway, waiting. Omar had better return. She'd hoped and prayed for so long, and now he was here, back from the dead, but also back to being flighty. She wanted to talk to him. Needed to.

Someone knocked on her door. Omar! Good. "Come in." She smiled, glad that Nash had persuaded him to return.

But when the door flung wide, it was Tova who came inside. Stormed inside was a better description. The woman's face was red, her lips pinched in a snarl that bared her teeth.

"Good morning," Shaylinn told her. She caught sight of Omar behind Tova and her heart quickened. He *had* come back!

Tova swept into the room until she stood over Shaylinn's bed. "Don't be friendly with me, you little wretch." She held up a crumpled piece of paper. Shaylinn recognized the bits of blue handwriting. It was one of her messages.

"Hey! Don't talk to her like that." Omar wedged himself between Tova and Shaylinn's bed, held the woman back. "Just calm down."

"She's been writing letters to my son." Tova shook her fist, the paper still clenched inside. "She has no right!"

Omar looked down on Shaylinn. "You wrote to Nash?"

"Yes," Shaylinn said, but quickly added, "That was our agreement if he was going to deliver my messages."

Tova walked to the foot of Shaylinn's bed, uncrumpling the letter. "This is *not* to Katz." She held it up, turned it so Shaylinn could see the whole thing.

Ah. "That's to Tym."

Omar looked from the letter to Shaylinn. "Who's tha—?"

"You have no business poisoning a thirteen-year-old boy's mind with your worldly ideas," Tova said.

"I didn't. I was very cautious in what I wrote. Nash asked me to do it. He even asked Ruston's permission first, to make sure it was okay."

This only seemed to anger Tova further. "You encouraged Tym to write to Dathan!"

"They're brothers," Shaylinn said. "And writing letters is a good way to keep in touch."

"Dathan has been exiled. He's no longer a member of our family. We don't communicate with him."

"Who's Dathan?" Omar asked.

"Dathan is Zane's real name," Shaylinn said to Omar, then addressed Tova. "From what I read of Kindred policy in the library, if a prodigal returns and asks forgiveness, he's to be forgiven and welcomed back. It's *your* law."

"Not all the Old ways are practiced here anymore," Tova said. "Not when the thin plague is rampant. We cannot let offenders back into the community to spread the disease."

"I have the plague," Omar said, setting his hand on Tova's shoulder and offering her a wide smile.

The woman shrieked and flew back from Omar.

Shaylinn tried not to laugh. "Tova, you can't get the thin plague from touching someone."

Tova kept back against the wall, eyeing Omar warily. "You have no right to meddle in my family's business, Shayleen."

"You're right. I'm sorry. I just figured that everyone has a right to know they are loved, especially around Christmas. And Tym wanted to tell Zane that he loved him. What's wrong with— Ahh!"

Another ache surprised Shaylinn, squeezing, burning the back of her spine. She held her breath through it.

Omar leaned over her. "Shay, what's wrong?"

"I have a bellyache," Shaylinn said. "I think I ate something bad."

"What did you eat?" Tova asked.

"Just oatmeal."

"The kids ate the same oatmeal and they seem fine," Omar said.

He didn't understand anything. "But they're not pregnant. Everything about me is strange right now."

"How long have you been hurting?" Tova asked.

"Off and on since breakfast," Shaylinn said.

"Contractions," Tova said with a nod of certainty.

Cold fear flashed over Shaylinn at the very idea. "No, it's too early."

"They start in your back and wrap around you," Tova said. "Is that what you feel?"

Shaylinn shivered. They couldn't be contractions. She was only at week... She couldn't remember what week it was, but she knew it was much too early. She tried to sit and reach for her journal.

"What do you need?" Omar asked, hovering at her bedside.

She pointed. "That red book."

He handed it to her and she flipped to the calendar in the front, quickly located December 21. "Twenty-six weeks." Tears flooded her eyes. "It's way too early."

"I will help you, Shayleen," Tova said. "Though I have no obligation to do so."

Tova help her? Anything but that. "No, that's okay. Omar? Will you go find Ciddah, please?"

"You bet." He turned and ran from the room.

"You need crampbark and fennel," Tova said, walking toward the bed now that Omar had gone. "We grow it in the greenhouse. I'll send Katz to get some. Until then, roll onto your hands and knees. Rest your head on your arms. Put your backside up in the air. That will help the babies move closer to your lungs."

Shaylinn couldn't help it. She giggled. "Gravity?"

Tova started for the door. "To be certain. Now do as I say. I'll return shortly."

Tova left, but Shaylinn didn't roll over and put her butt in the air. She wasn't even certain she was in labor. It was likely only indigestion from the oatmeal.

Omar returned with Naomi and Ciddah, both of whom shooed him right back out of the room.

"Don't let anyone come in here until I say so," Ciddah said. "Do you understand? I'm going to check her."

Omar looked past Ciddah and met Shaylinn's gaze. "Check her for what?"

"To see if the babies are coming," Ciddah said.

Omar's face paled, and he inched back a step. "What, uh... How long will that take?"

"Not long. Now, out!" Naomi said.

One more glance from Omar, and he pulled the door shut.

"You poor dear." Naomi sat on the edge of Shaylinn's bed, swept the hair back from her forehead. "Are you all right?"

"I'm fine." Shaylinn would never get to finish her conversation with Omar at this rate. "Ciddah, I really don't think I'm in labor. Tova thought so, but—"

"Tova has birthed five children, Shaylinn," Ciddah said. "I think that gives her some level of expertise."

"I guess."

Ciddah examined Shaylinn, and halfway through, another cramp seized her body. This one hurt more than the others.

"Ohh, Shaylinn," Ciddah said. "Yes, you're in labor."

Shaylinn took long breaths through her nose to try and ignore the pain. "Really?

"I'm afraid so, but the contractions aren't close. I really need some meds! What if Levi took me to a Pharmco? We could steal some."

"If he won't trade you for Jemma, he won't take you out for meds," Naomi said.

"Then he's a fool!" Ciddah tucked Shaylinn back under the blankets. "I've never tried to stop labor without meds or equipment."

"I'll fetch Chipeta," Naomi said. "She might have some ideas. She's miscarried several times."

"Miscarry!" The word shot fear through Shaylinn's heart.

"Don't worry." Naomi jumped up. "I'm simply hoping she remembers what Tamera tried to stop early labor."

A knock sounded on the door.

Naomi was already halfway there and opened it herself. Tova swept inside, holding a fabric bundle. Omar was right behind her. Naomi slipped out and shut the door.

"Why are you lying down?" Tova asked. "Roll over, Shayleen. Now!"

"What do you mean roll over?" Ciddah asked.

Tova explained how the position could help the babies fall away from the birth canal.

"It's worth a try," Ciddah said, nodding to Shaylinn. "If the babies come now, they'll be too little, and I have no way to help them."

Shaylinn didn't want to obey Tova, but Naomi's mention of miscarrying made her compliant. Tova instructed Ciddah and Omar to help Shaylinn roll onto her face, then supervised how to get her into the correct position. Shaylinn felt so fat and heavy and embarrassed that Omar was seeing her like this. She wanted him to leave, but she was afraid that saying so would hurt his feelings.

"Fifteen minutes, four times a day," Tova said. "I'm going to make you some tea that will also help."

"What kind of tea?" Ciddah asked.

"Crampbark and fennel."

"You grow those here?" Ciddah asked

"For medicinal purposes, yes," Tova said.

Shaylinn could only listen—she could see nothing from her position. The door opened and closed. Had someone arrived or left?

"Omar, will you watch Shaylinn?" Ciddah asked. "I need to find Levi. If he won't get me any meds, he needs to get an incubator. Preferably two, but we could make do with one."

"What's an incubator?" Omar asked.

"It's a special bed... box... for premature babies," Ciddah said. "It helps them stay warm and finish growing. I hope that Tova can help slow the labor, but if not, we need to have a place ready for those babies."

Again, the door opened and closed. "Who's still here?" Shaylinn asked.

"Just me." Omar. Weight shifted the left side of the bed, and Omar's head appeared on the mattress, peeking at her under her arm. "How do you feel?"

"Stupid."

"You? Never! Why?"

"Because I'm in a really strange position and all the blood is rushing to my head."

"I could draw you, Shay*leen*." He winked.

She reached out and tried to poke him. "Don't you dare!"

"I promise I'd make it favorable."

"Omar, no."

He chuckled. "Well, it would make you laugh, anyway. Things are way too serious in this room."

"Speaking of which, we never finished our conversation," Shaylinn said.

"The one about you dying?"

"Yeah, that one."

He took a deep breath. "I don't know if now is the best time."

"Of course it is!"

He set his hand on the back of her head. "Hey, listen. We're both really young, and weird things are happening to us. There's no one I'd rather spend my life with than you, Shay, but we don't need to rush into anything."

What did *that* mean? "You have someone else? Someone in the Lowlands?" A thought occurred to her with a jolt. "Was Kendall there?"

"Kendall is dead, Shay. There's no one for me but you. And that's how I want it. I swear."

Tears welled in her eyes. "Really?"

"Yeah. But what about you and Nash?"

She blinked quickly to banish the tears. "I think he likes me. But he's only my friend."

"Yeah, he likes you. A lot." He gave her a strange smile. "Okay, then. I like you and you like me. So, let's get you and the babies safe and get through this rebellion, and then if you're interested, maybe we can see if Levi will mentor us."

Longing filled her chest. But again, all she could say was, "Really?"

"You may not want to after going through labor. I've heard my mom tell stories."

"As long as you give up the PV. Do you think you can?"

"I told you, I already have."

"But for good?"

He laughed. It was soft and breathy. "Am I so unbelievable today?"

They sat together quietly for a time. Shaylinn felt peace with him here. She liked that they didn't have to decide anything today. And she liked the feel of his hand in her hair, scratching softly.

The door opened. "You can roll over now, Shayleen," Tova said. "It's been fifteen minutes."

Omar helped Shaylinn get settled upright in the bed.

Tova handed her a steaming mug. "Drink this."

Omar stood at the bedside opposite Tova. He tucked his hands into his pockets. "Can I get you anything, Shay?"

She wanted nothing more than for him to be around. "An incubator, I guess."

He leaned close and kissed her forehead. "You got it."

Chapter 24

Jemma sipped her water just have something to do. Again, the task director general had required her to attend dinner with him at Champion House, his palace in the forest. The same place Mason and Omar had come to rescue Shaylinn, Ciddah, and Baby Promise.

Tonight, Mr. Renzor was dining with the new enforcer general who had taken over after General Otley's death. General Stimel was tall and thin with dark hair, thick eyebrows, and large lips. He and Mr. Renzor had been discussing the general's plans to visit fight clubs to recruit for the enforcer training program. Jemma had long ago stopped listening.

She had been here twice before in the last few months. She and Mr. Renzor were never alone, thankfully. These were business meetings, and Jemma was his date. He wanted important people to see them together as the Vow Exchange grew closer.

Jemma didn't plan to be around when it finally took place.

She and Alawa had been plotting ways to escape. And while they had yet to find any possibilities that would work, they hadn't given up.

Mr. Renzor sat back in his chair. "Well, if there's nothing else, why don't we—"

"Actually, sir, there is one more thing," General Stimel said. "Well... It's just... There's been a development in the Lowlands, sir."

"What kind of development?"

He glanced at Jemma. "I hesitate to discuss it here."

"Should I be concerned?"

"Oh, I doubt it, sir. The new SimTags should solve all our problems. There's just one person who went missing, that's all. But he'll turn up. Probably hiding out in a dumpster with a PV. But I do need to discuss it further with you in, um," he glanced again at Jemma, "private."

"I see. Why don't we go to my office?" Mr. Renzor pushed back from the table and stood. "Ms. Levi, if you'll excuse us a moment."

"Of course," she said, smiling.

The men walked out of the dining room. Jemma watched their backs through the doorway as they crossed the sitting room and, eventually, walked out of her line of sight. She heard a door close in the distance, then silence.

She sighed, looked around the room, bored, wondering how long she'd be sitting here by herself. Something bleeped, drawing her gaze to the tabletop. Mr. Renzor had left his portable Wyndo device sitting beside his plate across from her.

Jemma's mind raced with thoughts of what it might contain. This might be the chance she and Alawa had been waiting for. The task director had information on that device, she was certain. Should she pick it up? Instead, she stood and walked around to his chair. She swiped her finger over the logo and a password box popped up.

Drat! She'd never be able to guess his password. She returned to her chair and sat down, took another sip of water.

Footsteps behind her made her glance over her shoulder. Kruse entered the room from a different doorway than the one the task director and General Stimel had taken. He stopped beside Jemma's chair, and she glanced up at him.

He kept his focus across the room. "There are cameras in this house." He spoke in such a low voice, Jemma had to strain to hear him. "We can hope that the surveillance department did not notice your interest in the task director's Wyndo."

Kruse's words made Jemma's heart skip. She didn't know what to say, so she focused on controlling her breathing, remaining calm.

"It was likely a message from his contact in Wyoming," Kruse said. "It seems the task director is thinking about moving there. That's top secret of course. He doesn't know that I know. I hope you won't tell him." He looked at her then, his eyes intense.

Why was he telling her this? "Not if you won't tell about the Wyndo."

He smiled wide, perfect teeth gleaming. "Agreed. Don't take such a risk again, femmy. You're a fighter. And I admire that about you. But I can't keep you safe if you take unnecessary risks."

"You? What do you mean? Safe from what?"

"I know you have no reason to trust me, but I am your friend. I won't let his plans succeed."

"You're a rebel?"

"No."

"But—"

"They're coming back. Remember what I said. I can only help you if you're alive."

"He won't kill me. He wants—"

The task director stepped through the doorway, Stimel behind him. "Are you finished, my dear?" he asked.

Jemma took a quick breath. "Yes, of course."

Mr. Renzor continued through the room, never stopping, headed for the front door. "Then let's return you to the harem."

Kruse pulled out Jemma's chair. She stood and followed Mr. Renzor out.

As always, on the ride back to the harem in the limousine, the task director spent the entire ride in silence, fiddling with his portable Wyndo. Jemma wondered if he had received word from Wyoming, as Kruse had suspected. She tried to catch the assistant's eye, but he too was busy with his own device.

It wasn't long until Jemma was back in her room in the harem. Alawa was already asleep, so she changed out of her fancy dress and into comfortable pajamas. She stood in front of the mirror to inspect her growing stomach. At twenty-four weeks along, it looked like a small melon was growing inside her.

Not a melon, though. A boy. Medic Vallen had told her just yesterday. If she couldn't be with her family for Christmas, she could think of no better gift than the new life within her.

And Kruse, as well. A new ally. Even here, there was much to be thankful for. It reminded her of an Old hymn.

"Count your blessings;
Name them one by one.
Count your many blessings;
See what God hath done."

Chapter 25

"Well?" Cadell asked when Mason arrived at the GMC the morning after Omar's balloon escape. Reena had not yet arrived, so they were the only two there.

"We're pretty sure he made it," Mason said, joining Cadell in his office.

"Pretty sure?"

Mason sat down on the chair in front of Cadell's desk. He knew how his answer had sounded, but he could only guess what had happened with the balloon. From what he'd been able to see, Omar had gone too far. They'd tried to pull him back, but he'd cut the tether. He wouldn't have done that unless he'd had to. "There's nothing to do but wait and see."

"Wait." Cadell's posture slumped. "I'll be sixty-two in three weeks. I've already been waiting a very long time."

"What's another week in the grand scheme of things?" Mason said. "There's more we can do, you know. We could try and find some answers."

"You said there hasn't been a natural pregnancy in years?" Cadell asked.

"That's right. Not in the Safe Lands," Mason said. "Ciddah said infertility started showing up five years ago and spread rapidly."

"What changed, do you think? The thin plague has been around since the Great Pandemic. Why, after so long, would fertility problems suddenly become rampant? Something must have happened five years ago. A new antibiotic, perhaps? Or a mutation in the disease?"

Maybe that was when they started putting stimulants in the meds. "I don't know. I'll ask Lonn."

"Richark Lonn?"

"He used to be a medic," Mason said.

"I know him. Fastest twenty rank in the history of medics. He's here?"

"In my bunkhouse. He was liberated a rebel, so that makes him a striker. He tasks in the cattle slaughterhouse."

"Richark Lonn in a slaughterhouse." Cadell shook his head. "That's really something. No one saved more lives than that man. Until he became a rebel, I suppose."

"He's still trying to save lives." Saved Mason's life every night in their bunkhouse.

"It was never reported why he was reassigned from the MC," Cadell said. "But word got around. They wanted us to know his behavior wasn't acceptable. Still, I used to dream about finding a cure. I was too scared, though. After what happened to Lonn. But I'm old, Mason. And I'm not afraid anymore. Back then, there was the threat of premature liberation to keep me in line. Now, what can they do to me?"

They could do plenty. "Move you to the strikers' bunkhouse and make you task in the cattle slaughterhouse."

Cadell winced. "True, that. I suppose they might. I've tended enough patients from there to know how dangerous it is." He tapped his fingers on his desktop. "I wish I would have taken more risks back then. I might have made a difference."

Mason sat up a little straighter at the idea of gaining a new rebel asset. "It's not too late. If Omar made it... If he got word to the right people..."

"I asked about compounding my own meds. I was told no." Cadell withdrew a vial of meds from a drawer. He reached across the desk and set it in front of Mason. "Thought maybe you'd like to mix this with your blood and see what's in it."

Mason picked it up and studied the clear liquid inside. "Is it yours?"

Cadell nodded. "We rarely use exam room two, so you could set up shop in there. You might also prepare an extra vial of meds for the patient in bed five to get yourself another sample to test. There's an extra blood meter in the cupboard above the sink by bed six."

Mason stared at the man, shocked in more ways than one. "Thank you."

Cadell stood and walked toward the door. "You just make sure you share your results. I'm curious to see what you find out."

As the day wore on, between patients, Mason set up his laboratory in exam room two. Before he could start, he needed to draw his own blood. But that wasn't going to be easy while he was working. When his lunch break arrived, he got a veggie sandwich from the GMC cafeteria and brought it back to his lab. He spent the rest of his lunch drawing his own blood and eating his sandwich while he rested. By the time lunch was over, he was ready to start testing.

He made two mixtures: One with his blood and Cadell's meds, and one with his blood and the meds of the patient in bed five. He tested Cadell's blood first. The tick, tick, ticking of the blood meter drew out the suspense.

Then it beeped. Mason read the display to identify the stimulant.

Inergia.

He'd never heard of it. He wrote it down on a slip of paper and tested the second sample. Xiaodrine, like Ciddah.

He recorded his data, frustrated that he had nothing more to test today. He cleaned up his mess, stored his blood samples in the mini fridge, and went back to work.

If he was going to do this well, he needed to get a lot more meds.

Mason had barely lain down on his mattress on the floor that night when the sounds of a fight made him sit up.

Shadows danced on the tile wall in the shower. He couldn't see who it was, but Lonn had gone over there. Surely Lonn could beat any man in a fight, though. That was why no one bothered him. Right?

Mason prayed Lonn would be safe, but he felt like a hypocrite, knowing he was truly afraid for only himself.

Then he heard it, the sound of SimAlarms stunning their victims. The SimAlarms made no real sound, of course, but the sounds of the fight ceased and were followed by soft grunting and some sort of a keen.

Someone on one of the bunks snickered.

Mason looked up to Hobbles. He was lying on his side, his eyes wide and fixed on the showers. Mason looked back just as the door to their block pushed open and enforcers ran inside. Six of them, all holding stunners in hand.

Finally. What had taken them so long?

"Everyone stay in bed or you'll be stunned," one of them yelled.

Mason didn't move. No one did. But someone was still snickering.

Four of the enforcers carried two big men from the showers. One was Strongboy. Mason didn't know the other's name. They carried them into the hallway, then came back in and carried out two more. Mason didn't know the names of these two, either, but he did know that they were Scorpion's lackeys. Four against Lonn? Why?

Lonn was the last to be carried out. As two enforcers dragged him past where Mason sat on the floor, Lonn wrenched free and grabbed hold of the end of his bunk bed, clearly unstunned.

"Hit me," he growled at Mason. "Now, you stupid shell!"

A third enforcer ran inside the room and pried Lonn's hand off the bunk.

"Attack one of the enforcers, then, boy!" Lonn yelled. "Do something."

Attack an enforcer? Mason didn't understand. The enforcers managed to get Lonn out the door before he could offer any more clues.

Why would he tell Mason to attack anyone?

The outer doors closed with a bang. Mason could hear the footsteps of the enforcers in the hallway, retreating from bunk 2C.

That's when they came for Mason.

Like the shadows of hawks they soared across the room, flew toward his place on the floor, looking to devour him. He understood Lonn too late. If Mason had joined the fight, he would have been stunned and taken to the warden. Now he was alone with evil men and no protector.

Mason slid underneath Lonn's bunk and grabbed the bedsprings above. Big hands snaked under the bed, grabbed him, pulled.

No, no!

His body slid out from under the bed. He wrapped his arm around one leg of the bed, bent his elbow, and clutched his opposite wrist with each hand.

Still, they pulled until the bed slid out from its place and hit the one in the next row over. Someone grabbed Mason's waist, squeezed and yanked. Mason felt like he might rip in half at his hip bones.

"I got this," a deep voice said. And suddenly the bed tipped up, and Mason lost his anchor.

They lifted him then, like the enforcers had lifted the others. Only Mason was not going to see the warden. Mason was going to the opposite corner of the room. To Scorpion.

He thrashed, kicked, bit someone's hand, but they did not release their hold. Suddenly, they tipped him on his feet so that he was standing in the gap between the bunks that belonged to Scorpion and Wicked. Scorpion was sitting up in his bed, looking surprised. His foot was still in a cast from when the cow had stepped on him.

Wicked had a hold of Mason's right arm. Mason didn't know the names of the others. He didn't recall ever seeing some them spending time with Scorpion *or* Wicked, though for the right price in this place, almost anyone could be bought.

"What's this?" Scorpion asked.

"You wanted him," Wicked said. "I got him for you."

"You arranged this?" Scorpion asked. "Even the guards?"

"It took some careful negotiations and plenty of credits," Wicked said, "but I figured if Rock Fist was gone, we could get the boy without too much trouble."

A smile stretched across Scorpion's tattooed face. "I'm impressed."

The guards were involved? Why? Mason wanted to die. *God, take me to heaven. Don't make me live through this. Please.*

"What shall we do with him?" Wicked asked. "We have all night."

Save me from these wicked men. Have I not tried to serve you? Have I not done my best?

Scorpion pointed over Wicked's shoulder, across the room. "Take him back."

"Back where?" Wicked asked.

"To his bed," Scorpion said. "Take him back."

"What? Are you crazy?" Wicked's eyes flashed. "Do you know how many credits it took to pay off everyone?"

Scorpion studied Mason, expression stoic. "There's no way you could've known it, Wicked, but I'm in Raven's debt."

Wicked's voice raised an octave. "Since when?"

Raven? That was Mason! The name Scorpion called him. He perked up, clinging to a shred of hope.

"You helped me," Scorpion said to Mason. "Now I'm helping you. This time, you go free. We're even now. Next time, I'll owe you nothing."

Vomit squeezed up Mason's throat. He swallowed it, trying not to let his emotions show. "We're even," Mason said, surprised at the sureness of his own voice when he was a pool of quivering fat inside.

"Good." Scorpion waved his hand at Wicked. "Let him go."

Wicked practically threw Mason across the room when he released him, which was just fine. Mason forced himself to walk back to his mattress on the floor like he wasn't completely terrified and about to collapse. His bunkmates were all staring. Mason doubted anyone had ever gotten away from Scorpion like that before.

Mason lowered himself to the floor and pulled the scratchy blanket over his body.

Hobbles whispered and it barely reached Mason's ears. "How did you do that?"

But Mason couldn't answer. He was too busy thanking God through his tears.

Chapter 26

"Ciddah, just say it plainly. What do you want me to do?" The woman had called for Levi yet again, ranting about Shaylinn's condition like it was his fault. He didn't like feeling attacked. It was a good thing Jordan wasn't here right now. Naomi had the baby in her room, and there was no sign of Ciddah's parents, so it was just Levi and Ciddah, standing in Jordan's living room.

"I need to get her out of here," Ciddah said.

"Not happening." Levi knew it sounded mean, but he couldn't risk moving Shaylinn.

"Then take me to a pharmacy where I can get her what she needs to save her babies."

He fought back a sigh. "I can't take you to a pharmacy."

"If it was Jemma, you'd do it," Ciddah said.

Low blow. Was he being coldhearted? What would Jemma say? "Ruston said his wife has things under control."

"Yes, but for how long? If those babies come this early, they'll die."

"What do we need to help them live? Meds?" Maybe the Owl could break into a pharmacy and get whatever meds were needed.

"Meds might keep the babies from being born early," Ciddah said. "But if they do come prematurely, I'll need an incubator."

Levi didn't understand that at all. "Like for baby chicks?"

Ciddah nearly growled at him. "An incubator is a bed for a premature infant. It's enclosed and the temperature is regulated. It also monitors the baby's heartbeat and internal temperature. It filters the air and protects the baby from infection."

Oh-kay. "Where would I find one?"

"Various places. Certainly, in the MC. And in the nursery. And I suppose they must build them somewhere."

If Ruston could find invisibility suits, he should be able to dig up an incubator bed. "I'll get one as soon as I can."

"Get two if possible, since Shaylinn is having twins."

Determined woman. Levi didn't understand how Mason could put up with her. "Two. I'll try and get two."

"Thank you, Levi."

"Sure." And he left.

He headed down the corridor, back toward his place. He could hear distant laughter from the children in the park. He should go find Ruston now and ask about the incubators, but he wanted to get Omar involved in this. A leader should delegate.

He opened the door. "Hey, Omar." He slipped inside the house and was started to find Kosowe sitting on the couch.

She stood to greet him. "*Behne*, Levi. Only I am here."

He stayed by the front door, keeping his distance. Clearly being subtle or ignoring Kosowe wasn't going to get her to back off. "What are you doing here?"

"I wanted to talk to you. I brought some food." She motioned to the table where a covered bowl and a loaf of round bread sat.

"You don't need to keep bringing us food, you know."

"I owe you a debt."

He inhaled. "No, Kosowe. You don't owe me anything. Go back to your tribe and live your life."

"I should have done something to stop Mia when she took Jemma."

That gave Levi pause. Why hadn't Kosowe helped Jemma?

"But she is gone," Kosowe said. "We should both move on with our lives." She walked toward him slowly. "I can help you move on."

A chill ran over Levi. Something about that night in the harem bothered him. He strained to remember what it was.

"I would make a good wife," Kosowe whispered.

It hit him suddenly. The whispering. Kosowe had lingered at the stairs, stalling Levi. And that was when Mia had taken his gun. But Mia would have had to sneak up on him to do that. Kosowe would have seen her coming. And then, after Mia had stunned him, she and Kosowe had whispered about something. If Kosowe had been so concerned for him, why had she taken the time to whisper before she went to get Jemma's help?

Because Kosowe had helped Mia stun Levi and Jemma. They'd planned it.

"I think a lot about that night," he said.

Kosowe stepped closer, grinning slyly. "The night we were together in Jack's Peak?"

He fought to keep his expression bland. "No. The night Mia stunned me and Jemma."

"You miss her."

That made him smile. "Yes, I do. But I will get her back, despite what you and Mia did to keep us apart."

Her eyes flashed wide, and she stopped her advance. "I don't know—"

"You stalled me so Mia could take my gun and stun me. Then you ran after Jemma and brought her back so Mia could stun her. Mia had her prize. You had yours."

Kosowe stared at him for a long moment, eyes intense. Then she practically snarled and said, "She is wrong for you."

Levi had to close his eyes to keep his temper in check. He'd been right. If it hadn't been for Mia and Kosowe, Jemma would have been safe. He opened his eyes and the front door, holding it wide. "Stay away from me. I'll speak with Beshup to make sure you do."

"Beshup is not my master."

"Please leave."

Her chin jutted out and she folded her arms. Was she really going to fight him on this? Make him drag her out of the house?

But she stomped her foot and stormed out the door.

He slammed it behind her.

There were twice as many men as usual at Thursday's rebel meeting, and all of the newcomers were Kindred. Levi wondered if they'd come because he was related to Seth McShane or because they wanted to get out of here too. Maybe both.

Maybe neither.

Levi had taken Beshup aside and told him what had happened with Kosowe. Beshup apologized profusely for Kosowe's behavior and promised to see that she was kept away from Levi's household.

The whole thing made Levi so angry, but there was nothing to be done about it now. Besides, it was time to start the meeting.

"Operation Lynchpin won't work without access to the Lowlands, which we now know is where everyone goes when they're liberated," Levi said. "No offense to Omar's plan, but I don't think taking control of the food and water is the best idea anymore. If we can instead get people in the Midlands and Highlands to see the truth of liberation, they'll be upset, and maybe protest or riot."

"It's still the same idea," Omar said. "Only instead of food and water being the lynchpin, it's the truth that will make everything crumble."

"So, we put the Owl on the ColorCast and let him tell the people the truth about the Lowlands," Jordan said. "Done."

"It's too wild," Levi said. "They're not going to believe it if they can't see it."

"We could send someone back with SimSight lenses," Zane said. "I can record their feed and show that on the ColorCast."

"That's good," Levi said. "And Lonn gave us some options of what they can do to help from down there."

"What kind of options?" Beshup asked.

"It's very specific stuff," Levi said, pulling out the papers. "They could hijack the Lowlands/Midlands gate, but only if we were attacking on the other side. They could riot. They could start fires. There are more ideas, but the point is, whatever they do, Lonn's idea is to do it at the same time as we do something up here. To attack all at once."

"We send a guy to the Lowlands wearing SimSight lenses," Zane said, "then we do something in both places. And I put it all on the ColorCast."

"That should work." Levi was getting excited. They might actually get out of this place. "The question is, can we send someone back?"

"Can't someone rappel down the wall or something?" Nash suggested.

"If they did it at night, it should work," Jordan said.

"No, they've got motion detectors on the walls," Omar said. "Maybe if we took out the power like you did before, shot out the transformer. But we'd still have to get up the side of the wall, and it's not easy."

"What's it like down there, Omar?" Levi asked. "Can one of us blend in? Or does it have to be you?"

His little brother sighed. "It would be faster if it was me, but I've gone missing down there, so they're probably looking for me. One of you might not be noticed during the daytime, but you could wander into trouble trying to get to Lonn."

"It shouldn't be Omar," Nash said. "Shaylinn needs him."

Levi gritted his teeth. Nell, of all people, had informed him that Nash and Omar both liked Shaylinn. Levi didn't have time for that kind of drama right now. "It would be best if Omar went back since he knows what he's doing."

"But how will we know if he gets the message to Lonn?" Ruston asked.

"Because I'll be listening." Zane tapped the place where his ear once was.

"I thought SimTalk doesn't work in the Lowlands," Levi said.

"It does for reputables," Omar said. "Just not strikers."

"I could fix that," Zane said. "I can hack their system if I can get a cube down there."

"Which is?" Levi asked.

"A portable terminal. In fact, once I hack it, I could enable the strikers' SimTalk and switch them all so that they can communicate with everyone up here."

"I don't like that," Ruston said. "What if people start tapping old friends and telling them they're alive and slaving away in the Lowlands before we can make our move?"

"If we're going to riot anyway," Omar said, "that would only help us."

"I agree," Zane said. "Do they see the same ColorCast as the people up here?"

"Yeah." Omar grinned. "They even know about the Owl."

"Perfect," Zane said. "If I can get a cube down there, I could hack the ColorCast and tell people in the Lowlands that their SimTalk implants are working again. So just as we reveal the truth, people in the Lowlands can start making taps and verifying what we've said. Total anarchy."

Silence filled the room, but it seemed to Levi that everyone liked the idea. "Let's do that. But we still need to figure out what we're going to do up here. Let's think on this some more. Hopefully, we'll come up with a decent solution. And once we know what we're doing, we can pick something from Lonn's list and send Omar back to set it up."

Most of the men left then, then Levi and the smaller team went over the plan to rescue Jemma. The day had almost arrived, and Levi didn't want to make any errors.

When Levi felt confident that everything was set for Jem's rescue, he looked down at his agenda and saw the last remaining item: Shaylinn. "We have a problem with Shaylinn. Ciddah is worried that the babies are going to come any day and she doesn't have an incubator to put them in. She says without one, they probably won't survive. Zane? Incubators?"

"Shouldn't be too hard to find. They're big, though. On wheels, most of them, from what I've seen on the cameras. But we could take it to the dumpsters and bring it down that way."

"I'd like to help," Nash said.

"No, I've got this," Omar said.

"*I've* got this," Jordan said.

"Great," Levi said. "If you three are going to argue over Shaylinn, then you three can work together to get the incubator."

Jordan and Omar glared at each other, and Nash simply looked sheepish.

"Can I make a suggestion?" Zane asked.

"Always," Levi said.

"Send Nash and Beshup to get the incubator at the same time you and Jordan go after Jemma. While Omar the Owl distracts enforcers in another part of the city."

"I don't want to complicate Jemma's rescue," Levi said.

"It won't," Zane said. "Dusten can drive for you instead of Nash. It's a simple switch. And the Owl's distraction should keep the enforcers away from you."

That could work. Anything to help Jemma's rescue go smoother. "Okay," Levi said. "Let's do it."

The remodeled Prestige building sat halfway down Anthracite Drive. From the Highlands, the harem car would pass through Gothic Gate and into the Midlands. Levi and Zane both figured the harem driver would take Gothic down to Winterset, then circle back to Anthracite. But there was a chance they'd weave their way through the old town area, taking Gothic to Belleview to Cinnamon Mountain and then come up Anthracite from the other direction.

There was no way of knowing which way they'd go. But that didn't really matter. Since Zane had no way of controlling the door locks on the car, they had to wait for Jemma to get out before grabbing her, anyway.

It was dark, and Levi, Jordan, and Dusten were waiting in the parking lot of the Prestige, sitting inside one of the DPT trucks. Once Levi heard from Zane that Jemma's car was almost there, he and Jordan would get out and walk into the lobby. That way they could exit just before Jemma entered. They'd grab her. And the moment Dusten saw them, he'd drive past and pick them up on his way out of the parking lot. Two blocks away, he'd drop them in an alley and continue on.

"Her car just passed through the gate," Zane said, through Levi's earpiece. "It's staying on Gothic."

"They're coming from Gothic," Levi told the others.

Dusten tapped his fingers on the dash. "Won't be long now."

Levi was nervous. The last two months had been torture, waiting for this day, ignoring the new threats that Renzor's people kept leaving in theater nine. Levi had wanted to trade Ciddah so badly. It was foolish, he knew. He couldn't trust that Renzor would give him Jemma. It would be a trap. Better to do things his way than kowtow to any demands from City Hall.

"How far along is Jemma?" Jordan asked. "Pregnancy wise?"

"I don't know." Levi didn't even want to think about the fact that these people had made his wife pregnant.

"I'm just wondering if she'll have trouble in the tunnels," Jordan said.

Levi would help her. "You helped Naomi through the tunnels when she was almost due. Jemma's not that close."

"Right," Jordan said. "That's right."

"They're on Winterset now," Zane said in Levi's ear.

Agony. Levi just wanted it over and Jemma back in his arms. "Where's Omar?" he asked Zane.

"Wreaking havoc on Villa Bonita. Enforcer 10 just got their first complaint from a resident. Shouldn't be long before they send someone to check it out. The car is on Anthracite now. Better head inside."

Levi and Jordan got out and walked across the lot. The night was chilly, the asphalt icy underfoot. Levi's breath clouded out through his lips. His gaze flickered between the lobby doors and the driveway to the theater, watching each set of headlights, wondering if they belonged to the harem car.

They reached the building and went inside, where warm air greeted them. The lobby was packed with people in fancy green and silver clothes, eager to celebrate the opening of yet another place to party. Levi hated them all. These people valued nothing that he did: family, hard work, honesty, sacrifice. These people did what they wanted for their own sakes, to please themselves, and their greed and selfishness showed with every flake of their skin. No amount of paint or fancy fabric could hide the truth. They were reaping what they'd sown, and Levi wanted no part of it for him or his people.

"The car is stopping," Zane said. "Doors opening. I see Luella Flynn and Finley Gray. They're coming inside. I don't see Jemma."

Levi's stomach flipped. "What do you mean?"

"The car is driving off to park," Zane said. "No Jemma."

No! She had to be there. "Why not?"

"Levi, how should I know?" Zane said. "I'm sorry, peer."

Sorry? Levi started toward the entrance. The automatic doors opened just as Luella and her partner started inside, dressed in green and silver.

Levi stopped directly in her path. "Where is she?"

"Where is who?" Luella had green glitter on her eyelids, lips, and cheeks. She blinked, looked him up and down. "Do I know you, trig?"

"Jemma was supposed to be with you," he said.

"Queen Jemma, yes. I'm sorry, Valentine. She was going to come, but she isn't feeling well today. Maybe next time." She patted his arm as she walked around him, waving to the crowd that had formed.

Next time? What next time?

Jordan tugged on his sleeve. "Levi, we need to go."

Levi let Jordan drag him out to the pickup zone where Dusten was waiting. As they rode back to Zane's house in frustrated silence, all Levi could think was *What if there isn't a next time?*

Chapter 27

Omar loved everything about his costume: the fit, the texture, the stretch, his paint job, the mask, the way the spray cans and stunner in his holster belt jangled as he ran, and especially the way the cape soared behind him like wings.

He'd missed being the Owl.

He darted from alley to alley, careful to stay in the darkness as much as possible. Villa Bonita was tonight's target. For Midlands housing, it was about as upscale as one could get. Some complained that only people in Renzor's favor were permitted to live there. It seemed like a place that most Midlanders would appreciate seeing the mark of the Owl.

Omar made his way out of an alley and onto 7th, lurking along the wall, hoping not to be seen just yet. Villa Bonita was on the corner of 7th and Winterset, just the right distance from the Prestige. Enforcers should get tied up chasing both parties.

He came to Winterset and waited until there were no cars, then ran across the street, imagining himself to be a real owl, trying to make his steps smooth. He held out his arms and admired the shape his shadow took on the street. He even skidded gracefully over an icy patch on the asphalt.

Omar set to work immediately and sprayed the words "Hoo is the Owl?" on the wall. Then he slapped up his stencil, filled it in, and ripped it quickly away. Around the corner he painted another owl, then wrote, "The Owl sees all." On the sign to Villa Bonita, he used white to cover the word "bonita" and stenciled an owl on the Wyndo that flashed images of happy people in their apartments. He went back and sprayed "Owl" over the white paint so that the sign now read "Villa Owl." Nice.

His thoughts drifted to the other missions tonight. Nash had better be able to get the incubator for Shay. And Omar also hoped Levi would succeed in rescuing Jemma. This night felt like a practice before the real thing. Operation Lynchpin was really going to happen, and Omar couldn't wait. But he had to. First, tonight. A small victory before the big one.

"What are you doing out there? Hay-o!"

Omar glanced up. Someone was leaning out their window, looking down on him. Good. Hopefully they'd call Enforcer 10.

"Zane? What's the status?" Omar asked.

"Levi and Jordan are in the lot. The harem car is just now turning on Winterset."

Omar looked down the road, as if he might actually see the car in the dark three blocks away, turning the opposite direction from him.

Levi's waiting for you, Jemma.

A siren pinged. Omar's heart jolted. He turned around, looking for the red and blue lights.

Nothing.

Movement out on the street. A car with all its headlights off. It had stopped a few yards behind him. What was that all about? Did they think they'd sneak up on him this time? Interesting.

Omar had two options for escape. The nearest crossway gates were either a half block down to 8th or two blocks up to Prospector Drive.

"Zane? Any taps for Enforcer 10?" he asked.

"A tap went out, but I've yet to see a response from Enforcer 10. It's like they didn't get the tap, even though I saw it go through."

"That's weird." Really weird. Time to go. "I'm heading back."

"See you soon."

Eighth was closer and Omar knew that crossway better. He took off, straight across the street, right in front of the mystery car. The vehicle started up and came after him, lights sending his silhouette long and massive on the street before him.

The Owl.

Awesome.

He darted into the alley that would lead to another alley that cut back out to 8th a few yards before the route that led to the crossway. It was a maze of nameless streets, and Omar loved it.

He wondered again why no enforcers had come. They'd come every other time. So, who was in that car?

He slipped around the corner where his alley met the next and...

Whack! Something struck him in the chest.

He fell flat on his back, the wind knocked out of him. *Breathe,* he told himself. *Get up!* He needed to run. Keep moving.

Before he could manage, two shadows loomed over him, reached down. Omar moved without thinking, but it was too late. There was a pop, some sparks, and a stunner ended his chances altogether.

No! This wasn't part of the plan. If he was caught tonight, Operation Lynchpin was over before it even began.

They picked him up and carried him. He tried to take note of where they were going so he could tap Zane the first change he got. Back out the alley the way he'd come. Pushed up against the black car. They cuffed his hands behind him. Swiped cold metal past each of his ears and pulled a fabric sack over his head. Shoved him into the car.

The car started and pulled away. The way he was almost sitting on his hands made the metal cuffs dig into his wrist. Omar had no idea where he was being taken. To the RC, probably, back to a cell, then before the Guild, who would liberate him again.

Lonn and his mother would be pretty disappointed. Shaylinn too.

Forgive me! I didn't mean to get caught.

On the ride, Omar beat himself up with a tirade of self-depreciation for his carelessness. It felt like the car drove long enough to cross the Midlands and Highlands both. They stopped several times, though Omar had no way of knowing if they'd gone through one of the Safe Lands gates. Feeling came back into his limbs and he tried to speak.

"SimTalk: Tap: Zane."

"We disabled your SimTalk," a male voice said.

Of course they had. "Who are you? What do you want?"

His captors ignored him.

Finally, the vehicle stopped and shut off. Omar was led inside a warm building. Over soft carpet. Across hard floors. A staircase down. The temperature dropped. The floor was still hard, but no longer as smooth as upstairs. They walked about twenty paces. Door hinges squeaked.

"Sit." A different man's voice.

Omar squatted carefully until his hands behind him felt a hard surface. He sat on a metal chair.

A door closed.

"Hello?" Omar said.

No answer.

"Hey? What's the deal? You're just going to leave me here?"

Nothing.

He thought about trying to leave, but that would be stupid when he couldn't see where he was going. He shook his head and tried to get the sack to slide off. He leaned forward and tucked his head between his knees. Shook his head again. Felt the bag slide a little. He shook harder until his head filled with pressure.

The bag slid off and plopped to the floor.

Excellent.

He sat back up and looked around, his face tingling with gravity's effect on his blood flow. It was a plain room. Sheet-rocked and taped but not painted. Omar had spent a few weeks tasking on a crew that painted rooms like these every day. Why had no one bothered to paint this one?

He got up and walked to the door. Turned around and tried the knob with his hands that were still cuffed behind him. Locked. If he wasn't cuffed, he could probably get out of here, break through the wall. Sheetrock was pretty brittle and thin.

Maybe he could do it anyway.

He locked his hands against each elbow, braced forearm to forearm, then tried to elbow the wall. That didn't work, though, and he ended up hitting his funny bone.

He stepped back and gave the wall a good side kick. His foot dented the sheet rock. Nice. He kicked it again. Again. Now that was progress. He turned and kicked with the other leg. Good. He walked up to the hole and peeked through.

The room on the other side was dark. Powdered chalk misted the air around the hole and made it harder to see. He sneezed. Backed away and breathed in some clean air.

A noise outside sent him scrambling. Should he sit? Get behind the door?

The door opened. Two men in black suits. Omar lashed out with a kick to the first man's chest. The guy stumbled back into the second man, who pulled a stunner from his buddy's belt.

The next thing Omar knew he was back on the chair, hooded again, and unable to move. They tied his ankles together with some kind of rope.

So much for getting away.

His captors left. Hours passed. No one came back. Omar's eyes started to sting from lack of sleep.

He'd almost given up when he heard footsteps outside the door. He straightened in the chair. Whoever this was, the Owl had to give his best.

The door hinges squeaked. Footsteps. Some scuffy ones, some that clicked.

"You really did it." A woman's voice. "Take that off."

Fingers tugged at the hood over Omar's head. Pulled it off. Before him stood the two men in black suits he'd seen before and a woman in a formal gown.

Omar couldn't believe it. "Luella Flynn?"

Lips painted green stretched into a beaming smile. "Caught you."

Chapter 28

“Shay? You up?” Jordan peeked through the cracked open doorway.

Shaylinn was up. She’d barely slept since the men had left the previous night. And now her heart sank heavily. “You didn’t get Jemma.”

“What makes you say that?” Jordan asked.

“If you’d gotten her back, she’d be here right now instead of you.”

Jordan pursed his lips. “Can’t fool you, can I?”

Tears filled Shaylinn’s eyes at the knowledge that Jemma was still lost. “What went wrong?”

“She wasn’t in the car. Just Luella Flynn. I guess we misread the calendar or they changed it or she really wasn’t feeling well. That’s what Luella Flynn told Levi—that Jemma wasn’t feeling well tonight.”

Shaylinn wasn’t feeling well, either. Between her inactivity, lying in Tova’s strange position, and Tova’s herbal teas, the contractions had gone away for almost a week. But she’d been in bed for two months. She wanted the pregnancy to be over. She wanted to be able to walk around.

“Nash brought back the incubox,” Jordan said. “Ciddah’s got it in my kitchen right now, washing it. Said it needs to be clean. He only found one, so your kids are going to have to sleep head to toe or something.”

“I’m sure they’ll manage. I’m glad Ciddah is here.”

“Yeah, she’s not half bad,” Jordan said, coming to stand at the head of her bed.

“Did something else happen? You’re hovering.”

“How am I hovering?” he asked.

“You’re standing over me. If you were relaxed, you’d have sat down by now.”

He sat on the edge of her bed.

“Too late. Out with it, Jordan.”

He sighed and rubbed his face. “Omar didn’t come back, kid. He got caught, actually. Zane saw it on the street cameras.”

“Oh.” Shaylinn shuddered and folded her arms. Omar caught? Again? Why?

"The little maggot was finally starting to grow on me too, the way he got out of the Lowlands like that—though I guess that was really more Mason's brain than Omar's brawn."

"It was enforcers?" Shaylinn's voice cracked, watery. She heaved in a breath.

"Zane thinks so."

"What does that mean? Will he go back to the Lowlands?"

"We don't know." He took hold of Shaylinn's hand and squeezed. "You'll be okay?"

She shook her head and tears blurred her sight. She blinked to wash them out of her eyes, but they were instantly replaced by more. So many tears for the girl who didn't cry.

Jordan scooted closer and pulled Shaylinn into his arms. He held her tightly and rocked her. "It's going to be all right. Know how I know?"

Shaylinn shook her head.

"Because you deserve every good thing. And I'm going to see that you get it."

Shaylinn wanted to argue with him, remind him that very few good things had happened to any of them in the past six months, but tears overwhelmed her and all she could do was cry.

Jordan must've stayed with her until she fell asleep, because when she awoke, he was gone and the room was dark. She couldn't see the clock without the lights on, and she didn't feel like getting out of the warm bed just to know that it wasn't time to wake up yet—not that she *could* get out of bed. So, she cried herself back to sleep.

She awoke the next morning to a knock at her door. Ciddah came in, pulling something behind her. The incubator bed.

"The boys got our incubator."

Shaylinn forced a smile. "I heard."

Ciddah rolled the clear plastic box around the foot of Shaylinn's bed and up against the wall on Shaylinn's left. She crouched and plugged it in.

"I think we should keep it ready just in case. How do you feel?"

"Angry."

"I know, femme. I'm so sorry. And I know it's hard for you to hear this, but you have to let it go for now. Find a way to relax. Severe emotional stress can trigger preterm labor. So, try not to think too much about it. I guess that's impossible, though, huh?"

"Have you stopped thinking about Mason?"

Ciddah sighed and fell into a slouch. "I see your point."

"I'll think I'll go back to sleep for a while," Shaylinn said. "Then I don't have to think about anything."

"Okay. Send Nell or one of the boys if you need me."

"I will," Shaylinn said, and Ciddah left.

But sleep would not come to Shaylinn that day. She got up to use the bathroom and found her bed sheets spotted with blood. Was it the same problem she'd had before? Or something else?

Panicked, she pulled the bedcovers over the stains to hide them and walked to the door. She opened it. Could see two heads on the couch. "Hello? Is Ciddah still here?"

The heads moved, and the faces of Joey and Weiss peeked at her over the back of the couch.

"She left," Joey said.

"I need her," Shaylinn said. "Can you have someone fetch her for me?"

"We can do it. Let's go, Weiss."

The boys ran to the front door and were soon gone. They'd left the door wide open, though. Shay crept out from her room, inching over the old rug. She closed the door, then started back to her room. Halfway around the couch she felt the familiar, slow spasm of a contraction.

Oh no.

There was very little pain. No more than a minor headache, and it was soon gone. Still, Shaylinn hobbled back to her room and climbed onto the bed, arranging herself in the position Tova had taught her. "Not yet, babies."

But the contractions didn't stop. Another came just as Ciddah arrived with Naomi and Aunt Mary.

"Oh, honey," Naomi said, taking in Shaylinn's position.

"It helped last time," Shaylinn said.

Thirty minutes later, the contractions were still coming and Shaylinn gave up trying to stop them. They were stronger now too, like the pulsing throb of a migraine around her waist. Ciddah helped her roll to her back and tucked her in.

"We should check you," she said. "And, Naomi, please help me keep track of the contractions."

"Shay, where do you keep your paper and pencils?" Naomi asked.

"In the drawer."

Naomi whisked out writing utensils and Ciddah set about "checking" Shaylinn to see whether babies were on their way or not.

"Well?" Naomi asked, pencil and paper ready.

Ciddah looked pale. "Not yet."

"What do you mean?" Shaylinn asked. "What's wrong?"

"Oh, nothing, Shaylinn, don't worry. It's just... With Kendall, the baby was already coming. To be honest, I'm not sure what I'm looking for. They don't teach this in medic school, since birth in the Safe Lands is a simple surgical procedure."

Ciddah didn't know what she was looking for? She was joking, right?

The door opened and in came Penelope and Nell, squealing about babies to hold. Shaylinn stopped worrying for a while, and soon her room was a flurry of noise. More had come: Chipeta, Eliza, and Aunt Mary. Which made it five women looming over her bed, arguing over who should "deliver" the babies, while Penelope and Nell played with the incubator.

"I'm delivering them," Ciddah said. "I am her medic and have been from the start."

"But you just said you've never done this before!" Aunt Mary said. "And you admit you don't even know what to do."

"I know what to do. Just not how to gauge when things will happen," Ciddah said. "I've assisted before. With Elyot."

"You should have seen Harvey and Elyot today," Naomi said to Chipeta. "We had them on the floor and they were cooing to each other."

"I think Chipeta should do it," Aunt Mary said.

"Well, I've never done it either," Chipeta said. "Eliza, why don't you run and see if any of the Jack's Peak women have experience birthing babies."

Shaylinn wanted to cry, but the pain was distracting her. She rolled onto her side, which felt the most comfortable. She heard the clump of the door, which must have been Eliza leaving. But all she could see from her position was a wall of women circling her bed.

"We already decided." Shaylinn panted, surprised that uttering only three words would leave her winded. "Ciddah is going to."

"But that was when we thought Jemma would be back," Aunt Mary said. "Jemma and Ciddah as a team is perfect, but alone..."

"I *am* capable," Ciddah said. "Once they start coming, I know exactly what to do."

Shaylinn didn't like this at all. They'd made a plan, but without Jemma, everything was messed up.

The door opened and closed again. "I'm here, Shayleen. Let me see you." Tova. She pushed through the crowd and up to Shaylinn's beside. She smiled down at Shaylinn, and brushed her hair back from her cheek. "Oh, yes. They are coming today, aren't they? Now you will see, Shayleen, with all of your letters. Pfft. Now you will learn the real hard work of a woman."

Shaylinn wanted to spit back an angry retort, but another contraction came, this one surprisingly strong. It felt like a giant had picked her up and squeezed.

Tova took her hand. "You must breathe. In and out. That's right." She brushed her hair back again. "Medic. How far along is she?"

"We don't know," Ciddah said.

Tova straightened, but kept her hold on Shaylinn's hand. "What do you mean?"

"I don't know how to tell how close she is." Ciddah winced. "I missed that part of Elyot's birth."

"Okay, listen up!" Tova yelled. "Everyone leaves but the medic and one other." She looked to Shaylinn. "Who do you want to stay?"

"Naomi," Shaylinn said.

"Okay, Naomi, fetch two large bowls of warm water and towels. Ladies, help her. Medic, you have some materials? Show me." Tova let go of Shaylinn's hand.

The room cleared out. Ciddah pulled a box up on the foot of the bed. Tova looked through it, selected a few things.

Naomi returned with one bowl of water and a pile of towels draped over her arm. Chipeta held the door for her as she carried them in and set the bowl and towels on the desk. Naomi left and shut the door behind her.

"Medic, we wash our hands first." Tova waved Ciddah to the bowl and washed and dried her hands. Ciddah did the same.

The door opened again. Naomi back with more water.

"Put that one here on the floor." Tova showed Naomi where. "And please empty that one and bring a new one." She waved at the hand-washing bowl.

Naomi obeyed and was soon gone again.

"Okay, now we check," Tova said. "Medic, come learn."

Shaylinn couldn't see the clock. She didn't know how long she'd been doing this. But it seemed like days. Her whole body ached to the point that she really wasn't sure where the pain was coming from anymore.

Time and again, Naomi had been sent for more bowls and towels. Shaylinn didn't know why. She didn't care. She just wanted the pain to stop.

"Here comes another, Shayleen," Tova said. "Soon. It will be soon."

Shaylinn gritted her teeth as the pain swarmed, burning and deep. She hated the Safe Lands for doing this to her. She hated Ciddah! And Omar too. Omar, who had abandoned her over and over.

And then the contraction was gone. But not like before. Not completely gone. Now when the contractions ended, she was left feeling bruised and beaten, like she was trying to recover but couldn't. Another would come. It would never end! She would probably die.

What if she died?

"Shay." Naomi took hold of her hand. "How are you? You want some water?"

Shaylinn shook her head.

"You're doing good, sweetie. I'm so proud of you."

"I don't want to die."

"Oh, no, Shay. That's not going to happen. You're doing great. Almost there, Tova says. Aren't you glad she's here?"

Shaylinn was.

The contractions came faster, seeming to possess her body. The agony was so intense she could barely breathe.

"Time to push, Shayleen!" Tova said. "Push, girl. Now! Push, push!"

Push? Shaylinn tried, swallowed with the effort. A faint moan slipped past her lips.

Naomi's face remained calm. "Good, Shay. You're doing great." Her voice was soft and soothing, her eyes focused on Shaylinn.

As the pain grew more intense, so did the voices. Louder, excited. A chorus of demands.

"Push! Push!"

Squeals of joy.

A light cry. An infant's cry.

"Okay, medic. You watch for the second baby." Tova stood, holding a grayish pinkish squirming thing.

Shaylinn saw blood. "It's bleeding? Is it okay?"

"Oh, yes, Shayleen. This is a strong boy." Tova picked up a pair of scissors and cut the gnarly cord, then brought the baby to Shaylinn. "See your precious boy, yes? See how much you love this one. Just one look and see if you don't."

A boy? It looked inhuman. An ugly doll covered in too much pinkish-gray skin that was slimy with blood and something white. Floppy arms and legs. Slimy black hair. Wrinkled slashes for eyes. A frowning mouth. His whole body fit in Tova's hands, head in one, rear end in the other.

He scared her.

"Is he okay?" she asked.

"Yes, love. He's just fine. A fine boy."

He didn't look fine. He looked weird.

Tova handed the boy off to Naomi, who oohed and ahhed as if he looked just like a sweet little puppy. Then it was time to push again. Soon a girl arrived, but she looked as strange as her brother, though she was redder, it seemed, and louder too.

But it still wasn't over. Shaylinn had to push again to expel the things that her babies had been living in all this time. Then Tova called Aunt Mary and Chipeta to hold the babies while she, Naomi, and Ciddah cleaned Shaylinn up. Once Shaylinn was settled in a new nightgown and a bed of fresh blankets, Aunt Mary gave her the boy to hold.

He looked much better now that he was dried off. He had a tiny little head the size of her fist that looked to be all eyes. Deep brown eyes the size and shape of almonds. Those wide eyes locked onto hers, and Shaylinn smiled and touched her thumb to his cheek. His skin was so soft. Tears filled her eyes. She'd brought life into the world. This little person had come from her.

So strange.

The women started to argue. Tova wanted Shaylinn to try and breastfeed the boy. Chipeta said it was too early. Ciddah wanted to give him formula. But Tova said that breast milk was not merely food, it was medicine for the babies' little bodies. Ciddah said that she was fed the formula and turned out fine.

"Can I see the girl?" Shaylinn asked.

Naomi was holding her now, and she sat on the edge of Shaylinn's bed and helped Shaylinn take the girl in her other arm so that Shaylinn was holding both babies. The girl was even smaller than the boy. She looked better too now that she was dry, but her skin was still very pink. She had even more hair than her brother, but her face seemed perfectly proportioned. Little brown eyes, a tiny nose, small lips. Shaylinn looked from one to the other.

"I like them." And she did. Her heart felt full yet completely frail at the same time.

Naomi laughed. "I'm sure they're glad to hear it."

"Do they have the thin plague?" Shaylinn asked. The question made her eyes brim with tears.

Ciddah broke off from her argument with Tova. "I don't think so, Shaylinn, but I have no method of testing them down here. You should only hold them a little while, then put them in the incubator to sleep. They'll need to spend a lot of time in the incubator. Several more weeks. You can take them out to feed and hold them, but they need to go right back in. They both look perfectly healthy, but there's no fat on them. The incubator will help keep them warm until they bulk up a bit."

Shaylinn kissed her babies, then allowed them to be put in the incubator. She submitted herself to Tova's lessons on how to hand pump breast milk so that the babies could be tube fed until they were old enough to learn to latch on.

So much work still, and she was so tired.

Shaylinn realized then that her childhood was over. She was a mother now, and her only concern was for her babies. It wouldn't change for the rest of her life. That was okay because these two were part of her, and she must do what was necessary to see that they were healthy and safe.

She would need to name them.

Would they ever see their father?

Chapter 29

Mason and Lonn sat by themselves at a table near the strikers' cafeteria doors. Mason had gotten toast and orange juice. Lonn was eating a pile of scrambled eggs and bacon that looked to have more fat than meat.

Lonn had returned to bunk 2C the morning after Wicked's attack. The yellowed remains of a bruise still showed under one eye. They'd had no more trouble since. Wicked probably was saving up credits for another try.

"I've been telling Cadell about you," Mason said.

Lonn frowned, his cheeks full with a bite of eggs. "Telling him what?"

"That you're here. He knows who you are, of course. I told him he should ask for you to be reassigned as a medic."

"It won't happen," Lonn said.

"Maybe not, but he's been helping me. He let me build a lab, and I'm testing the meds. Cadell's meds didn't contain Xiaodrine but Inergia."

Lonn chewed thoughtfully. "That's another amphetamine. For insomnia."

"That's what Cadell said. He asked his superior about compounding his own meds and was told no."

"Not surprising," Lonn said. "But, Mason, you're far too trusting. What do you really know about this man?"

"That he fought to get me moved from the feedlot to the GMC. That he's still fighting to get my housing changed."

"So he says."

"He helped us get Omar out of the MC." Was Lonn right that Mason shouldn't trust Cadell? He thought it over. "Sometimes you have to trust people."

"But are you certain you must trust *him*? Absolutely certain?"

"I am. He didn't tell anyone about Omar. And now he's letting me test meds in the GMC. He's a good man, Lonn."

Lonn sighed and nodded in resignation. "Then I'll trust him too, if given the chance."

Cadell slipped into exam room two and closed the door. "How's the testing coming along?"

Mason read the name of the stimulant from the blood meter. "This one has Focastat XR."

"That's a new one," Cadell said, coming to read the result for himself.

"Another amphetamine?"

"Yes, actually. It's prescribed for patients who can't focus. Try this one." Cadell handed Mason a vial, then picked up Mason's chart and made some notes. "Okay, I'll be back." He set the chart on the counter and left, shutting the door behind him.

Mason's lab had grown. He'd taken the padding off the exam table and spread his experiment out over the metal surface and all along the counter. Cadell had sent him here the moment he'd arrived this morning with instructions to test another seven vials he'd gotten from patients. Since then, he'd brought Mason the meds of every patient he'd seen that morning. Mason had tested a total of fifteen so far.

Mason had made a chart of his results. He'd put the patient's ID on the far left, then listed the stimulant found in that person's meds. The chart had two more columns: one for the reason the patient had come into the MC and another for the patient's overall health. Cadell had been filling those in as he came in and out between patients.

Mason studied the results. Of the fifteen, three had the same Xiaodrine that had been found in Ciddah's original meds, three had Centralin, three had Excitare, four had Inergia, one had Validum, and one had Focastat XR. Mason could not yet see any patterns in the patients' health, needs, or stimulant. They'd need to test many more meds to get such results.

Tedious. But at least he was doing something. There had been no message from Omar yet, and Mason couldn't just worry that his brother was hurt or dead. He needed to keep working.

The door opened. Cadell set a vial on the counter. "Come out. Quickly. Two enforcers just arrived."

Mason left the room with Cadell and walked to bed three. "How are you feeling, Ms. Silver? Is the pain still there?"

The elderly woman looked up at him. "Oh, it feels much better, medic. Thank you. I just hate that my hands don't want to work for me anymore. It's the most frustrating thing. But the pain makes it so much worse."

Mason nodded and, as the woman told him again how the pain made her drop things, he glanced toward the lobby. Sure enough, two enforcers were walking around the counter now. Coming toward Medic Cadell.

Mason's heart thudded. They knew! How? There were no cameras in the private exam rooms. Could Lonn be right? Had Cadell set him up?

"I demand more information than that!" Cadell yelled. "Besides, you can't just take my assistant and give me no replacement."

They'd come for Mason? Why? There was nowhere to run, so Mason walked toward them. "Is there a problem, Medic Cadell?"

"These men have orders to take you into custody."

Stay calm. "On what charges?"

"No charges," the enforcer said. "The liberator wants to speak with you."

That didn't fit with any of Mason's fears about Cadell. "Why?"

"You think the liberator tells us his business? How'd you get to be a medic?"

"Very well," Mason said. "Before we leave, would you give me a moment to inform Medic Cadell about my patient's needs?" He gestured to Ms. Silver's bed. "In private, please. Only a moment."

"Yeah, fine." The enforcer jerked his head toward the lobby, and the two walked back that way.

"Richark Lonn," Mason said to Cadell. "He's in the strikers' bunkhouse in sector five. Room 2C. If I don't come back, see if you can get him to be my replacement. He knows way more than me, anyway."

"What makes you think you aren't coming back?"

Mason grimaced and glanced at the enforcers. There was only one other reason he could think of as to why they would want to talk to him. "Omar."

"This has never happened," General Dannen said. "Not as long as I've been liberator, and that's been"—he frowned and looked off to the side—"close on to thirteen years now. I don't know whether to shake your hand or write you off as dead."

"What exactly is happening that's so rare?" Mason asked.

"The task director wants a word with you."

Lawten Renzor wanted to talk? "Write me off as dead." Mason should have expected it sooner. Omar's disappearance from the MC could not have gone unnoticed forever, and now that Mason was tasking there, they'd assume he had something to do with it.

Fine. He only hoped they'd leave Medic Cadell alone so he could continue the experiments.

Mason sat with the liberator until two enforcers arrived. It was the same two he'd met when he'd first entered the Lowlands.

"Take him to the turnstile," General Dannen said.

"Yes, sir."

Both men looked terrified, as though Mason were an explosive device. Or maybe they simply knew that where he was going could not possibly be pleasant.

Mason entered the turnstile like before, and when the door opened on the other side, two younger enforcers were waiting with Colonel Stimel, a man who worked for Lawten Renzor.

"Step forward," one of the enforcers said. "Hands above your head."

Mason complied. The enforcers cuffed his hands behind his back and led him out the long hallway. They passed the room where he'd been scanned and two more just like it.

"No scan this time?" he asked.

"You're not returning to the SC to task, Mr. Elias," Stimel said. "Nothing you might have brought out from where you've been could cause any trouble. Not where you're going."

"Knowledge is a powerful thing," Mason said, eyeing the enforcers. "Do these guards know what's through those doors?"

"If he speaks again, stun him," Stimel said.

"Yes, General."

General? Mason regarded the patches on Stimel's uniform.

Stimel noticed Mason's appraisal and smiled. "Someone had to replace General Otley."

The enforcers loaded Mason in the back of a transport vehicle similar to the one he and Omar had arrived in. This time he had no ankle cuffs, so he merely sat on the bench on the side wall.

Eventually the truck started moving. It traveled a very long way, stopping and going again and again—at traffic lights, perhaps? Mason could only guess that they were taking him to the Highlands Rehabilitation Center.

But when the transport finally stopped and the back doors were opened, they were inside a building again, so Mason had no way of knowing if his guess had been correct.

The enforcers led him down white painted hallways to a small room and locked him inside. The room was a cement cube. Gray floors, walls, and ceiling. No bed, chair, toilet. This wasn't a cell. Just a room in a place that no one could hear or see.

That thought sent his gaze searching for the yellow camera. He found it behind him, in the corner above the door.

So, someone could see after all.

His hands were still cuffed behind him, so he sank into a cross-legged position on the floor in the near middle of the room right beside a drain. That's when he noticed that the floor wasn't level but gradually sloped toward the center.

The realization made his stomach tighten. This was the kind of room that could be hosed clean. How much blood had been washed down that drain? Would any of his follow?

He supposed they'd left him here to worry, so he tried to use the time more wisely and prepare himself for the coming interrogation. He needed to give as much truth as he could. Creative lies would be difficult to remember if pain became a factor. They'd undoubtedly ask about Omar. As far as any cameras had recorded, Mason had last seen his brother in the MC when he was comatose. Perhaps if he kept that qualification in his mind, it would make the statement true if they used a lie detector. But if they asked about—

The door opened, the rubber sweep on its bottom brushing dully over the concrete. General Stimel entered along with two enforcers. One carried a lie detector box. The other a molded plastic chair with metal legs. He set the chair beside Mason, then the enforcers each grabbed one of Mason's arms, pulled him up, and dropped him on the chair.

The enforcer with the lie detector crouched at Mason's side and reached for his bound hands.

"It's not there," Stimel said. "It's in the back of his neck now."

The enforcer paused as confusion swept over his face. He slowly stood and moved behind Mason. Cold plastic pressed against the back of his neck. A beep.

"All set," the enforcer said.

"Thank you."

Such manners from the man about to interrogate him. So different from Otley. In looks too. Stimel was Otley shrunk by 5 percent, which might not sound like much, but it made a big difference. The man just wasn't as scary. A strong wind could knock him down.

"Mr. Elias, where is your brother?"

"Which one?"

"Omar Strong."

"I don't know."

A glance to the enforcer holding the lie detector. A nod.

"When was the last time you saw him?"

That a camera recorded, Mason added to the question. "In the MC."

Another nod.

Excellent. Maybe Mason was smart enough to beat the box.

"Was your brother awake the last time you saw him?"

Awake? "Uh, no. He was in a coma." But the hesitation had been costly. The enforcer shook his head.

"Try again," Stimel said.

This man was smarter than Otley had been.

"I don't have to answer your questions," Mason said, annoyed he'd become flustered so soon.

Stimel cocked an eyebrow. "Are you sure?"

What a way to word things. Mason eyed the second enforcer, who was leaning casually against the door. He noted the definition of the man's arms beneath his shirtsleeves, then looked back to General Stimel. "I'm sure." Sure that he was about to experience a great deal of pain.

"I don't suppose you'll tell us where Ciddah Rourke is, either?"

"I don't know where she is," Mason said.

A nod.

"And the location of the survivors from your village?"

"Some of them are in the Lowlands. I can't be sure about the others. I've been gone for months."

"Will you tell us where they once were?" Stimel asked. "Those who were in the Midlands?"

"No."

Stimel nodded. "So much for my asking nicely, then." He stepped back and motioned to the enforcer by the door. "Hadley, it seems he'd like to try things your way."

Mason's gaze locked with the enforcer's. Hadley pushed off the door, walked toward him, stopped in front of his chair. Mason glanced down at the man's hands. No gloves.

The man lifted one hand to Mason's face. Mason winced. But the man merely scratched his cheek as if Mason had an itch he couldn't reach. Grinned. "You scared?" Hadley kicked the side of Mason's foot.

"There's certainly no joy in my anticipation," Mason said.

Hadley swung his fist towards Mason's face.

Mason squeezed his eyes shut and winced.

Nothing.

He looked up to see Hadley's fist inches from his cheek. The man chucked. Tapped Mason's jaw.

"Enough," Stimel said. "I have other things to do. You've been briefed on the questions. If he starts talking, tap me." The man walked to the door, his retreating steps a countdown that brought Mason ever closer to extreme pain.

The door swung open and closed. Stimel was gone, leaving a fading gust of chilled air behind him.

"Time to cry," Hadley said. And this time, he landed his punch.

Chapter 30

Levi sat between Ruston and Zane in the nest and stared at the Wyndo wall screen. "When did you get this?"

"Enforcers put it in theater nine this afternoon," Zane said. "I sent Dusten to fetch it."

"Could this have been doctored?" Levi asked.

"I'm sure it *could* have," Zane said. "I don't see why they'd need to bother, though."

Sure. Why bother pretending to beat someone up when you could just do it?

"Need me to play it again?" Zane asked.

"No." Seeing Mason beaten to unconsciousness once was enough for him. "What do you think?" Because at this point, Levi didn't know what to do.

"I think Renzor really wants the girl," Zane said.

"I'm sorry, Levi," Ruston said. "I know this can't be easy."

"We still have the same problem," Levi said. "We can't trust her. Though she hasn't done anything untrustworthy since she's been here."

"True," Zane said.

"It's too big a gamble," Ruston said. "We can't risk the Kindred on a hunch that Ciddah might actually be trustworthy."

"Maybe you should show her this video," Zane said. "See how she reacts."

"How would that help?" Ruston asked his son.

"Well, she claims to love Mason, right? Let's see what she does when she sees this."

"Kind of cruel, isn't it?" Levi asked.

"Kind of cruel to leave your brother to die," Zane said.

That was for sure. "Okay," Levi said. "You want me to bring her here?"

"Upstairs," Ruston said. "We'll put it on the Wyndo up there."

"All right." Levi stood and headed for the exit. "I'll go get her."

He went into the basements and brought Jordan and Ciddah back up to the living room of Zane's house. Ruston and Zane were already there, sitting on one of the couches.

"Are you going to trade me for Jemma?" Ciddah asked. "I'm willing, but I don't believe for a second that Lawten will give her to you."

"This isn't about Jemma," Levi said. "There's been a new development." He nodded to the Wyndo wall screen. "Zane?"

"Wyndo: power. Play."

The video started. Mason on the chair being pummeled by some enforcer minion.

"Mason!" Ciddah cried out and walked toward the screen, reached for it.

Every three or four punches the enforcer stopped hitting Mason long enough to ask a question. "Where is Omar Strong?" More punching. "Where are the rebels hiding?" More punching. "Where is Ciddah Rourke?"

Levi hadn't wanted to watch it again, though this time he couldn't help feel a surge of pride for how well Mason had held up under such force. He never would have believed Mason could last so long. He felt badly to have misjudged his brother's strength.

"Shut it off," Ciddah said, turning her back to the screen. "I can't watch it anymore."

"It's almost over, and you need to see the end," Levi said.

One particularly loud punch knocked Mason off the chair. The camera zoomed in on his unconscious face, then switched to Lawten Renzor, sitting at a fancy desk.

"Had it not been for the need to protect my unborn child, we would have taken this approach with Jemma Levi long before now. Since Mr. Elias does not suffer the complication of pregnancy, he's a logical candidate for such questioning. What you have seen today is only a glimpse of what we can do. I assure you that Mr. Elias *will* tell us what we want to know. Unless"—he smiled, which looked wrong somehow on his face—"you bring me Ciddah Rourke and Baby Promise. I will trade Mr. Elias for Ms. Rourke and the infant, no strings attached. You have twenty-four hours to reply."

The screen went black.

Ciddah whirled around to face Levi. Her flaking face was streaked with tears. "Trade me," she said. "There's nothing to think about."

"There is, actually," Levi said. "It's the same problem we've had all along in deciding not to trade you for Jemma."

"It's not the same at all," Ciddah said.

"How do you figure?" Levi asked.

"Don't you see? He's not hurting Jemma, and he won't hurt her. But he'll kill Mason. You have to try to get him back. It's the only chance he has. Lawten is desperate. And if he sees he's going to lose..." She shook her head, sniffled.

Levi had no reason not to believe her. She certainly looked like she cared for Mason.

"What do you mean that Renzor thinks he might lose?" Ruston asked. "What does he want so badly?"

"Me." Ciddah sighed, wiped her eyes. "He turns forty on March twelve. He fears liberation. Plus, there are no openings on the Safe Lands Guild, and they haven't given him another alternative. I think he plans to leave the Safe Lands. He's traveled to Wyoming before on various political matters. He once said Wyoming has strict immigration policies, that they only accept family units. I think he's trying to create a family so that Wyoming will give him residence."

"Don't they have a policy against infectious diseases coming across their borders?" Zane asked.

"I don't know," Ciddah said. "This is only a guess on my part."

"If we return Elyot, he won't need Jemma to leave," Levi said.

"He'll keep her close until he's certain he has me back," Ciddah said. "My guess is that she's his backup ticket into Wyoming. That must be why he insisted on being the donor for her child."

That comment put fire in Levi's veins. "Trade them," he said. "Elyot is Lawten's flesh and blood. Of all the kids we rescued, he's the one that we truly don't have a say over. And if Ciddah is willing..."

"You would give a child to that man?" Ruston asked.

"I wouldn't give just any child," Levi said. "But this one is his."

"We can't give him the baby," Ruston said. "He's better off here."

"Yes, but my point is, a child belongs to his parents. Kendall is dead. Lawten is alive. And Renzor won't kill the kid. But he will kill my brother. Please, this is the only way. Unless you have another idea?"

Ruston rubbed his hand over his mouth.

"But what about what she knows?" Jordan gestured to Ciddah.

"What does she really know?" Levi asked. "She was brought here blindfolded. She knows we're underground, which Renzor already knows. She knows the entrance is through a house. But there are a lot of houses in the Safe Lands. I'm not worried that they'd find us. But I'm even less worried that Ciddah will tell them anything. I don't believe she's the traitor we feared she might be. And even if she is, we still have her parents."

A knock at the front door.

A hush fell over those in the living room.

The doorknob shook. Another knock.

Zane got up and walked to the door, looked through the peephole. "Unbelievable!" He jerked open the door. "Maybe Fortune does exist. You seem to have nine lives."

Omar slipped inside the house, wearing regular clothes. He pulled a second person with him, a person wearing a hood. "Maybe I'm just a cat."

"Brother!" Levi had thought he'd lost Omar for good this time. Yet he didn't like the hooded guest. What was he up to?

"Have you caught a mouse, Mr. Cat?" Zane asked.

Omar grinned. "Sort of."

Ruston didn't seem so excited to see Omar's guest. "Why do you insist on bringing people here without asking first?"

"This is a special situation," Omar said. "Anyone who doesn't want to be seen should leave."

"What does *that* mean?" Jordan asked.

Omar gestured to his hooded guest. "Just what I said."

"I saw you captured," Zane said. "I saw enforcers cuff you and put you in a car."

"Not enforcers." Omar looked around the room, an eager expression on his face. "Everyone is staying? All right then." He pulled off the hood.

Levi's jaw dropped. "Luella Flynn? Are you mad?"

"We weren't followed," Omar said.

Luella's gaze bounced from face to face, landed on Ciddah, and her eyes widened. "Oh, Ciddah Rourke. Hay-o, femmy. You *are* a rebel."

"Luella," Ciddah said.

"Who needs to follow you when they can just track her?" Levi said, angry that Omar had risked them all.

"I checked her for trackers, and I cut out her SimTag," Omar said. "She's clean."

"Being a rebel is all very exciting," Luella said, holding up her bandaged hand.

Levi wasn't buying any of this. "*You're* a rebel now?"

"I'm a reporter, trig. I bring truth to the people of this nation. And certain stories have eluded me for far too long. Liberation, for example. And the Guild Intelligence League."

"The what?" Levi asked.

"She caught me," Omar said. "She wants to interview the Owl. But I think she can do more than that. She can help us. She's the lynchpin."

"I thought truth was the lynchpin," Jordan said.

"How can she be the lynchpin?" Levi asked. "We can't trust her." He trusted Ciddah ten times more than Luella Flynn.

"She's the lynchpin because everyone *does* trust her," Omar said. "The people, anyway. And she wants to show the people the truth. She's the link that will make all our plans happen."

"I can help you," Luella said. "And you don't even have to tell me your plans. Just let me broadcast it."

Zane crossed his arms. "How?"

"Think about our plans," Omar said. "Zane can hack the ColorCast for thirty seconds tops. But Luella can show it for hours. She controls the ColorCast. She'd show Operation Lynchpin to everyone, live. And everyone will know the truth *as it happens*."

"I'm tired of the lies the Guild tells its people," Luella said. "I've been a tool in Lawten Renzor's drawer long enough. I want answers. I saw this man liberated." She nodded to Omar. "I thought that meant death. But here he is. Back from... where? The people have a right to know."

"You haven't told her about liberation?" Ruston asked.

"Not yet," Omar said. "I had to have something to bargain with. But I did tell her our original plan for Operation Lynchpin."

"Don't blow the dam," Luella said.

"*Omar!*" Levi glared at his brother. This just kept getting worse.

Omar glared back. "Just listen to her!"

"The dam is the only clean water source we have," Luella said. "And yes, clean water is still an issue for our nation. Wyoming hasn't been willing to trade the secret of their purifier. They'll sell us water, but at a very steep price. We want freedom for Safe Landers. Without the dam, we'll only put ourselves in a position to be exploited."

"But we need to take control away from the Guild," Ruston said. "He who controls the resources controls the people."

"In theory, yes," Luella said. "But I control the majority of the people. Whether or not they should trust me, they *do* trust me. Forget the dam. Instead, we interrupt the Guild meeting. We demand the truth from the Guild. Then we call for new leadership."

"Why would that work?" Levi asked. "Why would they tell you anything?"

"Because minutes before we interrupt the meeting, the Owl will reveal the truth about liberation in his interview on the ColorCast." She smiled at each of them. "Then I'll enter the Guild meeting demanding answers. Yes, there will be enforcers on hand, but most will be too shocked to follow orders. Omar said the truth about liberation is *that* shocking."

"It is that," Zane said. "But instead of the interview, let's stick with our plan. We send the Owl you know where, and she could broadcast that."

"Better yet, we do both," Omar said. "She can pre-record the interview, show it, and at the end of the interview, the Owl reveals what liberation is, then we go live to show it."

"Oh, I like that, trig! Won't you tell me now?" Luella asked. "I promise I won't ruin your plans."

"No," Levi said. "You wait. Then you won't have to *pretend* to be shocked when Omar shows you the truth." And there would be no time for her to betray them.

Luella heaved a sigh, but her eyes were sparkling. "It's going to be wonderful to do this with the Owl. He'll be the true hero of the Safe Lands. He'll have made good on his promise. I think we should reveal his identity at the end."

"My identity is not important," Omar said. "But since I won't be with you at the guild meeting, I want three things to happen: I want the harem disbanded, I want the doors to the outside opened so that people can come and go from the compound as they please, and I want the task oath lifted so doctors and scientists can work together on a cure."

"I think we have found a new leader, boys." Luella winked at Omar. "Don't his words send a shiver up your spine?"

It *did* sound like a solid plan. Better with her help than on their own, but Levi wasn't sure Ruston would go for it.

Then Ruston surprised him. "We also want SimTags abolished. They need to stop tracking everyone."

Omar pointed at Luella. "We should also demand a new election for the Guild. Let the people elect the members."

"The Guild *is* elected," Luella said.

"It's always a yes or no ballot," Ruston said. "This time, run elections for what names go on the ballot, and don't make it yes or no. Majority wins."

Luella beamed. "Yes! Let the people choose. The same way they've been voting for what kind of tribal SimArt Horgan Blost will get on *C Factor*."

"If that helps you," Omar said.

"All right," Levi said, "but let's sit down and plan out exactly how we're going to do this. And trading Ciddah for Mason too. We need to make sure everything is just right." And, if he could manage it, include a plan to rescue Jemma.

Because they wouldn't get a second chance, Levi felt. This was it. Operation Lynchpin was about to commence.

Chapter 31

Shaylinn stood in the kitchen washing out baby diapers. Her twins ate nothing but milk, so she was surprised how messy their diapers could be. Ciddah was right that they were still too little to breastfeed, which meant Shaylinn's life now consisted of trying to extract enough milk so the babies could drink it through their feeding tubes. It didn't sound like much, but it was exhausting.

"You really should let me do that for you," Nell said.

"Thanks, but I'm tired of being in bed. I needed to get up and do something." Even if it was washing out dirty diapers.

"Maybe we could walk to the park later?" Nell suggested. "Or you could go visit Nash."

"I have no need to visit Nash, but a walk to the park sounds nice."

"But he likes you. And I think..."

The sound of the front door opening cut off Nell's words. Shaylinn couldn't see the entrance from here. Nell was staring, though, and looked embarrassed for some reason. Shaylinn hoped it wasn't Nash and that he hadn't overheard what Nell had said.

"Is Shaylinn in her room?"

The blood drained from Shaylinn's face at the sound of Omar's voice.

"She's there." Nell pointed at Shaylinn in the kitchen. "We thought you were dead for sure this time."

"Turns out I'm not so easy to kill," Omar said.

Shaylinn still couldn't see him.

"I should go somewhere else." Nell stood up, turned, shot Shaylinn an overly dramatic surprised face, then turned back and vanished around the other side of the entryway wall. "I'm glad you're okay, Omar."

"Yeah, me too. Bye, Nell."

The door clumped shut.

Something wet fell on Shaylinn's foot. She was clutching a baby diaper in her hands, and it was dripping water all over the floor. She tossed it back in the sink, dried her hands on a towel, all while watching the edge of the wall for his appearance.

Omar stepped into the kitchen. He looked okay. Really good, actually. He was wearing jeans and a green shirt. Emerald green, he'd probably call it, or pine.

"Hay-o, Shay." His bluer-than-blue eyes locked onto hers.

She swallowed. “Hi.”

“I heard you had the babies.” He glanced at her belly.

His scrutiny made her cheeks burn. “It takes time to lose the weight.”

He took a few steps toward her. “I'm sorry I wasn't here.”

Something tickled her face and she brushed it aside. A tear. Why was she always so blubbery? “I thought they'd caught you.”

“Luella Flynn caught me. She didn't turn me over to the enforcers, though. She was just trying to learn the identity of the Owl.”

Oh no! “And she let you go?”

“Yeah.” Omar grinned and Shaylinn melted just a bit. “She's going to help us get out of here. She's the lynchpin.”

Shaylinn wasn't sure what he meant by that. “So, it's not over?”

“No. Soon though. Tomorrow, actually.”

Shaylinn stiffened at that news. “You're going back out?”

He winced and held up his hands. “I have to. This is our chance—to get our mothers back, to be free again. I've got to do my part.”

He was so brave to keep going out where enforcers could shoot at him. “I'm proud of you.”

“Thanks." He shoved his hands into his pockets. "Uh, Shay? Could I see them?”

She stared at him a moment, wondering what he was talking about, then it hit her, and she gasped in a breath. “The babies. Of course.” *Duh, Shaylinn.*

She walked slowly across the kitchen and living room to her bedroom door and opened it. The lights were off and she left them that way, but she flicked on the bedside lamp, then sat on the edge of the bed and motioned for Omar to sit beside her.

The lamp illuminated the incubator and the babies inside. They were dressed in little sack-like outfits that Shaylinn and Naomi had sewed out of some of the fabrics Omar had brought. The boy wore the red-and-brown stripes with white dog-bone shapes. He lay on his back, arms stretched above his head. The girl was dressed in the purple-and-yellow plaid with smiling duckies. She lay beside her brother on her belly and knees, her little rump up in the air.

Shaylinn glanced at Omar, watching the expression on his face.

He was staring at them, eyes liquid with tears that had yet to fall. “They're so small.”

“They came early.”

He glanced at her. “But they're okay?”

She looked at her children then, studying the way their little bodies rose and fell with each breath. “They seem to be. They can't eat on their own yet, so that's been a challenge.”

“Did you name them?”

“I accidentally named the girl Rosie because of how pink she is. I know that's kind of close to Rosalie, so now Rosalie thinks one of the babies is hers.” She shrugged. “I'm not set on it. And I hadn't named the boy yet because I was trying to think what you might name him.”

He took hold of her hand. “What had you thought of?”

Shaylinn's heart beat so fast to have Omar beside her, caring about the twins. "Well, I thought maybe Eli after Papa Eli, but I know Papa Eli didn't like anyone naming their kids after him."

Omar nodded. "He thought everyone deserved a fresh start in the world with no expectations to live up to."

"I thought maybe Nicolas, after the Owl from the comic book you like so much."

He laughed, a low and surprised chuckle. "After Detective Nick Terry?"

"Yeah."

"How do you even know who Nick Terry is?"

All these years he really had been oblivious to Shaylinn's infatuation with him. "You left your comic in the meeting hall once. I read it."

"Wow. Okay. Yeah. Let's name him Nicolas, then. It's a good name."

Yay! Shaylinn felt happy that they had agreed on that. "And Rosie?" She wrinkled her nose.

"I like Rosie, but, like you said, we already have a Rosalie. What if that's her middle name?"

"Okay. Does Nicolas need a middle name too?"

"Elias, whether Papa Eli likes it or not." He winked.

Shaylinn squeezed his hand. "Then what will be her first name?"

"What about Coraline or Cerise or Carmine? Those are shades of pinkish red. Or we could call her Ruby."

"Ruby Rose?" Shaylinn shook her head at that one. "I like Cerise. That really means pink?"

"More red than pink. It's French for cherry."

"It is? Oh, I like that. She's a little cherry. Just look at her nose." Shaylinn leaned close to the incubator.

Omar leaned with her. "She's beautiful. Just like her mama."

Shaylinn turned her head fully to face Omar. "I'm fat again."

"Hey, don't say those things." He gripped Shaylinn's shoulder, closed his eyes, leaned toward her, and kissed her... forehead?

He pulled back, staring into her eyes, then leaned in and softly kissed her lips.

Shaylinn's insides caught fire. "Omar."

"I know. I don't have the right. I should have asked first."

"It's not that. But I'm afraid you'll disappear again. I don't think my heart can take it. And I don't want you to feel like you have to be with me. Like you're obligated or something."

"That's not how I feel."

His words gave her hope, and she asked the question she needed an answer to. "Then how do you feel?"

He sighed and looked at babies. "I'm uncertain. About everything." He glanced at her. "I want to be a good father. But I'm afraid I'll mess it up. I want to take care of you, but I'm... well, afraid I'll mess it up. Tomorrow, I'm going to be the Owl one last time, because someone has to go back to the Lowlands to expose liberation for what it really is. And that's going to be dangerous. But if everything works out, well, I have some plans. And I don't know if you'll like them."

"Tell me."

He took a deep breath. "Even if they let us leave, I'm going to stay inside the Safe Lands."

Oh no. The words seemed to make everything fall. "You are?"

"If I can. Shay, I didn't tell you, but… I tried to kill myself when I was in the Lowlands. Not that long ago, actually. It was dumb, but I was tired of hurting, tired of making bad choices. And, well. I didn't die. So, I figure God gave me another chance to do something important."

Kill himself? Shaylinn's eyes flooded with tears. "What are you going to do?"

He blushed then, from his cheeks and down his neck. "Don't laugh, but I was thinking of starting a counseling center."

In a million tries, Shaylinn never would have guessed that. "Like, for people addicted to the stims?"

He squirmed a little. "That's part of it. But also, I don't know, just a place where people could come for encouragement and support. I don't think I can do it by myself, though. I'd like your help."

"*My* help? Why?"

"Because you see people, Shay. And I want to create a place where people can come and be seen. To feel accepted no matter what. And to get help and support if they need it."

"So I'd… talk to people?"

"Yeah. And maybe, if they're open to it, you can also tell them about God's love. I haven't really thought it through. Only that I wanted your help. If you wanted to, of course."

She looked at her babies. "I think I'd like that."

He smiled, leaned in to kiss her again.

Shaylinn pulled back. "Omar. Don't you want to ask me how I feel about you?"

His hair fell in his eyes, and he pushed it back over his head and grinned. "How do you feel about me, Shay-Shay?"

She pursed her lips, trying to look tough. "I'm crazy about you. But I'm a mother now, and I have to be smart and look after my children. I've seen so many good things from you. But I've also seen a lot of poor decisions. Like trying to kill yourself!" She slapped his arm. "Really? I just… I need to know who you really are before I make any commitments."

"I understand."

Really? "You do?"

"Yeah. And I'll win you, Shay. Just see if I won't."

She glanced back at the babies. "We'll see."

Chapter 32

A kick to Mason's solar plexus jerked him from sleep.

An enforcer loomed over him. "Get up."

Mason's body ached. His hands were still cuffed behind him, so he used his elbows to push himself up off the concrete. His shirt made a ripping noise as the fabric peeled away from where it had stuck to the floor with his dried blood. As he sat upright, fluid drained down his throat. He coughed to clear his airways.

The enforcer kicked his thigh. "Up, I said. We're moving you."

As Mason stood, an ache throbbed in his head. He followed the enforcer out into the hallway, where a second enforcer was waiting. The three of them walked to the elevator, which they rode to the eighth floor. Mason recognized the interior. This was the elevator in City Hall, where he used to task. Lawten Renzor's office was on eight.

Sure enough, the enforcers led him from the elevator to the fancy penthouse office. Lawten was sitting behind his desk. As always, Kruse stood beside him.

When Kruse saw Mason, his eyes lit up in surprise. "What have they done to that pretty face, Mr. Elias?"

"Broken blood vessels, likely," Mason said.

"That will be all." Lawten pierced the enforcers with a stare that sent them scurrying from the office, leaving Mason standing alone in front of Lawten's desk. Then he turned those beady eyes on Mason. "Did you enjoy your time in the strikers' bunkhouse?"

"Not really, no," Mason said.

Lawten grunted a wheezy chuckle. "I know what they do to each other down there. As task director general, I've seen many unpleasant things, especially in the bunkhouses."

"There are plenty of unpleasant things down there," Mason said, "though I managed to avoid most of them. If you had a conscience, you'd do something about it."

"Where is your brother?" Lawten asked.

"I don't know where either of my brothers are. And if I did, I wouldn't tell you."

"You've put me in an unpleasant situation, Mr. Elias."

Mason almost laughed at that. Yes, Lawten was the one in an unpleasant situation.

"But fortune must be smiling on you," Lawten said. "Don't think you'll get everything you want. In fact, you're about to find out exactly what you lost." He nodded to Kruse.

Kruse called back the enforcers, who took Mason out of the office and back to the elevator. This time, Kruse came along.

"You're going to beat me again?" Mason asked.

"Mr. Elias," Kruse said, "much to my dismay, you're leaving us. We can track your SimTag, of course, so do keep that in mind when you run off to your rebel friends."

Mason twisted around to look at Kruse. Was the man warning him?

One of the enforcers picked up on it as well. He shot Kruse a glare. "Why'd you say that? He might have forgotten and we could have tracked him to the rebels."

Kruse sighed, as if the enforcer had a very small brain and often exasperated him with stupid questions. "Mr. Elias is a genius. He doesn't need me to remind him how SimTags work."

The enforcer's eyebrows sank low over his eyes. "But—"

"Please don't hurt yourself," Kruse said.

The elevator stopped on the ground floor, and the enforcers took Mason outside through the front entrance to City Hall. A sleek black car was waiting. They loaded Mason into the backseat. Kruse climbed in beside him. The enforcers got in front.

The car didn't go far. Three blocks later they stopped at Champion Park. The enforcers got out and dragged Mason from the vehicle. Kruse led the way across the dark, wet grass to where two other enforcers were waiting in the middle of the park.

This all seemed very strange. "What are we doing here?" Mason asked.

No one answered.

They stopped when they reached the enforcers.

"Have they given the signal?" Kruse asked the new enforcers.

"Yeah, they're waiting."

"Then let's get this over with." Kruse raised his eyebrows at Mason, who had no idea what to make of any of this. What had Lawten said again? Fortune must be smiling on him?

One of the new enforcers tapped the Wyndo watch on his arm. His voice amplified through the watch speaker. "Levi Justin, we're ready."

Mason's heart rate spiked. What *was* this?

And then, about fifty feet away, Ciddah appeared, holding a baby.

Her name came from Mason's lips involuntarily. "Ciddah."

An enforcer pushed Mason's back. "Go on. Walk toward the girl."

Walk? Mason started to run, which was awkward with his abdominal bruising and his hands cuffed behind him. They met halfway across the expanse.

"Ciddah," Mason said. She looked different without Roller Paint. Her skin was flaking terribly, but Mason still thought she was beautiful. "What's going on?"

"Are you hurt badly?" She reached up and lightly touched his cheek.

Her touch increased his adrenaline. He wanted to hug her, but his arms... "I'll live."

The baby started to cry, and Ciddah bounced him. "Mason, I love you. I've never really loved anyone before."

"I love you too," he said.

She beamed. "You do?"

"Yeah."

"I'm sorry." She raised up onto her toes and quickly kissed him.

"I don't understand."

"Keep moving!" the enforcer yelled through his amplified Wyndo watch.

Ciddah stepped past him. Mason turned with her. The baby was still crying.

"Shh." She bounced him. A tear rolled down her cheek. "He's trading you for me and Elyot."

"No! Ciddah, please. I never asked to be rescued. I got caught in the first place because I wanted you to be free."

"I know. But I want you to be alive. And he'll kill you, I know he will. He won't kill me." She continued on, so Mason walked alongside her.

Two enforcers approached them, and the amplified voice said, "Mr. Elias, turn around or you will be shot."

Mason stopped, and his right foot slid on the wet grass. "We tested more of the meds," he called after her. "A dozen before I was taken. Some had Centralin, some had Focastat XR. Uh..." He struggled to remember the others. "There was also Validum, Inergia... uh... Excitare! Lonn thinks they might be experimenting on the population, to see what works best."

She turned around and stopped. "Only nothing seems to be."

"Exactly."

"This is your last warning," the enforcer called. "We will shoot."

The distant lamplight made her tear-streaked cheeks glisten. "I'll never forget you, Mason."

"Hey, now. I'll get you back."

"Mason, please don't risk your life for me. He's obsessed. He'll have you killed."

"I'm not afraid of him."

"Well, you should be."

Two enforcers reached Ciddah and took hold of her arms, dragged her so that she nearly dropped Elyot.

"This isn't over," Mason yelled, not wanting to stop talking to her.

Someone grabbed his arm.

He pulled away and yelled, "Ciddah!"

"Mase, it's me." Jordan's voice. "We've got to move quickly because they're going to follow us."

Mason felt like someone had ripped his heart out of his chest. He stumbled alongside Jordan for ten feet before he stopped cold. "I can't go with you. My SimTag."

"Don't worry about it."

"It's in my neck. You can't cut it out. They'll track me."

"We know, okay. Calm down. Omar told us. We've taken precautions. They can track you all they want. They won't find you until we want them to."

"The Technology Research Organization building?" Mason asked, thinking of the lead walls.

Jordan snorted. "You think too much. No, this place is even better."

Mason stumbled alongside Jordan to the edge of the park. There they got into a car, which drove them around a corner and into a dark alley where three white vans were parked in a row. They got out and climbed into the back one.

"What is this?" Mason asked.

"We've got ourselves a new rebel," Jordan said. "Luella Flynn. And these vans are painted with lead on the outside so SimTags can't be tracked. We're going to pass you around town until we've confused them, then you're going to another place that's painted in lead."

"What place?"

"Luella Flynn's house."

Jordan used a pair of bolt cutters to remove Mason's handcuffs. As the van carried them across the Highlands, Jordan filled him in on what had been happening with the remnant from Glenrock.

Shaylinn had given birth to her twins early, a boy and a girl. Ciddah's wisdom to find an incubator was likely the reason they were alive and growing. Jemma was in the harem, pregnant with Lawten Renzor's child, which Mason could not fathom a logical reason for, though Lawten had never been a very logical man. Levi had taken over Omar's Owl patrols. Omar had returned safely. And finally, Luella Flynn was going to help the rebels.

"You're certain we can trust her?" Mason asked.

"Doesn't matter," Jordan said. "We're not telling her anything yet. That means you have to watch what you say. Don't tell her the truth about liberation. You get me? That's very important. We can't have her going live with it until we're ready."

If it worked as they were hoping, the idea of using Luella to broadcast the truth was brilliant. The people would eat up any word that woman said. "I won't tell her. But once we go live with the truth, I'll need help to get Ciddah back."

Jordan hummed as if he just remembered something important. "Ciddah thinks Renzor is going to take her to Wyoming. Said he mentioned that once before—that Wyoming accepts family units as immigrants or something. He's going to be liberated in a few months, and Ciddah worries he's going to run, use her and Elyot as his family in order to get into Wyoming."

Ciddah to Wyoming? "Then we've got to stop him!"

"Calm down. We'll figure it out, okay? But first, Operation Lynchpin."

Mason took a deep breath. He was tired of waiting. He wanted to help Ciddah now. What if Operation Lynchpin made Lawten run? What if he was leaving for Wyoming with Ciddah right now?

Then Mason would find a way to get to Wyoming and get her back.

Luella Flynn's home was located in the same neighborhood as Champion House. Though the place wasn't nearly as large, it was still massive. The van drove inside a garage and Mason and Jordan climbed out the back.

Luella herself answered the interior door. "Hay-o, trig! Come on in." She waved Mason inside.

Mason glanced at Jordan, who was already walking back to the truck. "How is this a good idea?"

"It's the only idea," Jordan said. "Zane gave her an off-grid Wyndo. We'll tap you later through that and let you know where you can help tomorrow."

Mason nodded and turned back to face Luella. The woman was wearing a black tent dress that looked like a trash bag.

"Come in! You're letting out all the heat. Don't you know it's the middle of winter?"

Mason stepped inside the house and kicked off his shoes. The floor was gray stone. The walls a light peachy color. As he followed Luella into a fancy sitting room, he took in the rusty brown drapes, dark wood furniture with pearl gray upholstery. The home was tastefully decorated, despite what its owner was wearing.

Luella leapt into a recliner, feet first, and sat on her knees, her dress crinkling. "Have a seat, trig. You look terrible. Did Lawten's people do that?"

Mason lowered himself gently into a wing chair. "Yes."

"Not very chatty, are you?"

"Just shaken. Being here. It's not where I expected to end up today."

A wide smile broke out on her face. "I suppose not. You're likely star struck. It happens all the time." She clapped once. "So, what shall we talk about? Not liberation, of course. Though I have to say, in the history of the Safe Lands, no one has ever returned from being liberated. And now you *and* Mr. Strong have both returned in the same week. It's quite extraordinary."

"Yes, well, how did this arrangement with you and the rebellion come to be?" Mason couldn't imagine that Ruston or Levi would have thought to ask Luella Flynn for assistance.

"I caught the Owl. Mr. Strong. That's his true identity, though I assume you already knew that. Had him in my basement here for several hours." She said all this as if it were the juiciest secret of the year. "He wouldn't tell me the truth about liberation, but he promised me a video exclusive."

"Meaning?"

"He's going back to..." She waved her hand around as she searched for the right words. "Wherever it is you go when you're liberated. And when he does, I'll be recording through his eyes."

Mason wondered how Omar was going to get back. Maybe he still had the hot-air balloon. "Tomorrow?"

"That's right. And you're going to accompany Mr. Neil and me to the monthly Safe Lands Guild meeting. We'll show the Ancients and Lawten our footage of the Owl exposing liberation, then we'll issue our demands. We'll be a voice for the people. It's going to be astonishing."

Mason didn't doubt it. "I have something to add. The monthly blood draws all nationals must get. It's only a theory at this point, but Rich—" Should he tell her that Lonn was alive? Why not? "Richark Lonn and I believe that the bio—"

"You spoke to Richark Lonn?" Her eyes were round, amazed.

"I'll give you a hint, Miss Flynn: Liberation is not death. Yes, I came to know Mr. Lonn quite well. He and I are looking for answers in hopes of finding a cure."

"There is no cure," she said as if everyone knew that much.

"Are you so sure? We feel there has been no cure yet because of the task oaths everyone is required to take. The task oaths, we feel, were set in place to keep people from learning about the things the government was hiding. But if the doctors can work *with* the biochemists, instead of separately, if there's no more need to keep secrets, we think that will enable scientists to make progress toward finding a cure. As is, our theory is that the biochemists have—without patient consent—turned every Safe Lands national into a test subject as they search for a cure."

"That's preposterous." But she fidgeted, like she was wondering over his words.

"Is it? I've been in the Safe Lands for six-and-a-half months, and I've seen people in terrible health. Surely in your profession, you have too."

"Of course we're in terrible health. We have a terminal disease."

"Yes, but Lonn and I, we think the biochemists are doing more harm than good. One of your demands on the air should be that doctors and biochemists work together toward finding a cure. And that they stay accountable to the public with their findings."

"You're saying that my meds are hurting me more than helping me?" Her voice was high-pitched, borderline hysterical. "That they're *doing this* to me?"

"I don't know that for certain, Ms. Flynn, but I do know that something in your meds is harmful. And that should be disclosed. You should have the choice whether or not to further harm your health."

Luelle huffed and folded her arms. "Well, we agree on that much, trig. Heartily."

Chapter 33

Jemma's car stopped outside the front entrance to the ColorCast building. She broke out of a daydream about Levi and looked at Kruse, waiting for him to get out and open the door for her as he usually did, but he remained seated. When she looked at him, she found him holding out a slip of paper, a finger held up to his lips.

She took the paper and read it.

Rebels are about to make their move against the Safe Lands. Today, in your interview, Luella will ask you to tell the truth about your situation in the harem. This will not be edited, and I'm sure that Levi Justin will see it at some point. Use it wisely. This is your one chance to let Safe Landers and Mr. Justin know your true story.

Jemma stared at Kruse, and he winked and took back the note. "We've arrived, Ms. Levi. Shall we?"

Was Kruse a rebel? Was that why he'd warned her before? "Yes, I'm ready."

Kruse opened the door and helped Jemma out. She couldn't believe how big she felt already, and she was only twenty-five weeks along. She wondered how Shaylinn was feeling with two babies in her belly.

Kruse led her inside the building and into the theater. As usual, the couches were already arranged on the stage. But there was no one in the audience today. In fact, the entire building appeared to be deserted.

"Isn't anyone here?" Jemma asked.

"Only a few of us today," Luella said, coming at them from the back booth. She was wearing a tight black dress that looked to be made out of a rubber tire. "I hope Kruse briefed you on today's twist."

She glanced at Kruse. "He did."

"Excellent. Then let's get started, shall we? I've been waiting years for a day like today. So much excitement." She squealed and hopped a few times on her spiky heels. "I can hardly wait."

A day like today. What had Luella meant by that? Jemma followed the woman up onto to the stage, wondering if she could really say that her baby was Levi's. Wouldn't Luella Flynn's people just edit that out?

"Why don't you go ahead and get comfortable on the sofa, femmy?" Luella said. "It's a new one. Just replaced. The Owl ruined my last ones, that trickster. I'll join you in a minute."

"I don't have to walk out from the side?"

"Oh, not today. This is a special interview! New things are happening." Luella took Kruse by the arm and dragged him to the side of the theater.

Jemma walked up onto the stage and settled herself in the middle of the little white loveseat to wait. Luella and Kruse looked to be discussing something important, then Luella turned around and ran backstage on her high-heeled shoes. How could she move so fast in those things? Jemma could see her behind the curtain, just offstage, checking her makeup.

My, this *was* a special day!

A few minutes later, Luella joined her onstage. She sat on the sofa across from her, and Alb said, "We're rolling."

Jemma relaxed a little. Luella was an easy person to talk to when you weren't worried that she was twisting every word you said. Not that Jemma was certain she still wouldn't.

"Jemma, our lovely queen, welcome. We have a very serious topic to discuss today, and I'm so thankful that you've been brave enough to come forward. My guess is that you aren't the first who has had to deal with this, but it's my fervent hope that you will be the very last. Tell us the truth, Ms. Levi: Are you and Lawten Renzor really lifers?"

Jemma couldn't speak. Tears flooded her eyes, and she cursed the hormones the medic at the SC kept giving her.

"This must be very traumatic for you," Luella said. "Take your time."

Jemma met Kruse's gaze where he was sitting in the front row. He nodded for her to speak. "No, we're not lifers." She paused for another breath, having worked up her emotions too high. "The people who edit the interviews made it look that way. But I never said those things to him."

"But your baby...?" Luella leaned close. "I thought Lawten was the donor."

"No! He wasn't," Jemma said.

"This is all very shocking," Luella said. "How did you come to be in the harem, Ms. Levi?"

"The first time or this time?"

Luella leaned back on her couch. "Both, if you're willing to share."

"Well, the first time, Safe Lands enforcers came to my village and killed many people. They captured the survivors and brought all of the women to live in the harem and told us we had to be surrogates."

"Our Guild killed your people and kidnapped the survivors? Outsiders? I'm so sorry. That must have been a terrible shock."

"It was. We found out that the people in the Safe Lands are dying because of the thin plague, and that's the reason it's been so long since a baby was born here. Your government was worried about the declining population, so they went looking elsewhere for uninfected people."

"Yes, but Kendall Collin," Luella said. "Don't forget Baby Promise. Things are changing now, aren't they?"

"Baby Promise," Jemma said, "as dear as he is, was a failure to your Guild. Kendall Collin was uninfected when she came here, but her donor was an infected Safe Lander, which means Baby Promise is also infected."

"That's terrible news. We had thought Baby Promise was our hope for the future."

"He's a sweet baby, but he's infected with the thin plague."

"How did you come to leave the harem?" Luella asked.

"I was rescued by men from my village. We lived underground with Black Army rebels until we came back to free more captive women from the harem. It was then that I got caught and put into the harem the second time. That was when the task director general told everyone that he and I were lifers and that this baby was his own."

"And that's not true?"

"No. I'm not going to exchange vows with the task director general because I'm already married to Levi Justin. I'd like everyone to know that I was pregnant before I was captured this second time. The medic confirmed this on my first appointment in the SC. Lawten Renzor wanted you to think the child was his, but that's a lie, like so much of what he says. The child belongs to me and my husband, Levi."

"Even now, you're still a captive in this place. What do you truly want?"

"I want enforcers to open the gates and let me and my people go home. I want to be with my husband and family. And I want to keep my child."

Luella looked at the camera. "There you have it, Safe Landers. The truth. It's hard to believe that this has been going on in our fair city. But as promised, today we'll discover many ways we've been lied to by our task director general and the Safe Lands Guild. Next up, an exclusive interview with the Owl where he'll tell us what liberation truly is!"

"We're clear," Alb said.

"Wonderful." Luella set her hand on Jemma's knee. "We pre-recorded this, but I promise you it will air unedited. We just don't want to be here when it does."

Jemma wanted to believe her. "When will it air?"

"Tomorrow. Early afternoon. The Safe Lands Guild meeting starts at two. I plan to show this first, then the Owl's interview right after that. And if I'm not mistaken, when the Owl tells the nation the truth about liberation, that's when your Levi will be coming to the harem for you, so be ready."

Chapter 34

Everything was set. They'd had to wait until Tuesday for Omar to make the trip back, since that was the next day Lonn would have someone watching for light codes. The Owl had given Luella Flynn an exclusive interview which she would show Wednesday afternoon, and tonight Omar was going back to the Lowlands. Zane had programmed two pair of SimSight lenses—one of which Omar was wearing. And Ruston had prepared a crossbow that would shoot a grappling hook and rope up to the top of the Midlands/Lowlands wall. This was how Omar would get back. At least... that's what they all hoped.

Omar left around six that evening. He rode the Midlands train all the way through the manufacturing district and got off at the very last stop. Things were closed down, and it was already dark. It was an extremely cold night, and Omar was thankful for the layer of clothing he was wearing over his Owl costume. Hopefully that layer and the climb would keep him warm. The night was silent but for the swish of his pant legs, the crunch of each step over the snowy sidewalk, and the occasional clink of the items in his backpack.

Snodgrass Road ran parallel to the Midlands/Lowlands wall. Omar followed the road until he stood about halfway between the first and second northern turnstile towers. Then he cut down an alley between two buildings. He could see the chainlink fence that ran about ten feet out from the wall he had to climb. The wall loomed above, a black shadow but for the red lights that ran along the top. Omar looked behind him, up the alley. He looked to his left, his right.

No one.

"SimTalk: tap: Zane."

"Where are you?" Zane asked through Omar's SimTalk implant.

"Between the first and second turnstile towers. Standing right in front of the fence."

"Hold on and let me find you."

Omar slipped off his backpack and pulled out the wire cutters.

"Got you," Zane said. "Just let me figure out where to shut off the fence and you'll be on your way."

While Omar waited, he pulled his pack back on and gripped the cutters. He could hear Zane's fingers tapping dully over his GlassTop.

"Okay. You're going to have to go fast. Are you ready?"

"I'm going now."

Omar ran up to the fence and started cutting. He only needed a space big enough to squeeze through, but this was chainlink, and that meant a lot of cuts. He snipped the links up in a straight line and stopped about three feet from the ground. Then he took a big side step and made another line of cuts. When he finished, he pushed his back up against the fence. Like the flap of a pet door, he was able to push through the chainlink. Once he was on the other side, the fence snapped back in place, jangling. Hopefully that would make it difficult to notice any holes if anyone came looking.

"I'm through," he told Zane.

Omar turned and looked up at the wall. It had been fairly easy coming down, but going up... He shook off his fear and traded the bolt cutters for the crossbow in his backpack. The moment his hand closed around the crossbow's grip, Levi's words came back to him.

You can't afford to miss.

And he couldn't. He had one shot to get this right.

"You ready?" Zane asked.

"Yeah, I'm ready."

"The motion detectors in the section in front of you should be off. There's a patrol truck passing by on the wall above. So, hold up for a minute before you shoot."

Omar looked back to the wall. The little red lights were out now in a six-yard strip. He took a deep breath. His father's words came to him, the day he'd missed the buck and scoped himself between the eyes.

"How could you miss that? He was four yards away!"

Omar touched the bridge of his nose. His fingertips came away bloody. But it didn't hurt nearly as bad as his pride. "Maybe I should try the crossbow."

"Crossbow?" Father snorted his exasperation. "If you can't shoot a rifle, you can't shoot a crossbow. Go home and have your mom look at that. Levi! We're going to see if we can chase down that buck Omar scared off."

Omar rubbed his scar.

Enough stalling.

He removed a pillowcase from his pack, then carefully withdrew the coil of rope. He set it out in front of his feet where he wouldn't accidentally step on it. All the little knots made it look tangled, and Omar checked it to make sure it was still perfectly wound. It was. The hook should carry it right up into the sky with no difficulty.

"The patrol is gone now, Omar," Zane said. "You can go ahead."

"Okay." Omar raised the crossbow and forced himself not to think about Levi or his father. He aimed, exhaled, aimed again, and fired.

The hook soared into the dark sky, the rope lassoing out in coils in its wake. He stepped back, lowered the crossbow to his side, and watched the pile of rope continually shrink as the hook carried it higher and higher.

He bit his lip as he watched. *Please, please, please...*

The rope stopped ascending. It fell, lax, against the wall. Yes! Omar ran to it, lifted it carefully, and pulled slowly, hand over hand, hoping for the tug that would secure the hook so he could climb.

"I see your hook," Zane said. "You're pulling it across the road. You should have no problem catching it on the guardrail."

"That's the hope." Omar pulled slower now, hand over hand, staring up at the black wall.

"A little more," Zane said.

Omar pulled another arm's length.

"It's caught. You got it!"

Omar pulled again. And again. "It doesn't feel like I—" But the rope went taut. "I do. I've got it." He sighed his relief and smiled to himself.

"Now get going," Zane said.

"Yeah, yeah. I'm going."

Omar put the crossbow and pillowcase back in his pack, put on the pack, then started to climb. Two months in the Lowlands GMC had wasted away what little muscles he had built up lifting weights, but he hoped he had strength enough to climb the wall.

Because it was a very tall wall.

But that's why they'd tied the knots. To give him a rest every few yards. When his hands passed the first knot, he tried to watch it as he climbed, to see when his feet reached it. He didn't spot it again until it was past his feet though, so he gripped the rope between his feet and slid down a little until he felt the shape of the knot press into the arches of his feet. He held himself there, testing it. He let go with one arm. Shook it out. Grabbed the rope again and shook out his other arm.

This might actually work.

Up he went, hand over hand, taking rests when he needed to. Zane kept him company in his ear, and the rest of the journey went without a hitch. Omar reached the guardrail and climbed over.

He sat on the rail to catch his breath. "Zane? I'm up. I made it." He detached the grappling hook and started pulling the rope up onto the road.

"I see you. Well done. No sign of the patrols, so you're good to keep going."

"Okay." Omar took a deep breath and carried the hook across the road. The inner partition wall was only about two stories high. He lobbed the hook up and over the wall, then slowly pulled the rope until the hook caught.

Again, he climbed. The journey was much shorter this time, but when he reached the top, there was no easy way to rest. He swung one leg over and sat there a moment, looking at the view. The Lowlands were dark, but he could see the greenhouses and a collection of lights around the Lowlands/Midlands Gate.

"The patrol is coming back on the Midlands side," Zane said. "You need to get that rope off the road."

"I'm on it." Omar straightened himself, straddling the wall, and clutched it with his knees. He wrapped a section of rope from the hook end around his arm to anchor it, then pulled the slack quickly over the wall, letting it fall on the Lowlands side. He had just finished moving it all when the patrol passed on the Midlands road. He watched it go, wondering if the enforcers ever thought to look up.

He searched for the patrol on the Lowlands side but didn't see it. "I'm going down," he told Zane.

"Okay. If I lose audio, stick with the plan. Hopefully the Lowlanders will see the same ColorCast as everyone else."

"Yeah, hopefully." Omar placed the hook on the top of the wall and started his descent. He quickly reached the roadway, but getting the grappling hook to come off the wall wasn't as easy as he'd thought it would be. He repeatedly tugged and pulled and threw the rope, trying to dislodge the hook, and didn't realize when it finally came free until it almost hit him in the head.

Omar carefully gathered the rope and the grappling hook and carried it all across the road. He hooked it to the guardrail. "Zane? You still there?"

"I hear you loud and clear, peer, so it looks like the cube is going to work. Time for me to start hacking."

Relief settled over Omar at that news, but he wasn't on solid ground yet. "What time is it?"

"It's 8:04. You're right on time."

"Okay, good." From where Omar stood, he looked down on the Lowlands. He couldn't tell one sector from another in the darkness. But he easily found the grid of glowing greenhouses. He removed the flashlight from his pack and flicked it on and off, giving the light code in the direction of the greenhouses. Hopefully someone would be down there to see it.

He finished the light code, which communicated that he was about to come down the wall and needed a distraction since Zane had no way to shut off the motion detectors on the Lowlands side of the wall.

Omar stared at the greenhouses, waiting. "Nothing yet. How about the patrols?"

"Nowhere near you, so we're good there."

A light flashed once. Twice. Three times. "Three flashes, Zane. What does that mean?" Omar could dig out his copy of the paper from his pack, but this was easier.

"It means they got your message."

"What now?"

"More waiting, I guess."

So, Omar waited. Zane warned him when the patrol was heading back, and Omar hid behind the guardrail by a lamppost. The light made him feel like they could surely see him, but Zane promised he was hidden.

When the hum of the electric engine had faded away, Zane said, "Okay, you're good to come out again."

Omar climbed back onto the road and looked to see what, if anything, was happening below.

Smoke swelled above two of the greenhouses and flames spat at the dark sky.

"Nice," Zane said. "I see the fires through your eyes."

"Yeah, but only two." And they were relatively small. Two of the four dozen greenhouses. "Think I should wait?"

"No, that might be all they can do. You've got to go now. Plus, another patrol is headed your way. You've probably got five minutes."

If Omar accidentally set off the wall's motion detectors, hopefully the fires would be distraction enough. He set his grappling hook in place and carefully lowered his coil of rope, hoping that it wouldn't swing and hit the wall. The wall curved out about twelve inches along the top, creating a very small overhang for Omar to try to stay under. He climbed over the rail, got a good grip on the rope, and lowered himself down. He squeezed the rope tightly, slipping down inches at a time, trying not to touch the wall. Once he had descended ten feet or so, he went hand over hand, but his arms were tired and soon he was sliding down. The friction made his hands warm beneath his thick leather gloves.

Another thing he didn't know: whether the motion detectors monitored just the surface of the wall or the area in front of it as well.

It didn't matter. The Owl was going down, motion detectors or not.

By the time he'd reached the halfway point, at least a dozen greenhouses in sector one had caught fire. Flashing red and blue lights of the fire enforcer vehicles lit up the night below his feet.

"They're getting a bunch of them put out," Zane said.

Yes, they were. "I've got to get down there while there's still a distraction."

"Jump," Zane said. "I think you could make it the rest of the way. Rumor has it the Owl can fly, so..."

"Ha, ha." But Omar let his hands slide a little faster, letting three knots pass through his grip before squeezing again. He was only about three levels up now.

Keep going.

He stopped himself just above the top of the chainlink fence. Time to see just how well the supposed motion detectors worked. He took a deep breath and resituated himself with his feet facing the wall. The smell of marijuana made him pause. Not grass in juice form. Fresh marijuana. Like someone was smoking it, the way they used to in Jack's Peak.

The greenhouses must have been growing it. And now they were burning.

"What are you doing?" Zane asked.

No time to think about the smell. He glanced behind him at the fence. This was probably going to hurt.

He stretched his legs until they touched the wall. Pushed off with his toes. No alarms went off—that he could hear, anyway. The push got him swinging. The next time his feet touched the wall, he gave a good jump. He came back to the wall hard and jumped again.

One more time.

On the last jump, he kicked out with all his strength and eased up on his grip on the rope. As he sailed out, he slid down. At the apex of his swing, he let go of the rope. His body flew over the top of the barbed wire fence and toward the ground. He bent his knees and tried to land in a crouch, but his momentum was too high and he fell backward and rolled right along his spine. He tried to stay in a ball. His backpack got in the way and the tools inside beat against his ribs. But it also helped slow him down, and on his second turnover, he stopped rolling.

He hurt. His back and his head throbbed. He lay there, panting, trying to decide just how badly he was injured.

"Omar, you okay?" Zane asked. "I can't see anything. Open your eyes."

He did. The sky above was dark. He shifted, straightened his legs, then managed to sit up.

"There you are," Zane said. "Speak to me, peer. You hurt?"

"I think I'm okay."

"Then get up and run! Someone might have seen you."

Omar groaned and tried to stand.

Someone grabbed him from behind.

No! Omar elbowed the person, pulled away.

"Hey! Calm down. It's me. Lonn. I got you."

Omar relaxed and leaned on Lonn for a moment.

"How are you, you maniac? That fall looked rough."

"I'm okay. Is there someplace I can sit a minute?" Omar asked.

"Yeah, sure. It's not like every enforcer in the Lowlands isn't out tonight. But we'll get you to a nice place to sit. Would you like some lemonade too?"

Zane chuckled. "Oh, I've missed Lonn."

"Shut up," Omar told them both.

"That's the spirit," Lonn said.

"What's the time, Zane?"

"Twenty minutes until nine."

Omar took a long breath—a marijuana-filled breath. Panic gripped him, and his breathing became short and shallow. He shouldn't inhale the smell, right? He'd get hooked again.

He pinched his nose and took several deep breaths, trying to calm his nerves. But when he let go, he could still smell the marijuana.

"What's wrong?" Lonn asked.

"The smell. What if it gets me hooked again?"

"What smell?" Lonn looked to the greenhouses. "The plants?"

"That's marijuana," Omar said.

"Yes, but you can't get high from smelling the plants like this. The chemicals have to reach your brain, and you're leaving right now."

"Okay." Omar let himself breathe normally. "Where are we going? I've got a lot to tell you before curfew."

"Let's go to your mom's place."

"Sounds good."

With all the fuss over the fires in sector one, Lonn and Omar easily made it to his mother's apartment.

She embraced him, then helped him take off his coat. "Mason is gone. I don't know where. We haven't seen him for days."

"Cadell said enforcers took him from the GMC," Lonn said.

"Yes, he's okay," Omar said. "Renzor beat him up trying to get answers about where I went. But Levi traded him for Ciddah and Kendall's kid. So, he's fine but probably not happy about it. I didn't get a chance to talk to him."

"What does that mean, traded?" Mother asked.

"Renzor wanted the medic. Bad. So bad that he gave Mason back to Levi."

"The medic is the one Mason's likes?" his mom asked.

Omar barked a laugh. "You could say that. He told Levi he wanted to marry her."

Mother frowned at this. "Does she feel the same about him?"

"Who knows? She might."

"And how about you? Did you see Shaylinn?"

Omar grinned. "She had the babies, Mom. A girl and a boy. They're so little. We named them Nicolas and Cerise. You're a grandma."

Mother mirrored Omar's smile with her own. "But are they all right? Isn't it too early?"

"I think they're going to be fine. Shay seemed to think so. They've got them in some kind of special bed to keep them extra warm. I forget what Shay called it."

"An incubator," Lonn said.

"Yeah, that's it."

"Congratulations, son," his mother said. "I'm glad you got to see them."

He stood a little taller then. "Me too. So, listen. We've got a lot to do tomorrow." Omar sat down on the couch and told them the plan. He'd brought an extra pair of contact lenses for Lonn to wear, so they could team up. "We've got to show as much as we can as fast as we can. And Luella will broadcast it. I'm hoping that when the Lowlands enforcers see that this is on the ColorCast, they'll realize that everything it out in the open and let us be."

"We can hope," Lonn said.

Twenty minutes later, they had a quick plan for the next day. They'd start indoors at the GMC and share what Lonn, Cadell, and Mason had uncovered about the meds. Then they'd go to the bunkhouse, then the slaughterhouses. After that, if they hadn't been apprehended, they'd just keep going and show as much as they could, maybe even interview people along the way.

And since Luella Flynn didn't want them to start until noon, they decided to spend some time the next morning spreading the word. Lonn would inform the men in his bunk—try to get Scorpion and his crew to start some riots. And since Lonn didn't want to risk Omar to Prav's uncertain reaction, Lonn would send a man to Omar's old bunk with a message asking Prav to get some of the enforcers on their side. If they could somehow take over the Lowlands surveillance, then they wouldn't have to worry about SimAlarms slowing them down.

At ten minutes until ten, Lonn left to get back to the bunkhouse before curfew. Omar's mother made him a bed on the couch, then, like he was a little boy, tucked him in and kissed his cheek.

"Goodnight, Omar," she said.

"Goodnight. Mother, tomorrow will..." He blew out a deep breath. "Tomorrow is everything."

She brushed back his hair from his forehead. "Worry doesn't take away the dread of tomorrow. But it does take away today's strength. Get some sleep, my son, so you can be strong for the battle ahead."

Chapter 35

The next day, Omar met Cadell at the GMC. The medic sent Omar into exam room two, where he changed into his costume.

The door to the exam room cracked open. "You've got my contacts?" Lonn asked.

"Yeah," Omar said. "Come on in."

Lonn slipped inside and closed the door. He turned to face Omar and whistled. "That's some getup. Let's see it with the mask."

Omar picked up his Owl mask and put it on.

Lonn hooted. "Oh, that's good. And a cape too. You're sure going to draw attention to yourself out there."

"There's no way around that." Omar handed Lonn the contacts case. "There's fluid in the container, so be careful they don't slip out when you open it."

Lonn put the contacts in his eyes like he wore them every day. "These really recording?"

"Tell him yes," Zane said. "I've got you both visually now, and your audio is still good, Omar. I think I've hacked the Lowlands SimTalk too. Have Lonn tap 268-73 so I can see if it's working."

Omar relayed Zane's instructions, and while Lonn tapped Zane, Omar shoved his clothes into his backpack.

"Okay, I've got audio on you both now," Zane said. "This is great. So, Lonn, you're going to be my cameraman to start this out. I need to you look at Omar and try not to blink too much."

"I can do that," Lonn said.

"Good," Zane said. "And, Omar, when you introduce Lonn, you keep your eyes on him so we can see his face. This is live, so do your best. I'm going to patch in Luella now."

"Hay-o? Anyone there?" Luella asked.

"Yeah, Owl here. I hear you," Omar said.

"Oh, I see you now too!" Luella said. "Thanks for bringing me— Is that Richark Lonn?"

Lonn winked at Omar. "Hay-o, Luella."

"Walls! I can't believe this! Mason said so, but..." Luella sounded slightly hysterical.

"Okay," Zane said slowly. "So, Luella will listen in and ask questions."

"We're ready when you are," she said. "I'm juicing to see what you're going to show me. I can't believe you're with Richark Lonn!"

"Omar, whenever you're ready, give us the report," Zane said.

"Okay, here goes." Omar stood against the portion of the wall that was bare and looked into Lonn's eyes. "This is not an error. The Messenger Owl has truth to deliver to the people of the Safe Lands. Truth brings freedom. Listen well. Today on this ColorCast, I will expose liberation for what it really is. You deserve to know. You deserve freedom. Trust the Owl."

"Luella Flynn, Safe Lands ColorCast. Owl, can you tell us the secret of liberation?"

"For those still living," Omar said, "liberation is a short trip to the Lowlands where you will task the rest of your days. You will grow old. And you won't be allowed to leave."

"That's... Task? How can that be?" Luella asked. "Do you have any proof?"

"I'll show you, but first, I urge you to tap friends who have been liberated. The Owl has repaired the SimTalk frequencies. Tap now to verify that I'm telling the truth."

"I can tap my friends who've been liberated and you think they'll answer?" Luella asked.

"Some will," Omar said, hoping it was true. "If you have no one to tap, let me introduce you to someone you should recognize." Omar kept his eyes on Lonn and tried not to blink. "This is Richark Lonn, alive and well. He served faithfully as a medic in the Highlands until he was caught trying to seek a cure for the thin plague. After that, he started the Black Army and became a rebel. Lonn, tell the people about the Lowlands."

"It's like the Owl said, this place exists so that those who live in the Highlands and Midlands don't have to do much work. Until you get three strikes or you turn forty, that is. Then you move down here. Since I was a rebel, I've got it pretty bad. I live as a prisoner. This orange jumpsuit is what I wear every day. And I—"

"Lonn, it's so good to see you, trig," Luella said. "This is all so shocking. You really have to wear that orange jumper all that time? You can't even enjoy mimic styles?"

"That's right," Lonn said. "But not everyone is so bad off. Those we call reputables are the people who made it to age forty without striking out. They get to live fairly decent lives, really. They can even watch your ColorCast. But they're forced to work very hard. And they can't leave. Ever."

Omar took over before Luella asked another fashion question. "There's someone else Lonn and I would like to introduce you to. He's just outside this door."

Lonn and the Owl left exam room two and walked over to where Cadell was talking to a patient.

"This is Kam Cadell," Omar said. "He tasks here in the General Medical Center in the Lowlands. There aren't a lot of medics down here, so he's very busy. Plus, he's been working with Lonn to expose a secret about the thin plague meds all Safe Landers take. Medic Cadell, can you tell us more?"

"Sure, Mr. Owl. What it comes down to is that there are stimulants in the thin plague meds that are doing more harm than good. The only explanation we can come up with is that your meds aren't given only to help you, but to run experiments. The Safe Lands

Guild owes everyone an explanation as to why they've been using us as test subjects. The next time you see your medic, demand an answer."

"This is outrageous!" Luella said. "Are you saying that my meds have stimulants too?"

"That's our theory, yes," Cadell said. "We suggest that all Safe Landers have their meds checked to verify the contents."

"Medic Cadell, you're old," Luella said. "Tell us how this came to be? How did the Safe Lands Guild manage to separate the young from the old in the first place?"

Cadell chuckled. "Well, I'm not quite *that* old, Ms. Flynn, but I've heard enough stories to give you some explanation." He went on to explain about the fake outbreak and how the old Guild had sorted the people.

"The airborne strain was a trick?" Luella asked.

"That's the rumor," Cadell said. "And it seems like a logical explanation."

Logical, maybe, but also completely underhanded. "Thanks for your help in seeking the truth, Medic Cadell," Omar the Owl said. "Now, we'd like to show you what the Lowlands looks like. Follow me."

Omar went to the windows in the waiting room that looked out over the exterior of the Lowlands. On his left the sector one fields were nothing but huge patches of snow and dozens of charred greenhouses. On the right, the dairy pens sat side by side, stretching into the distance as far as he could see. Luella asked what went on in each, so Omar explained how the Lowlands was broken up into eight sectors and went over them in detail.

Then they left the GMC and Lonn stayed behind Omar to keep him on camera. They took the elevator to the underground level and walked into Cibelo: the city below the Lowlands. It was mostly deserted an hour after lunch. Luella remarked over the outdated clothing she saw on people and in store windows.

Lonn and the Owl ran all over the Lowlands, capturing footage and answering Luella's questions. They went to the strikers' bunkhouse where Lonn lived, then down through the car wash where they explained how the strikers were required to wash and change clothing once a week. After that they went to the feedlot, then the poultry slaughterhouse.

Shortly thereafter, Luella said farewell. She told viewers that she'd continue to show the Owl's exposé on the Lowlands and would return in an hour with a program they didn't want to miss, which Omar knew would be her barging in on the Safe Lands Guild meeting.

Omar and Lonn walked from the slaughterhouse toward Cibelo, stopping people as they went and asking about their lives. A mob formed around them, drawn no doubt by Omar's costume. Some enforcers approached, and Prav was with them.

"That you, Omar?" Prav asked. "I got your message, but didn't actually believe you were the Owl."

"Believe it," Omar said, "and believe that we can get out of this place for good."

"How?" one of the enforcers asked.

"Lonn and I are wearing SimSight lenses. And what we see and say is being recorded for the ColorCast."

Prav snorted. "And I'm Finley Gray."

"It's true!" a man said. "I saw it in the cafeteria."

"I got a tap from a friend in the Highlands," another man said. "Our SimTalk implants are working again. Try to tap someone. Try it!"

Prav frowned at Omar, but said, "SimTalk: Tap: Fawke."

Several of the enforcers also tried to make a tap. And soon voices all around were telling old friends about the Lowlands.

"Let's find a Wyndo screen," Prav said to one of the enforcers.

"It will be on in the strikers' cafeteria," Lonn said. "Why don't we go there?"

So, Lonn and the Owl led a parade of strikers and reputables into the strikers' cafeteria in sector five. And there they all were, on screen.

"It's the Owl!" someone yelled.

Cheers rose up from the men in the cafeteria, and they rushed toward Omar. Prav and his enforcers formed a wall around Omar and Lonn.

Omar climbed on the table. "You see now?" he yelled to those around him. "You see what's happening?"

The men cheered.

"Some of you have gotten taps today, haven't you?" Omar said. "The SimTalk implants are working again. What I see—what you see on that screen—" He pointed at the wall screen. "It's being shown right now in the Highlands and the Midlands."

Roars of appreciation filled the cafeteria.

"It's time they learned the truth about liberation. If you know people, tap them and tell them. They need to know that liberation is not death. It's prison. It's slavery!"

The men hollered in agreement.

"For decades, the liberated have worked so that the people in the Highlands and Midlands can play."

The men booed.

"That's not Bliss," Omar said. "And there's little *pleasure in life* when most of your choices are taken away."

Another yell.

Omar looked into Lonn's eyes. "Safe Landers, if we don't change this, you will all join us here someday. Don't let this continue! We must elect a new Task Director General."

A cheer rose up.

"We must elect a new Safe Lands Guild."

Another cheer.

"And we must insist that the doors to this place be open for good, so that all can come and go as they please."

The prisoners jumped to their feet, applauding, cheering, some with arms thrust in the air, Prav and his enforcers among them.

Omar grinned at Lonn. They had done all they could. The rest was up to Mason and Luella Flynn.

Chapter 36

"I'd like everyone to know that I was pregnant before I was captured this second time," Jemma said. "The medic confirmed this on my first appointment in the SC. Lawten Renzor wanted you to think the child was his, but that's a lie, like so much of what he says. The child belongs to me and my husband, Levi."

"*Mine?*" Levi jumped up from his chair in the nest where he'd been sitting on one side of Zane, watching Luella Flynn's interview with Jemma. His chair clattered to the floor behind him, knocked over in his excitement.

"You okay, brother?" Jordan stood up and righted Levi's chair.

"Mine!" Levi said again. He embraced Jordan, who thumped him on the back a few times.

"Best news I've heard since you told me Harvey had been born," Jordan said.

Jemma was still on the screen, so Levi released Jordan and stared at his wife. His amazing, beautiful, precious wife.

He was going to be a father!

But that was the end of the interview. Luella said something about revealing what liberation really was, then the screen went to a commercial.

Really? A commercial? Today?

"Congratulations, peer," Zane said. "No wonder they were able to make her a queen so fast."

"Yeah," Levi said. "Yeah! Why didn't I think of that?" He glanced at the time on the Wyndo wall screen. Twenty minutes before they were supposed to leave to get Jemma.

He wanted to go now.

He was going to be a father!

He managed to sit back down on his chair and watch Luella Flynn introduce the Owl's "Liberation Exposé." It started with the Owl in some medical building. Omar even had his creepy Owl voice working.

"This is not an error. The Messenger Owl has truth to deliver to the people of the Safe Lands. Truth brings freedom. Listen well."

Omar went on to tell the people the truth about liberation. Levi got chills. His little brother had come to this place a fool who'd believed every lie the Safe Lands had to offer.

But he'd learned—the hard way, sure—but he'd turned all that around. Now, he was taking this place down. He was one sharp kid.

Then his little brother introduced Richark Lonn, who Omar pointed out was very much not dead, and Medic Cadell, who warned viewers about stimulants in the meds. After that, Omar and ran all over the Lowlands, capturing footage and answering Luella's questions.

It was all fascinating and shocking, but Levi was distracted and kept a close eye on the time. The moment the clock said 1:00 p.m., he stood. "Time to go."

Zane tested Levi's earpiece one last time, and he and Jordan set off to free Jemma, once and for all.

He hoped.

With Luella distracting the entire nation, Levi felt confident that their plan would work, but his head kept saying that such an attitude was foolish. How many times had they gone through this before? Could the ColorCast truly be *that* powerful? Could it keep enforcers from doing their jobs?

He and Jordan went through the storm drains into the Highlands, picked up a truck that Dayle had left for them, and drove right up to the drop-off zone in front of the harem. No one came out to meet them.

"That's a good sign, right?" Jordan asked.

"Let's hope so." Levi got out, left the truck in front of the building, and walked inside, Jordan at his side.

People stood in clusters around Wyndo screens, staring. No one even so much as looked at them as they walked to the elevators.

"I guess they're all pretty shocked," Levi said.

"Can you blame them? It's mad. Their whole lives have been a sick joke."

Levi was thankful that his great-great grandpa Seth had sacrificed himself all those years ago so that Papa Eli and his friends could escape. He'd always been thankful, but he was more thankful today. He hoped the truth would truly set these people free.

The elevator quickly took them to the sixth floor. They stepped out into a gaudy hallway with a vaulted ceiling.

"This place is fancier than Renzor's office," Levi said.

"I think it's hideous," Jordan said.

"This carpet sure is." Levi paused and looked both ways.

"To the right, peers," Zane said through the earpiece.

They walked up to a garish door with some kind of hybrid creature sculpted on the surface. Levi tapped his glove against the SimPad beside the door. It didn't open.

"Zane? Can you open this door?"

"Not that one," Zane said. "The SimPad is actually a doorbell. Just wait there. Someone should come and open it. Be ready in case it's the enforcers."

Levi drew the stunner from inside his coat. Jordan drew his as well.

Sure enough, some ten seconds later the door opened. A maid.

"We've come to make a pick-up." Levi showed her his stunner and pushed past her.

"You can't come in here," the woman said from behind him.

But she didn't try to stop him, so he and Jordan walked inside the fancy living room. It was dark, the massive wall of windows turned into a screen where a handful of women sat watching the ColorCast. Good.

"Intruders!" the maid yelled.

A chorus of gasps went up at once. A man stood from one of the couches, reached for his stunner. Jordan fired first and the man went down.

The women screamed.

"There should be another one," Levi told Jordan.

"Here." A second enforcer stood and tossed his SimScanner toward them. "I won't fight you. Not now."

Jordan shot him with the stunner anyway and the women screamed again.

"He'll be fine," Jordan told them. Then to Levi, "It wasn't worth the risk."

Levi supposed that was true. "Yeah, I'm looking for a Jemma Levi," he called out.

"I'm here!"

On the far side of the room, Jemma stood up. He could hardly see her in the darkness, but her voice was unmistakable. She started toward him. He ran. They met behind a couch. He swept her up in his arms and twirled her in circles, breathing her in. She felt wrong in his arms though. It was her belly. Large and firm, it separated them in a wonderful way.

He kissed his wife.

"Matron! Call Enforcer 10!" some woman yelled. Not the maid. The maid was still standing over by the door, staring at the Wyndo screen.

"Shhh!" This from someone watching the ColorCast. "Did you see how they have to take showers?"

"Let's get out of here," Jordan said from behind him.

Levi released Jemma and took her hand, pulling her toward the front door.

Jemma let go of him. "Not without Alawa." She walked back into the collection of couches, and Levi followed her like a shadow to a group of chairs. "Alawa, come."

"Shut up!" someone yelled. "We can't hear." On screen, the Owl was still in the car wash.

A pregnant girl approached Jemma. By her coloring, she must have been the missing girl from Jack's Peak. "We can really go?" she whispered.

Another pregnant girl rose from her seat on the couch. "You can't leave!" She circled the couch and stopped between them and the exit.

"Mia!" someone yelled. "Stop talking!"

Mia. Levi gritted his teeth at the sight of so many problems.

"You're welcome to come with us," Jemma said in a low voice. "Your mother too."

"Oh, Mia, let's go with them." Another pregnant woman came to stand beside Mia. Levi barely recognized Jennifer in the darkness.

Time to go. Levi grabbed Jemma's hand and walked toward the exit. The pregnant Jack's Peak girl trotted alongside Jemma. Jordan pushed open the front door and held it.

They walked into the gaudy hallway. Free.

Almost.

"You can't just leave," Mia said from behind them.

Jordan pushed the elevator button and it opened right away. He stepped inside and held the door. Alawa went in.

Mia and her mother followed them to the elevator. They both looked to be about as pregnant as Jemma.

"Come with us," Jemma said. "There is no life here."

"That stuff on TV?" Mia scoffed. "That will blow over."

"Their government has been lying to them, and now they know the truth," Levi said. "Life here is going to change. And first chance we get, we're going home." Levi maneuvered Jemma to his other side, urging her to go into the elevator.

Mia stepped into Jemma's path, but she was looking at Levi. "You lied to Jemma. You're no better than they are."

Levi flexed his jaw. "I never lied to her." He turned Jemma to face him. "But I didn't tell you everything either. Mostly because I was afraid."

"I don't care what you did two years ago," Jemma said, eyes misty. "I just want to get out of here."

"Right this way." He escorted her into the elevator.

Jordan let go of the door, but Mia caught it. "How can you not even care what he did?"

"Mia, why do *you* care so much?" Jemma asked.

"Because I'm the prettiest. Everyone always said so. My whole life. Yet no one chose me." The haughty tone of her voice had changed to anger.

"The fairest of them all, is that what you think?" Levi asked.

Mia sniffed and raised her chin. "I know it."

"There is more to beauty than appearance, Mia," Levi said. "I've always thought Jemma was beautiful, but what made me choose her above every other girl was who she is. How she can make everyone she speaks to feel better about themselves."

"Mia, come with us," Jemma said. "You're my friend."

"I don't want your friendship. Mother and I will stay here."

Levi nodded at Mia. "Fine. Let go of the door, then." He wanted to push her hand off it. But Jemma was crying, and he didn't want to upset her further. He focused his attention on Jennifer. "We don't know what will happen with the Guild, but you're both always welcome in our home. Please come visit someday."

"Thank you, Levi." Jennifer tugged Mia away from the elevator, and the door slid closed.

They met no trouble leaving the harem. Their truck was still parked outside. Levi was tempted to try and drive back to Zane's house in the Midlands, but Zane told him the Highlands/Midlands gate was too risky and to stick with the plan.

It took a while to walk through the icy storm drains with two pregnant women, but they eventually made it back to Zane's Midlands house. Naomi and Tova were waiting with blankets to help the girls get warm, but first had a tearful reunion. Then they all sat around the Wyndo wall screen to watch the rest of Operation Lynchpin unfold on the ColorCast.

Even though it was well after 2:00 p.m. when the Guild meeting should have started, the ColorCast was still airing the Liberation Expose. The Owl was standing on a table in a cafeteria of some kind. The tables were filled with men wearing orange jumpsuits, and Omar had them all riled up. Again, Levi got chills as Omar ended his speech and received a standing ovation from the prisoners.

So far, it looked like Operation Lynchpin was going to be a success.

The camera suddenly switched to Luella Flynn, sitting on a fancy chair. "Safe Landers, I'm appalled. To see my fellow nationals in prison? To discover that Bliss is a lie? That we don't have multiple lives but only one? And that our own government has been using us as test subjects without our knowledge. The Owl is right: We must not let this go on another moment. Today is the monthly meeting of the Safe Lands Guild, and I think it's time we asked the Ancients and Lawten Renzor a few questions, don't you agree?"

The footage flashed away from the stage to show Luella Flynn's back as she walked down a wide hallway. Mason followed on her left, Ruston on her right. They reached a set of double doors that led to the Champion Auditorium. Ruston grabbed one door handle, Mason the other. They pulled them open at the same time, and Luella Flynn walked inside.

Chapter 37

Mason and Ruston entered Champion Auditorium side by side behind Alb, who followed Luella Flynn with a camera on his shoulder. The audience seats were empty, but the hooded Ancients of the Safe Lands Guild sat up on the dais, as did Lawten Renzor and General Stimel.

Lawten stood at his place in the center of the front table. He was wearing a black suit. "What is the meaning of this interruption, Ms. Flynn? You can't bring a camera into this meeting." His voice was amplified and rang out from all sides of the room.

"Have you not been watching the ColorCast, Lawten? It's been quite a day." Luella's voice sounded soft in comparison to Lawten's, but she was speaking into her handheld microphone, so viewers likely didn't notice the difference.

"While I know how entertaining your program is," Lawten said, "we have serious work to do."

Mason couldn't believe no one had brought the news to the Ancients. Luella reached the witness box and climbed the steps to the top. Alb stayed on the floor and walked to a place in the front of the room where he could get both Luella and Lawten in his shot. Mason and Ruston followed Luella into the witness box but stayed behind her.

"If you haven't seen the ColorCast today, you don't really know what kind of 'work' you have to do." Luella pointed to the Wyndo wall screen behind Lawten. "Can someone get that screen on channel two?"

"Ms. Flynn, I won't ask again," Lawten said, eyeing Mason warily. "Vacate this auditorium at once."

"Mr. Task Director General, I don't think you understand *me*," Luella yelled. "The Owl has taken over the ColorCast. And for the past hour and a half, he has showed Safe Landers what liberation really is. You—this entire Guild—are finished."

"Preposterous." Lawten sat back in his chair. "That vigilante is nothing but a liar."

"If he's a liar, he's a very good one," Luella said. "He's in the Lowlands, Lawten. He and Richark Lonn have shown us the strikers' bunkhouses, the fields, the feedlots, and the slaughterhouses. We've seen our liberated friends slaving away in Bliss. Though the Lowlands really aren't Bliss, are they?"

Lawten tapped his fist against the table. "I need some enforcers in Champion Auditorium. Now." He tapped his fist again. "Hay-o? Get me Enforcer 10."

The Ancient beside Lawten stood, his black robe billowing around him. "Wyndo: power. Channel: two."

"Don't give in to her," Lawten said. "This is a hoax."

But the theater went silent as everyone stared at the wall screen. It slowly came into focus. The Owl was standing in the middle of a crowd, but the screen was quiet.

"Volume: sixteen," the ancient said, and Omar's voice broke the silence.

"Do you have SimTags down here?"

"Yes," a man said. "But they just started implanting them in our necks since rebels have been cutting them out."

"But these SimTags work differently than those in the Highlands or Midlands, isn't that true?" the Owl asked.

A woman pushed up on Omar's right. "One thing that's different is if you miss your curfew, they're programmed to stun you, wherever you are. You'll go down."

"Stunned?" the Owl asked.

"Yes, and they also give a curfew warning. Just a little tweak to remind you it's ten minutes 'til."

"'Til what?"

"'Til you'd better be in your bunk."

"And what happens if you miss curfew and are stunned?" the Owl asked.

"Enforcers take you to the RC," the first man said. "Unless you get a bad bunch, then they might steal your credits and beat you up. They're not supposed to do that, but it's happened to more people than you'd think."

"I'm sorry," Luella said from her place in the witness box, "channel two is showing footage we all saw this morning, but channel one is live. Perhaps we should see what the Safe Lands people are watching right now?"

The Ancient who had turned on the Wyndo said, "Wyndo: channel one."

The screen changed to show the feed from Alb's camera: Champion Theater and the members of the Guild staring at the wall screen of themselves.

Lawten jumped up, hands on the table, leaning toward Luella in the witness box. "Turn that camera off this instant! I need some enforcers in here!"

"You have no more servants," Luella said. "Your enforcers want answers like everyone else. The people are watching. They know you've been lying. And they'd like to know why."

"You'll get no answers from us," Lawten said, "not like this. Not under threat. Give me a private interview, Luella, once I've had time to prepare."

"I'm a reporter," Luella said. "It's my job to uncover the truth. And I won't give you time to prepare any more lies."

"What are your demands?" a grizzled voice on the left wall asked.

"Excellent. I'm very glad you asked." Luella waved Ruston to the front of the box. He moved up to stand beside her. "Safe Landers, this is Seth McShane II, also known under the rebel name of Ruston Neil. He's the leader of the Kindred, who are known to us only as Naturals."

Gasps and whispers from the Ancients.

Luella turned around. "Mason, step up here, please?"

Mason moved to Luella's other side. It felt strange to have the attention of the Safe Lands Guild again. It hadn't been all that long since he'd stood here with Omar. Since this same group of people had liberated him.

"This is Mason Elias," Luella said. "Mr. Elias is from Glenrock, an outsider village that our enforcers destroyed this past June. The Guild liberated Mr. Elias a few months ago, but he's back. Mr. Elias is named after his tribe's founder, Elias McShane. These two men have a connection in their past. A similar donor, if you will. Ruston, can you tell us why Mason and our Task Director General both bear the number nine?" She held her microphone out to Ruston.

"I can," Ruston said into the mic. "It's the same reason that if I was to be assigned a number, it would be a nine as well. It's because we have similar DNA or genetic code. That's because, for Mr. Elias and myself, generations back, we had a donor in common. Mr. Renzor, however, he and I have the same donors on both sides. He is, after all, my little brother."

Mason leaned out of the box, trying to see Ruston around Luella. "What?"

"We don't have to listen to this talk," Lawten said.

"I'd like to hear it," the Ancient beside him said.

"As would I," said the grizzled voice.

"Lawten is a Natural," Ruston said. "Our mother went into labor early with him. We had no technology to help her. My father was worried that she or the baby would die. So, he took her to the Midlands MC where she delivered Lawten. The medics took him away, of course."

"Did you know this, Mr. Task Director General?" Luella asked.

When Lawten didn't answer, Ruston did. "He knew. After he graduated from the boarding school, I found him and told him. He didn't want to believe me, but I could tell he knew I spoke the truth. He wanted nothing to do with me, of course. Promised he'd turn me in if I ever came to see him again." Ruston looked to Lawten now. "So, I've not bothered you, my brother. But times change, and this city is changing. The people will demand trust from its leaders from now on. And the people will only trust those they elect themselves."

Mason stepped behind Luella and leaned between her and Ruston so that he could reach the mic. "And your meetings must be shown on the ColorCast where the people can watch."

"That's an outrageous demand," an Ancient in the back corner said.

"That's our offer," Ruston said. "We'll open nominations today, and you, distinguished members of the Guild, are welcome to make nominations—even nominate yourselves. However, the nominating committee will accept no more than six incumbent nominations, so decide amongst yourselves whom you will nominate. Also keep in mind that just because you make a nomination, it doesn't mean the Safe Lands people will vote for you."

"Ruston," Luella said, "could you explain what you mean by the people voting? Safe Landers have voted for our task director general for years. How will this be different?"

"This will be very different, Ms. Flynn. First of all, a nomination page has been set up on the grid. You can find it on the page for *The Finley and Flynn Morning Show*. Make your nominations from now until next Saturday evening at six o'clock, January 15. At that time, we'll post the results and Ms. Flynn will begin interviewing the candidates."

"Finley will help me, of course," Luella said.

"Interviews will run as long as necessary," Ruston said, "and they'll be recorded here so you can come and listen in person if you don't trust ColorCast. Once every nominee has had their chance to speak, the people will vote. The top nineteen candidates will be our new Safe Lands Guild. And they will choose the new Task Director General of the Safe Lands from their ranks."

"I would like to speak." An Ancient stood from his seat in the middle of the row on the left-hand side of the auditorium. He pulled off his hood.

And there stood Bender.

"You?" Ruston looked as shocked as Mason felt.

No wonder they hadn't found him in the Lowlands.

"May I have the floor?" Bender asked. "I'd like to explain and make some recommendations."

No one said a word.

"Twenty years ago, this Guild discussed a terrible bit of news. Biochemists told us that the thin plague had mutated, that it was progressing yet again, this time aging people faster than normal. They claimed not to know why. So, I started an investigation. What I learned... it wasn't pleasant. In their search for a cure, the biochemists inadvertently made things worse. It was accidental. And there was nothing to be done but to try and fix it."

"By making every Safe Lands national a test subject without their consent?" Mason asked.

"Yes," Bender said, "I'm afraid that's true."

"So, the stimulants in the meds slow the aging process?" Mason asked. It was all that made sense in his mind.

"That's right," Bender said. "But it also weakens their bodies, literally 'thins' them out. It's a no-win situation right now. We've been trapped for years. Caught in our own lies. And that's true for other departments as well. There's been so much corruption, to try and change things would have meant revealing the truth to the public. None of us were brave enough."

"You were." Three places down from Bender, another Ancient removed his hood. He looked to be in his mid-seventies, but with the thin plague, who could make a fair guess? "The Guild Intelligence League kept most of us in line."

"I merely tried to keep us from making things worse," Bender said. "But the people are right to demand a change. We have failed them."

"What's the Guild Intelligence League?" Luella asked in an excited voice.

"It's a secret organization I started to gather intelligence on the Safe Lands government," Bender said.

"Then who gathered intelligence on you?" Luella asked.

"The taskers in my office monitored me as much as any other member of this Guild," Bender said.

"But you pretended to be a rebel," Mason said. "You killed Chord."

"Oh, I'm a rebel, Mr. Elias. I was born in a Kindred home. I left, came back, left again."

"But you didn't betray us," Ruston said. "Our homes in the basements."

"I was never your enemy, Ruston," Bender said. "I was merely trying to do the most good the only way I knew how. I simply hoped that we might stop Mr. Renzor from—Where are you going?"

While everyone had been focused on Bender on the side of the room, Lawten had left his seat. He was walking down steps in the front corner of the amphitheater that were hidden by the tables on the dais.

"He can't go far," Luella said. "Please, continue, Mr. Bender."

But Mason knew just how far Lawten could go. He wanted to leave the Safe Lands and might already have a plan to do so. Plus, he had Ciddah. Mason descended the platform steps.

"What about Chord?" Ruston asked. "I suppose his death was for the good of all?"

"Chord stumbled onto the truth, yes, though he didn't understand it," Bender said. "I accept full responsibility for his death and surrender myself to the Guild for questioning."

A door opened in the front corner of the amphitheater, one that was painted green to match the walls. Lawten went through it.

"I too would like to surrender," the grizzled voice said.

Mason ran up to the dais. He lifted the tablecloth and crawled up underneath the table onto the platform floor.

"What's the matter with you?" someone else yelled. "Ancients of the Safe Lands don't surrender. We are the law."

"That's over now."

"And who will rule in our stead? Luella Flynn?"

"Why not?" Bender said. "She has as much right as any of you. In fact, I nominate Luella Flynn and Seth McShane as temporary co-task directors until a new one might be elected."

Mason crawled to the other side of the table and slid down the stairs to the mystery door.

"We still have a motion on the floor that hasn't been voted on."

And that was all Mason heard as he ran out the door, and it slammed behind him. There was only one way to go. A hallway that led to an exit on the side of the building. Mason ran through it and just caught sight of Lawten entering the next building over. City Hall.

Mason raced into City Hall and pressed the elevator button. One elevator was on five, going up. The other was on two going up. He couldn't afford to wait. Where Lawten Renzor went, Ciddah would be.

Mason ran for the stairwell. He had just reached the fifth floor when someone entered the stairwell above him.

"Up, quickly." Lawten's voice. And a crying baby.

"Why? Where are we going?" Ciddah!

Mason kept climbing, trying to make his steps soundless.

"Don't ask stupid questions," Lawten said. "They're going to arrest us. Do you want to spend the rest of your days in the RC?"

"I've done nothing wrong," Ciddah said. "You're scaring the baby. Please, give him to me."

"He's *my* child. I'll carry him."

Hinges squeaked and light flooded into the stairwell from above, as did the sound of a motor of some kind, which muted whatever Lawten said next.

Mason could see their ankles now. Ciddah's and Lawten's as they walked out the door and onto the roof. The door clumped shut behind them, making the stairwell dark and quiet again.

Mason ran up the last flight, wishing he'd thought to find a weapon of some sort. He pushed open the door and peeked onto the roof. A helicopter! That's what was making all that noise. The blades on top were already a spinning blur. An enforcer was helping Ciddah inside. Lawten passed her the baby and climbed in.

"Stop!" Mason ran toward the helicopter. No one seemed to have heard him. The enforcer reached for the door, but Mason arrived just in time. Grabbed the door. Pried it back open. "Ciddah, get out!"

Her eyes widened. "Mason!"

"Shoot him!" Lawten yelled. "Pilot, take off."

The enforcer drew a stunner, and Mason ducked. The door opened farther, and the enforcer leaned out and aimed for Mason again. Ciddah screamed.

Mason dove under the helicopter. A stunner cartridge hit the roof and slid past Mason's feet. He lunged back out and yanked the enforcer's leg. The man fell out the door, landed in a crouch on the roof, then tumbled forward into a somersault.

The helicopter lifted off the roof just a few inches. Mason threw himself down on the right landing skid. The helicopter continued to rise, and gravity made Mason's body twist around the skid until his back faced the roof. Oh, dumb! What was he thinking? He wrapped his arms and legs around the skid, holding on with the joints of his elbows and knees.

As the helicopter rose into the air, he looked down on the roof. The enforcer was sitting, holding his ankle, watching as Mason was lifted higher and higher.

The helicopter banked sharply to the left, steering out over the city.

"Oh, God!" Mason squeezed the skid, which pushed his head to the side. He watched the ground beneath them with squinted eyes. They flew over the tall buildings of downtown, past the wooded area where the mansion homes were. Mason caught a glimpse of Champion House.

They must not be going there. He wondered if the pilot had any idea that his helicopter carried another body underneath.

The air was so cold that Mason could feel ice crusting his eyelashes together. His fingers were already going numb, and the wind was extremely powerful. He couldn't hold on like this much longer. The helicopter flew right over the Safe Lands walls and the foothills of Mount Crested Butte. The snow-covered slopes and trees would give him a quick death if he were to fall.

He caught sight of a large white flag hanging off the branches of a barren willow tree. No, not a flag. His balloon. Omar must have cut it loose.

The helicopter banked hard left again, and Mason clung to the skid with all his strength. They passed over more frozen terrain. A frozen lake. Then he saw the runway in the distance, a charcoal slash through the white, snow-covered land on the south side of the mountain. It was the old Crested Butte Airport, not more than a ten-minute flight from the top of City Hall. Mason had heard Papa Eli and his father talking about the planes that came and went from here, wondering where they'd been flying to.

Wyoming. Lawten was trying to leave with Ciddah and Elyot.

Mason had to stop him.

The helicopter flew to the far end of the runway and made to set down in the cul-de-sac there. Mason needed a plan. He could see a plane waiting about fifty yards from the cul-de-sac, facing away from the helicopter, pointed up the runway like it was ready to take off. The side door was down, forming a set of steps up into the plane. If Mason were quick, he might be able to make it inside the plane without being seen.

He didn't wait for the helicopter to land fully. The moment the ground was within six feet, Mason let his legs drop. His feet hit the icy asphalt and he let go of the landing skid and skated out of the way. His first few steps were pretty wobbly as he could barely feel his feet, but soon he was running.

He reached the plane and grabbed the rail on the steps. His momentum sent him skidding past, over ice and tiny pebbles, but he held on until he stopped, then ran up the steps and entered the cabin.

Mason knew little about airplanes. This one was like stepping into an apartment house. Against one wall, four beige leather seats sat two on each side of a dark wood table. Across from them were two more seats, one behind the other. Farther down the aisle, six more seats faced the back of the plane and a Wyndo wall screen on one side of a narrow doorway. Mason ran to the doorwawy and passed through an area with a kitchen counter on one side and a bathroom on the other.

A curtain covered the end of the aisle. Mason slipped behind it. His shins struck a full-sized bed that filled the tail end of the plane. It was covered with a white blanket and cinched across the middle with a long, black seatbelt. On the wall behind the bed, another Wyndo wall screen hung on a wood panel that closed off the rest of the tail.

He heard voices outside. A crying baby. Hide! Where to hide?

He squeezed in between the curtain and the partial wall that held the bed in place. He pulled some of the excess folds of the curtain around his body.

The baby's cry grew louder. It was inside the plane now.

"Put her in the back seat," Lawten said, his voice somewhat muted. He was up near the front of the plane. "And make sure you buckle her in."

"Yes, sir." This voice was male, soft and young.

The plane trembled as people walked around. Mason held his breath. He could hear movement just past the kitchen/bathroom area. Was the "her" Ciddah? If so, why didn't she speak?

"The woman is secured, sir," the young man said.

"Good," Lawten said. "Now go ask the captain what I should do with the baby." Elyot was still crying. "And you, get me some coffee."

"I don't know how to make coffee, sir." This voice was deeper and somewhat offended.

"Then get me some wine, water, whatever you can find."

"Yes, sir."

Footsteps carried someone back toward the bed. Mason could hear someone opening cupboards and drawers.

"The captain said someone needs to hold him or we could strap him down on the bed." The young voice again. "At least until we're in the air."

"Then put him on the bed," Lawten said. "Maybe he'll go to sleep. Be sure and strap him in, though."

"Yes, sir." Silence followed but for Elyot's screaming until, "What are you doing?"

"He wants coffee. Do you know how to make it?"

"I don't even drink it. Let me past, will you? This kid won't shut up."

Something pushed against the bed curtain. Mason pinched the fabric around himself so that no one could see him.

The curtain shifted again. An enforcer leaned into view and laid baby Elyot on the end of the bed. He reached up and fumbled with the seatbelt. Once he got it apart, he moved the baby to the center of the bed and buckled the belt over Elyot's middle. The baby continued to scream. Hadn't they brought any food for the kid? Ciddah would know what to do, but where was she?

The enforcer walked back to the kitchen area. "I don't understand why he's traveling without his assistant. He always takes his assistant."

"He said it was a vacation for him and his lifer."

"That woman didn't sound like she wants to be here," the younger one said. "And who orders an enforcer to stun their lifer?"

"She was going to make us crash, trying to get the door open like that."

"I'm just saying she wasn't acting like Mr. Renzor's lifer. I think he's taken her against her will."

"That ain't our business, so you just be quiet about it."

"Yeah, but what about that tap from Pep? He said that liberation is—"

"What's taking so long to find me a drink?" Lawten bellowed.

"Be right there, sir!" Then he lowered his voice. "Pep was messing with you. How could liberation be in the Lowlands? People would know. Now, let's get out of here."

The enforcers' footsteps faded as they approached the front of the plane. Mason stayed put. Elyot was still crying, fussing and kicking his legs with great force for one so small.

They'd stunned Ciddah. She'd been trying to get to Mason. She must be in the back seat. He wanted to lean out and see, but he didn't dare. Lawten's raised voice caught his attention.

"Well, one of you is coming with me. I need help on this flight. Decide now."

"I'm off at eight," the deeper voice said. "I have plans with some of my peers. We're going night skiing."

"I have a shift in the City Hall lobby tonight from six to ten," the younger enforcer said.

"You're both coming," Lawten said. "Grab a seat and buckle up."

"But, sir, I—"

"I don't want to hear another word out of either of you. Buckle up!"

Silence gripped the plane. Even Elyot's crying had softened to whimpers.

"I'll shut the door and we'll be on our way." This from a new voice.

Mason wanted to look, but he stayed put. The fact that Ciddah had been stunned was a problem. He didn't think he could incapacitate both guards and Lawten without her assistance. But if he waited until they were airborne, the odds of escaping would shrink drastically.

The plane rolled forward, ending Mason's debate on the subject. He held onto the top of the half wall, but as the plane increased speed, he fell back and landed, sitting, on the bed just below Elyot's feet. He carefully pulled the curtain across the doorway so that it completely hid the bed from view.

His body slid back on the bed toward the tail. He lay down beside Elyot and grabbed hold of the seatbelt. The boy had started to cry again. Mason stuck his finger in the baby's mouth, and the little guy clamped on and began to suck.

The plane lifted off the ground. It wasn't like the helicopter. The sensation was similar to the feeling of riding to the top of City Hall in the elevator without stopping.

Mason had no doubt that they were headed to Wyoming. How long did it take to get there? From the Old maps he'd seen, Wyoming had been directly north of Colorado. Planes flew at high speeds. Anywhere from sixty to six hundred miles an hour, depending on the type of aircraft. He had a feeling that the flight wouldn't last long. An hour, maybe?

Plenty of time for him to be discovered. And what if he was? Would they kill him? Not likely on an airplane. Planes traveled much higher than helicopters and had pressurized cabins. A gunshot might only create a small leak in the hull, but there was also the danger of breaking a window, which could depressurize the cabin in seconds. Or the bullet could hit wiring on the instrument panel in the cockpit, or hit the pilot.

Or it could hit the fuel tank.

Surely enforcers knew better than to fire a gun on an airplane. They might not even be carrying dual action pistols. If Mason were caught in flight, they'd most likely stun him and deal with him later.

Maybe he should stay put, wait until they landed in Wyoming, and steal Ciddah away when Lawten let down his guard?

Elyot had fallen asleep, so Mason got down on the floor and peeked out from the curtain. Ciddah was sitting in the chair closest to him. At first glance, she looked to be unconscious, but her eyes shifted, looking up at the ceiling. Her fingers tapped against her legs. Stunned, but quickly recovering.

In the front of the plane, the enforcers were sitting across from each other at the table, the younger one facing the back of the plane but deep in conversation with his partner. Lawten occupied the front seat across the aisle from the table. Mason could barely see the top of his head over the seat back.

What to do?

There was nothing to do but wait for Ciddah to recover. Right? He looked back to her and met her eyes. She stared at him, no expression on her face at all, which was weird since he was almost positive she must be glad to see him.

He smiled at her, then slipped back behind the curtain. Better not press his luck. He would wait for her right here. She wasn't restrained. Once she could move again, she'd let him know. He felt fairly confident that no one would bother him as long as Elyot was sleeping. As it was, the other men had been letting him cry. Clearly, they weren't all that concerned with his care.

While Mason waited for Ciddah, he thought through as many scenarios as possible to subdue the men. It would be best to divide them. If he and Ciddah tried to face them all at once, they'd be overpowered. But if they could immobilize one at a time, they might stand a chance.

"Hey, little peer," the enforcer with the soft voice said, suddenly close. "Mr. Renzor says there are blankets in a drawer under the bed back here. You hogging all the blankets?" The curtain shifted and the younger enforcer appeared. Mason was already moving before their gazes met. He swiped the enforcer's SimScanner, leaned back on the bed, and fired.

The enforcer grunted and collapsed on the bed. Mason dropped the SimScanner and pulled the enforcer all the way up, fixing the curtain so that it hid the man's feet. The movement jostled Elyot awake, who shared his displeasure with a wailing cry.

Mason stuck his finger in Elyot's mouth and whispered to the enforcer. "I'm sorry I stunned you. Listen, your friend Pep was right about liberation. That's why Renzor is running. The Guild wants to arrest him. And he kidnapped Ms. Rourke and Baby Promise because Wyoming only accepts family units. But I'm here to stop him. He needs to answer for his crimes against the Safe Lands. And taking Ms. Rourke against her will isn't right."

The young enforcer merely stared at Mason. Hopefully that had been information enough to convince the guy. Mason took his finger out of Elyot's mouth and removed the enforcer's handcuffs. He secured the man's right hand to a metal ring on the wall that could be used to pull back the curtain, but he couldn't find anything to gag him with. He hoped the stun lasted long enough for him to finish his task.

Mason examined the weapons on the enforcer's belt. There was a stunner, the SimScanner, a dual-action pistol, and an expandable baton. Mason removed them all. He checked the dual-action pistol for ammunition, left the sleeper slugs in the gun, but removed the bullets and flipped the action to sleeper mode.

First, do no harm. No one was dying, if he could help it.

Mason tucked the SimScanner into the back of his pants and shoved the bullets and the baton into his pocket. He took the stunner in his right hand and the pistol in his left. That way, he could stun the enforcer but put Lawten to sleep. He wanted Lawten to be out the longest.

A deep breath and he was ready.

He peeked out the curtain. Ciddah sat staring out the window. Lawten and the other enforcer were in their seats, facing the front of the plane.

Might as well move as quickly as possible and get this over with.

He stepped through the curtain. Two more steps and he pressed up against the kitchen counter. Ciddah looked at him, eyes wide. But she didn't move her limbs, so she might still be incapacitated.

Mason stepped out into the main cabin, walking slowly past the seats.

"Check on the baby while you're back there, will you?" Lawten yelled.

Mason froze, gripped the guns tightly, slid his fingers over each trigger. Heat washed over him. Adrenaline. He'd never been a very good shot, and pistols were harder to aim than rifles. But the entire cabin couldn't be more than forty feet in length. He just needed to get a clean shot at each of them, which meant he'd need to walk right up to them or they needed to be standing.

"Go see what's his problem," Lawten said.

"Yes, sir." The enforcer stood.

Mason shot the stunner at the enforcer's back, but since the man had been moving, the cartridge flew past his side and struck the wall.

"Hey!" The enforcer reached for his own gun, so Mason aimed the pistol and fired. A hit! The enforcer kept coming, eyes bulging. He drew his pistol, which Mason knocked out of his hand. It dropped beside Mason's foot, and he kicked it behind him. The enforcer fell to his knees. Mason glanced at Lawten, who was glaring over the top of his chair.

The feeling was mutual.

Once the enforcer had passed out, Mason grabbed each weapon from the enforcer's belt and tossed them toward the back of the plane. Then he stepped over the man, heading toward Lawten.

"Mason, no!"

Ciddah was on her feet, holding the enforcer's pistol. She took slow steps, but Mason couldn't tell if that was because she was weak or being cautious.

He also had no way of knowing if she had the gun set on sleeper or kill. "Ciddah, put that down."

"This is my fight, not yours," she said. "I'm going to finish this."

Mason stepped toward her. "Ciddah, you can't fire a gun in an—"

She raised the gun at his face. "Mason, look out!"

He spun around and ducked. Lawten had been coming his way, but the airy pop of the pistol stopped him. Lawten cried out. Then a second shot. A third. Fourth. Fifth. Ciddah was screaming, firing every bullet in the gun. Lawten moaned, and a strange whistling sound filled the cabin. Ciddah continued shooting.

Mason had to stop her. He spotted the enforcer's stunner under the nearest chair. He dove for it, rolled onto his back, and shot Ciddah.

The cartridge struck her against her neck. Mason winced and jumped to his knees to catch her. A horrible cracking sound inspired him to push Ciddah into a chair by the wall and buckle her in. He leaped in the chair beside hers and buckled himself.

Then he looked for the damage.

He could still hear the whistling. He and Ciddah were sitting in front of the Wyndo screen, in the seats facing backwards, so it wasn't easy to see from his position. He looked over his shoulder. The enforcer lay in the aisle one seat away. Up by the table, Lawten sprawled on the floor. Mason could see no blood. He spotted a hole in the wall above the first window beside the door. And another one above the second window. Likely the cause of the whistling. He scanned the rest of that wall. Everything looked okay. Then what had made that breaking s—?

Crraaack.

He twisted around and peered between his and Ciddah's seats at the other wall. A window above the table had splintered like a spider's web.

The fuselage was breaking open.

Mason unbuckled himself and lunged for the sleeping enforcer. He dragged the guy down the aisle, pulled the handcuffs off the man's belt, and cuffed him to the leg of Mason's chair. Then he ran for Elyot.

He was halfway back to his seat carrying the baby when the window shattered.

Mason jumped into his seat, settled Elyot on his lap, and buckled them both, pulling the strap as tightly as he could. Then he reached over and cinched Ciddah's seatbelt.

Besides the shrieking of the wind and Elyot's anguished cry, at first nothing seemed wrong. Then an alarm beeped above him and oxygen masks fell from the ceiling. Only two were within his reach, right above their seats. Mason pulled down Ciddah's and put it over her head, fixing the mask to cover her mouth and nose. Then he put on his own. He breathed deeply, then held his breath and positioned the mask over Elyot's face.

The plane went into a dive, throwing Mason hard against the back of his seat. The guns slid across the floor. Things fell past him. Napkins from the kitchen area, fluttering by like a flock of doves. Cans of soda pitched right over his head.

Mason tried to remain calm. He continued to share his oxygen mask with the baby, but there was nothing more he could do for the enforcers or Lawten.

The plane rattled and jerked up and down like an isoelectric line. Mason feared that any moment it might fall out of the sky and kill them all. When the plane finally bumped against the ground, Mason yelped. The breaks grated, the tires skidded, and the plane twisted from side to side. Yet slowly, blessedly, they came to a stop.

Where had they landed?

Mason remained seated at first, letting his heart rate come down. He left the oxygen mask over Elyot's face and tried the air. It seemed fine, so he released the mask, which bounced back up toward the ceiling where it was still attached. Mason unbuckled himself and leaned over to check on Ciddah. She glared at him, which meant she was fine, so he stood up, cradled Elyot in the crook of his arm, and took in the interior of the airplane.

There was a hole in the side of the plane where the broken window had been. It wasn't a big hole, maybe the size of three of the round airplane windows. The enforcer on the floor was unconscious, so Mason set Elyot in Ciddah's lap and pulled his oxygen mask down and over the man's face. He ran into the bedroom and was surprised to see the enforcer there wearing an oxygen mask and fumbling with a key and his handcuffs.

Maybe Mason should have thought to find the key from his enforcer belt.

Mason backed out of the bedroom and scanned the floor for a stunner. There were none. Everything had been sucked out the window when the cabin had depressurized. He walked toward the front of the plane and the cockpit door opened.

Two pilots stepped out. The first took a step toward the cabin.

"What *happened* back here? Why did we lose pressure?" the second pilot asked. "Is anyone hurt?"

That's when Mason realized that Lawten Renzor was not on the plane. He crouched and glanced under the table, but no Lawten. His gaze went to the hole in the plane. He walked toward it. Looked out and said, "I think Lawten Renzor is dead."

CHAPTER 38

Levi, Zane, and the rest of the rebels remained underground for the next few days, watching the ColorCast. There were many riots, but the majority of the enforcers quickly fell in line with Luella Flynn and Ruston's temporary leadership and managed to bring order back to Safe Lands streets.

Many nationals were campaigning for seats on the new Safe Lands Guild. Levi quickly grew tired of watching speeches from strangers promising change. He didn't much care what happened so long as they opened the doors and let him go back to Glenrock.

But Jemma was back in his arms, so he felt as close to home as he could for now.

They did not yet open the Midlands/Lowlands Gate, but Luella announced over the ColorCast that they'd created an application on the grid for Lowlanders to apply for relocation. Reputables would be permitted to return to the Midlands first, then they'd review striker applications carefully, as many were criminals. Reputables might be permitted to return to Midlands or Highlands housing, though they might also be required to continue tasking in the Lowlands as the tasks there were necessary to the welfare of the nation.

However, Luella saw to it that the Owl was brought back to the Highlands for a follow-up ColorCast interview. She wanted Lonn too, of course, but he refused to return without Levi's mother and remained in the Lowlands until such time when her application might be approved.

Luella was supposedly working on it. But she had lots to work on, so Levi didn't expect to see his mother any time soon.

Omar returned to Zane's Midlands house with Mason and Ciddah in tow. There was a great celebration in Kindred Park, attended by the remnant from Glenrock, Jack's Peak, and many Kindred, including Tova. The woman appeared by no means cheerful, but Levi did see her speaking to Zane in a hospitable manner and wondered if her heart might be softening.

The entire time Ciddah regaled the crowd with the story of how Mason rescued her from the airplane, Mason hid behind Levi and Jordan, who thoroughly mocked him for his blushing face.

It looked like his brother was going to stick with this Safe Lands girl. Levi figured he'd better get used to the idea.

Six weeks later, on Tuesday, February 22, 2089, all the gates in the Safe Lands were opened, including the one leading outside. Levi, Jemma, and Jordan were in one of the first few vehicles to leave. Beshup and Mukwiv followed in a truck behind them. The remnant from Glenrock and Jack's Peak were going to keep living in the basements until Levi and Beshup could check the villages to see if they were habitable. It was the middle of winter, after all.

Right after that first attack on Glenrock months ago, Levi had used up all the firewood he'd been able to find to create the funeral pyre. It would take time to cut more wood for heat and cooking. No doubt Jack's Peak would face a similar problem. As much as they wanted to leave, they needed to be smart about it.

There were about two dozen vehicles leaving the Safe Lands that morning, way fewer than Levi would have expected. The people seemed to be afraid to leave. But maybe more would go out when summer came. Levi would have to encourage it somehow.

He wondered at that thought. Why should he care about helping any Safe Landers? Yet strangely, he did care. He had skills that Safe Landers did not. And if people wanted to find another way of life, Levi would be happy to show them.

The roads weren't plowed so they were difficult to see. Levi was thankful that Dayle had loaned him the bigger truck. He went slowly, though, having no desire to get stuck in the icy cold forest with his pregnant wife. The closer they got to Glenrock, the stranger Levi felt. It was like coming back to both life and death. Memories of his childhood mixed with what he'd experienced the last time he'd been home. So many dead bodies. His father, his uncles, little Sophie. Papa Eli dying in his arms. Digging the graves. Moving the other bodies to the funeral pyre. Lighting it.

"The forest always looks so pretty in winter," Jemma said. "I've missed it."

His wife's words cleared the solemn thoughts from his mind as he took in the beauty around him. He would just have to make new memories to replace the bad ones.

"There's a buck!" Jordan said. "Aww, man. I wish I had a rifle."

"He'll be there later," Levi said, glad to see a sign of wildlife. There was no reason to think there wouldn't be any, but the buck affirmed his decision to come back to Glenrock.

They *could* live here again. Life *would* get back to normal someday. He knew it. Though "normal" would be a little different from now on with the changes going on in the Safe Lands.

He drove the truck into the village square and could barely see the remains of the funeral pyre, jagged pieces of snow-covered wood in the middle of the roundabout. He was careful to steer clear of it, hoping he was staying on the actual road. He parked on the far side of the square, closest to his and Jordan's homes.

Jordan jumped out before Levi had completely stopped the truck. Levi shut off the vehicle and watched his friend bound through the snow to the Zachary tribe's home.

"The place looks okay," Jemma said.

"It's only been eight months," Levi said. "As long as the doors and windows stayed shut, the houses should be fine." Should be. They were all well-built cabins, that much he knew.

Levi got out, went around to help Jemma. Only when he had her steady on her feet did he shut the door of the truck. Zane had loaned him gloves with a ghoulie tag so he could drive the vehicle. Levi wondered if he'd always need to keep a ghoulie tag on hand from now on.

Jemma took a long breath and sighed, a smile claiming her face. "It smells so good out here. The pine and the fresh air..."

Levi took her hand, and they followed Jordan's footsteps so that Jemma could see her family's home. They found Jordan in the living room, sweeping up a snowdrift on the floor under a window.

"The place is in pretty good shape," Jordan said. "All but this window. A bullet must have broken it during the raid."

"Good thing no squirrels thought to come inside," Levi said.

Jordan shrugged. "Not that we know of anyway."

Levi and Jemma inspected Jemma's room, and she exclaimed joyfully over the presence of several childhood dolls that she showed to Levi. He faked joy at the recovery of the toys, but he was truly glad to see her so happy. When they finished at her house, they went to Papa Eli's, the house Levi had grown up in. The original house of the Elias tribe.

It wasn't in as good of shape as the Zachary home. The front door had been left open, and the place looked to have been ransacked by several hungry critters. There were jars all over the floor, but only a few were broken. Hungry as the animals might have been, it didn't look like they'd found all that much to eat. No broken windows, at least.

After that, Levi and Jemma started up the hill to the little cabin he'd built for them to live in once they were married.

Jemma waddled beside him, looking like a brown bear on its hind legs the way she took tiny steps, arms held out to keep her balance. Her layers of coats wrapped over her huge belly and made her look twice her size. She probably shouldn't have come in her condition, but she had wanted to. And so long as Levi could help it, he had no intention of being apart from her ever again.

He helped her up onto the porch. The mounds of snow on each step came up to their knees and kept them from slipping. Levi kicked it away from the door as best he could.

"I never got to see the inside," Jemma said, bouncing on her toes beside the front door.

"Of course you didn't," he said. "Only my wife is allowed in here."

"Then open the door," she said. "Your wife wants to go in."

He grinned and knocked the snow off the latch. "Looks shut up tight. That's a good sign." He hit the latch with his fist until it slid out of the notch. The door popped open a few inches. Levi grabbed it with two hands and pulled it against the snow on the porch, inches at a time until the door cleared an arc that they could walk past.

Jemma stepped toward the entrance.

"Wait!" Levi put his arm in front of her. "I'm supposed to carry you inside."

She grinned and sniffled, her cheeks rosy with cold. "Well, hurry up and carry me then. I want to see my house!"

Levi swept her and his unborn son into his arms and walked sideways through the door. It was fairly dark inside as the windows—besides being covered with the curtains his mother had made—were coated in frost and snow. Levi set Jemma on her feet in the middle of the rug her mother had made for them. Shanna had given it to Levi for the living room floor, and he'd put it exactly where she'd told him to.

It took a moment for his eyes to adjust. The place didn't look any different from how he'd left it. Just cold. He walked to a window and tried to push the curtains aside, but they were frozen to the glass.

"They're stuck?" she asked.

"Frost," he said.

"Levi, I love it."

He looked at her, standing where he'd left her in the middle of the rug, her breath clouding around her face. "Do you?"

"Yes." Their gazes met and held until she smiled. He always won their staring wars. She wandered toward the rooms on the back half of the house and peeked in the first one. "What's this room?"

He walked up behind her and set his chin on the top of her hat, then wrapped his arms around what passed for her waist these days. "Your mom was going to give you one of her sewing machines. I was going to put it in here. But maybe this should be the baby's room."

"Naomi says Harvey is too little for his own room," Jemma said.

"Well, he won't be forever."

"But for a while we'll have to keep the baby with us."

"Okay." He took hold of her shoulders and turned her around. "So maybe this will be our room for when the baby is sleeping." He kissed her. Their noses were cold, and their breath made their faces moist.

She broke away first and looked up at him, her brown eyes searching his. "Will we live happily ever after now?"

He searched his memory for one of the stories she loved. "If we promise to outlive each other," he said, "which I promise this very moment."

She put her arms around his neck, grinned, then delivered her line. "Oh, my sweet Westley, so do I."

He tried to remember the alternate ending from the book and added his own twist. "But that was before Mason's gunshot wound reopened, and Omar fell back to vaping, and Shaylinn's children turned into owls and flew away, and Zane lost his other ear to frostbite. And the forest around us was filled with the sound of Lawten's pursuit..."

"Peace! I will stop your mouth." She kissed him again. He thought about telling her that she was mixing up her stories, but the kiss was more pleasant than teasing her would be.

They didn't stay in Glenrock. Just long enough to look around and for Levi and Jordan to assess the amount of work it would take to get everyone in their homes again.

Two or three weeks, tops, they figured.

They piled into the DPT truck and started back. Levi really didn't want to return to the Safe Lands, but until he could get out here and cut some firewood, they'd have to spend their nights in the city.

"It's weird that so few tried to leave today," Jordan said.

"Where would they go?" Jemma asked. "To someone who's never left the walls, outside would look like a frozen wasteland. I don't blame them for staying where it's warm."

"I guess," Jordan said. "I'd just think they'd want to get out, you know? Now that they know they've been prisoners."

"Maybe in the spring," Levi said. "It will have to happen gradually. It's the price of paradise. People who live in such a place go soft. They have no reason to learn to survive on their own. And a little bit of work completely overwhelms them."

"They're lazy," Jordan said.

"They've never had to be anything else," Jemma said.

"Now they'll have the opportunity," Levi said. "It will be interesting to see how much things change."

As much as Levi didn't want to care how things in the Safe Lands would change, he did care. Not only would he help anyone who wanted to live outside the walls, he'd also go back often to visit his brothers, who, he knew, weren't planning to come home.

Chapter 39

"Watch the steps. The middle one has a crack. I'll have to fix that." Omar grabbed Shaylinn's elbow as she climbed the steps to the cabin, Cerise in her arms.

"I'm fine, Omar." Shaylinn cast him an exasperated smile.

Shanna followed, holding Nicolas. Omar ran ahead of them all and opened the door. The cabin still smelled musty inside, despite him having aired out the place all week. Ruston had told Omar that he could have the cabin, and so Omar had offered it to Shaylinn since it felt similar to home but was still in the Safe Lands.

He'd already brought over two cribs that Zane had helped him get from the nursery in the Medical Center. He'd put them in the room that used to be Naomi and Jordan's and set up Shanna in the room that used to be Shay's.

Omar walked inside first, straight back to the bedrooms, and opened the door to Shay's new room. "The cribs are already here," he said. "I got new blankets for your bed too."

Shaylinn stepped inside and gasped. "Omar! It's lovely."

Shaylinn's bed had a lavender comforter. Cerise's crib was pink. And Nicolas's was green. Omar had also painted the room's walls yellow and covered them in his own paintings, save one. *The Starry Night* by Vincent Van Gogh was hanging on the wall opposite Shaylinn's bed so she could see it when she drifted off to sleep and when she woke each day.

She stopped to look at it now. "Omar, wasn't this painting hanging in Champion House?"

"You saw it?" He was surprised she'd remember such a thing. "It's a present from Luella Flynn. I asked her if I could have it. She said she thought it looked like a kid painted it." He laughed at that. "I didn't bother to tell her that it was priceless."

"I think it's beautiful."

"Thank you," Omar said, as if it was his own work.

Shaylinn walked to the pink crib and laid Cerise inside. "Are you staying for lunch?"

"I'm staying all day, if you don't mind," Omar said.

"Really? I thought you'd be at the Yellow House."

"Hope House," Omar said. "I changed the name. It's being painted today."

"Painted yellow?" she asked.

"The inside is being painted. White, actually."

"I like Hope House better than the Yellow House. You don't have to pay to use the building?"

"Luella said it's mine. For as long as she's task director, anyway." And Omar hoped he'd be able to make a difference in that place, to offer something to other broken people.

Shaylinn shot him a wide-eyed smirk. "Luella Flynn, the Task Director General. I still think that sounds a little scary."

Omar had to agree. "The rest of the Guild will keep her in line. And she might find that politics isn't for her."

"I'm glad Lonn got elected. And Ruston. And you."

"It's only because I was the Owl and we were on TV. They don't really know us."

"They will. You're all good men."

Omar walked over to her until they were standing side by side, looking down on Cerise. "I'm glad you decided to stay here with me," he said.

"Not with you exactly," she reminded him. Again.

"Not yet, anyway."

She looked up at him with only her eyes, so it looked like she'd rolled them and they'd gotten stuck. "*Omar...*"

He grinned and bumped his side against hers. "I know. But I swore I'd win you, and I'm not giving up until I do. Where is *Nash*, anyway?"

"I haven't seen him since the day Levi moved everyone else back to Glenrock."

"Good. Maybe he moved out there with them."

"*Omar!*"

"I just like to know where my competition is, that's all."

She took hold of his hand and squeezed. "You don't have any competition, and you know it. We're your family."

For one insecure moment, all Omar's failures flashed through his memory. He didn't deserve this family. Their love. They'd made it too easy on him. He should have to work harder. Then he remembered that forgiveness was a gift. He had accepted Shaylinn's continued forgiveness and had finally started to forgive himself.

He just forgot sometimes.

Omar pulled Shaylinn into a hug. "Then I'm a lucky man."

Chapter 40

"How is he?" Ciddah asked.

Mason sat in the chair in front of Ciddah's desk in her office in the SC. He studied the results of Omar's blood test on the CompuChart. "Better. His red blood cell counts are up. The white too."

"But it's not a cure."

"No." And maybe there never would be a cure. This was a virus, a living organism that mutated quickly and continually. Even if they did someday find a cure, they'd likely have to change the vaccine again and again to keep up with different strains.

As things were, the stimulants had been keeping metabolic rates somewhat normal, but they'd also been doing more harm than good, causing the virus to mutate faster. What they needed to do was to find a new type of stimulant that didn't have such terrible side effects. One that would keep people alive longer and keep the virus from mutating so quickly. There must be a way.

Mason had shared some ideas with Lonn, Medic Cadell, and the biochemists in the compounding lab, but his knowledge consisted primarily of natural remedies. Lemon oil stimulated white and red blood cell formation. Grapefruit oil was said to increase metabolism. There were herbs that could help promote blood cell production: echinacea, dandelion extract, licorice root, and even deer antlers. Certain herbs increased metabolism, as well. But nothing that would likely cure the thin plague.

He sighed and clicked off Omar's page on his CompuChart, set it down on a stack of folders on Ciddah's desk. He made sure the stack was steady before he let go.

Ciddah leaned on her elbows on her desk, her electric blue eyes fixed on him. "What's wrong?"

He shrugged. "I enjoy being a part of the team that's researching a cure, but sometimes I feel totally inadequate."

"You're not inadequate."

"Maybe. But it pains me to remember how arrogant I was when I first came here. Thinking I could find a cure for this plague that's been here almost since the Great Pandemic. Me, not even a fully trained doctor. Even now, what do I know?"

"Mason, you know lots of things our doctors and scientists don't know. You're invaluable."

"I don't know about that," Mason said.

"You are. Plus, you believe in the possibility of success. And you care about people. The others had no concern for the individual patients. They were focused on trying to cover up their mistakes. But you're honest and eager and willing to try anything. We will succeed because your faith and enthusiasm is contagious."

Mason swallowed, slightly embarrassed by her high praise. "I still think it has to do with the water," he said. "The water in this mountain was never tainted with the original strain. If they could find the progression, then they'd be able to reverse it."

"I agree that the water is an excellent place to start, but it's going to take time."

Time. Mason sighed deeply and studied Ciddah's face. He'd moved back to his apartment in the Westwall. Ciddah had moved back to her place in the Westwall too. And they'd both come back to task in the SC, working hard to make sure their patients were getting the safest meds, and helping the Cure Committee in their spare time.

But there was still no cure, though Lonn and Cadell were confident that one would be found now that they were free to search without restraint.

Mason was being impatient. That was the problem. Time wasn't passing by *that* quickly. He just hadn't decided what to do about Ciddah yet. He wanted to marry her, but he thought it would be wise to wait until a cure was found.

"You never said whether you were going to come to dinner," Mason said.

She straightened her posture and started looking through papers on her desk. "No, I didn't."

"Well?"

She pierced him with a steady gaze. "I still haven't forgiven you for stunning me."

He laughed at that. "Ciddah, you were shooting a gun on an airplane. We all could have died. I was trying to save us."

She rolled her eyes. "You're always right, aren't you?"

She had shot out a window! The plane had a hole in it. But Mason held his tongue.

Ciddah hadn't been dealing well with having killed Lawten Renzor. She'd confessed that she'd been having nightmares about that moment on the plane. She had to appear before the Safe Lands Guild in a week to answer for it. And Mason would be called as a witness.

Luella Flynn assured them that Lawten's having kidnapped Ciddah would help her case, but Mason was still worried.

She folded her arms and leaned back in her chair. "I think I should get to stun you. Fair is fair."

Oh, really? "You're absolutely right, Ciddah. Fair is fair. But you forget I already got shot with a stunner when I rescued you from Champion House. *And* I got shot in the leg with a real gun too. If anything, I should get to shoot you in the leg."

She faked a shocked gasp. "Mason!"

"How about we call it even and you come to dinner with me?"

She twisted her lips like she was considering it. "Where are we going?"

"To the cabin. Shaylinn invited us over. Omar too. And Shanna."

"Do you think it's fair that I asked her to watch Elyot while I'm at work?"

"Shanna loves it. Jordan, Jemma, and Shaylinn are all grown now. And she wants to help Shaylinn with the twins. One more doesn't make a lot of difference, I don't think."

"And you know that because you've raised so many babies yourself."

She would truly try and distract him all day with sarcasm. Mason stood up and walked toward the exit.

"Wait! Where are you going?"

He opened her office door and turned back to face her. "To dinner. Are you coming or not?"

"You're not going to shoot me, are you?" she asked.

"You're in luck. I've quit using guns. As it turns out, they're very dangerous."

"Oh, well, in that case, let me get my coat."

Mason and Ciddah took a taxi to the cabin in the Midlands, where Omar, Shaylinn, and her mother had dinner waiting in a home filled with the sounds of new life and love.

THE END

About the Author

Jill Williamson is a multi-passionate creative who loves the arts. She has written over thirty books for readers of all ages. Her debut novel, the medieval fantasy adventure *By Darkness Hid*, won an EPIC Award, a Christy Award, and was named a Best Science Fiction, Fantasy, and Horror novel of 2009 by VOYA magazine. She considers herself a "storyworld first" novelist, as she starts new projects by first building the world, then characters and plot. Jill loves working with other writers and encouraging them to respect their dreams. She speaks and gives writing workshops at libraries, schools, camps, and conferences. She is most recently a producer of films, working closely with her writer/director husband and other creatives in the Pacific Northwest.

To be notified of new releases and to get a free short story (ebook or audio), visit jillwilliamson.com/sanctum and subscribe to her email newsletter. You can support Jill and her writing on her Patreon page at patreon.com/JillWilliamson. You can also find Jill on the following social media platforms:

WANT TO KNOW HOW IT ALL BEGAN?

Find out how Eli McShane and his friends ended up forming the village of Glenrock in the Thirst Duology.

A waterborne disease has sprung up in every corner of the globe, decimating the human race. Seventeen-year-old Eli McShane and his friends flee the chaos and violence in Phoenix and journey north toward the rumored location of a safe water source. They add several to their number, including a mysterious girl named Hannah, who, unknown to Eli, is being hunted by a dangerous man.

Desperation brings out the worst in many of the travelers, infecting even those closest to Eli. When division comes, will he be able to hold his group together or will each fall victim to their own thirst for survival?

DISCOVER THE WORLD OF THE SAFE LANDS
BY JILL WILLIAMSON

THE SAFE LANDS TRILOGY

Brothers Levi, Mason, and Omar find their entire lives changed after they are made to live behind the Safe Lands' walls. Each must navigate the challenges before them, and somehow rescue their loved ones who remain alive.

THE THIRST DUOLOGY

When a waterborne disease wipes out the majority of the earth's population, an introverted teen must lead his friends out of the chaos and violence in Phoenix to the rumored location of a safe water source before desperation drives them apart.

AWARD-WINNING FANTASY FROM JILL WILLIAMSON

"Wonderfully written with a superb plot, this book is a sure-fire hit with almost any reader. An adventure tale with a touch of romance and enough intrigue to keep the pages turning practically by themselves."
–*VOYA* magazine

"This thoroughly entertaining and smart tale will appeal to fans of Donita K. Paul and J.R.R. Tolkien. Highly recommended for . . . fantasy collections."
–*Library Journal*

"Williamson crafts a complex and vividly portrayed epic fantasy reminiscent of George R.R. Martin's *A Song of Ice and Fire* series but less edgy."
–*Library Journal*

"[*King's Folly*] is an intense drama of biblical proportions... Wilek, Mielle, and Trevn in particular are intriguing, and the ending leaves readers wondering what adventures await this group of young people searching for truth."
–*RT Book Reviews*

TO LEARN MORE VISIT
WWW.JILLWILLIAMSON.COM

www.ingramcontent.com/pod-product-compliance
Lightning Source LLC
Chambersburg PA
CBHW011620030826
48979CB00039B/2823/J

* 9 7 8 1 9 5 5 8 4 3 4 7 8 *